A Good Clean Fight

Derek Robinson is a policeman's son from a council estate who crossed the class barrier by going to Cambridge, where he got a degree in history and learned to write badly. A stint in advertising in London and New York changed that. In 1966 he moved to Portugal, wrote two unpublishable novels, returned to England flat broke, and finally got it right when *Goshawk Squadron* was shortlisted for the Booker Prize. This novel of the Royal Flying Corps led to a sequel, *Piece of Cake*, which told the story – 21 years later – of an RAF fighter squadron in the first year of World War Two. *A Good Clean Fight* follows that squadron to North Africa. The desert war was unique: in the absence of civilians, there was nothing to harm except the sand, the enemy, and yourself. Hence the title, which is also ironic, since there is nothing either good or clean about violent death. Robinson's novels contain a streak of black humour and a certain debunking of the myths of war. The desert campaign was sometimes brutal but it was never glamorous and rarely glorious. There were major cock-ups, and there was great courage. *A Good Clean Fight* aims to do justice to both.

Derek Robinson lives in Bristol. When he's not writing, he's either publishing his best-selling guide to the local underground lingo known as 'Bristle', or playing much squash, against everybody's advice.

A Good
Clean Fight

Derek Robinson

CASSELL

Cassell Military Paperbacks

Cassell
Wellington House, 125 Strand
London WC2R 0BB

First published by Harvill 1993
This Cassell Military Paperbacks edition 2002

British Library Cataloguing-in-Publication Data
A catalogue record for this book is available from the British Library

ISBN 0-304-36313-8

Printed and bound in Great Britain by
Cox & Wyman Ltd, Reading, Berks.

To Squadron Leader Bob Spurdle, DFC,
to Squadron Leader R. W. 'Wally' Wallens, DFC,
and to their comrades of the RAF
in the Second World War

Also by Derek Robinson and published by Cassell

KENTUCKY BLUES
DAMNED GOOD SHOW

and in Cassell Military Paperbacks

WAR STORY
HORNET'S STING
GOSHAWK SQUADRON
PIECE OF CAKE

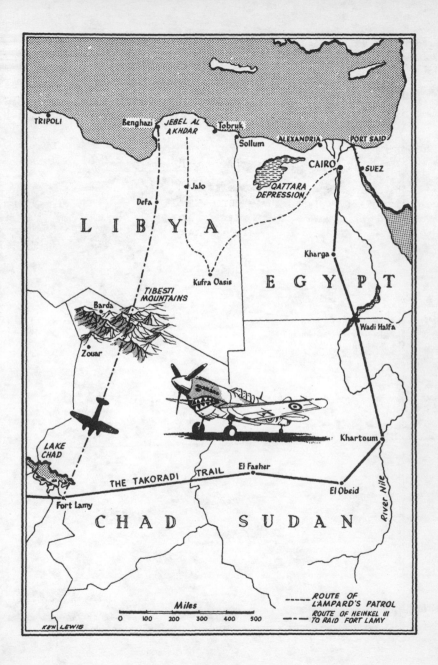

TRIPOLI Benghazi *JEBEL AL AKHDAR* Tobruk ALEXANDRIA PORT SAID
Sollum SUEZ
CAIRO
QATTARA DEPRESSION
Jalo
Defa
L I B Y A
E G Y P T
Kharga
Kufra Oasis
TIBESTI MOUNTAINS
Barda
Wadi Halfa
Zouar
LAKE CHAD
Khartoum
THE TAKORADI TRAIL El Fasher
Fort Lamy El Obeid
CHAD S U D A N River Nile

Miles
0   100   200   300   400   500

ROUTE OF LAMPARD'S PATROL
ROUTE OF HEINKEL III TO RAID FORT LAMY

KEN LEWIS

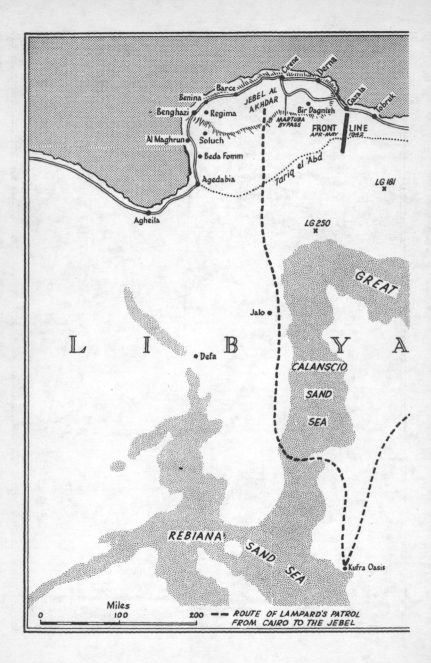

Cirene
Derna
Barce
Benina
Gazala
Tobruk
Benghazi • Regima
JEBEL AL
AKHDAR
Bir Dagnish
MARTUBA
BYPASS
Al Maghrun •
• Soluch
FRONT LINE
APR-MAY 1942
• Beda Fomm
• Agedabia
Tariq el 'Abd
LG 181
x
Agheila
LG 250
x
GREAT
Jalo •
L I B   Y A
• Defa
CALANSCIO
SAND
SEA
REBIANA
SAND
SEA
• Kufra Oasis
Miles
0   100   200 — — — ROUTE OF LAMPARD'S PATROL
                                        FROM CAIRO TO THE JEBEL

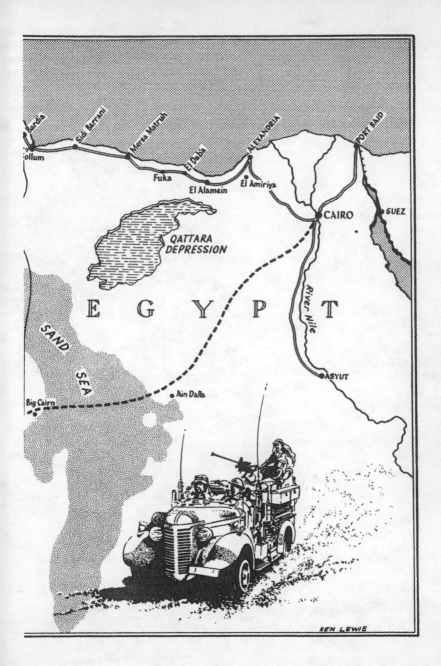

Bardia
Sollum
Sidi Barrani
Mersa Matruh
El Daba
Fuka
ALEXANDRIA
El Amiriya
El Alamein
PORT SAID
SUEZ
CAIRO
QATTARA
DEPRESSION
E G Y P T
River Nile
ASYUT
SAND
SEA
Big Cairn
Ain Dalla

KEN LEWIS

CHAPTER ONE

Walkover

It was good to be alive and young and flying Messerschmitt 109s from Barce airfield in April 1942.

Barce was in Libya, near enough to the comforts of Benghazi and far enough from the Gazala Line, which was a couple of hundred miles to the east, near Tobruk. Beyond the Gazala Line (which existed on the map, but was mainly minefields, and so invisible) were the enemy: British, Australians, New Zealanders, Rhodesians, South Africans, Indians. So you were usually safe enough at Barce. If you were a Me109 pilot you flew every day – training exercises, mock combat, gunnery practice – just to keep yourself tuned-up. When you landed you could go for a swim in the Med, maybe drive into Benghazi for a meal. It was a good life. Rewarding by day and relaxing by night. It would come to an end soon. One more big shove by the Afrika Korps and Rommel would be in Alexandria. Where would the British go then? India, probably. That was somewhat beyond the range of a 109, even with drop-tanks.

The only thing conceivably wrong with Barce (and the half-dozen other airfields along the coastal strip between Benghazi and Tobruk) was a range of mountains just to the south, called the Jebel al Akhdar; and even the Jebel wasn't much of a problem because as mountains go they were more like high hills: in fact they had to work hard to reach a couple of thousand feet. Nevertheless, if the weather suddenly closed in – and it could rain like a bastard in this part of Africa – then a bit of careless navigation could lead you to try to fly slap through the limestone escarpment of the Jebel. So far nobody had succeeded in achieving this feat, although a couple of scorched wrecks marked the sites of brave attempts.

* * *

Captain Lampard and Sergeant Davis came across one of the wrecks just below the rim of the escarpment and sat in the shade of what was left of a wing while they looked down on Barce. It was midday and the heat was brutal. Lampard had chosen to leave their camp, hidden five miles back in the Jebel, and come here at midday because he reckoned nobody down there would be looking up. And even if someone did look up, all he would see would be dazzle and shimmer and, if his eyesight was phenomenally good, the army of flies that followed Lampard and Davis everywhere. If they followed Lampard rather more faithfully it was not because he was the officer but because he was six foot two and there was more of him to overheat.

Each man examined the airfield through binoculars while the flies walked around their ears, lips and nostrils.

"See the wire?" Lampard said.

"Yes. Concertina, the usual stuff." Davis spat out a reckless fly. "We can cut it, easy."

"Might be an alarm wire running through the middle. Cut that and bells start ringing."

"Doubt it," Davis said. "Look at the length of the perimeter. Bloody miles. Think of the current you'd need."

Lampard thought about it while he went on looking, and then said: "Doesn't matter, anyway. There's a damn great gap. See? Far right."

Davis found the gap in the wire. It was where the coastal road passed closest to the airfield. As they watched, a truck swung off the road and drove through the gap. "That's daft," he said. "Why string up miles of wire if you're going to leave a hole? I can't believe it."

"Maybe they shut it up at night," Lampard suggested.

"Can't see any spare wire lying around. No sentry, either. That's sloppy, that is. Not like Jerry at all." Davis was a Guardsman; he disapproved of sloppiness, even German sloppiness.

But Lampard had already lost interest in the unfinished wire. He had turned his binoculars on the built-up area of the airfield and he was watching the arrival of a large staff car, an Alfa-Romeo with the top down. Three officers and a dog got out. The dog was enormous, as big as a young pony. It cantered around the car, skidded to a halt in front of one of the officers, reared up, put its paws on his shoulders and licked his face. He stumbled backwards and the dog fell off him. Lampard saw the silent laughter of the other men. One of them clapped his hands, soundlessly. The dog bounded amongst them and the man whose face it had licked shook his fist, then took a little run, swung his leg and kicked it on the rump. "Did you *see* that, Davis?" Lampard gazed wide-eyed at the sergeant. "First they invade Poland, then they go around kicking dogs. People like that have got to be taught a lesson."

Lampard booted the blistered wreckage of the German aeroplane, hard, as they went back up the escarpment. "That's blindingly obvious," he said.

"I wonder how much one of these costs, new," Davis said.

"Ten thousand pounds, I think. Twenty, by the time they've got it all the way out here."

"So there must be about half a million quid standing around down there." Davis paused to take a last, backward look. "I hope they got good insurance." Lampard was already at the top, striding hard, rapidly moving out of sight. Lampard knew only two speeds: asleep, and apace.

*   *   *

They came back at ten o'clock that night with three more men: a lieutenant called Dunn and two corporals, Pocock and Harris. Apart from desert boots and black stocking-caps, they wore normal British army battledress, so dirty that it was more charcoal-grey than khaki. They were all bearded and their faces were sunburned to a deep teak that merged with the night. Each man carried a rucksack, a revolver and six grenades. Lampard also had a tommy-gun. There was no moon. From the top of the escarpment, Barce airfield was a total blank. Even the road that ran past it was lost in the darkness.

Lampard could find only one track down the escarpment so he led his party down it. The track wandered aimlessly and took them into clumps of scrub or across patches of scree. The scrub grabbed at their arms and tugged at the rucksacks. The scree collapsed beneath their feet and sent them slithering, hands raked by the broken stones. Before they were halfway down it was obvious that the track had lost them, or they had lost it, or maybe it had never meant to go all the way to the bottom anyway. Lampard waited while they gathered round him. The starlight was just bright enough to let him count them. "Any damage?" he said. Everyone was scratched and bleeding, but Lampard meant something serious, a broken leg or, even worse, a lost rucksack. Nobody spoke.

He followed the contours until he met a dry streambed. At least that's what it looked like; it was certainly a gully that seemed to take the shortest route down the hillside. He stepped into it and dislodged a rock that made off at great speed, leaving small, rattling avalanches behind it.

"One at a time down here," Lampard said. "Allow a decent interval. No point in stopping a rock with your head. This is liable to be a bit steep."

He went first. It was more than a bit steep. By sliding on his hands and backside and braking with his boots he made fast, painful progress. Pebbles scuttled alongside him.

Then it got steeper and the pebbles were beating him. He glimpsed a looming boulder blocking the streambed, got his feet up in time and flexed his legs; even so, the shock jarred all his joints and left him sprawled over the boulder with the gun-muzzle poking his ear and the grenades making dents in his chest.

When his breath came back he stood on the boulder. It looked very black on the other side. He tossed a stone and it told him his future: the gully dropped thirty feet straight down. Maybe more.

The others arrived at safe intervals. He led them round the boulder and tried to get back into the streambed lower down but, perversely, there was no streambed. Evidently the water went underground. There was, however, a new track. It wandered, but it always wandered downwards. In five minutes they were on the plain. Fifteen minutes later they reached the road and they were looking at the gap in the wire and at notice boards stuck in the ground at each end of the gap. The notices said *Achtung! Minen*. They also carried a skull and crossbones. "That's all balls," Lampard said softly.

They eased their rucksack straps and waited. The starlight was slightly brighter now, and the notice boards, stencilled black on white, were big and obvious.

"Well, you're the boss," Lieutenant Dunn said. They were grouped closely together.

"Hang on," Davis said. "Let's think about this."

"It's all balls," Lampard said. "Put up to scare off the Arabs."

"I don't remember seeing them this afternoon," Davis said. "In fact I'm sure I didn't."

Dunn said: "You don't think they might have mined the gap this evening, Jack?"

"Not a chance. Jerry transport uses it as a short-cut to get on and off the airfield. We saw them do it."

Corporal Pocock, who had gone forward, came back

and said: "You can see the tyre tracks, sir. And plenty of footprints too. No sign of mines."

"What sort of sign did you expect to see?" Davis asked.

"Dunno. Disturbed earth, that sort of thing."

"The entire bloody gap is disturbed earth."

"Listen," Lampard said, "they haven't mined it for the blindingly obvious reason that they're going to need it again tomorrow. Satisfied?"

"You're the boss, Jack," Dunn said. "I hope you've reckoned the odds, that's all. I mean, it's just possible that Jerry's decided not to use it any more. In which case –"

"In which case he'd close the gap with wire, which is ten times faster and cheaper than mines. Agreed?"

Short pause. "Unless he ran out of wire," Davis said.

"For Christ's sake!" Lampard said, pointing. "It's *concertina* wire. It's made to stretch, isn't it?"

Corporal Harris had been tossing pebbles into the gap. "If we had some prisoners we could send them through to find out," he said.

"Right, that's enough talk," Lampard said. "I go first." He turned and strode into the darkness.

The others retreated rapidly to the edge of the road and lay flat. Lampard's figure was a dim blur. "What if it really is mined, sir?" Pocock muttered to Dunn.

"I suppose that will become blindingly obvious, Pocock."

Lampard reached the gap, crouched and stroked the biggest and freshest of the tyre tracks. They were clean-ribbed and firm. He surprised himself by being reminded of the last time he had touched a woman. He was twenty-four, and women were fun, but war was better. He stood and stared. His body was pumped-up with energy. All his senses were supremely alert, competing to serve him best. He went across the gap in a rush of long strides, heels digging into the tyre track. Nothing exploded. He wanted to laugh and cheer and throw grenades; now he *knew* he

16

was unstoppable. *Achtung! Minen*, what a lot of balls! He strolled back, casually and a bit jauntily, hands in pockets, to the middle of the gap. "No problem," he said. He jumped up and down. "Safe as Oxford Street."

"My old granny got knocked down in Oxford Street," Harris muttered.

They followed Lampard in single file.

"Mind you, she was pissed as a fart at the time," Harris said. Lampard ignored him. They set off, in line abreast, widely spread.

Corporal Pocock was the first to find an aeroplane. They converged on him and walked around the Me109, touching its skin and sniffing its expensive aromas, the fruity tang of aero-dope and the faint, fairground stink of once-hot oil. Now they could see the silhouette of another 109, and beyond that a smudge of darker darkness that promised a third. Lampard jogged down the line and counted ten fighters. He left Davis and Harris to take care of them and moved on with Dunn and Pocock at a brisk run.

Pocock found the second line of fighters, too. A thin mist was rising, enough to absorb the starlight, but a faint reflected gleam from a cockpit canopy caught his eye. He set down his rucksack and hurried on to find out how many more aircraft were parked here. Dunn and Lampard examined this one. "Pretty new," Lampard said. "The paint's still smooth and shiny." He was standing on a wheel and feeling the engine cowling. "It gets sand-blasted damn fast. What are you looking for?"

Dunn was fiddling with the side window of the cockpit. It clicked, and half the canopy swung open. "I had a thought on the way down that bloody mountain," he said. "Why not stuff the bomb beside the seat? That way you get the fuel tank. It's L-shaped, the pilot sort of sits on it. Make a lovely bonfire."

"If it's full. Might be empty. Anyway, we want the airframe. That's the expensive bit."

"You know best."

Pocock returned, gasping but triumphant. "Twelve of the buggers," he said.

"Marvellous. Tell you what," Lampard said to Dunn, "put half the bombs in the cockpit and half on the wing-roots."

"A controlled experiment," Dunn said. "The spirit of true scientific inquiry."

"Wait for me here." Lampard jumped off the wheel and made off into the darkness. *This is too easy*, he thought. *Where's Jerry? No sentries? No dogs? It's a pushover. A walkover. A cakewalk. A piece of cake.* There was benzedrine in his pocket, but benzedrine would be wasted on him now. He saw the massive shape of a bomber. His blood was thumping like jungle drums.

It was a Junkers 88, twin-engined and huge. "You beauty," he whispered. He decided to place a bomb on each wing, between the engine and the fuselage, but the wing was high above his head. He ran to the tail, took two bombs from his rucksack, and used his elbows to heave himself onto the tailplane. He began to walk forward, but the curved fuselage was wet with mist and he slipped and fell, knowing that he was falling and kicking off so that he landed on his feet and rolled over. That seemed enormously funny. For a few seconds he lay on his back and laughed without making any sound except for a bit of wheezing. "All right, you slimy bastard," he said. He put the bombs inside his shirt.

Next time he sat on the fuselage, straddling it with his legs, and heaved himself towards the wings. Then it was easy. He stuck pencil-fuses into the bombs, planted them and jumped down. It was all so simple. The more he did, the easier it got.

He found a three-motor Fokker transport with a ladder leading to its cockpit. That got a bomb. Moving fast, he put bombs on the wings of two small aircraft, probably spotter planes, and in the cabs of three massive petrol bowsers which reeked of fuel.

He sat on an oil drum and checked his watch: twenty-three minutes since they came through the gap. The first pencil-fuses had been set for an hour, with the later fuses being shortened as time passed. The night was pleasantly chilly: a night made for action. Lampard felt pleased yet also oddly discontented, almost resentful. He had come a very long way to give the enemy a bloody nose and they were nowhere to be seen. "Pathetic," he said aloud, and got up and walked back to Dunn and Pocock.

"We've done all these fighters," Dunn said, "and we found something that looked like an ammo dump, so we did that too. Also a great stack of boxes. Probably spares."

"Good," Lampard said. He kicked a wheel. "I suppose we might as well go home, then."

They returned to the first row of fighters. Davis and Harris were sitting on the ground, back-to-back, eating some chocolate they had found in a cockpit. "Any luck?" Davis asked.

Dunn said: "Two dozen planes in all."

"And a sentry," Davis said. "Harris found a sentry."

"That's that, then," Dunn said. "Home for cocoa."

"What's the rush?" Lampard asked. "I've still got some bombs left."

The others were shrugging on their rucksacks, ready to go. Lampard took his rucksack off.

"Look, sir: we've done the job," Davis said. "Let's not push our luck."

"Wouldn't dream of it, sergeant." Lampard was counting his bombs. "Two. Anybody else got any left-overs?"

"This place is going to be hopping mad in twenty minutes, Jack," Dunn said.

"I should hope so. Well?"

"One here," Pocock said reluctantly.

"I've got a couple I was saving to leave in the gap," Davis said.

"That makes five. Let's see if we can find some nice big hangars and blow 'em up."

"There isn't time, Jack."

"Then we'd better hurry." Lampard set off, half-running and half-striding, and the others scrambled to follow before they lost him in the gloom. "This is fucking lunacy," Davis whispered. Dunn grunted: he knew he needed all his breath to match Lampard's pace.

Lampard hustled them along for about two minutes, gradually slowed to a walk and finally stopped. "There," he said. A fine sliver of light appeared, no more than a hairline crack in the blackness. Dunn marvelled at Lampard's night vision while he despaired of his judgement. Light meant people. "Onwards," Lampard murmured.

It was a hangar, a steel shell as big as a bank. Davis pressed his ear against the side. Sometimes a muttering of voices could be heard, and the faint click of metal on metal. "Occupied," he whispered. Lampard led the patrol around the corner. The sliver of light came from an ill-fitting blackout around a huge sliding door. Lampard peered in, but saw only a pile of paint tins. Using the tips of his fingers, he felt his way across the sliding door until he found a small hinged door set into it, and grunted with satisfaction: hangars were much the same the whole world over. Dunn was beside him, tapping his luminous watch. "Fifteen minutes to detonation," Dunn whispered. Lampard took a deep breath. The air tasted sweet and exhilarating, delicately laced by some aromatic desert herb. Before his mind made the decision, his fingers had turned the handle. It opened inwards, as he knew it would. He knew everything, and the knowledge made him smile with delight. The enemy was there to be beaten. All it took was nerve and Lampard had nerve galore.

He sneaked a glance around the blackout curtain hanging inside the door and saw bright lights over broken aircraft and deep shadow elsewhere. Lovely. He slipped off his rucksack and primed all the bombs with fifteen-minute fuses. He put three in his tunic, took a bomb in each hand and strolled into the shadows. His rubber soles made no sound on the concrete. For a long moment he watched Germans in white overalls doing things to the guts of the engines of two 109s. In another area, men were fitting a new propeller. They seemed relaxed and happy in their work. He strolled on and came across an aircraft with no wings or wheels, supported on wooden trestles. He left a bomb in its naked engine. Nearby was a stack of wooden crates, each stencilled with MB and a serial number. MB had to mean Mercedes-Benz. He found a gap in the stack and left two bombs deep in the middle. Someone shouted a challenge. Lampard ducked and stopped breathing. *Now we fight!* he thought; but the shout went on and on and became the opening phrase of a snatch of opera. Other men joined in, until they were all thundering out the Toreador song from *Carmen*. Lampard planted his last two bombs, one on a mobile generator and one on a tractor, and strolled back through the shadows to the door, pom-pomming along with the singers because he didn't know the words.

Dunn had the door open, ready for him. "Jerry's getting jumpy. He had a searchlight on, sweeping the field."

"We might as well leave, I suppose."

"Through the gap?"

"Where else?"

"We've only got eight minutes."

"Ample."

"They'll see us when the bombs go off."

"They'll panic when the bombs go off."

"You know best, Jack."

The rest of the men began moving as soon as they saw the officers coming. Lampard used a luminous compass to find a bearing to the gap in the wire. After a hundred yards they reached a tarmac road. "Good," Lampard said. "This is faster." His eyes were feeling the strain of looking five ways at once, but his legs and lungs were strong, and he enjoyed marching fast on the smooth surface. He could scarcely hear the faint tread of boots, but he knew exactly where his men were. They were spread behind him in a loose arrowhead. Dunn was on the far left, Davis the far right, Pocock at the rear. Harris was nearest. High time Harris got made sergeant, he decided. A decoration would be wasted on Harris, but he'd like the extra stripe. And the pay. That thought flickered through Lampard's mind while he glanced at his compass. He reckoned the time remaining on the fuses. He pictured the gap waiting ahead and the steep escarpment of the Jebel. At that point he strode into a dazzle of headlights that stopped him like a blinding brick wall.

For a few seconds the only sound was the panting and heaving of the patrol. Sergeant Davis spat. Faint shreds of mist drifted across the dazzle. Lampard squinted hard and began to make out three sources: probably headlamps and a spotlight. "Good evening, gentlemen," said someone in a voice that was urbane and confident, like the head waiter at Claridge's. "Weapons on the ground immediately, please. Then take two paces forward and lie flat." Nobody moved. Lampard cocked his head. Five hundred miles away an orchestra was playing Mozart. Very faint, but quite unmistakable.

"Naturally you are surrounded." A tiny click, and Mozart died. "Unless you surrender, I regret that you must be shot where you stand." The regret sounded formal but genuine, like Claridge's turning away a gentleman without a necktie.

Still nobody moved. The initial blindness had gone, but the dazzle was painful and it made the surrounding darkness twice as dense.

"I'm going forward," Lampard announced without turning to the patrol. "If I am fired upon, you will blow this vehicle to bits. Understand? Never mind me. One shot, and you destroy the vehicle totally and immediately." He had the sensation of being outside himself, watching and hearing these orders being given. He stepped forward and the sensation vanished.

It was an Alfa-Romeo open tourer, very big. A Luftwaffe major sat behind the wheel. Nobody else was in the car. Lampard stood on the running board and looked around. Empty ground. "You don't half tell whoppers," he said. "Now kill the lights and jump out."

The major pressed switches and the night flooded back. "I may take my stick?" he asked.

Lampard opened the door. The major had some difficulty getting out. By now Sergeant Davis and Corporal Pocock had moved out wide to guard the flanks. Harris searched the German for weapons: none. Dunn said: "I make it three minutes, Jack."

"More than ample. We'll take this splendid car."

"We can't leave *him*," Dunn said.

"Let me kill him," Harris said.

Lampard said: "Yes, why not? Silly sod's no use to anyone. Completely unreliable."

"To escape, you need me," the German said. Harris had his fighting knife ready, its point denting the man's tunic just below the ribs. "Go without me," the major said, "and all will be killed by the mines." His voice was calm and steady, as if to say: Take it or leave it.

"Nuts!" Dunn said. "We got in, we'll get out again."

"I think not. When you got in, our minefield was *ausgeschaltet*." He frowned for a moment. "Off-switched. Switched off. You see, our mines are activated by electricity. Now the minefield is active since ten minutes. I myself have turned the switch."

Lampard nudged Dunn. "What d'you think?"

23

"It's possible."

Lampard stared down. The German's face was nothing in the night, but his voice had been firm. "Why bother?" Lampard asked him. "What's the point?"

"Two minutes five," Dunn said.

"I shall require more than two minutes five to explain our system of airfield security," the major said. He sounded slightly amused.

"Okay, forget it." Lampard turned away and plucked the car's radio aerial. It vibrated noisily, so he stopped it. "You said you could get us out of here."

"I said that I can try."

"Oh-ho. You can try. Now why would you want to do that?"

"Jesus Christ." Harris was sheathing his knife. "Who cares?"

"I care, corporal. I'm not accustomed to being helped by the enemy."

"It is better than death," the major said. "Even to a German officer, death is not welcome."

"Those fuses aren't tremendously accurate, you know," Dunn said.

"What's your idea?" Lampard asked.

"We go in this car and depart through the main gate," the major said. "I drive. The guards never stop my car."

"No. I'll drive. You sit beside me. Let's go."

"No. Not a good idea." Davis and Pocock had come in from the flanks and were scrambling into the back seats, but the major did not move. "Better I drive."

"If you drive we might go anywhere. Straight to the guardroom, for instance."

"And then you shoot me."

"Anyway, I can drive faster than you can."

"I well know the road. Do you well know the road?"

"Fuck my old boots!" Harris muttered. "*I'll* drive and you two can stay here and argue."

"Take that man's name, sergeant."

"This car is mine," the major said. "The guards see you driving and at once they think, hullo, something smells of fish."

Lampard opened the door and helped him get in.

"That is good." The major started the engine.

Lampard vaulted in and sat beside him, tommy-gun across his legs. "Fishy," he said. "The word is fishy." The car moved off.

"You agree, then."

"Faster," Lampard told the major. The car swung right and left, found a straight, picked up speed. "I may shoot you anyway when we get out," Lampard said. "Just to calm my nerves."

"He's frightfully nervous," Dunn said to the major. The major smiled.

He drove fast, on dipped headlights. In much less than a minute they were approaching a pair of striped poles across the road. A guard stood in the soft, yellow light of a hurricane lamp; behind him the guardhouse was dimly visible. The guard had a rifle, but he slung it on his shoulder when he recognised the car, turned away and leaned on the counterweight to raise the pole. The major slowed, gave an economical wave, and accelerated through the gap. "Too easy," Davis said. "Let's go back and do it again." The major worked up through the gears with familiar ease. A mile away, a flash blew a golden hole in the night, and then a bang like a thousand fireworks caught up with the car. The men in the back turned to watch. Lampard watched the major. The major watched the road.

A mile and five explosions later, Lampard said: "This is far enough. Get off the road and drive towards the Jebel." The night was dancing to the flames of blazing aircraft.

The major slowed, but only slightly. "You wish seriously to walk up the Jebel?" he asked. Two trucks raced past them, sirens screaming, heading for the field. The rapid thumping of anti-aircraft guns began. "Just do it!" Lampard shouted. The major changed down a gear. "I know a track," he said. "A motor track." A brilliant flash that exposed all the countryside was followed by a dull boom like the slamming of a castle door. "A good motor track," he said. The entire castle collapsed and the wallop of its destruction washed over the car so violently that everyone flinched. "Bomb dump," Pocock said, pleased. Lesser thuds and crumps followed. The major changed down again. "I myself have used this track in daylight," he said. "But you perhaps will rather climb into the Jebel on foot." He changed down again. Now they were crawling.

"All right," Lampard said, "we'll try this amazing track of yours. No lights. I don't want the Afrika Korps watching to see where we go."

"Alternative illumination has been provided," the major said. The sky over Barce aerodrome pulsed and flickered with a red and yellow glow that grew steadily brighter.

He crossed the plain and found his track. The ruts did not match their wheels, and the potholes were as big as buckets. The major charged the car at the hillside as if it were a challenge. Rocks jumped up and savaged the chassis, and the springs groaned under cruel and unusual punishment. The track twisted as it climbed, twisted as it dipped, twisted as it twisted. Later it got worse. Long before that, Lampard had dropped his tommy-gun and was working hard to protect himself from the rush of shocks.

When they topped the crest of the escarpment he shouted, and the German let the car run to a halt. Lampard reached across and switched off the engine.

Corporal Pocock wiped blood from his nose, mouth and chin. "You tryin' to start a war or somethin'?" he demanded thickly. Blood continued to flow.

"Stop whimpering," Dunn said.

"Boots off," Lampard told the major.

"You fear I will run off?" The major got out and took his boots off and gave them to Lampard. "There is little risk of that." Lampard looked. The heel of the left boot was built up about three inches.

"Why don't we let him go?" Corporal Harris said. "Let him walk down the mountain in his socks?"

"Search him," Lampard told Davis. The sergeant rummaged in the German's pockets, and a small heap of papers and possessions accumulated on the ground. "Back in the car," Lampard ordered. He scooped everything up and examined it, piece by piece, in the soft light of the dashboard. "You're a major in the Luftwaffe," he said.

"So? I feel like a prisoner of the British army."

"Schramm. P. D. Schramm. What does the P stand for?"

"Paul." He slumped in his seat, rested his head and shut his eyes. "And your J stands for Jack, I think."

Lampard ignored this; he was preoccupied with a sheet of typewritten paper. "What d'you make of that, Mike?" he asked.

Dunn stared where Lampard's finger was pointing. "*Abt 5*," he said. "That's got to be Abteilung 5, hasn't it? Luftwaffe Intelligence."

"Lovely grub. That's the cream on the strawberries, that is. He goes straight to Egypt."

"Do you intend to introduce yourself?" Schramm asked. "Captain Lampard?"

"Can't resist showing off, can you?" Lampard stuffed Schramm's belongings into a rucksack. "Just for that you can come and watch the show."

They joined the others, who were looking down at the fires on Barce airfield. Even now, there were occasional explosions. An improbable nursery-pink glow was reflected from immense clouds of oily smoke, and the stink of burnt fuel and explosives drifted with the midnight breeze. "What d'you think Abteilung Funf will make of that little lot?" Dunn asked the German.

"Can't resist showing off, can you?" the German said, which amused the rest of the patrol.

*　　*　　*

The top of the Jebel was rolling hillside. It rolled for about a hundred and twenty miles from west to east, and twenty or thirty miles from south to north. Sometimes it rolled vigorously and the terrain became rugged, with deep valleys and steep cliffs. It was a blend of the Cotswold hills and the Scottish Highlands; not so green, but plentifully supplied with stunted trees and shrubs, wandering Arabs and herds of goats, and just right for hiding in.

Sergeant Davis drove the Alfa. In half an hour he found the dry wadi where they had left the jeep. Corporal Harris drove the jeep. At one a.m. they reached the main camp, five miles further south in the Jebel. Three vehicles were waiting there: an armed jeep, a wireless truck, and an armed Chevrolet truck, all loaded and ready to move.

The rear party – six men – had started a brew-up as soon as they heard the engines. Everyone got a pint mug of thick, sweet tea with a tot of rum in it while they discussed the raid. Schramm too was given a mug. He tasted the drink and asked if he might have the rum without the tea. "Don't mind him," Davis told the soldier who had made the brew-up, "he's foreign, he doesn't know any better."

"You'd better get used to it," Dunn told Schramm.

Schramm took another sip, and winced. "I have only one cousin and he lives in Leipzig," he said.

"Yes? So what?"

Schramm sipped his tea, and recoiled fractionally. "Next of kin," he said.

"Cheeky bastard!" Pocock said.

"Take that man's name, sergeant," Schramm said.

"You're very frisky," Lampard said, "for a prisoner-of-war with a gammy leg and no boots." The German smiled. He had a very broad smile which bunched up the skin over his cheekbones and, despite all the arrowhead wrinkles, made his eyes look quite boyish. Lampard smiled back. *What a nice chap*, he thought. *Just waiting for a chance to kill us all and do a bunk.*

* * *

By daybreak the patrol had moved ten miles further south and the vehicles were tucked away in the curve of a winding valley, beneath an overhang of tall limestone cliffs. The shape of the trucks was lost under camouflage nets, spread wide and held down with rocks. Schramm watched while pretending not to watch. He knew that even the most low-flying aircraft would never find them. It was difficult enough to find somebody who *wanted* to be found in the Jebel.

The sun rose with its usual abruptness: from grey-green dawn to full daylight in fifteen minutes. Schramm could feel the temperature start to climb, baking the dew-damp out of his clothes. He sat, resting his back against the cliff, and admired the way they worked. Nobody gave orders, each man knew his job. Nobody hurried, but nobody stood and scratched himself and waited to be told what to do. A bit of quiet joking went on, not much. Lampard ducked under the camouflage netting and came out with a jerrican of water, carrying it as lightly as a briefcase. Someone was whistling. Bacon was frying. Schramm thought: *They are three hundred kilometres behind our lines and they are at home.*

He awoke when Corporal Pocock shook his shoulder. "Breakfast," Pocock said. For a second or two, the German was in the wrong world and nothing made sense. Then he remembered, and groaned. "You'll feel better after a nice mug of tea," Pocock said. "And Mr Lampard says you can have one of your boots back."

It was the boot with the built-up heel. Schramm put it on and limped after Pocock.

Breakfast was a lavish fry-up: sausage, bacon, steak, potatoes, beans; all out of tins. There was tea by the pint and tinned apricots. Schramm looked at his loaded mess tin. "*No sauerbraten mit knödels?*" he said. "No *rahmschnitzel mit champignons?*"

"You catch us on a poor day, I'm afraid," Lampard said. "But when we reach Cairo I can promise you lots of egg and chips."

"Egg and chips!" Harris said, and his eyelids drooped at the thought. "I'd kill for a plate of egg and chips." A few men laughed, but only a few; evidently it was an old joke.

"Tell you what," Lampard said to Harris. "If our prisoner tries to escape, you kill him and I'll buy you egg and chips in Cairo for a week."

Harris looked at Schramm. Harris had flat grey eyes, as flat as buttons, and they narrowed and widened as he chewed a piece of steak. He swallowed it, sucked his teeth, and said: "You look like a sporting gent. I'll give you a kilometre start and I bet I kill you inside twenty minutes." He stabbed a sausage and twirled his fork.

Schramm ate a fried potato and studied the sergeant as if sizing him up. Then he ate another potato, still looking at him.

"Not interested?" Harris said. "Don't blame you."

"Oh, it interests me. Not as a piece of sport, because for me war is not sport. I am thinking, what is the possible stake? What do you own that I want to win, maybe?"

Harris unbuttoned a pocket and took out a very old and dirty rabbit's-paw. "Lucky charm?" he suggested.

"If I win it," Schramm said, "it will not have been lucky, will it?"

"He's got you there," Pocock said.

"Only bloody time he will get me."

There were caves in the cliff, and the men carried their bedrolls into them. Schramm expected to have to lie on the ground, but he found that the back seats of the Alfa had been removed and taken into a cave for him to sleep on. "Most kind," he said.

"Our pleasure," Lampard said. "Tell me: do you think your people are out looking for us?"

"Yes." Schramm made a pillow of his tunic. "Hundreds. Thousands."

"Jolly good. Where?"

"Here, naturally. The Jebel."

"Why naturally? For all they know we came by submarine. Or we could be hiding out in Benghazi."

Schramm covered a yawn with his hand. "If you please . . . Could we discuss this later? I am not so young as you. I tire more rapidly."

"My dear major, I do apologise. Shocking manners." Lampard straightened the car seats and brushed dust from them. "By all means get some rest. You are, after all, our guest. And if there's anything you need, anything at all . . . um . . . I'm afraid you can't have it." He smiled with such charmingly fake regret that Schramm, already drowsy in the growing heat, thought: *He wants me to believe we're all playing a game. All in fun.* Beyond Lampard, standing silhouetted in the mouth of the cave, was Corporal Harris. Nothing funny about Harris. Schramm shut his eyes and tried to ignore the squadrons of wheeling, buzzing flies, and very soon succeeded.

*   *   *

By mid-morning the rocks were frying. By midday the air had had all the guts baked out of it. You could breathe it, given that there was nothing else available, as long as you kept it out of your lungs.

By mid-afternoon, the blaze of noon was just a cool and enviable memory. By mid-afternoon, the sun was dumping a massive glut of heat on the Western Desert. The sun had beaten everyone, beaten them to the ground, left them for dead. The sun was, yet again, undisputed champion of the solar system. And then, thank Christ, it relaxed. The heat eased. Men breathed again.

Schramm had slept, on and off, for most of the day. Now he came out and sat in the shade and watched the patrol get on with the chores of desert life: cooking food and cleaning weapons, refuelling the trucks, checking the tyres, double-checking the radiators, and a dozen other details. Schramm noticed that the camouflage nets were still in place. And there was a lookout on top of the cliffs.

Lampard sat beside him and began cleaning his tommy-gun. "I'm awfully sorry we can't offer you shaving water," he said.

"My dear Lampard." Schramm half-raised a hand to dispel any anxiety.

"Satisfy my curiosity." Lampard squinted down the barrel. "Does everyone in Abteilung 5 speak such good English?"

"I think so." Schramm rubbed his chin. He quite enjoyed not having to shave. "Each one of us specialises, of course."

"Really? What is your speciality?"

"Central London. The Knightsbridge area. But only as far as Harrods."

Lampard cleaned a spring. "Bloody sand . . . You do talk a lot of balls."

Schramm took off his right sock. Already there were holes in the heel and toe. He stuffed it in a pocket. "You grew up in Norfolk. Am I right?"

Lampard stared. "You can tell all that from my voice?"

"Oh no. Everything is on your file. What more can I remember? Your middle name is . . . wait a moment . . ."

He frowned at his bare foot and clenched his toes. "Roger?"

"Richard."

"*Richard*, yes. And two years ago there was an officer you had a fight with. Hooper. Captain Hooper."

"Good God. Any more?"

"Um . . . Captain Hooper lost."

Lampard got on with cleaning his gun. "Where *did* you learn your English?" he asked.

"Oh well," Schramm said. "It is not a military secret. In 1917 your Royal Flying Corps shot me down. I was for a long time a prisoner of war, very boring, the camp had no books in German so I read books in English, hundreds of them. Dickens, all of Dickens, all Thackeray, Trollope, Kipling, Hardy, Stevenson. And some Americans: Mark Twain, O. Henry, Edgar Rice Burroughs. Others, I forget the names. The Tarzan stories I enjoyed the most. No doubt they symbolised escape, and freedom, and so on. Do you like books?"

Lampard aimed at the sky and tested the trigger action. "I don't really like anything except fighting . . . After the war?"

"Here and there. This and that. A little teaching. Tour guide for Americans. Some journalism in London. Reuters man in Berlin." He watched Lampard empty a magazine and clean the bullets. "I find this strange," he said. "Why do you use a clumsy gangsters' weapon when you could use the Sten gun, which is half the size?"

"It makes me feel like James Cagney. What were you doing in that car?"

"Listening to Rome radio, on . . ." He tapped his ears.

"Headphones."

"Yes, headphones. When I saw you I removed them. But you could see nothing, could you? I think you made a great gamble."

"So did you, old chum. One hiccup out of you and my

chaps would have put half-a-dozen grenades into that Alfa."

"Thus killing you too."

Lampard slotted the magazine onto the gun and put the gun inside a dust-proof bag. He did not close the bag. "You don't think that would stop them, do you?"

Schramm tried to grip a pebble with his toes, but it was too big. "It seems an excessively violent way to fight a war, that's all."

"Excessive violence is what they enjoy."

"Especially Corporal Harris?"

"Oh no, not Corporal Harris. Corporal Harris is bored with excessive violence. What Corporal Harris enjoys is some really ferocious homicidal thuggery."

"And plates of egg and chips."

Ten feet above their heads, an empty food tin on a string jerked and rattled against the cliff face. "Aircraft," Lampard called, "aircraft." Unhurriedly the men left their jobs and sat in the deep shadow. After a while they heard the thin, lazy buzz of its engine, but the noise came bouncing off the valley walls and only the lookout on top of the cliff knew where the plane was. "Harris has a passion for egg and chips," Lampard said. "He and Pocock got lost after a raid, decided to walk home, about two hundred miles. Ran out of food, so they found one of those Road Houses you've got all along the coastal road. Casa something."

"Casa Cantieri."

"It was night-time. They tossed in a couple of grenades and killed everyone except the cooks. Pocock wanted to grab some grub and skedaddle, but Harris made the cooks fry him egg and chips. They were all Italians, by the way. The place looked like a slaughterhouse, blood and guts splashed everywhere. Cooks were terrified, and the odd Italian soldier kept arriving. Harris stood by the door with a meat cleaver and chopped them down as they came in.

Pocock wasn't enjoying this very much, but Harris was in his element, in a quiet sort of way. The cooks, of course, couldn't think straight and they made a nonsense of the egg and chips, so Harris told them to try again. While they were doing that he chopped a couple more late arrivals. Finally the cooks managed to do him his egg and chips the way he liked them. By now Pocock couldn't eat anything, so Harris ate his share too. Then they left. I don't think I've done full justice to the occasion, but no doubt your imagination can fill in the gaps."

"I have no imagination," Schramm said. "It surrendered, in the face of overwhelming reality."

The tin above them rattled twice. "All clear," Lampard said. "Your chaps don't seem to be making much of an effort to find you, do they?"

Schramm gave a sad smile. "You know what German soldiers are like," he said. "Slack, lazy, disorganised and irresponsible. I expect they're still finishing lunch."

*　　*　　*

The patrol stood around in a loose circle and ate from their mess tins. It was easier to wave away the flies when you were standing, but the flies never gave up. They too had been waiting all day for this meal. It was rich and rewarding: salmon, ham and tongue, sausages, mixed vegetables, chutney, apricots, cheese. All tinned. The only untinned protein to be eaten was the odd, unwary fly.

The wireless officer, a young and balding signals lieutenant called Tony Waterman, said: "If it's not a rude answer, which part of Germany are you from?"

"Leipzig."

"Ah." Waterman nodded, and kept nodding while he thought about that. He was short and thickset, with a very round face that settled naturally into an expression of placid goodwill. "I saw a bit of Hamburg and Hanover, but oddly enough I never got to Leipzig."

"Yes, I know."

Waterman smiled his gentle agreement with Schramm's agreement.

"What d'you mean, you know?" Gibbon asked. Gibbon was the navigator for the patrol. His beard, under the dust, was as red as oxblood. He squinted suspiciously at Schramm, but then Gibbon squinted at everyone. Too much desert sun.

"Major Schramm has a file on each of us," Lampard said. "In fact he has a file on the entire SAS. You haven't met Captain Gibbon." He waved his mess tin by way of introduction.

"How do you do," Schramm said.

"Intelligence knows nothing," Gibbon said. "That's the first rule of war, the one they don't teach you in Staff College."

"Corky is right," Schramm said, which amused everyone except Gibbon. "And congratulations on your Military Cross."

"See what I mean?" Gibbon said to Dunn.

"Corky hasn't got the MC," Dunn told Schramm.

"Soon he will."

"Really? What for?" Lampard asked.

Schramm licked a bit of chutney off his upper lip. "I am afraid I am not at liberty to tell you," he said. Even Gibbon laughed at that. Schramm blinked and smiled. "Sorry," he said. "Accidental pun."

Corporal Harris scuffed his boots and kicked a small stone towards Schramm. "What have you got on me in your files?" he asked.

"Oh . . ." Schramm thought hard. "I feel sure the records indicate that you are a scholar and a gentleman who would never blow his nose on the tablecloth if he could reach the curtains." This was said so blandly that it surprised them. Corporal Pocock choked. Everyone else laughed, everyone except Harris. He took a swig of tea, swallowed, took another swig and expertly sprayed it through his teeth. "I don't think he's a bleedin' Jerry at all," he said to Lampard. "He's too clever by half. He's one of ours who's sold out."

"*Es war sehr schön. Ich danke Ihnen. Ich muss jetzt gehen*," Schramm said.

Lampard looked at Dunn. Dunn said: "I believe that was 'Thank you for having me, I've got to go now'."

The lookout's tin rattled. "This must be my bus," Schramm said. "Shut up!" Lampard snapped. Already the patrol was moving into the deeper shadow of the cliff, trailed by a long streamer of flies. Above their indignant buzz came a distant drone, like a small power-saw in the sky. "Just a Storch," Dunn said. "Nothing to worry about." The Storch was a small high-wing plane which the German army used for search or reconnaissance or taxiing generals about the battlefield. It could fly as slowly as an old crow and it could turn inside its own length, but usually it had no guns. Lampard and Dunn settled down on either side of their prisoner and got on with their meal.

"This is the second visit by an aeroplane in less than an hour," Schramm said. "Perhaps you have been . . ." He searched for the word. ". . . rumbled."

"I expect he's seen our tracks," Lampard said, "but not for the last quarter of a mile because we went back and wiped them out, so now he doesn't know which wadi we might be in."

"In any case," Dunn said, "he daren't come down really low to look for us in case he finds us. You saw what we've got: three lots of twin-mounted Vickers machine guns. Make a lovely mess of him, they would. Aren't you going to finish your apricots?"

"Yes. But the guns aren't manned."

"He doesn't know that."

"How can you be sure?"

"Look," Lampard said, "I'm in command here. Now shut up and eat your apricots, or I won't take you to see General Cunningham in Cairo."

"He is in Alexandria," Schramm said. "And General Auchinleck now commands your Eighth Army."

Lampard uttered a cry of exasperation and threw up his hands, losing a boiled potato from his fork. "For God's sake *stop showing off!*" he cried.

"Sorry. I thought you would wish to know."

"Now look what you made me do." Lampard sucked his empty fork. "That spud came fifteen thousand miles, all down the Atlantic, round South Africa, up the Indian Ocean, through the Canal, across miles and miles of burning desert, scorched by day and frozen by night, just to give me strength to fight the horrible Hun, and you've gone and ruined it."

"If you know so much," Dunn said, "how come you didn't know we were going to raid your place last night?"

Schramm ate his cheese. Lampard reached across him and gave Dunn a congratulatory slap on the leg. "Blindingly obvious," he said. "Well done, Mike."

Nobody spoke for a while. The note of the aeroplane engine hardened and softened as it turned, invisibly. Dunn flicked a couple of drowning flies from his tea, and drank fast before the mourners could arrive. Lampard yawned and stretched his arms until his ribcage creaked. "Sergeant Davis!" he called.

"Sir?"

"Has the lookout had his meal yet?"

"No, sir."

"Send up a replacement. This shufti plane is being a bit of a bore. It'll be dark in an hour and I want to move pronto."

"Sir."

Dunn scratched his beard vigorously and examined his

38

fingernails. "What were you listening to, in the car?"

"Music. Mozart. Reception is better away from the buildings."

"My sister plays the piano. She won a prize for playing the Moonlight Sonata. Mozart wrote that, didn't he?"

"Beethoven."

"Oh, well. Same difference."

"The English are not a very musical race," Schramm said.

"Dunno about that. We've written some damn good songs. 'Yes We Have No Bananas'. 'Roll out the Barrel'. All that stuff Vera Lynn sings, like 'There'll Be Blue Birds over the White Cliffs of Dover'. And you should see our chaps listening when Lili Marlene gets sung on Radio Belgrade: dead silence, nobody moves. Anyway —"

"Shut up a minute," Lampard said.

The lazy buzz of the Storch had strengthened and deepened. The sound came bouncing off the walls of the wadi, confusing the ear. Then suddenly the plane appeared, grey as a moth, strolling along, ludicrously slowly, trembling in the last of the waves of hot air. It was low, about three hundred feet, and it was exploring the valley where the patrol was hiding. Lampard was unworried. The trucks looked like scrub and the men looked like the rocks they sat among. The pilot was up in the glare of the setting sun, searching for detail in shadow as dark as a cellar. As long as nobody moved nobody would be seen. "Good heavens. That is a British plane," Schramm said. As Lampard and Dunn shaded their eyes and tried to make out its markings, Schramm heaved himself up with both hands and began running.

Sergeant Davis got off the first shot. The act of drawing his revolver left him sprawling awkwardly and he missed. Harris fired next, but he had been staring at the plane and he couldn't focus fast enough on the shadowy figure and he too missed. Dunn got closest. Dunn got a bullet between

Schramm's feet. By then Schramm was twenty yards from the foot of the cliff and dodging briskly, not to make himself a more difficult target but because the stony floor of the wadi hurt his bare right foot, and in any case his boot made him lopsided. He stumbled, almost fell, saved himself with both hands and kicked forward like a sprinter in his blocks. Ten strides took him out of the shadow and into the sunlight, both arms waving like a shipwrecked sailor at a passing sail. Lampard was bellowing: "Hold your fire! Stay where you are! Cease fire! Do not move! Let him go!" Schramm heard nothing. He was prancing along the valley floor, strenuously signalling his existence to the Storch, forcing his limbs into violent action despite the pain in his lungs and the fiery protests of his damaged bare foot. The Storch dipped. Schramm cheered and waved his handkerchief. The Storch lost a hundred feet and circled.

Davis called: "There's a rifle in the jeep, sir. I can get him with that, easy."

"No, sergeant. Now everyone listen to me. I don't want that prisoner killed until the aeroplane has gone. I don't want him *touched*."

By now Schramm was a hundred yards away, heading for the mouth of the wadi.

"You know best, Jack," Dunn said quietly. "Personally I'd put a bullet through the bastard p.d.q. That little shufti plane can't land here, and it wouldn't even if it could."

"*Think*," Lampard said. "The pilot sees a man. The man wants to be seen. He's not an Arab. He could be this Luftwaffe major the pilot knows is missing, probably pinched by enemy raiders. And all of a sudden — bang! — somebody shoots the bloke. Now what does that tell the pilot?"

"See what you mean."

"If you got a radio message from that Storch saying, 'Here's a funny thing: I've just found your missing major, but would you believe it, somebody down there's just shot him', what would you do?"

"I'd say . . . um . . . 'Give me the map reference and I'll send a dozen Stukas to work it over'."

"Right. Think how many airfields Jerry's got within range of here. There's time for him to make an attack before the light goes. Ever been Stuka-ed?"

"Once. Bloody murder." Dunn and Lampard watched Schramm trotting away down the wadi, while the Storch made wide circles above him. After a while Schramm turned a bend and was lost to sight. "The sensible thing for that Storch to do would be to go home and refuel," Lampard said. But the Storch continued to circle for several minutes. "Buzz off, for heaven's sake!" Lampard said. And this time it did, climbing to a thousand feet, levelling off and flying north.

"Harris!" Lampard called. Harris trotted over. "He's crippled in one foot and by now he must be half-maimed in the other, so he can't have got far. Go and kill him, fast. Get back in ten minutes and I'll make it *double* egg and chips for a week." Harris was already on his way. They watched him go. He ran leaning forward, as if into a stiff breeze.

Gibbon the navigator had joined them. "Given a million soldiers like Harris," he said, "the war would be over in a week."

"No, you're wrong," Lampard said. "Given a million soldiers like Harris the war would never end." That made no sense to Gibbon, but he didn't care enough to argue. "Sarnt Davis!" he called. "Just time for a brew-up, I think."

* * *

Schramm had been limping to spare his right foot. Occasional smears of blood showed behind the toe-prints, while the left boot kept stamping its pattern in the dust.

One stride by Harris covered two by Schramm. Harris

reckoned the German must be slowing all the time. Schramm was twice as old as Harris, unarmed, slightly disabled and almost certainly not trained in hand-to-hand combat. If Harris had been capable of pity he might have felt sorry for him. As it was he looked forward to the pleasure of a quick knifing and then the reward of Captain Lampard's praise.

By now the wadi had taken a bend to the left and another to the right. Still the footprints limped ahead. Harris wondered where the hell the German thought he was going: not to a landing strip, that was certain; too many rocks everywhere; the wadi was strewn with them, many as tall as tombstones. Now the smears of blood were getting bigger. Something lay on the ground ahead: a handkerchief, or part of a shirt. Maybe Schramm had tried to bandage his foot and failed. Harris put on speed until he was running hard, chasing his own shadow. That shadow was Schramm's piece of good luck. Schramm was squatting behind a rock, hearing the running footsteps get louder and watching the shadow magnify until he took the only chance he was ever going to get and he dived at Harris's legs. A boot smacked Schramm's mouth and pain flowered through his head, but Harris suffered much more because he was travelling fast when he tripped and his face skidded along the wadi floor. Schramm lurched to his feet, a rock in each hand, missed with the first and cracked Harris's head with the second. It was a sharp rock and it dented his skull like a badly parked car. Schramm turned to see who was following; who would fire the squirt from the tommy-gun that would cut him down before the rattle could reach his ears. Nobody followed. *Bloody fools*, he thought. *They don't deserve to win.*

Harris's right boot was too big for Schramm, so he pulled off Harris's socks as well, both of them, and took his tunic and his revolver and grenades and knife, then he scuttled down the wadi until he was safely around the next bend. His fingers trembled and his lungs heaved as he dragged on the socks and laced up the boot. He heard himself laugh and didn't like the sound: too shrill, too triumphant. He had never killed a man before. He stamped his right foot. The boot felt good. He grabbed the weapons and ran.

*   *   *

After fifteen minutes, Sergeant Davis and Corporal Pocock went to find out what was keeping Harris. Davis brought back the body, carrying it slung over his shoulder, the head wobbling and the hands flapping at every stride. Behind him came Pocock, carrying the left boot and walking backwards in case the German had decided to follow them and fling a grenade.

Lampard went forward and met Davis. "This was all my fault," he said. The body slipped a little. Davis shrugged it back into place.

The rest of the patrol came to look. All they could see of the back of the head was a thicket of flies. Nobody spoke. Someone got a blanket and spread it on the ground. Davis knelt on the edge of the blanket and let the body fall. The flies rose in fury, and at first everyone thought the strange, high-pitched sound came from them; until they realised that Lampard was weeping.

Some men were surprised, but no one was embarrassed: Captain Lampard commanded the patrol, it was his privilege to weep if he wanted to. They withdrew and left him to it.

"What d'you think happened?" Lieutenant Dunn asked Davis.

"Harris must have took his boots off to kick the Jerry officer to death," Davis said, "and he got a whiff of his own feet and dropped dead."

"It's no joke, sergeant."

"Course not, sir. It might have happened to any one of us. I shared a tent with him, I should know."

Captain Gibbon strolled over to them. He nodded at the sky, which was primrose-yellow fading to blue-black. "I hope he gets a move on," he said softly. "Dark in ten minutes." They glanced at Lampard, who was standing motionless beside the corpse, his arms folded and his head bowed. "Attitude to be adopted, other ranks, for the mourning of," Gibbon said. "Brigade of Guards drill book, Appendix 'F', Active Service, Foreign Parts, matinées Wednesdays and Saturdays." Dunn turned away. He, like Lampard, was a Coldstream Guard, and so he felt a loyalty to him; yet now that Gibbon had pointed it out, Lampard's attitude did look too formal, too posed. There was a lot of Lampard – he had powerful features, an icebreaker of a nose, wide and determined lips, a thrusting jaw – and merely arranging his hefty limbs, finding places to put those considerable hands and feet, gave him mannerisms and attitudes that might seem posed. Dunn was sure that none of this was for effect; Lampard just behaved naturally and it ended up *looking* like an act.

Lampard knelt and neatly folded the blanket over Harris. "Right, gather round," he called.

They gathered round.

"Schramm has gone," he said. "Question is, how far and how fast? Mike: what would you do if you were Schramm?"

"Beat it for home," Dunn said. "And hope I ran into a search party on the way."

"You wouldn't lie up and wait for daylight?"

"Not bloody likely. Sooner I get back to base, the sooner base can scramble some Stukas to catch us in the desert."

"So maybe we shouldn't dash off into the desert." Lampard shut his eyes so that he could massage the lids. "Sergeant Davis looks unhappy."

"He's got Harris's knife and revolver and grenades, sir," Davis said. "And he's got a bloody nerve, too. He might just be daft enough to come back in the night and try to do more damage."

"He's made a pretty good start at that," Gibbon said.

"I'm not going to spend the night here," Lampard declared. Grunts of satisfaction all round. "Assuming the enemy comes after us, which way will he expect us to go? South or east?"

"South," Dunn said. "Back to Kufra."

"Yes? Why? It's seven hundred miles to Kufra. A thousand from Kufra to Cairo. Why should he expect us to make an enormous detour?"

"Because that's the way we came," Corporal Pocock said.

"Does he know that?"

"He seems to know everything else," Dunn said.

One of the fitters broke wind. "Beg pardon," he muttered. "Bloody cheese."

"If he thinks we know he knows, maybe he'll think we'll go east instead," Lampard said. "Run parallel to the coast. Less than half the distance. Refuel at Siwa. By far the best route. Blindingly obvious."

"There's only one thing wrong with the east route," Gibbon said. "It's lousy with aeroplanes, so we get shot up."

"No danger of getting shot up," Lampard said. "We just destroyed half the Luftwaffe, remember?"

"I'm not worried about the Luftwaffe," Gibbon said, "I'm worried about those lousy bastard Beaufighters who used the Rhodesian patrol for target practice."

"Human error."

"Just as dead."

Nobody wanted to discuss it. The Rhodesian patrol of the Long Range Desert Group had been driving across a stretch of sand so flat and so wide and so empty that you could see a lost jerrican at twenty miles, when a pair of RAF Beaufighters found them. There were recognition signals for just such a situation, but the Beaufighters kept attacking despite the recognition signals. Human error. Human dead.

"We bury Harris and then we beat it south," Lampard said.

*   *   *

Paul Schramm walked all night and reached the top of the escarpment just before dawn. He stopped there and waited for daylight so that he could find a way down to the plain. His entire body ached with fatigue and his feet felt as if they had been tenderised with steak mallets, but he commanded himself to keep moving, to keep limping up and down, to stay awake.

A couple of hours earlier he had paused for a few minutes. He had stretched out on the ground and rested his feet on a bank of earth because he remembered reading somewhere that infantry on the march always did this when they fell out for a break: something to do with letting the blood drain away from the legs. Schramm was not an infantryman. He was a middle-aged intelligence officer with a bad limp, and when he tried to stand, even the limp was a lost skill. His legs were a wash-out: his feet didn't want to take his weight and his knees disowned any responsibility for anything. It took him a long time to persuade the leg joints to bend again and the leg muscles to carry his weary body along the broken tracks of the Jebel.

His legs' readiness to quit surprised him. Thereafter he did not trust them. He kept them working all the way to the edge of the escarpment, and then he refused to sit down, although his knees were wobbly and the soles of his feet were hot with blood.

It had been an interesting walk, probably far longer than it need have been because at first he kept losing his sense of direction in the moonless gloom. The wadis wandered and divided and tried to lead him in circles, so he climbed to the highest spot – a ruined tomb, as it turned out – and tried to identify some stars. While he was at it he decided to dump the grenades, which were heavy and awkward. He left them in the tomb. He set off, looking at the stars but thinking of some inquisitive Arab boy getting blown to bits (or, even worse, half-blown to bits). He went back and retrieved the grenades. For the first time since he had killed him, he thought of Harris.

And with pleasure. Schramm was not a violent man. He rarely allowed himself to lose his temper. Given the chance, he would sidestep to avoid treading on an insect. Yet there was something symbolic about whacking Harris on the head. Harris's weakness had been his brain. His body was splendidly trained to do its job, but his brain was small and weak, too small to consider the possibility that his victim might have the nerve to wait in ambush.

Now, as he trudged away from this high and lonely tomb, wearing Harris's right boot and stuffing Harris's grenades back in the pockets of Harris's tunic, Schramm was amazed at, and appalled by, his own audacity. One attack: one chance. If he had failed, Harris would have caught him in ten seconds and knifed him in twelve. But he hadn't failed! And how many unarmed middle-aged gammy-legged German officers had cracked the skull of a young thug of a Commando? Schramm shivered with pride. Then, almost at once, he sneered at himself for being such a caveman. To celebrate killing Harris was to come down to Harris's level.

Ah, but there was also Captain Lampard. Schramm had made a fool of Lampard, too. Furthermore, he had discovered a few useful things about him. Lampard was quick-witted and intelligent: he had let Schramm run away rather than alarm the Storch. He was cocky to the point of arrogance: he should have kept Schramm blindfolded or at least shut away in a cave, instead of allowing him to watch the patrol at work. And the decision to send only one man to catch him was significant. It was as if Lampard had been showing off to Schramm, minimising his escape. Lampard's nerve was strong, but sometimes his judgement was weak. That was worth remembering.

Soon Schramm forgot Harris and Lampard and the rest of them. It took all his attention to concentrate on walking north. He was not convinced that he was steering by the right stars. Then he had a stroke of luck. The British began bombing somewhere – probably another airfield, maybe Benina or Berka, which were near Benghazi; it was unlikely they would go for Barce again so soon – and he saw the wandering stab of searchlights, which he used as a guide. The raid ended; he trudged on and had a stroke of bad luck: he blundered into an Arab camp and set the dogs howling. He backtracked and made a wide detour. Too wide: he roused another camp. The alarm spread and every dog aroused another dog. The night was slashed with howling. Schramm zigzagged miserably through it all, wishing he had a stick to defend himself; Harris's revolver wouldn't be much use if some rabid cur tried to savage his legs. Then, for no reason, someone on a hilltop fired at him. The flash and bang so startled Schramm that he stumbled, fell, and cut his knee. Indignation and pain made a powerful cocktail. He dragged Harris's revolver from its holster and exploded three colossal, deafening shots at the night. He sprawled on the ground and massaged his right wrist, which had suffered from the recoil. The echoes died and even the dogs were silenced by his fit of rage. He crawled away, cursing. But not loudly.

The rest of his trek was a blur of memory. Sometimes he couldn't remember where he was going, sometimes he remembered where but not why. Fatigue fogged his brain and left his body plodding on in a state of pointless, pig-headed obstinacy. In the end, arrival at the escarpment came as a small shock.

Then dawn, too, came with a speed that surprised him; or perhaps he had dozed off as he ambled up and down. Anyway, there was no sign of a track down the hillside and no sign of Barce airfield below. He was miles and miles off course.

Full daylight arrived before he found a track. Going downhill made his knees ache and cramped his thighs. He told his legs to stop complaining, they should think themselves lucky they weren't going up. Somehow or other he reached the bottom. Feeble and wet with sweat. He knew the sun was shining because he couldn't see it. Already the whole sky was one great roasting dazzle.

The obvious thing to do now was to walk across the plain. Schramm squinted and saw no end to it. His legs got this message and threatened mutiny. Everything he looked at shimmered in the heat. Even he was shimmering; trembling more and more violently. *Come on*, he told himself petulantly, *you are an officer, now demonstrate your powers of leadership, you idiot.* He demonstrated his powers of leadership. He got rid of the hand-grenades. One by one he pulled the pins and flung the grenades quite a long way. They exploded with very impressive cracks and crumps and pillars of smoke. *Total waste of time and effort*, he told himself, by now in a thoroughly bad temper.

As it happened, the grenades did a lot of good. A battalion of infantry, eating breakfast at the roadside a mile away, heard the bangs and sent a squad of men to investigate. They found Schramm trudging unsteadily in the wrong direction. An hour later he was on a bed in the hospital at Barce airfield and a Luftwaffe doctor was extracting bits of sock from the ragged soles of his feet. "How far did you walk?" he asked.

Schramm opened his eyes, then shut them. "Only the

first two metres," he said. "I skipped the rest." He groaned as more skin came away.

"See what happens to you when you tell bad jokes," the doctor said.

The station commander, Oberstleutnant Benno Hoffmann, came in. "Well, I tried," he said. "They say there isn't a spare aeroplane within a hundred kilometres." Hoffmann had a camera. He began taking pictures of the feet.

"What's that for?" Schramm asked.

"Cookhouse. I want it clearly understood that this meat is unfit for human consumption. And even if they had a spare plane they still wouldn't send it. Smile for daddy." He took a couple of full-length shots.

"Why not?" Schramm asked. Apart from an occasional twitch as the skin came off, he lay as still as a log.

"Oh, lots of reasons," Hoffmann said. "They're at least a hundred and fifty kilometres from here by now, so they're somewhere in the Sahara, and the Sahara is the size of France, and it's only four trucks and a dozen men, so if you don't know where they are you'll never find them." He sat at the bedside and felt Schramm's wrist, seeking the pulse. "Forget about them, Paul. Just think about getting your strength back."

"I know exactly where they are," Schramm said. "They're driving south, fast as they can. They want to squeeze through the gap between Jalo Oasis and the Calanscio Sand Sea. After that it's wide open desert and they're safe."

"Radio the garrison at Jalo," suggested the doctor, whose name was Max.

"Italians," Hoffmann said.

"Don't we talk to our glorious allies?"

"They don't always listen. They especially don't always listen if it means going out looking for huge, ferocious, British Commandos."

"Special Air Service," Schramm corrected.

"Shut up, you, you're dead." Hoffmann frowned at the doctor. "At least, my bit's dead. How are your bits?" Max left Schramm's feet and repositioned Hoffmann's fingers. "Ah!" Hoffmann said. "You nearly slipped away, there, Paul. Try to pay more attention."

"They'll go through the Jalo Gap at midday," Schramm said.

"For all you know they're still hiding in the Jebel."

"They're not hiding in the Jebel." Schramm's voice was low but firm. "They've used up all their bombs. Soon they'll be getting low on fuel and food. They want to go home."

"They told you all this?"

"They told me I was on my way to Egypt. And their trucks are half-empty. I could tell that from the suspension. Too much bounce in the springs."

"I've finished stripping the wallpaper," Max said. "Now I'm going to paint some magic muck on your feet before I bandage them. This may sting a bit."

"Oh Christ," Schramm said. "I know what that means. Give me something to hang on to." Hoffmann offered his hands and Schramm gripped his wrists. "We've still got that Storch, haven't we?" Schramm asked. "The one that found me?" Hoffmann nodded. He wished Paul would shut up. The grip on his wrists was tightening and sweat was popping out of Schramm's forehead like rain on a windscreen. "Give me the Storch," Schramm said. "I can show the pilot where to look." Now the sweat was chasing itself down his face. "Nearly done," Max said. They could hear his fingers slapping on the magic muck. "If I find them," Schramm said, "you can persuade Operations to send a bomber or two, can't you?"

Hoffmann found himself nodding. "This is pure black-mail," he said.

"Done," said Max. Schramm's grip slowly relaxed.

"You're not fit to fly," Max told him.

"He's not going to fly," Hoffmann said. "He's going to sit beside the pilot and look. He's fit to look, isn't he?"

*   *   *

Lampard's patrol was less than halfway to Jalo Oasis when dawn broke. There had been trouble with the trucks: first a puncture, then dust clogging a carburettor, then another puncture. They drove without lights, not knowing who might be out searching for them. It was a moonless night. Once they left the Jebel the country was low-lying desert; neither flat nor hilly, dotted with scrub, very boring; but it was always possible to buckle the steering on a very boring rock. And there was the Tariq el 'Abd to be crossed.

The Tariq was an ancient camel trail. The Jebel formed part of a great two hundred-mile bulge into the Mediterranean, and the Tariq was a short cut across the base of that bulge. German and Italian generals felt uncomfortable at the thought that anyone could so easily travel so close to their flank, and all along the Tariq they had scattered tens of thousands of 'thermos' bombs: anti-personnel bombs designed to look like vacuum flasks. Unscrew the cap and it blew your arms off. Drive over one and it blew your wheel off. Maybe more.

Lampard halted his patrol a few miles short of the Tariq el 'Abd when he reckoned dawn was still half an hour away. Within a minute, a fire was lit and a dixie of water was set to boil. To brew up in the desert, all you needed was a large tin filled with sand and soaked in petrol. It burned cleanly and steadily, and for a surprisingly long time. Soon bacon was frying alongside the brew-up.

They had stopped in a hollow. Lampard didn't care if he was seen by passing aircraft – a fire in the desert wasn't worth a bomb or even a bullet, there were always Arab fires twinkling on the horizon – but he cared about German armoured cars. After all that havoc at Barce the enemy must be out hunting him. Of course the desert was vast, it was easy to vanish into it, but if you were found there was nowhere to run to and nothing to hide behind. In fact you were lucky if you could run. On his first patrol Lampard had discovered what it was like to have to run: they had been chased for an hour, flat out, by vehicles that might have been German armoured cars or might have been a roaming unit from the flank of the Eighth Army. Nobody could identify them and nobody wanted to let them get close enough to be identifiable, so the patrol just turned and ran, trying not to think about punctures and hoping that if there were any soft sand about, the other lot would get stuck in it. In the end they out-ran them and never found out whether it was a great escape or all a waste of time. That's what happened when you were lucky. If you were unlucky and they jumped you, it would probably be a very brief fight. In fact it probably wouldn't be any kind of fight, just a sudden storm of heavy machine-gun fire laced with cannon shells, and the patrol vehicles, being soft-skinned, would get torn to bits. What would happen to the members of the patrol, being even more soft-skinned, wasn't worth thinking about.

Lampard, Dunn and the navigator, Gibbon, walked to the top of the nearest hillock. After hours of engine-roar, the silence was so total that it was almost painful. The desert had the same kind of crystalline stillness you get on nights of intense frost. The stillness and the silence formed a powerful presence: to break them was to reveal how great they were, how little you were.

The three men stood and listened. Nothing.

"Various possibilities," Lampard said. "Jerry has no patrols out looking for us. Jerry has patrols out, but not near here. The patrols are near here, but they're hiding in a wadi, waiting for daylight."

"Is there anything we can do to alter any of those possibilities?" Gibbon asked.

"No."

"That's what I thought."

They walked back to the fire. "Jerry won't try to jump us before dawn," Dunn said. "He hasn't the faintest idea how strong we are."

"Mr Schramm will tell him," Gibbon said.

"Schramm's still hiking across the Jebel. Anyway, nobody knows we're the same outfit that attacked Barce. We could be a completely different patrol, lousy with mortars and bazookas and pom-poms plus a couple of anti-tank guns in the boot."

"I wish we were," Gibbon said.

"I don't," Lampard said. "If you want to slug it out, go and join the Tank Corps. Ah, bacon!" He rubbed his hands and leaned over the fire to sniff the aroma.

"He always says that," Gibbon said to Dunn. "Every morning he says *Ah, bacon!* What does he expect? Jam sandwiches?"

"I think he likes bacon," Dunn said.

"If there's one thing I like," Lampard said to Sergeant Davis, "it's bacon."

"One day we'll have scrambled eggs," Gibbon said, "and he'll still say *Ah, bacon!* You mark my words."

"Got any eggs?" Dunn asked the cook.

"Only dried." The cook was busy forking bacon into mess tins.

"Don't like scrambled eggs," Lampard said. "They remind me of my prep school. The headmaster's brother kept a chicken farm. We used to say that if you eat eggs all the time, you feel down in the mouth."

A fitter called Blake said: "I wouldn't send any kids of mine away to boarding school." He spat out a bit of rind. "Not natural."

They were standing in a circle around the fire. The air was as warm as a sunny English summer afternoon, but the night was still black.

"Oh, I don't know," Dunn said. "After ten years at boarding school, the rest of life comes as rather a pleasant surprise."

"Who's to say what's natural?" Davis asked.

"Joe Harris wasn't natural," Corporal Pocock said, and took a quick swig of tea as if to wash away the taste of the words.

Tony Waterman, the signals officer, happened to be standing next to Pocock. "Mustn't speak ill of the dead, old chap," he said.

"Yes, sir?" Sergeant Davis stopped eating a biscuit and gazed at Waterman. "Why is that, sir?" Waterman was startled. He picked his teeth with his tongue while he tried to think of an answer, and failed.

"Eat too many *eggs*," Lampard said, talking to the fire, "and you feel *down in the mouth*."

"We got it the first time, Jack," Dunn said.

"Ask me," Pocock said, "the only safe time to speak ill of Harris is now he *is* dead."

"I thought you were his friend, corporal," Lampard said.

"Harris had no friends. He didn't get on with people, except when it came to killing them. He was bloody good at that."

"Good, but not perfect," Gibbon said.

"Killing the enemy is an admirable pastime," Lampard said. "I myself quite enjoy it."

"How many d'you reckon you killed at Barce?" Waterman asked.

"Hard to say. I expect quite a few went up with the ammo dump. Couple of dozen?"

Waterman nodded. He was Signals, he knew nothing about combat. "Seems reasonable. More than enough to avenge Harris, anyway."

Gibbon said, looking at the sky: "Can you avenge someone before he gets the chop?"

Most of them let the question pass. It was too complex

and uncomfortable; and anyway, who cared? But the idea interested Gibbon. "Premature retaliation," he said, still studying the sky. "Vengeance in advance. By gum, there's a lot to be said for it, Tony. It solves so many problems! Strike first and beat the rush! Draw blood now and avoid disappointment later! Revenge is sweet, so why wait until you need some? Shop early while stocks are plentiful."

"You do blather on," Waterman said.

"I might recommend Harris for a decoration," Lampard said.

"His feet smelt worse than any man I know," Davis said.

"Perhaps a Mentioned in Despatches would do," Lampard said.

There was a soft grey tinge in the sky. Soon the sand would be touched by shades of delicate pink and green and purple and, for a few minutes, the desert would look beautiful, before everything got roasted white again. The patrol busied itself, topping up fuel tanks and emptying bladders. They wanted to reach the Tariq el 'Abd while the thermos bombs would still be casting long shadows. If they were exposed, that is.

*   *   *

It had not been easy to get the Storch: the plane was over-due for overhaul, the fitters actually had it in the hangar, with the engine cowlings off and the tanks drained, when Hoffmann told them to put it all together and fill it up.

As the plane was being pushed out of the hangar, Major Jakowski's car arrived, brakes screeching, horn blaring. Jakowski was in charge of airfield protection at Barce and he had just returned from a large meeting in Benghazi where he had been made to describe the disaster that had happened two nights ago: twenty-seven aircraft destroyed, six men dead, twelve wounded, one missing, five large vehicles burned out, also much fuel and ammunition lost, extensive damage to buildings ... When he stood up at the meeting and heard his own voice, the list sounded dreadful. It *was* dreadful. It was like the toll of some massive air battle, without the consolation of enemy losses. Those present had then asked a lot of hard questions of Jakowski. Jakowski had few answers to give. The general who chaired the meeting had not spared him. Next time, Jakowski knew, it would be the Russian Front.

So he had raced back to Barce, thinking hard of all the men whose backsides he would kick. Trouble was, they were nearly all up in the Jebel, searching for the British raiders. Then he saw the Storch. "I want that," he told Hoffmann. There was a brisk argument which Jakowski lost. He lost because he had no good reason for using the Storch; he just wanted to create the impression of activity by flying hither and yon, seeking out his patrols one after another. That was not what he said. What he said was that he needed the plane so he could effectively liaise with and integrate the units carrying out his clean-up operation in the Jebel. The Storch would give him an essential overview of this. "I've got to have it," Jakowski said. His shirt was black with sweat.

"Wrong place," Schramm said. He was in a wheelchair. "The British raiding party is not in the Jebel. Not any more."

By now the pilot of the Storch had arrived. "You want an overview of the Jebel?" he asked.

"Yes," Jakowski said.

"Well, you won't get it from this box of bits. She hasn't got the ceiling. I flew her yesterday. She's tired out, she needs a new engine. And look at this." He took hold of an aileron and worked it up and down. "Soft as shit," he said.

"How can I do my job without proper support?" Jakowski demanded, but the steam had gone out of him.

"She'll fly, won't she?" Hoffmann asked the pilot. The

man shrugged, but he didn't say no. "Fly her today and we'll service her tomorrow," Hoffmann said.

"You're absolutely sure there are no British in the Jebel?" Jakowski asked Schramm.

"I didn't say that. The men who came here two nights ago have left the Jebel, I'm sure. But there may be others."

Jakowski took off his cap and slashed at the flies. "This isn't war," he said. "They didn't teach us anything about this at Staff College."

Four medics lifted Schramm out of the wheelchair and hoisted him into the cockpit. They packed cushions around his bandaged feet and fastened his straps. While the engine was warming up he showed the pilot where to go. The pilot folded the map and stuffed it down the side of his boot. "It's none of my business," he said, "but if you're so sure you know where these Commandos are going, isn't it possible they know you know, in which case they won't go there?"

"Not Commandos." Schramm yawned. "SAS." For the first time since he had escaped, his body was allowing itself to relax completely. "They think that because I know that they know that I know what they intend to do, then I'll think they'll change their plans. That would be the obvious thing to do, which is why I'm sure they won't do it."

"Why not?"

Schramm's sleepy brain struggled to explain why not, and eventually succeeded. "Because," he said, "it would be pointless for us both to do something different." Now that he heard his explanation it seemed not quite right, but he couldn't spot the fault. "Too confusing," he said, and yawned.

"You know best," the pilot said. "But if you think we'll see much of anything in the desert at midday, you'd better think again." He tested the engine until the Storch shuddered against its brakes, and then he let the revs fall to a grumble. "I'm told they built this thing out of what

58

survived from three wrecks," he said. "Sometimes she feels as if perhaps they lost a few bits. But you're not interested in that sort of technical detail, are you? No. We might as well leave before one of you has a small heart attack."

The Storch groaned and stumbled up to three thousand feet, hitting thermals that felt like hump-backed bridges. But once they were above the Jebel the air became cooler and smoother. The cockpit canopy had a canvas screen that kept the sun out; with the cabin ventilation wide open it was really quite pleasant. Schramm let his head rest against the side window and looked down on the landscape he had so painfully limped across: dusty green scrub and grass, red earth fields, grey stone outcrops, all of it split by hundreds of wrinkled wadis. It looked a bit like a very old, stained camel-blanket, dropped and forgotten. The window vibrated gently. It was a pleasant sensation. Schramm relaxed and enjoyed it.

* * *

Crossing the Tariq was a walkover.

Gibbon found the tracks the patrol had made when they came north and now they drove south, fitting their wheels into the same ruts. Dead easy. On the other hand there was a dead camel a hundred yards away providing breakfast for a dozen birds and a million flies, which probably meant it had trodden on a thermos bomb. Mike Dunn studied it through his binoculars and reported no evidence of the camel-owner. "I expect the birds ate him first," Pocock said. "Bloody tough meat, camel."

"Where on earth do the birds come from?" Dunn wondered.

"Same place as the flies," Lampard said. "Nowhere and everywhere."

"I wish something would eat the bloody flies," Pocock said.

"My brother-in-law sold flypaper before the war," said Blake, the fitter. "He could've made a fucking fortune out here."

"Give me his address," Dunn said. "I'll get him flown out."

"Too late. Fell down a hole in the blackout. Broke his neck."

"Ah. Pity."

"Flies didn't think so. Best thing ever happened to them."

It was about two hundred kilometres to Jalo. By mid-morning they were more than halfway there, which pleased Lampard. The more distance he put between the patrol and the Jebel, the greater would be the area that the enemy had to search. There was a danger in speed, in fact several dangers: the trail of dust announced their presence; the broken ground gave the tyres and springs a continual beating; and men who had already driven through the night had to take the heat that came pounding down from the sky as well as the heat that hammered back from their engines, along with the eternal, smothering sandy dust that sought out their eyes and ears and nostrils like a plague of grit. Lampard took the risk of speed because he knew he must have the luxury of time when they crawled past Jalo Oasis. No plumes of dust near Jalo; no bellowing engines. The Italians who garrisoned Jalo were not famous for their aggression, but if they knew how small this patrol was, they might be tempted to come out and chase it. An Italian bullet could be as fatal as any other kind.

At the approaches to the Jalo Gap, Lampard called a halt for a brew-up. The rambling, uneven terrain that spread south of the Jebel was behind them now; they were back in desert, pure and simple, and the land was almost featureless. Heat hit the sand like a punishment and the sand just lay there and absorbed it, too dead to be killed any further.

The flies flew in from all quarters, buzzing with approval. These were the first white men for a week to sweat here. Lampard took a shovel, walked a hundred yards, dug a hole and squatted over it. His personal bodyguard of flies went berserk. He ignored them; he had long ago learned that you could never win the battle with the flies; the only sane thing was to forget them.

He was pleased to note that even from here the vehicles looked slightly soft and vague. The heat-haze that settled on the desert at midday was doing its stuff. It would get worse than this, until visibility fell to less than half a mile. Splendid. He filled in the hole and five hundred flies went to an early grave.

Sergeant Davis gave him a mug of tea, black as tar. Lampard added condensed milk, lots of it, and watched the colours swirl and jostle and blend. He drank. It tasted wonderful. "In the words of the poet," he said, looking into his mug, "Earth has not anything to show more fair."

"Oh, I dunno," said Davis. "I knew a girl in Rotherham. Tits like coconuts."

"What, all brown and hairy?" said Blake. He wrinkled his nose. "That's not very nice."

"How did he know?" Corporal Pocock asked Lampard.

"How did who know?"

"This poet bloke."

"The name was Wordsworth," Tony Waterman said.

Davis shook his head. "Not her in Rotherham, no. Her name was Prendergast, Maureen Prendergast."

Dunn said: "Jerry must have told the Eye-ties at Jalo to watch out for us in the Gap. It's the obvious thing to do, isn't it?"

"How did Wordsworth know?" Corporal Pocock persisted.

"Jerry must have told him too," Blake said.

"If the Eye-ties come out from Jalo to get us, we run for it," Lampard said. "Flat out."

"I mean, it's just his opinion, isn't it?" Pocock said. "Just Wordsworth's opinion, that's all. I mean, he didn't know everything, did he? Earth has not anything to show . . . How the hell did Wordsworth know what Earth had to show? Probably never been east of Hackney in his whole life."

"They wouldn't see anything from Jalo," Dunn said. "Not this time of day."

"I bet Wordsworth hadn't seen Jalo, for a start," Pocock said.

"I tell a lie," Davis said. "Her name was Pickering. Her in Rotherham. Maureen Prendergast lived in Barnsley. I preferred Muriel Pickering, myself. Tits like melons."

"People shouldn't make sweeping statements," Pocock said. "Not unless they got proof."

"I suppose we ought to make allowances for Wordsworth," Waterman said. "He never knew when to stop. He was the bloke who wrote: 'and then my heart with gladness fills and dances with the daffodils'."

"He wouldn't have liked it here," Davis said. "Too hot to dance."

"I knew a Pickering once," Blake the fitter told Davis. "Not Muriel, though."

"I reckon anyone who dances with the daffodils must have a few tiles off his roof," a trooper called Smedley said.

"You're thinking of Doris. Muriel's sister. Went to live in Pontefract. Doris Pickering," Davis said. "Tits like turnips."

"Let's go," Lampard ordered. The fire was out, the gear was loaded.

"Tell me, sergeant," Gibbon said. "Purely for my information: given the choice, would you prefer tits, or fruit and vegetables?"

"That's what I ask myself every night, before I go to sleep," Davis said. "Tits or turnips? Turnips or tits? I could murder a nice juicy turnip now, but on the other hand . . ." He stopped because they had all stopped.

Aeroplane.

Nobody spoke. The easy-going buzz, too thin to be a bomber, too slow to be a fighter, could only be a Storch, dribbling along at three or four hundred feet, and it had to be looking for them.

"Let's knock it down if we can," Lampard said, "but if anyone fires he's *got* to hit it. Otherwise we leave it alone." The men hurried to their vehicles and peeled the dust covers from the Vickers twin machine guns.

The buzz approached, altered its tone, faded, returned, changed tone again. "Box search?" Gibbon said to his driver. "Sounds like it," the driver said. In a box search the aircraft flew a series of rectangles, each one butted against the last, slowly working its way along a route.

And then they saw it, soft as a moth, all detail fogged out by the heat-haze.

"Too high," Lampard said to Dunn. "He can't see anything from up there, not through this soup. That's blindingly obvious."

The noise dwindled and the silhouette dissolved to nothing. "Fathead," Lampard said. "Right, off we go. Five miles an hour and keep it quiet." The patrol moved off.

⚓   ⚓   ⚓

In the Storch the passenger sat behind the pilot. Paul Schramm leaned forward and pointed at the altimeter. "Lose some height," he said. "Lose a lot of height, in fact. I'll never see anything from up here."

"You'll see even less if I go into that muck."

"Let's try, anyway."

The pilot turned the plane through a right angle as easily as if he were swinging on a lamppost, and levelled out, but he did not lose height.

"They're down there somewhere," Schramm said. "I know it. What are you afraid of?"

"I don't trust this squalid altimeter," the pilot said.

"For Christ's sake! It got us over the Jebel! Besides, there's nothing near here to fly into. It's all just desert."

"Maybe. This wreck was being pulled apart in a hangar only an hour ago. I bet they bust the altimeter. Bet they forgot to reset it."

"Looks good to me."

"Anyway, there's desert and desert. I've seen dunes a hundred metres high in the Calanscio." He meant the Sand Sea that formed the eastern side of the Jalo Gap. It did indeed look like a sea: a succession of monstrously heaving waves and swells.

"We're nowhere near the Calanscio," Schramm said. "We're in the Gap, aren't we?"

"I don't trust that squalid compass," the pilot said. "There's something peculiar about it." He swung onto another leg of the search and watched the compass react. "Damned mechanics," he muttered. "First thing they do is bust the compass."

Schramm lost patience. "Get down there," he ordered. "Or I'll have you court-martialled."

The pilot sighed and eased the control column forward. The haze gradually thickened until it was like flying through industrial smog, yellow-brown, quivering with dust. Visibility was so bad that it was impossible to tell where the haze ended and the desert began. The horizon wasn't much help: just a blur where brown-yellow turned to yellow-brown. "We're down," the pilot grunted. "Hope you like it."

For ten minutes they searched and saw nothing. By then they both knew they were through the Gap and on the edge of the open desert, with the Calanscio receding to their left and Jalo Oasis falling behind to their right. Schramm realised now what a barren idea this search had been.

Guessing where the enemy was didn't necessarily mean you could do anything about it.

"You know this wreck flies on fuel, don't you?" said the pilot.

"I know." Schramm glanced at the gauge. Low.

"You can't trust that," the pilot said. "First thing they do is bust the fuel gauge."

"All right. Since we've got to go back, let's stay down and look for wheel tracks."

"Is that all you want? Christ, if that's all you want I can show you dozens of them, hundreds. It's like an autobahn down there, next exit five hundred kilometres south, Kufra. Our Latin comrades used to have a garrison down at Kufra, you know."

"I know."

"That was before the British turned up."

"I know that too."

"First thing the British do is bust the Italians."

"I've heard enough from you," Schramm said. "Just drive the bus."

The plane flew north. The pilot had been right: tyre tracks were everywhere. Some were obviously old, partly smoothed by the wind, but many were new. Or looked new. Schramm despaired. A month, a week, five minutes; who could tell the difference? Then the pilot nudged him. Schramm looked where the pilot was looking, away to the left. Five square blobs on wheels. "Get closer," he said.

The pilot circled, edging slightly inwards. The vehicles were moving very slowly.

"Could be an Italian patrol," Schramm said. "I can't tell from here."

"British trucks. Look at the silhouettes."

"That proves nothing. We captured hundreds of them. Get closer."

"If I get any closer and they're not Italian, we're dead." Schramm tried to focus his binoculars on the hazy shapes, but all he got was bigger hazy shapes. "It's got to be them," he muttered. "I'm not going back without . . ." But he couldn't complete the sentence. He felt slightly sick. Maybe the doctor's injection was wearing off; certainly the pain had come back, as if an electric fire had been brought too close to his feet. Or maybe the sickness was the effect of all this circling with no clear horizon to cling to. For a wretched moment, Schramm suffered the illusion of hanging motionless while the rest of the world swung hugely and helplessly around him. He shut his eyes.

"Fifty-fifty that's an Italian patrol looking for your British friends," the pilot said. "Fifty-fifty it isn't."

"All right." Schramm was too weak to argue. "We'll report it to Barce as a possible target and go home. Let them make the decision."

"Send the message now?"

Schramm opened his eyes. "Yes, now."

"I'll have to take her up five hundred metres. This isn't the greatest radio in the world."

"So do it."

Schramm's body was angled back as the nose came up, and his head got gently tilted until it rested on the seat top. The position was soothing. Nothing more to be done. Over to the professionals now. "Oh, you bitch," the pilot muttered. Schramm compelled his mind to alert itself, and grudgingly his mind responded. "What's wrong?" he asked.

The nose was going down again. The pilot was fussing with the controls, nudging the throttle a fraction forward and half a fraction back, cocking his head to test the engine note as he glanced up at the wings. "She won't climb," he said. "We nearly stalled. I can't get any lift."

"You mean there's a fault somewhere?" Schramm heard the foolishness in his words and struggled to recover control of himself and his situation. "Forget the signal," he said. "Make for Agedabia. We can land there." Agedabia was about a hundred kilometres south of Benghazi. The land between Jalo and Agedabia was fairly flat. The pilot was shaking his head, not in answer to Schramm but as a verdict on the performance of the Storch. "She is not a happy aeroplane," he said. "People have not been kind to her, and now she doesn't want to fly any more."

*   *   *

The five vehicles of the patrol had stopped and their engines had been turned off. Nobody spoke. They all sat and looked at the haze, which was beginning to lift, but still it was like looking at a hot and hazy nothingness. They listened to the sound of the desert, but this was a hopeless mismatch because the desert had been practising its silence for tens of thousands of years. The desert was a master of silence. They were novices.

Dunn got down from his truck and walked over to Lampard's armed jeep. The scuffing of his boots was noisy. Lampard sat upright, only his head moving as he hunted for sound. Dunn waited. He could feel sweat trickling inside his ears.

"That's never happened before," Lampard said. "Normally, when a shufti-kite flies away, you can still hear it for a minute or two. Especially if it's climbing."

"Beats me," Dunn said.

Lampard stood up and rubbed his backside. "If we didn't hear it fly away," he said, "that means it hasn't flown away."

"Logical," Dunn said.

"If it hasn't flown away, it's on the ground. Nearby."

"Fancy that," Dunn said.

"I do fancy it. Go due west one mile," Lampard told his driver. "That's where he faded out."

*   *   *

The pilot switched off the engine before the Storch had rolled to a halt. Already the desert heat was hammering at the cockpit and Schramm was sweating hard. Part of this was panic. "That was a very stupid thing to do," he said. "What if we can't get it to start again?"

"If I have to crawl over this wreck," said the pilot, "I would prefer not to do it behind a prop that is throwing desert at me like a small sandstorm." He opened the door and stepped down. "Don't touch anything," he called. "It might be booby-trapped."

Schramm slid his side window back and felt the desert breathe its heat at him. He hated it for wanting to bake him to death and hated it even more for being such a faceless murderer. There was nothing out there to focus his hatred on. Everything to see and nothing to look at. Just a trembling blur of sand. After a while Schramm realised that his head was doing the trembling and he closed his eyes. Slashes of purple and scarlet flickered and merged, vanished and popped back. His imagination re-positioned him high in the sky, looking down on himself, a speck inside a bigger speck lost in a flat wilderness that didn't give a damn for either of them.

When the pilot climbed in and shook him awake he was sunk in such a deep fatigue that the man's words meant little. "Trouble with the elevator. Maybe a pulley's jammed somewhere and trapped a cable, I don't know. All I know is the elevator won't elevate us. Also the engine hasn't been giving full power. I found a cracked fuel line, which means dust and dirt got in, so now we've got dirty fuel. I told you this wreck was a wreck."

"Yes," said Schramm, and felt pleased with his achievement.

"If they've got any brains in Barce they'll come looking for us."

"I'm the brains in Barce," Schramm said.

The pilot sighed. "I think I'll have a little sleep," he said;

but instead he put his head out of the cockpit. "Hear that?" he asked. Schramm held his breath and listened. Beyond the thump of his own pulse he heard the low mumble of engines.

"Nothing in sight on this side," the pilot said. All the cockiness had left his voice. Schramm squinted at the haze, much thinner now, saw nothing and said nothing. The pilot heaved himself across the cockpit and got his head out of the other window.

Five seconds later he dropped back into his seat. "The trucks we were chasing seem to have found us," he said. Already he was priming the engine, setting the throttle, thumbing the starter.

The Storch was still hot: she fired instantly, dirty fuel or not. Within thirty yards she was flying. The pilot got her ten feet off the ground and failed to make her climb an inch higher. "Any idea how fast they can go?" he asked. Schramm took too long thinking. "Never mind," the pilot said. "We'll soon know."

*   *   *

Lampard led the patrol at a brisk, bumpy twenty miles an hour through a shallow depression and around a patch of rocks, and stopped. Before he could raise his binoculars he saw the Storch, half a mile to his right, just as it left the ground. "Tally-ho!" he shouted. "After the bastard!" But his driver had already seen it and Lampard's words were lost in the bellow of the engine. The jeep jumped away from its own dust.

The rest of the patrol joined in the chase with more or less enthusiasm. Mike Dunn, in the armed truck, urged his driver on. He knew the contest was absurd: any plane could out-run a truck, never mind out-climb it, but where Lampard led, Dunn followed: simple as that. Sergeant Davis, in the other armed jeep, did the same. In the wireless truck Tony Waterman left it to his driver to decide the pace. Waterman's job was to remain operational, send and receive signals, not get mixed up in combat. Captain Gibbon, the navigator, had taken over the Alfa-Romeo, and he made no great effort to keep up. The desert surface was patchy and in parts treacherous, the Alfa's tyres were losing their tread, and Gibbon believed that Lampard was simply frightening the German plane away, so why take chances?

After a quarter of a mile Gibbon saw that he was wrong. The Storch was flying, but only just. It was not climbing and it was not escaping. As the Alfa bucketed over some unexpected corrugations, Gibbon saw the red pulse of tracer leap from the machine guns in Lampard's jeep and arc high towards the plane. The burst fell short. But not all that short.

Schramm heard the stammer of the guns. He felt curiously unworried. Flying like this was like travelling on a gentle fairground ride, dipping and rising and dipping again. It took his mind off the pain. "Can you see them?" he shouted.

"Ever been to Jalo?"

"No."

The pilot saw the glint of an outcrop coming towards them and he nursed the machine over it. "Oasis, right? Palm trees, yes? Hundreds. Thousands, probably."

"Are you going to Jalo?" Schramm asked. It was *you*, not *we*. Schramm was just a passenger now. Excess baggage.

"She won't go over any palms," the pilot said. "They're much too high for her."

Schramm looked out and saw the odd palm tree, its fist of leaves well above their heads. The corner of his eye caught the flicker of tracer, as hot as neon. "I know you can't climb," he said, "but can't you go faster?" He could see there was plenty of throttle waiting to be used.

70

"Faster is slower. Watch." The pilot opened the throttle a fraction. At once the speed increased but the nose went down. He closed the throttle by the same fraction and the nose came up again. "Slower is faster. Know why? Fly slow and there's not much airflow over the elevators. We stay up. Fly faster, more airflow for the elevators to bite on, so they send us down. It's a balancing act."

"They'll catch us if you don't go faster."

"They'll catch us if we do. Catch us with our nose in the sand."

Lampard braced himself to fire another burst and as he squeezed the triggers the jeep cornered so sharply that he got swung sideways, lost his footing and shot the sky instead. "God's bowels!" he shouted. When the jeep straightened, he looked to see what the driver had avoided. The sand was brown in places, so brown it was almost chestnut, but tinged white. "Salt marsh?" he said. The driver nodded, too busy searching the land ahead to speak. Lampard looked for the Storch, no longer dead ahead, then looked for the rest of the patrol, strung out behind, and he made his decision. "Stop!" he said. "This is no damn good."

The jeep turned and cruised back, skirting the long patch of salt marsh. Dunn's truck saw them coming and waited.

"Nasty bit of bog," Lampard said. "By the time we found a way around it, we'd have been too late."

"Pity," Dunn said. "You were gaining on him, too."

"I was indeed. How far away d'you reckon those palms are?"

"Which palms? I can see about five thousand." The skyline to the north and west was black with trees. Some seemed to float on lakes of light.

"Two miles at most." Lampard answered his own question. "More to the point, where's Jalo garrison? It could be on the other side."

"Don't know," Dunn said. "Doesn't matter, does it?"

71

"Correct. Doesn't matter a toss. Not a tiny toss." They looked at each other and laughed with the suddenness of broken tension. The chase was over, Jerry had won, it was all a joke. Jolly funny joke. Davis's jeep and Waterman's wireless truck arrived while they were still laughing. Corporal Pocock was sitting on top of the truck. "Captain!" Pocock shouted. "That sodding Storch is down again."

Lampard scrambled up beside him. Far off, beyond a patch of scrub, half a wing could be seen sticking out. The ground where the plane had landed fell away in a slight depression and this had hidden it from view unless you were Pocock, up high. "Brilliant!" Lampard said, and jumped down.

He couldn't wait for the Alfa. He called the rest of the patrol around him for orders. "Stroke of luck," he said. "Whatever's wrong with that shufti-kite is getting worse. I shall go back in the jeep and try to find a way around the salt marsh. Mike, you follow. The rest wait here. Any questions?"

Sergeant Davis said: "There's Eye-ties in those trees, you know."

"What makes you think so?"

"Flies." Davis waved an arm through the buzzing black aura. "Smell the garlic on their breath." He was not happy.

"Why hasn't someone come out to help those idiots in the plane?"

"Dunno."

Lampard looked through his binoculars at the stretch of palms, but it was only a gesture, and they all knew it. "It'll take us three minutes, maximum," he said. "I've never known an Italian who could put his pants on in less than three minutes."

Gibbon arrived in the Alfa as Lampard and Dunn left. "What's the score?" he asked; and when Waterman explained, Gibbon merely sniffed. "Not impressed?" Waterman said.

"We should be on the trail, not on the spree."

"It's only three minutes, Corky."

"What if it takes longer?"

"Then we've got time for a brew-up."

Gibbon turned away and tried to find some shade. Waterman climbed onto his wireless truck and settled down to watch the attack. Trooper Smedley sat beside him. "If you ask me, this is plain bloody silly," Smedley said.

"Ours not to reason why."

"First we go to all that trouble to try to sneak through the Gap, then we go chasing butterflies till we're nearly in Jalo. What's so special?"

"You know what he's like when he gets his teeth into something," Waterman said. "British bulldog."

"I had a mate had a bulldog," Smedley said. "Ugly as sin. Dog wasn't much to look at, neither."

Schramm leaned forward and tried to see what the pilot was doing to the engine. Waste of time asking: he got no answer except metallic clinks and thumps that made the plane shiver. All he could see were hunched shoulders, moving as if the arms were using a spanner. The stink of petrol was so strong that it shimmered.

"Go and get some soldiers from the garrison," Schramm shouted, but it came out as a weak shout. "They can tow us in."

No reply. Schramm gave up. He was an Intelligence Officer; he was not trained for combat, he was trained to use his brains to help others succeed in combat. The last forty-eight hours had proved what he already knew: combat was a young man's game. He rested his head against the baking-hot leather of the seat and thought of cold steins of beer until he could almost feel and taste the wonderful stuff and he had to swallow in order to meet the illusion; but he had no spare saliva and the swallow was a failure. The pilot, looking pleased, climbed into the cockpit. "Problem solved," he said. "I have emptied half the Sahara out of the bowels of this poor old cow. Now she'll sing like a bird."

"And fly like a bird?"

"No, she'll fly like a grand piano, but even a grand piano can fly if you lash enough power to it."

The engine fired willingly enough; after that it coughed and roared alternately. The pilot knew he had to cut and run before it overheated. He ran, trying to taxi between or around the stones, some as big as melons, that dotted the ground. Three times out of four he missed them. Fourth time, the plane rocked and the wheels suffered. There were also palm trees and patches of scrub to avoid. He leaned far forward until his nose almost touched the windscreen. The rudder never ceased wagging.

Lampard's driver had found a track. It wasn't much of a track, but it was definitely not salt marsh and it seemed to lead somewhere near where the Storch had been last seen. Lampard told him to get a move on, and the jeep hammered along at a good twenty-five miles an hour. It felt like seventy. Behind, the armed truck charged into the jeep's dust with blind faith.

Waterman watched the progress of the interception through binoculars from the top of his wireless truck. It had the inevitability of gradualness: the jeep was travelling at more than twice the speed of the Storch; the gap between them closed like slowly shrinking elastic; you could plan the point of meeting. That point was never reached. When the range was still two hundred yards, the jeep slowed, the truck came alongside it, and both began firing.

As if these shots were starting signals, four armoured cars charged out of the oasis in line abreast and sped towards the attack. They were less than half a mile away. Very soon they too were firing, brief ranging shots of heavy cannon laced with tracer. The shots fell close and kicked up sand. Immediately the armed truck was reversing at speed up the track, its gearbox screaming, its driver searching for a turning place. Lampard fired a second, longer burst at the zigzagging Storch. Then his driver spun the jeep round and chased the truck.

The Storch kept going. Schramm had felt bullets whacking into it and he had heard them fizzing past. He was helpless, just as liable to be killed if he jumped out as if he stayed inside. The pilot was cursing the aeroplane, the British and the desert, and his face was screwed into a vast grimace that anticipated each crash of wheel against rock. The engine kept cutting out for an instant and then picking up with a harsh and painful roar, as if it had to take breath each time. *Like a bullfight*, Schramm thought, *it's like a wounded bull*. He told himself not to waste time on fantasies. So what else could he do? Tighten your seat belt! Get your head down! He did both those things. *Fatuous*, he told himself. *Futile*. There was more firing. The pilot sighed. The Storch seemed to trip. It fell on its nose and smashed its propeller: Schramm clearly saw some of the bits spinning away and bouncing off a red rock. The tail kept coming up until Schramm was hanging in his straps, looking down at a boiling cloud of dust and dirt. The door beside him sagged open, a clear invitation. He punched the release button on his straps, fell helplessly and lay with his face in the sand, moaning. Nobody responded. "Oh, Christ, that hurt," he said weakly. No answer. If it hadn't been for the flies, everything would have been very quiet. Ten thousand flies. All sopranos. How odd. "They can fly," Schramm told the pilot. "Why can't you?" He examined the flies and saw instead a remarkably regular pattern of black specks, thousands of black specks. The noise was inside his head. "No flies," he said weakly.

Lampard heard the pounding of the Bofors gun, solid and steady as a bass drum, before he saw the armed truck through the cloud of dust it had thrown up as it reversed. Dunn's driver had found a half-circle of rocks, probably an old goat-pen, enough to give the truck some protection, and before Dunn could jump down from the cab his crew had the Bofors in action, pumping 37 mm shells at the Italian armoured cars. By the time Lampard's jeep stopped in the lee of the truck, the Breda 20 mm was firing alongside the Bofors. The clatter and bang were deafening. Lampard grabbed Dunn by the arm. They ran clear of the dust and the noise.

"Three," said Lampard. "I can see three. There were four. Where's the other gone?"

"Maybe it went back," Dunn said. "For God's sake, let's get down." The three armoured cars were at the extreme limit of the Italians' range, but spent rounds were plopping into the sand and Dunn felt conspicuous.

"Why should it go back?" Lampard was searching the scene through binoculars. "Makes no sense. Tell you what makes sense. Outflanking makes sense. Those three keep us busy while number four sneaks round behind us and duffs us up."

"That's all salt marsh," Dunn said, waving towards the left. "So he can't get through there, can he?"

Abruptly all firing ceased. The armoured cars had pulled back. For a while both sides stood and looked at each other through air that twitched and shivered and baked.

"Let's get out of here," Dunn said. "What are we waiting for?"

"What are *they* waiting for?"

"The heavy brigade. Stukas. Who knows? Tanks. Artillery."

Lampard made one last search through his field-glasses, knowing that every second was risky and enjoying every second of risk. "All right, let's go," he said, but he took a final look at the wrecked Storch. Nose down and tail high, it made a silhouette like an English market cross. Someone tumbled from the cockpit and fell out of sight. Dead or alive? Probably alive. Less than totally satisfying, that. Pity

76

the kite hadn't burned. Nothing beats a nice pillar of flame. His jeep came by and he swung into the front seat.

Dunn was relieved when the three armoured cars made no attempt to follow. He guessed that the sudden presence of a Bofors on an ordinary-looking truck had alarmed and discouraged them. Now the only danger lay in covering the next five or six miles of patchy going before the Italians could whistle up an air strike; after that it was all hard, flat desert where you could really put your foot down and sprint for home. A dull thudding pounded the air. At first Dunn thought it was a flat tyre beating itself to bits, but the truck ran smoothly. More thudding sounded, then a pause, then a long and gloomy crump. "Jesus!" he said.

His driver pointed. "Wireless truck," he said. Black smoke, rich as oil, was gushing into the sky.

A fold in the land hid the truck from view: the same fold that, earlier, had concealed the Storch from Lampard's jeep. Dunn knew his driver was right. Only the wireless truck could have burned like that. Now they knew where the fourth armoured car had gone, although how it got there was a mystery. The armed truck rounded the salt marsh and they saw more of the burning vehicle. It was gripped by vivid red flames that jumped and swayed like dancers, all wrong for the desert, far too lively; nothing should be so wildly active in such stifling heat. Another crump shook the wireless truck, or perhaps that was just the shuddering of the afternoon air. Fresh smoke boiled up, thrusting the old smoke higher.

Lampard's jeep got there first. He stopped for ten seconds to check out the area, seeking any trace of the enemy. Then he made a fast circuit of the burning truck. Two men came out of a patch of waist-high scrub. They were Corporal Pocock and Trooper Smedley.

"Where's the Alfa?" Lampard demanded. "Where's Davis?"

"Gone." Pocock pointed eastward. "And bloody lucky to do it."

"Anyone hurt?"

"Mr Waterman's in there." Pocock looked at the wireless truck. Only its shell was left, looking curiously frail through the flames. As the wheels burned out, the chassis settled, like an animal making itself comfortable.

"Jump in," Lampard said. Dunn's truck had arrived. "Time to beat it for home, I think." He got out and went over to Dunn. "Looks like Tony got the chop," he said.

Dunn was beyond caring. All he knew was that he was sitting next to the biggest smoke signal in Libya. "Too bad," he said. When Lampard remained looking at him, he added: "Could have been you or me, I suppose."

"More likely you or I."

Dunn stared. "Come again?"

"You or I, not you or me. Verb *to be* takes the nominative, not the accusative." Lampard nodded in approval of himself.

"Drive on!" Dunn said loudly. Death he could take. Death and grammar, no.

If he had used his brains, Schramm would have crawled into the shade of the Storch's wide wings and waited to be rescued. Instead, he got to his heavily bandaged feet and tried to walk to the headquarters of Jalo garrison in order to tell them to radio Barce airfield. It would be a simple message, merely informing Hoffmann where to find (and destroy) the British patrol, and so Schramm thought it must be a simple walk. That wasn't sensible, but Schramm was sick and tired of acting sensibly. He had acted sensibly when he got captured, and when he escaped, and when he walked across the Jebel, and when he acquired the Storch; and look what acting sensibly had got him: an escort of flies. He stumbled bravely in the wrong direction. When he reached a palm tree he clung to it and had a rest before aiming for the next palm tree. He had no hat. He walked

78

with his mouth wide open, wheezing the superheated air over his bone-dry tongue.

When the Italian armoured cars were sure the British patrol had gone, they checked out the Storch and extracted the body of the pilot. Someone noticed blurred footprints and quite quickly the Italians found Schramm, who had almost completed a full circle.

At Jalo hospital the doctor didn't even try to understand his croaking and grunting. When Schramm had sipped a little milk, some of his voice returned, but his Italian was jumbled and the doctor knew little German. Schramm kept getting out of bed and trying to use the telephone. Eventually the doctor gave him a swift injection when he wasn't looking and Schramm fell peacefully asleep, which gave the doctor a chance to examine his feet. Schramm's feet greatly impressed the doctor.

Lampard and Dunn raced back along their own tracks and found the Alfa and the other jeep waiting at the point where the patrol had turned off to hunt the Storch. There was no pause, no discussion. Lampard waved at Gibbon, pointed south, and the patrol began the long sprint across the serir to Kufra.

Serir was the best going in the Sahara. It was a fine, smooth, gravel plain and it stretched without bump or blemish from horizon to horizon. It was so good that you could almost take your hands off the wheel. Unless a mirage appeared there was nothing to see, nothing to look at except the other vehicles barrelling across the flat, empty, beautiful landscape. The patrol loved it. Every hour took them another fifty miles from the enemy. The racing air hustled around their bodies and for the first time in many days they were almost cool.

Near the end of the serir the Alfa began to complain. Its exhaust pumped smoke and the engine developed a painful clatter. A couple of miles later there was a small explosion and the engine dumped its oil on the desert. One of the trucks took the Alfa in tow, but within minutes that truck had a puncture. As soon as they restarted, a jeep stopped. The engine was healthy but the clutch had quit. Lampard looked at the sun. Kufra was still a good hundred miles away, with some sharp rocks and then a nasty little neck of the Sand Sea to be crossed. He glanced at his driver. The man had eyes like a lizard with a hangover. Lampard had been sharing the driving. He knew how the man felt. "We'll stop here," Lampard announced.

Nobody talked much. The cooks got cracking. The patrol was a long way from the enemy, but all the double-Vickers were cleaned just the same. The loads were checked for leaky water tins or jerricans. The fitters peered into engines that were still too hot to touch, or squatted by the tyres, looking for tomorrow's trouble.

Meanwhile: food.

Compared with the average soldier in the Western Desert, the men of the SAS ate like kings. Lampard's patrol lined up for sardines, meatloaf, fried onions, tinned potatoes, pickles, tinned vegetables, tinned peaches, cheese and biscuits. Each man got two pints of tea. There was jam and syrup and, if the patrol commander said so, an issue of rum.

Lampard looked at his men. Nobody had washed in two weeks. Hair, beards and uniforms were filthy from a blend of desert dust and Jebel dirt and the greases and oils applied to weapons and vehicles, all of it evenly distributed by the action of sweat. The men took their loaded mess tins and moved away and ate the food steadily and blankly, not looking at each other, certainly not looking at the sunset, which was releasing a sudden flood of startlingly lovely colours, greens and pinks and mauves. "Rum," Lampard said to the cook, who nodded. But even that word failed to turn any other heads.

When they had finished eating, Lampard collected his second pint of tea (the one with the reward of rum in it) and took Sergeant Davis aside. "What went wrong?" he asked.

Davis cleaned his mess tin in the sand. He held it up to the fading, spilled-paintbox light so that he could see into the corners. He murmured, "Dear, dear." He cleaned it again, checked it again, turned it upside-down and banged it with his hand to shake the last few grains loose. "Difficult to know where to begin," he said.

Lampard slowly walked away. Twenty paces. Davis counted them. He turned and walked back. Nineteen paces. "You lost a pace somewhere," Davis said. "My old drill sergeant wouldn't have liked that. He'd have sent you back to find the bloody thing."

"Suppose we start again." Lampard sipped his tea. "What went wrong?"

Davis was ready this time. "Not for me to say, sir. But I can tell you what *happened*. One of those wop armoured cars got around the salt marsh somehow, and it clobbered us."

"Why didn't you see it coming?"

"I've wondered about that myself. Two reasons. One is, as soon as their cars came out of the oasis and started firing, we decided to pull back. So we weren't watching them all that closely, especially as we had a bit of trouble turning the wireless truck. The other reason is the armoured car that hit us didn't come flying across the bog. It came sneaking up a little wadi on the other flank."

Lampard folded his arms and let his heavy head sink until his chin would go no further while he absorbed this information. "What next?" he asked. His voice was so gruff it was almost a growl.

"Next . . . Well, next the Eye-ties fired a burst and hit the wireless truck. Hit the tyres, front and rear, so I knew that was that, and we decided to get out quick. That was when Mr Waterman got upset about leaving his code books in the truck, so he went off to get them, and while he was inside the truck the Eye-ties gave it several squirts and I reckon they hit the petrol tank. Like putting a match to a gas-ring. Whoosh! Up she went."

The sun had almost gone. The temperature was falling in a rush; soon it would be time for a woollen cardigan. "It must have been an extremely small wadi," Lampard said.

"Big enough."

"What I mean is, there was no reason to expect an attack from that quarter."

Sergeant Davis said nothing. Enough light remained for Lampard to see the look in his eyes: a look that said *Not for me to say, sir.*

"On the other hand," Lampard said, "on this sort of job there's always reason to expect an attack from any quarter."

Davis said nothing in the same expressive way.

"On the *other* other hand," Lampard said, "no risk, no win. And we did get the Storch."

"So we did," Davis said. "We got the Storch."

Normally everyone sat around for an hour or two, talking, maybe listening to the BBC. Not now. After driving all night and all day they wanted only sleep. A couple of fitters worked on their vehicles for an hour or so, but by eight p.m. they too were wrapped in their blankets. Nothing moved in the desert; it was as still and silent as the sky. For the best part of twelve hours the members of the patrol slept like dead men, which in some cases was good practice.

Soon after dawn, Gibbon saw Dunn stowing his blankets in the truck, and walked over. "You're a clever chap, Mike," he said quietly. "Maybe you can explain what we were supposed to be up to, yesterday."

Gentle flattery from Gibbon put Dunn on the alert. "What d'you mean?" he asked. He knew what Gibbon meant.

"Of course, I'm only the bloody silly navigator," Gibbon said. "What do I know about the art of war? It seemed to me yesterday that we were in the wrong bloody place at the wrong bloody time, risking the whole bloody patrol for the sake of a twopenny-ha'penny target that wasn't worth five rounds rapid. But of course I could be wrong."

"We did hit the plane," Dunn said.

"Bang goes tuppence-ha'penny," Gibbon said. "Yippee."

"It's not as simple as that."

Gibbon twitched his nostrils. Bacon was frying. "Burnt pig!" he said. "Nothing like it, is there?"

"That's not very funny," Dunn said.

"Nobody ever caught the pig laughing," Gibbon said, "so I'm sure you're right."

They walked to the fire and watched the cook at work. Lampard joined them. "Ah, bacon!" he said.

Gibbon cleared his throat. "I was just thinking about yesterday's little battle," he said.

Lampard stretched and yawned and waited.

"Hot stuff," Gibbon said.

"Just a skirmish."

"I bet the Italians claim a major victory. Big British attack repelled with heavy casualties."

"No doubt. But it was still just a skirmish."

"No heavy casualties?"

That made Lampard look sharply at Gibbon. "You know the score," he said. "We had a spot of bad luck."

"Ah, is that what it was?" Gibbon asked. "A spot of bad luck?"

Dunn said: "For Christ's sake, shut up, Corky."

"Just trying to put myself in the picture, Mike."

Lampard snorted to blow some flies off his beard. "I bet I could find a fuel dump in Jalo Oasis at night," he said. "And an ammo dump. How about it, Corky? You and me in the jeeps with a couple of chaps. You navigate and I steal some fuel, and then we go marauding around the Jebel. Are you on?" Lampard slapped his hands and infuriated the flies.

Gibbon tried to think of a good reason why not, and couldn't. He was saved by Sergeant Davis. "The tyres won't stand it," Davis said.

"Oh well," Lampard said. "Another time, perhaps."

Davis was right. They had to mend six punctures to cover the remaining two hundred kilometres to Kufra, which was a big, sprawling, well-found oasis with plenty of stores, including new tyres. Kufra was an SAS base, so Lampard was able to radio HQ in Cairo and report his arrival. Cairo ordered the patrol home.

CHAPTER TWO

More Bright Breasts

"Ping-pong is not an Olympic sport," Henry Lester said. "What you've got here in the desert is a ping-pong war. That's why the public don't buy it. It's not box-office."

"For Pete's sake, Henry," his wife said. "Put a sock in it and eat your ice cream."

They were in the Gezira Sporting Club in Cairo, having dinner with a mixed bunch of journalists and army officers, and all night Lester had been trying to provoke a winnable argument. He was forty-one, shortish, chunky, with a receding crewcut, and he represented a Chicago newspaper whose readers like to be told just what the hell was going on in the world, short and sharp, without a lot of tap-dancing and blowing bubbles. So Lester held short, sharp, strong opinions about almost everything. "I'll say this for Cairo," he said. "They make good ice cream, and that's the only single, solitary thing to be said for the place."

"Glad you enjoy it," said a lieutenant-general called Saxon. "Just remember you wouldn't be sitting here at all if the British Army hadn't stopped Graziani's attack in 1940."

"Ping!" Lester said. "Wavell counter-attacks, gains a thousand miles. Pong! Rommel arrives, the British lose it all. Ping! Auchinleck attacks, *he* gains a thousand miles. Pong! Rommel attacks and wins half of it back. Ping! Did I forget anyone?"

"Only a few dead men," said a brigadier named Munroe. "A few hundred thousand, that is, counting both sides. Pity they're not here to argue with you, isn't it?"

He was next to a lanky, grey-haired Reuters man, Shapiro. Shapiro said: "Somehow it seems worse, out in the desert. I mean, you look at the bodies and you think: They died for what? For *that*? That sand?" He shrugged.

"Casualty figures don't matter any more," said Saxon. "Not since the last war."

"You can't mean that," Lester said. "Tell me you don't really mean that." Saxon shrugged.

"Arrows on maps," Shapiro said. "Joe Public opens his newspaper and he sees arrows on maps, and he thinks, 'Hey, that's the same as this time last year. *And* the year before. What's goin' on out there?'"

"An extremely difficult war," Munroe said. "That's what's going on."

"Which you make more difficult for yourselves by keeping everything so damned secret," Lester said. "I talked to more generals and admirals and air marshals in Poland and in France than I've ever *seen* here."

"Poland and France fell rather quickly," Saxon said. "As I recall."

"Yes, but Henry's got a point," Shapiro said. "You're never going to win here unless you get big reinforcements. You're fighting Rommel and you're also fighting London and Washington. You've got to get your Western Desert back on the front page."

"They've had victories here," Mrs Lester said. She was sick of the subject.

"We have indeed," Munroe said. "We've won plenty of tank battles, for instance."

"See one burning tank, you've seen 'em all," Lester said. "I've seen fifty burning tanks. Theirs, not ours."

"Me too," Shapiro said. "I took pictures but they were no good. All smoke. Black on black."

"That's a frightful shame," Saxon said, "but we don't actually destroy the enemy in order to make attractive illustrations for the world's press. If you had been in Sidi Barrani when we took it, you would have seen . . ." He paused. "Well, perhaps it's better not to pursue that theme at the dinner table. Suffice it to say that the scenes were unforgettable."

"I believe you," Lester said. "The trouble is, Sidi Barrani has changed hands so often, it's a joke." Saxon drank his coffee and studied the dregs. "You think I'm being unfair, don't you?" Lester said. "The fact is, people in England make jokes about Sidi Barrani. And it's even worse in Chicago. In Chicago they think Sidi Barrani's one of the chorus in *The Desert Song*."

"That's certainly box-office," Mrs Lester said. "I saw it three times."

"Well, I don't know," Munroe said. "You don't want tank battles and you don't want Sidi Barrani. What *do* you want?"

"First choice?" Shapiro said. "A storming advance, a massive victory, and no ping-pong."

"That may take a little time to arrange," Saxon said. "Second choice?"

"Action!" Lester said. "Gung-ho slam-bang excitement. Hollywood's making a monkey out of the Nazis, it's easy, Errol Flynn does it every week. Why can't you?"

"Because it's not the same as victory," Munroe said comfortably.

"No," Shapiro agreed, "but it'll do until victory comes along."

"Otherwise the public is really going to lose interest," Lester said.

"You know, there *are* other wars," Saxon told him. "You're not obliged to stay here. Go to Russia. Go to the Pacific. Go to China."

"I did. I spent two years covering China. Lousy war. Did you know the Chinese have twenty-six ways of spelling dysentery?"

Saxon said: "Is your husband always as dissatisfied as this, Mrs Lester?"

"Henry was born miserable. He came down the birth canal shouting for Customer Complaints."

"They were closed," Lester said. "Typical incompetence. I couldn't even reach my lawyer! Can you believe it? Half-past four in the morning, here I am, stark naked and held against my will in this squalid hospital, and my lawyer doesn't answer his phone!"

"Nothing went right after that," his wife said. "Nothing." The others smiled. She didn't. It wasn't funny to her any more. "Dance with me, Sydney," she said appealingly to Shapiro, "or I'll have the Mafia break both your legs."

"Well, if you're going to use flattery . . ." he said, and led her to the dance floor.

*　　*　　*

The patrol got four days' leave.

All of them spent a lot of it in water. They had dreamed and daydreamed about water all the time they were in the desert: rivers, streams, cloudbursts, running taps, blue-green swimming pools ten feet deep. Fire hoses spouting. Spring showers. Mountain lakes. The spray from watering-cans. Melting ice. There were countless ways to dream about water when the temperature was a hundred and twenty, when the ration was eight pints per day and you felt you were sweating nine pints an hour. During their leave in Cairo the members of the patrol caught up on their fantasies and wallowed in the stuff.

After that, they ate and drank. Rommel's Afrika Armee was waiting beyond the border, but Egypt was technically neutral and there was no rationing in Cairo. The patrol gorged itself on fresh fruit: melons and pomegranates, peaches and grapes, oranges and figs, cherries and pears and plums. Not dates. They'd seen enough of dates. Above all, they ate ice cream. There were places in Cairo that sold ice cream that was such a silky, swift-melting masterpiece of chilled flavour that even the passing thought of it in the depths of the Sahara made a man salivate. The patrol ate a lot of ice cream. Also many plates of egg and chips. Forget Harris. You couldn't beat egg and chips.

At night they drank. The officers drank, in the main, gin and tonic; the other ranks drank beer. Most got drunk but none got dangerously drunk. The worst thing that could happen to a soldier in the SAS was to be kicked out: 'returned to unit', as the official phrase had it. Nobody got drunk enough to risk that.

Sex – which, in the desert, quickly receded in the face of such heavy competition as survival and combat – emerged again in Cairo as a major preoccupation. However, very few of them took a chance on the prostitutes who were making a killing out of the war. This had little to do with any high moral tone in the SAS but a lot to do with avoiding being returned to unit. Those with an irresistible itch for sex simply scratched it and then went for another swim, another dish of ice cream, another plate of egg and chips.

Captain Lampard – unlike many of his fellow-officers – did not rent a flat or a house in Cairo; he preferred to live in his tent in the SAS camp just outside the city. He spent the first morning of his leave writing a report of the raid on Barce and subsequent events. He left it with the adjutant's office to be typed up, took a shower, changed into a fresh lightweight uniform, signed out a jeep, and set off to call on some old chums in a part of British Army Headquarters known as Department SU. Here they had the safe if mournful task of recording the names of those who had fallen in battle, or laid down their lives, or made the supreme sacrifice, or even – modern war being a mechanical and impersonal affair – been killed. Someone with an eye for symbolism had brought back from Benghazi an Italian road sign which said SENSO UNICO, meaning one-way street, and stuck it on the department's door. It soon got taken down, but the name stuck. Lampard was heading for Department SU.

*   *   *

"There you go," said the Army Censor. "Best I can do, I'm afraid."

Henry Lester took the typewritten pages from him and flicked through them. Almost at once he felt a stoniness in his stomach. He recognised the sensation and he hated it. Even after two years of reporting this war he was still not immune to its horrors. He shuffled the pages into a bundle and fanned himself with it. He had expected losses, you always got some losses, but this was a massacre. Blue pencil ran from end to end. Whole paragraphs were wiped out. The bastards hadn't censored his story, they'd carpet-bombed it. "I can't send this," he said.

"That, of course, must be your decision."

"It won't mean a damn in Chicago."

"Possibly not. I've never been to Chicago." That sounded as if it might possibly be construed as a somewhat harsh comment, so the Army Censor added: "I must say I did enjoy your little reference to the Poles."

"So why kill it?"

"Ah . . . policy, old chap, policy."

Lester felt his heart begin to pound. That piece about Polish troops had cost him two days' research. "I want to see your boss," he said.

"Colonel Knibbs? I'll *try*, but . . ." He picked up the phone.

Lester waited an hour and ten minutes outside the Chief Censor's office while, inside, a foul-tempered argument simmered and occasionally boiled over. At last, two disgruntled officers, both much-decorated and deeply sunburned, came out and Lester was shown in. Colonel

Knibbs, tall and thin with half-moon glasses propped on his forehead, was standing by the window, drinking tonic water from the bottle as he looked down at the crowded street. "If you were to shut your eyes and chuck ten bricks out of this window," he said, "I bet you'd hit one enemy agent on the head. Possibly two."

"Can I quote you?"

"Alas, no."

"No." Lester sat down but the seat was hot, so he found a cool one. "Looks to me like I can't say anything." He held up his censored story by the corner, letting it dangle like a small dead animal.

"Well, you certainly can't send *that*. It amounts to an explanation of our loss of Benghazi." Knibbs spoke sharply.

"None of which will come as a surprise to Rommel."

Knibbs finished his tonic and let the bottle drop into a waste basket. "Let me tell you what those two officers were so angry about, Mr Lester," he said. "They got out of Benghazi before it fell. Now, there were many reasons why Rommel was able to take Benghazi so easily, and most of them are in your excellent but doomed report. Superior armour, shorter supply-lines, poor British communications, and so on. But, as I'm sure you know, everyone in the desert listens to the BBC news, and the morale of our men was considerably damaged when some idiot in London announced on the BBC that Benghazi was indefensible, that as a battleground it was impossible to hold."

"Yeah, I heard something about that," Lester said.

"Those officers heard *all* about it. They were desperately trying to organise a confused jumble of men who were tired and hungry and who had lost half their weapons, and who were getting bombed by the Luftwaffe every twenty minutes and shelled by the Italians every ten, and to put the tin hat on it, every hour on the hour the BBC came in loud and clear saying Benghazi hadn't got a hope."

"Not smart."

"They blame me," Knibbs said. "Understandable. I'm the nearest censor. Nothing to do with me, of course. I don't control the BBC. Nevertheless, I think it's time we gave Benghazi a rest."

"What about the Poles?" Lester asked. He pointed to the censored paragraphs. "They weren't there. I put them in for contrast. The Poles fight like hell."

"And if they get captured, the Germans promptly shoot them. Not always, but often enough. So, for the Poles' sake, no tales of Polish ferocity. Not for a while, anyway."

Lester went home. His wife took one look at him and returned to her book. "And you can shut up, for a start," he said.

*   *   *

Lampard sat at a desk in a spare room at Senso Unico and carefully scanned the typewritten sheets listing the names of officers recently killed in action in the Western Desert.

He paid no attention to anyone above the rank of captain; nor was he interested in New Zealanders or Australians or Indians. He was looking for junior officers in English regiments (not Scottish) and only in certain regiments at that – the closer to London, the better. He might accept the Gloucestershires, at a pinch, but not the Durham Light Infantry, and certainly not the Lancashire Fusiliers.

Then he looked at the next-of-kin. Most of the addresses were in England, but a few were in Cairo or Alexandria. After all, Egypt was a neutral country; you couldn't stop somebody's wife living there if she could wangle the passage. India was full of officers' wives, and when their husbands got posted to Egypt the wives sometimes followed. And occasionally a chap met an English girl in Cairo working as a secretary at GHQ or the embassy, and married her.

Lampard made a short-list of nine, all first-lieutenants or captains from decent regiments, with next-of-kin living in Cairo. He studied the addresses and crossed out two. Wrong parts of town. He stared hard at the remaining seven names: Benson, Challis, Fitzroy, d'Armytage, Tait, Spencer and Cox. He didn't like Tait, it looked hard and unpleasant, but he couldn't think why. He crossed it out. There was something wrong with Cox, too. Lampard frowned and rolled the pencil between his fingertips. Of course. There was a Cox in his patrol. No relation, but Lampard was superstitious about such things. Cox was deleted. That left five.

He returned the lists to the sergeant who had produced them, thanked him and left. It was tea time. Perfect.

*   *   *

Most people considered Cairo in midsummer too hot for tennis. After the stupefying, relentless, furnace-heat of the desert, Dunn and Gibbon found Cairo quite mild. They played a couple of sets at the Gezira Sporting Club in order to work up a sweat and go for a swim. The luxury of diving into a few hundred thousand gallons of water had the same appeal as an open brewery to a drunk: they kept climbing out for the sheer pleasure of jumping in again.

They were sitting on the marble edge of the pool, legs in the water, skin glittering like fresh paint, when Dunn said, "Funny thing. All the time we're in the desert I dream about getting back here, and now I'm back here –"

"You can't wait to go out on patrol again."

Dunn thrashed the water to a foam. "Oh well," he said. "I suppose it's not a very bright remark."

"Don't get all depressed, Mike, for Christ's sake," Gibbon said. "You're right, it wasn't very bright, but that's nothing to be ashamed of because after all you're not very bright yourself, are you?"

Dunn stood up, jumped in, heaved himself out and said: "I think I'm fairly bright."

"If you've got to think about it," Gibbon said, "don't bother."

"I passed out tenth from top at my OCTU. Lots of chaps failed OCTU. That shows something, doesn't it?"

"Shows you're a good soldier. Good soldiers aren't bright. Quite the opposite. Good soldiers advance into a storm of withering fire when someone orders them to go and capture something. And guess what happens?"

"They bloody well capture it," Dunn said stubbornly.

"No, they get withered. It's what withering fire does. It withers people." Gibbon looked into the pool and followed a young woman swimming underwater, silver dribbles of air escaping her mouth. "I still haven't got my MC," he said. "It's a swindle."

"Who do you blame?" Dunn asked. "Luftwaffe Intelligence, or our admin?"

"Keep still." Gibbon got up, stood on Dunn's shoulders, balanced for a second, and dived in. The kick-back sent Dunn sprawling.

*　　*　　*

The two Curtiss P-40 Tomahawks were on their way home when they met six Macchi 202s flying in the opposite direction.

The Italian machine was a more advanced fighter, with a greater rate of climb. The Tomahawk was more rugged, could take more punishment, and at lower levels it could out-turn the Macchi. The Tomahawk had six machine guns; the Macchi had two, plus two cannon. Both formations were at about eight thousand feet; at that height the types more or less matched each other in performance. So it came down to the calibre of the pilots. In general, Macchi 202 pilots were good.

Flight Lieutenant Michael Melville led the pair of Tomahawks. He was a Canadian who had flown with the Desert Air Force for nearly a year and he had scored five kills. His wingman was Sergeant-Pilot James Blunt, from Scotland. Six months in the desert, no kills. Destroying enemy aircraft was not his prime job. He was there to guard Melville's tail and leave Melville free to do the damage.

The Italians divided. Three climbed steeply. The other three made straight for the enemy.

Both Melville and Blunt had experienced a flutter of fear when they first saw the pattern of dots and knew what it meant. Melville's heart began a runaway pounding, while Blunt's stomach lurched towards sickness. The sensations were familiar and they vanished quickly. When he first flew on operations, Blunt had been worried by this fact of fear, but Melville had told him that every pilot suffered a bit of twitch before combat, and now Blunt no longer worried. His stomach settled down as the dots began to magnify.

This happened fast. The closing speed was over six hundred miles an hour and the sleek, slippery shape of the 202, like a Spitfire crossed with a 109, soon became clear. Melville's reflector sight was switched on, the gun-trigger on his joystick was set to fire, his straps were tightened, his seat slightly lowered to create more protection from the back-armour. No need for him to tell Blunt anything. They had flown as a team too long for that. Now the enemy colourings were visible: sand-brown with olive-green splotches, white spinner and wingtips. The three climbing fighters showed blue-grey undersurfaces. Blunt automatically searched the rest of the sky. Empty. The odds were six-to-two, but Italian pilots were not famous for long air battles. They usually scrapped briskly and departed. Anyway, if the fight went badly for the Tomahawks the answer was to shove the stick hard forward. The Tomahawk could dive like a truckload of bricks.

Melville led Blunt into a head-on attack which was

calculated to test the Italians' resolve. For a couple of seconds the air sparkled with tracer and then the enemy had whipped past. Melville was bending into a hard left turn and as Blunt followed he felt his machine bounce a little on the Italians' slipstreams.

The turn tightened, dragging his guts down and sucking the blood from his brain. This was all very familiar. Up ahead, Melville's eyes were browning-out too, but he forced the turn until his fingertips prickled and the aircraft was flirting with a skid. When he straightened out, the three Macchis were a mile away, still turning.

The skid that Melville had avoided caught Blunt. Briefly his controls felt sluggish and he knew the wings had lost some of their grip on the air. When he could see clearly again he had drifted far from his leader. At once he searched the sky above. Nothing. That was wrong. He looked at his leader and saw two Macchis pull out of a swooping dive and close on him from beneath. "Break left!" he shouted. And turned hard into them, to scare them off with a long-range burst. He fired, the whole scene blurred and shuddered. When he released the trigger the enemy had gone but the other Tomahawk was in his gun-sight and it was ablaze.

Blunt was so shocked that for a moment he could only stare. A long moment, perhaps four or five seconds. Long enough for an Italian pilot to swing behind him and pump two or three cannon shells into the left wing-root of the Tomahawk. The wing detached itself as if perforated. The rest of the aircraft fell in a fast and giddy spin that nailed Blunt to his seat.

The six Macchis resumed their original formation and circled the columns of smoke while their leader noted the time and place for his combat report. Then they cruised home.

The adjutant waited two days before he emptied Melville's and Blunt's tents, just in case they walked in from the desert. He waited two more days and then sent all their belongings to the Committee of Adjustment in Cairo. He didn't know what happened to the stuff after that and he didn't care. He was just glad the whole sorry affair could be forgotten. In James Blunt's case that was not easy: he had been bright and amusing and on the edge of promotion. However, the adjutant had won his wings in the Royal Flying Corps in 1917, and so he had considerable experience in how to forget men.

The squadron he had joined then was called Hornet Squadron and it was called Hornet Squadron now. It was led by a New Zealander, Squadron Leader Fanny Barton. On the day the two pilots' belongings were packed off to Cairo, Barton got a telephone call from Wing HQ. An hour later he was in the wing commander's office, which was a captured Italian army trailer, slightly bullet-holed, previously owned by a small general. The doors and windows were wide open and a teasing breeze wandered through from time to time, swapping static heat for moving heat. It rattled the papers on the table, papers held down by the nose cone of a shell or a hunk of shrapnel or an infantry dagger, and then it faded away as if exhausted by its own tiny effort. "I was at a meeting yesterday, Fanny," the wing commander said, "and if a vote had been taken, you would have got the chop."

It took a few seconds for the full meaning to sink in. "I'd have lost the squadron?" Barton said.

"You'd be flying a desk in Cairo. The Desert Air Force has a small glut of chaps eminently qualified to do your job and itching to get their hands on it, this being the only fighter war of any consequence outside Russia. Or the Pacific, I suppose. Would you like to go back there? Defend New Zealand from the yellow peril? No, I thought not. And I can tell from your cross-eyed expression that you wish to know why the chop should fall on you."

"I certainly bloody well do."

"It's because your squadron hasn't scored in a month. And the month before that wasn't very brilliant either. Don't kick the table, Fanny," the wing commander said patiently, "you'll only spill the ink."

"Sorry, sir," Barton said. "I meant to kick the waste basket. Must have missed."

"Yes. That's your problem nowadays, isn't it? Missing things."

"We can't hit what isn't there."

"Other squadrons seem to manage it."

"My boys have seen exactly four enemy aircraft in the last three weeks, fired their guns once, couldn't get anywhere near the rest. Jerry's got the legs of us whenever he likes."

"That's not quite the full story, is it?" The wing commander scrabbled among some papers and found a crumpled carbon copy. "I take it Melville and Blunt can be written off?" Barton nodded. "And a couple of weeks ago you lost . . . who was it?"

"Shepherd and . . ." Barton squeezed his face to make his memory work. "Pelican. No, not Pelican, that's what the boys called him. Pelligrin. He was French. They collided on take-off. Sheer bad luck."

"Some squadron commanders are unlucky. At least, that's what yesterday's meeting seemed to think. And the meeting wasn't in a mood to hang around waiting for your luck to change. My guess is you've got a week, at most."

"Jesus Christ," Barton said. He looked as he felt: as if an old friend had kicked him in the ribs. "I'm doing my best, sir. What more can I do?"

"Get lucky." The wing commander screwed up the carbon copy and threw it away. "Nobody's blaming you, Fanny. It's just that we do need results."

Barton usually drove fast, flogging the engine, spinning the wheel, slamming the gear-changes. Not now. Now he drove slowly back to the airfield. Bitterness had sapped his strength and he felt slightly ill.

He had been with Hornet Squadron, off and on, since the war began. He'd taken charge in France when the CO was killed. He'd commanded it in the Battle of Britain and he'd led it on some very hairy sweeps over northern France in 1941 until German flak made a mess of his Spitfire and he'd just scraped home over the white cliffs of Dover, demolishing some farmer's barn in the process. Four months in hospital, then two months as a flying instructor at an OCU, during which he'd nagged and nagged until he got sent to Africa to rejoin the squadron.

At first there had been bags of trade. Lately things were quiet. That wasn't his fault. Men got killed. So what? What did the silly bastards at HQ expect: all profit, no loss?

"They've got scrambled eggs for brains," he told Kellaway, the adjutant.

"Ah. You've heard, then." Kellaway was emptying sand from one of his desert boots. "How the devil does the stuff get in?" he wondered.

"Heard what?" Barton asked.

"Takoradi." Kellaway saw Barton frown, and explained: "The Takoradi flap. Cairo's cocked things up as usual and all of a sudden they've got more kites than pilots at Takoradi. Didn't you know? I thought that's what Wing wanted to see you about."

"Me? No. Why? Nothing to do with us."

"Chum of mine says he heard that the solution to the problem is to send a squadron of fighter pilots to Takoradi, lickety-split."

"Wing said nothing about that."

"He says he also heard we're top of the list."

"Oh, *shit*." Barton slumped into a chair. "If the boys get sent to Takoradi we can kiss goodbye to the squadron. We'll never see them again."

"Well, that's the gen according to my chum, and he should know."

Barton stared at Kellaway's brass buttons. They had been polished so often that the little eagles were worn down to a blur. He must have cut the buttons off his old uniform and sewn them on his tropical tunic. Buttons like that said more than medals. They had seen a lot of service, all through the twenties and thirties. Kellaway had chums in all sorts of useful places, and they helped each other. If one of Kellaway's chums heard Takoradi linked with Hornet Squadron, he would let Kellaway know. Lickety-split.

"I don't suppose your chum had any magic answer to the curse of Takoradi?"

"No." Kellaway curled his forefinger behind his thumb and flicked a large and hairy centipede off his desk. "It's like Whipsnade Zoo in here . . . If I were you, Fanny, I'd try and have a word with Baggy Bletchley."

Barton told Prescott, his signals officer, to find Air Commodore Bletchley as soon as possible. "He's got an office in Alex," Barton said, "but he won't be there." This was true. Prescott's men hunted Bletchley from one airfield to another and reported at last that he was visiting a Hurricane squadron south of Sidi Barrani. When Barton landed there forty minutes later, Bletchley had gone to see some Australians near Buqbuq. Barton followed fast and got him.

They sat under a canvas awning and drank tea made the way the Australians liked it: strong enough to stun a tapeworm.

"You surprise me, Fanny," Bletchley said. "I'd have thought your boys would have jumped at the chance to see a different bit of Africa." It was 110 degrees, and even in sweat-stained khaki drill he still had something of the sleekness of the good career officer.

"From Cairo to Takoradi is nearly four thousand miles,

sir," Barton said. "Which means it's nearly four thousand back again. That's not a fun trip."

"Dear me. And I thought you New Zealanders liked to travel." Bletchley had a gentle, slightly twisted smile which made Barton feel like a schoolboy who had disappointed his teacher. "Ever been to Takoradi, Fanny? On the Gold Coast. Aptly named. Golden beaches, sparkling sea. You fly down the coast to the Niger — one of the truly great rivers of the world — and then turn east over land as green as emerald to a place called Kano. Kano! Not just an ancient African town but a fortress city that lives behind its own battlements! On to Fort Lamy in Chad. A piece of France set down in the heart of the dark continent. To Khartoum, where the two Niles meet and great history has been made. From there it's a doddle, you just follow the river past the splendours of Luxor to the fleshpots of Cairo. Do you realise, Fanny," Bletchley said, "before the war, Imperial Airways flew the rich and the powerful along this route? And now you can have the same unforgettable experience *and be paid for your pleasure?*" He threw up his hands at the wonder of it all.

"What would we fly?" Barton asked. "Hurricanes?"

"Yes. Brand-new."

"And hung with long-range tanks like a bull's balls. You left out a few stops, sir. It's five hundred miles over emer-ald-green jungle to Kano. After Kano there's Maiduguri, *then* Fort Lamy, Geneina, El Fasher and El Obeid, *then* Khartoum. After Khartoum it's still a thousand miles via Atbara, Wadi Halfa and Luxor before you reach Cairo."

"Goodness," Bletchley said. "You've done your homework."

"I met a guy in Tommy's Bar once who'd just done a ferry job from Takoradi. Took him more than a week."

"Ample time to view the scenery."

"He said every stop is a dump. He said Kano to Khartoum is seventeen hundred miles of bugger-all.

Nothing grows, nothing lives. Not a nice place to have engine-failure."

Bletchley finished his tea. He swirled the dregs and looked at the leaves.

"He told me ten per cent of the kites never make it to Cairo," Barton said. "He told me you could navigate by the wrecks."

"Slight exaggeration," Bletchley murmured.

"Takoradi is a bitch, sir."

"Of course it is. But it's the only way we can get fighters to Egypt, short of sending them around the Cape and that takes forever. The Takoradi route is working wonders, Fanny, but it needs more pilots and I've got the job of finding them."

"Don't look at my squadron, sir. We're fighter pilots."

Bletchley read his tea-leaves again. "From what I hear, not everybody is totally convinced of that."

"Things will change, sir. You watch."

"Oh, I shall," Bletchley said. "Believe me, I shall watch very closely."

Barton flew back to his airfield, thinking hard all the way, and sought out his intelligence officer. Schofield was about thirty, a hardworking young architect until the war came along. He was a good listener. Barton said nothing of the risk to his own job, but he spelled out the Takoradi threat. It was essential, he said, that the squadron rapidly made itself indispensable.

Schofield sharpened a pencil. All his pencils were as sharp as needles. "You know the form, Fanny," he said. "This is one of those long pauses in the fighting while we all get our breath back. Our army's not strong enough to attack. Rommel's not ready yet, either. So he's not about to risk his lovely Messerschmitts in the sky. Why should he? He needs them for his next battle. I'd do the same if I were Rommel."

"Wing reckons the other squadrons are making kills."

Schofield shrugged. "They prang the odd bomber, now and then."

"I'd give a crate of Scotch for the odd bomber, now and then."

"You can't shoot them down if they won't take off."

Barton took one of Schofield's pencils and tested it on a fingertip. It was very sharp indeed. He pricked his skin, jerked his hand and snapped the point. "Sorry," he said. Schofield took it from him and began re-sharpening it. "Looks like a dead end," Barton said. He sucked his finger.

"Well," Schofield said, "unless you know a way to get the enemy off his backside, you're somewhat stymied, aren't you?"

Barton went away and brooded over it. Next day he called on the wing commander again. "I know how I can give my boys a crack at the 109s, sir," he said, "but I need your okay."

The wing commander looked and waited.

"It involves doing a bit of strafing," Barton said. "Rather like Ray Collishaw. Wasn't he AOC Western Desert when Italy came into the war? May 1940?"

"June," the wing commander said.

"Now, correct me if I'm wrong, sir, but didn't the Italian Air Force have him hopelessly outnumbered? Five to one? Six to one? Something ridiculous like that. And Collie simply ignored the odds. The RAF went on the attack and never stopped."

"He used to say 'We'll fox 'em'," the wing commander said. "Collie was a great one for foxing the enemy."

"And didn't it work? The poor bloody Italian infantry never knew where they were going to be bombed next! Collie used to look at the map and say, 'We've just attacked here and here, so they'll expect us to hit there and there next, but we won't do that, we'll hit this, that and the other instead'. And the Eye-ties got so twitchy they screamed for their air force to come and protect them."

"Standing patrols," the wing commander said.

"Exactly. Dawn-to-dusk umbrella over the troops. A wicked waste of good fighters and it wore them out like ninepins."

"I don't think ninepins wear out, do they?" the wing commander said. "Still, the Italians certainly gave themselves big servicing problems. They ended up with more kites in the hangars than in the air."

"Collie foxed 'em," Barton said brightly. "So can I."

"What with? The Tomahawk's not a bomber."

"But we can ground-attack the buggers, sir. We can strafe them every ten minutes. Strafe 'em from arsehole to breakfast! They won't like that! They'll scream for fighter cover. Standing patrols of 109s! Then at last my chaps can have a decent scrap."

The wing commander thought that if Barton grew any more enthusiastic, smoke would come out of his ears. "I'll put it up to Group," he said. "Don't hold your breath."

*　　*　　*

Group disliked the idea.

"Barton's bored, is that it?" the group captain said. "Tough titty. We're not here to amuse Barton and his boys." The group captain was suffering from dhobi itch, a form of athlete's foot in the crotch that prickled maddeningly. He could barely restrain himself from scratching.

"Exactly what I told him, sir," the wing commander said.

"There are fundamental flaws in his proposal," said the group captain. "This isn't 1940, Barton's not Collishaw, and the Luftwaffe is not the Regia Aeronautica."

"There's another thing, sir. Barton's squadron is almost out of range of the enemy ground forces."

"That's no problem. I can move him forward. Far forward." The group captain wriggled his backside as hard as he dared. It did no good; if anything it aroused the dhobi itch; but sometimes you had to act whether it worked or not.

"I've been strafed once or twice," the wing commander said cautiously, "but never day-in day-out. They say it's a bit of a bind."

"Do they? Then they're farts." The group captain got up and walked stiffly to the window. "Constant strafing is utterly demoralising. Worse than bombing. Far worse."

"I suppose the Tomahawk is quite good at ground attack."

"Not bad. It certainly *looks* ugly enough, with those bloody silly shark's teeth." The group captain squinted at the bleached-out glare and watched a little dust-devil whirl across the sand, tottering like a drunk, until it spun out of view. "What it boils down to," he said, "is giving Barton a free hand to make a complete bloody nuisance of himself in the hope that he scares up a few Me109s."

"That's about it, sir."

Group decided to sleep on it. Next day he telephoned Air Commodore Bletchley. "Look, sir," he said, "you've known Squadron Leader Barton a long time. What d'you think of him?"

"I like him. He's a typical New Zealander. A blood-thirsty young bugger with precious few scruples. Admirable."

"And this plan of his?"

"Well, it raises two simple questions. What's the worst that can happen? And what's the best that can happen?"

"The second's easy: we get a chance to thin out Rommel's 109s now. Worst? I suppose the absolute worst is bang goes a squadron of Tomahawks."

"Which are obsolete."

There was a pause.

"I've a feeling I've overlooked something," the group captain said.

"Don't get sentimental," Bletchley told him. "Spare me that."

The group captain hung up. He locked the door, took off his shorts and spread some new anti-fungoid cream all over his hectic crotch. He had no faith in the treatment. This was Africa, and Africa always won. Standing in his shirt, with his legs wide apart, he telephoned Wing and gave his decision: transfer Barton's squadron to LG 181 immediately and tell him to begin strafing operations a.s.a.p.

"Right, sir," the wing commander said. "Who knows? This might solve all Barton's problems."

"I expect it will. One way or another."

Delicately, the group captain stepped into his shorts. He winced as he pulled them on. War was tolerable, but war plus dhobi itch was beyond the call of duty.

*   *   *

Major Jakowski's desert-brown open-top Mercedes swept across the parade ground in front of the Italian army barracks in Benghazi and stopped next to the main entrance. Captain di Marco stepped forward with six men and a sergeant. He was the wrong side of fifty, too old for combat, but he knew the desert, he spoke adequate German and therefore he had been made a liaison officer. He was tall, with grey hair turning silver and a serious, unblinking face whose skin was lightly pockmarked like an unripe orange.

Two of his men hurried to open the rear doors of the Mercedes while another two manoeuvred a wheelchair into position for Major Schramm to use.

Di Marco saluted. "Good morning, major."

Jakowski returned the salute with the minimum effort. It was ten a.m. and he was sweating already.

They processed through the barracks. Soldiers stopped

what they were doing and stiffened to attention until the group had passed. Finally it reached a large room, draped with Italian flags and regimental pennants. There were captured Arab swords on the walls and a dais with a twice-life-size bust of Mussolini. A laurel wreath lay around its neck. A dozen chairs upholstered in red leather surrounded a table of polished oak.

"We're a little early," di Marco said. "Would you like some iced lemonade?"

"I'd like some blood," Jakowski said. He wandered off and looked at a photograph of cavalry.

"They raided us again, two nights ago," Schramm said. "Not Barce. Tmimi, near Derna. Just a landing-ground, but they caused a lot of trouble. Could you make it iced tea for me?"

The captain looked at the sergeant, the sergeant nodded at one of the soldiers, and the soldier went out. Jakowski came back. "Horses are useless in the desert," he said.

Time passed. The soldier returned with the iced drinks. A little later, four army officers came in and di Marco made the introductions. The senior Italian officer, a brigadier, invited everyone to be seated. Schramm's wheelchair was eased into place beside the table.

Jakowski had asked for this meeting. He had heard that the Italian army was making its own plans to counter the SAS raids. It made sense to co-ordinate his operation with theirs, whatever it was. He sat back and let the brigadier open the discussion.

Jakowski's knowledge of Italian went little further than restaurant menus. The brigadier had no German. After a couple of minutes, di Marco gently stopped him and began to translate.

"The Italian High Command has examined the concept of maintaining a mobile column in the Sahara in order to intercept enemy patrols, and it has decided that this is not the most efficient way to use its resources."

"Why not?" Jakowski asked.

"Because its resources are small, while the desert is big."

"They'll never succeed if they never try. How can —"

"Be quiet," Schramm said. "Let him finish."

"Instead," di Marco said, "a combined operation of the Italian air force and army is being planned. Long-range reconnaissance aircraft will search the desert all day, every day. When they find an enemy patrol, a unit of Italian paratroops will be flown immediately to that spot."

"They'll be dead before they touch the ground," Jakowski said. "Those SAS jeeps carry heavy machine guns."

Di Marco spoke to the brigadier, and the brigadier replied.

"The paratroops will not be dropped within machine-gun range of the enemy patrol," di Marco said. "They will be dropped several kilometres away."

"In that case they will never catch the enemy," Jakowski said, "no matter how fast they run."

This time the brigadier did not wait for di Marco's question. He rattled off a confident statement as he opened a folder and spread out some large photographs. A jeep-like vehicle was shown descending beneath a cluster of three parachutes. It landed on its wheels, the silk canopies collapsing. Men drove it away.

"You need specially adapted aircraft to do that," Jakowski said. "How many has he got? And how many search aircraft?"

Di Marco came back with the information. At that moment, only one search aircraft was available but more were promised. As for aircraft to deliver vehicles by para-chute: several large troop-carriers were being adapted as a matter of urgency. They would be delivered at the earliest possible opportunity.

"That's too late," Jakowski said. "The threat is *now*. We must act *now*."

The brigadier understood his tone of voice and spoke a few crisp words. "You believe in confronting the enemy," di Marco translated. "We believe in outwitting him."

There was little more to be said. After a few minutes the meeting ended.

On the way out, Schramm said: "I know it's not your style, but I must say their solution seemed to have a lot of merit."

"Too much machinery. Too many things to go wrong."

"Air power can be valuable," di Marco said.

"Look: there's no easy way to do a difficult job. You can't fight the battle from some remote operations room. You've got to get out in the desert and track down the enemy and blow his damned head off, five hundred kilometres from anywhere. It'll take sweat and guts and sheer bloody persistence. Jumping out of aeroplanes is no short cut to success."

They passed yet another garlanded bust of Mussolini. Schramm said, "How often do you change the laurel wreaths?"

"Once a week," di Marco told him. "Fresh laurels are flown in from Italy every Friday, without fail."

"Victory through air power," Schramm said. Jakowski gave a bleak smile. He could afford it. He knew he was right.

*　　*　　*

Lampard involved himself as little as possible with the administrative side of the SAS. He realised that it performed an essential job – men had to be paid, promotions approved, casualties treated, supplies organised, vehicles replaced, records kept – and he was grateful that competent, conscientious officers took care of all that dreadful boring routine stuff. For himself, Lampard wanted none of it. He wanted to return to the desert as soon as possible and start causing more havoc.

However, although he wanted none of it he recognised that he must have some. On his second day back in Cairo he handed his written report on the Barce raid to Captain Kerr. One of Kerr's jobs was to debrief the incoming patrol leaders. Lampard rather liked Kerr. He was a Scot who seemed always to be half-smiling, or on the point of doing so. You felt Kerr was glad to see you again.

It took Kerr two minutes to read Lampard's report and five minutes to reread it. Meanwhile Lampard sat in a corner and flicked bits of broken matchstick at the flies.

"Twenty-seven aircraft destroyed," Kerr said. "That's a fine figure."

"Glad you like it."

"The old man was very pleased. He's away in the desert again, otherwise ... And you got an Italian motor-car to boot. A great big Alfa-Romeo. Tell me more about that."

"What's to tell? We found it, so we snaffled it. Better than walking home."

A bit of matchstick had landed on Kerr's desk. He poked at it with his pencil, cautiously. "Keys in the dash, I suppose," he said.

"What? Oh no. No fear. Corporal Harris fiddled some wires. One of his civilian skills."

"Of course." Kerr squeezed down hard on the end of the bit of matchstick and made it hop. "Too bad about Harris. Was there no warning sign?"

"Well, with hindsight maybe he did look a bit knackered, but then I suppose we all looked a bit knackered."

"Odd that he didn't tell anyone. Knife wound in the stomach, you'd think he'd say something."

Lampard shrugged. "Maybe he didn't want to slow us down. Heart like a lion, Harris. Bags of pride."

"Yes." Kerr sat back. Lampard got up and perched one

buttock on a three-drawer filing cabinet and folded his arms. "Presumably Harris was on his own when he got the wound," Kerr said.

"Seems likely. I reckon he went hunting for Jerry sentries in the dark."

"Ah." Kerr made a note.

"You remember what Harris was like. Extremely fond of blood sports."

"So he was. You don't mention any sentries here."

Lampard yawned and covered his mouth. "Excuse me. Cairo always feels a bit sluggish after the desert ... Sentries. No, I don't mention sentries because I didn't see sentries, probably because Corporal Harris found them first, for which I am very, very grateful."

"Ah." Kerr scribbled. "And you're in no doubt about the cause of death."

"Tony Waterman confirmed it." Lampard rubbed a finger along his jaw. Being clean-shaven still felt strange. "No doctor. Bloody ass of a doctor fell ill at Kufra on the way out. Tony knew a bit of first aid, so I asked him to take a look."

"And where was the wound?"

"Oh ... about here." Lampard pressed his stomach to the right of where a belt-buckle would have been. "Does it matter?"

"It might, it might. You're recommending a decoration, after all. They'll want to know what killed him."

Outside, the endless racket of crowds and traffic and street-selling rose above Cairo in a fog of noise. Inside, a distant telephone rang and rang with the maddening persistence of an idiot child. Nearer, a man coughed.

"Too bad about Waterman," Kerr said.

"Bloody Stukas," Lampard said. "Once they find you it's all a matter of luck. Tony was unlucky."

"The fortunes of war." Kerr never lost his half-smile. Sometimes it was sad, sometimes not, but it was always there. "Tell me about the Stukas. How did they attack you?"

"Normal way. They fell on us from a great height." Now Lampard had found a rubber band and was playing with it like a catapult. "We got dive-bombed by the pilot and when he pulled out we got strafed by his rear gunner. Standard practice. Remember?"

"Happy days," Kerr said. He too had been a patrol leader until severe jaundice put him in hospital. He flicked through the pages of the report again. "Only the wireless truck was hit, I see. That was lucky, wasn't it?"

Lampard stretched the rubber band too far and it snapped. "Sorry," he said. "Don't know my own strength."

"It matters not." Kerr reached in a drawer and tossed a small handful of bands onto his desk. "How many Stukas were there?"

"Oh . . . several. If you can count the flies in this room while I chase you with a club, you've got your answer. I had other things on my mind."

"So Jerry hammered you pretty hard," Kerr said. Lampard grunted. "But he only got the wireless truck," Kerr said again.

"Everybody else found some cover. They jumped us in the open and we ran like hell. Went tearing up this wadi and got inside some little cliffs. Under the overhangs. Tony was a bit slow, I suppose."

Kerr straightened the pages and banged a staple through the corner. "Twenty-seven kites," he said. "Bloody good show."

Lampard placed two letters on the desk. "Next-of-kin," he said. "Will you forward them?"

"I'll forward one," Kerr said. "Harris's family is in London. The other you can deliver yourself, if you wouldn't mind. Mrs Waterman lives quite near here." He wrote on the envelope and handed it back. "Nice lady, so I'm told. Rotten luck for her."

Lampard read the address and nodded sombrely. He picked up his cap and spun it on his finger. "No fun for me, either," he said.

*　　*　　*

Even in North Africa little children like to play in the sand, which was why the infants' school on the outskirts of Derna had a sandbox. The building had lost half its roof, and two walls were ventilated by shell-holes big enough to drive a tank through. This was proved by the remains of a burned-out British tank inside a classroom. But the remains of the infants' school suited General Schaefer's staff. They kicked out an Italian signals unit and took over. A few tarpaulins made a discreet tent over the sandbox, and the sandbox – fifteen feet by six – was perfect for a multicoloured sand-map of seven hundred miles of coast-line, with Derna more or less in the middle.

The sand-map was a work of art. It began with Alexandria (big black blob) on the extreme right and traced the coastline westwards through El Alamein and all the old familiar battle honours, Mersa Matruh, Sidi Barrani, Sollum, Bardia, Tobruk and Gazala, which marked the line that separated the opposing armies. West of Gazala came the most populated part of Libya, the Jebel el Akhdar, which means Green Mountain. It was peppered with bases and aerodromes and landing-grounds: Bomba and Tmimi, Martuba and Derna, Slonta and Barce, all across the Jebel to Benghazi with the airfields of Benina and Regima and Berka clustered around it; then southward down the bulge, past Beda Fomm and Antelat to Agedabia, which was about as far as the British got on their last offensive, until Rommel caught them off balance and shoved them back to Gazala. (Tripoli, Rommel's big supply port, was a further four hundred miles westward.) The Mediterranean was blue sand, the Jebel was a bump of green sand, and all along the coastal strip there were more red stars and blue squares and silver circles than you could count, each telling part of the recent history of Rommel's Afrika Armee. It was a hell of a good sand-map.

General Schaefer had ordered this conference on behind-the-line security, which everyone knew meant insecurity. He had summoned the officers responsible for protecting sections of the seven-hundred-mile stretch of coastline. They numbered thirty-seven, and they sat on ammunition boxes while Schaefer stood beside the sand-map and put them in the picture.

"It's simple, gentlemen," he said. "While we are preparing to win at the front, we are losing at the rear."

That got their full attention. Schaefer was a hard, unsmiling man. He had a small silver plate in his skull, compliments of a French artillery attack at Verdun in 1916, and his work-rate occasionally drove his staff officers to a state of collapse. It was said that he had been transferred here from Russia because of a row with Hitler. Schaefer had won the debate but (inevitably) lost the argument. Now he was telling them they were losing in Africa! Major Jakowski (third row, second from left) was impressed.

"Losing does not mean lost," Schaefer said. "It means the enemy is doing far better than he should. And that must stop." An aide handed him a clipboard. "I am aware that the enemy has been raiding behind our lines for a long time. But this year the raiding has intensified." He handed the clipboard back. "I won't waste time with statistics. Aircraft destroyed. Fuel-dumps destroyed. Vehicle parks destroyed. *Men* destroyed. Look down here. Each red star is an airfield raid. Each blue square is a fuel-dump raid or, worse still, a fuel-tanker destroyed. Each silver circle is a raid on an ammunition-dump. Of course the enemy raiders have suffered losses too. But *they* are losing a few jeeps and a handful of men while *we* lose a squadron of fighters.

So it must stop. And you are here today to help me find a way to stop it."

It turned out to be a long day.

Many officers had prepared proposals in advance and they submitted these ideas along with plans, maps, charts and graphs to support them.

The first man up proposed a total sunset-to-dawn curfew all along the coast road; during curfew, heavily armed motor patrols would be free to shoot anything that moved. At first this appealed to many, but then the questions began. What happens when something is needed urgently at the front? What about our Italian allies, notorious nightbirds? How many motor patrols would you need to be sure of catching every raid? Enthusiasm faded. The next suggestion was for the floodlighting of all aerodromes and similar targets. It was pointed out that the RAF would enjoy bombing illuminated targets. Yes, the officer agreed, that was a factor; but on radar warning of incoming bombers the lights would of course be switched off until . . .

Until the SAS co-ordinated its raids with RAF attacks?

"I never claimed it was perfect," the officer said.

"Very wise," General Schaefer said. "Thank you."

Next up was a newly-arrived officer with a plan to recruit all the Senussi Arabs as a well-paid corps of observers and informers. Imagine the effect of two hundred thousand informers and bounty-hunters, and all for what? A couple of million marks?

He stopped because Schaefer had raised his hand. "Butcher Graziani conquered these people in the twenties by slaughtering them. The Arabs loathe the Italians and they hate us because if we win the Italians will stay here. The Arabs will take your money and still help the British. So would I, if I were an Arab. Next?"

Next came electrified barbed wire plus packs of Rottweiler guard dogs. After that, a proposal to build a string of big, raid-proof compounds for all Axis forces in the coastal strip. Then a plan for standing patrols by the Luftwaffe, dusk to dawn. Someone asked: "How can the Luftwaffe find a raiding party in the dark, let alone identify it?" This led to a discussion of airborne searchlights and the use of paratroops. The idea died.

Slump. Only the flies remained brisk.

Jakowski had ignored all this chatter and concentrated on the sand-map. He had never liked it. The thing was perfect, but it was all wrong.

There were a couple of buckets of sand on the floor behind General Schaefer, left over from the map-making. Jakowski had always been impetuous; it was one reason he was still only a major among these colonels and brigadiers. He walked behind Schaefer and grabbed a bucket. "With your permission, sir?"

Schaefer waved him on. Jakowski stepped into the Mediterranean. "We've all been looking in the wrong place!" he declared. "*That's* where the trouble comes from!" He swung the bucket and shot the sand over the top of the Jebel el Akhdar and out of the sand box. It spread wide and fan-like, lapping the boots of the front row. There was silence as he got the second bucket and flung out a further forty thousand square miles of Sahara. "The way to stop these raids is to hunt them down in the desert *before* they can do any damage. Give me five hundred men and fifty vehicles, sir, and I guarantee results."

General Schaefer almost smiled. "What is your name, major?" he asked.

An hour later Jakowski flew back to Barce. In the mess he met Schramm, propped up on his new crutches. Jakowski described the conference. "Don't say he's given you five hundred men," Schramm said.

"No, that wasn't possible," Jakowski said, "but he's given me a hundred and fifty, plus thirty desert vehicles. It's a start. In fact we start tomorrow. Into the desert."

"Would you like some advice?" Schramm asked.

"No." It was an impulsive reply, but now Jakowski couldn't take it back.

"No," Schramm said. "I didn't think you would."

Jakowski linked his fingers behind his back, squared his shoulders, pulled in his stomach and made his knuckles crack. "Schaefer asked me who would be in charge of airfield security here while I'm away. I recommended you."

"What a kind thought," Schramm said. "Hurry back, won't you?"

*   *   *

Captain Kerr could smell the presence of a serious lie; literally smell it. It smelled to him like bad fish, like fish that had begun to rot. This is a foul and disgusting smell and he had learned to control and conceal his instant revulsion. Nevertheless, the smell was indisputable.

Kerr was rational and intelligent and he resented being bullied by his senses when there was no obvious cause, so he consulted the family doctor. "Olfactory hallucinations," his doctor said with the utter confidence of a man who, by lucky chance, has read all about it in a new book only the night before. "Some people hear things, some see things, others taste things. You smell 'em. Perfectly harmless."

"Good God," Kerr said, weakly.

"Jolly useful in your line of work, I should think."

Kerr was a solicitor and he defended a lot of criminals. *Alleged* criminals. Like all solicitors he was an officer of the court with an obligation to the truth. If a defendant came to him and said, "This is the story I'm going to tell in court," Kerr refused to represent him. He was a serious young man and a good lawyer, and word soon got around that if you wanted Mr Kerr to defend you it was smart to assure him you were telling the truth.

As a result Kerr made a living and heard a lot of lies.

Small lies didn't worry him. It was the gross distortions

of fact, the lies that stood truth on its head, which made him angry. He usually knew them when he heard them: most people are bad liars. And quite soon he began to notice this sudden whiff of stinking fish in his office as a new client told his tale. He trusted his judgement. When the case came to court, Kerr had a way of slightly lowering an eyebrow, or sometimes he might put a slightly different inflection in his voice. It was enough. The magistrates knew. He knew they knew. He had done his duty by his client and by the court.

Came the war. As soon as he put on khaki the olfactory hallucinations stopped. Kerr had almost forgotten what bad fish smelt like until he sat listening to Jack Lampard describe the deaths of Corporal Harris, stabbed by a German sentry, and Lieutenant Waterman, bombed by Stukas. The stench of dishonesty was in his nostrils again. He actually recoiled an inch, so great was the shock; and then he disguised the movement with a sympathetic nod.

After Lampard had gone, Kerr sat and wondered what to do. He could always question Mike Dunn or Corky Gibbon, perhaps even Sergeant Davis or Corporal Pocock. What if their answers proved that Lampard had been lying? What then? If he took no action it was all a waste of effort. If he took action, the trust between Lampard and his patrol was badly damaged. Obviously something peculiar had happened out there in the blue. On the other hand, the raid on Barce airfield had been highly successful: aerial reconnaissance showed many burnt-out wrecks. So Lampard had told the truth about *that*. Kerr tossed Lampard's report into his out-tray and put the matter out of his mind.

But it refused to go; it drifted back and made a quiet nuisance of itself. He opened a desk drawer and took out a battered copy of *The Seven Pillars of Wisdom*. He found the story of the battle at Tefila, with T. E. Lawrence's account of how he got a DSO on the strength of a report he himself had written 'mainly for effect'. Someone had underlined Lawrence's final remark: *We should have more bright breasts in the Army if each man was able without witness to write out his own despatch.* Kerr grunted. He took the report from the out-tray and stuffed it in his briefcase.

*   *   *

It took Jack Lampard ten minutes to walk from Captain Kerr's office to Mrs Waterman's address. He hated every minute of it. Unpleasant people kept trying to sell him things: fly whisks, Arab chewing gum, sun glasses, perfume, shaving brushes, cigarettes, hand-tinted pornography and twenty other sorts of rubbish. They ran backwards in front of him, shouting upwards, they smiled with broken and blackened teeth, they shoved and kicked each other and, worst of all, they *touched* him, pawing his arms and stroking his shoulders until their dirty little hands infuriated him and he struck out. But they were almost always too quick. He hit only one, an insistent, whining cripple whose nose had been half eaten away by disease. Lampard's knuckles smacked his nose and sent him sprawling, and Lampard strode on, feeling stained and contaminated.

If the Arab street-salesmen were bad, the general noise was worse. Cairo was always clogged with traffic. Cars with broken exhausts revved and roared as they tried to fight their way through tangles of foul-tempered camels and overloaded donkeys and stinking motor-bikes and people, people, always too many people, all of them shouting to make themselves heard above the racket of the shouting of the rest. Those with horns or hooters or whistles used them ceaselessly. Radios blared. Lampard didn't like noise, filth or tradesmen at the best of times. Cairo was loud and squalid and a constant pest. He clenched his teeth and thought of the purity of the desert.

Mrs Waterman took a long time answering the doorbell of her flat. When she did she was barefoot, her black hair was tousled and she was wearing a white cotton frock misbuttoned down the front. "I beg your pardon," Lampard said brusquely. He hadn't wanted to come in the first place.

She held the door handle while she rubbed the back of her right calf with her left foot. "You're the best-looking man I've seen all day," she said, "but then you're the only man I've seen all day so don't get excited about it." Her voice was Home Counties English, pleasant enough but with a touch of huskiness that added strength. She looked twenty-three.

"Captain Lampard. I've come —"

"Don't tell me why you've come, I shan't remember and I honestly don't care." She walked away, arms outstretched for balance because she was on the balls of her feet. It brought out the best in her legs. "I've already had the chaplain and a man from some benevolent fund and a rather grim type who asked if Tony kept a diary and two army widows who seemed to want to form a *club*, God help us, so you see I've been thoroughly taken care of. Debriefed. Isn't that the word?"

Lampard felt awkward, left standing in the doorway, so he came in and shut the door. "Yes. Debriefed."

She sat on a couch and tucked her legs under her. "Very silly word," she said. "You couldn't debrief me if you tried, could you?"

"Couldn't I?" He found a chair.

"Certainly not. I haven't worn any briefs since the really hot weather began. It was one of the things that used to make Tony very nervous. One of the many things."

"Oh?" That reply seemed inadequate, so he said, "Your husband was a brave and conscientious officer, Mrs Waterman. He will be much missed."

"Not by me." It was said flatly.

"I see." But all that Lampard saw was her good looks. Although she didn't smile, hadn't smiled since she opened the door, Mrs Waterman – grey eyes, clear white skin, neat, square-boned features – was attractive. "This has been a very painful time for you, Mrs Waterman," he said.

"Look, if you can't talk like a normal human being you might as well buzz off. In the past few days I've heard enough platitudes to stuff a sofa. What's this?"

Lampard, now thoroughly rattled, had got up and given her his letter. "I've brought it, so you might as well read it," he said. He went past the couch and stood at the french windows.

She read the letter. "You make him sound like Lawrence of Arabia. Tony wasn't like Lawrence of Arabia. *Florence* of Arabia, perhaps. Old Flo. Dear old Flo." She stood up and gave him back the letter. "Tony was a bit of an old woman, really."

This angered Lampard. "The man was a gallant comrade," he said sharply, "and a splendid servant of king and country."

"And a lousy husband."

Lampard tore the letter in half, and then in half again.

"Bet you can't do it three times," she said. He tore the letter again. "Now give me the pieces," she said.

"Go to hell," Lampard said.

She grabbed his hand and tried to prise the fingers open, but he squeezed harder until she suddenly stooped and bit him on the wrist. "You bitch!" he shouted in a curious thin, high-pitched voice; but his grip had relaxed and now she had the pieces of paper. "Happy New Year!" she cried, and flung them in the air. "Goodbye, Tony, it wasn't nice while it lasted, so thank God it didn't last long."

Blood was running down Lampard's fingers. "Well I'm damned," he whispered.

"That looks nasty," she said. "You're lucky I'm a nurse. Come this way."

ingly he followed her into the bathroom, where filling the basin with hot water. She added anti- and ordered: "Stick your hand in there and don't it." He obeyed. They stood and looked at each other in the mirror for the best part of a minute. "I don't know why you're so angry," she said. "I didn't kill him."

"It took me two hours to write that letter," Lampard said.

She pulled down his head and kissed him on the mouth. He took his hand from the water. "You'll probably die," she said. "You know what nurses' teeth are like. Riddled with plague."

"In that case I might as well die in bed."

They spent much of the day in bed. He bled a little onto the sheets, but not much.

Before he left, he asked: "Why on earth did you marry Tony if you didn't like him?"

"Because he kept asking," she said, "and I got sick of saying no."

*   *   *

In April 1942 the British were losing badly, the Americans were still stunned by Pearl Harbor and the Russians were in the most terrible mess. It was, as has been said, Hitler's finest hour.

His allies the Japanese weren't doing badly, either. They had just conquered an empire that reached from the boundaries of India to within striking distance of Australia, and they had done it all in three months, at virtually no cost. They had taken Hong Kong in December, Malaya in January and Singapore in February. The fall of Singapore was the biggest single surrender in British military history. The Japanese also sank a battleship, the *Prince of Wales*, and a battle-cruiser, the *Repulse*; destroyed an entire Anglo-Dutch fleet; and sent a fleet of their own marauding into the Indian ocean. This was not good for the prestige of the white man.

In Cairo, that prestige had already taken several hard knocks. Three months earlier, in January 1942, the new and exciting German general, Rommel, had surprised the British with a sudden assault that sent them scrambling back through Libya until they had lost two-thirds of all the land gained in *their* previous offensive. Rommel was now at the Gazala Line, getting his breath back, but nobody expected him to stay there long. Egypt was his goal; Egypt and the Canal. Britain would fight, of course, but Britain's recent record was not encouraging.

In 1941 British forces had failed to save Greece – their withdrawal was another Dunkirk – and then failed to hold Crete. The Royal Navy had lost command of the Mediterranean. Italian frogmen sank two battleships in Alexandria harbour and German U-boats sank the carrier *Ark Royal* and the battleship *Barham*. Malta was under siege, battered daily by the Luftwaffe.

Meanwhile, there were no lessons to be learned from the poor bloody Russians. At the start of 1942 their generals had launched several counter-offensives. Stalin knew no flexibility; his orders were to advance at all costs. The attacks failed disastrously. This left the German army dominant. It besieged Leningrad in the north, it was poised to take Moscow in the centre – at one stage German troops reached the tram terminus and actually saw the golden domes of the Kremlin – and it threatened the oilfields of the Caucasus in the south. A glance at the map showed that, once he had the Caucasus, Hitler could swing south through Persia to Iraq and deprive Britain of an enormous amount of oil. It was no daydream. Iraq had rebelled against British control in the summer of 1941, and British forces had had to be sent from Egypt to put down the revolt.

All these developments were watched with great interest

by those Egyptians who could spare the time from toil (probably no more than one in a hundred). Egypt was neutral. The British were there strictly according to treaty agreements. Thanks to the war, some Egyptians were making fat profits, but that didn't mean the British were especially welcome and they certainly weren't universally popular. It even happened that when street demonstrations took place, the name of Rommel got shouted.

In these troubled times there was not a lot the British embassy could do to enhance prestige, but it did what it could. It held a reception to show the world that, contrary to rumour, everything was business as usual. Black tie and decorations.

Mr and Mrs Henry Lester got an invitation. He was in a foul temper and didn't want to go. She did. They went, and when they arrived at the embassy gates he had forgotten to bring the invitation.

"Bonehead," Mrs Lester said, and didn't care who heard.

The embassy official was polite but unshakeable and, with some Royal Marines behind him, certainly immovable. Entry was by printed invitation only. No exceptions. A matter of security, you understand.

They stood aside and watched a stream of guests go in while Lester hunted through pockets he had already hunted through. "Why didn't you ask me if I had it when we left?" he complained.

"Same reason I didn't brush your hair and take you to the bathroom."

He gave up. "It's no damn good."

"Pure Freud. You never wanted to come, and now you've got your wish."

"Shut up and let me think."

"News flash: Henry Lester thinks. The world holds its breath."

A white Bentley pulled up with no more sound than the

purring of a well-fed tiger and the chauffeur went around to open the rear door. Lester hustled forward. The man who got out was about forty, sleek as a shark in a white dinner jacket, but with a chubby face, cheeks like polished apples and wide-awake eyes. He wore a discreet row of medal ribbons. Lester said: "Listen, you don't know me, I'm Henry Lester, special correspondent, Chicago *News*, but I wonder —"

"How do you do? How *do* you do. What an enormous pleasure and privilege to meet one of our American chums." They were shaking hands and the chauffeur was getting back in the car. "Ralph Malplacket. You must come and have a drink. Is that your wife? Delightful —"

"Sure, but I was wondering, you see I forgot the goddamn invitation so if you could lend me your car for ten minutes just to —" The Bentley purred away. "Oh, forget it," Lester said.

Malplacket had a large and impressive nose, hooked like an eagle's, which buttressed the rest of his face. He tipped his head back and looked at Lester as if trying to get him in clear focus. "Stay there," he said. He strode over to the embassy official and in a high, clear voice, said: "You haven't let Chubichov through, have you?"

"Chubichov?"

"No, no. Chubi*chov*. Chubichov with an f, not a v. Or he may call himself Bulstrode. You know who I mean?"

"Um . . ." The embassy official glanced at a Marine, who held all the invitation cards of guests so far admitted. "Actually, I'm not sure —"

"Good God, man." Malplacket gazed down his craggy nose. "You mean you don't know? You know *me*, I hope. My father's Lord Blanchtower, I'm seconded to MI at MEHQ." He took a document like a miniature passport from his breast pocket, half-opened it and then thrust it back. "Chubichov? Yes or no?"

More guests were arriving. The official felt the pressure

of Malplacket's fog-lamp stare. He pointed to a Marine. "This man has a record of all the guests who've been admitted, sir," he said hurriedly. "Good evening madam, good evening sir . . ."

Malplacket waved away the Marine's clipboard with its typed lists of names, some ticked, some not. "Give me the *actual invitations*," he said. "I am in no mood to be trifled with . . . Thank you." He took the large bundle of cards and turned aside. For half a minute he flicked through them, occasionally selecting and scrutinising, once or twice holding a card up to the light. He returned the bundle. "Very lucky," he told the embassy official. "*Very* lucky. But you will not forget that name?" He cocked his head.

"Um . . ." The man had to think. "Chubichov."

"Chubi*chov*. With an f. And now if you will be so kind as to admit my good friends Mr and Mrs Victor Stanhope of the Standard Oil Corporation . . ." He took an invitation card from his pocket and waved the Lesters forward. The official's eyebrows went up. "I thought . . ." he began. "Misunderstanding, dear boy," Malplacket said. "Not doing terribly well today, are you? Try and pull yourself together and I'll say nothing to the ambassador. Bulstrode. Have you made a note of that?"

Strolling about the embassy gardens were the brightest and the best of Cairo society, plus quite a few of the worst if they were powerful enough (this was no time to be nitpicking about your friends; the big thing was to make it look as if you had lots of them). A regimental band played Gilbert and Sullivan. (Rommel? Who's he?) Malplacket signalled a waiter and distributed champagne. "Well, we certainly have to thank you, Mr Malplacket," Mrs Lester said. ·

"Not a bit. My pleasure. Hands across the ocean."

They drank to that. "May I ask you a question?" Lester said. "Who is Chubichov, pronounced Chubichof?"

"My tutor at Oxford."

"Oh. Is he dangerous?"

"If he were here now, you would find him absolutely terrifying. He died in 1935. I say: there's Evelyn Waugh. I need him for my cricket team. Excuse me."

They watched him stride away, foxtrotting between the clusters of guests and delicately waving a silk handkerchief at someone out of their sight. "The English nobility," Lester said. "Ten centuries of inbreeding. Perfect manners and scrambled brains."

"Is that so? Your brains weren't winning any prizes five minutes ago."

"Okay, so I made a mistake. You never made a mistake?"

She gave him a short, hard stare and turned her back on him. He realised what a mistake that question had been. The day itself had been depressing, long and sweaty and full of failure, and now he was ready to hit someone. "Cricket is a *man's* game," he said, speaking to her back as if it were a dartboard, "and Evelyn is a *woman's* name. Dumb I may be, but in any language that doesn't add up. Right?"

"It's a man's name too, in England. Evelyn Waugh happens to be a famous English novelist. Why don't you go and interview him?"

"Oh, sure." He turned and stared at the bandstand. "He can tell me how the British got onto this sticky wicket. That's gonna fascinate them in Chicago, isn't it? A pansy foreign novelist with a fountain-pen bigger than his dingaling, lecturing the American people on cricket." Lester found himself talking to a passing brigadier and his wife. "Don't blame me," he told them. "It was her idea." He gestured towards his wife, but when they looked where he gestured, nobody was there.

"Can we be of any help?" the brigadier's lady asked.

"My wife just ran off with the ambassador's cook," Lester said. "Little runty Arab, black teeth, no hair, bad squint, drags his right leg. You seen him hanging around?"

The brigadier shrugged. "Cairo's full of chaps like that, isn't it?" he said.

Lester didn't look for his wife; he knew she would be with the people from the American embassy, probably talking about the latest Hollywood movies. Instead he found the bar. Amazingly they had bourbon. At last something had gone right on this day. It was only a small thing, so he made it as big as the glass would hold and settled down to drink the evening to death.

Meanwhile, in another part of the forest of guests, Lieutenant-General Saxon was strolling with Brigadier Munroe. They found a couple of chairs under a shady tree and relaxed.

"What a grisly mob," Munroe said. "Half of them are racketeering crooks and the other half are the more degenerate, backstabbing relatives of King Farouk."

"And that's only the women," Saxon said.

"I find this sort of thing very heavy going. Sooner be out in the desert making enemies than stuck here making friends."

Saxon grunted agreement. They sprawled, in an officer-like way, and watched the chattering guests. "My God!" Saxon said. "See that chap? There . . . Waving his arm. Nose like a parrot."

"Parrots don't have noses," Munroe said.

"He was a priest at Dunkirk."

Saxon got up and walked across to Ralph Malplacket. "Excuse me, Father," he said. "My friend over there is feeling a little run-down. I wonder if you could bless him."

"For fifty guineas I'll sanctify him." Malplacket stared at Saxon's face, and then looked away. "You were on the beaches, weren't you? You shared your omelette with me."

"Half an omelette, actually. Stone-cold, too."

"But quite delicious. How did you get home?"

"Destroyer. And you?"

"I didn't. Oh dear . . . Forget I said that. I wasn't really there, you see."

Saxon introduced him to Brigadier Munroe. "This isn't Father Oliver," he said, "and he wasn't at Dunkirk giving supreme unction or whatever it's called to a lot of dying soldiers."

They shook hands and sat down. "I'm Ralph Malplacket. Actually it was rifle oil," he said. "I flatter myself that those who were still conscious died a little happier for my imposture."

"You certainly knew the script," Saxon said.

"I drew on my old college grace a good deal. Ten seconds of Latin is enough for anyone, isn't it?"

"If you weren't a priest," Munroe said, "what were you?"

"Can't say, I'm afraid. Deathly secret."

"Ah." Connections formed in Saxon's brain: tiny electrical circuits responded to demands he did not know he was making: memory raced through ten million images and discarded all but one, enlarged it, sharpened it, offered it. "Of course," he said. "You're Lord Blanchtower's son."

"I believe there was some debate about that, at the time. But yes, I shall inherit. If I'm not shot first."

"He's in the government, isn't he? Your father," said Saxon.

"Blanchtower is Minister for Enthusiasm. Not really. His proper title is Minister for Public Affairs, but that is generally thought to be one of Winston's little jokes. Anyway, his task is boosting the enthusiasm of the British people. Good news would help. The War Cabinet believes there is always good news somewhere, if you look hard enough."

"Rubbish," Munroe said.

Malplacket nodded. They were near a tree. He got up and reached into its branches and brought out a bottle of champagne, half-full. "I knew the ambassador's drink would run out early," he said.

"Desert war isn't like any other war," Munroe said. "London hasn't got the foggiest idea. They think it's all golden sands up the blue. Precious little golden sand in the Western Desert, I can assure you. Mainly dust, grit and flies."

"Also heat," Saxon said. "The heat can be quite hot."

"Dust, grit, flies, heat, sweat and bits of dead soldier," Munroe said. His face was completely expressionless.

"You've forgotten the wind," Saxon said.

"I'll never forget the bloody wind. It's the bloody wind that blows the dust and the grit and the flies and –"

"You're absolutely right," Malplacket said briskly. "Nobody in London understands. All they see is two armies each on the end of a piece of elastic."

"Rather like a yo-yo, would you say?" Saxon asked.

Munroe cheered up fractionally. "Or ping-pong? More like ping-pong, surely."

"You should meet Henry Lester, Mr Malplacket," Saxon said. "Henry Lester has tremendous enthusiasm for the desert war."

"Lester? I believe I've met him, here, tonight."

"Hank the Yank," Munroe said. "He can split an infinitive from twenty yards with his eyes shut. Henry's the man for you."

*   *   *

Flight Lieutenant Patterson had never trusted Air Commodore Bletchley. He had never been required to trust him: when they first met, in France in 1939, Patterson was a mere pilot officer, saw Bletchley only on his occasional visits to the squadron and rarely spoke to him. But there was something too suave about Bletchley for Patterson's comfort. Patterson came from a wealthy Glasgow family and he had had a privileged, protected childhood; nevertheless he was Scottish and the wealth came from coal mining, so he had no time for anyone who looked as if he might have a soft handshake. In France, Patterson had watched Bletchley take sherry with his squadron leader and had thought: *smooth bastard, that one*. But then Patterson had never really trusted anybody over the rank of group captain. He suspected that you had to be very suave to climb so high.

In fact Bletchley had a firm, dry handshake. Patterson discovered this when he got invited to lunch at Shepheard's Hotel in Cairo. He also noticed that Bletchley had aged ten years in the past two. The smooth face was now cracked by sun and worry and the sleek brown hair now was cropped and showing grey. But the smile hadn't changed.

They ordered drinks. The table was set for three, but if Bletchley wasn't going to explain then Patterson wasn't going to ask. Instead he said: "This is extremely kind of you, sir."

"Not at all. Thank our well-beloved sovereign King George the Sixth, he's paying for lunch. Perhaps I'll provide the tip. D'you know, Patterson, my conscience has never been easy about you, ever since I lost a bet with a fellow called Roberts. Titch Roberts. That was during the Battle of Britain. Your lot were taking a bit of a pasting and Titch Roberts made some fatuous remark about how it was always darkest just before the dawn. Words to that effect. Anyway it annoyed me. I hadn't had much sleep for days, chasing around trying to get blitzed airfields operational again, and I knew how bad things really were, so I bet him that come Michaelmas there wouldn't be an original pilot left flying in your squadron. Bet him a tenner. Gruesome thing to do, wasn't it? Makes me ashamed just to think of it."

"When's Michaelmas?" Patterson asked. Their drinks arrived.

"September 29th."

"You nearly won, then."

They touched glasses and drank.

"I never got the chance to pay up," Bletchley said. "Titch fell off his roof one night when he was trying to put out an incendiary bomb. Typical piece of incompetence. How that man got to be a group captain is beyond me. On the other hand, if he hadn't been such a fathead he would have left the bomb to the fire brigade, so perhaps it all makes a kind of sense."

"Natural pruning, sir."

"Exactly. And here, from the land of the prune, comes Captain Hooper. Now we can eat."

The man who joined them was a pilot in the United States Air Force. This did not surprise Patterson: he had noticed several American airmen in Cairo and there were a lot of American aircraft, especially bombers, in Egypt. Hooper was a small, neat man whose exact age was hidden behind a broad and very black moustache that lay across his upper lip like a neatly clipped hedge. Patterson rather envied that moustache. Twice he had tried to grow a decent moustache, but the results made him look furtive rather than virile so he shaved them off. Hooper's moustache made him look like a Western lawman. His expression was watchful and he had unusually clear eyes. Patterson noticed that he rarely blinked.

After the introductions Bletchley said: "Captain Hooper is going to fly with us."

"Yes?" Patterson said politely.

"I need desert combat experience," Hooper explained. "Have you had any?"

"A bit." Evidently Hooper wanted to hear more, so Patterson said: "All I can tell you is the sun fills half the sky and it's usually lousy with Huns."

"Ah." Hooper seemed quite satisfied with that.

During lunch Bletchley chatted about the latest war news

until he suddenly said to Patterson: "I'm rather surprised you're still a flight lieutenant after all this time and effort."

"Maybe I prefer effort, sir."

"But you were in line for promotion recently, weren't you? After your last tour of ops?"

Patterson looked away. "Somebody hinted that there was another stripe waiting if I went down to Rhodesia and did some instructing."

"Rhodesia! Wonderful country," Bletchley told Hooper. "Chance of a lifetime," he told Patterson.

"Damn good chance of getting stuck there for a lifetime," Patterson said. "It's three thousand miles from here. I wangled a job at the Fighter School just down the road instead."

"Where, I'm told, you've been invaluable," Bletchley said.

Patterson shook a few grains of salt onto his plate, dipped his finger and licked the tip. He said: "I served my time, I paid my debt to society and now I'm ready to come out, sir."

"Back to combat?" Hooper said.

Bletchley smiled at them both. "Take a tip from an old lag," he said. "Don't push your luck. Know when to fight and when to run away. That's what Eddy Rickenbacker told me in the last show, when I was young and eager, a damned sight too eager." Patterson still sat hunched over his plate, tapping the salt grains and brushing them off his fingertips. Hooper got on with his steak. "There's no shame in knowing when to quit," Bletchley went on. "Quite the reverse, because there's no merit in death. Not a bit. That stuff about *dulce et decorum est pro patria mori* is all balls, you know. Death in action is neither sweet nor fitting, and God knows I've seen enough of it to know."

"Me too," Patterson said, not looking up.

"Of course I grieve for every man we lose," Bletchley said. "That doesn't mean to say I measure each man equal, equally valuable, equally expendable. Certainly not. Some men must be protected. Their worth is greater. Simple as that."

Patterson raised his eyes. "Are you still talking about me, sir?" he asked.

"I've been given a roving commission," Bletchley said. "Stooge about from squadron to squadron, talk tactics and equipment, find out what's cooking in the kitchen and then spread the good word. Sharpen the cutting-edge. Sort of thing we should have done in the Battle of Britain and didn't. We had no flow of information then, neither upwards nor sideways, so a lot of decent chaps got killed for nothing. *This* time we'll get it right. There's a place on my staff for an intelligent young fighter pilot."

"I've applied to go back on ops," Patterson said. He disliked Bletchley too much to look at him.

"I'm looking for someone who's flown in the desert and who knows what questions to ask. He'll be a squadron leader this year and, if he plays his cards right, probably a wing commander next."

"Excuse me, sir," Patterson said. He got up and walked towards the lavatory.

He washed his face, scrubbed his nails, brushed his hair, let his pulse-rate slow down, and went back. Hooper was eating ice cream. Bletchley was watching a waiter peel an orange for him. "You've given it some thought, then?" Bletchley asked.

"Not for a second," Patterson said. "I want to join a fighter squadron in the desert, sir. I want to get back on ops."

"Of course you do. But first you want some of that splendid ice cream. A double portion for Mr Patterson," Bletchley told the waiter. "Where he's going, his memory of the stuff will need all the help it can get."

They moved to the terrace for coffee.

"You might like to know," Bletchley told Patterson,

"that if you had shown the slightest interest in joining my staff I would have been on the phone this afternoon and your posting up the blue would have been killed stone dead. Up the blue," he told Hooper, "means into the desert."

"I'm flattered, sir," Patterson said.

"Don't be. I wouldn't have you on my staff under any circumstances. You're a total fighter pilot and as such completely useless for anything else."

Patterson was startled. "Then why offer me the job, sir?"

"To make absolutely sure. But if you'd so much as blinked, you know where you'd be tomorrow?"

"No idea, sir."

"Rhodesia. Wonderful country. You'd hate it." He drank his coffee in three gulps. "As it happens I'm going your way tomorrow, so you can have a lift up the blue. Cairo West aerodrome, 0600 hours. No, don't get up."

They watched him stride away, upright and confident as a good RAF officer should be. "Bastard," Patterson said. "Did you see his dirty little game?"

"I saw it before you did. Kind of took you by surprise, didn't he?"

Patterson scowled at Bletchley's empty chair. "You'd think he'd have something better to do in the middle of a war than talk a pilot into flying a desk."

"Well . . ." Hooper looked at Patterson's left hand. The thumb was constantly worrying the fingers, pressing and flicking, chasing and snapping. Patterson put his hand in his pocket. "How many tours have you done?" Hooper asked.

"Two." Patterson stared him in the eye. "Just two. One in the UK, one out here. The way that old bastard was going on you'd think I was over the hill."

"Don't get mad at me," Hooper said. "I'm just a poor harmless Yankee boy who got sent in to make up the numbers."

"I'm going for a swim," Patterson growled. "D'you want to come?"

Hooper was slightly amused. The ends of his moustache went up a fraction. "I read a book about how to make friends," he said, "and I have to tell you, you're doing it all wrong."

"I don't want to *make friends*," Patterson said. He made it sound like a disease. "I made a lot of friends once and they all turned out to be bloody idiots, every single one of them." His stare was now a challenge for Hooper to argue the point.

"I just had a great idea," Hooper said. "Why don't we go for a swim?"

They walked across the terrace.

"What about this evening?" Hooper said. "Any plans?"

"I think I'll murder my wife," Patterson said.

"Yeah," Hooper said. "Well, I can see how that might make you feel better."

CHAPTER THREE

A Few Desert Sores

The Tomahawks landed at LG 181 in the late afternoon when the air was calm and the light from the west made lengthening shadows of the machines until the wheels touched and created high plumes of dust that ran down the strip and fogged everything.

LG stood for landing-ground. Most of the Western Desert was one enormous LG. All you needed to do was pick the rocks out of the sand. In England the fighter airfields were given friendly names: Biggin Hill, Tangmere, Middle Wallop, North Weald, Hornchurch, Bodkin Hazel. No names in the desert. Nothing to name.

The squadron had flown fifty miles from LG 158 to LG 181. This did not mean there were twenty-odd landing-grounds between the two. The war was not as neat as that; the war had bounded and rebounded across the desert, sometimes charging in hot pursuit, sometimes lurching into uncertain stalemate, sometimes backing off in a strategic withdrawal that degenerated into a galloping rout. As the armies moved, so the air forces abandoned or seized airfields which were often already familiar to the new owners because they had been seized or abandoned more than once before. If the airfields became crowded there was always more desert for a new LG and always a new number to identify it, sand and numbers being very cheap in North Africa.

The ground crews had moved to LG 181 by truck during the day and the pilots found more or less what they had left: a fringe of tents, a couple of dozen vehicles, a fuel dump, an ammunition dump, four Bofors ack-ack guns, cooks' wagon, signals truck, latrines and half a million flies. In case of enemy attack, everything was widely dispersed.

Barton landed first. He dumped his parachute on the wing and strolled across to the signals truck. Prescott and Schofield were sitting in its shade. "Christ, you look lousy," Barton said to Schofield.

"He feels lousy," Prescott said.

"I didn't ask you," Barton said.

"I know you didn't," Prescott said, "but at the moment all messages are being relayed through me. I expect you want to know what's wrong with him."

Barton squatted and examined Schofield's face. Beneath the tan, Schofield's skin was slack and grey and his eyelids drooped, pouchy as a frog's. Schofield licked his lips and breathed through his mouth, almost panting, then licked his lips again. Apart from that he sat quite motionless, as if he'd been dumped there. "What's wrong with him?" Barton asked.

"Gyppy tummy. The Doc's gone to get some stuff."

Barton touched the intelligence officer's cheek. "He's freezing," he said. "Get a blanket."

"Five minutes ago he was sweating buckets."

"Just get a blanket."

Prescott went. Barton stood and looked down at Schofield. The squadron MO arrived, carrying a bottle of water. "Dysentery," he said. He knelt and got Schofield to swallow a tablet, holding the bottle to his lips to wash it down. "Well done," he said. "Now for God's sake *keep* it down."

For the first time, Barton noticed the smell.

"We can't wait for the ambulance plane," the doctor said. "The troops are refuelling the blood wagon now. I'll go with him."

Barton took the bottle and had a swig. "What am I supposed to do for an intelligence officer?"

"Beats me. This one's no good to you. He's discharging at both ends and leaking through every pore. If he goes on dehydrating like that in this heat he'll be dead in twenty-four hours."

The ambulance bustled across the sand and pulled in downwind, so that its dust would not blow over them. Prescott arrived with a blanket, in time to see Schofield lifted aboard and driven away. "Tough luck," he said. He was wearing the blanket draped over his head and shoulders.

"Don't stand there looking like Santa Claus," Barton said. "Get on to Wing, tell them –"

"I already told them, Skip," Prescott said. "They'll organise the ambulance plane and it'll rendezvous with the Doc, if not tonight then first thing tomorrow."

"Yes, but –"

"And Wing is also finding us a new IO with utmost speed. The adj sent off a signal half an hour ago."

"Oh."

"We're not complete dummies down here, you know. You flash boys may be hot stuff upstairs, but the ground staff does its share of work too."

"Sure." Barton scuffed the sand to cover the stain where Schofield had been sitting. "What have you done about the view?"

"View?" Prescott turned through a full circle and everywhere he looked was empty and flat and desolate. "What view?" he asked.

"Exactly," Barton said. "It's perfect. Don't touch it." He trudged off to his quarters. As squadron commander he was privileged to live in a trailer. Everyone else had half a tent, except for flight commanders, medical officer, intelligence officer and adjutant, who had a whole tent each.

By now the squadron had landed and the pilots had moved into their tents. Moving in took only a couple of minutes; you put up your camp bed, unrolled your bedroll and dumped your personal kit in a corner. Personal kit amounted to a few clothes, toilet kit, perhaps a book, sometimes a souvenir such as an Italian officer's dress sword or a pair of German binoculars. One pilot kept a pet tortoise. Most tents had lucky charms kicking around somewhere: a mangy rabbit's-foot, a pair of dice, a celluloid toy won at a fair, a twisted bullet prised from a cockpit, a girlfriend's scarf, now torn and sun-bleached and streaked with sweat stains, but still treasured like the last five-pound note on earth.

The youngest pilot on the squadron was Kit Carson. He was twenty but looked eighteen. He had been christened Tarquin Borrowdale Delahaye Carson, but from the day he went to school he was called Kit. Because he had an uncle who was a bishop, and because he wore a little gold crucifix on a fine chain around his neck, Kit considered that he was not superstitious; yet he was interested in other people's superstitions. He wandered from tent to tent, asking questions and writing the answers in a spiral-bound notebook he had scrounged from the orderly room.

Tiny Lush, dozing on his bed, muttered obscenities at him so Carson moved on. He found Billy Stewart sitting motionless in the doorway of his tent with his hands eighteen inches apart as if describing the length of a fish. Occasionally the hands clapped and Stewart did or did not kill a fly; then the hands returned to their first position. "Got a minute, Stew?" Carson said. "I'm finding out if people are superstitious. Have you got a lucky charm?"

Stewart did not look up. "The little buggers know I'm here," he said. "When I kill one, the others all get a really bad case of the twitch for twenty seconds. But they never go away. Not stupid, see? But not bright either. You've got a brain like a fly, Kit. What d'you think they think I think they're up to? And vice versa?"

"Dunno. Is this a superstition of yours? Killing flies?"

Stewart was silent for a good minute. Then he said: "I have only one superstition, Kit. I never talk about my superstitions. I'm very, very superstitious about that. Write it down."

As Kit Carson wrote, Stewart abruptly banged his palms together. Carson said: "You can't kill them all, Billy."

"Ah, but they don't know that, do they? And I think I've got them on the run. They're showing signs of panic."

Fifty yards away, Pinky Dalgleish watched from his tent. He was 'B' Flight Commander and he had been called Pinky because his little finger stuck out like a bowsprit when he drank tea. This was a misleading characteristic: Dalgleish was an aggressive pilot who hated coming back with unfired ammunition, and he had a sometimes black and brooding temperament which made Kit Carson nervous of him, even though Kit was not in 'B' Flight; but now he saw Dalgleish watching and decided to go over.

"I heard," Dalgleish said, "and I've got twelve superstitions. I always fly with my lucky acorn stuck in my navel. I always whistle 'Annie Laurie' while I'm sticking it in. Then I always piss on the left wheel of the aeroplane, spit on the prop, kick the adjutant, and how many's that?"

"Five," Carson said. "I think."

"I can't tell you the other seven superstitions, they're disgusting, you'd puke all over the carpet. What's all this in aid of, anyway?"

"I'm writing a book," Carson said. "Like that chap Hillary. He wrote a thing called *The Last Enemy* and it's sold thousands and thousands. All I need is lots of stuff about superstitions and so on. You know. Anyway, thanks very much."

"It was all lies and I deny every word of it," Dalgleish said. "You print it and I'll sue."

"Hey, that's good." Carson was scribbling hard. He looked up. "Got any more?"

"Kit, you're an arsehole."

Carson sucked his pencil. "No," he said, "sorry. Can't use that."

*　　*　　*

Bletchley's personal Avro Anson landed an hour before sunset. It was a curious machine, made from the remains of two crashed Ansons plus the wheels off a Blenheim. He called it the Brute. Its wings were warped in opposite directions, the rudder was a bit off-centre, the engines were old and frail. Bletchley was the only man who knew how to make it go. He came over the horizon at seventy feet and seventy miles an hour, that being the way the Brute preferred to fly.

The sergeant cook watched three men climb down and ordered three more tins of bully-beef to be added to the stew.

By then Fanny Barton had beaten the dust out of his other cap (the one without oil stains), collected Flight Lieutenant Kellaway, and driven down the airstrip in a captured VW desert-wagon.

"Unexpected pleasure, sir," he said, saluting.

"Well, I was in the neighbourhood," Bletchley said, "So I thought I'd deliver your new flight commander. Also Captain Hooper of the US Army Air Force." The two men came forward and saluted. Barton returned the salute. "Good God, it's Pip," he said.

"Guilty," Patterson said.

"I thought I told you, sir," Kellaway said to Barton. The *sir* was because Bletchley was there. "I'm sure I told you."

"You said it was someone called Patterson, but there are dozens of Pattersons . . . Still, it's nice to have you back, Pip."

"It's nice to be back, sir." Patterson had expected Barton to shake hands and when Barton didn't he felt uncomfortable, so he looked around. There was little to see and nothing to comment on. He ended up looking at Barton again and realised how much the man had changed since the days when he had led the squadron during the Battle of Britain. Then, he had been vigorous and determined, sometimes anxious but usually cheerful. Now he looked like a man who took power in his stride and who enormously enjoyed shooting things down or blowing things up. In his smile there was something of the smile of the tiger. Patterson found the smile disconcerting, because he suspected that Barton was sizing him up for the job of leading others in the work of destruction and killing and general mayhem. It made him a little uneasy.

"Well, look here," Kellaway said. "We'd better get you two into some tents before the light goes."

"I'll sleep in the Brute," Bletchley said.

"Welcome to our war, captain," Barton said. He shook hands with the American. "I'll see you later. Did you bring any of that special engine oil, sir?" he asked.

"Come and see."

Patterson and Hooper threw their kit into the back of the VW as Bletchley and Barton went up the steps of the Anson. The air commodore had brought a case of tinned beer. He opened two cans, which frothed and foamed vigorously. "Your health, and by God you're going to need plenty of it," he said. They drank.

"I take it we're off the hook as far as Takoradi goes," Barton said.

"Probably. We may have found some Poles to do the job. Very keen, which means they'll smuggle gold or diamonds up from West Africa. You know what the Poles are like: mad gamblers. Suits me. It gives them an incentive to get the Hurricanes to Cairo, and that's what matters. The Takoradi run is our ace of trumps."

"Absolutely, sir. Splendid news."

"What a hypocritical young thug you are, Fanny. You don't give a tiny toss for Takoradi, do you?"

Barton wiped froth from his chops. "I'd sooner be near the action, sir."

"Somebody gave me a definition of strafing, the other day," Bletchley said. "Russian roulette at three hundred miles an hour and zero feet, he said it was." He finished his beer. "Quite exhilarating, if you like that sort of thing."

*   *   *

Captain Hooper came from a base in the Delta which had hot and cold showers, a pool, laundry, dry cleaners, barbershop, and an eager twenty-four-hour service of Arab shoeshine boys. He knew that life in the desert wasn't going to be like that, but he was startled to discover just how dirty everyone in Hornet Squadron was. Dirty and smelly.

Kellaway had put him in Tiny Lush's tent. Lush was six foot three and fourteen stone. He wore Arab sandals, dirty shorts and a dirty shirt. He hadn't shaved for a month; above his short, red beard was a big moustache. His hair was a tangle of curls that reached his collar. Parts of his body seemed more sunburned than others, but Hooper soon recognised these as old oil stains. Lush gave off a soft, ripe smell, like a farm horse at the end of a hard day.

"Life is very simple here," Tiny Lush told him. "We get up with the sun and have breakfast, which is always porridge, jam and tea. In the morning some of us patrol the skies and usually find a lot of nothing. Lunch is at twelve. It's always biscuit, tinned sausage and tea. In the afternoon some of us patrol the skies and find what's left of the morning's nothing. At six we eat supper, which is always bully-beef stew. By seven the sun has long since set and we stooge off to bed. Very, very simple."

"No shaving?" Hooper said. "I thought the RAF didn't permit beards."

"This is five o'clock shadow," Lush said. "The water ration here is one pint per man per day, not counting what the cookhouse uses. You shave if you like. Wash your socks too, if you're really fussy. Most of us just let nature take its course. Anything else I can tell you?"

Hooper thought. "The guy who had this bed before me. What happened to him?"

"You don't want to know that. Might put you off your supper. Shall we wander over to the mess?"

The mess was a large canvas roof over some trestle tables and benches. Half a dozen pilots were already there and more came ambling across from their tents. Hooper was wearing his everyday uniform of slacks and tunic, somewhat crumpled after the trip in the Anson, but amongst this crowd he felt dressed for a parade. They were in uniform in the sense that they looked alike, but it was a uniform of motley. A few wore battledress tops, unbuttoned, but most preferred cardigans in varying shades of khaki, or sleeveless pullovers, or sweaters tied loosely around the neck. Their khaki shorts or corduroy trousers were baggy and creased like concertinas. Most wore calf-length mosquito boots; a few were in sandals or shoes. Hardly anyone was wearing RAF headgear, but Hooper saw several Luftwaffe caps, one Australian slouch hat and an Arab fez. Everybody's clothes looked stained and scruffy. Several pilots had shaved within the past week and one or two actually looked clean-shaven; however at least half were on the way to having recognisable beards and more than half had grown moustaches. Hooper saw no moustache that was neat and tidy, like his. All their moustaches seemed to be reaching for their ears.

Squadron Leader Barton and Air Commodore Bletchley joined them for supper. Lush was right. It was bully-beef stew. Hooper got introduced to everyone and soon forgot nearly all their names, but that didn't matter because nothing seemed to matter. It was all relaxed and cheerful. Once, in England, Hooper had visited a fighter wing based at a pre-war aerodrome where there were lots of large brick buildings and an officers' mess with white pillars flanking the entrance. What he remembered most clearly from that visit was his host's warning not to stand in front of the fire. There was, he explained, a strict pecking-order about who might warm his backside first at the anteroom fire on that (and many similar) RAF stations. LG 181 was a million miles from there.

Before the meal was over Hooper had been given a nickname. Someone – inevitably – said he had a cousin in New York. Hooper said he had never been to New York, which surprised them. "I've been to Manhattan," he said. "Manhattan, Kansas, that is."

"I met James Cagney once," Bletchley said. "Awfully nice fellow."

"It's a big country," Hooper said. "Me, I'm just a hick from the sticks." They liked the phrase. From then on he was Hick Hooper.

The sun went down with its usual sudden rush at six-thirty. By seven the night was as black as the inside of a coal sack. Lush took Hooper to their tent; he found it by walking from Tomahawk to Tomahawk, counting until they reached the fourth, D-Dog; their tent was fifty paces further on. Hooper stumbled on a guy-rope. "If you have to get up in the night," Lush said, "don't go far. People have been known to wander off for a wee-wee and never find their way back."

"Thanks. I'll stay right here."

Nevertheless, after they got into their bedrolls and the candle was put out, Hooper found the atmosphere heavy with the smell of Lush and Lush's clothes. He tried to ignore it, but the enclosed space seemed to trap and concentrate the aroma. After fifteen minutes Hooper found himself breathing through his mouth and he decided to take action. "Look," he said, "d'you mind if I sleep outside?"

"Not a bit," Lush said. "Most thoughtful. You do stink

a bit. Like Harrods' soap department. Not to worry, old chap. After a couple of days you'll smell quite normal."

*   *   *

Next day began at six, prompt.

Dawn in the desert was like a slow-motion explosion in a paint factory. Beautiful floods of colour washed across the sky and by touching the desert transformed it into a glorious field of delight. Tiny Lush crawled out of his tent and saw Hick Hooper watching it. "Wasted on the wogs, isn't it?" Lush said. "Sleep all right?"

"Yeah. I thought I heard a rooster."

"That's Geraldo. Bloke called Moffatt bought it from an Arab, didn't have the heart to kill it. Then Moffatt got the chop over Tobruk. Now Geraldo's the squadron mascot." Lush scratched and yawned. "Thank Christ, here comes tea."

The tea-wagon was a former Italian army van, much bullet-holed. The driver gave them each a mug of tea and a mug of water. "Bloody awful weather," Lush said.

"Might get a bit of sun later," the airman said. He drove on.

"We've been saying that to each other every morning for three months," Lush said. "Very reassuring. A fortress in these fickle times."

"I notice he didn't call you 'sir'."

Lush sipped his tea and sighed with pleasure. "We save the sir-stuff for big occasions. Coronations, state funerals, deliveries of beer."

"Didn't realise you guys were so democratic."

"Democratic?" Lush took another swig and found sand in his tea; he collected the grains on his tongue and spat them out. "We're not *democratic*, Hick. Fanny's king here."

"I guess I say 'sir' to Fanny."

"Everyone says 'sir' to the CO first thing in the morning and last thing at night. In between . . ." Lush shrugged. "Play it by ear and watch his eyebrows."

"Yeah? For what?"

"For when they meet in the middle. That means Fanny's hopping mad, so stand clear."

"What is he? Australian?"

"New Zealander. Came halfway round the world to fight. Very keen. We've also got a Greek and a Pole. Mick O'Hare's Irish. Fido Doggart was born in Kenya or Uganda or Shangri-La or some bloody place. The rest of us are normal. More or less."

They finished their tea. Hooper looked at his mug of water. "This is really all I get until tomorrow?"

"Enough to clean your teeth."

A hundred yards away, a Tomahawk coughed and its propeller jerked stiffly through a half-circle. A sergeant fitter shouted something to the airman in the cockpit. His voice was instantly eaten up and swallowed by the immensity of the desert. The Tomahawk coughed again, repeatedly, more deeply and fruitily until greasy black smoke jumped from the exhaust vents and the engine roared. The sergeant fitter stood with hands on hips, his head tilted, listening as the revs slowly built and the fighter trembled against its chocks. He had the air of a lion-tamer, watching the animal sit because it had been ordered to sit and not because it liked the position. All around the landing-ground, engines were kicking and jerking into noisy life. Much dust was being thrown up. Dawn had ceased its extravagance and the sky was a hard, hot blue again.

On their way to the mess, Tiny Lush said: "If you desperately want a bath, you can always save up your ration, you know."

"How long would that take?" Hooper asked.

"Dunno. Six months, probably. It'll be raining by then."

"It rains in the desert?"

"In winter. Tips down. You wake up swimming."

Breakfast was porridge, biscuit, margarine and plum jam, with more tea. The biscuit was like ship's biscuit, thick and hard and perforated. The cock Geraldo strutted around the table, grabbing fallen fragments.

Pip Patterson, at another table, said hullo to Hooper, but otherwise nobody paid him much attention; after all, this was his second day on the squadron, so by now he was part of the furniture; people got used to a lot of comings and goings in the Desert Air Force. A dozen conversations were competing with each other. "How's old Schofers?" asked a flying officer called Fido Doggart. "Any news?" He got no answer. Doggart's shaggy moustache was stained the several colours of bully-beef stew. For someone who was only twenty-two his face looked battered and grubby; but the eyes were eager. The eyes were those of the head boy who is blackmailing the school matron for fornication and is taking his payment in kind.

"Bloody biscuit again," Tiny Lush complained. "Boring bloody biscuit."

"Give the grease a shove," someone said. The tin of margarine slid along the table.

"Pay attention, Uncle," Doggart said to the adjutant. Kellaway looked up from his clipboard, still mentally adding columns of figures. "Carry nine, carry nine," he muttered. "What's wrong, blast you?" he asked.

"Bread," Lush demanded. "When are we going to get bread?" He banged a biscuit on the table, hard, so that crumbs flew.

"Stuff your bread," Doggart said, "What about Schofield? Has he bought it, or what? I need to know."

"How can you stuff bread?" Kit Carson said. "You can't stuff bread."

Kellaway shut his eyes. "Carry nine," he told himself.

"I bet they get bread at Wing," Pinky Dalgleish said.

"Bread's what you stuff stuff *with*," Carson said.

"Stuff-stuff?" Kellaway opened his eyes. He looked baffled. "What d'you mean, stuff-stuff?" But by now Carson had his mouth full.

"Schofield owes me forty ackers," Doggart said. "He bet me five to two Geraldo couldn't fly, silly man."

Kit swallowed hard and gestured with his mug. "When I said stuff-stuff, I meant like stuffing birds, Uncle," he explained. Kellaway still looked blank. "You know, like Geraldo," Kit said.

"Nobody stuffs Geraldo," said a Greek pilot called George. He had just sat down. "Geraldo is my friend. You want to stuff Geraldo, you have to stuff me first."

"Queue forms on the left," said Doggart.

"Schofield's in hospital, that's all," Kellaway told him irritably. "It's only gyppy tummy, for God's sake. Nothing to get worked up about."

"Not like bread," Dalgleish said. "I get very worked up about bread, especially since we never get any."

"Geraldo's not your friend," Kit Carson told Greek George. "He bit you the other day. How can —"

"I forgive!" George said. "All Greeks forgive and love everyone."

"You love Huns?" Tiny Lush asked.

"We love dead Huns very much, yes."

"Oh, bugger," Kellaway grumbled. "Now I've gone and forgotten the bloody number I was carrying."

"Seven," Doggart said firmly. Kellaway frowned at him, unbelieving. "Or possibly twelve," Doggart said.

"Fido, you're a berk," Kellaway said crossly. He had drunk too much of Baggy Bletchley's whisky last night. He really didn't like whisky, but when the air commodore offers you whisky you drink the stuff. That was part of the adjutant's job: keeping the CO company on a whisky-binge. Fanny liked whisky too much and sometimes he liked too much whisky. That wasn't good for the squadron. A hundred yards away, a mobile generator started throbbing. Kellaway's head throbbed too, but not in synch with the generator. That annoyed him. The whisky had left him thirsty, so he made himself drink tea. It tasted like paint. Warm, sweet paint. What he wanted was milk, chilled milk, pints and pints of lovely chilled milk, so wonderfully white and wet and cold that it would wash him clean and quench his thirst for ever and ever . . . He shook his head, hard, to get rid of this torturing image. Sweat dribbled into his eyes and stung them.

Tiny Lush leaned across the table and showed Hooper a biscuit. "See these holes?" he said. "Know what they're for?"

"Beats me."

"To let the weevils out. You have weevils in America?"

"Sure. The best." Hooper rapped the biscuit with a spoon. "Any weevils in there?"

"No. Little bastards deserted when they heard we were going up the blue."

Dalgleish said: "The weevil has a tiny brain, but he uses it all the time. That's the main difference between your average weevil and Kit Carson."

"Which one is Kit?" Hooper asked Dalgleish. "I've forgotten."

"The one with jam on his chin."

"I'm writing a book," Kit told Hooper. "It's going to make everyone here famous. You wait and see."

"I knew someone died from gyppy tummy," Greek George said. "He was running to the latrine and he tripped and broke his bloody neck."

"Pilot?" asked Doggart.

"Air-gunner."

"No loss, then. He wouldn't have hit the bog anyway."

Tiny Lush stood and stretched. "What a dump," he said. "Half a million square miles of sod-all. I don't know what you did to get sent here," he told Hooper, "but let this be a lesson to you."

"I came here to learn air combat," Hooper said. "So far it's the only thing nobody talks about."

"What's there to tell?" Lush said. "Try really hard and you might die of boredom."

"No action?"

"Kit wet the bed last week," Doggart said. "That was pretty exciting."

*   *   *

Barton had briefed his flight commanders the night before. He had called them to his truck and shown them a map of the sector of the desert within range of LG 181. "Fun and games tomorrow," he said. "Ground attack! Nothing but ground attack. What a treat, eh?" He was smiling like a boy who'd been promised an air-gun for his birthday; Pip Patterson thought he could even see a sparkle in Barton's eyes, though it might have been the glint from the oil lamp. "No more climbing and stooging about and finding nothing upstairs," Barton said. "This is guaranteed action! We'll fly in pairs. Six pairs, six targets." He waved at the map. Six crosses were widely scattered. "Take your pick, except for this one." He pointed to the most northerly cross. "That's mine. Lovely juicy battalion of kraut infantry under canvas. Yum-yum."

"What are these others?" Dalgleish asked.

"Troops, supply depots, fuel dumps, transport parks, the usual rubbish. All on this list."

They studied the list. "Take off at 0800 hours?" Patterson said. "This is all a bit sudden, isn't it, Fanny? I haven't met half my Flight yet."

"Brief them after breakfast. They're all old sweats, they'll know what to do. Don't worry about the kites, they'll be ready. I've given the ground crews their orders." His smile broadened until he burst into laughter. "I do enjoy a good strafe. The little buggers run like rabbits until bingo! They all fall down, rows and rows of them." He drummed his fists on the table in a rapid tattoo. "Wizard sport. Wizard!"

"Why eight o'clock?" Dalgleish asked. "I thought dawn was the best time."

"They're all in bed at dawn. I want them on their feet with their bellies full of breakfast."

"Breakfast," Patterson said flatly.

"Yes. See, most blokes feel like death when they get up, so you don't want to kill them then, do you? They wouldn't notice the difference. But prang 'em when they've begun to come alive and it's a much bigger disappointment. See?"

"No," Patterson said.

"Well, you never did have any imagination, Pip. What was it Moggy Cattermole used to call you?"

"For Christ's sake . . ." Patterson hunched his shoulders. "Bloody Moggy. Why d'you have to bring him up?"

"*Pathetic Scotch dwarf*," Barton said, delightedly. "That was it."

"Charming," Dalgleish said.

"It was the way he said it," Barton told him. "Like . . . I don't know . . ."

"Like a dog shitting on the carpet," Patterson said. "Moggy was the squadron shit."

"You must be at least six foot," Dalgleish said.

"Forget it. Forget Moggy."

"He was a character," said Barton.

"He was a shit and he got the shittiest chop you can get," Patterson told Dalgleish. "Clobbered by a Spit. When would that have been?" Barton shrugged. "September '40, probably," Patterson said. "Towards the end of the Battle, anyway."

Barton folded the map and gave it to Dalgleish. "Maybe it wasn't a Spit," he said. "I mean, that was just a rumour."

"I heard Moggy yelling blue murder at the other kite on the RT," Patterson said, "and the Observer Corps said they saw a Spitfire attack a Hurricane. When the post mortem opened him up they found enough three-oh-three ammo to fill a two-pound jam jar."

"These things happen," Barton said jauntily. "I should know. I got a Blenheim once."

Dalgleish had reopened the map. He was estimating the various bearings and times to the targets. "I'd much sooner do this at dawn, Fanny," he said. "That way we'd have the glare behind us. Dazzle the buggers, right?"

"But you'd have to go in *low*," Barton said. "Lousy view of the target. Better later. Sun's still in their eyes, it's twice as bright, you arrive at five hundred feet, see what's on offer, nip down, piss all over them, crack off home. Beats working for a living, doesn't it? Right, I'm off to drink Baggy's booze."

When he had gone, Dalgleish said, "Did he really get a Blenheim?"

"It was the squadron's first kill of the war," Patterson said. "Mistaken identity. We all thought they were Ju88s. Awful boob. Fanny had to go and apologise."

That amused Dalgleish. "You wouldn't catch Fanny apologising for anything nowadays," he said. "You'd get a kick in the slats before you got an apology out of him."

Patterson found the list of targets. He spiked it on a pencil and twirled it like a parasol. "I suppose all this gen came from Intelligence," he said. Dalgleish nodded. "So it's probably three days old," Patterson said. "A day to take the snaps, a day to collate all the gen, a day to get it sent up here."

"So what? It doesn't matter what we hit, as long as we hit something."

Patterson twirled the paper in the opposite direction. "Done much ground-strafing?" he asked.

"As little as possible," Dalgleish said. "The whole point of flying is to get away from all that unpleasantness."

*　　*　　*

Barton's information was wrong. His target was not a battalion of German infantry living under canvas. It was two battalions of German infantry and they were on parade.

This was pure chance. One battalion was being replaced by the other and it chanced that a general on a tour of inspection decided to see them both at once. The men had scrubbed and shaved and polished and pressed, and now they were drawn up in columns of four with their unit standards planted in the sand and their officers strolling about, chatting, sweating and wishing the old bastard would for Christ's sake come. He was forty minutes late.

The only soldier not on parade was a corporal with a sprained ankle who was manning a forward observation post, five miles out in the desert. The British army was a long way off, but you never knew when some armoured-car patrol might come looking for trouble or prisoners or cheap glory; and there were always aircraft to watch out for.

The corporal had been on duty all night. He was weary, with the grubby fatigue that comes from hours of doing nothing, seeing nothing, hearing nothing. He had to keep a log, and now he was bringing it up to date: *0500 hours – nil*, he wrote. *0600 hours – nil. 0700 hours – nil.* He heard the noise of aircraft and jerked his head up, but his eyes flinched against the glare and refused to change focus fast enough. By the time he found the two planes a mile away they were leaving him, too low to reveal their wing markings. He got the binoculars on them at the second attempt, but his grip was tense and their speed was great: they kept slipping in and out of view. Still couldn't see the markings. Looked Italian. Italian air force had a new fighter, Macchi 202. These were Macchis. Probably.

He knew about the general's visit. It took him five seconds to worry whether he should telephone the camp and maybe disrupt the entire parade with a false alarm and lose his stripes. Then he grabbed the phone. It took eight seconds for a sergeant to answer it. "You sure?" the sergeant asked. "No," said the corporal. "Maybe they were ours, maybe they weren't. All I know is they were going fast and low."

"Major!" the sergeant shouted, and ran. It took him twelve seconds to find the major and another six seconds to give him the information. The major thought hard. "He's not sure?" he asked. He could see the general's car approaching, entering the camp, motorcyclists leading. "No sir, not sure," the sergeant said.

The major did a brave thing. He dismissed the parade. He shouted the order to dismiss as loudly as he could. "Air attack! Air attack!" he bawled. "Take cover!" He was ten seconds too late. Barton and his wingman, Stewart, arrived in a storm of noise and a blast of gunnery. They began firing before they reached the camp, the aircraft slightly nose-down and the bullet-strikes always racing two hundred yards ahead, so that most of the men they killed were dead before the shadows of the Tomahawks rushed across them. Barton was amazed and delighted. What a mob! What a score! Stewart was so startled he could not quite believe it was happening. The flaming, juddering racket of his guns made his eyelids flicker, and briefly he saw the scene of scattering men and collapsing bodies like an old cinema film, badly projected.

Then the camp was behind them. Some red tracer chased the planes. Barton weaved a bit to spoil the gunners' aim. Soon they were out of range. Barton climbed and turned for home. Stewart followed, covering his leader's tail as a good wingman should. The strafe had been over so quickly, he couldn't take it seriously. He found himself chewing hard on the inside of his mouth. He'd fired one long burst, that was all, and it had ripped through those men, flattened them like a gale of wind. Stewart was as keen to score as the next fighter pilot: he knew the exultant surge when an enemy plane exploded or spun down and crashed. But this was different. This wasn't fighting. The old reassuring .phrases slid through his mind: *They started it. They'd kill you like a shot if they could. The only good Hun is a dead Hun.* He was not reassured. He tasted blood and stopped chewing. *Forget it*, he told himself. *It's over. Forget it.*

*   *   *

Dalgleish took Hooper as his wingman.

Their target was a transport park. The good thing about this was the fact that trucks — unlike tanks or artillery — were soft-skinned and burned easily. The bad thing was that, because of the good thing, transport parks were heavily defended. When he was two miles away, Dalgleish saw that this park was empty. But the flak batteries were still there. They all opened up and soon Dalgleish was flying through a field of black blots. He called: "Break left!" and they turned and fled. It was the first time Hooper had experienced flak and he was impressed by its intensity. One moment you were in clear sunlight, the next you were bounced about by a storm of black smoke balls. Shrapnel rattled on his Tomahawk. He was glad to escape.

Dalgleish went up to three thousand feet, cruised south and found what looked like a German army signals unit. Soldiers ran for cover as the two planes dropped, but they could never run fast enough. The Tomahawks went in side by side and sprayed the site good and hard. If there was any answering fire from the ground it soon gave up. The planes made a tight half-circle and came back and savaged what was left of the trucks and trailers, the aerials and the technicians. It was only a small unit and they left it burning fiercely.

Tiny Lush and Greek George flew a hundred and forty miles on dead reckoning and found their target exactly where it ought to be, an Italian infantry camp, neat rows of tents all lined up for destruction except that half the tents displayed big red crosses.

They prowled around it at a respectful distance and argued over the radio. Greek George didn't believe it was a real hospital, or even half a real hospital. Lush said: "Forget it, George. If we start strafing their hospitals they're going to come over and hit ours."

"Let us go down and beat the place up," George said.

"That's crazy. What good would it do?"

"Might draw flak. Can't be a hospital if they got flak guns."

"Who says?"

They argued some more. Lush grew bored. He had a cousin in the Medical Corps and there was no way he was going to strafe this camp. They left it and flew on. Far away in the biscuit-brown wastes of the desert a speck of bright red glowed and slowly faded. Lush dropped a wing to give himself a better view. Now a tiny spot of green came into existence at the same place. "Shut up, George," Lush said. "I've found something better."

The specks of colour were signal flares and the flares had signalled the start of an infantry training exercise, complete with mortars and anti-tank guns. The two Tomahawks arrived at ground level and made a great nuisance of themselves, completely ruining the exercise. On the other hand, the German troops got in some practice with intensive small-arms fire. Greek George flew into a long burst from a machine gun and came out bucking and twisting and without much of a right wingtip. Something whacked Lush's tail unit and sent him into a violent skid that raised a gush of sweat all over his body. But both survived and they flew home while German medics scrambled fast between the wounded and the dying, and the dead got heaved onto a truck, and the colonel in charge of the exercise picked himself up and used a handkerchief to clean his right ear of sand.

Kit Carson flew as Pip Patterson's wingman. Their objective was supposedly a fuel dump, but they never found it. Many miles short of the target they crossed paths with a force of German tanks and artillery which had probably received warning and was certainly on the alert. The flak was suddenly so dense and furious that Patterson heaved the Tomahawk onto its side and kept turning tightly until he browned-out, his head and arms feeling remote and empty. When the blood had completely forced its way back up his body, he searched for Kit and found him tagging along faithfully, a couple of lengths behind.

Patterson made a long detour, and when he was sure they were safe he was also sure he was lost. No fuel dump today.

He found a narrow-gauge railway, but it was empty. He found a cluster of light tanks, but they were broken and burnt wrecks left over from the last battle. In the end, he found a convoy of trucks, if three could be called a convoy. The drivers baled out and ran. Patterson and Carson took it in turns, battering the vehicles into blazing scrap. It seemed an expensive way to fight a war, sending two fighters nearly three hundred miles there and back to duff up three trucks.

The last two pairs to take off were O'Hare with Doggart, and Ostanisczkowski with Bailey. O'Hare was an Irishman from the Republic; Doggart was English. Ostanisczkowski was Polish and he was always called Sneezy. Bailey was a Canadian who was usually called Butcher.

O'Hare and Doggart had been given a target marked simply 'troop concentration'. They arrived at about five thousand feet, got very briskly peppered by enemy flak batteries, and fell through the black fluffs like a suicide pact going off a cliff. At a thousand feet, red and yellow tracer built a bright bead curtain all around them and they opened fire, sprayed the ground in long shuddering bursts, flattened out when they could see the shadows of their Tomahawks rapidly magnifying, and beat it for home.

"See any troops?" O'Hare asked.

"Saw a lot of shit," Doggart said.

"Christ," O'Hare said. He sounded disgusted. "We didn't strafe them, Fido. They fucking strafed us."

"Fuel dump," Doggart said. "Betcha."

"Shit in spades," O'Hare said.

They flew in silence for a few miles while they thought about it. With flak like that, flak at every height, spread all across the sky, layered black flak waiting ahead of you, streams of coloured flak spilling across the air towards you, it was pure luck if you got through.

"Fuel dump," Doggart said again. "They always protect their lousy fuel dumps."

"I don't want to think about it," O'Hare said.

Sneezy and Butcher Bailey chose to fly low, no more than a hundred feet, all the way to their target. The decision nearly killed them before they got halfway.

Sneezy led. Bailey followed a length or two to the right, outside the slipstream. After about ten minutes, Sneezy tried to increase speed and found his throttle was sticking; it refused to open smoothly. He told Bailey to lead, and he fell back while he fiddled and fussed with the throttle lever. There was a variable-friction device designed to hold the lever steady; maybe that was on the blink. Sneezy kept one eye on the racing blur of the desert as he checked the throttle, but he needed a third eye. At the last split second he saw his propeller-arc about to hack into Bailey's tail-plane. He shoved the stick forward and instinctively slumped deep in the cockpit as Bailey's Tomahawk wandered carelessly backwards only a few feet above him, so near that he could see its tail wheel shivering and feel the shove of massively displaced air. Then he snatched the stick back as the desert floor jumped at him. For a few seconds he was so low that he sensed the thin cushion of air holding his plane off the sands. His muscles tensed for a crash that never came. The Tomahawk eased upwards and he levelled off at five hundred feet, where he felt safe enough to breathe again. Bailey had had the same idea. "Dumb bastard," Sneezy said to him. He was still too frightened to be angry. He looked at Bailey again and saw that his wheels were down. "Bloody stupid thing you did," Sneezy said. Now anger began to soak through him like heat. The angrier he got the more Polish he sounded. "Kill yourself, you bloody dumb lousy idiot, but don't kill me too."

"Didn't do a damn thing, Sneezy," Bailey said. "It just happened."

What happened had been a quick shudder followed by a couple of heavy clunks and thuds, the wheels-down light came on and a sudden drag cost the Tomahawk twenty, thirty, forty miles an hour.

Bailey had grabbed the throttle, but too late: he glimpsed Sneezy's aircraft sliding under him, insanely close. He shut his eyes and hunched upwards, away from the collision. No crunch came. He had opened his eyes and climbed for safety.

"Get your wheels up," Sneezy said.

"I tried," Bailey said. "No go."

Sneezy drifted sideways under the other plane and looked. The wheels seemed firmly locked down. "Chuck her about," he said.

Bailey went up and chucked her about, not violently because the Tomahawk was not designed for wild aerobatics with the wheels down. But he gave her a good, brisk shake and a couple of hard bumps. Nothing made any difference. "Must be duff hydraulics," he said. "What now?"

"*Na miłośća, Boska!*" Sneezy said.

"Don't you dare talk to me like that," Bailey said.

"You can't strafe," Sneezy said. Bailey didn't argue. The Tomahawk felt sluggish and clumsy. "Stay up here," Sneezy said. "I find something to hit, we bugger off."

They cruised about for a long time before Sneezy noticed a plume of dust that had to mean transport. It turned out to be an enemy tank-recovery unit, giant tractor-trailers loaded with damaged tanks. The column saw him coming and made a smart U-turn back into the fog of its own dust. Sneezy went in and blazed away, but he couldn't see what he was hitting, or even if. Somebody could see him, though. As he left he felt the smack of heavy machine-gun bullets and saw splashes of raw metal on the engine cowling.

Bailey's ground crew knew there was something wrong when he came in sight with his undercarriage down. He landed cautiously, taxied to dispersal and stood around, mopping the spit from the radio-mike in his oxygen mask, while they went to work.

"Look at that," the sergeant said. "Some bastard shot you in the plumbing."

Bailey went and looked. "Probably an Arab. Or a German with a tea-towel on his head."

"Not a nice thing to do."

"That's what Sneezy told them. Hullo, here's my taxi."

Barton arrived, driving the VW at high speed. He stopped by locking the handbrake and jumping out (there were no doors) while the VW was skidding broadside. It was still drifting across the sand as he spoke to the sergeant: "Can you fix it?" He meant the undercarriage.

"Might take an hour, sir."

"Right. Hop in, Butcher. You're late for the briefing."

"What briefing? We haven't had debriefing yet."

"No time." They got in the VW. Barton revved the engine hard and set off with a howl of wheel spin. "Lovely day," he shouted. Bailey clung on with both hands. It was the same old day, nothing but heat, sand and flies. Barton thought it was lovely. Bully for Barton.

The rest of the squadron had landed. They were in the mess tent, drinking tea, sprawled in canvas chairs, dozing, playing poker, scratching, yawning. Only Pip Patterson seemed at all interested in the recent sorties. He was talking to his Flight, asking if they had hit their targets. "We hit *some* bloody thing," Doggart said.

"So what was it?"

"Sewage farm," O'Hare said. "Bloody great German sewage farm." He yawned and massaged his eyes.

"Turds everywhere," Doggart said. "Colossal exploding German turds."

Patterson gave up on them and turned to the Pole.

"Was cock-up," Sneezy said. "I strafed a big cloud of dust. Maybe tank transporters in it, I don't know."

Patterson looked at his list of targets. "Nothing about that here."

Sneezy took the list, read it and gave it back. "List is cock-up," he said.

Pip Patterson folded his list of targets and put it away. He glanced around, saw Pinky Dalgleish watching him, and shrugged. "Oh well," Dalgleish said. "Just another day on the factory floor."

Barton came bounding into the mess tent as the VW went skidding by with Butcher Bailey still in it. Only Hooper was surprised by this; everyone else had seen the trick before. "All here?" Barton said. "Good, fine, splendid. Now tell me, in five words or less, how you enjoyed yourselves. Pinky?"

Dalgleish counted off the words on his fingers. "Flak, flak, flak, flak, flak."

"Same here," said Lush, "only more so."

"Beats me how all that shit missed us," O'Hare said. Bailey wandered in and belched. They all looked. "Just punctuation," he said. Nobody even smiled. Bailey's belches were part of the furniture.

"Went up, came down," Sneezy said to Barton. "Butcher

had wheel trouble. Me, I blew holes in a cloud of dust."

That left Patterson. "Had a row with some panzer," he said. "Didn't win."

"Oh, for Christ's sake don't do *that*," Barton said brightly. "Don't bloody well *win*. We need the enemy to kick and scream and bleed all over the desert. So far today we've got five or six Jerry army commanders shitting bricks and they haven't had their mid-morning schnapps yet. I like that. It gives me a rich, warm feeling inside."

"Stew tells me you hit your target," Dalgleish said to him.

"Bashed it. Silly buggers were lined up on parade! We shot about five hundred." Barton's attempt at a modest smile came out crooked and gleeful. "Couldn't miss!" he said. "I got all mine in the belly-button."

"So they got a rich, warm feeling inside," Doggart said.

"I didn't hit my target," Dalgleish said. "Duff intelligence, Fanny."

"Don't worry about it, sport. Plenty more where that came from." Barton gave him a map. "Six more lovely targets. I don't care who hits which, or how, or when, as long as you're all back for lunch." Nobody moved.

Patterson said: "Another strafe *before* lunch?"

"That's the general idea," Barton said, "and if you get it right we'll do two more this afternoon."

Everyone watched his face and tried to guess whether or not he was joking. In their static silence, the slap and creak of the mess tent roof in the desert breeze was suddenly loud. Barton enjoyed their attention and his genial grin told them nothing.

*   *   *

Schramm was on the phone when Hoffmann and Jakowski came into his office.

Balsa-wood models of enemy aircraft hung on threads

from the ceiling. Hoffmann blew softly and made them turn. Jakowski reversed a chair and straddled it.

Schramm cut short the call and hung up. "No news," he said. "I've checked with every intelligence officer I know, up and down the coast. Nothing."

"I don't believe it," Jakowski said. "No patrol activity at all? That's unbelievable."

"No *incoming* activity. Three patrols are going home."

"You'll never catch them," Hoffmann said. "Once they've finished raiding, they go flat out for Cairo."

Jakowski rested his arms on the top of his chair and frowned at Schramm's telephone. "I've been working around the clock to put this new unit together. My men believe they're going to hunt down the enemy and hammer him. If I tell them we haven't even got a target, their morale will fall like a stone."

"Give them a week's hard training in the Sahara," Hoffmann suggested.

"They don't need *training*. They're seasoned soldiers. They need *action*."

"Look," Schramm said. "I can only tell you what I know – three SAS patrols are going home. What I *don't* know is how many patrols might still be hiding in the Jebel."

"Might? Why do you say –"

"Because military intelligence is not an exact science. We lost track of a couple of British patrols last month. Maybe the trucks broke down. Maybe they all died. Maybe they linked up with another patrol. Who can say?"

"I don't believe the enemy has stopped raiding," Jakowski said. "Not after such success. Why should he?"

"Perhaps his patrols need a rest," Hoffmann said. "After all, he's got other ways of making a nuisance of himself."

"Yes? What?"

Schramm picked up a teletype print-out. "Ground-strafing our troops at the southern end of the Front.

Camps, supply dumps, vehicle parks have been getting sprayed every ten minutes. The generals are livid. They want standing patrols of 109s."

"Not a hope," Hoffmann said. "Standing patrols just drink fuel and wear out pistons."

"Strafed," Jakowski said. "By what?"

"An aggressive squadron of Curtiss Tomahawks," Schramm said.

"Based where? It must be an advanced airfield."

"We don't know. We're looking."

"It could be a diversion," Jakowski said. "While these Tomahawks are hammering on the front door, another patrol sneaks in through the back. Yes?"

"Well," Hoffmann said, not at all convinced but not wishing to discourage him. "Just stay away from any Tomahawks."

"Stay away?" Jakowski sprang to his feet. "Why? They're vulnerable, aren't they? If you can find their location, I can smash them. All I need is a map reference."

"Good God!" Hoffmann said, quite startled. "That's a brave idea."

"It's no more than what the enemy has been doing to us. Get me that location and I'll strafe the strafers, and then raid the raiders." He strode out, looking pleased.

"What a fire-eater," Schramm said.

"He likes to make things hot, doesn't he?" Hoffmann said. "He's going to the right place for that."

*   *   *

They did another strafe before lunch, but only part of a strafe in the afternoon. Half the Tomahawks were being repaired: guns had jammed, engines misfired, controls failed to respond, bits of aircraft had been blown away by ground fire. When the remaining Tomahawks landed, most of them were suffering too. Barton scrubbed the fourth strafe. "Too bad," he said to the adjutant. "Just when the boys were getting into the swing of things."

"A bit rough on the kites, though," Kellaway said. They were sitting on the sand on the shady side of his orderly room, which was a tent.

"Well, they're rough old kites. They were clapped-out when we got them, weren't they? The sooner we bash 'em to bits, the sooner we get given something better."

"Did Baggy Bletchley promise that?" Kellaway asked.

"Sort of." Kellaway grunted. Barton looked sideways. "Have you heard something?" he asked.

"Just a rumour, Fanny. Don't get your hopes up. Hurricanes galore, so it said. All brand-new. Mark Fives."

Geraldo strutted past, came back for a closer look at Kellaway's left boot, pecked it once and went on his way.

"Hurricanes would be nice," Barton said. "Spitfires would be even nicer."

A brisk westerly wind had sprung up and the tent canvas bellied against their heads.

"Funny thing about camel dung," the adjutant said.

Prescott came over to them, leaning into the wind and holding a big buff envelope with both hands. Spurts of dust fled from his feet at every step. He sat next to Barton, glad of the shelter of the tent. "If I'm interrupting anything special I'll buzz off," he said.

"Uncle was about to tell a funny joke about camel dung," Barton said. His eyes were half-shut.

"I just passed Billy Stewart," Prescott said. "He's killing flies again."

"As long as he's happy. What you got?"

"Signal from Group." Prescott gave him the envelope. "Tomorrow's targets."

"Filthy habit," the adjutant said. "And he never washes his hands."

"Schofers reckoned Billy was mad," Prescott said. "But then, Schofers thought you were all a bit cracked." He scratched his stubbled jaw and stared at the hazy, wobbly horizon. "Mind you, Schofers wasn't exactly normal, was he? Anyone who plays himself at chess, and loses, has to be a bit peculiar."

"We had a chap like Billy when the squadron was in France," the adjutant said, "only in his case it was butterflies. Chased butterflies all over the aerodrome. Chap was a Hindu — white man, not an Indian, got converted in India — and according to the Hindu faith when you die you come back as something else, and because this chap's brother-in-law had snuffed it he was convinced he would come back as a butterfly, if only he could find the right one."

"Wait a minute," Prescott said. "Who was convinced? The brother-in-law, or your chap?"

"Our chap," Kellaway said.

"Who was also a brother-in-law," Barton pointed out sleepily. "He was the brother-in-law of the other brother-in-law."

"I expect they were both convinced, in the circumstances," Prescott remarked. "I mean to say, if you're dead and you find you've turned into a butterfly, there's not much point in arguing the toss, is there?"

"Nobody would listen to you anyway," Barton said. "Not if you were a butterfly."

That seemed to end the discussion. They sprawled in the windy heat and allowed their various preoccupations to drift through their minds. Prescott thought about his girl-friend Susan, back in England, and wondered whether or not she was looking after his car, a Bull-nose Morris he'd won in a poker game shortly before he got posted overseas. Susan had a wonderful body and a brain still in its original wrapper that she was saving in case she needed it when she got old. He had told her what to do. The car was in her father's garage, resting on wooden blocks to save the tyres, and every other month she should run the engine for a few minutes to keep the rust at bay. It was the first car he had owned. She'd forgotten. He was convinced she'd forgotten. Not her fault. Cars weren't important to her. Prescott thought of her delightfully curving body and forgave everything. Then he thought of the Bull-nose Morris rusting into a corroded hulk and his shoulders hunched. Bloody women.

The adjutant was thinking of the latrines and his sister and his will, more or less simultaneously. His sister had just married, big surprise, she was five years older than he was and he'd assumed she'd given up the hunt. Now somehow she'd snared this barrister fellow. Amazing. So she was taken care of, which was more than you could say for the blasted latrines; he could smell them without even trying. Kellaway had a keen nose, which could be a curse as far as latrines were concerned. Bloody pits hadn't been dug deep enough. So she wouldn't need his money now, would she? He'd have to change his will. Maybe endow a scholarship at his old school. The Kellaway Scholarship. That had a nice ring to it. Yes. What a stink.

Fanny Barton wasn't so much thinking as remembering.

He was remembering the ranks of German soldiers breaking and running, still in lines as they ran, ragged lines that were ludicrously slow although the legs and arms raced like clockwork toys. He remembered the simple joy of squeezing the pistol-grip on the joystick and seeing the rows of running men fall as if they had tripped over their own feet. They were always two hundred yards ahead, always falling. He heard the machine guns' racket, he felt their recoil, he saw in the edge of his vision the flames at the gun-ports, but the big impression was one of magic. The bullet-stream was a magic force like a great invisible bow-wave that constantly surged ahead and flattened any little obstacles. Strafing wasn't like ordinary battlefield killing. Strafing was fun and Barton enjoyed it, and then enjoyed remembering how much he enjoyed it, over and over again. The memory was so rich that it made him sleepy, as if he'd done a long hard day's work. Again his mind replayed the image of the falling men. Magic.

"Aren't you going to open that?" Prescott said. He meant the envelope.

"Maybe. Maybe not," Barton murmured.

A scrap of paper blew across the landing-ground, hustled along by the west wind, with nothing to stop it between here and Egypt. In a couple of months, Barton thought, some poor bloody wog might pick up that bit of paper in Cairo and find himself reading Standing Orders that blew off the wall of some Luftwaffe unit outside Benghazi a fortnight ago. If he could read. If he cared. If he didn't get knocked down by a British army three-ton truck, like a lot of dozy gyppoes did. They wandered into the road without looking and rapidly got converted into a pound of raspberry jam. It happened all the time, Barton had hit an old fellah one night on the road to Alex; no point in stopping, the chap was obviously stone dead. Bloody idiots.

Something began bothering Barton. "This bloke who chased the butterflies," he said. "I don't remember him, Uncle, and I was with the squadron in France almost from the start."

"Not *this* war, Fanny," the adjutant said. "The last one."

"Oh." Fanny lost interest. Uncle's flying had been with the Royal Flying Corps, in aeroplanes that had too many wings and the same top speed as a Bugatti. Also no parachute. Loonies, the lot of them.

"Come to think of it, he might have been a Buddhist," Kellaway said.

"How about the butterfly?" Prescott asked. "Could it have been a seagull?"

"Unlikely," Kellaway said. "Seagulls are Church of England. Well-known fact." He went to get the latrines sorted out before he caught dysentery and his sister inherited everything.

*   *   *

Henry Lester and Ralph Malplacket agreed to have lunch and pool their information about the prospects for newsworthy military excitement.

They went to the Chinese restaurant in the Prince Albert Hotel. This was Lester's idea. None of the other correspondents ate there and he wanted to keep Malplacket to himself. "I guess you know your way around this town," he said. "I mean, in our line of business, who you know is what you know. Isn't that right?"

"Actually, I've only been out here a week," Malplacket said. He poured tea for them both.

"Still, you don't get a chauffeured Bentley for nothing," Lester said, with a small smile of admiration.

"That, alas, belongs to the ambassador's wife. I only borrowed it. Now she has it back."

Dishes were placed before them: roast Canton duck, prawns with straw mushrooms, chicken with bamboo shoots, crispy noodles, water chestnuts, beansprouts, fried rice.

"Well, that's a shame," Lester said.

"Not really. I don't need a Bentley to take me to the right people. You see, before I left London, father gave me a list of names of valuable contacts, chaps in high places who keep their ear to the ground. Blanchtower used to be political adviser to the Governor-General. Even wrote a book about Egypt." Malplacket took out a sheet of paper and unfolded it.

Lester read it carefully. "I expect you know them," Malplacket murmured.

"I heard of them. Some, anyway. When was your father here?"

"1932."

"That explains it. Everyone on this list has died or gone

home, bar two. One of those is permanently drunk and the other's a recluse."

"Ah." Malplacket ate a prawn. "Blanchtower sometimes shows a curious sense of humour."

They ate in silence for a while.

"Look here, old chap," Malplacket said. "This is my first experience of seeking large publicity for anything. Hitherto my main concern has been to avoid attention at all costs."

"Yes? Tell me more."

"Can't, I'm afraid. Sworn to secrecy. Awfully dull, anyway, and no use to you. I seem to have spent half my life sitting in European cafés, waiting for blokes who never turned up. Jolly rough on the kidneys, I don't mind telling you, but it's not exactly headline material, is it?"

Lester helped himself to more noodles.

"Therefore I'm at a bit of a loss when it comes to knowing where one goes to find the news," Malplacket went on. "If I need a pound of coffee I usually go to Fortnum and Mason's. Now that I need a juicy chunk of war my instinct is to go to the War Department. But you say the powers that be are rather tightlipped at present."

"Verging on lockjaw," Lester said.

"But doesn't the army employ information officers, or the like?"

Lester thought about explaining and quickly abandoned the idea. "Look," he said, "why don't you come with me next time? See for yourself."

"That's very kind. It does seem rather strange, to have a war and not brag about it. The army is costing Britain an absolute fortune, you know. Absolute fortune! Blanchtower showed me the figures before I left: the noughts just went on and on and on. Hard to believe all that money isn't buying a spot of action *somewhere*."

*   *   *

There was no time to recruit volunteers. On General Schaefer's authority, Major Jakowski took one hundred and fifty men from a reserve regiment of German infantry and led them into the desert in a convoy of forty vehicles, which was ten more than Schaefer had promised, but Jakowski decided he needed the extra margin of safety. The desert was big and he planned to be away for at least two weeks, maybe three.

"Leadership and discipline," Jakowski told the men when they assembled, back-lit by the orange glow of dawn. He was standing on the tail-gate of a truck and wearing a soft cap with goggles pushed up onto his forehead, just like Rommel. "Leadership and discipline can defeat anything and anyone, and that includes the Sahara desert and the British raiding parties." He spoke quietly but firmly. "You and I, we're going to secure this territory with the same guts and determination that have made Germany the master of most of Europe and half of Russia. Leadership and discipline will always beat pirates or cowboys or outlaws, which is what the enemy raiders are. So far the desert has been their shelter. No longer. From now on the desert is our property and the enemy our prisoner."

Jakowski's delivery was good but his timing was bad. These troops had all had experience of battle. As they dispersed to their vehicles, one soldier said to another: "He talks as if we've won before we've started."

"Not worth going then, is it?" said the other man. "Will you tell him, or shall I?" But they spoke cheerfully. After the sweat of training exercises and the grind of guard duties and the tedium of kit inspections, this was an adventure. With extra rations, too.

The column barrelled briskly along a good road that skirted the western edge of the Jebel el Akhdar. Most of the vehicles were short-wheelbase canvas-topped trucks, Fiats or Mercedes with the odd Ford, each armed with a heavy machine gun mounted on a swivel; moreover,

Jakowski had chucked General Schaefer's name about pretty freely in the motor parks around Benghazi and he had collected a heavy breakdown truck (with a big winch), a petrol bowser, three supply trucks to carry food, three water-tankers, a radio truck, an ambulance, a command vehicle in which to hold briefings, and a small mobile bakery. After he took the bakery he had doubts; but then he told himself that a hundred and fifty men would need a lot of feeding. And certainly when they saw it, the men were pleasantly surprised. Fresh bread in the desert was a great luxury.

By eight a.m. the column had rounded the Jebel el Akhdar and the road was turning into a track. It had been much battered by the tank-treads of both sides, and some of the tanks lay about, fire-blackened, holed, capsized. "They remind me of the pieces moved to the sides of the board in a game of chess," Major Jakowski said to his driver, who nodded. They looked to him more like a damn good reason to stay out of panzers, but you couldn't tell an officer that. He wiped his hands on his trousers. The palms were sweating so much that they kept slipping on the wheel. If it was this hot now, what would it be like at noon?

"Turn here," Jakowski ordered.

The column bumped over the broken edge of the road. A broad, shallow gully pointed roughly south-east, which should take them into the desert, where Jakowski hoped to find evidence of the British raiding patrols. Even if he didn't find evidence, his men would get valuable experience of searching the desert. At best, of course, they would intercept a raiding party and wipe it out.

The gully forked, and forked again. It deepened too: they were still in the edge of the foothills of the Jebel and these wadis had been scoured out by the flash-floods of a hundred thousand years. It was possible to pick a path down the middle and after forty minutes Jakowski was reasonably pleased with their progress when a harsh metallic twang made him jump. Bright metal showed through the camouflage paint two feet in front of his driver. They were being shot at. "Stop!" he shouted. They stopped.

The order took a full minute to work its way back up the column. Long before then, Jakowski's driver was spraying machine-gun fire against the right-hand side of the wadi. It made a furious, stuttering racket that echoed and re-echoed. The trouble was he couldn't see what he was firing at. All the dust raised by the vehicles behind him was drifting forward, thickened by exhaust fumes. He aimed from memory, upwards at where the skyline had been. The gunner in the truck behind joined in; the infection spread; gunners throughout the column were sprinkling little bursts amongst the invisible rocks, believing they must be under attack because everyone else was firing. Meanwhile Jakowski, thinking hard, realised that the bullet could as easily have come from the left as from the right, and he ordered the driver to hit that side, too. He swung the gun, rattled off fifty rounds into the drifting haze, and looked to Jakowski for fresh orders. "Cease fire," Jakowski said glumly. He walked to the next truck and shouted at them to stop. "You," he ordered. "Go back and tell all those idiots to cease fire." The man set off, moving very carefully and shouting very loudly.

The dust drifted away. The air cleared. No attackers were to be seen. Everything was silent. The drivers had switched off their engines: overheating came fast in this temperature. The column sat in the wadi like a parade waiting in a side street.

Jakowski found the nearest lieutenant and told him to see what damage had been done. While that was happening, he climbed the wall of the wadi and looked at the terrain. It told him nothing. It was all hillocks and ravines, and the hillocks were all lumps and bumps, dotted with rocks, spotted with thorn-bushes, fringed with silvery grass. Everything else looked grey-brown. It looked dead: baked to death. Nothing moved except the grass, and that had a constant, nervous shimmer, as if flinching away from the hot wind.

The lieutenant was waiting below. Jakowski scrambled down.

"One bullet-hole, sir," the lieutenant said. "In the canvas. Driver swears it's new, I'm not so sure. No casualties."

"That's all?"

"Yes sir." He thought: *Now the old bastard's pissed-off because nobody got killed. Can't win, can you?*

"We must have fired off five thousand rounds," Jakowski said bitterly. "Just for one lousy sniper. And I bet he was out of sight before we even started."

The lieutenant said nothing. There was nothing to say.

"For God's sake, let's get out of this bloody dump." Jakowski waved at his driver to start up.

"One truck has a puncture, sir," the lieutenant said quickly. "They're mending it now."

"Get the other officers," Jakowski ordered. "I want them here. Now."

The lieutenant returned with two captains and two lieutenants. Jakowski led them down the track, out of earshot of the troops. His driver strolled over to a friend, who said: "What's happening?"

"They're getting pissed on from a great height," the driver said.

"I wouldn't mind getting pissed on, in this heat. Bloody old Jacko can piss on me every hour on the hour, if he likes."

Jakowski said to his officers: "Leadership and discipline. Remember? One smelly Arab takes a pot-shot at us and everyone goes berserk. We must have wasted ten thousand rounds on these damn rocks."

"I honestly thought we were under attack, sir," a captain called Rinkart said. "It certainly sounded like it."

"Those were all our guns, you bonehead."

"We couldn't tell that, sir," said the other captain, whose name was Lessing. "Not in all that dust." Jakowski gave him a hard, wide-eyed stare. One of the lieutenants murmured: "The fog of war." Jakowski switched the stare to him. "Figure of speech, sir," the lieutenant said.

"Fog of intelligence," Jakowski barked. "From now on, nobody opens fire unless I give the order."

"We'll never hear it," Lessing said. "Not over the noise of the engines."

"Red signal flare," Jakowski said. The officers looked at each other. "I take it we did bring signal flares," he said heavily. His nostrils twitched like a rabbit's.

Rinkart said: "I think I saw a box being loaded, but God knows which truck they're in."

"Find them," Jakowski told a lieutenant. "Meanwhile I'll give the signal to open fire by sounding the horn of the vehicle I'm in. A loud continuous blast on the horn. Think you can hear that? Short blasts mean cease fire."

"What if we get fired on, sir?" Lessing asked. "And you don't hear it?"

"Use your initiative."

The drivers restarted their engines, all except one of the water-tankers, which whined and kicked but would not start. Major Jakowski ordered it to be towed. The column moved on. After a mile it began to leave a thin trail of water. The air was so full of dust that nobody noticed.

*　　*　　*

God got the blame for the first casualty.

Major Jakowski knew all about the Tariq el 'Abd; his map clearly indicated those stretches which had been sown with thermos mines (by the German army, so the map ought to be accurate); and he kept well to the north of it until he met a camel track that crossed his path. It was a broad, well-trodden track, and several vehicles had followed it too. He turned right. By now his column was out of the broken foothills and into something that looked like real desert. The heat was cooking up mirages. A palm grove shimmered. A rock apparently as big as a hotel trembled in the distance. Jakowski was not fooled.

It was about ten or twelve miles before they reached the Tariq. They saw it from a long way off. On the bare and barren desert, the skeleton of a camel stood out like a monument. A dozen skeletons littered the Tariq.

Jakowski put down his binoculars. "Go easy," he told the driver.

Further on, the tyre tracks and the camel tracks all converged. "This must be the place to cross," he said. "Go where they went. *Exactly* where they went."

The last vehicle in the column, several hundred yards away, was a food truck, packed high with cases of tinned stuff plus three soldiers. Two were veterans of the Afrika Korps, Oskar and Bruno, aged twenty-two or twenty-three; the third was a recent replacement, aged twenty. His name was Caius. Oskar and Bruno were whiling away the time by educating Caius. "You don't want to worry about those British Commandos, kid," Bruno said. "They're not so bad."

"Right," Caius said. He hunched his shoulders.

"Well . . ." Oskar spat out a date-pit. They were all eating from a box which Oskar had discovered was broken open after he kicked it hard. "Depends, doesn't it? *Some* aren't so bad. I mean, I personally don't believe that story Sergeant Nocken told."

Bruno picked his teeth with his tongue. "You mean the one about the British Commando who tore off the stormtrooper's arm and beat him to death with it? That story?"

"No, no," Oskar said irritably. "He had witnesses for

that, didn't he? I mean the story about the little Commando who stood on the oberstleutnant's feet and screwed his head round and round until it . . . You know."

"Well, it's possible," Bruno said. "Don't you agree it's possible, kid?"

"No idea," Caius said, and looked away. He really didn't know, and he didn't want to think of it. He had heard of men, infantrymen, who had gone all through the last war without having to fire a single shot at the enemy. Not one.

"I suppose it's no different from taking a stiff cork out of a bottle," Oskar said. The truck moved. "Off again," he said.

"Anyway, what I meant was the Arabs are a bloody sight worse than the Commandos," Bruno said. "You want to watch out for the Arabs, kid."

The first three vehicles made the narrow crossing over the Tariq without difficulty. Then the driver of the breakdown truck paid too much attention to the NCO standing in front and waving him on. He made a bad gear-change and stalled the engine. It restarted promptly enough, but the driver was angry with himself and he punished the engine by over-revving it. The wheels spun and dug twin pits in the sand. Hot rubber smoked. The NCO shouted. The driver whacked the gear-lever into neutral and cursed.

"Brilliant," the NCO said. "Now see if you can get it out backwards."

The driver tried to reverse and merely lengthened the pits. Eventually, by rocking the truck back and forth he lengthened them so much that he could charge forward and smash his way up and out of trouble.

A couple of men shovelled sand back into the holes. Waste of time. The next few drivers, determined not to make the same mistake, went hard and fast into and out of the crossing, and made the holes worse than ever. Soon they merged into one sharp dip. The harder the trucks hit it, the deeper it got. And vice versa.

"Extremely cunning, your Arab," Bruno said. "I mean, take those things they carry water in."

"Goatskins," Oskar said.

"He knows that. He's not stupid. *You're* stupid. He's very intelligent. He's got brains written all over his face."

Caius ducked his head to hide a blush. He was very conscious of his boyish good looks and what's more Bruno had been wrong: Caius hadn't known that Arabs carried water in goatskins.

"Last time we took Tobruk," Oskar said, "I saw a New Zealander with brains written all over his face. He couldn't have been very clever, because they were his brains."

Bruno waved this reminiscence away. "Question is, how do they do it?" he said. "How do the Arabs get the goat out of his skin without slitting him up the belly?" He raised his hands in wonder at this native trick.

"That's why you never want to get caught by the Arabs, kiddo," Oskar told Caius. "They'll do the same to you."

"Very clever fellow," Bruno said, "your average Arab."

"I heard they pour ants down your throat and let them eat you up," Oskar said. "Those desert ants, they've got jaws like crabs."

"I had crabs once," Bruno said. "They had jaws like sharks."

Caius said suddenly: "I had a shark once. It had jaws like . . . like . . ." He couldn't think of a good ending. "Like nutcrackers," he ended. The others laughed. "Any Arab gets a grip of you, kid," Oskar said, "he'll crack your nuts and eat the meat too."

Major Jakowski tried not to show his impatience. It was common sense to halt the column on the southern side of the Tariq until all the vehicles had crossed. Forty vehicles couldn't be rushed, not with that hole in the middle deepening with the whomp of every wheel. He wanted to get on fast, but he didn't want his men to think he was the sort of commander that always nagged and moaned, never smiled or joked. He walked over to the two captains, adjusting his walk to a saunter. They were looking at the sky.

"It's not going to rain," Jakowski said lightly.

"We were wondering whether we ought to disperse the vehicles, sir," Rinkart said. He was dark, almost swarthy, with a stocky build. As far as Jakowski could tell, thick black hair grew all over him. All the same, Rinkart had a sharp brain and he was good in battle: Jakowski had taken the trouble to check his records. "Whoever he is, he's seen us," Rinkart said. "He's been circling for five minutes."

"Where?" Jakowski could see nothing. Rinkart pointed at the speck in the blazing blue. Jakowski searched and still saw nothing, but he didn't admit it. "If he's Luftwaffe, they already know we're here," he said, wiping his eyes. "And the RAF wouldn't send one plane this far."

"They might if it's a Beaufighter," Lessing said. He didn't look like a soldier: too tall, too slim, his voice slipped too easily into a drawl and he had an actorish way of standing, all the weight on one leg and the hand propped high on his waist. Yet he too had a fine combat record. "If that's a photo-reconnaissance Beaufighter, Cairo will know all about us in a couple of hours."

"We shan't be here in a couple of hours," Jakowski said. "Further south it's like an autobahn three hundred kilometres wide."

Another truck came roaring and bucking through the gap.

"I'd be happier if we weren't all bunched-up like this," Rinkart said.

"No point in dispersing now," Jakowski said. The last truck was making its approach.

"You're lucky, you are," Bruno said. "The Arab men won't harm you. Not you."

"Why?" Caius asked.

"Because their women will want you."

"Blond," Oskar explained. "Highly prized by Arab women, a tasty young white blond boy."

"Lucky me," Caius said. He wished they would stop.

"If you call having to perform twelve times a day being lucky," Oskar said.

"Seven days a week," Bruno added.

"That's what they want from you," Oskar said. "All day long. Dawn to dusk. If you can't deliver the goods, they get nasty."

"You've insulted them, you see," Bruno said. "Out come the knives. Off come your sweetbreads."

The truck swayed as it put on speed. It lurched and bounced so hard that all its load rose up and crashed down. "Jesus Christ!" Oskar said. He had spilled the dates. At once there was a second crash, more muffled than the first, and Caius fell forward so that his face was in Bruno's lap. Bruno shoved him upright and he fell again, sideways. One boot struck Oskar on the knee. He began to curse, but stopped when he saw Caius's hands. They were trembling vigorously, as if trying to shake off something wet and distasteful. After twenty seconds they stopped and lay still.

The doctor's examination was brief.

"First, he's dead," he told Jakowski. "Second, the only damage I can find is a small hole in the back of the skull. No exit wound, so it almost certainly wasn't a bullet."

"Dig a grave," Jakowski told Captain Lessing. Lessing, standing with his arms crossed, aimed a finger at a small rise. Men were already digging there. "Ah," Jakowski said. "Good."

Captain Rinkart joined them. "Several men heard an explosion. One says he saw a little spurt of flame near the truck as it hit that damn hole. So it looks like a thermos bomb went off."

Jakowski said: "I thought those bloody things were safe unless you tampered with them."

"That's the theory," Lessing said.

"If it was lying near the crossing," Rinkart said, "we've been tampering with it. Every time a truck hit that hole the vibration gave it a good hard shake."

Jakowski sat on his heels and looked at the calm young face. "His war didn't last long, did it?" he said.

"It's only a skull," the doctor said. "A man's skull is quite thin. It won't keep out fragments of shrapnel travelling at high velocity."

"An act of God," Jakowski said.

One of the lieutenants took charge of the burial party. He read out the short funeral service from his field service manual and when he came to the dead man's name he mispronounced it. Bruno and Oskar looked at each other. Typical. Buried the wrong man.

"Put plenty of rocks on him," Lessing advised. "The vermin in these parts are very persistent."

Ten minutes later the column began to move south. Oskar saw some dates lying on the floor of the truck and he kicked them over the tail-gate. Let the vermin enjoy them instead.

*   *   *

"Cleopatra had the right idea," Elizabeth Challis said in her high, clear, expensive voice. "One has only one true love in one's life. When that love dies, one's reason for living goes." She trailed her fingers in the Nile.

The other hand held her glass. Jack Lampard, sitting opposite, put an inch of wine into it, and said: "But think what a tragedy that would be for us poor men. Without beauty such as yours to worship, we might as well all go back to the desert and simply kill each other."

They were in a felucca, at night, sailing past Zamalek Island, where the Gezira Club's lights blazed. Somebody's band was playing a foxtrot, 'Dinah'. The music rose and fell with the breeze.

"I'm sorry," Lampard said. "I shouldn't have said that. Incredibly crass of me, in the circumstances."

"*Tais toi*," Elizabeth Challis said. "I'm not a porcelain doll, you know."

"Gerald was frightfully brave at the end." Lampard ate a few strawberries and drank some wine. "Of course I wasn't with him, I was nearby, still fighting off the fearful foe, but they told me he spoke of you."

She turned her splendid head on its splendid neck, straight off the cover of *The Tatler,* and looked at him. *My stars*, Lampard thought. *The face that sold a thousand tubs of Pond's skin-cream.*

"They say he said he didn't want you to mourn his passing," Lampard said. He tried to see the look in her eyes, but the little lantern in the boat cast too many shadows. "I mean, not excessively."

"Dear Gerald."

"He was never a man to think first of himself."

"He made the supreme sacrifice." She sipped a little wine and uttered soft, appreciative noises with her lips. "What a frightfully good year this Chablis was."

Lampard raised his glass. "To absent friends."

"Yes." She sighed, and he observed her silk dress slip sleekly across her breasts. "Yes. Isn't it dreadful? There are moments when I can't remember what he looked like. His face is just a blur."

"Perfectly normal reaction, my dear."

"Actually, Gerald was a brandy-and-soda man. He could be frightfully stuffy in some ways. I mean, this wine would have been wasted on him. Utterly wasted."

"Mustn't let it get warm, must we?" Lampard refilled their glasses.

He put both hands on her waist when he helped her ashore, and he tipped the boatman quite generously. They took a horse-drawn gharri back to her house in the Garden City. He liked riding in a gharri. Its ironclad wheels made a splendid clatter. If it had to stop in traffic, the driver could be relied upon to use his whip on any hawkers or beggars who tried to bother them. Lampard gave him a good tip, too. She noticed. "You spoil them," she said.

"You spoil me," he said. She had taken his arm for the walk to the front door. She gave him the key. Opening doors was a man's job.

They danced to a stock of records that dropped, one by one, from the arms of her modern American record-player: 'Blue Room', 'We'll Meet Again', 'Dancing in the Dark', 'Stardust', 'A Foggy Day in London Town'. She hugged him and asked: "What makes your uniform crackle like that?"

"Light starch," he said. "Or perhaps static electricity."

That amused her. "Might one be scorched by you?" she asked.

"You are in terrible peril," he said gently. "Strike the slightest spark and there will be a colossal explosion."

The record ended. "Stay," she said, and went out. She came back dressed in silk pyjamas and carrying another pair. "These were too big for Gerald," she said, "but they should fit you."

Lampard left the house at dawn. *Played two, won two*, he thought.

*   *   *

Strafing continued all next day.

The ground crews had worked throughout the night and Hornet Squadron was fully operational again. Barton had the pilots awoken at four-thirty a.m. Briefing was to be at five, take-off as soon as possible afterwards. The night was still very black at four-thirty. Black and cold. Hick Hooper forced himself out of bed and was immediately shivering. He pulled his uniform over his pyjamas and walked around the tent, stamping and slapping to get his body going, and he tripped over a guy-rope. "Holy Moses," he said. The tent swayed.

"You're allowed to swear," Tiny Lush told him. He was giving his chest a good two-handed scratch.

"My own fault," Hooper mumbled.

"So what? Never sit on your emotions. Gives you terrible piles. Well-known scientific fact." Lush put on a sweater and pulled a knitted stocking-cap over his ears and headed for the mess. Hooper followed. The sky was thick with icy stars.

By then the two flight commanders had already met Barton in his trailer.

"We'll hit Fritz before he's had time to put his teeth in," he told them. "And we'll bash the Eye-ties while they're still looking for their hernia belts." He was clapping his hands, not for warmth but to release his exuberance.

"You're bloody chirpy," Patterson said, "sir."

"Dawn is a bloody chirpy time," Barton said. "If you're a bird, that is." He spread his arms wide and flapped his hands. "Think of the worms. Wrapped in their blankets. Waiting to be strafed." He smacked his lips.

"Yesterday, sir, you said breakfast was the best time," Dalgleish said.

"No, no. Dawn. *Daaaaawn*." Barton turned it into a long, theatrical groan. "Worst time of day. Everyone feels rotten. Mouth like an Arab's armpit. Then, before you can properly wake up, some bastard *Englander* comes along and blows half your head off." At times like this, Barton had a cheerful, boyish face. He raised his eyebrows and turned down the corners of his mouth. "Be fair," he said. "You wouldn't like it."

"Dawn." Dalgleish looked at his watch. "We'd better get cracking."

"Hit 'em low," Barton said. "Below the belt."

"I'm not flying a hundred and fifty miles at night at zero feet," Patterson declared. "I had enough of that insanity over the English Channel."

"Suit yourself," Barton told him. He gave them each a list of targets. "Just get over there and make bloody nuisances of yourselves."

As they were leaving, Patterson stopped. He was reading his list. "This can't be right, Fanny," he said. "We hit these yesterday."

"You're surprised?" Barton twitched with pleasure. "Good. That means they'll be astonished."

The mess tent was filling up with yawning pilots. Pip got his mug of tea and sat next to Dalgleish. "Hell of a gamble, isn't it?" he said.

"Maybe. Tell you at breakfast."

"I might not get back for breakfast."

"Then you'll know the answer, won't you?"

"That's a great comfort." Pip drank. "Shit," he said. "There's sand in this tea."

"You're a lucky lad," Pinky told him. "Usually you get tea in your sand." He went off to brief his Flight.

The squadron took off in pairs as soon as the first grey tinge in the east gave a hint of the horizon. It was full daylight when they came back and landed, engines crackling and snapping as the power came off and the wheels touched and set off instant streamers of dust. All twelve Tomahawks came back. Only one pair had met a defence that was obviously hotter and stronger than the day before, and that was Barton and Stewart, so everyone felt good. "You wanted me to tell you something," Pinky Dalgleish said to Patterson. They were standing in line for fried tinned bacon and tinned tomatoes. "Can't remember what. Can you?"

"Who killed Cock Robin?" Patterson was feeling marvellous. He and Kit Carson had found some trucks that blew up with a gratifying shower of pyrotechnics and they had chased a bunch of infantry like panicking sheep. "How many beans make five? Did your mother come from Ireland? Who were you with last night, out in the pale moonlight?" He was ravenous. The aroma of fried bacon made him salivate.

"I remember now," Pinky said. "Something about a hell of a gamble."

"Everything's a gamble," Pip said. "Why worry?"

"I'm not worried, Pip. If you go for a Burton today, can I have your bacon tomorrow?"

"Not a funny joke."

"Who said it was a joke?"

Fanny Barton's second-guessing of the enemy's mind gave the squadron a good day. The dawn attacks, with pairs of Tomahawks arriving at high speed from the eye of the sun, achieved surprise everywhere except at Barton's own target. "Flak as thick as pig shit!" he told Kellaway, who was acting Intelligence Officer. "Billy would have got out and walked on it, but he didn't like getting his boots dirty. Did you, Billy-boy?" Stewart smiled and nodded. The flak had been terrifying, a sudden storm of hate that flooded the sky, but they had bashed through it all and survived. Billy Stewart had total faith in his CO. Where Fanny went, Billy followed. Their fighters were ripped and slashed by shrapnel, but so what? The Tomahawk was a tough old kite, the troops would slap on some patches. And look at Fanny, pleased as sixpence. Billy smiled. Kellaway smiled. He liked a happy squadron.

They strafed again at midday, swooping through the hot and dusty haze on a different set of targets. And again at sunset, when they circled wide to the west, put themselves between the dazzle and the eyes of the German gunners, and then raced home.

Night fell at six-thirty prompt.

Supper was bully-beef stew with biscuits and tea.

"What d'you make of it so far?" Fido Doggart asked the American politely.

"Good place for a war," Hooper said. "Nothing but sand and flies, and the flies seem to enjoy the company."

"It's a funny thing," Mick O'Hare said, "but I've been in the blue now man and beast for nigh on forty years come Shrove Tuesday, and I know every fly by name and by face, yet I've never seen a fly land on Butcher Bailey. Isn't that an odd thing?"

"Even flies draw the line somewhere," Fanny said.

"Flies have got some respect," Butcher told them. "They recognise Norman blood."

Kit Carson had been about to eat some stew. Instead he aimed his spoon at Butcher. "You telling us your ancestors came over with William the Conqueror?"

"Don't point that thing at me," Butcher said. "It might go off."

"You should have seen the flies in France in '40," the adjutant said. "Big as sparrowhawks."

"This stuff went off last week," Kit said, eating it.

"Polish air force was very aristocratic," Sneezy announced. "My squadron commander, a genuine Polish count, brave as a lion. One day a pilot tries to land, forgets to lower his wheels, nasty prang. My squadron commander takes pilot behind hangar and shoots him. In the head. With a pistol."

"That's not very nice," Pinky Dalgleish observed.

"Did he get court-martialled?" Pip Patterson asked.

Sneezy was amused. "How could he? He was dead! Shot through the head! Besides, no time for court-martial. Germans invade."

"Well, it's one way to fight a war, I suppose," Barton said.

"Aristocrats got no time for peasants," Sneezy said. "Pilot behaves like peasant, doesn't deserve to be pilot."

"Remember that in future, you lot," Fanny Barton said.

"You can't shoot me behind the hangar if I prang," Fido Doggart said. "We haven't got a hangar."

"Uncle: order a hangar," Barton said. "A small portable hangar."

"What we really need is a portable gramophone," Kellaway said wistfully.

A vehicle arrived, headlights burned in the blackness, doors slammed. The doctor came in and dumped a couple of cardboard boxes. "Onions," he said. He looked and sounded very tired. "I hope there's some grub left." He found a space to sit at the table and looked around until he found Fanny Barton. "Schofield's dead," he told him. "Dead and buried."

"I'm sorry to hear that," Barton said. The adjutant nodded and grunted a sort of confirmation. Nobody else spoke. This interested Hick Hooper. An American squadron would have reacted differently: somebody's fist would have slammed the table, heads would have swung towards the doctor, there would have been passionate remarks like *Jesus, can you believe it?* or *What a lousy deal.* But the RAF didn't go in for that sort of thing.

"I brought the new IO with me," the doctor said. A cook put a plate of stew in front of him. "Old pal of yours. Skull Skelton."

That startled Barton. "Tall bloke? Glasses, big forehead? Always disagreeing with everyone?" The doctor, spooning down stew, nodded. "Well, I'm buggered," Barton said.

"Baggy Bletchley must have fixed it," the adjutant said.

"Skull was Intelligence Officer when the squadron was in France," Barton told the others. "And all through the Battle of Britain. Then he had a row with an air vice-marshal and got posted to the north of Scotland."

"What was the row about?" Kit Carson asked. To him, arguing with an air vice-marshal was inconceivable.

"Something to do with putting extra-long-range drop tanks on the Spits," Barton said, "so the kite flew a very very long way, but the trouble was it behaved like a constipated brick. Remember, Pip?"

Patterson shook his head at the memory. "You get jumped by a Focke-Wulf 190, there's no time to fart about with drop tanks," he said.

"So the AVM turned out to be wrong," Barton said. "But Skull had gone north by then. And several good pilots had gone west."

A few minutes later Skull came in, carrying a portable gramophone and some records. He paused and sniffed appreciatively. "The aroma has something of the barnyard bouquet of a truly fine burgundy," he said. "And is that Limburger cheese I detect?"

"My stars," Kellaway said. "You're a squadron leader now."

"That's desert feet you can smell," Tiny Lush said.

Skull put the gramophone and records down. "They tell me you can't even get *The Times* delivered here," he said to Barton. "They say this is the worst posting in all Africa."

"Takoradi is far worse," Barton said happily. "Anyone doesn't like it here can go to Takoradi."

"Even the flies hate Takoradi," Pip Patterson said. "Or so I'm told."

"What have you got there, Skull?" Kellaway pointed to the gramophone records. "Bloody Beethoven, I expect."

"No fear," Skull said. "Lots of Al Bowlly singing 'Empty Saddles in the Old Corral' and other classics. Wonderful stuff." He picked up a record and carefully wiped it on his sleeve. "Al Bowlly is the English answer to Bing Crosby, you know," he said.

"A crooner," Kellaway said emptily. "Couldn't sing 'Land of Hope and Glory' to save his life. Sorry I asked."

*   *   *

Henry Lester took Ralph Malplacket to see an amiable major who was a press liaison officer at Middle East HQ.

"Nothing much on the books at present, I'm afraid," the major said.

"My editor is convinced I'm goofing off," Lester said. "He's been holding the front page so long, his arms ache."

"War is never continuous. There are lulls. This is a lull."

"Newspapers can't lull. Those that do, die."

"Well, if it's death you want to cover I can steer you towards several excellent military hospitals. Or military cemeteries, come to that."

Lester shrugged. He got up and drifted away to the window.

"It's all a matter of degree, isn't it?" Malplacket said. "We realise that it would, of course, be premature to expect a full-scale battle as such." He twirled his Panama hat on the end of his forefinger. "For myself, any item of news would be welcome, provided it put fresh heart into the munitions workers of England as they toil in their factories. Not a swingeing defeat of the Hun, just a refreshing taste of success." He twirled too hard and his hat spun off his finger.

Lester came and picked it up. "British Commandos use tommy-guns, don't they?" he asked the major. "Chicago *makes* tommy-guns. Now there's a hell of a good story just waiting to be written."

"Think what it would do to the morale of our gallant American cousins," Malplacket urged.

The major made a short telephone call.

"I can get you attached to a tank exercise," he told them. "People like reading about tanks. All that dashing about the desert. Live ammunition, too."

"It's not tommy-guns, though, is it?" Lester said.

"It might be. Some infantry will be training alongside the tanks. The odd tommy-gun might appear. You never know your luck." The major was adjusting the things on his desk, squaring off the blotter, the files, the ink stand.

"So kind of you to chat with us." Malplacket got his

hat back from Lester. "If, by chance, a Commando raid should materialise, you will bear us in mind, won't you?"

The major almost smiled. "Nobody tells me anything about Commando raids, and if they did I wouldn't believe them. If you're looking for a really good scrap, I recommend the Black Cat Club."

"It's gone downhill lately," Lester said. "I've seen more blood on the floor at the Chicago Chrysanthemum Show."

"Best I can do," the major said.

They went out and sat in a big Buick. Lester had borrowed it from Shapiro, who was in Syria looking for a story.

"I feel sluggish when there's no news," Lester said. "I mean, news, that's what life is all about, right?"

"It's a point of view," Malplacket said.

"The way things are now, it just depresses the hell out of me. I was in Spain in '37 and people from both sides were falling over themselves to give us their news. Most of it was crap, but at least they were *willing*. In China, for God's sake, they'd lay on a battle if you promised them ten bucks. Even in Berlin there was always news, provided you knew which stone to turn over. But here ... It's like I'm not speaking the same language because I didn't go to the right school, or something."

"Funny you should say that," Malplacket said. "Yesterday I bumped into a chap called Craven, Sticky Craven, hadn't seen him since Eton. He couldn't spell to save his life and now he's an air vice-marshal! With a little squadron leader to carry his briefcase."

"Did this Craven tell you any military secrets?"

"Um ... No. I didn't actually ask him about the war. Forgot, I suppose. We talked about cricket, mainly."

"Eton," Lester said thoughtfully. "D'you reckon you might find a few more of your old school pals in high places, if you went around and looked?"

"Oh, dozens. Scores, probably."

Lester started the car. He was beginning to feel slightly better. "Thank God for privilege," he said. "Cheaper than corruption, and you meet a better class of person."

*   *   *

Jakowski halted the column at noon so that the cooks could make a meal and the fitters could service the trucks. Both tasks proved impossible. The vehicles were too hot to touch and it was idiotic to light a fire in an atmosphere like the breath of a furnace. Jakowski settled for bread, dates and water. The column sat in the middle of the empty desert and fried. The men tried to sleep. The flies cruised from truck to truck, pausing only to refresh themselves with an occasional sip of sweat.

At mid-afternoon Jakowski reckoned that the heat had relaxed a fraction and he decided to move on. First, everyone was to get a third of a litre of water. That was when the leak was discovered. One of the water-tankers was half empty.

The news shocked him so much that for a few moments he felt ill: his chest hurt and he seemed to have forgotten how to breathe. This feeling of illness came as a second shock. He did not want the sergeant who had reported the leak to suspect anything, so he squatted on his heels and traced meaningless symbols in the sand. His father had died of a heart attack a year ago. Maybe it ran in the family. He forced his lungs to do their job and he felt his heart thudding too fast, too hard; but at least it was thudding.

"Lead on," he said. He smoothed out the symbols as if he had solved a piece of algebra, and stood up. "Captain Rinkart!" he shouted.

The sergeant showed them the hole, low down on the tanker. It was about the size of a thumbnail and it was blocked by a metal plug. "Bullet," the sergeant explained. "Ricochet, I expect, sir."

"It's not leaking," Major Jakowski said, and felt foolish because the remark sounded like a complaint. He thumped the side of the tanker with his fist.

"Beg pardon sir, but it only leaks when it moves. When the truck moves, that is, sir. That's how I spotted it. Driver brought it up here so we could issue the ration, I saw the dribble coming out. Truck stopped, dribble stopped."

Jakowski straightened up. "I don't believe it," he told Rinkart. "It's a conspiracy." That was meant as a joke, but nobody smiled.

"Water is very heavy," Rinkart said. "The truck hits a bump, it sloshes about, the tank distorts, the bullet doesn't fill the hole, we lose another mugful."

"And nobody noticed."

"It's the dust, sir," the sergeant explained.

"Get it repaired," Jakowski said. He walked away. "Five pfennigs-worth of ammunition fired by some scrofulous Arab," he said. "Makes you sick, doesn't it?" He was beckoning to the other officers.

"We still have the other two water-tankers, Major," said Rinkart.

"That's like saying we still have two-thirds of a chance of finding the enemy." Jakowski waited until Captain Lessing and the two lieutenants joined him and told them what had happened. "Right, assume you're in command," he said to Lessing. "Assume I trod on a mine like that poor bastard we just buried. What's your plan?" Inexplicably, he yawned.

"That depends on what your original orders were, sir. I mean, what is the object of the operation? Unless I know that —"

"Yes, sure, agreed. Our immediate object is to get through the Jalo Gap, into the wide open spaces where there are no hiding places and where we stand an excellent chance of intercepting an incoming patrol of British raiders."

"In that case, sir, I'd send the water-tanker to Jalo Oasis and get it repaired and refilled."

"Which will take how long?"

"A day. Day and a half."

Jakowski grunted. It was the right answer, but he still didn't like it. "I see," he said. "Meanwhile this force sits on its fat backside, eats, drinks and plays cards for a day and a half."

One of the lieutenants got in fast. "Not necessarily, sir. The force can move south and rendezvous with the water-tanker at a prearranged map reference."

"Do it," Jakowski told Lessing. "Did you find those Luftwaffe compasses? Good. Make sure every truck has one. Now let's get out of here, this place bores me."

As he walked to the head of the column, men everywhere were moving and shouting, truck doors were slamming, motors roaring, black exhaust smoke gusting. The action made him feel better. As long as the column kept moving he felt strong and confident. When it stopped, things went wrong. Men died. Water got lost. The trick was to keep moving.

*   *   *

Paul Schramm looked like a thoughtful, patient man and half of him was. He spent hours and days studying intelligence reports, and he had an endless appetite for detail. Lampard's was not the only SAS patrol operating in the desert — far from it — and Schramm had files on them all; but he took a greedy interest in Lampard. Within twenty-four hours of the patrol's return to Cairo, Schramm knew about it. In due course he knew about Mrs Waterman and Mrs Elizabeth Challis, too. He even knew that Lampard had probably not used a condom.

"Interesting," he said to Oberstleutnant Hoffmann. "Significant, even."

They were in the station commander's office at Barce aerodrome.

"I don't see why," Hoffmann said. "I'd sooner know the calibre of his guns than the size of his weapon."

"I'm interested in his character. Perhaps his lack of character."

"You think he'll come back here, don't you?"

"I *know* he'll come back here."

"There are plenty of other airfields. Berka, Mersa Brega, Antelat, Slonta, Derna, Martuba. Dozens of them."

"He wants his revenge. I made a fool of him, didn't I? He'll be back, because he can't resist it. Not in his character."

Hoffmann strolled over to the window and watched a pair of Messerschmitt 109s sprint side by side until their tails lifted and almost at once they were flying, the dust trails collapsing behind them, wheels retracting; the raw, tearing racket fading to a soft thunder as the fighters made height. He grunted with envy. "I'd give a year's pay to fly one of those. Once a month they let me take up a Storch, just to keep my flying pay, and once a year, if I'm lucky, some Heinkel pilot lets me have a feel of the controls. But it's not the same."

"I know," Schramm said. He had heard it before.

"They say a 109 is too precious to risk on a crumbling ruin like me. They're saving them all for the next shove."

"I know that, too. In fact I told you."

"So you did . . ." Hoffmann turned away from the window. "What else have your ten thousand busy spies been able to tell you?"

"They say Takoradi has turned into a gold mine."

"They're probably right." Hoffmann thought about it. "But what good are spies if you can't use their information?"

"It's infuriating," Schramm said. "If only we could plant bombs in the enemy's Hurricanes the way they plant bombs in our 109s."

"You would need very long arms indeed."

Schramm got his crutches and went back to his intelligence reports. There was nothing new so he reread the old stuff. When he had exhausted that, he sat and stared at the telephone, wishing someone would call him. This was the other half of Paul Schramm. With no work to do, he had a very low tolerance of boredom. Eventually he grew thoroughly irritated with himself and clumped along the corridor to see the station doctor. "I wondered whether you might want to take a look at my desert sores," he said. All the cuts and scrapes he had collected during his escape across the Jebel had become infected and needed regular painting with gentian violet.

"I checked them this morning," the doctor said. "Do they hurt?"

"No." Schramm hung on his crutches and searched the room for entertainment or distraction.

"I know what you need, Paul," the doctor said. "You need a second opinion."

"No, I don't. There's nothing wrong with me."

"There's something wrong with me, though. I'm sick and tired of your ugly face." He scribbled something. "I'll make an appointment. Believe me, you'll be amazed by the results. Now go away."

*　　*　　*

Lester did his best with what little he could find.

The Chicago *News* got some smart professional stories about American bombers hammering Axis bases deep inside Libya, full of good detail regarding waist-gunners shouting "Three o'clock high!" while German fighters came plunging from the sun and oily plumes of smoke surged into the blue skies as the bombs found their targets. Lester worked hard, but with the Doolittle raid hitting Tokyo for the first time, while Japan conquered Burma, he knew his stuff would be lucky to make page five.

He kept in touch with his sources and spent much of his time with Ralph Malplacket, partly because he enjoyed his company and partly because he thought it might pay dividends. The son of an English lord who had the ear of Prime Minister Winston Churchill, and here he was prowling around Cairo looking like a rich refugee from a Sydney Greenstreet movie. There must be a story in him.

They usually met at Groppi's for iced coffee or tea at mid-morning. Groppi's was the coolest, cleanest teashop and bar in Cairo, probably in the Middle East; and when they came back from the desert most officers took several luxurious baths and then went to Groppi's for ice cream or cocktails. Sometimes Malplacket recognised old friends, or the sons of old friends, and a conversation developed. It was never very successful. He wanted an account of life in the desert; they asked about horse-racing at Ascot and salmon-fishing in Scotland. "Hasn't changed," he would say. "Much the same as ever." What they craved, of course, were images of lush turf and of roaring, foaming, peat-tinted rivers: the things they had dreamed of as they squinted into the painful glare that bounced off the desert or suffered the sandy dust that blew into every corner and opening of the body. "Now tell me about your war," he would say eagerly. "You have had a thrilling time, I hope?"

The desert warriors, tanned as dark as teak, found the idea amusing. "Not exactly thrilling," one of them said. "Thrilling isn't the word that first springs to mind."

"Tedious," suggested another officer. "Also grubby."

"It's empty, you see," the first officer said. "There's nothing out there. Terribly difficult to be thrilled by a lot of empty nothing. When you've captured it, what have you got?"

"Sod-all," the second officer said. "That's an Arabic phrase which means my camel has farted."

"Camel farts are pretty exciting events in the desert," the first officer said. "People talk about them for days on end. That's because there's bugger-all else to talk about."

"Bugger-all," the second officer said. "That's an Arabic phrase meaning two dead Italians and half a million flies."

Lester and Malplacket had lunch at the Union-International Hotel, which was rich with high-ranking officers. "The gabardine swine," Lester said gloomily.

"I say, that's rather good," Malplacket told him. "Did you just think of it?"

Lester considered lying and decided against it. "Old Cairo joke," he said. "Why don't they fight the war right here? Look at all the fascists you could kill."

"That's a bit strong." Malplacket glanced about the room. "I mean, take Boy Duff-Mannering, over there in the corner. He's not a fascist. He's all in favour of restoring the Holy Roman Empire. Told me so himself."

"Let's order," Lester said. "So I have something to throw up."

They ordered chilled cucumber soup, followed by curried shrimp with salad and a bottle of Bordeaux blanc on ice. After that they had trifle. "Trifle is one of the old country's great gifts to the Empire," Malplacket said. "You can judge a colony by the quality of its trifle."

"The British Empire's a racket." Lester felt better with good food inside him.

"Tell me," Malplacket said, "have you always been a war correspondent?"

"Sure. I covered baseball, football, hockey, tossing the beanbag; it's all war. I covered the conventions, Republican and Democrat both, and believe me that is war to the *death*. The only thing I've covered that turns out not to be war is this war. Right now this war is out to lunch."

"Not entirely," Malplacket said. "The old-boy network has come up trumps. I have made several promising appointments."

They drove across Cairo in the big Buick with the top down, to a Victorian house standing in its own grounds. Royal Marine sentries scrutinised their papers. "The colonel is expecting me," Malplacket said.

They were escorted to his office. Maps and photographs littered his desk. He was tall and languid, with a handshake that brought tears to Lester's eyes. "Glad to meet you," Lester said. "I'm a special representative to the Governor of Arizona, who of course is one of President Roosevelt's right-hand men."

"Ah," said the colonel.

"Philip and I are cousins," Malplacket told Lester. "He's in charge of all the Commandos in these parts, and if anybody can get us on one of their raids, he can."

"Second cousins," the colonel said. He had a pure, dry, Scots accent. "And I do not control the Commandos. Even if I did, I wouldn't send either of you on one of their raids because the odds are ten to one that you would be killed, and that would be a blow to the State of Arizona."

"Sure would," Lester said. He knew from the colonel's tone that the meeting was as good as over.

"Nevertheless," Malplacket said, "could you not release a sliver of information about the startling achievements of your Commandos?"

"What startling achievements?" the colonel asked.

"If I knew that, Philip, I wouldn't have to ask," Malplacket said. "Now please don't be tiresome. It's far too hot."

The colonel looked up and watched the ceiling-fan rotate like an old, tired windmill. He said, "We did have a corporal who saved an Arab from drowning in the Canal." He turned, found his reading-glasses, put them on, looked over the top at Malplacket. "But he was a very small

Arab," he said, "and probably not startling enough for your purposes."

Back in the Buick, Lester said: "He wouldn't tell us the time of day if he had a dozen watches and a two-bell alarm clock."

"Philip always was a selfish boy. Never shared his gobstoppers. Do you really know the Governor of Arizona?"

"Never met him. Neither has anybody else. Sounded good, though, didn't it?" He flexed his fingers. "Guys who try to bust your hand make me mad." He leaned on the horn and blew a bunch of donkeys aside.

Their next stop was an office block off Ramses Street in the New City.

"I'm Senator Mackenzie of Illinois," Lester said to a sentry before Malplacket could speak, "and we have an appointment with . . . Who are we seeing, Sir Ralph?"

"Admiral Blackett."

"Blackett, right." Lester gave the car keys to the sentry. "Make sure it doesn't get scratched, won't you."

As they entered the building, Malplacket said softly, "I wish you'd cut out these impersonations. They're not necessary, you know."

"Scared?"

"Not a bit." Malplacket rebelled at the way Lester was taking charge.

"Breathe deeply. Smile."

"I'll tell you what. I'll stay down here. You go up and interview him, Senator."

"No, no. The admiral will have tea waiting for us." Lester steered him towards the lift. "Your Royal Navy makes great tea, so I'm told."

They were not offered tea; in fact a civilian secretary had to get the admiral out of a meeting. He was stocky, pink-faced and cheerful; he was unimpressed by Senator Mackenzie; and he could give them exactly three minutes.

"We too are in a tearing hurry," Malplacket said. "How is my godson, by the way?"

"James is fine, and that's twenty seconds you've wasted. Come on, Ralph. What the devil d'you want?"

Malplacket explained his mission to Cairo. "Blanchtower feels the Navy's not getting the kudos it deserves."

Blackett was grimly amused. "Oh, yes? For what exploit in particular?"

"Your Small Boat Section, for instance. Very cloak-and-dagger, so I'm told, and just —"

"Never heard of them."

Malplacket was taken aback. "I understand they use little ships and sneak behind enemy —"

"Ships or boats?"

"Um . . . Does it matter, frightfully?"

"It does in the Royal Navy. A ship is not a boat. A *ship* is a large sailing vessel with three or more square-rigged masts, or by extension from that, a vessel of some appreciable size that is propelled by engines so that it may navigate across the high seas. That is a *ship*. A *boat* is not a ship. A boat is a *small* vessel propelled by oars or paddles, perhaps sails or a motor, but not fit for the high seas. That is a *boat*." Blackett was enjoying this. "It might help you to appreciate the distinction if you remember that a *ship* can carry a *boat*, but a *boat* can never carry a *ship*. There is a sub-definition by which a 'ship' means a ship's crew, but I don't suppose that's what you had in mind."

"No."

"It's probably much the same in the US Navy, Senator," Blackett said, so that their American guest should not feel excluded.

"Exactly," Lester said. "Word for word."

"Getting back to the heart of the matter," Malplacket said, "Small Boat Section or Small Ship Section: which have you got?"

"Neither," Blackett told him. "Not in the Royal Navy. And that's three minutes. Goodbye." He shook hands. The civilian secretary took them downstairs.

"See what I mean?" Lester said. He took the car keys from the sentry. "This war is out to lunch."

"He was lying," Malplacket said brusquely. "I always thought my godson was a dishonest little brute; it's obviously an inherited quality. He's at Oxford now, writing bogus poetry and walking with a limp to look like Byron."

"Since we're not getting anywhere," Lester said, "you might as well drive." They got in.

"The little blighter's malingering. I shall cable Blanchtower and have young Blackett conscripted into the Pioneer Corps at once, it will do him the world of good." Malplacket drove straight across a stop sign. A gharri swerved and hit a roadside fruit stall.

"Smart work," Lester said. "You just caused an accident."

"This entire city is an accident. All I did was make it more interesting."

They drove past Ezbekiya Gardens. "Are those zinnias?" Lester asked. "My wife was always trying to grow zinnias."

"Those are chrysanthemums," Malplacket said.

"Horseshit," Lester said.

"No, I think you'll find that on the rosebeds," Malplacket said.

"Listen, I know chrysanthemums. I *covered* chrysanthemums, for God's sake. They're very big in Chicago. I can do five hundred words on chrysanthemums at the drop of a hat."

Malplacket took his hat off and dropped it in Lester's lap. "Go," he said.

Lester put on the hat. "I only write for money."

He slumped in his seat. High above, kites slid along air currents, waiting for something to die. Cairo's Sanitation Department. Always on duty, never on strike, a credit to the city. Maybe there was a piece for the paper in that. Anyway, why weren't these stinking birds out in the desert? That's where the real work had to be done. No ambition. Henry Lester couldn't understand people without ambition. Even birds.

Malplacket drove over the Kasr Al-Nil bridge to Zamalek Island and turned north, into what was probably the best part of Cairo to live. The small block of flats at the end of a cul-de-sac was half-hidden by tamarisk and eucalyptus, and its balconies foamed with the red of bougainvillaea and the blue of morning glories.

"You'll like James," he said. "He's a group captain in RAF Intelligence. Not awfully bright – at school I had to help him with his Greek."

"You check him out." Lester slumped in his seat and pulled his hat over his eyes. "I'll stay here and get some rest."

The front door opened as Malplacket approached it. "James!" he said. "How kind of you to come and meet me. But then you always were the soul of courtesy."

The group captain did not offer to shake hands. He was big. When he leaned against the doorframe it creaked a little, and he filled most of the space. "Philip just phoned," he said. "You're trying to scrounge secrets, he says. With some gloomy Yank."

"He's in the car, decoding a few cables from Washington. The fact is, James, that Blanchtower wants me to report on the Special Air Service, so I came straight to you."

"Don't know why. Nothing to do with the RAF."

Malplacket breathed deeply and tried to smile. "With a name like 'Special Air Service' it can scarcely be anywhere *but* the RAF," he said. "Can it?"

"Nothing to do with us. Goodbye." The group captain stepped back, hooked his foot around the door and shut it.

"You struck out again," Henry Lester said.

"It's a delicate matter, very technical and, of course, highly confidential." Malplacket started the Buick. "He'll do his best. He was noncommittal."

"Yeah, you struck out."

They drove south and crossed to the mainland. Malplacket was subdued. The traffic was bad: he got behind a tram and followed it, stopping when it stopped. During one stop, Lester said: "My wife left me yesterday."

"Gone for good, you mean?"

"That's what it looks like. Took a boat to South Africa. Or maybe it was a ship. Yeah. Must have been a ship."

"What a shame," Malplacket said. "I'm very sorry."

"Well, it's been a long time coming, so I can't say I'm surprised. Still . . ."

"It's always a bit of a shock. Always."

"This might be a good day for getting very drunk," Lester said.

"I was thinking along similar lines."

"Suppose we start at Shepheard's. Then the Cecil Hotel, the Metropolitan Dugout, then Dolls', the Excelsior and Pastroudi's. After that –"

"How about the Black Cat Club?" Malplacket suggested.

"Sure."

"Is it a truly frightful dive?"

"Babylonian," Lester said. "Even the cockroaches go about in pairs."

*   *   *

For the third day of strafing, Fanny Barton made some changes. In the dawn attack, the whole squadron flew as one unit – a different unit. Overnight the aircraft had been painted blood-red on the wingtips and nose, with a red band around the fuselage just forward of the tail. The shark's teeth had gone.

"Striking, isn't it?" Barton said.

"Reminds me of the yellow-nose 109s we used to meet over France," Patterson said. "Very nasty, they were."

"Stuck in your memory, didn't it, Pip? That's the whole idea. Let the Afrika Korps think there's a brand-new red-nose Tomahawk squadron operating. Gives them something fresh to worry about."

"I miss the teeth," Dalgleish said.

"Relax, Pinky. It'll come off as soon as we get back."

That was in the grey of pre-dawn.

Barton waited until he saw the first curve of golden-orange sun nick the horizon, and led all twelve fighters in a booming, ripped-edge charge across LG 181.

There wasn't enough space to get everyone in line abreast, so Pip Patterson's Flight made the second rank. Pip had never done this before, not in the desert, and he had brooded over it during Barton's briefing. There would be a crowd of kites making a great cloud of dust, all at high speed. His Tomahawk was in the middle. It wandered to its left on take-off unless you corrected it. How could you correct it properly when you couldn't even see your wingtips? Fido Doggart was on his left. What if Fido wandered to the right? With full tanks and a full load of ammo, nobody would win that argument. Nothing left to bury but the fillings in their teeth. "This is a bit hairy, isn't it?" he had asked Fido. "How can you see when you can't see?" His stomach didn't like the pint of tea he'd sent it, and he was sweating already.

"Take off on a compass bearing. That's what I do," Fido said. "Treat the shit with the contempt it deserves."

It was like night-flying. As he raced into the deep-brown fog of dust flung up by the Flight in front, Pip stared at the compass needle and every time it twitched he corrected with a shove on a rudder pedal until at last he felt the tail come up and the jolting stopped. Suddenly the dust cloud fell away and he looked up into clear air. His Flight was neatly aligned to left and right, fifty feet off the deck, wheels tucking themselves away. Fido gave him a cheery wave. Pip nodded. He thought the red paint made the Tomahawks look like parrots. Not very warlike. At least the shark's teeth had looked tough.

Barton led them in the same take-off formation, Flights astern, except that Pip let his Flight fall back so as to escape the wash of the aircraft ahead. Barton liked to cruise at a height of a hundred feet, and that left little room for error. He steered them south of west for about half an hour, then turned north-west for fifteen minutes. By now everyone knew they were deep inside enemy territory and all their heads were turning, searching for the high glint, the microscopic gleam as sunlight bounced off alloy and perspex. Earlier, Hick Hooper had asked Mick O'Hare what was the most dangerous moment in combat. It sounded like a foolish question, but he couldn't think of a better one and he was prepared to sound foolish if he learned something. "It's when your neck starts to ache," Mick had told him. "So you give it a little rest. Only a few seconds, maybe ten or twenty. After all, doesn't it deserve a little rest? A small reward for all the hard work, twisting and turning. Nobody will notice. Nothing terrible's likely to happen in a few seconds, is it? During which time a tiny little 109 has fallen like Lucifer from the heavens above and all your worries are over, Hick." O'Hare had squeezed his shoulder. Now, as the squadron turned north, and then north-east, Hooper's neck ached. But his head kept turning. The sky was so vast and empty, his eyes hungered for something to focus on, a bird, a cloud, anything to cut this damned wearying infinity down to size.

Nobody spoke. The desert skimmed below, a soft beige blur.

Barton signalled: a quick waggle of his wings. Patterson

lost a little speed. His Flight dropped further back. The
target was a minute away. He widened the gap until the
Tomahawks ahead were six small blobs, trembling like
quicksilver against the brilliance of daybreak. Then Patterson opened his throttle. As he did, he felt sweat dribble
down his spine, although the cockpit was cool and he was
wearing only shirt and shorts. His Tomahawk surged
forward. The others matched him. He took them down to
fifty feet. Now the blur was a streak. Far ahead, red tracer
stabbed the daylight.

The target was a large tented camp. Its anti-aircraft
defences had recently been strengthened with extra flak
batteries and heavy machine guns; but the Tomahawks
swept in so low that most of the gunners were afraid to
fire in case they blew the heads off soldiers caught in the
open. The fighters smashed through a tangled net of vertical tracer and left behind a shambles of collapsing canvas
and sudden death. The German gunners chased Barton's
flight, too furious now to care if any soldier was in the
way, and so were surprised by the arrival of Patterson's
flight from behind. Men were picking themselves up, glad
to be alive, or climbing out of slit trenches, when a second
rush of bullets cut them down. Before they could fall, the
Tomahawks had gone, their bellowing engines fading to a
distant drone. The entire attack had lasted twelve seconds.

The two flights came together and Barton took them up
to five thousand feet. Now he could break radio silence.
"Hamlet leader to Hamlet aircraft . . . Bloody good show,
Hamlet aircraft," he said. "Piss on the Afrika Korps, right?
Okay, Hamlet aircraft, we've spoiled their breakfast, let's
go and get ours." All this was for the benefit of the Luftwaffe's listening posts, who monitored the Desert Air Force
frequencies. "Hamlet leader, out."

Skull was waiting for them, with his clipboard and his
fountain pen. He knew they had fired their guns: all the
canvas patches that kept out the dust had been blown

away. As the Tomahawks drifted down, the air made a wistful song in the open muzzles.

Barton landed first. "Did it work?" Skull asked.

"Worked a treat. They never thought we'd be daft enough to arrive from the west. Not at sunrise. So they must have been squinting into the sun, looking the wrong way. Anyway, we blasted the living daylights out of them."

"Infantry?"

"Used to be. Dead men now, half of them." Barton beamed with satisfaction.

Pinky Dalgleish strolled over, swinging his flying helmet. "What was all that crap about Hamlet, skip?" he asked.

"New squadron call-sign," Barton said. "Goes with the red noses. See? Something for Luftwaffe Intelligence to chew over."

"Not Hamlet," Skull said. "Falstaff. Hamlet wasn't a drunk, for God's sake. Falstaff is the one with the red nose."

"Oh." Barton tried to take it seriously but failed. "Is that what you said? All I could remember was it came from Shakespeare, and the only bloke I know in Shakespeare is Hamlet. He is in Shakespeare, isn't he?"

"Never mind, Fanny," Dalgleish said. "I expect Hamlet liked his beer as much as the next man."

"There's no textual evidence of that," Skull said. "On the other hand, I suppose there's no textual evidence against it, either."

He went off to debrief all the pilots. An hour later he took his notes to the CO and said, "I don't suppose you will welcome this news, Fanny, but all the information I have collected leads me to the conclusion that your dawn strafe did much less damage than you had hoped."

"Don't talk balls. It was a bloody good show, we duffed them up. Who says we didn't? I want the bastard's name."

"It's not a question of what people say. It's more a matter of what they don't say. For instance, nobody remembers seeing German transport in any quantity. The most any pilot noticed was the odd vehicle. Yet a camp of that size merits a hundred trucks at least. Nobody saw any radio masts. A big infantry unit should have a signals section. Nobody saw smoke from cookhouse fires."

"Everyone saw smoke from flak. No shortage of that."

"Nevertheless." Skull took his glasses off and cleaned the dust from the lenses. In five minutes they would be just as bad: Africa always wins. Barton watched and wondered why every intelligence officer had bad eyes. Maybe it was an Air Ministry regulation: four-eyed nit-pickers only need apply. Skull put his glasses on and saw the scowl bunching up a corner of Barton's mouth, and wondered why every fighter-squadron commander had such a poor capacity for bad news. Maybe it went with the job: anyone who thought a lot about it wouldn't do it. "Nevertheless," he said again, "all the evidence indicates that the vast majority of those tents were empty."

"Cock." Barton turned his back on him. "How do you know? Could you see inside them?"

Skull counted silently to five, and asked: "Could you?"

"I saw several hundred bodies."

"Half of whom were almost certainly very much alive. They fell flat when they saw you coming. Very natural."

"Half." Barton's voice was slack with contempt. "You're very precise, Skull, considering you were safely tucked up in bed at the time."

"Half is generous. A quarter is more like it. I've been doing this job for a long time, Fanny. All pilots exaggerate. They're excited. Who wouldn't be? Their claims get duplicated. That's inevitable. They multiply, I divide, we end up somewhere near the truth. Heavens above, I've known cases where –"

"I don't give a toss what you've known." Barton faced him again. "I'm not interested in history. I want to scare up some 109s so we can shoot the buggers down. Nothing else matters." He took Skull's notes and tore them in half.

"If they don't matter," Skull said, "why have you destroyed them?" He didn't wait for an answer. Barton watched him walk away until he was just a trembling blur. A few minutes later the pleading tones of Al Bowlly throbbed across the baked air of the landing-ground, with Roy Fox and his Orchestra suavely lending support:

When you don't care . . .
I'm bound in iron bands,
When you don't care . . .
I'm lost in desert sands.
In this wilderness, with none but you to guide me,
I'm in heaven with your tenderness beside me . . .

"Sarcastic bastard," Barton said aloud.

*   *   *

Paul Schramm's feet had begun to heal. He could drive a car, provided he didn't stamp on the pedals, so he drove to Benghazi Hospital to keep the appointment which the station MO at Barce had made for him. Schramm didn't want a second opinion, but he could do with a haircut and the Officers' Club would have the latest newspapers.

An orderly led him to the office of Dr Grandinetti, who turned out to be female. Well, why not? She looked to be about forty. Her face was a slim oval, no make-up. She had short black hair, very curly, and a straight gaze, with one eyebrow slightly cocked. He did not like the look of her, and he decided to make it as brief as possible. "It's just a few desert sores," he said.

"That's not what Max told me. Max is quite worried about you."

"Max is an old woman." He made a little throwaway gesture. "Sorry."

She spent an uncomfortably long time looking at him, and then said: "Sleeping well?"

He thought three times before saying: "As well as the British bombers let me." She kept watching him, so he added, "I don't need much sleep."

"Lucky you," she said. Schramm thought she looked slightly amused. Bloody woman.

"Well, if that's it, I'll be leaving," he said. "Thanks for your time."

"Suppose I asked you to take your clothes off, major," she said.

"Suppose I asked you to do the same," Schramm snapped. He felt the blood rush to his head. *This is ridiculous*, he told himself. *She's trying to provoke you and you're just helping her.*

"Suppose we examine this situation." She opened a bottle of acqua minerale and poured two glasses. "You come here for treatment. In the last three years I have seen ten times as many naked men as you have. Twenty. I see a dozen naked men before breakfast. Not all alive, of course." She sipped the fizzing water and pushed the other glass across her desk. "So why are you in such a rage?"

"I'm not in a *rage*, for God's sake. It's just that . . ." He shrugged. "This is all such a waste of time. Mine and yours."

"Don't concern yourself with me," she said sharply. "Be honest: you don't give a damn about me. Do you?"

Schramm felt trapped. If he agreed, she scored. If he disagreed, she scored double. Bloody woman. "Agreed," he said. "I think you stink." It was such a childish remark that he surprised himself. On the other hand he enjoyed it. "Don't feel offended," he said. "I think the whole damn world stinks."

"In that case it's no wonder you're depressed," she said.

"Who says?" He was peeling bits of dead skin off his fingers. He hunched his shoulders. He stared at a corner of her desk, analysing the joinery, the way the various pieces of wood fitted together. His eyes felt tired, his eyelids were heavy, he had to keep blinking. This wasn't right, it wasn't fair. He'd come in for somebody to check his desert sores, that's all, and now he'd be lucky to get his hair cut ... Bloody, bloody woman. What the hell was the matter with her? "Maybe I got a touch of sunstroke a couple of weeks ago," he said wearily. "There's really nothing wrong with me." He looked up. How could she be so cool? Why didn't she speak? Why didn't she tell him what was wrong with him?

"Sunstroke," she said. "That was careless."

"I got captured by the British. That's all I can tell you, and I shouldn't even tell you that."

"But you escaped." She made a fist of her left hand and propped her chin on it: a small but touching gesture. "That's not a secret," she said. "I worked it out by myself."

"I escaped." Schramm didn't want to think about all that. "I escaped, that's that, it's over, happy ending, welcome home, Paul. Have a medal, take two, take a dozen, give them to your friends if you can find any." He got up and took off his tunic. There was sweat on his face. He wiped his face with his hands, wiped his hands on his trousers. "Brilliant. Everyone's proud of you."

"But the whole damn world stinks," she said flatly.

"You've noticed it too, have you?" he said. "That's reassuring." He slung his tunic over one shoulder. "You don't want to look at my sores, and I don't want to look at you."

"Come back tomorrow, please," she said. "Same time."

*   *   *

David Stirling created the Special Air Service in 1941. At a time when everyone else regarded the vastness of the Sahara desert as an obstacle, and an impassable obstacle at that, Stirling saw it as an opportunity: a golden opportunity. The war was being fought up and down the coastal strip because that's where the road was, plus the occasional length of railway. Thus the battlefield was a thousand miles long but only fifty miles wide, and most of it was empty desert. No civilians to worry about. No property to protect. No pernickety neutrals whose borders had to be respected. It was a tactician's delight and a quartermaster's nightmare. Given enough supplies, you could fight wherever you liked. Given enough supplies: that was the rub. Harbours were few, so the man who allowed commanders to fight was the truck driver. Tens of thousands of truck drivers, German and Italian, British and Commonwealth, brought food and water, ammunition, medicine, mail, petrol and spares and God and the quartermasters knew what else, and hauled their loads hundreds of miles to the Front (which of course did not exist in the traditional sense, being only an interim stretch of desert where you were perfectly free to walk if you didn't mind getting your head blown off by some invisible gunner). At the time of the stalemate in May 1942, each side was trucking its supplies five or six hundred miles.

Long before this, Stirling had shown how vulnerable to attack the enemy supply system was. But first he had had to overcome two massive, ancient, faceless obstacles: the Sahara and British Army HQ. Of the two, the army proved harder to beat.

Stirling's sin was that he was proposing an irregular operation, led by himself; and he was only a second-lieutenant at the time. By instinct the staff at Middle East HQ, Cairo, rejected irregularity of any kind. They had been trained to fight orthodox battles on battlefields: find the enemy and biff him where it hurts, before he can biff you. That's what it came down to. They didn't like cocky young subalterns with nil experience who proposed to poach the best men from the best regiments and then swan off up the blue where they could run their own show, all togged up like the chorus from *The Desert Song*, no doubt. It was flashy and it was fun to go and play cowboys behind enemy lines, but it didn't win wars. If you allowed one freelance operation, soon everybody would want to do it. "I blame that bugger Lawrence," a major-general said. "He started this irregular carry-on. *Very* irregular, according to his version. Personally, if I got deflowered by a fat Turk the last thing I'd do is write a damn great thick book about it . . . Who is this fellow Stirling anyway? What's his game?"

Stirling won. He went to the top, or as near the top as he could reach. Being six foot five he was never inconspicuous; what's more he was on crutches, the result of an accident in parachute training which had badly damaged his back and temporarily paralysed his legs. Nevertheless, he bluffed his way into Middle East HQ without a pass, and before he got caught and thrown out he had managed to talk to General Ritchie, who was deputy to the Commander-in-Chief, General Auchinleck. It says much for Ritchie's and Auchinleck's intelligence and imagination that they recognised a good idea even when it was presented by a crippled subaltern. Stirling got permission to recruit sixty-six men and form a detachment of the Special Air Service Brigade, which did not exist but the title might persuade the Germans that it did.

The first SAS raid went in by parachute, at night, and was a disaster. The aircraft met gales and rain, the parachutists fell into a sandstorm, some were killed or injured, some simply vanished. Of sixty men dropped, twenty-two survived. No damage was done to the enemy. The survivors were brought out by a patrol of the Long Range Desert Group.

Parachuting wasn't the way to deliver the SAS. But if the LRDG could bring them out, Stirling reckoned it could also take them in.

The job of the LRDG was to patrol deep behind enemy

lines and collect information. They could take their trucks across five hundred miles of empty sands and arrive within two hundred yards of their planned destination, even if it was just a cross on the map. Which it often was.

In December 1941 the LRDG escorted three small SAS patrols to within walking distance of several German air-fields near Benghazi. Some fields were empty but others were not. Twenty-four aircraft were destroyed at Tamit, thirty-seven at Agedabia. The next night, Stirling's men went back to Tamit, found some replacement aircraft standing there and destroyed those too. Elsewhere, much enemy transport got blown up. The patrols marched back into the desert, rendezvoused with the LRDG, went home to Cairo.

Stirling had found the formula for success: small patrols of very physically fit, highly-trained men, completely self-contained, able to arrive from nowhere, create total havoc in the night and vanish the way they came. The SAS grew rapidly and raided ceaselessly. Eventually it trained its own navigators and became independent of the LRDG. The SAS was more than a thorn in Rommel's side: it was several thorns. They didn't always draw blood. Some patrols got badly knocked about, but that was the price of audacity. If, as Lampard's raid on Barce showed, you could wipe out a fighter squadron at the cost of two lives, in the crude arithmetic of war that was damn good value.

*   *   *

Lampard found a signals lieutenant called Sandiman and a trooper called Peck to replace Waterman and Harris. There was no shortage of volunteers to join the SAS, and both men had seen a lot of fighting in the desert, but Lampard wanted to be sure they had the strength – physical and moral – to survive the extreme tests that SAS raiding would impose.

He called the patrol together and began training. At first they marched across the desert near Cairo with heavy loads. They covered ten or twelve miles, did some weapons-firing, marched another five miles, made a dummy raid on an imaginary airfield, then five more miles and met the truck that took them back to a shower, a meal, a bed. Soon he extended the daily distance and cut down the water ration. Peck and Sandiman kept up with the others.

"Are they good enough?" Lampard asked Lieutenant Dunn.

They were sitting in cane long-chairs outside Lampard's tent. It had been a roasting day and Dunn's aching feet were hugely grateful to be at rest. "They haven't cracked up, cocked up or thrown up," he said. "What more d'you want?"

"I want to see them drink their own blood."

Dunn thought about it. "When they've done that," he said, "should they go on and drink yours too?"

"Yes. Provided they ask permission first. I keep wishing I'd shot that German, you know. That chap Schramm. Shot him before he had a chance to escape."

Dunn was accustomed to Lampard's abrupt changes of topic. He leaned back and waited.

"Not dead," Lampard said. "Too valuable for that. But I should have shot him in the leg, so he couldn't run."

"Water under the bridge, Jack. Besides, it's not as if he got away with any secrets. We didn't tell him any-thing."

"Let's go back and bump him off."

"Tonight?"

Lampard looked him straight in the eyes and held the stare until Dunn had to blink. "No, not tonight." he said.

"Good." Dunn was pleasantly drowsy. "Not tomorrow night either, if you don't mind, Jack. I'm taking my popsy to the flicks." He let his eyes shut. "It's *Snow White*. Utterly terrifying. She holds my hand during the worst bits."

Lampard left him dozing and went off to make some telephone calls. When he got back, Dunn was very awake and talking to Gibbon, the navigator. "Corky's got a gong!" Dunn announced. "He's got an MC for . . . What's it for, Corky?"

"Usual shit," Gibbon said. "Stealing pencils, not getting caught." They knew he was pleased because he looked gloomier than ever.

"Maybe Major Schramm put in a word for you," Lampard said.

"Bugger Schramm! He was only guessing," Dunn said. "We're all going to have a drink or seventeen, to celebrate. The whole patrol! You coming?"

"I've got to go to a conference first. Hold out your hand." Lampard scribbled on Dunn's palm in indelible pencil. "Call me at this number and I'll join you after, say, 2100 hours."

An hour later he was being let in to the penthouse flat of Mrs Joan d'Armytage. This was the third time they had met and he was impressed by her smallness. The previous times they had met at Groppi's, where she had been seated and it was crowded. Now, in all this spaciousness, she seemed doll-like. And yet she was a very grown-up doll: a lot of womanliness was packed into that little figure. She wore a black dress, sleeveless, simple. They shook hands. Lampard was afraid to squeeze, so he compensated by taking her hand in both of his. She added her other hand to the clasp. Lampard experienced a sudden tightening in his throat.

They went onto the balcony and drank cocktails. "Very Noel Coward," he said. "What is this drink called?"

"It's a sidecar. Brandy, Cointreau, lemon juice. Quite drunk-making."

He looked down at the street. The traffic was fighting its usual civil war. "God, isn't Cairo *loud*!" he said.

She nodded, and looked at the early stars.

"You'd think they'd get fed up with shouting at each other," he said. "Arab mentality, I suppose."

She said *Mmm* as she worked on her drink.

"Still, I expect they think we're pretty peculiar too," he said.

The sidecars had come from a cocktail shaker. She gave it a flourish, and the ice cubes chattered. "Look," she said, "we don't need to go through all that junk again, do we?" It was a statement, not a question, and a pretty brisk statement at that. Lampard said: "Um . . ." She poured more drinks, and did it with a snappy action that suggested impatience. "The first time we met you were kind enough to tell me how Desmond got killed, frightfully brave, trying to save somebody else and so on, and you produced the large masculine handkerchief as required."

"Never got it back, though."

"You will. Second time, we talked about Desmond a bit, London a bit more and Cairo a lot. A hell of a lot. Good. I'm not complaining, but we've done that. Haven't we?"

Lampard pressed the chilled glass against his chin.

Thirty miles his patrol had marched since dawn that day, on a bottle of water: a ration which the British Army considered fatal, and yet everyone had survived. Tongues like raffia place-mats, maybe, but they survived. Now he had inside him this thrilling drink, which made him feel as happy as he'd felt since he'd strolled about the hangar at Barce, leaving bombs like clues in a treasure hunt, and here was the startling Mrs Joan d'Armytage looking at him with one eyebrow cocked and half a smile. It made *him* feel small, that look of hers. A porcelain doll, yet she made him feel small. Amazing. "I'm sorry," he said.

"Oh, stop being so bloody English. I'm widowed and you might be dead next week. Why apologise? It's such a waste of energy." She turned and went inside.

Lampard counted to ten and followed her. She was standing in a dark corner, looking at gramophone records.

"Anyway, you're not a bit sorry," she said, "so why lie? I hate this tune." She smashed a record against a table, casually. "Desmond's favourite," she said. "Now it's in as many bits as he is."

"Don't get mad at Desmond," Lampard said. "It's not his fault he's dead."

"I'll be mad with anyone I want to," she said calmly. "You really are utterly useless, aren't you? You can't be relied upon to do the simplest thing." She left her gramophone records and walked over to him. She took his hands in each of hers and raised them to her shoulders. She slipped his fingers beneath the straps of her dress. "Up," she said. She raised her arms as he raised his. The dress came off as easily as shelling peas. Easier. Underneath was nothing but skin. "Well, it's a hot climate," he said. "Have you a coat hanger?"

"I do," she said, "but if you have a cock I think that might fit better." He looked shocked. She looked pleased. She took his hand and led him into the bedroom.

*　　*　　*

The water-tanker and its escort failed to meet the rest of the column at the rendezvous.

It was late afternoon before the column arrived at the map reference point, exactly one hundred kilometres south of the Jalo Gap, and found nothing but empty serir. The map had promised vast areas of serir, an Arab word meaning a flat gravel plain, and it was right. To the horizon in any direction no stone was bigger than an egg.

The surface made for fast, accurate driving, and on the way south Major Jakowski had taken the opportunity to hold a couple of training exercises.

"Suppose we were to meet an enemy force, here and now," he said when they stopped for the midday meal. "What would we do?"

"Depends on its size, sir," Captain Rinkart said.

"Ten vehicles. No armoured cars."

"So they are almost certainly not going to attack us. I would approach them and find out if they out-gun us."

Jakowski was disappointed: Rinkart sounded awfully cautious. "Look: you're strong enough to surround them and hit them from all sides at once," he said. "While you're thinking it over, they're escaping." He turned to Captain Lessing. "Aren't they?"

"Yes, if they possibly can. However, if we make them stand and fight they might be carrying light howitzers in their trucks. Say, six shells a minute from up to five or six kilometres. Just imagine, sir." Lessing shook his head. "They might even hit *you*."

"No artillery," Jakowski ruled.

"Well, there's still the possibility of heavy-calibre machine guns," Rinkart said. "I hear they've got twin point-five-inch Vickers on their trucks. RAF surplus. The Vickers is a brute of a gun. It can blow a truck to bits at three thousand metres. It's still lethal at four or five thousand. Six, maybe."

"That's that, then," Jakowski said. "Let's all turn round and hurry home."

"No, sir," Lessing said. "Let's call in the Stukas."

Jakowski shook his head. "Radio silence. I made that clear before we left. We'll never catch the enemy if we keep telling him where we are."

Lessing thought: *But if we've found him he knows where we are, you dummy*.

"All right," Jakowski said. "All right. No doubt the options will clarify themselves under the pressure of actual combat. Meanwhile you, Rinkart, take three fast trucks and disappear and make some mock attacks on the main column. Lessing, put a lookout on every truck. The men are dozy. They think because this desert's empty it's safe. Well, it's not empty and it's extremely dangerous."

Rinkart cheated. He took six trucks, split them into pairs and came at the column from three different directions, sometimes breaking off and retreating, sometimes running parallel, sometimes racing in and aiming a burst of machine-gun fire high above the column. It enlivened the afternoon and it pleased Major Jakowski. Thus he was not too upset when his navigator told him they had reached the rendezvous and no water-tanker was waiting. "I expect they had a puncture, sir," one of the lieutenants said. Jakowski ordered a truck to be placed with its headlights aimed at Jalo, as a beacon for the missing drivers. By dawn the truck's batteries were flat and nobody had arrived. By midday Jakowski was worried, angry and impatient; but mainly impatient. "Can't wait any longer," he growled, and left a sergeant and two men with two trucks at the rendezvous. As soon as the water-tanker turned up, they were all to chase after the main column, damn fast. Meanwhile water rations were cut by a third.

*　　*　　*

Before the war, Skull was a junior don at Cambridge, teaching the history of the Protestant sects in Tudor England. Often he challenged the accepted version of events. As he said in his lectures, the truth was always the truth, no matter what men preferred to think.

When war came and Skull was rapidly commissioned into the RAF as an intelligence officer, he brought his awkward Cambridge interest in the truth with him. It often upset people. Even in the RAF there were men, quite high-ranking men, who grew quite indignant when foreign journalists questioned the official figures for enemy aircraft destroyed. Skull was present when an air marshal said to some sceptical war correspondents: "If you think so little of our claims, why don't you go to Berlin and check theirs? The Luftwaffe's scores are absolutely preposterous!"

"With respect, sir," Skull said, "what the Luftwaffe claims is beside the point. Proving them wrong doesn't prove us right."

"Wait outside, Skelton," the air marshal said stonily. When the journalists had left, still unconvinced, he recalled the intelligence officer and blasted him for his interfering stupidity. Skull was unmoved. "I'm sorry if I embarrassed you, sir," he said. "But if we believe our own lies we deceive ourselves and, by so doing, we aid the enemy. Surely that's self-evident."

"Don't preach to me, flight lieutenant."

Skull twitched his nose so that his spectacles bounced. "Preaching assumes moral alternatives, sir. War allows us no such choice. We cannot award a fighter pilot his kill just because we feel he *deserves* it. The truth —"

"Get out," the air marshal rasped. "Stay out. I never want to see you again."

That was shortly after Dunkirk. Later, Skull upset more people and got posted out of Fighter Command; made enemies in Bomber Command, and was eventually posted to Egypt. When his Uncle Stanley heard where he was going he gave Skull his old rowing blazer. "Just the thing for the desert," he said. "Don't suppose I shall need it again. Holidays thing of the past for us. Lucky you."

As it happened the old buffer was right. His blazer was a size too large for Skull, and its stripes of dove grey, pillar-box red and royal blue, with gold piping, had faded to soft pastel shades, but its cool looseness was just the thing for the desert. Skull wore it with a pair of corduroy bags bought in Cairo, and he carried an old golf umbrella that doubled as a shooting-stick, which he'd found in a flea market.

Dressed like this, he was walking around LG 181, examining the Tomahawks one by one. A senior flight sergeant went with him.

The adjutant saw this little parade every time he looked

up from his desk in the orderly room. Eventually he gave in to his curiosity. Intelligence officers did not usually go about in the heat of the day, scrutinising the undersides of aeroplanes. Kellaway put his cap on.

"This one looks as if it's been flown through a barbed-wire fence," Skull said to the flight sergeant. He ran his fingers over a rash of patches that spattered the fighter's belly. "Several fences . . . Who's is it?"

"The CO's, sir." The flight sergeant pointed at the letters F.B. on the fuselage. It was the squadron commander's privilege to have his initials on his aircraft.

"Yes, of course." Skull fingered some bullet-streaks on the engine cowling. "I thought the CO always took the best kite."

"He does. Engine's perfect. He can't keep away from ground fire, that's all. You should see the armour under his seat. Taken a right hammering, that has."

"Hullo, Uncle," Skull said. "Thank you, Chiefy." As the flight sergeant walked away he said: "The ground crews are working miracles, as usual."

"Yes?" Kellaway looked at the aeroplane and saw nothing new: just an oil-stained Tomahawk with lots of scratches around the cockpit, black streaks below the exhaust stubs and smoke trails on the wings behind the guns. "Jolly good," he said. Of course the ground crews were excellent; they always were; why comment on it? "What does 'effulgent' mean?" he asked.

"Shining brightly. By extension, splendid or brilliant. Why?"

The adjutant looked disappointed. "I'm trying to put together a letter to poor old Schofield's next-of-kin. Something for Fanny to sign. He's hopeless at that sort of thing, all he can think of is *He pressed home his attack without thought for his own safety*. I don't suppose anyone pays much attention to these letters, but you can't honestly say that sort of thing about a blasted intelligence officer, can you?" He went and sat in the shade of the wing, leaning against a wheel.

"I take it Schofield wasn't effulgent," Skull said.

"Don't say I said so, but he was a bore."

"Ah."

"Kept rattling on about the temperance movement. I think his father died of drink. Not very appropriate, though, was it? Not here."

Skull closed his umbrella and sat against the other side of the wheel.

"All the same, the man wasn't a complete failure," Kellaway said. "It would be nice to trot out something different for a change." He turned his head and sniffed. "Smell anything?"

"Petrol."

"Oh." Kellaway relaxed. "What if I said his work was at all times thoroughly meretricious? That has a nice ring to it."

"Meretricious is a damn good word."

"Yes. I saw it in a crossword once. It sort of stuck."

"It means cheap and nasty. From the Latin, *meretrix*, a harlot."

Kellaway tossed a handful of sand at some flies who were lazily dogfighting in the shade. They ignored him. They knew all about sand.

"I thought it had something to do with merit," he said.

"No doubt the harlot would say it has," Skull said; but he knew at once that it was too hot for that sort of discussion. "You could always say he set an example to the rest of the squadron," he suggested. "You don't have to say what he set an example *in*."

The adjutant nodded sleepily. "Exemplary conduct," he murmured. "That'll do nicely."

"Come on." Skull got up and opened his umbrella. "I'm going to harangue Fanny, and I might need a witness."

Kellaway paused when they were halfway to Barton's

truck and sniffed the air again. "I knew I could smell it," he said bitterly. "Damn. Sometimes I wish God would strike us all down with permanent constipation."

Barton was sprawled on his bunk, looking at a map of central Libya. He had a fistful of coloured pencils. "Any new targets from Group?" he asked.

Skull shook his head. "I dropped in to ask about my leave."

"Leave? You only just got here."

"True. But I shan't be here much longer if you keep up your strafing campaign."

"Oh yes?" Barton was barefoot. He folded his legs and began stuffing pencils between the toes. "What's wrong with it?"

"Every machine in the squadron has been hit by ground fire at least four times. Sometimes minor damage, sometimes not."

"They all got back." Barton wiggled his toes and made the pencils ripple. "All profit, no loss."

"That's luck."

"Tough old kite, the Tommy," the adjutant said. He was thinking about the best spot for the new latrine pits.

"Luck runs out," Skull said. "Three sorties a day, day after day, all strafing runs, somebody's bound to get hit where it hurts. At that height, at that speed, chances are he'll dig a big hole. Sandbags in the coffin, as we used to say."

"No coffins in the blue," Kellaway said. "Can't get the wood."

Barton found his cap and put it on. He tipped it forward so that he had to lift his head in order to see the Intelligence Officer under the peak. "You've gone all gloom and doom, Skull," he said. "You were never like this in the good old days. Court jester, that's what you were. Kept us all merry and bright, didn't he, Uncle?"

"Look, Fanny," Skull said quietly. "I've seen squadrons

come and go. I watched one squadron nearly disappear in less than a *week*, for Christ's sake. On Sunday it looked fine and by Thursday there were only five kites and six pilots left, and two of them were zombies. By Saturday they were all posted, the CO with them. The only thing left was the squadron number. Less than a week."

"Bomber Command," Fanny said, with a slight shrug.

"And they had four engines to your one, and they didn't go looking for trouble like you do. Now, I've had a guided tour of your Tomahawks and by my reckoning sixty-seven per cent of them had a ninety-four per cent chance of taking lethal damage on forty-one per cent of these strafing missions."

"Golly," Kellaway said.

"You made those figures up," Fanny said.

"Of course I did. Look at any machine and you can see where enemy fire just missed coolant or hydraulics or controls or fuel. It won't last."

"The fuel tanks are self-sealing."

"And the enemy's bringing up more flak batteries all the time. That's what you want, isn't it? You're deliberately provoking them. Flak makes holes too big to seal, Fanny."

"I'll fox 'em. We'll go where there isn't any flak."

Skull had been standing. Now he found somewhere to sit, and he looked hard at Barton's face, the open and healthy face of a New Zealander who had grown up on a farm and travelled halfway around the world to fight for Britain, the kind of face the Air Ministry liked to put on its posters: not too handsome, but resolute, warm-hearted and true. Merely looking at that face depressed Skull. He had been meeting variations of it for the past two years and most of those men were dead. Or missing. Or, in a couple of cases, mad. "It's a misuse of the aeroplane," he said. "The Tomahawk wasn't made for ground attack. You know that."

"Do I?" Barton began plucking the pencils from between his toes. "What a rotten shame."

Kellaway had begun to feel left out. "It was the same in the last show," he said. "They made us do a lot of trench-strafing then. Bloody dangerous, I can tell you."

"War *is* dangerous," Barton said. "That's the whole point."

"I see," Skull said. "So the object is to make it as dangerous as possible, is it?"

The adjutant said: "I don't see how anyone could have made it more dangerous." He heard his own grimness and added, cheerfully, "Still, we did win."

"Thanks for this little chat, Skull," Barton said. He dropped the pencils into a shell-casing. "Just like old times."

"Mind you, I sometimes wonder." The adjutant gestured at the desert. "If this is what you get for winning, what's second prize?"

"Takoradi," Barton told him.

"It's nothing like old times," Skull told Barton. "France was a nonsense, England was a battleground. This looks more like a playground. Your playground."

"Hey, hey!" Kellaway said. "Watch your words, man."

"Why? It's time for a little truth, Uncle. We all know this strafing campaign is Fanny's idea. We all know it's bloody dangerous. Who are we going to blame when some poor devil flies into a flak barrage and doesn't come out? God? Rommel? Nobel, for inventing TNT? Tell me, I'd like to know. I'd like to have my excuses all ready and polished well in advance."

"Out," Barton ordered. "Out, out!"

He followed them. The three men walked in silence to a piece of nowhere, a patch of sand splattered with oil stains where a Tomahawk had once stood. Barton stopped, so the others stopped. They formed a wide triangle. The desert brooded hotly to the horizon. "If any other

229

Intelligence Officer had spoken to me like that," Barton said, "I'd have kicked his bollocks until they rang like the bells of St Mary's. You've now exhausted my goodwill. Next time, ding-dong. I run the operations in this squadron. You stick to your little bits of paper. I didn't ask for you, I don't want you, and if you get in my way I'll hit you so hard you'll feel like twice the square root of fuck-all." He turned and left.

Kellaway walked with Skull to another part of the landing-ground. It was nowhere in particular: just remote from the CO. Skull looked about him, at the bleached desolation, more grey grit than white sand, doing nothing as far as the eye could see and doing it in blank silence. Not so much a desert as a waste. "Poor show," Skull said.

"You asked for it," Kellaway said.

"I meant the landscape. God lost his crayons that day, didn't he? Still, you're right, I asked for it. The funny thing is, I didn't plan to say any of that stuff. It just came out."

"Is that a fact?" The adjutant's whole career had been in the RAF. Hornet Squadron was his life. Skull's behaviour amazed and offended him. "Your rank may be squadron leader," he said, "but Fanny's the boss here. If he says north is south, then south it is."

"That's absurd."

A red golf ball landed twenty yards away and skipped past them. Someone shouted: "Fore!" and a second red ball fell out of the sky.

"You talk about absurd," Kellaway said. "Just watch this."

Mick O'Hare and Tiny Lush strolled towards them. They shared two clubs: a driver and a putter. O'Hare was consulting a tattered booklet describing, with maps, the course at Royal St Andrews, and they were talking loudly, ignoring Kellaway and Skull. Greek George tagged along behind. "Fine shot, Tiny," Mick said. "Look – you're bang in the middle of the green."

"Damn lucky, Mick. I got a nice bounce off the heather."

"Well, I was quite fortunate at the waterfall."

"Tricky shot, the waterfall. It's what I call a tricky shot."

"All that spray."

"And the salmon," Tiny said.

"The club professional killed a fifteen-pounder there last Tuesday. Hit it square between the eyes with his brassie."

"How odd," Tiny said. "I'd have used a niblick." They reached the balls. "Your honour," he said, and gave Mick the putter. Mick attempted a very long putt at a non-existent hole and shook his head in dismay. "Your hole," he said.

"Who is winning?" Greek George asked. Nobody paid any attention.

"The next is the short dog-leg," O'Hare said. He consulted his booklet. "The tee is by that big oak tree." They set off. "It's near that stag," he added.

"What is stag?" Greek George asked.

"You got wolves in Greece?" Lush said.

"Sure, we got wolves."

"Well, it's nothing like a wolf." Their voices faded.

"Not much truth there," the adjutant said. "Plenty of sanity, though."

"They're all sane when it doesn't matter," Skull said.

"You were never a fighter pilot, Skull. You don't understand."

That happened at mid-morning. Barton led the squadron on another strafing mission at noon. When they landed, two aircraft were missing: Butcher Bailey and Greek George. Nobody had seen what happened to them. Visibility had been lousy: the usual heat-haze made worse by a gusty wind that sent dust spiralling into the sky. The squadron had split into four sections for the strafe. When they regrouped they were minus two machines. Simple as that.

"Well, you told us so," the adjutant said to Skull. The pilots had been debriefed and gone to their tents. The airfield was silent and still except for the odd hiss of sand snaking across the ground.

"I told you what you already knew," Skull said stiffly.

"And you were right. Dead right. Double-dead right."

"What's that? A joke?" When Kellaway did not answer, Skull poked his shoulder. "Explain the joke, Uncle. I don't get it."

But Kellaway walked away. The wind gusted and made his khaki drill trousers flap and snap. They reminded Skull of Charlie Chaplin. He realised that the adjutant was quite small; or maybe he had lost weight in the desert. Part of Skull felt sorry for Uncle, stuck in the blue, shuffling documents as pilots came and went; and another part hated him. *You told us so*: that had been a cheap thing to say. Skull went to his tent and wound up the gramophone.

"Empty saddles in the old corral," Bowlly crooned, *"where do you ride tonight?"* Nobody offered an answer.

* * *

Jack Lampard took a fresh sidecar with one hand and the telephone with the other. Half an hour ago he had felt so stunned by sex that he could scarcely keep his eyes open. Now, as Joan d'Armytage turned away, her silk pyjamas swung open and showed him a glimpse of shining white skin, a sway of breast, the ripple of nipple on silk. He knew it was a deliberate act of provocation. First Mussolini in Abyssinia, then Hitler in Poland, now Joan d'Armytage in Egypt. It couldn't be allowed to go on. Somewhere, sometime, somebody had to make a stand. All she was wearing was the pyjama jacket. He looked at the way it was tucked up by her neatly rounded rump. *You've already made a stand*, he told himself. Too late. The new mobilisation orders had gone out. *Jesus*, he thought, *don't you ever have enough?* "Hello," he said into the phone.

"That you, Jack? Mike here. You wanted me to call you.

Sorry I'm a bit late." Glass splintered and crashed. "*Christ!* That was close . . ." Dunn's voice became distant. "My advice, old chap, is to sit down before you fall down," he told someone. Hoarse shouting could be heard. "I'm afraid I don't speak Polish," Dunn said. Furniture smashed. "Now look what you've done to yourself," he said. The line crackled like blazing twigs, then cleared. "Sorry about that, Jack. Bloody Poles never learn, do they?"

"Sounds like trouble."

"Well, they started it."

"Where are you?"

"Sitting under the bar at the Hole in the Wall. Quite safe. No beer, though. We're moving on soon. The Poles seem to have lost interest." A bang that made Lampard's head jerk was so loud that even Joan d'Armytage heard it. "Soda-syphon," Dunn explained. "Two syphons, actually."

"Any casualties?" Lampard asked. He knew she was watching and listening, and he creased his brow.

"Not that I know of. We went to the Pyramid Club first, full of smelly sailors so we chucked a few in the Nile, seemed the best place for them. Ran out of beer, went to Pat's Bar, all the lights failed, total panic, couldn't see to drink. Went to the Drum, full of RAF types too drunk to fight, ran out of beer, came here. Dull evening so far." Somewhere a window shattered.

"Too bad." Lampard shrugged at Joan d'Armytage. He didn't enjoy pub-crawls, but this was his patrol and he felt left out. On the other hand, Mrs d'Armytage was stripped for action. Semi-stripped. Would she wait? Perhaps he could dash out, have a quick drink and dash back. "What's your plan?" he asked Dunn.

"Black Cat Club. Worst belly-dancer in Cairo."

"Meet me there. Ten minutes." He hung up. "Duty calls," he told her as he pulled on his underpants. "Small crisis. You know how it is."

"Bloody silly war. It ruins everything." She buttoned her pyjamas: a sad little action that almost made him stay. "Damn, damn, damn." She shivered, and hugged herself. "I hate drinking alone. And I know I shan't sleep."

"This won't take me long. An hour at most. You can wait an hour, can't you? Of course you can." He kissed her on the forehead. She held his arm and said, "You never told me what that shoulder flash stands for." He squinted at it. "SAS?" he said. "Sex and sidecars." It amused her. He went out smiling.

*　　*　　*

Running a nightclub in wartime Cairo was a risky business. The city was stiff with customers eager to spend their accumulated pay before they went back to the desert, but they were a volatile mix of nationalities and services. Some were suspicious or jealous of others, and many were fighting men who couldn't get out of the habit of fighting. A nightclub could make a lot of money fast and then lose it even faster if the customers grew impatient and wrecked the place.

The Black Cat had been wrecked twice already. Its new owners learned from those mistakes. They moved the club to a small two-storey warehouse. By knocking an enormous hole in the ground-floor ceiling they made it possible for the customers upstairs to watch the floor show going on downstairs. This doubled the capacity and the profits, but it also made the place as hot as a steam house; so they removed most of the roof to let the body-heat out.

The ground floor had a small stage for the belly-dancer and another for the band. If the dancer was bad the customers usually pelted the band, so it performed inside a cage of wire netting. When people upstairs grew bored they usually threw things at people below, so a layer of wire netting was strung between them. On each floor the bar ran around three walls, the management's policy being that nobody should ever have to wait for a drink. They painted everything pink or gold, they engaged fifty youngish ladies who got paid on commission only, they watered the booze and jacked up the prices, and they hired black bouncers who could sometimes be knocked down but could never be knocked out. The Black Cat made money. The belly-dancer was no great shakes, but the bouncers were a great attraction. Some people went to fight them. Others went to watch the fights.

Lampard met Mike Dunn and the rest of the patrol outside the club. He felt slightly peculiar: a bit lightheaded; and not only his head, his limbs too seemed to wish to float. "Right," he said. "Drinks are on me. Don't get into a fight without my permission. That's an order."

The Black Cat was comfortably full and most of its customers were in uniform. Conversation made a steady roar, and steel-blue cigarette smoke rose to the sky like heat made visible. Lampard stopped and looked around. "Can't say I fancy drinking standing up," he said.

"Maybe someone will leave," Dunn said.

No one left. A hostess, not young and not pretty, walked by and smiled. Lampard smiled back. At a nearby table a large and drunk pilot officer said: "Bet you she's got legs like bloody nutcrackers." Some of his friends laughed. One said: "Give her fifty ackers, she'll squeeze the milk out of your coconuts." The pilot officer said: "Fifty? Don't I get any change?"

Lampard kicked his chair. "Get up," he said.

The pilot officer turned and looked. "Did you kick my chair?" he asked. He was a very large young man. The rest of the patrol hung about in the background. "A bloody pongo!" the pilot officer said. "All boots and no brain." Someone chuckled, which pleased him.

"Get up *now*," Lampard ordered. The pilot officer made

a sad-clown's face. "Oh dear," he said. "Pongo wants to tango." Everyone at the table laughed.

"Get up and apologise to that lady," Lampard said. His voice was bleak as midwinter. The pilot officer blinked. "What lady?" he asked. The hostess had long since disappeared.

"The lady about whom you made a foul and offensive remark."

The pilot officer thought, and remembered, "Oh, *her*. The one with legs like nutcrackers. That's no lady, that's just a buckshee bint."

Lampard took him by the ears and lifted. The chair toppled, the pilot officer howled, his knee hit the table and all the drinks fell over. Lampard released his ears and punched him three times, left-right-left, on and about the heart, so fast that it sounded like one blow. When the bouncers arrived, Lampard was holding him by the collar. His face was the colour of raw pastry. "This officer is unwell," Lampard said. "His friends will take him home."

The table emptied. The patrol moved into the seats. The Arab band finished playing 'Yes Sir That's My Baby' and began 'Stormy Weather', charging into it at double-time.

"Somewhat extreme, Jack," Corky Gibbon said. It was his MC, so in a sense it was his party. "He was only a Brylcreem Boy. They can't bloody march, let alone fight."

"He holds the king's commission," Lampard said. "He should behave like a gentleman. I gave him the opportunity to apologise. That's why we're fighting this war: for the sake of decency and chivalry and the sanctity of womanhood."

"I must remember that," Sergeant Davis said. "Next time I blow some bugger's brains out."

"Please do," Lampard said. He was serious.

"Right now I'd kill for a plate of egg and chips," Corporal Pocock said. Everyone laughed except Sandiman and Peck. "Family joke," Pocock told them. "Explain later."

Bottles of champagne – Egyptian champagne – were arriving. A smiling hostess, not young and not pretty, joined them.

"Good evening, madam," Lampard said. "I apologise for the brutish behaviour of my fellow-officer. I can assure you that he now regrets it as much as I do. We in the British Army have the utmost respect for decency, chivalry and the sanctity of womanhood."

She heard this with widening eyes. "No shit," she said. Lampard looked away. The band finished 'Stormy Weather' and without pause played 'Yes Sir That's My Baby' again.

"They get it from the Americans," Mike Dunn told him. "Damn Yanks are all over town."

"I suppose one shouldn't expect gratitude," Lampard said.

"Not in her case. This isn't the same woman as before."

"You like more champagne?" she decided, signalling to a waiter.

The band abruptly dropped "Yes Sir That's My Baby" in mid-bar. The lights dimmed. A drum roll grew big and faded to a whisper, a spotlight picked out the tiny stage, and the band slipped into the more comfortable world of Arab music. The belly-dancer appeared, and got on with her job of feeding the sexual fantasies of men who would soon be living in the desert on bully-beef and erotic memories for weeks or months on end.

Three minutes was enough for them. She was a veteran, and hardworking, but the lissom slither of the true dancer was missing. "Ars est celare arse," Corky Gibbon murmured to Dunn. The rough soldiery didn't know much about the art of the dance, but they knew when their desires were not being aroused. The roar of conversation returned. Soon bottles and glasses and ashtrays began to crash against the wire barrier protecting the band. Lampard yawned, and as his head went back he caught a glimpse of a white beret at the back of the upper floor. "Hullo!" he said. "Snowdrops. What luck."

Upstairs, Henry Lester was talking to a soldier with a white beret tucked under his left shoulder-strap. He was writing down what the man said. The American was too drunk to see straight, but not so drunk that he couldn't use his shorthand. "Okay," he said. "I got the bit where you blew up all the Stukas. Then what?" His shorthand was fuzzy. He held the notebook at arm's length. Everything separated into two wandering images. "Ralph, does this look okay to you?" he asked. "Lovely, lovely," Malplacket said, not looking. He had his own conversation going. Another man with a white beret and SAS shoulder flashes was telling Malplacket about the time his raiding party had run out of food so they joined an Italian brigade of infantry that was queuing up for dinner and they got hot pasta and fresh bread and oranges and red wine, and then they beat it into the desert.

"After the Stukas," the first soldier told Lester, "we got chased by Messerschmitt 109s, so the next night we went back and found what airfield they were at and we sneaked in and we blew them up." He finished his drink and gestured with the glass to make his point. "And that's not all, believe me."

"Bartender! Same again," Lester said. "What next?"

"Tell him about Kufra," Lampard said.

The soldier half-turned. He was in truth a lance-corporal in the Pioneer Corps. When he saw Lampard looking down at him, his bladder clenched and a single squirt of urine wet his left thigh. He tugged the white beret from his shoulder strap and stuffed it in a pocket. "Time we got back to camp, sir," he muttered. "Come on, Tom."

"You've been to Kufra, of course," Lampard said. "Every SAS patrol goes through Kufra."

"Sir." He was trying to stand at attention, but one knee kept defaulting.

"Remember the lakes at Kufra? Amazing colour, weren't they?" Lampard put his arm around the man's shoulders. "Emerald green, wouldn't you say?"

"Yes sir."

"And delicious! Sweet as milk, that water! I bet you always filled your jerricans at the lakes."

"Yessir."

"No. The lakes at Kufra are blue as sapphire and bitter as sin." Lampard cuffed him lightly and knocked him into the next table, which capsized with a crash.

Lester was outraged. "You just hit my exclusive," he said. Malplacket too was upset. "No way to treat a comrade in arms," he reproached. The second soldier was encouraged by their support. "I wouldn't do that if I was you," he warned Lampard.

"Wrong," Lampard said. "I wouldn't do that if I *were* you." He seized the other soldier by the lapels and threw him away. Another table went over.

"What's the matter? You crazy?" Lester yelled.

"Subjunctive mood follows a conditional clause," Lampard informed him.

"Correct," Malplacket said grudgingly. It was the last coherent word spoken for a long time. Men whose drinks had been spilled began throwing chairs at Lampard. The rest of the patrol arrived in a rush and the fighting spread. Malplacket and Lester found safety on the other side of the bar. They saw Lampard grab the first bogus SAS man, heave his dazed body off its feet and toss it over the balcony. It bounced on the screen of wire netting and rolled to the centre. The other man tried to crawl away, but Lampard found him and threw him after his friend. Mike Dunn and Corporal Pocock got a glimpse of this as they beat back various attackers. They picked up a stunned sailor and flung him over the edge. The netting split beneath the weight. Bodies began to drop onto the loaded, crowded tables below. The bouncers who had been heading for the upstairs fight turned and hurried towards the greater uproar downstairs. A manager hustled the belly-dancer offstage. The band struck up 'Yes Sir That's My Baby'. "Time to go!" Lampard shouted.

Malplacket watched the patrol disappear through the exit, the crowd falling back to let them through. "My stars!" he said. "What was that all about?" Lester didn't answer. Lester had gone too.

*   *   *

The door to the penthouse flat was unlocked. Very little had changed inside. Mrs Joan d'Armytage was still drinking sidecars and she was still wearing only her pyjama top. There were more broken gramophone records on the floor. "Well, Jack," she said. "Have you tidied up your silly war?"

"Slight misunderstanding, that's all. I got Rommel on the phone. We soon straightened things out."

"Really." She walked into the bedroom. Bits of records crunched beneath her bare feet.

"No, not really. That was all lies. I couldn't get Rommel. Line engaged." He followed her. "I'll try again tomorrow and —"

"Never mind, I don't care. I really don't. I cared about the war when Desmond was alive, but now it's not important who wins. He was a nice man, Desmond, not much good in bed and absolutely no sense of humour, but kind, very, very kind. Men don't understand kindness, do they?"

"Don't they?" Lampard smiled, but he was impatient. He didn't want to talk about the late Desmond d'Armytage. He didn't really want to talk at all, he wanted to get on with it. If he'd come all the way back here for nothing, that would be a very poor show. "I do my best," he said.

"I suppose you do." She began unbuttoning his shirt.

240

"Anyway, who cares?" She punched him in the stomach, and her fist bounced off the ridged muscle. "Sex comes first. Also fifth, second, fourth, third and ninety-ninth." He got rid of his clothes. She turned off the lights.

Sex was easy for Lampard: once given permission to carry on, his body simply followed the standard operating procedure while he enjoyed the heady pleasure which it brought. Sometimes sex led to a slight sense of abandon, and this disturbed him. He liked to be in total control. Yet good sex required a degree of surrender. Some instinct told him so. His mind had conjured up a curious way to discipline this abandon. It led him through the stations on the Central Line of the London Underground. When he was only fifteen and staying with an aunt at Holland Park, he had often visited a wonderful redheaded girl who lived far away at Woodford. She had kissed him a few times and then dropped him. Now the names of the Underground stations between Holland Park and Woodford surged through his mind in proper sequence as the slim fingers of Mrs Joan d'Armytage gripped his buttocks and controlled his tempo. *Holland Park, Notting Hill Gate, Queensway, Lancaster Gate, Marble Arch*: he was bucketing along, deep in a warm tunnel. *Bond Street, Oxford Circus, Tottenham Court Road.* Long way yet. Plenty of time. *Cairo, Khashab, Bawiti, Ain Dalla, Kufra* . . . Damn. That wasn't the Central Line. Mrs d'Armytage did something exciting with her loins. *St Pauls, Bank, Liverpool Street.* Better. *Bethnal Green, Mile End, Stratford.* Not far now. Get your ticket ready, Jack.

The lights blazed. "Charming!" an angry man shouted. "Fucking charming!"

"Oh, God damn it all to hell," Mrs d'Armytage said wearily.

Lampard glanced over his shoulder. An Australian major was glaring down at them. He was as square as a brick and he looked as hard. "Get your bloody clobber on and get out!" he shouted. He kicked Lampard's clothes across the floor.

"Do you know this man?" Lampard asked. Mrs d'Armytage sighed and wriggled out of bed. "What a bore you are, Freddy," she said, crisply, as if the major were a dull housemaid. "And so *loud*. You're not in the Outback now." She went into the bathroom. The lock clicked shut.

"Shift your arse," the major ordered.

"Not the behaviour of a gentleman," Lampard said. He was sitting on the side of the bed. "Barging into a lady's bedroom. Using foul language."

"Listen, you yellow streak of Pommy piss. I've just had two months up the blue. If you don't shift your arse and fast, I'll kick it through that door." Rage was making the major blink. A pulse in his neck was pounding furiously.

"No, I don't think so," Lampard said. He stood up. "I think the proper thing is for you to go away now. It's quite plain that Mrs d'Armytage doesn't want to see you, Freddy."

The use of his name detonated the Australian major's fury. He charged at Lampard, roaring obscenities. Lampard did what he was trained to do: he hit the most vulnerable part of the attacker's body as hard as possible. The edge of his right hand scythed through the air and whacked the major's throat just below his Adam's apple. It smashed his windpipe. That was that. The windpipe, being a collection of bits of cartilage held together by tissue and muscle, is far from indestructible, but it is vital. The crushed cartilage blocked the airways to the major's lungs. As he fell, pain flashed its emergency message to his brain, and his brain stimulated his adrenal glands, and those glands rushed adrenalin to his bloodstream, and it was all for nothing. The last thing he knew was that he was being strangled; but even that mistake lasted only a few seconds. No air to the lungs meant no oxygen in the blood. The brain must have oxygen. Quite quickly, the brain died.

Lampard stood for a long time with his arms folded, watching the sprawled body. He was naked and his skin was chilled, yet he had no wish to dress. When one of the major's feet twitched and surprised him, he cleared his throat. The noise made him realise how quiet the flat was. Mrs d'Armytage was silent in the bathroom. The silence began to bother him, and to break it he said the first thing that came into his head: "Yes Sir, That's My Baby."

A few seconds later a man in the next room said, "No sir, don't mean maybe." He came and stood in the doorway. It was Henry Lester. "Don't explain," he said. "I saw it all."

Lampard put on his trousers. "Why should I explain anything?" he asked.

"I'm a newspaperman. This looks like news."

"Excuse me." Lampard went past him and searched the rest of the flat. The outside door was open; he closed it. When he came back, Lester was testing the major's breath with a small silver mirror from Mrs d'Armytage's dressing table. "No soap," Lester said. "They do this all the time in the movies and it never makes a damn bit of difference. Same here. There's nothing stiffer than a stiff, is there?"

Lampard put his shirt on. "You were at the Black Cat Club," he said.

"I followed you here. You're SAS, aren't you? And those guys in the white berets were phoneys. Am I right?"

"The brigade abandoned the white beret some time ago. Too conspicuous." Lampard found his shoes and socks. "Word got around Cairo that wearing a white beret and SAS shoulder badges was a quick way to a free drink. Imitation warriors appeared on the scene. We discourage imitations." Using his foot he nudged the major's limbs straight. "You appreciate I had no choice whatsoever."

"This place Kufra," Lester said. "That's the big oasis, right? I guess you guys use it a lot."

"I have nothing to say about Kufra."

"No, sure, I understand. You said it all, back there at the

club." Lester glanced towards the bathroom. "She okay?"

"Probably taking a bath. Don't disturb her. I've got to get this thing out of here." They were standing by the body, the American at its head, the Englishman at its feet. "Any suggestions?" Lampard asked.

"What d'you usually do?"

"Dig a hole in the sand."

"Back in Chicago they dig a hole in the lake."

They looked like a pair of removal men, patiently working out how to get a big sofa through a small door.

"I don't suppose anyone saw him arrive," Lampard said.

"Only me." They looked at each other. "Sure, you could kill me too," Lester said, "but that would only double your problem. Why don't you just airmail this one?"

"Airmail?"

Lester got a grip of the major's armpits. "Take his feet," he said.

They carried the dead major through to the rear balcony. It overlooked a garden, six flights down. "Plenty of backswing," Lester said. "On the count of three." The body went sailing into the night. They waited, and heard a brief, crunching thud. "It's all roses and grass down there," Lester said. "Chances are he broke his neck."

The cocktail shaker held the makings of one last sidecar. Lampard split it between two glasses, and they drank. He looked about the flat. "Hard to believe," he said.

"Guy was drunk. Leaned too far. Lost his balance."

"Why did you follow me?"

"I'm interested in Kufra. Seems to me there's a helluva story in what you're doing."

Lampard thought about it. "Pity," he said. "You've been very helpful. Awfully sorry, old chap, but that's the way it has to be. Now: can you find yourself a taxi?"

"Why don't we share one?"

"I feel I ought to stay here a little longer. One doesn't like to leave a job half-done, does one?"

"One certainly doesn't," Lester said, "and I guess two don't like it twice as much."

When Lester had gone, Lampard tapped on the bathroom door. "Bedtime," he said. Mrs d'Armytage came out wearing a red silk nightdress that clung to her like a frightened child. "Good God, you've got your clothes on *again*," she said.

* * *

Major Jakowski's column kept radio silence, but his signals unit listened out at regular times for messages. He was hoping that Luftwaffe Intelligence would discover the location of the landing-ground used by the ground-strafing Tomahawks. That would be perfect – a long dash; a dawn assault; blazing aircraft and pillars of smoke; then a swift return to the patrol area, poised for more action.

What everyone needed was action. They were getting bored with making long sweeps across the serir, which was so flat and empty that no matter how far you drove you always ended up feeling you were back where you'd started. Action would be the test and the reward. It was time for some blood to justify all this sweat.

And then, in the middle of the afternoon, when they had paused to rest and refuel, the radio truck picked up a signal from Benghazi. It was the message Jakowski had not expected. It said that radio-traffic intercepts by Luftwaffe Intelligence indicated the possible presence of an enemy patrol at the following map reference.

He looked up. The sky was a soaring, intoxicating blue. Anything was possible under such a sky. Forget the Tomahawks! This enemy patrol was his real target. Let the aeroplanes wait!

He summoned his officers. "Where are we?" he asked Lieutenant Schneeberger. "And where are they?"

Schneeberger was the column's navigator. He had

trained as a Luftwaffe navigator for a few weeks until a defective eardrum made flying too painful and he had transferred to the army. Since the column set out, Schneeberger, with the help of a sergeant, had plotted its course by dead reckoning. They recorded the compass bearings it followed and the distance in kilometres it travelled on each bearing. Now Schneeberger unfolded his map and aimed his pencil at the end of the wandering line. "I calculate that we are here, sir." He looked at the signal. "And the enemy is . . . um . . . let's see . . . here."

Nobody spoke, but Captain Lessing gave a small, amused grunt. Schneeberger looked again. He was pointing at the middle of the Calanscio Sand Sea. "That's where the signal puts them," he said defensively.

"Ludicrous," Lessing said.

"The English are mad but not suicidal," Captain Rinkart said.

"Good, good." Major Jakowski liked an argument; it gave spice to his decision. "Be more explicit, gentlemen, please."

"Well, the dunes in the Sand Sea are too high and too steep," Rinkart said. "And there are tens of thousands of them."

"You can't get a truck across the Calanscio," Lessing said. "Even the Arabs have more sense than to go into it."

"No water anywhere," Rinkart said. "Heat like a furnace."

"You've been there, of course," Jakowski said.

They waited for each other. Eventually Rinkart said: "I've seen aerial photographs. If I'd been there, I wouldn't be here, sir."

"The English seem to have managed it."

"This map reference may be wrong, sir," Lessing said. "Benghazi says it got some intercepts. That just means a couple of our direction-finding stations took bearings on an enemy transmission and the bearings crossed in the

Calanscio. Maybe the transmission was too short to give a good fix. The bearings might easily be a few degrees out. That can alter the fix considerably. Ten kilometres? Thirty? Fifty?" He took his cap off and shook it. The answer was not there. All it held was a little sand.

"Heat makes radio signals wander too," Lieutenant Schneeberger said.

"When were these intercepts made?" Rinkart asked. "Benghazi doesn't say. Could be last night. Yesterday, even. The enemy's moved since then."

Jakowski clasped his hands behind his back and squared his shoulders. "And on the positive side?" he said.

Another lieutenant, whose name was Fleischmann, said: "If the enemy is in the Sand Sea, and we can catch him, he won't be able to escape easily, sir."

"Anyway, we can always call up the Stukas," Schneeberger said. Jakowski sniffed. Schneeberger added: "As a last resort, sir, of course."

"We're going in," Jakowski decided.

"It might be a decoy, sir," Rinkart said. "A couple of men planted in the Calanscio with a radio to distract us from their main patrol."

"I've considered that. I shall divide the column into Force A and Force B. Rinkart and Schneeberger will come with me as Force A into the Sand Sea. We'll take twenty vehicles and fifty men," he told Rinkart. "Go and pick the best." To Schneeberger he said, "Leave your sergeant-navigator with Fleischmann. He can teach him how it's done. Lessing, you're in command of Force B. Keep up the hunt. We all rendezvous here in forty-eight hours precisely. Right, let's see some action."

Twenty minutes later, Force A detached itself and drove eastward. Soon the vehicles were dots on the desert. After that, only their dust-cloud proved that they existed. Eventually it too was swallowed by the boiling horizon.

"So here we are," Captain Lessing said. Lieutenant

Fleischmann and Voss, the sergeant-navigator, stood waiting for orders. It was too hot to sweat; the sweat dried as soon as it formed on the skin. "Sergeant: if we leave here, can you guarantee to bring us back? I mean, to this very spot?"

"Do my best, sir." But Voss had been a lay preacher at home in Saxony and he could not tell an outright lie. "That's not to say you'll get an actual rendezvous."

"No? Why not?"

"Hard to explain, sir. You see, Lieutenant Schneeberger and me, we each had our own compass and we travelled in different trucks and we made separate records on separate maps. The idea was to keep a check on each other in case one made a mistake."

"Admirable."

"Yes, sir. Trouble was, it didn't work, sir. End of the day, the route on my map didn't look a bit like his route."

"Faulty compass," Fleischmann suggested.

"I changed my compass, sir. Changed it twice. Made no difference."

"So Schneeberger's compass was wrong."

"He changed his, sir. We still didn't agree."

"And by how much," Lessing said, "did you not agree?"

"Seventy-three kilometres, sir." Voss opened his map. "Mr Schneeberger reckons we're *here*. I reckon we're *there*, seventy-three kilometres to the south-east."

"It could be worse than that," Fleischmann said.

"Don't be bloody silly," Lessing told him. "How could it be worse?"

"Maybe they were both wrong. Maybe the truth is we're neither here nor there, but somewhere else."

Lessing stared at him. Fleischmann was right: it could be far, far worse. The implications spread through Lessing's mind like shock waves. "So that water-tanker we sent to Jalo," he said. "Maybe it wasn't late at the rendezvous yesterday."

Voss said: "By my reckoning, sir, the column stopped about twenty-five kilometres east of the real rendezvous point."

"How can all the compasses be wrong?" Lessing said.

The three men stood and worried, while the desert wind hunted tirelessly up and down the musical scale.

*　　*　　*

Captain Kerr liked to start work at six a.m., when the telephone was silent and he could concentrate on signals that had come in from the patrols during the night. Thus he was surprised to find Lampard waiting outside his office and looking, Kerr thought, weary and a bit anxious. "Come in, park yourself and get it off your chest, whatever it is," he said.

"I want to leave now. Today," Lampard said.

"You're not due to go on patrol until –"

"I know, I know. But everyone's fit, the vehicles are ready, we can draw stores in an hour. I want to go."

Kerr brushed some dead flies from his desk onto his blotter. "They got clobbered by the fan," he said. He opened a window and tossed them out. "Never learn, silly creatures. A lesson to us all to watch where we're going and to stay out of trouble."

"I know the colonel's in the desert, but you don't need his permission," Lampard said. "You can do this off your own bat."

"Has someone in your patrol not watched where he was going and got himself into trouble?" Kerr asked.

"No. Nothing like that. I just want to get in an extra couple of days' training. We can do it en route. More realistic."

"Ah." Kerr sat at his desk and folded his arms. He thought for rather a long time. Lampard watched. He yawned, once. Then his face resumed its old expression: hard, serious, tired.

Kerr unfolded his arms. He scrabbled through some papers, found what he wanted, read it, put it back. "No trouble, then," he said.

"There are too many mouths and ears in Cairo. Security's a joke here. I never feel safe until I'm in the blue. Sooner the better."

"The thing is, you see," Kerr said, "if somebody had got into trouble, it would be bound to come out. You wouldn't be here, but I would. And here is where the trouble would land." He took out a piece of chalk and marked a cross on the middle of his desk. "Here."

Lampard frowned at the cross.

"You're not the first patrol leader to do this," Kerr said. "Others have turned up here with a sudden craving for heat, thirst, sand, flies and all the delights of the desert." He worked hard with the chalk.

"It's not really trouble," Lampard said. "It's just a sort of an awkward coincidence. It involves a lady who is the widow of an officer killed in action, a Mrs d'Armytage. I called on her last evening to offer my sympathy. He was an Old Boy of my school, you see."

"I see nothing awkward so far."

"She lives in a block of flats. While I was there, an Australian major fell from the balcony. Broke his neck."

"Her balcony?"

"Heavens, no. Balcony at the other end of the building."

"Careless."

"Drunk. I mean, that's my guess. You know what these Australians are like." He had a short staring-out match with Kerr which ended in a draw. "I found the body when I was leaving. In a rosebed. If there's an inquiry they'll question me and then Mrs d'Armytage will get dragged in, and she's really not strong enough."

"You found this unfortunate Australian major lying in

a rosebed," Kerr said. Lampard nodded. "How did you know he had fallen from a balcony?" Kerr asked.

"It was obvious."

"It was pitch-black."

Lampard turned his head, deliberately, and looked out of the window.

"All right, let's put that aside for the moment," Kerr said, "while we take another look at Tony Waterman's death." That brought Lampard's attention back with a snap. "Refresh my memory," Kerr said.

"It's all in my report. The Stukas got him."

"Yes? Describe the scene."

"Oh, don't be so bloody silly." Bad move, Lampard realised. He got his temper under control. "They caught us in the open. We did the usual – spread out, dodged about, ran like hell. Most bombs missed. One didn't."

"A direct hit?"

"Probably. The truck got blown to bits, I know that."

"Small bits?"

"I didn't measure them." Lampard was having trouble with his temper again. "Yes, of course small bits."

"Including Waterman? No point in looking for his body?"

"He was dead. The Stukas were still very lively. If anyone had stopped to poke through the wreckage I'd have court-martialled him."

"Of course. But next day?"

Lampard sighed. "Nothing worth burying. Maybe the vermin got there first."

"Ah." Kerr seemed satisfied at last. He reached into a drawer and placed two small discs on the chalk cross. "Tony Waterman's dog-tags," he said. "As I believe the Americans call them."

Lampard examined them. One disc was scorched and twisted, the other was intact. He held the intact disc between finger and thumb, as if it were a rare coin. "Someone found these lying in the desert?" he said. "That's amazing."

"No. Someone found them in the cab of a burnt-out truck on the edge of Jalo Oasis," Kerr said. "Which is more than amazing. It's staggering."

"If true. I don't believe it. Who says he found them?"

"An Italian officer of the Jalo garrison. He sent them to Benghazi. One of our agents there arranged for them to be stolen, and he posted them here via the next Long Range Desert Group patrol, together with an order for a sack of tea. Apparently the Arabs will do anything for tea. Did you know that?"

Lampard carefully replaced the discs on the chalk cross.

"You had no orders to attack Jalo," Kerr said. "If Tony Waterman died on the edge of Jalo Oasis you have some serious questions to answer. Such as what you were doing there, how it went so sadly wrong, and why you invented a Stuka attack fifty miles away to cover it up. Compared to all that, the violent death of an Australian major is like an overdue library book."

Lampard said nothing. His eyes had the sullen, unco-operative look that Kerr had seen many times before, the look of someone who had been caught with his hands in the petty cash.

"I don't understand you," Kerr said. "Why do such a stupid thing? I don't mean the Jalo attack. I mean lying about it. We all make tactical mistakes, we all lose men, nobody gets upset about that, it's war. But a patrol leader who comes back and tells outright, downright lies, who pretends the losses were not his responsibility . . ." Kerr shook his head. "The British army takes a very dim view. That sort of thing simply cannot be ignored. You must know that."

Lampard mumbled: "I did my best." His shoulders were hunched defensively. Kerr had the feeling that if he shouted suddenly, Lampard might cry.

"Spare me your self-pity," he said. "It doesn't suit an officer of this regiment. If you're not strong enough to lead, then resign your commission and let better men lead *you*." He poked at Waterman's discs with a pencil. "And, who knows, maybe kill you too."

"Sorry," Lampard said.

Kerr got up and opened a wall safe, took out a heavily sealed envelope and dropped it in Lampard's lap. "Your orders," he said. "Open them after Kufra. I wish you a successful patrol. You may need all the success you can get."

Lampard left.

Kerr picked up the discs and rubbed out the chalk cross. He took a sheet of paper and wrote:

This officer has the potential to be an extremely successful patrol leader. He has already led raids that have inflicted great damage. (His reported score of aircraft destroyed at Barce has been independently confirmed.) He is successful partly because he is skilled and singleminded in attack, and partly because he is often totally lacking in consideration for the safety of others – or indeed himself. If he has a weakness it is that he is so obsessed with achieving success that he cannot tolerate any criticism of his failure, great or small. In future his patrol reports must be carefully scrutinised and doublechecked in every detail. On return from his current patrol the colonel should interview him. Promotion and/or decoration are due, but may not be advisable.

Kerr found Lampard's file, clipped the sheet to it, and tossed the file into his out-tray. On his blotter he scribbled: *Send Lt Pemberton to interview Mrs d'Armytage a.s.a.p.*

An hour and ten minutes later, Lampard led his patrol out of Cairo. They passed the Pyramids, skirted a little hill called the Gebel el Khashab, and headed into the empty sands. Lampard relaxed: his problems were behind him. The beauty of the Sahara was that you could vanish into it. He began to sing. Corporal Pocock, who was driving the jeep, thought it was something wrong with the transmission at first. Lampard had a truly terrible singing voice.

CHAPTER FOUR

Bad Form

Fanny Barton had briefed his squadron to strafe the target once only, break left and get out fast and low.

Greek George broke right. Something huge and hot exploded on the ground and its blast blew his Tomahawk squarely to the right. He was dazed; for a second or two the world was black on white. Then he saw the horizon trying to stand on its ear, and so his hands and feet automatically did the right things and the aeroplane completed its barrel roll. Colour leaked back into his eyes. Red and yellow tracer slid past the right wingtip, grew tired, fell away. George discovered that he was holding his breath, a bad habit in battle, so he let it go and filled his lungs a few times. Better, much better. So why was he shaking like a man in a fever?

He took the fighter up a couple of hundred feet and as it climbed he knew that he wasn't shaking. The aircraft was. By the time he levelled off he was sure he knew why. At least one propeller blade was bent or bust. Maybe more than one. He circled and tested all the controls, and they worked, so it had to be the prop. "Fucking prop," he said in Greek. That was a mistake: a pilot should never insult his aircraft before he has landed. Half a minute later, an angry bang came from the direction of the prop. At once the shaking became much worse. George had been trying to read his compass through the agitated blur of vibration. The frantic judder made it completely useless.

So he was lost. The midday sun cast no shadow. He could be flying east or west, north or south. Meanwhile, his Tomahawk was shaking itself to death. For all he knew he was hurrying deeper into enemy territory. He might as well get out, before a wing came off. The fighter would not climb, so he couldn't bale out. Too late to use his radio. Anyway, nobody would find him. He switched off the engine.

The racket ceased, the shaking stopped. He slid back the cockpit canopy and tightened his straps. The airstream sang its tuneless song. By now the Tomahawk was seconds away from its last touchdown.

As ever, it led with its chin. The desert came up and hit the gaping shark's teeth so hard that the aeroplane bounced, twice, and then stuck out a wingtip and, showing a kind of grim, suicidal fury, cartwheeled into a heap of boulders. The last thing George knew was he was hanging upside-down in a fog of petrol fumes. He whacked the strap-release buckle and fell on his head. The day ended.

Butcher Bailey also failed to break left.

He machine-gunned a column of trucks, leaped the column like a show-jumper and felt a massive thump that numbed his arms and hands. Two cannon shells had battered his back armour. The steel kept them out, but his spine felt the shock. For a long while he could not move the control column. The Tomahawk flew itself until life and pain drained back down his arms. By then the rest of the squadron was out of sight.

Butcher experimented. His arms ached as if they had been clubbed and his fingers had precious little grip, but they moved the column. He nudged the Tomahawk up a bit and then left a bit, until he reckoned he was on course for home. The Allison engine roared steadily. For fifteen miles, twenty, thirty, he kept turning his head to make sure nothing was chasing him. While he was doing this he saw his shadow on the sand. A long thin scarf spilled out behind the silhouette. It was coolant. The engine was losing coolant, a lot of it, fast.

The needle on the dial that measured engine temperature

was already edging its way into the red. Butcher put the undercarriage down before the engine boiled dry and seized up solid. The desert looked helpfully flat and there was no lack of it. He switched the engine off as the wheels touched. Immediately, he tried to call LG 181. All he could hear was a thick hum and his ears were manufacturing that. The radio was dead. Killed in action.

The Tomahawk ran and ran until finally its tail sank and it trundled to a halt.

Butcher undid his straps and stood on his seat-parachute. His back felt like a rucksack full of hot rocks. He turned slowly through a full circle and in all that space he saw nothing in the desert except his own wheel-tracks. He heard nothing but the soft sizzle and creak of his engine. He smelled nothing but the friendly, leathery aroma of the cockpit. Everything else, to the horizon and God knew how far beyond, had been baked to death a million times over.

Butcher wiped salt sweat from his eyes. He swore until the futility of his voice depressed him, and then he climbed down and sat under a wing.

*   *   *

Skull debriefed the pilots. Once the strafe had begun, nobody had seen what became of Greek George and Butcher Bailey.

"One is so frightfully busy," Tiny Lush said. "You know how it is." Skull cleaned his spectacles. "No, on second thoughts, you don't," Tiny said.

Hick Hooper was in the mess tent, drinking the remains of somebody else's tepid and dusty tea, when Pinky Dalgleish came in and said, "Your kite's operational, isn't it?"

"Sure. Got a few scratches, that's all."

"Right. If you're hungry, grab a slice of bully. We're off to look for those two."

"Good."

Dalgleish rubbed his eyes and blinked hard. "No, I wouldn't go that far, Hick. Eleven-to-three against is what I'd offer, and that's generous. Either they went down in the target area, or they didn't. If they did, they're in the bag. If they didn't, we've got about five thousand square miles to search. Still, it's worth a try."

"Suppose we find them. What do we do?"

"Land, if you can. Park the bloke in your lap and take off. He waggles the stick and you work the rudder pedals. Dunno who operates the throttle and the undercarriage. Toss for it, I suppose. Highly uncomfortable, but it's been done."

"And if we can't get down?"

Dalgleish sighed. "Make a cross on the map and give it to Fanny. He gets paid more than we do. Come on. Sooner we go, sooner we get back."

*　　*　　*

Fanny Barton sat in the shade of an awning fixed to his truck and watched his intelligence officer approach. The awning was canvas, so bleached and baked that the next sandstorm would split its fragile seams. Barton hoped that Skull's giant golfing umbrella would go too. He was sick of the sight of it. If Skull's great brain was too sensitive for the sun he shouldn't be here.

"I've debriefed them," Skull said. "D'you want to tear up my notes now or later?"

"Just tell me."

"Right. As usual, the significant item of intelligence is what did not happen. No burning vehicles, for instance. Every pilot reported hitting a truck, or several trucks. No pilot saw flames."

"So what?"

"Well, the target was supposedly a German army vehicle

park. Normally German trucks are fuelled-up. When strafed, a fuelled-up truck should burn. These didn't." He twirled his umbrella.

"You're paid to be so bloody clever," Barton said wearily. "Go on, amaze me."

"I think the target was phoney. All those trucks were cripples, probably British, probably abandoned in the last retreat. There must be a thousand of them scattered about out there. My guess is the Germans collected a couple of hundred, lined them up in a neat square, maybe painted the ones on the outside, planted a few flak batteries all around, and waited."

Barton thought of the reconnaissance photographs of the target he had studied. No sign of flak batteries on those pictures. He had known then that there must be flak, that it must be hidden, camouflaged, and anyway the recce aircraft was two miles high when it flew over. What he hadn't expected was such a savage barrage of flak. It had totally boxed the squadron and shaken it like soil in a sieve. "Bad luck," he said.

"I think not," Skull said. "You have said you will fox the enemy. On this occasion the enemy has foxed you." Barton was silent. "I take no pleasure in reaching that conclusion," Skull said. "Butcher Bailey and Greek George are not going to return, are they? Both must be out of fuel long ago."

"It's a setback," Barton said. "It's not a defeat."

*　　*　　*

Ninety minutes after they had taken off, Dalgleish and Hooper landed. Skull came to the door of his tent and looked. Dalgleish shook his head. Skull went back in.

They ate cold stew in the mess tent. Tiny Lush was there, feeding bits of biscuit to Geraldo. "I'm trying to teach him to sing 'Lili Marlene'," Tiny said, "but he only speaks Greek."

Hick watched the flies operate standing patrols beneath the canvas. His muscles were weary. He felt pleasantly scruffy: he hadn't shaved, his clothes were crumpled and sweat-stained, he no longer noticed Lush's ripe body smell. On the outside, he was comfortable. Inside, part of him was so discontented that it twitched like a bucket of eels.

"Plenty of light left," he said. "Maybe we just missed them."

"Yes," Dalgleish said. "Or maybe the whole squadron could search for a week and find nothing."

Hick shook his head.

"Why don't you go and read a good book?" Tiny said. "Fido Doggart's got half of *Lady Chatterley's Lover*. The fucking's fucking awful, but the weather's good. Lots of lovely rain."

Hick got up and went out. Geraldo followed. They walked to the orderly room, but the adjutant was not there. Hick found him a hundred yards away, watching two airmen dig a hole. Geraldo strutted around the scene, scratching and pecking at the loose sand.

"What's the form about George and Butcher, Uncle?" Hick asked. "I mean, what happens now?"

"Keep up the good work, chaps," Kellaway encouraged. A pickaxe struck stone. The airman using it cursed softly and Kellaway winced. "Well, do your best, anyway," he told them. He led the American away, out of their hearing. "Bloody rock everywhere," he said. "I can't get any damn depth ... Look, old boy: as far as any search goes, ops aren't my pigeon. You really ought to see Pinky, or Fanny. But I can tell you what they'll say."

"Those guys might be alive."

"And then again they might not. Even if they are alive, and supposing we found the kite, it might be empty because the pilot had buggered off fast before the Hun turned up and popped him in the bag." Kellaway's voice was gently calm and reassuring, the voice he had used a hundred times at Guest Nights when a blotto officer needed to be steered to his bed before he broke something he couldn't afford, such as an arm or a leg. "See what I mean?"

"I hear what you say," Hick said. He scratched his stubble, hard, using both hands. "It's still hard to take."

"Hick, old boy, *every*thing's hard in this war. You'd think in all of Libya a chap could find a place for some proper latrine pits, wouldn't you? Honestly, I don't know where to dig next."

They walked back to the hole. The American still felt stung by everybody's apparent indifference. He had braced himself to face death when he came into the desert, but he had assumed that death would stiffen resolve, or even revenge. When they got one of yours, you got two of theirs, or five, or ten: that's how a war was won, you kept knocking the bastards down. Not here. On this squadron, two good pilots failed to return and everyone behaved as if they'd simply missed the train.

"Hard as bloody concrete, sir," one of the airmen said. He was standing on bare rock. The hole was less than knee-deep. He swung his shovel like a tennis racquet and a dozen flies pinged off its blade.

"You see my problem," Kellaway said to Hick Hooper.

Geraldo climbed onto a small heap of excavated sand, looked about him, and thoughtfully made a tiny deposit of shit. "And you're not helping neither, mate," the other airman told him.

"Well, let's try somewhere else," the adjutant said.

Hick left him. It was late afternoon. Yet again Skull was playing 'Empty Saddles in the Old Corral' on his gramophone. Skull sang along with Al Bowlly.

> *Empty saddles in the old corral,*
> *Where do you ride tonight?*

Are there rustlers on the border,
Or a band of Navaho?
Are you heading for the Alamo?

He saw Hick walking to his tent and waved a lazy hand. Hick nodded. A slick crooner and a smooth dance band scratching out a phoney cowboy song in the middle of all this endless African godawfulness. For the first time he began to realise that the Desert Air Force was slightly off its head. Not completely mad: survival in the desert demanded self-control. Just mad enough to score a point or two against the sky and the Sahara. That was the real war. You couldn't win, of course. The trick was to lose with style. Like Skull.

*   *   *

Paul Schramm went back to see Dr Grandinetti in Benghazi hospital because his sores were not healing and he didn't trust the medical officer at Barce airfield. Also there was something wrong with his liver, or perhaps his kidneys: his blood felt thick and sluggish. Food had no appeal. Twice he had woken up, slick with sweat, unable to breathe, heart pounding. His feet itched and ached all the time. Something had to be seriously wrong with him. All this he told her, in clipped and gloomy phrases. "No energy," he said. "Teeth hurt."

"Take your clothes off."

He stood in the middle of the room while she worked him over with her chilly stethoscope and her warm, strong fingers. She did not hurry. At first he was impatient; then he conceded that she was in command and he relaxed. The coolness of the marble floor helped. His sexual organs, briefly aroused by contact with the fresh air, soon lost interest and withdrew. He wondered about this. She was, after all, an attractive woman. Perhaps it was an additional symptom that he ought to mention . . .

"Get dressed," she said. "Your age?"

"Forty-four."

"You have a problem." She began washing her hands. "One leg is much longer than the other."

"That's where you're wrong. The other leg is too short."

His fingers were making such hard work of fastening his shirt buttons that he gave up.

"I am a surgeon. I could operate."

"No thanks."

"Don't you want to be a balanced, upright citizen?"

"I want to be able to eat and sleep, so that I can do my job properly."

She dried her hands and watched him put his shoes on. "Come," she said. "You can see how this hospital works."

Schramm wanted to know what was wrong with him, but if she persisted in being mysterious he was damned if he was going to ask. "I've seen hospitals. Hospitals stink."

"Ah, but I have to do my rounds of the wards. And I might need you to translate. My German is not perfect. Come." She took his arm.

An hour later they were back in her office and he was standing at her handbasin, splashing cold water on his sweaty face. "Men are just meat to you, aren't they?" he said.

She sat on a windowsill where she knew there was a pleasant draught and watched him dry himself.

"Let them all die," he said. "Who cares? You don't really care. This is just a dump, isn't it? Just a dump for the useless by-products of war. You'll never catch up, you know. The war's faster than you. Anyway, let someone else sweep up after the stupid generals. Why do you bother?"

"It's your war," she said. "You tell me."

He flung the towel into a waste basket. "I'd better get out of here before I damage something," he muttered.

"Come back tomorrow," she said. "If you like."

*   *   *

263

Malplacket was in Groppi's, treating his hangover, when Lester brought in a fellow-American. "Oscar Flynn, flight lieutenant," he said. "One of those gung-ho types who likes the RAF so much he won't leave it." They shook hands. Flynn was thin and balding, aged about twenty-five, elegant in two-tone shoes and a seersucker suit. "Is that black velvet?" he asked.

"It claims to be," Malplacket said. "Alas, the stout is not Guinness and the champagne is not French, and the mixture is not strong enough to knock the pennies off the eyes of dead Irishmen, as it should. But it is infinitely better than Egyptian gin." They ordered another jug.

"Oscar has flown virtually every type of Allied plane in the Middle East except a Halifax bomber," Lester said.

"Just a matter of time," Flynn remarked.

"Admirable ambition," Malplacket said. The speech about black velvet had taken all his strength.

"And he's flown everywhere," Lester added. "Abyssinia, Palestine, Aden . . . All over the place." He seemed paternally proud.

"I ferry stuff," Flynn explained. "I ferry aircraft, people, cargo. Great way to see the world."

"Tell Ralph about Persia."

An hour later, Flynn left. Lester walked with him to the door, stood chatting, shook his hand, slapped his back, and returned to their table. "Great guy," he said.

"I'm sure Transport Command is proud of him," Malplacket said, "but his is not exactly an epic tale of guts and gallantry, is it?" He resented having had to listen to so much tedious talk about flying.

"Air power. That's what this war is really about. Command of the skies." Lester was very pleased with himself.

"Are you going to fly to Persia?"

"I might. I might." He took a handful of nuts and munched them enthusiastically.

Malplacket gave up. "Go to Persia, then," he said. "I

shall go back to my flat and lie down in a quiet room, if there is such a thing in this bloody city."

"Air power," Lester said. "You watch."

*   *   *

The Calanscio Sand Sea was by far the most impressive piece of Africa that Captain Rinkart had ever seen. It was beautiful, immense and terrifying. That night, he wrote to his wife in Dusseldorf: "Imagine a photograph of the Atlantic Ocean taken during a great storm. The Sand Sea is like that, except the waves are twice or three times as big and absolutely smooth. You climb to the top of one and what you see is more and more, to the horizon. Nothing moves. I would tell you that these dunes are frozen, but of course they are as hot as hell."

Rinkart did not say in his letter that the Sand Sea frightened him. An hour before sunset he had driven into it with Major Jakowski. They went only a few hundred yards, then left the truck and climbed the highest dune they could see. From the top, the view made Rinkart feel weak. As the sun went down, it washed the Sand Sea with changing colours that were so pure, so rich and so vast, his eyes were overwhelmed: how could God waste all these oceans of gold and green and red and blue on a wasteland? And yet this was no random wilderness. The dunes made a pattern that ran north and south. Jakowski would have to find a way across that pattern, working against the grain of the dunes. Rinkart looked down into the purple gloom of the valley. He realised that he was breathing deeply, summoning up strength to tackle tomorrow.

"The SAS are in there," Jakowski said. "I can smell them." His head was up, his eyes were bright; he was as perky as a spaniel.

They descended the quick way, half-running and half-sliding. Jakowski drove back to camp in a blazing rush, the beams of his headlights bouncing off the dunes.

"It won't be easy," he told Lieutenant Schneeberger, "but if the British can do it, we can do it better."

"Yes sir. I'm a bit worried about my compass," Schneeberger said.

"So change it. We've got plenty more, haven't we?"

"Yes sir."

"Cheer up, Schneeberger. It's only a piddling compass, I'm not going to dock your pay for it." Jakowski could smell hot goulash and purple cabbage and fresh bread. He went off to inspect the weapons and came back looking pleased. "The great thing about the desert is there's nobody to kill but the enemy," he said. "Let's eat."

*   *   *

Butcher Bailey was asleep under the wing of his Tomahawk when the dust-storm reached him. He awoke in a panic, half-blind, half-smothered, all memory of his forced landing having been drowned in sleep. All he knew was what he saw and heard and felt: a blizzard of dark and dirty dust that howled with a kind of triumphant wretchedness and went after his eyes and ears and nose and mouth. There was no sky, no sun. He stood up to run and his head hit the wing. Then he remembered, and he knew it was pointless to run. He felt his way to the fuselage and climbed into the cockpit, got both hands on the canopy and kept whacking and heaving at it until grudgingly its clogged runners gave way and it slid almost shut. He was wet with sweat and the dust coated his skin like brown paint.

Butcher couldn't see as far as the propeller. Sometimes he got a glimpse of the exhaust stubs seven feet away. There was nothing to be done. He knew all about dust-storms. They were far more common than sand-storms, they were filthy and disgusting and wearying, and you just had to wait until they went away. Once, he had sat in a tent for three days and nights with a towel over his head, waiting. He didn't even want to think about that now.

The dust-storm did not trouble Greek George. He was many miles away, in a deep cave, and as the wind hustled past the mouth of the cave it made a soft, breathy boom like a bass saxophone. He found the sound quite pleasant.

It was all the more so because nearly everything else hurt.

It hurt to swallow. This was bad because he was thirsty and someone had tried to help him drink. Who this was, George didn't know. There seemed to be people in the cave, but if he turned his head, pain flared in his neck and back. Shallow breathing was good and he concentrated on doing that. The thing to avoid was coughing. Coughing was murder, it brought great pain all over his chest, pain like fire, and it took weeks and months and years to go away. His arms and legs did not hurt much. One elbow and one knee ached, but they did it quietly, not wishing to bother him with their small problems at such a time. George lay still and enjoyed the bass saxophone. Soon, perhaps, it would play a tune, a whole tune. He looked forward to that.

*　　*　　*

Hornet Squadron was airborne and halfway to its targets when Barton saw the dust-storm and turned away to avoid it. The muck stood several hundred feet high and it reached to the horizon, so that was the end of strafing for today. "Gunnery practice," he announced. "Shadow firing, and make it difficult. The Hun won't make it easy, will he?"

Shadow firing was the bright idea of someone in the Desert Air Force who wanted a target that looked and moved like an aeroplane, and who realised that the next best thing was its shadow racing across the side of a dune. Cheap, unbreakable, no working parts to wear out. The squadron split into pairs and found some dunes. Hooper went with Dalgleish.

"I'm a German shufti-kite," Dalgleish told him. "Very small, very slow. Make a beam attack." He brought his Tomahawk down to three hundred feet and let it waffle along at a bit above stalling speed, while Hooper curled around in a big circle and charged in. Dalgleish dropped a wing to make his shadow even bigger. Hooper aimed at the centre of the black shape flitting along the side of the dune and he fired. The shadow fluttered like a frightened moth. He eased the stick back and leaped the dune. "Missed me," Dalgleish said from above.

He climbed and waited for Hooper to turn and return. "Bloody awful," he said amiably. "Too bloody fast, and far too bloody soon. No bloody deflection to speak of. By the time your bloody silly bullets reached me I was elsewhere and they were too bloody tired to stay bloody up."

"Poor bloody show," Hooper said.

"Definitely no coconut, I can assure you."

"I'll get closer next time, Blue Leader."

"You do that, Blue Two. Okay, now make a quarter attack from the stern. Assume I'm an Me110."

Hooper's second attempt failed. He overhauled the other Tomahawk in a long and shallow dive, saw his bullets make explosions of sand a good length ahead of the racing shadow, and suddenly there was no shadow at all.

He climbed and rejoined Dalgleish.

"The bloody Hun's not going to hang about," Dalgleish said. "First shot and he's off, right?"

"Right, Blue Leader."

"So kill him quick. Stick your nose up his bum and blow his sodding head off. Okay, do a stern attack."

This time Hooper chased the shadow patiently, got squarely behind it, crept even closer and raked it so thoroughly that he ran out of ammunition.

They flew home. The landing-ground was loud with the snarl and grumble of taxiing fighters. Airmen sat on the ends of the wings, guiding the pilots through the dust the props threw up.

"Learn anything?" Dalgleish asked.

"Beam attacks aren't too easy," Hooper said.

"Beam attacks are a bitch. Even if you get everything right the bugger's still flying *across* your bullet-stream. In 1940 some boffin did his sums on an eight-gun Spitfire and he reckoned that in a perfect beam attack, if the enemy's doing three hundred miles an hour and you open fire at two-hundred yards' range, the best you can expect is to hit his machine with seven bullets."

"Seven hits?" Hooper said. "Eight guns, and only seven hits?"

"Seven *maximum*. Eight guns each firing twenty rounds a second, that's a hundred and sixty bullets a second, and they nearly all miss, because why? Because the enemy's in and out of your bullet-stream like *that*." He clicked his fingers. "Even those seven strikes are far apart. Did they teach you lethal density at flying school in America?"

"The phrase came up."

"In 1940 we reckoned it took sixteen strikes per square foot to blow a lethal hole in a 109."

"That was with .303 ammunition. We've got .50."

"And the 109 is tougher and stronger. Look, I'm not saying it can't be done. Some guys can do it, they attack on a beam and they lay off full deflection and they allow for bullet-drop and wobbly ammo and gun shake and hot flushes and Christ knows what else, and they blast the bugger to tiny bits. But those guys are special. What *you* do, Hick, is you get yourself *behind* the enemy. Right? Now he's flying in line with your bullet-stream and you can really hose him down." They walked towards the mess tent. "See anybody else up there?"

"Um . . . No, I guess not."

"Never guess, Hick. Use your eyes. Always look. The war doesn't stop for gunnery practice, you know."

"Sure."

"When I was a very small boy I was doing a test flight when I got jumped by a 109. If he hadn't been such a rotten shot he'd have killed me, and quite right too. The war doesn't stop for test flights."

"I'll remember that." But Mick O'Hare had given him the same advice, Hooper thought, and he had forgotten it. Throughout gunnery practice he had assumed Dalgleish was protecting him. Never once had he searched the sky. Delayed fright made the back of his neck cringe.

In the mess tent, the pilots were talking about drink. At midday they always talked about drink.

"Next time I'm in Cairo," Billy Stewart said, "I'm going to buy a chromium-plated bucket and keep it permanently filled with gin and tonic."

"Two buckets," Fido Doggart said. "One to drink while the other's being refilled."

"Can't stand gin," Tiny Lush said. "Gin's for tarts and sailors."

"My mother drinks gin," Fido said.

"And a bloody good bosun she is," Tiny said.

They sprawled on old ration boxes or petrol tins, their eyelids heavy with heat, their voices flat and slow. Nobody moved except, occasionally, to scratch. They were like cattle, drowsing through the hottest part of the day.

"Bugger gin," said Sneezy. "Vodka. And ice water. Rivers of it." His eyes closed. "I swim in vodka and ice water," he murmured. "I swim . . . And I drink . . ."

"The Romans had the right idea," Doggart said. "Fountains flowing with wine." Before he could stop himself he had licked his lips and tasted the salt of dried sweat. His tongue also collected a few grains of sand. He spat them out.

"Don't waste it, Fido," Lush said. "Spit on me."

Fanny Barton bustled into the tent and everyone woke up. "Too bad about the dust-storm," Barton said. "All ops are off for the rest of the day. Good news for tomorrow, though. No strafing. Bomber escort instead. Won't that be fun?"

"What height?" Pip Patterson asked.

"Oh ... the usual. The bomber boys won't want to be lower than ten thou, so we'll be at angels twelve or fourteen. Nice and cool. Wear your woolly knickers."

"What time?" Dalgleish asked.

"Take off 1500 hours. Back in time for tea. Special treat tomorrow: soft-boiled eggs and hot toast. If we can get the eggs. And some toast, of course."

"Target?" Tiny Lush said.

"Same as always. Front-line British infantry." Barton went out, whistling.

"That last bit's got to be a joke," Hooper suggested. Nobody answered.

"Angels fourteen," Dalgleish said to Patterson, "at three in the afternoon." His voice was flat as a mill-wheel.

"Look on the bright side," Patterson said. "Jerry will think it's a mirage. He'll never believe it."

Hooper looked at O'Hare. "Angels fourteen is bad news," O'Hare told him. "Above eight thousand the Tomahawk flies like a brick. At fourteen, like two bricks. Also, if you take off at three, sun's going down in the west, which is where the enemy lives. His 109s hide in the sun until a couple of bricks stooge by and they bounce them. The End. Kindly take your umbrella when you leave the theatre."

"You can't bounce a brick," Doggart said. "I've tried."

Ten minutes later, when the adjutant came into the mess for lunch, the pilots were silent. He asked what was up. Dalgleish told him. "We all want a crack at a 109," he said, "but . . . ." He made a sour face.

"I'm sure Group has its reasons."

271

"Oh, yes. They're brave at Group," Fido Doggart said. "By God are they brave."

"Don't blame Group for an operational necessity," the adjutant said sharply. "Anyway, it's not the first time the squadron's flown cover for our bombers. We did the same job at Maastricht in 1940. A very proud moment in the squadron's history."

Patterson caught Skull's eye. "Tell me it's not going to be like Maastricht."

"What happened there?" Hooper asked.

"What didn't happen? As Uncle says, a very proud moment. By the end of the day the pride was spread extremely thick, because there were precious few of us left to spread it on."

"And as it turned out," Skull said, "Maastricht didn't make a tremendous amount of difference anyway."

There was nothing that Kellaway could add to that. He chewed his food and tried not to think of a particular pub in Kent where the draught bitter washed away all the sins of this wicked world. The memory of the taste persisted. "Skull," he said, "what was that pub called, near Bodkin Hazel, where we used to drink? All the chaps put their footprints on the ceiling. Bloody good beer." The adjutant clicked his fingers. "*Red Dragon*! That's what it was called."

"No it wasn't." The answer had strayed into Skull's mind like a moth through an open window. "It was the *Spreadeagle*."

The adjutant knew immediately that Skull was right and he resented the fact. Clever sod. Bloody smart-aleck intelligence officers. Bloody heat. Bloody grub. He pushed his plate away: let the flies have it. "Anyway," he said, "I've solved the problem of the latrine pits. Got hold of some TNT. I'm going to blow enough holes in this lousy desert to accommodate all your bowel movements for the rest of the war."

Throughout the afternoon, the camp trembled to the crash of explosives. Cordite tinged the air. Neither the bangs nor the stink did anything to help the pilots relax. Skull put on a record of a slow fox-trot. Ray Noble's band got behind the crooner and urged him on:

> *Won't you make my life sublime,*
> *Darling, to the ends of time?*

A detonation jogged the needle. "To the ends of time, the ends of time, the ends of . . ." Skull ended it.

At the end of the afternoon the CO announced that the bomber-escort job was off. Scrubbed. Forget it.

Immediately, everyone's spirits revived. Life was suddenly better, brighter, brisker. "Back to normal tomorrow," Barton said. "Dawn strafe as usual." There was a rumble of satisfaction.

Skull watched this with something like amusement. Later he said to Kellaway, "One wonders whether there really was a bomber mission to be escorted."

The adjutant had mislaid a stick of dynamite, so his mind was elsewhere. "Of course there was," he said. "What are you suggesting? Fanny made it all up?"

"Morale has definitely improved since he scrubbed it."

"Morale was always perfectly sound."

"No. Too much strafing. The chaps were getting brassed off."

"Not nearly as brassed off as the Hun, I bet."

"Then where are his standing patrols?"

"You tell me. You're supposed to have all the brains."

It was a cheap way out, and they both knew it; but Kellaway didn't care. He had more pressing problems. Holes didn't grow on trees.

*   *   *

273

What was extraordinary was that Paul Schramm knew he was dreaming; and since it was only a dream he need not take it seriously. On the other hand, he'd better pay attention, because the music was Schumann's Third Symphony, the *Rhenish*, and he was first percussion. Indeed, he was the only player in charge of the drums and cymbals and bits of ironmongery. It was a very responsible position. Schramm knew that he was deeply honoured to hold it, him with one leg shorter than the other.

Listen, pay attention, he told himself, *this is Schumann, this is important. Concentrate.*

He took up the big padded drumsticks. The whole orchestra was spread below him, all solemnly working their way towards the end of the slow movement. You could tell it was the end because Schumann had put in a few slow drumbeats. Not many. Two or three. Maybe five. Seven at the most. Paul wasn't worried. It was only a dream.

The conductor looked up. He was Charlie Chaplin. That was fine: Chaplin was entitled to dream too. He aimed his baton and signalled the first drumbeat. As Schramm brought down his right drumstick it turned into a German infantry stick-grenade, so he whacked the nearest musician on the head with it and created a splendid explosion. Keeping strictly to the beat, he hit another head with the left-hand stick-grenade, and then kept on banging heads with grenades as the score said. It was marvellous fun. Schumann might not have liked it, but Schumann was dead. So was everyone within reach. What a performance! Someone was shaking his arm. Probably Chaplin, trying to take away his stick-grenades. Idiot! Didn't he realise it was only a dream?

"Better wake up if you want to get any rest," a man said. He was not Chaplin. Only one arm, and no moustache. Nice smile, though. He went away and came back with a mug of coffee.

Schramm swung his legs out of the bunk. "Dreaming," he said. He took the mug.

"Looked more like fighting."

The air had the stunned, sour smell of all concrete bunkers. Schramm sipped his coffee and new life trickled into him. He even remembered the one-armed captain's name. It was Mix. Karl Mix. Funny name, Mix. There was a Hollywood cowboy called Mix, but he had two arms . . . *Wake up, Paul, for the love of God.* "Anything happening out there?" he asked.

"No. The British bombed Benghazi as usual."

The bunker was in the corner of a satellite airfield near Soluch, about thirty miles south of Benghazi. Luftwaffe Intelligence had been told by an Arab informer that an SAS patrol would raid it that night. A few dummy aircraft and some good-looking wrecks had been placed as bait. Mix's men had some clever new night binoculars that let them see in the dark, or so Mix claimed. Their machine guns were on fixed lines of fire. Now it was nearly three a.m. and the gunners out there must be bored to death.

"Do you miss your arm?" Schramm asked. "Sorry. Very stupid question. I'm an idiot."

"My wife misses it," Mix said. "In bed."

"Oh."

"There are certain things that can't be done with the left hand. Or not as well. Are you married?"

"Technically." Schramm glanced at Mix. The man had a lean body that looked good in uniform, grey eyes with plenty of lashes, and rich chestnut hair. Given another arm he could have been an actor, or a model. As it was he looked improbable, like an adult who was hiding his arm in order to frighten the children. "Shoelaces must be a problem," Schramm said.

Mix nodded. "Also cuff-links, contraceptives, collars, flies, and corkscrews."

"I suppose your batman helps."

275

"Not with the contraceptives. He's Catholic."

Schramm laughed, and drank his coffee. "So was I, once," he remarked.

Mix waited. "God let you down?"

"I'd always been obedient, faithful, pure – well, fairly pure – and year after year I'd prayed and confessed, and I'd felt properly humble and contrite, as ordered, and then out of the blue a burst of machine-gun fire ruined an ankle and I was lopsided for ever."

"Not the eternal reward you had been hoping for," Mix said. "Protestant bullets too, probably."

"How about you? What's your faith?"

"I believe in luck. I tell people I lost my arm in Russia. Well, I didn't completely lose it. It got blown off and it ended up a tree. Froze solid. Like iron. Then one windy day by enormous good luck it fell off and hit one of our intelligence officers on the head. Knocked him silly. Or even sillier. Sorry, you're in intelligence, aren't you? Well, if they send you to Russia don't stand under any trees. If a breeze gets up, it rains frozen limbs. Arms are dangerous enough. Imagine the leg of a Prussian grenadier, hard as ice, whistling down –"

"Your telephone's ringing," Schramm said.

In fact its red light was blinking. Mix answered it, listened, hung up. "Visitors," he said.

There was a trench from the back of the bunker to the nearest gun-pit. The night was utterly black and silent. Schramm's eyes were so useless that they kept blinking for fear he might walk into something. Eventually the captain stopped him. He heard some soft shuffling. Schramm flinched when Mix put his lips to his ear and whispered: "They've crossed the perimeter." He moved away.

Schramm breathed deeply and smelt the oil of the weapon. It tasted sweet and sharp, and reminded him of his mother's sewing-machine. That was very unmilitary, and he suppressed the memory. Mix took his arm and steered him onto some duckboards. Schramm realised that he must be looking out at the airfield. It was like having a bucket over his head. Trust Africa to overdo everything. His eyes began to ache with blackness. Nobody was out there. Even the SAS couldn't move without light, could they? It was probably a herd of wild goats. Goats were nocturnal animals. Well-known fact. Or was that foxes?

"They've arrived," Mix whispered. "Just squeeze."

Schramm's right hand was lifted and placed on the pistol grip of the machine gun. The wood was smooth and shapely and warm: another man's hand had been there. Schramm knew that what he was about to do was forbidden and delightful, the greatest sin and the hugest pleasure, and so he did it, he squeezed the trigger and the night was ripped apart by flame and fury. Everything was a triumph of excess: the racket deafened, the stabbing flames dazzled, cordite fumes swamped the air. After a couple of seconds, Schramm became aware that somebody else was gently swinging the gun through a narrow arc, scything the night.

At last the weapon exhausted itself and he released the trigger. Elsewhere other machine guns ceased their rattling. High overhead, a flare burst, radiantly white, bleaching the ground, and hung on its tiny parachute.

"Wait here," Mix said.

Schramm looked hard and saw nothing, but his vision was still imprinted with blossoms of red and yellow and green.

He sat on an ammunition box. It was the first time he had consciously tried to kill someone who was not actively trying to kill him. He held out his hands and stretched his fingers. Not a tremor.

Nerves of steel. Guts of putty, but nerves of steel.

Mix and his men came back. The men looked pleased. Mix seemed detached, almost remote. "We got them all," he said. "Four. Want to see?"

The flare was fading, but a truck had been brought up and its unmasked headlights lit the bodies. They did not look comfortable in death. Limbs and heads were twisted into the kind of wrong and painful attitudes that can be achieved only by severing tendons and shattering bones and chopping ligaments. "Not like the cinema, is it?" Schramm said. "You can't pay actors to look like that."

Mix said nothing.

Schramm moved closer to the nearest body. He wanted to know if Lampard was here; but this body was too short. Half the man's face was missing: another truth you didn't see in war films. Schramm looked elsewhere and noticed the badges on the tattered tunic. "German uniform!" he exclaimed. "That's damn dangerous. They could have been shot for that." Mix cleared his throat. "Well, you know what I mean," Schramm said impatiently. He went to the next body. It lay on its back, wide-eyed and open-mouthed, like a ten-year-old boy who has just seen his first naked lady. "This one isn't SAS," Schramm declared. "Too small, too young. I mean, just look."

"In my opinion," Mix said, "none of them is from the enemy. I think they are all deserters. Two German, two Italian. They've been living in the Jebel and tonight they came down to see what they could steal."

Schramm knew that he was right. "It was all too easy, wasn't it?" he said flatly. "Far, far too easy."

"Well, killing people *is* easy," Mix told him. "Any fool can do it. I did it all the time in Russia."

Schramm drove himself back to Barce and slept until ten. He showered and shaved, went to his office and slogged through the heap of files that had come in from Tunis and Benghazi. It was weeks since there had been any real fighting on the ground, but the enemy was intensely busy, preparing for the next battle. New squadrons had reached Egypt, with new types of aircraft. Technically, the

Luftwaffe was still superior; the enemy still had no fighter to match the performance of the Me109G. Come to that, the Macchi 200 and 202 could outfly any Hurricane, Tomahawk or Kittyhawk, but the Italians never got enough of them in the air. Italian servicing was diabolical.

As usual, there was a sheaf of reports about SAS movements. Luftwaffe Intelligence had plenty of informants, both in Cairo and in the desert. The problem lay in deciding what to believe. Schramm disbelieved almost everything, although he looked long and hard at a report that Captain Lampard's patrol had left Cairo. It might be true. If true, the patrol might be in the Jebel al Akhdar in two or three days (allowing for some delay in receiving the report). But there were already several patrols allegedly operating in the desert – more patrols than actually existed. So this report could be bogus. Or perhaps a decoy. There was a risk of making the airfield defence units jittery with warnings of raiders who never turned up. That was bad for morale; and the SAS had frayed enough German nerves already.

It was lunchtime. Schramm had not eaten breakfast; in fact he had taken no food since the previous afternoon, except for coffee in the bunker. He felt empty, but not hungry. The Officers' Mess was a block away, full of hot food and cheerful colleagues. He put his cap on and glanced at a mirror. It reflected a pair of bleak and deeply distrustful eyes. "Don't give me that look," he said aloud. "I've never done you any harm, have I?" The eyes did not change.

He drove to Benghazi.

It was a slow, sweaty drive: army convoys everywhere; military policemen who ignored his rank and shouted about unexploded bombs and forced him to make detours along pot-holed lanes; dust; marching troops; security checks; dust, dust, dust. Finally he had to park a long way from the hospital because the streets around it were clogged with ambulances. And when he got to Dr Grandinetti's office the door was shut and a bald-headed orderly was sitting in front of it, reading a very old newspaper stained with what looked like very old blood. "Come back tomorrow," he said before Schramm could speak.

"I have an appointment."

"Not so loud." The man frowned severely. "All appointments cancelled."

"Why? What's wrong?" Fear shocked him wide awake. The orderly was waving him down to quieten him. Schramm grabbed the newspaper and flung it behind him. "If she's dead I'll kill you," he snarled. "Let me in." His pulse was hammering and he felt faint. He staggered slightly. He was too weak to kill anyone, even himself. The orderly saw him differently. The orderly saw a madman and so he picked up his chair to fend him off. Schramm seized its legs. A feeble struggle began. People came running. The door opened and Dr Grandinetti appeared, wearing only her slip. "Stop, stop, stop," she said. "One war at a time."

"Thank God," Schramm said. "I thought –"

"No, you didn't. Men never think." She kissed the orderly on the forehead, took Schramm by the necktie, towed him into her office and kicked the door shut. "Sit down."

She took his pulse, stared into his eyes, went away and came back with a stethoscope. While she was leaning over him he found that by tipping his head he could see much of her breasts. "Do you like them?" she asked softly. He was so startled that he could only grunt. The stethoscope slid. "Would you like to touch them?" she asked, smooth as steel.

"Not at the moment, thank you." He regretted his refusal as soon as he heard it. "Perhaps some other time," he added.

"You're not completely dead, then. Wash your face."

As he was drying himself he saw a folding bed with the sheets thrown back. "Were you asleep?" he asked. "I'm sorry if I woke you."

"Don't concern yourself. I had to get up to open the door. Old joke. Old and tired and not very funny." She was in her favourite place, on the windowsill that caught the breeze. "You look terrible. What's wrong?"

"This war is what's wrong," he said without thinking. "I can't do it. I can't go on with it." He sat on the floor and rested against the wall. He was as far from her as he could get. "Waste and suffering and pointless death. I hate it. Can't eat, can't sleep. It's just . . ." He shrugged. "You know."

"Not me. I'm involved in more pointless death than you are, and I eat like a horse and sleep like a baby."

"That's different. You clean it up. You don't inflict it."

"Neither do you."

"I did once."

"Why?"

"Because he was trying to kill me. And he was half my age and twice as strong, and well armed while I wasn't armed at all." Schramm was cracking his knuckles; he tugged too hard and hurt himself. He sat on his hands. "Damn," he said miserably, "I suppose you might as well know everything."

"That would make an interesting change."

He did not tell her everything. He told her about his escape from Lampard's patrol, about running painfully down the wadi until he was too exhausted to go on, about hiding and throwing himself at Corporal Harris's legs and then jumping up and smacking Harris on the back of the head with a rock. He made his account as objective and unemotional as possible, but he included every relevant detail and by the end his voice was trembling and tears were sabotaging his eyes.

"So he is dead and you are not," she said. Sitting on the

windowsill, one knee up and one leg hanging down, she looked as relaxed as a tigress in a tree. "What next?"

Schramm blew his nose. "I took his weapons and one of his boots. Also his socks, because his feet were bigger than mine. And I ran like hell." His voice was firm and steady again: the crisis was over. "Night fell, which helped. Then it was just a long, long walk over the Jebel."

The leg that was hanging swung gently, as if blown by the breeze, and her sandal swung by its toe-strap.

"Now you know," he said. He felt hugely relieved that he had told her all about the killing of Harris. All the tension had drained out of him. He was pleasantly tired.

"You sleep badly," she said. "Poor appetite." She was watching something happening in the street. "You feel . . . how?"

"Oh . . . Weary. Depressed. No energy."

"Why do you think that is?"

Schramm didn't want to think. He had worked hard; now he deserved to rest. She knew he was weary and depressed, yet she kept making him work. Why didn't she have pity on him? He groaned quietly. She ignored it.

"I can't forget the sound that lump of rock made," he said. "It was a kind of a thick *crack*, like what you hear when a golf ball gets hit just right . . . It was a terrible noise, horrible, sickening. And I can't forget the way he fell. One second he was an élite British soldier running like a stag, the next second he was flat on his face, and an instant later he was dead. Stone dead. The whole bloody business goes through my brain again and again. Here he comes, I kill him, here he comes again, I kill him again . . . It never stops. I hate it. Look at me: I'm no soldier. I'm supposed to be intelligent, civilised, all that nonsense, and I'm really prehistoric. Give me a rock and I'll smash a skull. It disgusts me. Best thing I can do is smash my own skull. I thought I was clever and I'm stupid. Primitive. Brutish. That killing makes me despise myself. I don't want to go on living with the person who could do that sort of thing. I hate it."

At last she turned her head from whatever it was in the street she had been watching. "You're lying," she said, quite evenly. "You don't hate it. You enjoyed it. Killing that man gave you pleasure, great pleasure. That is what you hate to admit. That is why you sleep so badly and eat so little. You tell lies to yourself, but they are not believed."

Schramm stumbled to his feet. He knew that his face was stiff with rage, but he could do nothing to change it. "Goodbye," he said.

"Come back tomorrow."

"Why should I?"

"I like you," she said, "and you need me."

It was another dreary, sweaty drive back to Barce.

When he got out of the car, the station commander was standing talking to a tall, thin Italian officer. Hoffmann beckoned Schramm over. "You know Captain di Marco, don't you? He tells me that something peculiar is happening to Jakowski's desert force. They've split up, and it seems they're all over the place."

"The pictures taken by our photo-reconnaissance aircraft," said di Marco, "indicate several sections moving in completely different directions."

"Maybe they're chasing several different raiders," said Schramm. Let Jakowski do what he liked. It was too hot and he was too tired. "Why don't you ask him?"

"He won't break radio silence," Hoffmann said.

"Well, that's up to him, isn't it?"

"The desert gives a man only one chance," said di Marco.

"What's that supposed to mean?" Schramm's manners were coming apart. He didn't care.

"Has Major Jakowski led an expedition into the Sahara before?" di Marco asked. "Has he any men with him who are experienced in long-range desert travel?"

"Don't know. Probably not. He reckoned that if the British soldier can do it, so can the German."

"Leadership and determination," Hoffmann said. "Guts and discipline. That's all it takes. So Jakowski said."

"And forty trucks," Schramm added. "Including a mobile bakery."

"It sounds like a head-on assault on the desert," di Marco said.

"That's how Jakowski operates," Hoffmann told him.

"My money is on the desert," di Marco said. He shook hands, and they watched him walk away.

"He's very full of himself," Schramm said, "considering what the Italians haven't done to help Jakowski."

"Well, di Marco knows what he's talking about. He made a lot of expeditions into the Sahara before the war. On camels, in cars, by plane. He's got a pilot's licence, you know."

"Oh!" Schramm said. "I just realised. He's *that* di Marco. Good God. The big explorer. Well, I'm damned. Why didn't he go with Jakowski?"

"Why didn't Jakowski ask him?"

Schramm gave it five seconds' thought. "Because Jakowski wants all the credit. Jakowski knows best, and what he doesn't know he believes he can find out without anybody else's help."

"That's what he's doing," Hoffmann said, "dashing off in four directions at once . . . I hear you were in the thick of the action yourself last night."

"I was very brave," Schramm said. "Hitler would have been proud of me."

* * *

Some time during the night the bass saxophone quit and a pair of flutes took over. They blew sad, breathy, wandering notes which hunted each other and never came together.

There were nine Arabs in the cave: two women, an old man and six children. During a rare moment when all the pain had left him, Greek George counted them. Later the pain came back and he couldn't even count his own fingers.

All the Arabs were quite small, as brown as walnuts, poorly dressed and very serious. If he smiled, they smiled back; but that was simple courtesy and their smiles quickly vanished.

Later still, when the pain had again drifted away, he wondered if they knew which side he was on. Maybe they thought he was a German. Somewhere sewn into his uniform were five gold sovereigns. Surely they must recognise a British sovereign. He moved an arm to search and ripped the scab of blood that glued his shirt to his damaged ribs. Pain raged. He lay still and tried to pretend it was happening to another person. That worked. He knew it worked because he could hear the other person sobbing.

Before all this, or after it, or both, the Arabs gave him liquid to drink, heavy bowls of stuff which foamed and smelled rancid. That was encouraging: at least his nose still worked. It looked like sweaty cheese and old piss, mixed up to a froth, but he drank it. One of the girls held the bowl to his lips. She was about twelve. She had high cheek-bones and clean sweet lips and he fell in love with her. It must be camel's milk. His mouth loathed it, but his body was grateful. He wanted to thank her. "Eff-hah-rees-toh," he whispered. She smiled. George couldn't believe his amazing good luck. He had been rescued by Arabs who understood Greek. Now nothing was impossible.

One thing was impossible for Butcher Bailey and that was to stretch his legs.

He had been inside his cockpit for over twenty-four hours, with only one brief excursion to empty his bladder and to grab the emergency food from its container near the tail unit. He shoved it inside his shirt, turned to lean into the howling wind, lost his footing and got blown over. In the end he crawled as far as a wing and dragged himself back into the cockpit. Dust had piled up on everything: the floor, the seat, the compass, the gunsight, everything. It took all his strength to ram the canopy home.

After that there was nothing to do but eat as little as possible, wait for the dust-storm to end, and try to find a comfortable position for his body. Butcher had long legs. The Tomahawk cockpit was not made to live in. Wherever he put his feet, eventually it gave his legs cramp. Meanwhile the storm whined and wailed and rocked the aeroplane.

There was an easy way to guess the height of a dust-storm. The higher the cloud, the lower the temperature on the ground. This was because the sun could not penetrate the dust. Butcher reckoned the temperature in his cockpit was thirty or forty degrees Fahrenheit below normal.

*   *   *

The sky was clear over the Calanscio Sand Sea. Its early morning periwinkle blue had been slowly baked to a milky white that was painful to the eyes. Down between the dunes the air was so saturated with heat that the sands seemed to swim. There was a pleasant little breeze off the Sahara, but none of Jakowski's men felt it because it blew from west to east while the valleys of the dunes ran from north to south. Looking up at the crest line, they sometimes saw feathers of sand being blown like snow. The only breeze they felt came from the movement of vehicles. Force A was making good time along the valley. Unfortunately it was not making good progress.

The wireless intercept had placed the enemy raiders to the east, deep inside the Calanscio. Late the previous night, the radio truck had picked up another signal from

Benghazi. Reception was poor, but the message seemed to give a new location for the raiders, and it seemed to indicate that they were moving north. The radio operator could not be absolutely sure. Important parts of the message had been distorted beyond understanding.

If the enemy was moving north, Force A was travelling parallel with him. Lieutenant Schneeberger was searching for a gap in the dunes that would give access to the next valley, where he hoped to find another gap, and so on eastward. The only alternative was to climb up the side of this valley, drop down into the next, and then repeat that process over and over again, which was plainly impossible. These dunes were steep. Some rose to five hundred feet. How could anyone drive up such mountains of sand?

Schneeberger found a split in the lines of dunes. It was a dead end. His vehicles turned and trailed back to the main valley. A couple of miles further on, another split appeared. This time Jakowski sent Schneeberger to explore it alone, while everyone else sat and stared at the great bleached billows that soared in silence on either side. After twenty minutes Schneeberger's truck reappeared, not from the direction in which he had gone, but dead ahead, in the same valley. The split had rejoined it.

The troops watched impassively as the truck returned to them.

"Schneeberger's back again," Bruno said.

"Forgot his handbag, I expect," Oskar said.

Major Jakowski had a brief conference with Captain Rinkart and Lieutenant Schneeberger. "I'm tired of this," he said. "We take the direct route from now on. The enemy's over *there*." He looked eastward. "That's where we go." His fists were on his hips, his cap was on the back of his head. "Up and over."

"I've never seen a truck climb anything as steep as that," Rinkart said. "Not even in bottom gear."

"Perhaps if the truck were unloaded first, sir," Schneeberger suggested.

"Then what?" Jakowski asked. "Do we carry the load up to it on our shoulders? Use your tiny brain, man."

Rinkart focused his binoculars on the upper reaches of the dune. It was as smooth as a snowbank and almost as white. He breathed shallowly, trying to keep the baking heat out of his lungs. There was sweat inside his ears; it slid about as he moved his head. "The conventional way to climb a mountain," he said, "is to zigzag up."

"Try it."

Sergeant Nocken was the best driver. He took a small, powerful truck with good tyres and made it climb across the slope from right to left. The lower part of the dune made a gentle rise, so the first leg was easy. He accelerated into the turn. The rear wheels flung out a fantail of sand and the truck swung onto the second leg. Now the climb was steeper and the truck began to drift sideways. Nocken gave it more revs. "Good man," Jakowski said. "Good man." The bellow of the engine echoed back and forth across the valley. "It's not going to work," Rinkart said. "The slope's getting steeper all the time. He won't make the next turn."

"Shut up!" Jakowski flung his cap at him, and missed.

"Don't fight me, major," Rinkart said. "Fight the desert."

Sergeant Nocken could feel the slope getting worse. The truck was leaning hard on its downhill wheels, which left the uphill wheels with little thrust. He launched a long, brave charge at the next turn, made the engine howl, spun the wheel and attacked the gradient, but the sand crumbled and gave no grip. Nocken was defeated. The truck stalled. So much for Rinkart's idea.

Schneeberger dusted the major's cap and returned it to him.

"If we could only get the salvage truck to the top," Jakowski said, "we could winch all the rest up."

"Captain Lessing has the salvage truck, sir," Schneeberger said. "We didn't bring it."

"I know that, you fool. Spare me your brilliant analysis of the impossible. I need a solution."

"The dunes might be flatter further on," Rinkart said. "Or lower. Or both."

"I'm not going where the desert *prefers* me to go. I'm going where I damn well *want* to go."

Sergeant Nocken backed, and turned, and let the truck trundle down to where the officers were standing. "Permission to try again, sir?" he said. Jakowski was impressed. He liked the man's spirit. "Granted." he said.

This time Nocken made no attempt to ease the gradient by zigzagging. He pointed the truck squarely at the dune and drove up it as fast as he could. He surprised the watchers by racing past the point where the truck had stalled; but soon his impetus faded to nothing. The roar sank to a growl. The truck was just a box on wheels, clinging to the face of the dune.

"If they wanted it to fly," Oskar said, "they should have put wings on it."

"Go and tell the major that," Bruno said. "It's the sort of thing he likes to know."

"Not me," Oskar said. "Let him work it out for himself."

Jakowski took the map from Schneeberger. He didn't want to look at it, but he was sick of looking at all this sand. It infuriated him with its conspiracy to force him to drive north (or south) when the enemy was squarely to the east. Rinkart was right, damn him: the desert was the enemy. And all these men were standing around, waiting for their orders. What orders? To retire? Quit? Admit failure? Even the thought brought a bitter taste to his throat. He spat, hard.

"Look, sir," Schneeberger said.

Sergeant Nocken had brought his truck back, had crossed the floor of the valley and driven far up the opposite dune. Now he turned and came barrelling down, the engine whooping and shouting as he slammed through the gears. The valley floor rose to meet him and the truck surged up the lower slopes on the eastern side. Nocken worked the clutch and the gears to preserve every ounce of momentum. He need not have worried. The truck climbed like a bird. It had power to spare when he stopped it on the crest line. He hooted his horn and waved. They waved and cheered. He looked around; to the east there was nothing to be seen but the Sand Sea. Its colossal waves repeated themselves to the horizon, utterly still, mountainous and painfully silent. Sergeant Nocken, who had about as much imagination as an adjustable wrench, was startled. He had never before seen anything so lovely or so frightening.

Dune-driving was a special skill. The big thing was the initial charge: if you could get up enough speed to rush the lower slopes, after that it was all a matter of not losing your nerve as the slope got steeper and threatened to turn the truck on its back. Even on the steepest sections, a dune gave remarkably good driving surface, provided you chose fresh, unbroken sand and got the most out of your engine. Above all, it was a matter of faith. Once Nocken had proved it could be done, the others did it too.
it too.

After they got to the top, of course, they used their descent to speed them up the next dune. Compared with grinding along in convoy, this was exciting stuff. The drivers began to challenge each other. The best drivers found that they could hit the top at speed and never need to stop, happy in the knowledge that there were no rocks or trees or obstacles of any kind in the Sand Sea. It was like a colossal, endless roller-coaster.

Only one truck could not be persuaded to climb the dunes, and that was the water-tanker. The men filled every water-bottle and spare container and left the tanker to be collected on the way back.

It was a minor inconvenience. By nightfall they had crossed twenty-seven rows of dunes. Jakowski was very pleased. "We're in striking distance," he said. "Tomorrow's going to be interesting." He ordered an issue of rum for everyone, with a double for Sergeant Nocken.

*　　*　　*

Butcher Bailey hid his water-bottle under his parachute so that he wouldn't be tempted to cheat. He was rationing himself to one sip every four hours. His body resented this decision. It wanted everything now, poured down its throat in one long gurgling, soaking rush; and when he refused, his brain retaliated with tantalising images of bubbling streams and splashing fountains. Meanwhile the dust-storm was an endless dreary brown-grey blur, slamming against the cockpit canopy, and his legs ached to stretch themselves.

It blew itself out after a day and a half. Bailey stumbled down from the cockpit. He took all his clothes off and beat them against the Tomahawk, but he could not clear the fine grit from his ears and eyes and nose. He celebrated his release with a double sip of water and a malted milk tablet. His body needed more, much more. Hunger and thirst nagged him throughout the weary night.

Dawn produced the usual silent extravaganza of colours on the usual empty stage.

He stood on top of the engine cowling and looked at mile upon mile of slightly undulating nothing, and despair seized him so that for a moment his breath got trapped in his throat. He couldn't walk his way out of this problem, not on the tiny amount of water he had left, not in this murderous heat. And even supposing he could, how far would he have to walk? Fifty miles? A hundred? Don't be stupid. "Is that all there is to life?" he said aloud. "All over, already?" To his surprise there were tears in his eyes. "It doesn't seem much," he said, and climbed down. At least the tears washed some of the grit away.

*   *   *

Three days after his forced landing, Butcher Bailey was lying underneath the Tomahawk, brooding on fate and the memory of Groppi's ice cream, when he heard the faint buzz of an engine. The buzz deepened to a growl, and out of the quivering heat-haze emerged a motorcycle with sidecar. It took many minutes to arrive, and when it did Bailey saw on it the sign of the Afrika Korps: a palm tree and some forked lightning in the shape of a swastika. The man in the sidecar got out and said, "You are our prisoner. Give me your weapons."

"Haven't got any," Bailey said. He was surprised how thin and husky he sounded. "Except for the machine guns, and they're a bit hard to get at."

They searched him and gave him a full water-bottle. He drank half of it slowly and felt enormously better. "This is a surprise," he said.

The sidecar passenger introduced himself as Hauptmann Winkler. The other man was a corporal; he spoke no English. "We saw your machine from a big distance," Winkler said. "We were part of a training exercise. Then the storm came. Now we are lost."

"That's jolly bad luck." Bailey poured a little water into his palm and washed his eyes. They were immensely grateful.

"You have a compass?" Winkler asked. "Good. You will . . . What is the word?"

"Navigate."

"Thank you. Yes. You will navigate us to the nearest German camp."

"It's the very least I can do," Bailey said.

* * *

Now that he was feeling slightly better, George the Greek noticed the flies. At some stage he had fouled his trousers and the flies thought he was the greatest invention since camel-dung. George couldn't remember doing it, but he wasn't surprised that it had happened. The crash was a long time ago. Nobody's bowels waited for ever.

The flies were a torment. When they got bored with his stinking trousers they went on walking tours of his arms and neck and face. They buzzed with gratification.

When the dust-storm died and daylight reached into the cave, he managed to show the old Arab man that he wanted to be rid of his trousers. The man tugged them off. He did it very cautiously, as if afraid of worsening some injury. George stood up to show everyone he was well again. His heart panicked and his legs wandered in various directions. The Arabs caught him as he fell.

Nevertheless he was able to clean off the filth, using handfuls of grit from the cave floor. One of the children brought him some fresh sand and he completed the job with that. The flies didn't like it. All but a few hundred left in disgust.

From time to time he heard the roar of engines. Some were low-flying aircraft; others he guessed to be armoured cars. None of the Arabs spoke English, but one drew a swastika in the dust and signalled the need for silence.

At the end of the afternoon, the serious little girl brought him more sour milk and a little bread. Then everyone helped to lift him onto a stretcher, a real army stretcher except that one corner of it was missing and his leg flopped down. The serious little girl held his foot. Dusk rapidly turned into night. They carried him out of the cave and along the wadi. There were no flies. Libyan flies were not qualified for night-flying. That was a blessing.

*　　*　　*

The German corporal drove the motorcycle-combination. That was his job. Everything else was not his concern. Hauptmann Winkler sat in the sidecar and watched Bailey, who was on the pillion with the Tomahawk's compass. Winkler had his pistol out, in case Bailey tried to attack the corporal with his compass.

They drove for two hours, due east. The going was good. If the corporal wandered off course Bailey had only to point and they swung back at once. There was no shadow. The sun roasted all colour from the world, but their speed created an agreeable breeze.

They stopped to refuel the engine.

"One travels and one goes nowhere," Winkler said, rubbing his backside. It was true. The desert here was no different from the place they had left. He gave Bailey a water-bottle. "How much further?"

"An hour."

"Any camp is good. German army or Italian. Luftwaffe, even."

"I know."

The corporal locked the cap on the jerrican. "*Drei liter, Herr Hauptmann,*" he said, tapping the can.

"Ample," Bailey said.

An hour later, Winkler suddenly shouted and the corporal stopped. The sun had moved on; there was a shadow. Winkler got out, looked at the tracks they had made, turned and looked at the shadow he cast, and said in a child's voice: "This is all wrong!" The safety-catch on his pistol clicked. "This way is east. We must go *north.*"

294

Bailey rested his arms on the corporal's shoulders and rested his head on his arms. "Too late," he said.

"You *lied* to me," Winkler said. "You are an officer and you *lied*."

"Awfully sorry, sir," Bailey mumbled. "And that's another lie."

*   *   *

Benghazi did rather well out of the desert war.

It was originally an Arab port, but by 1942 the Italians had been there for twenty years and it was like a little Naples in Africa. In the ping-pong war, Benghazi changed hands at least once a year, sometimes twice. This meant that there was always a fresh influx of thirsty men who had slogged east or west across the desert and who were delighted to find the comforts of civilisation. For its part, Benghazi was happy to serve them. Good pasta was good pasta, whether it was eaten by a German or an Australian. Inevitably the town got knocked about by bombs, but the target was usually the docks. If a bomb-aimer had a fit of twitch when searchlights coned his machine and he pressed the tit too soon, it might be the end of a decent little restaurant or a hardworking brothel; but that was an acceptable business risk. Like Londoners during the Blitz, the Italian colonists of Benghazi took pride in maintaining service as usual. War was hell, of course, but it was no excuse for badly-cooked spaghetti.

Maria Grandinetti told Schramm that he was taking her out for dinner. "It's time you started paying for your treatment," she said.

"All right." He thought hard for a few seconds and said, "There's a restaurant called the Sorrento which I sometimes pass . . ."

"Very wise."

"Oh." That flattened him. "I'll take you to the Officers' Club, then."

"No you won't." She picked up the phone and dialled. "It's full of boring uniforms and I see more than enough . . . *Ah, Pietro, come sta? . . . Benissimo, grazie. Per questa sera . . .*" Her rippling Italian was far too fast for Schramm. He moved away and took a seat, and watched her lively, intelligent face in a mirror, because he did not wish to be seen to stare but he enjoyed looking.

She hung up. "*Tutto va bene.* Dinner is arranged. Very expensive, but you have conquered Europe, you can afford it. Now it's time for me to go round the wards. Come."

"I hate your damned wards."

"Which just shows how dishonest you are." She took his arm and steered him out of her room.

As she made her way down the wards, moving from bed to bed, talking quietly with nurses and doctors, examining wounds, asking questions, Schramm stayed well in the background. He kept to the centre of the ward and looked to his front. Pain was a fact, but he didn't have to see its suffering face. Bad enough having to breathe the tainted air and hear the occasional groan. This is not your job, he told himself. Leave it to the professionals.

"Paul," she said. He strolled across and looked at her. There was something lying on a bed, but it was none of his business. "This I think is one of your men," she said.

Schramm took the clipboard holding the patient's record. Debratz, Kurt. Aged twenty. *Gefreiter*, which meant airman, lowest form of life in the Luftwaffe. The date he got his wounds was the day the SAS raided Barce. Kurt Debratz. Must be the lad who was working a fire hose when a 109 exploded and blew him over the fire truck. Burns, fractures, internal damage: the works. Recommended for a decoration, God knows why. All he did was point a hose.

Schramm returned the clipboard. "One of ours," he agreed.

"Perhaps not one," she said. "More like seventy per cent."

Now Schramm had to look. The head and chest were all bandages. One leg had gone and one hand. "That won't do his love life any good," he said flatly.

"It's not a problem any more. His love life was blown off with his leg." She was totally matter-of-fact.

"What do you expect me to do?" he asked. He tried to match her tone, but his voice sounded harsh.

"Enjoy yourself," she said. One of the nurses looked startled and immediately busied herself with tidying a loose dressing. Schramm frowned and hunched his shoulders, and felt the fire of guilt seep into his face. Dr Grandinetti moved on.

The afternoon was slowly ending: running out of heat and light and energy. He took her to her flat, only a couple of blocks away. She said she wanted to wash her hair. He knew that, if he asked, he could stay while she did it. That was what he wanted; but he was still stiff with anger and he produced a clumsy lie: he had to go to the Officers' Club in case there were any messages waiting that required immediate action ... She cocked her head and smiled. "Don't let the war get cold," she said. He turned and left her, trying hard not to march.

Since he had gone to the trouble of lying, he lived up to it and went to the Officers' Club, took a shower, shaved, had his uniform pressed, his shoes polished (a waste of time in the Benghazi dust) and his hair trimmed, and drove back to the flat feeling at least two ranks senior to himself.

She was ready. Green silk dress, scarlet scarf knotted at the neck, no hat, gold bangle on the right wrist. Maybe a hint of perfume, or perhaps that was the scent of some flower in the night.

"You look," he said, and cleared his throat, "all right."

Her mouth curled up at the corners. "I bet you've been

practising that all afternoon." She got into his car. "Hotel Garibaldi. Take the Benina road, it's on the left."

He drove ten yards and stopped. "We can't go there. That's General Schaefer's headquarters."

"Trust me."

The Garibaldi was hidden behind a mass of cypresses. Schramm's papers took them past the sentries at a checkpoint, and he drove up a white gravel drive that crunched like icing on a wedding cake. He stopped by an entrance of fake Moorish arches. The blackout was total. A soldier came from nowhere, opened the car doors, helped the lady out.

"What am I going to say?" Schramm muttered.

"Schaefer doesn't scare me," she said, quite loudly. "I've seen his X-rays. I wouldn't take those kidneys as a gift."

Inside, the lighting was soft and sympathetic, very old light that knew its manners and didn't stare at the guests. A tall, thin man dressed like an ambassador to the Court of St James came forward and received them. Maria said something that made him smile, and for a few moments they swapped silver trills of Italian like two songbirds after a fine breakfast. Then he escorted them into a dining room that was far too good for General Schaefer and his unhappy kidneys.

Wine appeared. Antipasto appeared. Olives, smoked ham carved so thin it dissolved in the mouth, cherry tomatoes, breadsticks, little pats of butter stamped to resemble Deutschmarks as a gesture from the hotel to its guests, of whom there were many. Schramm and Dr Grandinetti had been given the last table.

"Explain," he demanded.

"Not in that tone of voice." She took a spoon and cracked him on the knuckles.

"You sadistic bitch." He saw that she approved of this response. Now he was thoroughly confused. "Do that again and I'll strangle you with that horrible red scarf," he told her gloomily. He sucked his knuckles.

"Signs of improvement," she said, and lifted the spoon. He grabbed her throat with the undamaged hand, but at the first touch his fingers lost their strength. She made no move, simply sat and looked him full in the face, while his fingers slid down her smooth, strong neck and came to rest above her collarbone. His fingertips discovered a steady throb. "Pulse normal," he said. "What's wrong with you?" She tilted her head back to stretch the skin beneath his touch. "You're enjoying it, damn your eyes," he said.

"I enjoy everything. I enjoy life. That's what it's for."

"Pain? Blood? Death? Those too?"

"Yes, those too. They are all part of life."

"Gibberish." He took his hand away. "Death is shit. Nobody can enjoy death." But he had to look away from her.

A waiter came, topped up their glasses, and went.

"Absent friends," he said, and drank. "Where is the host?"

"General Schaefer is in Rome with his staff for a conference. After Rome, Tripoli. He will not need the Garibaldi for a week."

Baby veal cutlets in cream sauce arrived.

"So who's in charge? That smooth individual in the cutaway coat?"

"His name is Pietro. It's Pietro's hotel. When Schaefer commandeered it, he kept Pietro as manager. When Schaefer departs, Pietro returns to business. Pointless to waste a good hotel, after all."

"I don't suppose Pietro has any trouble getting anything he wants, not with Schaefer's weight behind him."

She shrugged one shoulder. "He's a manager. He manages."

"How did you get us in here? Blackmail?"

"Gratitude. Pietro had a hernia and I operated. Have you ever had a hernia? No? I'm not surprised, your lower torso is in very good condition, I especially enjoyed examining the abdominal muscles, flat as a washboard, a delight to the touch."

"I've been saving them for the right woman."

"Yes? Don't waste any more time. There are silver threads in your pubic hair."

Schramm had been about to eat his spaghetti. He put the fork down.

"I apologise," she said. "That was not an appropriate thing to say."

After that they spoke little. The meal was excellent. Pietro drifted by to ask if all was well, and Maria complimented him on the fish.

"Ah, the sole. You should thank the English air force for the sole."

"Really? Why is that?"

"Each time they raid the port, a few bombs land in the sea. Next morning your dinner is on the surface, waiting to be collected."

Schramm said, "You take war in your stride, Signor Pietro."

"War takes me in its stride, major. Six months ago an Australian colonel was sitting in your seat."

Schramm was amused. "And a year ago?"

"One of Rommel's staff, probably."

"And six months before that?"

"An Englishman, or perhaps a New Zealander. I should have to look it up. Two years ago? An Italian officer of some kind, or the archbishop of Benghazi, or the chief of the carabinieri: that sort of person. You are about to ask which nationality I prefer. I am about to ask which liqueur you would like with your coffee."

As they drove back to her flat, Schramm said: "Do you think General Schaefer is taking a cut of the profits?"

"Of course."

He turned a corner, and said: "I can't imagine General

Auchinleck or General Montgomery going into the restaurant business while they were fighting a war."

"You're such a Puritan." She thumped him on the knee and the car accelerated briefly. "What harm does it do?"

"It's crooked."

"So are you! Learn to enjoy your crooked life, Paul."

He parked the car and they went inside. She gave him a Greek brandy. "I am not going to make love with you," he said firmly.

"I should hope not," she said. "You might have some fun, and then you'd never forgive yourself."

His desert sores, healing fast now, began to itch. He longed to fling his clothes off and rub soothing ointment on them. "You're such a hypocrite," he said. "You pretend to be a doctor, full of care and compassion, but it's all just a joke, isn't it? That's why you made fun of that poor wreck of a kid this afternoon, Kurt . . . Kurt whatever-his-name was."

"You started it," she said. She was perfectly calm.

"No I didn't." But that was a lie.

"You said –"

"Never mind what I said." He slammed his glass down and spilled some brandy.

"You see? You can't even enjoy being in the wrong."

"Enjoy, enjoy, enjoy! What d'you think this war is, a carnival?" She nodded and smiled. He glowered. "Then you shouldn't be here." He got up from one chair and dropped heavily into another. "You have no right to get involved in a war unless you're prepared to take it seriously." He recognised that voice: it was his father's. For a couple of seconds he clenched his teeth. "Why didn't you stay in Italy and take out tonsils?" He made the word *tonsils* fly like a knife. He really enjoyed it.

"I didn't stay in Italy because . . ." She paused, and wrinkled her nose, and said. "No. I'm bored with telling that story. Ask Max."

"Max the MO at Barce?"

"Ask Max. He knows."

They sat and looked at each other. A portable gramophone was on a cane table next to her chair. Without looking, she stretched an arm and turned the record with her fingers, making the needle produce music at a lazy half-speed. She stopped and turned the record in reverse, so that the music sounded Chinese. Still they looked at each other.

"What makes you so angry?" she asked. "Is it that I made you pay for my dinner?"

"Oh, for Christ's sake . . ." He waved the suggestion away. "Anyway, I'm not angry."

"You're *furious*."

"Rubbish."

"Yes you are. You are full of rage."

"I am not angry!" he shouted. "And for the love of God leave that stupid record alone!"

She took her fingers off the record. "If you were to be angry," she said, "what would you be angry about?"

"Intelligence," he said before he could think what he was saying. "It's a lie. I'm supposed to be an intelligence officer. Right? Intelligence. Fighting the war with brains. God in heaven, if men had any brains they wouldn't *go* to war in the first place. War doesn't use brains. War *replaces* brains. There's no such thing as intelligent violence. Violence *kills* intelligence. That's what's truly disgusting about war." His shoulders were hunched, his face was twisted, his fists kept squeezing something that wasn't there. "The only thing that violence creates is more violence. Me, I'm superfluous, the generals keep men like me around so they can delude themselves that war is a science. Do you want to know what war is? War is getting behind some poor bastard and smashing his skull so hard his brains leak out. Those are the only brains I've ever used in this stinking war — that poor bastard's brains, and I can't think of a bigger waste of intelligence, his and mine, and it makes me so angry I want to vomit."

She let the echoes die. "Well, I believe you're angry now," she said. "But I don't think you were angry *then*, when you hit him. It was a great thrill, wasn't it? Very, very gratifying. You were amazed to discover how much you enjoyed it."

Schramm was leaning forward, elbows on knees, hands covering his mouth.

"How do you know?" he said. He was suddenly enormously weary.

"It's easy. Your words said horror, but your voice said delight. The way you described it, you obviously enjoyed yourself. But you couldn't admit that to yourself, because it wouldn't be nice, and you still think you are a nice man."

He rubbed his nose as if remodelling it. "What do you think?" he asked.

"I think you want to do some more killing."

"That's not possible," he whispered. "I'm a forty-four-year-old intelligence officer with a limp, and you tell me that what I want to do is to kill?"

"Why not?" she said. "They shot you in the foot. You've had twenty years to think it over. Now you're ready to get your own back."

"It's unbelievable." His hands were over his eyes. "How can I live with a monomaniac killer?"

"I keep telling you," she said. "Enjoy it. I do."

* * *

From Cairo to Kufra Oasis was the best (or worst) part of a thousand kilometres. The SAS liked the route because, once they went past the Pyramids and turned south-west, they were out of sight. For three, perhaps four days they would be driving through desert that was virtually empty of people. On Day One they might see an occasional Arab in the quivering distance, and there might be a couple of them at the spring of Ain Dalla where the patrol stopped to top up their jerricans with its pure, delicious water. But Ain Dalla was on the eastern edge of the Great Sand Sea, five hundred miles of soaring corrugations. Its breakers topped three or four hundred feet; at their highest, five hundred. Far to the south, long fingers of the Great Sand Sea reached down to the Gilf Kebir. This was a plateau whose cliffs fell a vertical fifteen hundred feet and ran for ninety miles. Together, the Great Sand Sea and the Gilf Kebir formed a pair of obstacles that had kept Kufra secret from the rest of the world for centuries.

It was possible to avoid the dunes and the cliffs, but this meant making a huge dog's-leg of a detour to the south; and the going below the Gilf Kebir was not good. The SAS usually took the more direct route to Kufra, across the Great Sand Sea. In 1940, the Long Range Desert Group had searched out a stretch that was passable and had marked the route with stones and empty petrol tins. It covered over a hundred miles and the driving could be desperately difficult. When the sun was overhead every trough became an oven and the roasting glare destroyed all sense of shape until, as one LRDG man put it, only the pit of your stomach told you whether you were going up or down. There was always the risk of sticking in soft patches of sand. At best that meant the slow, sweating toil of digging out the wheels, of easing steel sand-channels under them, of coaxing the sodding truck yard by yard to firm ground. At worst it meant unloading the bastard first.

The end of this crossing of the Great Sand Sea was marked by a triangulation point called Big Cairn. It stood five feet high and it deserved its name because there was absolutely no competition as far as the eye could see, not a rock, not a stone, not a bush, not a dead tuft of grass. After the Great Sand Sea the Sahara went to the other extreme and became a flat negation, a nothingness, a stale horizon. A wasteland of thin gravel spread westward for fifty miles until it got swamped by the next Sand Sea, which was the Calanscio. The SAS turned south by west at Big Cairn and crossed the invisible boundary between Egypt and Libya. From then on it was simply a matter of barrelling across the overheated desolation, maybe mending an occasional puncture, and counting the hundred and fifty interchangeable miles to Kufra and its amazing, miraculous fund of sweet water that almost made the long journey worthwhile.

Lampard's patrol made steady progress. He was in no hurry; he enjoyed this stage of the operation: it gave him the pleasure of knowing that a raid lay ahead without the burden of knowing when and where. His orders were to be opened after he had left Kufra.

The best time of all was at night. The chores had been done, the meal had been eaten, the men could sit around the fire and talk. If they didn't want to talk, they could always look at the stars. The desert sky had stars the way Wordsworth had daffodils.

*　　*　　*

Major Jakowski awoke an hour before dawn, confident and at ease. He lay in his blankets and looked at the stars. They too were in the right place at the right time and following the correct sequence of events, as prescribed by Providence. This inevitability was something he found reassuring. He knew that he drove himself and his men hard, perhaps too hard. Well, this was the reward for effort. He had searched his mind for hidden risks, and found none.

He ate breakfast with Rinkart and Schneeberger, and gave them his tactical appreciation of the situation.

"My intention is to continue driving eastward until we intercept the British raiding patrol," he said. "It is evidently travelling along a dune valley, going from south to north."

"Might it not be going from north to south, sir?" Rinkart suggested. "Benghazi's second signal wasn't much help to us."

"North to south makes no sense. There has been no recent enemy activity to the north of here. It is far more likely that this patrol is heading north, to start raiding."

"Why are they going up through the Calanscio?" Schneeberger asked. "Why make life so difficult for themselves?"

"Perhaps because the open desert has become too dangerous for them. Maybe they heard about us. I don't know, and I don't care. All that matters is that *they* are going north while *we* are going east. Eventually we must cross their tracks. Then it will be a simple matter of pursuit and, in due course, battle. The dunes that now shield the British will soon trap them. There will be no escape. You look unconvinced, Rinkart."

"Sir: suppose the enemy isn't exactly where we think he is. Suppose we go charging over a dune and find him waiting for us on the other side."

"I've considered that possibility. According to our information, this British patrol is at least thirty kilometres from here, so we can afford to advance with all possible speed for the first hour. After that, I shall send a single vehicle ahead to scout."

The valley was still in deep shadow when the drivers began starting their engines. Jakowski enjoyed the din; it made a rough, soldierly answer to the brooding silence of the Sand Sea.

"If we can average fifteen kilometres an hour," he said to Rinkart, "we ought to be on the enemy's tail by midday."

"If Benghazi is right," Rinkart said, "and if Schneeberger is right, and if the stars are right, then possibly yes."

"You should have been a tram driver." Jakowski poked him in the chest. "You want to know exactly where you'll finish before you start. War's not like that."

"Trams have their advantages, sir. They go backwards as easily as they go forwards."

Jakowski turned away and stared up at the crest line. It was edged a crisp black by the new day beyond. "You're concerned about getting out of here," he said.

"We might get into a fight and lose all our transport."

"In that case we shall have failed, and we shall deserve all the consequences. However, I don't intend to fail . . . Now what's happened?"

It was Sergeant Nocken, running towards them and shouting something about a puncture. "I hear you," Jakowski shouted back. "Now for the love of Christ run away and mend it!" Nocken was already on his way back.

While the wheel was off, three other trucks went sick: an electrical fault, a clogged carburettor and a cracked fuel line. "Just as well they happened before we set off, sir," Sergeant Nocken remarked. Major Jakowski looked at him as if he were the village idiot.

Fifty yards away, Bruno felt the first dribble of sweat wander down his ribs. "There's this waterfall near where I come from," he said. "Big waterfall."

"Yeah, you told me." Oskar said. "Don't tell me again."

"You can sit under it. Sit and soak."

"Don't tell me."

"Water never stops falling. Wouldn't think it possible, would you?"

Rinkart went looking for Schneeberger and found him inside a truck, grimly pencilling lines on a crumpled map. "Made any progress?" Rinkart asked.

"Lots." Schneeberger showed him a tangle of lines. "Take your pick. Any one of those could be yesterday's course, depending on which compass you prefer. Watch this." He picked a compass out of a box containing a dozen and waited for the needle to settle. "Magnetic north," he said. "Or is it?" He got out of the truck and walked ten yards. Rinkart walked with him. Now the needle had swung fifteen degrees to the east. "Maybe *this* is magnetic north."

Rinkart took the compass from him, breathed on it and polished it with his shirt. "For all we know, both those readings are wrong," he said. "Real north may be southwest on this piece of junk."

"It's neither here nor there," Schneeberger said, "as we master navigators like to say." He took the compass from Rinkart and hurled it as far as he could up the side of the nearest dune.

"Are all the rest like that one?"

"They vary. Some more, some less. Fickle, is what they are."

"It looks very much as if some fat Luftwaffe quartermaster has dumped his rubbish on us."

They walked back to the truck and sat on the tail-gate.

"How about the stars?" Rinkart asked. "Can't you fix our position with a sextant, or something?"

"That's sailors. Airmen use an astrolabe. I haven't got either, and I wouldn't know how to use it if I did. My celestial navigation was so bad, the school was getting ready to dump me when my ears did it for them."

"What it comes down to," Rinkart said, "is you're a failed navigator, and we're lost."

"I never asked for the job," Schneeberger said indifferently. "Why don't you take it? You know as much about it now as I do."

"Have you told Jakowski?"

"Would it make any difference if I did?"

"Probably not. As long as we keep crossing these damn dunes we must be going east, and that's what matters to him."

The repairs cost them an hour.

"That's an hour we're going to make up," Jakowski told his officers. "Nobody stops until I do. Not to blow his nose, not to eat his rations, and certainly not to admire the view from the top. Any questions?"

"What if a truck breaks down?" Rinkart asked.

"We pick it up on the way back." Jakowski glanced at Schneeberger, but Schneeberger was busy sharpening his pencils. "All right. The trick of this manoeuvre is for each driver to avoid another man's tracks. Broken sand gives no grip. We go up in line abreast. Order and discipline. That's the formula for victory. Let's go."

Everyone was glad to be on the move. Using Nocken's law of dune-driving, they first went halfway up the previous slope, turned and used the downhill rush to create enough impetus to charge up the facing dune. Nobody paused at the top: on the contrary, everyone knew by now that the faster you dropped, the faster you climbed.

At first they charged the dunes as one man, in line abreast. Then, inevitably, some trucks or drivers proved faster than others, and the formation became ragged. Jakowski waited for nobody. He had taken the best vehicle, a sporty little battle-wagon, and in Sergeant Nocken he had the best driver. The combination was exciting. "Put your foot down, Nocken!" he shouted as they went howling down over a dune. "What are you afraid of?" Nocken obeyed. The battle-wagon rocketed over the top. It was actually airborne for a few feet. Jakowski turned as they went racing down the other side and watched his vehicles come leaping into view, one after the other, like skiers on a mountainside. Excellent, excellent!

Rinkart, in the middle of the column, had stopped worrying. Jakowski's plan was set in motion; there was nothing anyone could do to alter it. He relaxed. Schneeberger, at the tail, watched his compass and continued to plot a course. The task might be pointless, but it was his duty and he did it.

Meanwhile, Sergeant Nocken had discovered a curious and encouraging thing. All dunes were not alike. Some were better than others for driving up. The curious part about it was that height and gradient were not necessarily an obstacle. Nocken had noticed that a low dune, not particularly steep, could be quite difficult to climb. On the other hand, a high dune with a much steeper face often seemed to welcome him. The difference, he realised, was the surface. For some reason the sand on a moderate dune didn't give his wheels much grip; it was soft and slack. The steeper the slope, the harder the sand. His wheels had something to bite into.

There was a limit, of course. Some dunes were just too steep. The trick lay in picking the right compromise. Nocken could look at a dune and know in his heart what was possible, and where, and how fast, because Nocken had a heart like a sixteen-cylinder Mercedes-Benz diesel engine.

His discovery pleased him. He decided to tell the major about it at the next stop. Then Nocken made another and even more important discovery about the shape and structure of the Calanscio Sand Sea.

As usual Jakowski was urging him to greater speed as they rushed to the ridge; as usual the battle-wagon bounded over the top like a great puppy just let off the leash. Then Nocken had perhaps a fifth of a second to discover that this dune was crescent-shaped at the top, that the crescent was hollow, and that the battle-wagon was flying horribly far out into space. Its engine screamed because its wheels met no resistance. That was the last sound Nocken heard. The battle-wagon crashed on its nose a hundred feet down the slope, bounced and rolled and flung him out with most of the steering wheel through his chest. Jakowski was already lying far behind him, his face between his knees because his spine had snapped.

The rest of the column followed. Order and discipline. The trucks came sailing over the top, sailed into nothing, plunged and smashed and made a stream of wreckage that rolled noisily down to the trough. Twelve trucks threw themselves after their commander, then an ambulance, then a radio truck, then one loaded with fuel. Rinkart was dead; Bruno was dead; Oskar was trying to breathe, but his lungs were crushed. The fuel truck exploded. The next truck driver heard the bang as he reached the crest, but he could not stop. Smoke boiled into the sky. The following truck skidded sideways and halted with five feet to spare. Its driver looked down and could not believe what he saw. Blazing fuel was trying to set the sand on fire. A ruined truck burst into flames and soon it began to spray ammunition. All the bodies lay still except one which, perversely, kept rolling all the way down the dune to the very bottom.

Lieutenant Schneeberger found himself in command of the remains of Force A: three trucks and five men. Nothing could be done until the fires went out and the ammunition stopped exploding. He ordered an issue of rum, clearly the best decision he had ever made, so he repeated it. Then they buried the dead, collected five wounded and drove back along their tracks. By nightfall only two of the wounded were still alive.

*　　*　　*

The strafing went on and still the Luftwaffe put up no standing patrols; nor did the Italian air force. No enemy fighter appeared in the part of the desert reached by Hornet Squadron. What the enemy did was strengthen his anti-aircraft batteries. Every day, flak fragments or heavy machine-gun bullets scarred the Tomahawks and every scar had to be patched. All the strafing was carried out at very low level and there was a running joke in the squadron about battle damage caused by German bayonets; but what all these missions were doing to the fighters' performance was no joke. Each new patch knocked another fraction off the speed; every hour in the air took a bit more heart out of the Allison engine and already the squadron's Allisons were growing old on a diet of dust and fine grit. The same abrasive mixture got into the guns, the undercarriage, the propeller-pitch mechanism, everything that required one surface to move against another. The desert was sand-papering the aircraft to death.

The only thing that worried Fanny Barton was his failure to provoke the Luftwaffe to action. He called a meeting of the flight commanders and the intelligence officer. "Any ideas?" he asked.

"What about night-flying?" Patterson said. "Spoil their sleep. That should make them pretty ratty."

"You mean on top of what we're doing already?"

"Yes. The Luftwaffe did it to us in France. We chased them all day, they bombed us all night, day after day, no rest. Sooner or later you get the jitters, I don't care how tough you are."

"I don't remember that," Barton said. He had been watching the adjutant approach with a sheaf of papers for him to sign. "Uncle, you were at Pont St Pierre when the balloon went up. Did we get the twitch?"

"Of course not," Kellaway said at once. "The chaps were first-rate. The whole squadron came through with flying colours." He gave Barton a fountain pen.

"That's balls," Patterson said. "Some blokes couldn't hold a mug of tea without spilling half of it."

"Hangovers," Kellaway said. "Bloody awful French plonk."

Barton scribbled and scribbled. "I can't remember losing any sleep, Pip. Too damn tired to bother about bombs."

Patterson watched him concentrate on making his signature, and saw how his face crowded together a lot of lines that had been absent in 1940. Patterson was about to say: *You were the one I remember spilling his tea, Fanny, and* that was at dawn, before the first sortie, so God knows what you were like after the last . . . But he thought better of it and merely shrugged.

"Can't strafe at night anyway," Pinky Dalgleish said. "Got to see to strafe."

"I wasn't thinking of strafing," Patterson said. He was tired of his stupid idea, nobody was listening, he was sorry he'd mentioned it. "Just flying about and annoying their flak. Keeping the buggers awake."

"Staunch," Kellaway announced. When everyone looked at him, he said: "That's what I'd call the way the squadron stood up to the Hun in France. Staunch. Damn staunch."

"Half the squadron," Skull corrected. "Half the squadron stood up. The other half got knocked down." He could see that Kellaway disapproved. "Truth doesn't go away just because it's unpleasant," Skull told him. "France was a shambles. We were —"

"I was damn proud of the squadron and I still am. Men died but they didn't die in vain."

"No? For all the difference they made, some of them might as well have cut their throats. It would have been far cheaper and a great deal less painful."

"That's a disgraceful thing to say."

"It was a disgraceful bit of war."

"Shut up!" Barton ordered. "I don't give a tuppenny toss for 1940. I want to know how we can get some results *now*."

"What would spice up the strafing," Dalgleish said, "would be a few bombs. Nothing like a nice two-hundred-and-fifty pounder up your chuff to start the day with a bang."

"Well, you know the Tommy isn't adapted for bombs," Barton said, "but I'll see if we can get the doings fitted. Good idea."

"I sometimes think Jerry might get more pissed off with us if we hammered his supplies," Patterson said. "Rations and water especially. I mean, how would we feel if our water-tankers kept getting shot up by 109s?"

"Bloody thirsty." Barton thought about it and smiled. "Big, fat, Jerry water-tankers. Soft target, slow, no escort probably. Lovely grub! Let's do it. Let's hit 'em where it really hurts."

"I'll get you map references for wells and water points," Skull said. "There can't be many, so the tracks should be obvious."

"Funny thing," the adjutant said. He shook his head. "We had exactly the same problem with the Boche during a spell in 1917. He wouldn't come up and fight. In the end one of our chaps flew over the airfield where that ghastly fellow Richthofen was based and dropped a challenge. Meet me in single combat over such-and-such a place tomorrow at half-past two, that sort of thing. Chap called Somerset, Tommy Somerset. Awfully good at conjuring tricks. Made things disappear. I could never . . ." Kellaway gave a gentle, perplexed smile.

"Did he turn up?" Barton asked.

"Richthofen? No, no. Complete washout."

"Right," Barton said firmly. "Thank you, everyone. See you all later."

"Tommy got knocked down by a bus in Piccadilly," Kellaway said. "Or it might have been Regent Street. There were conflicting reports."

"There always are," Skull said.

The flight commanders left. Skull remained. The adjutant looked at him, glanced at the CO, and decided to stay for a while.

"The Duke of Wellington . . ." Skull began.

"Wasn't a fighter pilot," Barton completed. "So the hell with him."

Skull turned to Kellaway. "The Duke of Wellington said that all the business of war is trying to find out what you don't know by what you do know."

"Too deep for me, old chap."

"Guessing what's on the other side of the hill. That's what he called it."

"I don't need to guess anything." Barton said. "I fly over the other side of the hill twice daily. I can see what Jerry's doing."

"But can you see what he's thinking?"

"Can *you*?" Kellaway asked.

"I can try," Skull said. "Suppose we begin with what we know. We know the Germans are no fools. When you start strafing them, all day every day, and it's not part of a larger offensive, they must ask themselves why. We know that the Afrika Korps is a very tough army. It's been strafed before. It's not going to collapse just because a squadron of elderly Tomahawks attacks it. And we know our attacks are having less and less effect."

"Rubbish!" Barton said. "They're running like rabbits."

"Debriefing tells me otherwise. One in three of your targets is a dummy, perhaps one in two. Jerry's twigged what you're up to, Fanny. He's put more observers out in the desert, and further out, so by the time you reach the target his troops are in their trenches. And you're flying through heavy flak."

"How do you know?" Barton growled. "You don't know."

"I suppose it's what we'd do," the adjutant said. "I mean, if we kept getting strafed."

Barton's eyebrows were one thick black line. "That just proves how much we're hurting them. And I don't believe all that cock about decoys. Bloody hell! What is this? A war or a duck shoot?"

The silence lasted so long that it began to trouble Kellaway. "I suppose we could always ask Group's opinion," he suggested.

"No! Never!" Barton slammed his hand on the table and made sand jump out of the cracks between the planks.

"That's fatal. They'll think we can't cope on our own. Next thing I'll be running a weather-station in Greenland. No!" Another whack sent the sand leaping again.

"Just a thought."

"It really doesn't matter what Group thinks," Skull said, "or what I think, or you think, or Baggy Bletchley thinks. All that matters is what the enemy *does*. That includes what he doesn't do. Let's face it, Fanny, he hasn't put up any standing patrols and he's not going to."

"You give in too easy. The game's not over yet."

"The game is *up*, Fanny. You've stung him and he hasn't jumped."

"I'll sting him a bloody sight harder yet. Then he'll jump. You watch."

"Or maybe you'll get stung. Badly. They're waiting for you now. You realise that, don't you? You know how lucky you've been, so far."

"A squadron makes its own luck," Barton said. The adjutant knew that clipped, flat voice. It meant the CO was fast running out of patience. Kellaway tried to catch the intelligence officer's eye, and failed.

"You can't manipulate the enemy," Skull said. "It's time to cut your losses."

"Horseshit. I'm nearly there. One more strafe and the sky's going to be lousy with 109s."

"Very well." Skull shoved up his glasses and rubbed his eyes. "Do as you please."

"Don't worry, I shall."

"Yes," Skull said, and for the first time a trace of anger sharpened his voice. "In a shifting and uncertain world, that's one thing we can all depend on, isn't it? You will do what pleases you."

"Oh, get out," Barton ordered. "You're a pain in the arse, Skull, you can't fly, you've never been higher than you can jump, and you sit there telling me my job? Go away, you make me tired."

"Ah-ha," Skull said. "I seem to have drawn blood."

"Meeting's over," the adjutant said firmly. He took Skull by the arm. "Come on, I need a second opinion on my new latrine pits." He led him out.

"Do it properly," Barton called after them. "Take all day. Write me a nice long report."

Not looking back, Kellaway waggled a hand in acknowledgement. "Let him have the last word," he murmured. "It's his squadron."

They did in fact walk to the nearest pit. A whiff of explosive still clung to the shattered stone. "You seem to be determined to get yourself sacked yet again," Kellaway said.

Skull thought about that and kicked a small pebble into the hole. "I haven't got your diplomatic gifts, Uncle," he said.

"Bugger diplomacy. Let me tell you something. If it wasn't for Fanny, this squadron wouldn't exist. I'd be shuffling bumf in Cairo, you'd be giving slide-shows on aircraft recognition and the pilots would be driving Hurricanes along the Takoradi Trail. Not a very glorious end to a squadron that cut its teeth in the Royal Flying Corps."

"Takoradi," Skull said. "Takoradi . . ." He sent another pebble rattling into the pit. "Was that really on the cards?"

"It was. And if you think the chaps would prefer flying a bunch of gash Hurricanes straight out of packing-cases, probably assembled with the wings upside-down, four thousand miles across bits of Africa so nasty that even the dimmest native won't live in them, and if the kite packs up and you survive the crash it's a hell of a long wait for the next number eighty-eight bus . . ."

"Which is almost certainly full anyway," Skull said.

"I've forgotten what I was saying." Suddenly the adjutant's mind was as blank as the desert. Its abdication alarmed him; he felt betrayed; this sort of thing happened too often nowadays. "What are we doing here?" he asked.

Skull misunderstood the question. "Too deep for me, old chap," he said. Another pebble was balanced on the toe of his boot and he lobbed it in. "You were speaking of what the chaps would prefer."

"Yes." Kellaway's mind cleared. "And it's not Takoradi. Ask any of them. They didn't join the Desert Air Force to become long-distance bus drivers."

"I see." Skull nudged one more pebble onto his left boot with his right, but it fell off. "Fanny saved the squadron from Takoradi by volunteering to let it strafe itself to death. Am I right?"

"No. Just give the CO credit for having the best interests of his squadron at heart. And for the love of God stop chucking stones into my latrine pits!" The adjutant had gone from calm reason to raging fury in an instant. He jumped into the pit and grabbed the pebbles and hurled them at Skull. "If you can't get anything right, you four-eyed fart," he shouted, "for Christ's sake don't make life more difficult for the rest of us!"

Skull dodged and eventually ran. He had never known the adjutant lose control like that. It shocked Skull, and it made him wonder what he had done to cause it. Maybe he was wrong about Barton's strafing campaign. The adjutant was a mature, sensible man. If he was upset, something was very seriously wrong.

*   *   *

After two days in another cave, the Arabs moved Greek George to some tents in a long, very wide wadi that actually had grass growing in it. By now he could walk, although his right knee soon swelled and locked solid if he worked it hard. And his ribs still weren't happy. If he coughed or sneezed they caught fire. He guessed that something had snapped or cracked and probably the bone was setting wrongly. Nothing he could do about that. Or about the many scabs and desert ulcers that marked his violent argument with the sharp bits of the Tomahawk's cockpit.

He walked a bit, collected scraps of desert thorn for the fire, sat in the sun until it burned his skin and then sat in a tent and played games with the serious little girl. She liked cat's-cradle; it fascinated her; her eyes would follow his fingers working the web of thread and finally she would look up at his face with such open admiration that his heart was touched.

Now that they could cook, the food was better. They gave him eggs, small but good, and meaty black olives. Sometimes they killed a goat or a sheep, and there would be a long, silent feast.

George could feel himself getting better. He learned some words. The sour milk was *leben*. A kind of porridge of barley flakes soaked in butter was *esh*. A guide was a *khabir*. *Nasrani* meant 'enemy'. A *basas* was an informer. Some words he knew already: a *bir* was a well, *kebir* meant 'big', a *gilf* was a cliff or sometimes a plateau. As the days went by he picked up more words. The one word that was always in the back of his mind was *basas*. He never used it but he couldn't forget it either.

*   *   *

Skull looked out the information concerning enemy wells and water points and sent it across to the CO. That left nothing to do. He put a fresh needle in the gramophone and played 'Empty Saddles'. Geraldo appeared, circled the apparatus a couple of times and stood with his head on one side, gurgling and clicking, watching the record go round. *Empty boots covered in dust* . . . Geraldo pecked the record. The voice hesitated but did not stop. *Empty guns, covered in rust* . . .

"Silly bird," Skull said. Geraldo strutted away. His

philosophy was if you can't eat it, fight it, or fuck it, then it's not worth your attention.

At 1100 hours Barton summoned Skull to attend a flight commanders' briefing.

"Take-off in half an hour," he told them. "I'll lead 'B' Flight with Sneezy as my number two. When we get there we'll split up into sections and go looking for ration convoys and water-carriers. Pinky, you take what's left of 'A' Flight and hit this bloody great fuel dump, here." He showed Dalgleish a cross on the map. "The troops are changing your ammo," he said. "You'll have three rounds of incendiary to one of armour-piercing. No tracer, you won't need it, the dump's too big to miss. Set the bastard on fire, it'll burn for a month."

"Not Sidi Zamzam again," Dalgleish said. "Not that damn dump again."

"This is a freelance sweep, right?" Patterson asked. "I mean, each section is on its own?" Barton nodded. "What if a section can't find any water-tankers? Is there an alternative target?"

"No!" Barton said."Find them! Look harder."

"Are you absolutely sure about this, sir?" Dalgleish asked. The 'sir' made Skull and Patterson turn.

"Sure I'm sure. What's up? Not thrilling enough?"

Dalgleish swivelled the map and leaned on his knuckles, arms stiff and straight. The hairs on his arms were so black that even the desert sun could not bleach them. He had shaved that day, which was unusual, and a fine sheen of sweat coated his face. Skull, looking at his profile, guessed his age as twenty-four. That was old for a flight leader. By twenty-four you were either dead or promoted. Skull lowered his head to get a better view and saw that Dalgleish was not looking at the map, he was looking through it: his eyes were out of focus. How odd. "We've been to Sidi Zamzam before," Dalgleish said, his voice as flat as glass. "We've been there . . . how often?"

"Three times in the last week," Barton said jauntily.

"Three times in five days, actually," Skull said.

"They're bound to be waiting for us," Dalgleish said.

"No, it's the last thing they'll expect us to do," Barton said brightly. "They'll never believe we'd come back again. Not with a hundred other targets waiting to be hit. We'll fox 'em. You watch."

"That dump . . ." Dalgleish heaved himself upright. "That dump is going to be filthy with flak."

"Not a chance," Barton said. "They've moved the flak. Now it's there, there, there, there and there." His forefinger stabbed at the map.

"The fourth strafe in six days," Dalgleish said. "It's not going to work, sir."

"It's a glorious opportunity, Pinky. One good kick in the slats and they'll burst into tears."

"Lousy with flak." Dalgleish's voice was still dead level. "Four strafes in six days. It won't work."

"If you're not tough enough for the job," Barton said, "then say so, but don't go on bleating at me." Dalgleish was silent. "Are you tough enough?" Barton asked.

"I don't know, sir." Dalgleish raised his head and looked Barton in the eye. "I suppose I'll soon find out." There was more sweat on his face, and for a moment Skull thought the wetness below his eyes was tears. Then Dalgleish went out.

Ten minutes before take-off he walked into the orderly room and handed the adjutant a small bundle of papers. "That's my diary," he said. "You'd better burn it, Uncle."

"Diary," Kellaway said. He recognised that empty, stony look on Dalgleish's face; he had seen it before, on other pilots. "Burn the diary. Right-ho, Pinky."

"Six blank cheques, all signed. I've got some debts in Cairo and there's my mess bill to be settled."

"I'll see to them all."

"Three letters, all for England. I suppose they'll need

stamps. Here are some snapshots. Pilots' names are on the back. Might be handy for a squadron history some day."

"Yes indeed."

"Everything else is packed. I want you to have this, Uncle." It was a small silver penknife.

"My stars! Thanks awfully. It's . . ." But already Dalgleish was walking away.

The ten Tomahawks got airborne with the usual massive battering of noise, made one thunderous circuit of the landing-ground and flew west.

Kellaway and Skull watched from their separate tents. When the last weak rumble had soaked into the sky, the adjutant strolled over to Dalgleish's tent. All his kit was neatly packed, his bedding rolled up and stowed in a corner. The tent looked very empty. *How can he be so sure?* the adjutant thought. Yet this was not the first time a pilot had come away from a briefing and put his affairs in order. By now, Kellaway knew better than to try to reassure the man, or try to turn it into a joke. A fighter pilot should know his own business.

He thought of asking Skull about the briefing, and he was actually walking towards his tent when he heard the melancholy opening bars of 'Empty Saddles'. He turned and went back to the orderly room.

*   *   *

For once, navigation was not a problem for Lieutenant Schneeberger. He steered by the sun. The map said the Calanscio Sand Sea ran north and south, so he made his little group follow the sun, westward. Once clear of the Sea he would turn north and run for home: simple.

Schneeberger's problem was getting his drivers to rush the dunes bravely enough to reach the top. It took strong nerves to keep the accelerator flat to the floor as the gradient grew worse, with the crest only seconds away; and everyone's nerves were still suffering from the memory of catastrophe. Schneeberger pointed out that they were retracing their tracks, so there could be no danger. His drivers agreed, but all too often they ran out of momentum short of the top and had to reverse, slowly and awkwardly, all the way to the bottom.

They were losing time and wasting fuel. Some of them abandoned the trail of tyre tracks and attempted to climb a lower dune, which looked easier. Each time they discovered, as Sergeant Nocken had, that the sand on a moderate slope gave a poor grip. Wheels spun and speed died. More fuel had been burned, more time used up.

The roller-coaster style of driving was not kind to the two surviving wounded. They died within minutes of each other and were buried together. Schneeberger read the brief form of words from his field service manual, and as he shut the book and looked up at the soaring arcs of silent sand that trapped him, he despaired.

Such bad luck could not go on forever, and they all felt a huge sense of relief when they came across the water-tanker which had been abandoned on the outward journey. With so few mouths left to drink, they could afford to swig as much as they liked. It was a gloriously drunken, orgiastic quarter of an hour. Men grinned and shouted and sang. Some even threw mugs of water at each other. Schneeberger did not interfere.

Spirits were high as they prepared to move on. The tanker had been left on the side of a dune and under the weight of the water its rear wheels had sunk deep in the sand. Reversing was impossible. The driver tried to climb and turn. The manoeuvre demanded a lot of power. The tanker lurched, and its load sloshed violently. All the weight was on one corner. There was a sharp crack.

It was a broken half-shaft and they could not repair it. They tried to tow the tanker and it very nearly capsized.

Schneeberger gave up. "Fill everything you can find," he said, "including your bellies."

* * *

It was too hot to work. The air moved sluggishly. Kellaway tried to read a list of recommended promotions among the ground crew. The sheets of paper stuck to his fingers. Skull's distant music ended; now the camp was silent. Kellaway rested his head on his sweaty forearms for a moment, and when he woke up he had no idea how long he had been asleep. Two minutes? Twenty? His watch would tell him. No, his watch wouldn't tell anyone anything. It had stopped.

Well, that wouldn't do. A chap had to know the time. The adjutant peeled bits of bumf from his sticky forearms and went out to look at the sun. Sun never stopped. Bloody reliable, the sun. He stared hard at it and learned nothing. There was nobody to ask, nobody nearby at least. Figures moved in the distance, but out there all humanity was overwhelmed by the endless waste of the desert: it turned men into feeble stick-figures, as unimportant as insects, shaped and reshaped by the casual distortions of the careless heat.

During operations, the squadron kept observers at various points beyond the perimeter of LG 181. Airmen sat on top of small pyramids of empty oil drums and gave advance warning of anything that approached, especially if it was a Tomahawk trailing smoke. Kellaway trudged all the way out to one of these observers and when he arrived he had forgotten what it was he wanted to ask.

"Not much of a view," he said.

"Bugger-all view, sir," the airman agreed.

He watched discreetly as the adjutant wandered all around his post and ended up staring at the simmering horizon.

"Binoculars all right?" Kellaway asked.

"Yes, sir. Very good, sir." He swept a patch of sky, just to prove it. "Nothing doing except the brag school behind the stores." He turned and focused on this. "Corporal Barber's got three kings, lucky bastard."

"What?" Kellaway clambered up the oil drums. "Where?" The airman pointed. Kellaway took his binoculars. The card game leaped into view: six men in the shade of a tarpaulin, squatting around a blanket. Money got tossed into the middle. Silent laughter brightened their faces. He scrambled down and set off across the sand. The airman called out, asking for his binoculars back. No reply.

As he marched, the adjutant talked to himself. "It's all very well . . . I mean, it's all very fine and good, but who carries the can? The poor bloody adj carries the can . . ." He stopped muttering when he approached the brag school and they all stood up. "Don't give a toss for King's Regs, do you?" he shouted.

"Beg pardon, sir?" Corporal Barber said.

"You're gambling, aren't you? Don't deny it, I saw you!" He waved the binoculars. "The only game of chance permitted on an RAF station is housey-housey when officially organised by a senior NCO. You're on a 252, all of you."

"Yes, sir," Barber said. Nobody else spoke. It was embarrassing to be threatened with being put on a charge by the adjutant, of all people. The finer points of Air Force law got forgotten in the blue. The adjutant knew the troops played three-card brag whenever they could, and they knew he knew. Why not? The pilots played poker, and nobody tried to stop them.

A couple of the men jerked their heads: the flies were a nuisance. "Stand at attention!" Kellaway shouted. The men stiffened.

He walked slowly around them.

"You are improperly dressed," he told an engine-fitter

325

wearing torn shorts and boots. He took a pace back and examined him, starting with his feet and working up to his head. "Your eyes are too close together," he decided. "Get them changed." If he heard their stifled laughter he ignored it. He was looking at their boots through his binoculars. "Foul. Filthy. Disgusting. Atrocious. Those are idle boots! Idle on parade, all of you. You're all too idle to be charged. Corporal! Fetch me a Bren gun. I intend to shoot these men."

"Yes sir." Barber hesitated. "I don't think we have any Brens, sir."

"Then fetch a rifle. Six rifles. And a spade."

"Sir." Barber hurried away.

After a while, Kellaway noticed that the men were standing at attention. "At ease, you chaps," he said. "Stand easy. No need for any bullshit here. I'm only the adj, after all. Only the poor old adj . . . Looking for Flight Lieutenant Dalgleish."

"He's flying, sir," one of them said. "They all are."

"Oh." Kellaway absorbed this unexpected piece of information. "Well, it's bloody inconvenient. How can I give him his letters if he's fart-assing about the sky?"

"Red flare, sir," one of the men interrupted, and pointed to the west.

High over the distant desert a scarlet blob fell in a slow curve. It was the signal that an observer had seen an unidentified vehicle, possibly hostile.

"Can't hear anything," the adjutant said.

"I can, sir. It sort of comes and goes."

"Oh, well. Better prepare for the worst." It was impossible to defend a place like LG 181 against even a small enemy force, so the standard procedure was to prepare to blow up all fuel and ammunition and get out fast. Already, trucks were being started. The brag school faded away, leaving Kellaway to search the horizon.

Corporal Barber found Skull and warned him that the

adjutant was in no condition to give orders. Skull took command. A look-out on the roof of Barton's trailer reported that the desert was empty of all activity except one very small, slow dust-cloud. Skull sent Barber to call off the demolition parties.

Two minutes later a German motorcycle combination came to a halt beside the adjutant. "Hullo, Uncle," Butcher Bailey said. "Look, I've captured the entire German army. Well, the first two, anyway. It's a start, isn't it? This is Hauptmann Winkler."

"How do you do?" Kellaway said. "Could you by any chance oblige me with the right time?" He got no answer; Winkler merely shook his head, overcome by dismay. By now everyone was hurrying to see the exotic arrivals. Entertainment was scarce at LG 181: this was like a three-ring circus. "Tell you what, Uncle, I could do with some tea," Bailey said. "Quite a lot of tea, in fact."

"Well, you certainly can't go into the mess looking like that. You're improperly dressed, man. Where's your hat?"

"My hat?" Bailey was, for a moment, baffled. "My flying helmet? I lost it, Uncle. It's back there, about a hundred miles away."

"Then you'd better damn well go back and get it, that's all." The adjutant was suddenly stiff with anger. He noticed a man with a rifle and took it from him. "You know the penalty for being improperly dressed in the face of the enemy, don't you?" He worked the bolt and cocked the weapon.

"Steady on, sir," a sergeant warned. "That's loaded." Men fell back on all sides.

That was when Skull and the MO arrived.

"Hello, Uncle," Skull said. "I say, are we under attack?"

"See for yourself," Kellaway said gruffly. He waved the rifle towards Bailey and the Germans.

"Well, you mustn't shoot any of them, really you

mustn't. I haven't debriefed them yet. It's contrary to King's Regs. You know that, Uncle."

"Oh." The adjutant looked deeply disappointed. "I'll shoot *him*, then." He took two steps towards the doctor and raised the rifle.

"Tell you what, I've got a better idea," the doctor said rapidly. "If you want to do some real damage to the enemy, why not shoot that ugly thing?" He pointed at the motor-cycle combination.

Kellaway turned on it and banged off five rounds of rapid fire. They all missed. The noise fled into the desert and was lost. "Well done, Uncle," the doctor said. "That showed them who's boss." He put his arm around Kellaway's shoulders.

"Have you seen Pinky?" the adjutant asked. "I'm awfully afraid his watch has stopped." As they strolled away the doctor took the rifle from his hands and passed it to the nearest airman.

Skull, Bailey and his prisoners went to the officers' mess. The Germans accepted mugs of sweet tea, but Winkler refused to answer questions. "He's got the hump," Bailey explained. "They were lost, and he thought that just because I've got a kind face I'd take them home. Now he's going to sulk until he dies, and then we'll be sorry, you wait and see."

"What a shame," Skull said. "He looks quite bright."

"No, he's an intelligence officer. Wouldn't know how to fall off a log unless there was a set of instructions on the inside of the box. Where *is* everybody?"

"Well, the squadron's on a job. Obviously. Greek George is missing. He didn't come back from the same strafe you didn't come back from." Skull noticed Winkler blink at the word *strafe*.

"Probably walk in tomorrow."

The MO arrived, smiling. "How do you feel, Butcher?" he asked.

"Fine. Terrific. Mind you, anything's bound to be an

improvement on yesterday. Yesterday I was sitting under the poor old kite, waiting for the grim reaper."

"Ten minutes ago I was standing in the sun, expecting the same thing." They all laughed, except the Germans.

"Where's Uncle now?" Skull asked.

"In my tent. I gave him a whacking great slug of rum and he went out like a light. He was almost asleep on his feet when he drank it. I don't think he's really ill, just . . . you know . . . doolally."

"Sand-happy." Bailey stretched out on a bench. "Been in the blue too long."

"*Wüstenkrankheit*," Winkler remarked unexpectedly.

"There you are," Skull said. "His lot gets it too."

"Why don't you go and take a nap, Butcher?" the MO said.

"Because I want to see the squadron land."

"Well, they won't be long." As Skull raised his mug of tea, the first faint groan of far-off aero engines made itself heard. "There you are. What did I say?" He stood, and the two prisoners got to their feet. Bailey jumped up, suddenly refreshed. "Come with me!" he ordered. The corporal trotted after him. Skull and the doctor followed. Winkler did not. "Come on," Skull urged. "I'll find you a tent."

"Someone must carry my bag." Winkler had brought a small zip-top bag from the sidecar. "I am an officer and a prisoner of war. It is my right under the Geneva Convention." He was quite serious.

"Who brought it in?" Skull asked, and answered himself. "The corporal. So he can take it out." They stared at each other. "Go ahead. Your German is better than mine."

"I have no authority. He is your prisoner."

"You want *me* to order him to carry *your* bag?"

"Him or another. It is not my responsibility."

"Leave the silly bag." By now Skull was having to raise his voice to counter the sound of the engines. "We'll get it later."

Winkler shook his head. "It is my right under the Geneva —"

He was stopped by an abrupt clamour: shouts, whistles, handbells. He cocked his head and listened. The engine-roar hardened and broadened. "Messerschmitt!" he bawled. Skull's head turned and he looked out at men sprinting so hard that their boots threw up long spurts of sand; while unseen anti-aircraft guns began a hectic, hammering series of *crack-booms*, until even their racket was swamped by the roar and rip of four Me109s streaking past in line abreast, strafing the field at zero feet. Skull had never been so close to so many enemy fighters: their gunports blazed red flame and trailed black smoke; the pilots had faces; the tailplanes twitched; all happening just yards away. And then they were gone. What beauty! What menace! What a raucous, murderous, ear-battering roar!

Skull turned to speak to Winkler and the tent was empty. "Hey!" he cried. A foot moved. Winkler was under the table. Skull felt relieved: how embarrassing to lose the prisoner! "They've gone now," he said. Winkler's face appeared. He pointed and vanished again. Skull turned back and saw the razor-thin silhouettes of four 109s coming straight at him. They were not a rigid line: each fighter wandered slightly up or down, as if a ripple had washed through the flight. They opened fire simultaneously. Twenty guns thrashed the desert so far ahead that Skull was astonished to see a man's body being rolled over and over by the impact. Oil drums bounced like ping-pong balls. A small truck was a small inferno. A row of tents fell as if tripped. Skull was too dazed to move until he cringed as finally the 109s bore down on him, bellowing like mechanical bulls, and flashed overhead. The mess tent danced in their backlash. Winkler grabbed Skull's ankle and Skull fell flat. "You wish to die?" Winkler shouted. Then another flight of 109s slammed across the landing-ground from yet another direction. Their cannon manufactured a stolid *womp-womp-womp* and something huge exploded. Skull tried to dig with his head. He got a mouthful of sand. He was grateful. He wished there were more.

The attack lasted a further forty seconds. Long before the end, most of the ack-ack gunners had stopped firing. A couple were dead. The rest were helpless. The German fighters had split into pairs. Every few seconds, a fresh pair bounced the airfield from a new and unexpected angle. They rocketed over the perimeter, did some damage and raced away before the sweating gunners could swivel and find them. As one pair left, another pair leaped in, strafed and climbed hard to make room for a third pair arriving out of nowhere at high speed. It was a brilliant display, packed full of courage, skill and confidence. When the 109s quit, re-formed out of range and droned away, they left LG 181 in tatters.

Ten minutes later, the first of the Tomahawks came drifting in. It was the pair flown by Pip Patterson and Kit Carson. As soon as they were refuelled and rearmed they took off and patrolled the airfield: the 109s might come back, and a squadron was most vulnerable when it had just landed. For the rest of the day, Hornet Squadron kept a section up as a standing patrol.

That left only three Tomahawks on the ground. Of 'B' Flight, Mick O'Hare had failed to return. Of 'A' Flight, Pinky Dalgleish, Tiny Lush and Billy Stewart were missing. Well, not really missing. Hick Hooper knew where they were. They were dead.

So was Butcher Bailey. His was the body that Skull had seen being rolled over and over by the gale of machine-gun fire. When the raid was finished, Skull had approached it and recognised its smashed and bloody face. The flies were already feasting. Skull spread his blazer over the head and walked away.

*   *   *

Captain Lessing was not surprised when Jakowski's Force A failed to return to the rendezvous. He knew that his Force B was at the right place because he had left a truck to mark the spot before he took his men off to hunt British raiding patrols. They found none, and Sergeant Voss struggled for half a day to find the rendezvous: he overshot it twice and would have missed it a third time if someone hadn't seen the truck, a tiny smut on the horizon. By then Voss was trembling so much with anxiety, he could scarcely draw a line on his map.

The cooks gave everyone half a cup of lime juice, a standard issue in the Afrika Korps. Lessing took his and went with Lieutenant Fleischmann where no one could hear them.

"A thousand to one Schneeberger's never going to find us," he said.

"Ten thousand," Fleischmann said gloomily. "Right now, Schneeberger's probably going the wrong way up a one-way street in Old Khartoum."

The image struck Lessing as very funny. He laughed until he had to lie on his back and recover. It was the laughter of stress. Fleischmann, pleased at his success, sat and smiled. Eventually Lessing wiped his eyes. "Oh dear," he said. "All the same, we've got to wait for them."

"How long? We've only got enough water for six days. Assume it takes three days to get back to Benghazi —"

"I know, I know."

"There's always the radio," Fleischmann said. "If we were to transmit non-stop, Jakowski's operator could figure out where the signal was strongest and then they could steer on that bearing."

Lessing stood up and stretched until every muscle felt used. The trouble with this sort of desert warfare was you never got any exercise. You just sat in a truck and worried. "Last resort," he decided. "What else can we do?"

In the end they created two landmarks. By night a truck's

headlights blazed towards the Calanscio; by day an oil fire pushed a thin black scarf of smoke into the sky. Schneeberger's men saw neither. They were in the wrong place, heading in the wrong direction.

*　　*　　*

The burning vehicles were towed into the desert and abandoned. The senior NCOs hunted all over the camp until they had accounted for their men, one way or another. Live cannon-shells were collected and made safe. Tents were re-erected. The doctor was up to his elbows in blood when Fanny Barton appeared at the doorway of the medical tent. "Ten minutes," the doctor said, not looking up.

"Don't rush anything."

"I shan't. Not much left to rush."

Ten minutes later he came out, wiping his hands with a towel that reeked of disinfectant. "Three dead, seven badly hurt. Two won't last the night. Plus a lot of cuts and scratches, not serious."

"Where's Uncle?"

"In his tent, sedated. I gave him some rum." The doctor thought about explaining and decided to let it wait. "Best to leave him alone."

"If you say so. Only five dead, then."

"Never say 'only'. Each one was somebody's son."

Barton grunted. "Doesn't say much for the Luftwaffe's gunnery, does it? A pack of 109s gets a free hand and they can't even reach double figures. Bloody pathetic."

The doctor found his words amusing. "Is that what you intend to say at the grave-side?" he asked. "Better than ashes to ashes, I suppose."

"I'm not saying anything. Uncle handles all that."

"Uncle's incapable."

"He'll be fit tomorrow, won't he?"

"He might. The corpses won't. My advice is, bury them

fast before they start to stink. Meat doesn't last in the desert, you know."

One of the two dying airmen stopped breathing ten minutes later. The other clung obstinately, perhaps pointlessly, to life. Thus there were four bodies to be buried. Each was wrapped in canvas cut from tents too badly shot-up to be worth saving. They were placed on tail-gates unhitched from trucks. Four men carried each tail-gate, not on their shoulders but held like a stretcher. When they were all ready, a flight sergeant said, not raising his voice, "Off you go, lads." They did not march but walked, in single file, the two or three hundred yards to where the ground had been opened.

The day was dying, too. Tremendously elongated shadows stalked ahead of the burial parties. In the background the final pair of Tomahawks came in to land, engines just ticking over. They lifted their shark-toothed snouts and flared their wings, touched down and rumbled away to dispersal. When their engines were cut a silence occupied the whole landing-ground as if all noise had been abolished for ever.

The ground crews and the other troops, the cooks, orderly-room clerks, batmen, signals staff, medics, had already gathered. The officers stood together. Everyone watched in silence as, one by one, the white bundles were placed in the ground. There was just enough room. Blood had soaked through some of the canvas. A few men took handfuls of sand and scrubbed their fingers. Then they joined the rest.

Fanny Barton stepped forward. "Flight Lieutenant Martin Bailey," he said, reading from a sheet of paper. "Corporal James Carter, Leading Aircraftman George Campbell, Aircraftman Victor Pettiman." He put the paper away. "These men were all our comrades and our friends. Now they are dead. They died in action, serving their country." He spoke slowly, stretching the words, because he had very little to say. "I don't need to speak of their bravery, their loyalty, or their devotion to duty. They gave what we all have to give. That is, our strength and our lives." He tried to think of some more, but his mind was empty. An evening breeze turned up and skittered loose sand into the hole, where it gathered in the canvas folds. "They were our comrades and our friends," he said again. A disturbance began behind him, with scuffling boots and harsh whispers, but he ignored it. "And now we must lay them to rest."

"No, sir." It was the adjutant, cap askew, tunic misbuttoned, and shaking with indignation. "Not in my latrine pit, if you *don't* mind, sir."

Barton was taken aback. "Oh, for heaven's sake, Uncle," he said.

"Heaven can make its own sanitary arrangements, sir. Those are mine."

"Dismiss the men," Barton told the senior NCO.

"Come along with me, Uncle," the doctor said. "We'll have a nice drink." But Kellaway was squatting on his haunches, staring at the bodies. "I know these men," he said.

Skull strolled towards him. "Time for supper, Uncle," he said. "Coming?"

"Have you debriefed this lot?" Kellaway demanded. Skull nodded, smiling. "Well, you'd better get your finger out, old chap," Kellaway said. "Some of them don't look too clever." He put one leg over the edge and prodded the nearest body with his boot.

"Don't worry, Uncle," Skull said. "I promise you that everything here was laid down according to King's Regs."

"That's different." The adjutant stood and frowned at Barton. "You didn't say that, sir. He didn't say that," he told Skull. "Makes a big difference. You're a good man, Skull," he said. They shook hands. "You can go to my school when I'm dead. You'd like that, wouldn't you? Lots of books and things . . ." They walked away, chatting.

Barton waited until Kellaway was safely out of earshot. "Right!" he said. "Let's get this bloody hole filled up fast, before the daft bugger changes his mind." Spades swung, and sand thudded onto the bodies.

Supper was bully-beef stew. After the stew came tinned apricots. Barton quickly ate his meal. "Pip and Skull," he said.

They went to the CO's trailer, and he poured three tumblers of rum. "I can't stand this stuff," Skull said. He drank a large mouthful. "War has ruined my palate. See?" He drank some more.

"Well, we did it," Barton said. "Here's to us." They joined in the toast, although Patterson hesitated. "I told you it would work," Barton said. "One good kick in the slats and they burst into tears. I told you so."

"No, you didn't, Fanny," Pip said. "You told Pinky."

"Who disagreed," Skull added. "Said it wouldn't work." He topped up his glass. "This stuff gets worse and worse."

"Seems he was right," Pip said.

"Rubbish! We got the Luftwaffe off its fat backside, didn't we? First time we've seen 109s in a month. See? Strafing works. It bloody well works!" Barton drummed his feet like a boy at a football match.

"I know it's a tedious point of fact," Skull said, "but you didn't see them. Everybody here saw them. You didn't."

"Thank Christ we didn't," Pip said. "If they'd turned up ten minutes later, or we'd been ten minutes earlier . . ." He sipped his rum, a sip that grew into a long swig. "I was out of ammo and low on fuel," he muttered. "I don't even want to think about it."

"Ah, but we foxed 'em, didn't we? They came all the way to have a showdown, and it was a fiasco!" Barton enjoyed that thought. "Hell of a long trip for a 109, that. Somebody over there takes Hornet Squadron very seriously." He grinned like a cartoon tiger.

"I shall miss Pinky Dalgleish," Pip said. "Didn't know him long, but . . . He was a good type." Being a good type was about the highest praise you could give a man in the Désert Air Force.

"I expect he'll walk in tomorrow," Barton said. "Or the next day. Look at Butcher."

"Funny you should say that," Skull remarked. "I did look at Butcher, and Butcher would have looked at me, except that half his head was missing. I can show you the shape of the other half, if you like." He found a rusty stain on the front of his blazer.

"Don't get sentimental," Barton said.

"Well, I won't if you won't. Pinky will never walk in. Nor Tiny Lush, nor Billy Stewart. They're all stone dead. Hick saw it. Hick saw three Tomahawks blown to bits inside ten seconds. He gave me a careful report which I totally believe. So can we please abandon all this romantic tosh about corpses walking in from the desert?" Skull took some more rum. "Excellent filth, this," he said.

"I'm definitely going to murder my wife," Patterson said. He was hunched over his glass, and he was not joking. "Soon as I get back to Cairo I'll kill the cow."

"Feel free," Barton told him. "Kill mine while you're at it."

"You're married?" Skull was amazed.

"Blame the booze. They took me off ops in England so I got permanently pissed and one day I woke up married to something called Enid. Legs up to the armpits and she banged like the shithouse door. But she hated flying. Hated it. Wanted me to quit. Nag, nag, nag. Christ knows where she is now."

"Good Lord." Skull was still struggling to absorb this news. "I have a cousin called Enid. She plays the organ rather well."

"Not half as well as my Enid." Barton emptied the bottle

337

into their glasses. "Don't worry, there's more," he said. "I've been saving the stuff."

"I think you would be ill-advised to murder your wife, Pip," Skull said.

"What's wrong with her?" Barton asked. "Is she ugly?"

"She's so lovely that it hurts," Pip said. He sat up straight. He had been crying and he didn't care who knew it.

"So what's the problem?"

"Bloke called Dumbo Silk . . ." Pip blew his nose. "Flew together, drank together. He blew a 109 off my tail that I didn't know was there. Best pilot I ever saw."

"Dumbo Silk," Fanny said. "Yes. I've met him in Tommy's Bar a couple of times. Face like a choirboy and he told me the funniest dirty story I've ever heard. He went over to Beaufighters, didn't he?"

Pip nodded. The tears were drying, leaving faint tracks on his dusty face. "One day I came home and she said I'd had a phone call. Dumbo had bought it. That knocked me flat. I never thought they'd get Dumbo, he was too . . . too *good*."

Fanny said nothing. He had heard others say much the same; sometimes he had been present when they got the impossible, unbelievable news and had watched them grow old in a matter of minutes. It had even happened to him, once, long ago.

"Not a nice experience," Skull said. "Not nearly as disgusting as drinking this liquid squalor, but all the same . . ." He washed some rum around his teeth and swallowed. "What happened next?"

"Well, I was useless, wasn't I?" Pip said bitterly. "I couldn't even stand. I sat on the silly bloody carpet and cried like a baby."

"All men did, up until the Middle Ages," Skull remarked. "Considered quite normal."

"She disapproved. She went out, went for a bloody

338

swim. When she got back I was in bed, knackered, half-asleep. She wanted sex, *now*. I wasn't up to it. That convinced her. I was more in love with Dumbo than I was with her." His eyes began to leak again. "By Christ, I think she was right."

Geraldo poked his head inside the truck. "Sod off," Fanny growled. He threw the empty bottle. "Go and find your own dung heap. I'm on top of this one."

"End of story?" Skull asked.

"Rows. Fights." Pip touched a scar on his cheek. "Her wedding ring did that. She screwed a captain in the Pay Corps, I chucked all her stuff out of the window, now she says she's pregnant and she wants all my money."

"The Pay Corps!" Skull made a face. "Dear me."

"It must be a relief to be back in a nice clean war," Fanny said.

"It is. It is." Pip took some more rum.

"Talking of which," Skull said. "Our hauptmann prisoner – thank you, just an inch or three to keep out the cold – Mr Winkler assures me that your strafing campaign disturbs the Wehrmacht not in the slightest. In fact, he says, the more you do it the less it hurts."

"That's exactly what you'd expect him to say, isn't it?" Fanny said blandly.

"Why?"

"He's lying, that's why. Why? Because he wants us to stop. Billy and I slaughtered an infantry battalion. Billy and I caught them on parade and we *massacred* the bastards! So don't tell me –"

"Yes, I mentioned that to the hauptmann," Skull said.

"What did he say?"

"No more parades in the desert. You and Billy won't catch them like that again."

"Billy won't catch anyone," Pip said, "poor sod."

"I believe Winkler," Skull said. "I think he's telling the truth. And I'll tell you why," he went on as Fanny's mouth

339

opened and snapped shut. "If he was really trying to trick us he would say the strafing had inflicted vast casualties, German morale is in their boots. *That* would encourage us to continue strafing."

"I don't need Winkler's encouragement," Fanny growled.

"Which is just what the enemy wants us to do."

"Bollocks."

Skull shrugged.

Pip was amused. "Got no answer to that, have you, Skull? See, brains aren't everything."

"I've foxed 'em," Fanny said dourly. "I've got them so they don't know winking from wanking."

Skull took more rum. "I used to think this muck was filth," he said, and drank. "But now that I penetrate the stench, I detect a hint of coarseness beneath the putrefaction."

"By God!" Pip said, impressed. "Wish I could talk like that." Fanny sneered. "Did you learn it at Cambridge?" Pip asked Skull.

"I don't *think* so. Nobody actually *learns* anything at Cambridge."

"Anyway, I got the buggers off their backsides," Fanny said. "Didn't I?" Nobody answered. "Didn't I?" he demanded.

"Yes," Skull said. Fanny grunted with satisfaction. "And no," Skull said.

"No standing patrols," Pip pointed out.

"They'll be up tomorrow." Fanny scratched his armpit so vigorously that he spilt his drink. "One good kick in the slats," he said as he scuffed the rum into the floorboards. "You watch."

Skull stood. "It's a pity Dalgleish can't be here to discuss the point with you." He finished his drink.

"He was a volunteer. He didn't have to go."

"*What*? You left him no choice."

"Bollocks."

"Sidi Zamzam was a deathtrap. You knew it, we all knew it. Pinky handed Uncle his will before he took off. The flak got him, but you killed him."

The punch was a huge haymaker that would have broken the intelligence officer's face, but as Fanny swung his fist he slipped on a pool of rum, blundered into Pip and trod on his foot. Pip cursed and struck out. Geraldo, airborne in panic, flew into them. For a moment there were arms and feathers everywhere. Fanny thrashed about and tried to beat off the bird, but hit the lamp instead. In the blackness, Skull decided it was time to slip away.

It took him some time to find his tent. His feet had difficulty walking in a straight line. The desert was a lake of black ink. The stars glittered brilliantly. When he admired them he tripped over his wandering feet, so he stopped admiring. They continued glittering. It occurred to him that they didn't give a damn if nobody looked at them, ever. He was thinking about this when he reached his tent and found Hick waiting for him. "Goodnight," Skull said.

"I've got something to tell you. I didn't tell you at debriefing because –"

"Tell me tomorrow, Hick old chap. I'm going to play a little music now, and –"

"This is serious."

Skull lit a stub of candle and sat on his bed. "Not as serious as 'Empty Saddles in the Old Corral'." He found the record. "This is a seminal example of the entire *oeuvre*. This is . . ." But by now Hick too was sitting on the bed. "I shan't remember it, whatever it is," Skull told him. "I've had rather a trying day."

"I blew up an ambulance this afternoon."

"Theirs or ours?"

"Theirs."

Skull put the record aside. "It could have been worse,

341

then. Begin at the beginning, as the King said." He saw that Hick wanted to know which king. "Never mind!" he said, waving his arms as if they could dispel curiosity. "It doesn't matter."

"I was Tiny Lush's number two," Hick said. Which had saved his life. Dalgleish and Stewart led the attack on Sidi Zamzam. Lush and Hooper followed, with Hooper last of all, two or three lengths behind Lush and off to his right. They all knew that there was no hope of surprise. Several times the formation had been forced to weave and duck as tracer reached up and chased them. Warning signals from those gunsites must have raced ahead.

Towards the end there was no need to navigate. All trails led to Sidi Zamzam. Just follow the tracks; any tracks. The target came up on the horizon looking like a dozen crates that had fallen off a truck. Soon each crate became a dump the size of a small warehouse, the dumps built far apart. Dalgleish was amazed: it was twice the size he remembered. No flak yet. He wondered if some of the dumps might be dummies. All were draped with camouflage netting. Which was which? Who cared? Still no flak. What a dump! Joke. Nearly there. Fifteen seconds. The target blurred in the prop-disc. In and out, fast. Ten seconds from now . . . Still no flak. Still no flak. Still no flak. Then he was blown apart.

A shell hit his cockpit with a ferocity that ripped the aircraft into large pieces and flung them left and right, so it had no difficulty in destroying Dalgleish. He knew nothing. He certainly felt nothing. If his eyes registered any part of the flash, his brain had only a millionth of a second to record the image before the explosion plastered his head all over the inside of the cockpit canopy, which was itself utterly shattered and scattered and lost. What happened to the rest of his body was of no importance. The Tomahawk's nose and engine flew on, screaming and dropping. It carved a spectacular scar in the desert floor and vanished under a boiling dust-cloud.

By now Billy Stewart was dead. The sudden storm of explosive that had boxed him in included a long burst of heavy machine-gun fire. This crept along his engine cowling with a noise like a maniac using a pickaxe. As Stewart snatched at the control column the bullets smashed through his ribcage. The impact whacked the column sideways. The fighter rolled obediently into the ground. It crumpled like cardboard and bloomed in flame.

Tiny Lush swore continuously when Dalgleish exploded and Stewart crashed and the box of flak came rushing at him, bigger than ever, blotched with shellbursts and laced with tracer. He flirted with turning away, knew he'd left it too late and decided to climb over the flak instead. The flak hounded him. A cluster of razor-edged shrapnel chopped off one tailplane and half the rudder, and the Tomahawk lurched into a spin. The faster it fell, the worse the spin. Lush was still cursing when it hit the desert and he hit the instrument panel and the entire fuselage compressed itself around him and through him until there was no cockpit any more.

Hooper had the advantage. He was a few lengths behind Lush, giving just enough extra space to let him break right and escape the flak. He fled. He dropped to zero feet, rammed the throttle wide open and raced for safety. He felt sick. His left leg had the shakes so badly that he took his foot off the rudder pedal. Something was wrong with his mouth: it wouldn't shut, and he couldn't breathe properly, and the inside was so dry that it hurt. He tried to swallow and there was nothing to swallow. His arms felt so weak that he was terrified of crashing the aircraft. If this was war he hated it and it hated him.

After a couple of minutes he recovered. He took the machine up to five thousand feet and circled while his heart stopped banging and his leg stopped twitching and his mouth summoned up saliva from somewhere. He was still frightened. He was alone, he was badly shaken, he was vulnerable. The intelligent thing was to go home. He was actually calculating his compass course when flak burst around him and ahead, so close that he saw a flicker of hot red in the heart of each ball of smoke, and he even heard the gruff *woof-woof*, exactly like some distant elderly dog.

At once he dropped a wing to the vertical and fell sideways, curling hard left. The desert stood on its ear and revolved right. His airstream howled strangely until the Tomahawk eased itself into a normal dive. He was strapped tightly to the machine, he trusted it to do what he wanted, and he was no longer afraid. He was enraged. They had killed his friends and now they had nearly killed him too. Find them and blast them: that was the answer. It was all very simple. Rage had cleared his brain. It lusted for a target.

He levelled out at three hundred feet and searched and searched. No target. No flak battery, nothing. Just empty desert. Rage became resentment and it soured him. He slumped and let the aeroplane fly itself. The aeroplane did this quite competently, and after a short while it found him something to kill: a travelling dust-cloud.

Inside it was a small convoy, probably five or six trucks, typical German supply stuff, canvas-topped, big wheels, desert camouflage. Hooper felt impatient to smash them, so that he could go on and smash something bigger. They were coming towards him, so he dipped and made a head-on attack. A shallow dive let him open fire on the first truck, then ease the nose up a touch and hammer the rest in turn. The last was an ambulance. Big red crosses everywhere. Hooper was so startled that he forgot to stop firing. The ambulance sagged under the impact. Briefly it became outlined in flame, like a firework show-piece; then it exploded with great violence. Hooper had a glimpse of jagged, blinding heat. He snatched at the stick and felt the Tomahawk being bounced by the shock waves.

"I went back to look for the ambulance," he said, "but it wasn't there."

Skull sighed, heavily. "It's not on, old chap. You really mustn't blow up enemy ambulances, even if they are full of ammunition. It's what the RAF calls bad form. Look: you forget you ever told me, and I'll forget I ever heard."

"So then I went and shot up four more German ambulances," Hick said. He made it sound like a perfectly sensible thing to do.

Skull fished out his handkerchief and blew his nose. As usual he found a deposit of desert dust. "Four," he said. "You strafed four more German ambulances." He rubbed his forehead, stretching and smoothing the skin. "This has been a truly terrible day," he said. "I thought it was over, I thought nothing more could go wrong. You strafed four more German ambulances."

"Two exploded," Hick said. "I reckon they must have been carrying ammunition. Hell of a bang, both times. I was looking up at bits of ambulance coming down."

"And the other two?"

Hick shrugged. "Maybe they unloaded their ammo already."

"Maybe they were full of wounded."

"You want me to apologise? I'm not going to apologise. I killed some of their people. They killed some of my people. Tomorrow will be the same. I like ambulance-busting. I'm good at it, and it makes sense. Not often that fun and profit get combined in a war."

"God help me, I'm beginning to think you're right," Skull said. "I must be as mad as the rest of you."

CHAPTER FIVE

Zig Zag

Schramm snatched at the Luger, bent his knees, squinted down the barrel and fired three shots. Each shot made him blink furiously. He lowered his arm. The sergeant sidled up and detached the gun from his fingers. "Perhaps we ought to practise first with an empty weapon, sir," he said.

"I think you hit the red flag," Hoffmann said. "Or if you didn't hit it, you certainly frightened it."

Schramm looked at the Luger. "That thing doesn't suit me," he told the sergeant. "It feels all wrong. I need a sub-machine gun, something I can get both hands on. A Schmeisser, or something."

"Intelligence officers don't carry Schmeissers, Paul," Hoffmann said.

"Well, you suggest something then. Thank you, sergeant." They strolled away.

"You're not a firearms man," Hoffmann said. "A club would be more your style. Look at the way you walloped that British soldier. Pure Stone Age."

Schramm grunted. "I told you Lampard's patrol has left Cairo, didn't I?"

"More than once."

"There must be other patrols hiding in the Jebel. Or near it. I've applied for more troops to guard the airfields. General Schaefer's in Tripoli, at a conference. Apparently he can't make a decision in Tripoli, don't ask me why."

"A week ago you said trip-wires around the perimeter were the answer."

"Trip-wires are good for twenty-four hours, maximum.

Then they break. See that man?" Schramm pointed to an elderly Arab in a distant field. "He's looking for a lost camel. At any given moment half the Arab population of Libya is out looking for lost camels. The camels break our trip-wires. If not camels, then goats, donkeys, sheep."

"Have you ever thought of planting decoy aircraft? Or dummies? You could booby-trap them."

"I'd certainly like to try. Can't get the resources. Wood, canvas, paint, skilled men – all are scarce. I thought of towing in some wrecked 109s and cannibalising them, but the salvage people got there first."

"Plenty of wrecked Hurricanes in the desert."

"I've tried, Benno. No transporters, no lifting gear, no spare fuel."

They walked in silence towards the admin block. A pair of 109s drifted in over their heads, and growled and sighed towards the point of touchdown as smoothly as if they were sliding down a pair of banisters. The spindly sets of undercarriage seemed to brace themselves for the shock, and then the aeroplanes were taxiing, blowing back the inevitable dust-clouds.

"Why have trip-wires?" Hoffmann asked suddenly. "I mean, what's the point?"

"To defend the airfield."

"You don't care about the airfield. You care about the air*craft*. Why not put trip-wires around the aircraft? And place a guard in each cockpit all night."

At once, Schramm saw the simple good sense of the idea. "Yes," he said. "We could rig the trip-wire to a warning signal in the cockpit."

"Twelve planes, twelve men. That's all you need."

"I should have thought of that," Schramm said. "Come on. You've earned yourself a large drink."

It turned out to be a very quick drink. The mess telephone rang: Hoffmann was needed in his office. But the medical officer, Max, was nursing a beer, so Schramm joined him. "Fallen in love with your consultant yet?" Max asked.

The question disturbed Schramm so much that he covered his feelings with a cough that sounded, even to his ears, dishonest. "Should I?" he said.

"Everyone does, sooner or later."

"Including you?"

Max smirked. "She and I are colleagues, so that comes under the heading of confidential information. Still, she's a darling, isn't she?"

Schramm nodded. It was the wrong word, far too happy and delightful, but the very sound of it jolted his senses. If he could utter that word to her ... Absurd. Impossible. "And remarkably well qualified," he said soberly. "For a woman."

"Not bad. First-class qualifications in surgery, pathology and psychiatry, that I know of. Probably more that I don't."

Schramm scratched his leg and thought of his piddling desert sores. "We're damn lucky to have her." And then he remembered what she had said to him: *Ask Max*. "So what the devil's she doing, stuck in Benghazi?"

"Exiled, Paul, exiled. Maria's been here since long before war broke out. You can't stop a woman like her from using her mind. Trouble is, she speaks her mind too."

"I noticed."

"So did Il Duce's government. Dr Grandinetti pointed out very clearly what she considered to be the failings of Fascism, and they said shut up, and she went on, so they arrested her. Next day she was on a boat. This would be in '36 or '37. They dumped her in a two-room clinic somewhere up in the hills, surrounded by Italian colonists who came here because they were too stupid to make a living back home."

"I'd heard rumours," Schramm said, "but this is the first case of exile I've actually met."

"Oh, they're all over the place," Max declared. "If you ever need a really tricky operation, very cheap, get yourself up into the poorest, filthiest mountain village in Italy. You'll find an exiled brain surgeon lancing the boil on a farmer's backside."

"Is that what Maria did?"

"Yes. Boils, childbirth, tonsils, ringworm, fractures, burns, amputations, dentistry: you name it. Then Mussolini decided to overthrow the British Empire and she was summoned to Benghazi to help repair the flower of Italian youth, which was beginning to arrive with alarmingly large holes in it."

"Extraordinary."

"Not at all. Quite routine." Max finished his beer. "Don't let her break your heart, Paul. She's not worth it. No woman is."

"Thanks. Have you got a degree in psychiatry too?"

Max stared at nothing, as if thinking hard, and produced a short, soft belch. "You agree it's a form of madness, then," he said. "Love, I mean. What I believe the army calls a self-inflicted wound." He left before Schramm could find an answer.

Maybe there was no answer, he thought. Maybe Max was right. While they had been talking, this war had killed several hundred men in various parts of the world. Women, too. Convoys were being torpedoed, factories bombed, whole cities fought over, and yet Paul Schramm, who couldn't even stand up straight, awoke every morning thinking of Maria Grandinetti. It was bizarre. She probably treated him as an amusing example of some middle-aged folly, the kind of thing psychiatrists talked about during the coffee-break at conferences. Bloody foot! It was all the fault of his bloody foot. He kicked it and made it hurt. Serve it right.

Hoffmann's return saved it from further pain.

"I can't make any sense of this," he said. He handed

Schramm some large photo-reconnaissance prints, still tacky with developing fluid. Some small areas had been circled in crayon. Inside the circles were clusters of tiny dots, tinier than pinheads.

Schramm peered at them. "The plane was high enough, wasn't it?"

"I told the pilot to stay high. If Jakowski's about to make a kill, I don't want the enemy scared off by an inquisitive aircraft. Anyway, these pictures were taken early in the morning, so the shadows are good and crisp. The experts with the magnifying glasses tell me those dots are Jakowski's force. Trouble is, twenty trucks are missing."

Schramm made the prints overlap to form a bigger picture. "Trucks don't get lost in the desert," he said. "Even if they got burned or shot-up, we'd still see the wreckage ... They might be in Jalo, I suppose. Under the palm trees."

"Why Jalo?"

"Why indeed? Jakowski won't find the SAS *there*."

"I don't like it," Hoffmann said. "I smell ... I don't know what I smell, but it stinks."

"Send him a signal. Ask him to confirm that all is well."

"Maybe I will." But Hoffmann didn't move.

"Is that the Sand Sea?" Schramm put his finger on a thick bank of ripples, strongly contrasted in black and white, running to the edge of the print.

"He wouldn't send twenty trucks into the Sand Sea, Paul. What's the point? There's nothing to find in there."

"True. Nothing but shadows." Schramm shuffled the prints together, made them square, and ruffled the edges with his thumb. "Twenty trucks is a lot of trucks to fall off the map."

"I'll leave it until tomorrow," Hoffmann decided. "I can't believe ..." He shrugged.

"Look: here's a suggestion. Why don't I go and pick

Captain di Marco's brains? He knows the Sahara inside out." Schramm spread his hands. "You never know."

"Take the prints," Hoffmann said.

*　　*　　*

Next morning, early, Skull told the CO what Hooper had done. Barton was amused. "Bless my soul!" he said. "Fancy that nice Mr Hooper being so beastly to the Hun! And to think he only came here to learn the tricks of the trade."

"If we shoot up their ambulances –"

"They'll shoot up ours. I know. Who gives a toss? Do you care how many pongoes get the chop? Neither do I. Sod 'em. Our bloody ack-ack does its best to kill us, doesn't it?"

Skull was silenced. He was also hungover. His brain throbbed and his eyes ached. Fanny, by contrast, was bright and brisk. He must have a head like a brass bucket.

"Coming to briefing?" Fanny said."You can tell them about the ambulances."

"You don't need a briefing. You've only got four pilots left. Just stand in the middle of the field and shout."

"That's a good idea." Fanny put his arm around Skull's shoulder as they strolled away. "You're good at words. Tell me what to shout."

Skull squinted at Fanny's hand. "What's this in aid of? Last night I pointed out a certain blatant cognitive dissonance within your claims, and you got blotto and tried to kill me."

"I can't shout all that, Skull. Especially the blatant bit, whatever it was. They wouldn't understand. I didn't. They're just decent, friendly, hardworking fighter pilots who want to be loved. Give 'em a bucket of blood for breakfast and they'll kick an orphan to death if you promise them a kiss afterwards."

Skull attended the briefing. All five aircraft would patrol at twenty thousand feet. Nothing was said about strafing or about ambulances and the pilots seemed quite cheerful.

After they took off, Skull went to the mess tent and found the adjutant chatting with Hauptmann Winkler. "Feeling better?" Skull said.

"Better than what?" Kellaway said.

"Nothing. Slip of the tongue." If Kellaway couldn't remember anything, there was no point in reminding him. Geraldo strutted in, took a long cold look at Skull, and avoided him. "This is Geraldo," Skull said. "Some say he speaks Greek, but I have tried him on Socrates in the original and his response was discouraging. Forthright, colourful and pungent, but discouraging."

"Did you know that our guest has read all of Sherlock Holmes?" Kellaway said. "Damn good show, I'd say."

Winkler cleared his throat. "I wish to speak of my sadness at the death of the young officer who . . . with whom . . . He was . . ." He shook his head, unable to find the words.

"Butcher Bailey," Kellaway said. "He was an awfully good type." There was a long, uncomfortable pause. "Tell you what," Kellaway said. "You can come to his funeral, if you like."

Oh double-buggeration, Skull thought. "We've done it, Uncle," he said gently. "Did it yesterday afternoon. Had to. Couldn't wait."

Kellaway's eyes flickered, but yesterday remained a blank. "We've been pretty busy lately," he told Winkler.

That was when the doctor came in, holding a printed form. "How d'you spell 'doolally'?" he asked.

"I should know," Kellaway said, and rattled it off. "We had an awful lot of it in India, especially during the hot season. Some chaps can't take the sun. Go haywire. You see it in their eyes. You look all right," he told the doctor. "Not so sure about old Skull here. Give him some

California syrup of figs, that's what he needs, a good purge to sort him out . . . Oh well. Time I got back to the office and did some bumf-shuffling. I keep asking Group for replacements, but the buggers never come." He took his mug of tea and went.

"Did you have to do that?" Skull asked.

"Yeah!" The doctor made himself look reckless. "Teasing the lunatics is the only fun I get in my job."

*   *   *

The sky was an icy blue at twenty thousand feet. The pilots were breathing oxygen, and the Tomahawks wallowed in the thin air like yachts on a mooring. Their Allison engines were toiling manfully and getting precious little reward. If someone made a hash of a turn, he soon lost half a mile and took five grim minutes to catch up.

Barton constantly looked down, searching for standing patrols of Me109s. The others looked up and around, heads always turning. Twenty thousand feet was nothing to the enemy. He might be two miles above them, a tiny metal splinter hiding in the sun. Pip Patterson did not spare his neck muscles. Once, long ago in France, he had been part of a squadron that had landed minus two, and nobody had noticed their absence until then. Chilling to think that while you were cruising along, your tail-end Charlies were getting picked off. Too much sky. Too many blind spots.

The patrol churned and turned, swapped their glimpse of the remote Mediterranean from right to left and back again. Elsewhere, the Sahara rolled to all the horizons like an old carpet worn right through to its biscuity backing.

After thirty minutes Barton grew impatient and took them down to twelve thousand, then eight, then five. The enemy refused to be provoked. The sun climbed higher. Hot air tumbled up and spoiled the formation-keeping. "Sneezy," Barton said. "This is as good as anywhere."

The Pole shoved his canopy back and peeled off. Holding the stick with his knees, he tossed out the golf clubs that had belonged to Tiny Lush and Mick O'Hare. "Take that, bloody Nazi bastard shits," he said. He rejoined the others. "What I hit?" he asked.

"Two Blenheims and a Liberator," Patterson said.

"No cigar," Hooper said.

They flew home. A Bristol Bombay transport was parked in a corner of the field, not far from the Brute. The Bombay had spatted wheels, twin engines on high wings and a blocky fuselage that looked as if it had been assembled from surplus packing crates. It was obsolete, slow and highly reliable.

Barton taxied to his desert-wagon and drove to his trailer. He could see Air Commodore Bletchley sitting on the steps, talking to the adjutant. Barton kept swallowing to suppress a sickness that attacked his throat. If they'd sent a bloody great Bombay, that meant he'd got the sack. It meant Takoradi had got the pilots and Hornet Squadron was dead. At first he'd thought maybe some replacements had arrived, but the Bombay was far too big for that. Anyway, they could have come in the Brute. It was all over. He got out and saluted: not a good salute, but his arm was weary. Bletchley stood and gave his old familiar half-smile: up one side and down the other. "I'll push off, sir," the adjutant said. "See you at lunch, I hope."

They went into the trailer. Barton dumped his stuff on his bunk: scarf, sweater, gloves, helmet, goggles, map. Half of it fell on the floor.

"Iced coffee?" the air commodore said. "Fresh from Cairo." He unscrewed the top of a giant Thermos. "Shepheard's best."

Barton found a couple of mugs and knocked the sandy dust from them. Bletchley poured. Ice cubes clinked. "Happy days," Barton said, miserably. Bletchley grunted agreement. They drank. It was blessedly black and chilled and it went down fighting. "Whisky?" Barton said. Bletchley nodded. Barton drank more. You couldn't have a good wake without good booze.

"I don't suppose you brought any replacements, sir," he said.

"No."

"Doesn't matter. We haven't got any kites to put them in."

"Well, the Tomahawk's seen its day, hasn't it?"

And so have I, Barton thought. "That sounds fairly final, sir," he said, and regretted it. Why do Baggy's dirty work?

"Nobody blames you for trying, Fanny. Nobody blames you for . . . um . . . not succeeding." He saw Barton's wry smile, and said: "That's how I see it. Not a question of failure, as such. Yours was a promising idea and in other circumstances it might have paid off. Handsomely."

Barton looked out of the window. Nothing handsome could ever have happened at dirty, dusty, duffed-up old LG 181, where even the graves were latrine pits.

Behind him Bletchley was going on about the risks of war and how every operation was a gamble, more or less . . . Barton nodded occasionally, but he wasn't really listening. The truth was, he wanted to leave *now*. If his job was over, then cut its throat and be done with it. No handshakes, no goodbyes, no clumsy speech of thanks to the squadron drawn up in a square while the wind chased dust between their legs and Uncle stood by to call for three cheers for the CO. Barton had heard too many such speeches, and more than once the man delivering them had been on the edge of tears; you could tell from his voice, from the way it faded and cracked and suddenly everyone was staring at the ground or the sky and wishing the bastard would *end*. Barton wondered whether tears would betray him like that. Fighter pilots weren't supposed to be emotional, and fighter *leaders* were supposed to be pure steel. It was all an act, of course, and many fighter leaders kept up the act with the aid of half a bottle of whisky a night. Failing that, success was a good stimulant. Fighter pilots were a fairly simple-minded crew; Barton had no illusions about that. They did a complex job, but ultimately it was judged by a brutally simple test: either you blew the other plane to buggery, or the adj wiped your name off the squadron board. There was no other reason to fly. If you couldn't do the job you were taking up space that another man wanted. Maybe he'd be luckier. Barton wanted to go *now*, in the Brute, back to Cairo. Let Uncle clean up this mess.

"If anybody's to blame," the air commodore was saying, "it must be the Luftwaffe. Not their finest hour. Remind me to talk about posthumous gongs, by the way. They can't all have one, but I might get a DSO for Dalgleish."

That was when Barton really knew he had failed; and for a moment he found it hard to breathe. A fly landed on his arm, and when he shook his arm it did not move so he became infuriated and banged his arm on the table and hurt himself. "You'd better talk to Uncle about that, sir," he said. "The sooner I get out, the better."

"Certainly not." Bletchley stared with astonishment. "You don't imagine I've gone to all this trouble just to taxi you back to Cairo, do you?"

"I thought . . ." Barton was too bewildered to know what he thought.

"For God's sake, Fanny, do you want your job or don't you? The other day you were fighting tooth and nail to keep it. Now you sound as if you don't give a tuppenny toss if your chaps go to Takoradi and you go into a nursing home."

"When you referred to my lack of success, sir, I assumed —"

"Christ Almighty, man, the Desert Air Force sacks a squadron leader every day and twice on Sundays! Believe me, nobody sends an air commodore to break the sad news and a Bombay to cart the chap away."

"No, sir. So why is it here?"

"Didn't you get my signal? Obviously not. Another cock-up. I sent it last night by despatch rider, so I expect he fell down a well and broke his neck, they're always doing it. Listen. The Bombay will fly fuel, ammunition and food, plus a skeleton ground crew, to LG 250. You will follow in five Kittyhawks which are on their way here now, as soon as they have been adapted for low-level bombing. Your task is to bomb and strafe German fighter airfields. You've proved that the 109s won't come up and fight – which frankly is no surprise, Rommel would be mad to release them before his next attack – so you'll destroy them on the ground."

"LG 250," Barton said. "Where is that, sir?"

"A long way behind enemy lines."

Barton went out of his trailer and took his shirt off. He let the sun dry the sweat that was running down his body. "Have I got any choice in the matter?" he called.

"No. Do it or don't do it." When Barton didn't answer, the air commodore said, "Don't be tiresome, Fanny. You know you're going to do it."

"It sounds bloody lethal."

"I certainly hope so."

"I mean, if Jerry finds an LG in his backyard, we won't stand a chance. He'll wipe us out."

"It's the last place he'll look."

Barton went back into his trailer and sat on his bunk. His eyes were still screwed-up from avoiding the sun and the dusty wind. "I'm getting too old for this game," he said.

"Bring it off and you'll be a wing commander with a DSO," Bletchley told him, "and nobody will be more delighted than I." The air commodore poured out the rest of the iced coffee and handed him his mug.

"You've got a really shitty job, haven't you, sir?"

"We can't all be heroes." Now that he had got what he wanted, Bletchley allowed himself to relax a little.

"I wouldn't know a hero if he came up and bit me in the arse," Barton said. "I've met plenty of killers, and a couple of suicides, and one or two poor sods who should never have been pilots in the first place, and a few blokes who were so thick they terrified the enemy without realising it, but never a hero."

"You're a hard man, Fanny," Bletchley said; perhaps mockingly, perhaps not; Barton could not tell.

Bletchley borrowed the battle-wagon and made a quick tour of the camp, talking to the troops and visiting the wounded. He said a few words at the funeral of the airman who had died during the night. Afterwards he walked to the mess tent with Hick Hooper. "I'm sorry you're not getting any combat experience," he said. "Blame the Luftwaffe."

"I've been good and busy, sir. Made a lot of friends."

"And lost a few yesterday, I understand." Hooper had nothing to say to that. "Still, that's how it is with strafing operations, I suppose," Bletchley said. "You'll let me know when you feel you've learnt enough, won't you?"

"I'd like to stay, sir."

"Stay? You mean for good?"

"Yes, sir. I'd like a permanent transfer to Hornet Squadron."

"You'll be dead before the bumf is cleared."

"So forget the bumf, sir." Hooper was perfectly calm. "I like it here. It's clean."

"I must say *you* don't look awfully clean."

"I feel clean. Sun, sand, sky and a bunch of fifty-calibre machine guns playing my tune. My idea of heaven, sir."

"Good show," Bletchley said automatically. "Keep on hammering the Hun."

He sought out Skull. "Fanny seems a bit twitchy," he said. "It hasn't anything to do with those damn fool ambulances, has it?"

"Ambulances? No. What ambulances? Oh, you mean *those* ambulances." Skull wiped dust from his spectacles. "How did you know, sir? They weren't in my report."

"No, but they were in several German reports, and our people have ways and means of eavesdropping that it's better you know nothing about." Bletchley looked pleased with himself. "What's your version of events?"

"Well, sir, Hooper says he hit an ambulance by mistake and it blew up like Krakatoa. That inspired him to strafe a few more. Half erupted with a colossal and gratifying bang. Half didn't."

"Mnnnnn." Bletchley squashed his lips together and made a disparaging noise through his nose. "Of course we have only Hooper's word."

"True. He seemed quite certain, though."

"Combat can do funny things to the mind. Hooper had just seen the rest of his flight destroyed before his very eyes, hadn't he?"

"Yes, but –"

"The man was in a state of terrible shock, wouldn't you say?"

"Not when he gave me his report . . ." Skull saw the air commodore raise his eyebrows. "Of course that was much later," Skull said tamely.

"Terrible shock. His mind was in turmoil, wasn't it? Overwhelmed by a primitive rage." Bletchley gave a sad smile. His voice was calm and reasonable. "I expect it was swamped by a wild blood-lust to take revenge on the brutal enemy. You'd be the same, wouldn't you?"

"Um . . . approximately," Skull said.

"So we can discount what Hooper said. After all, ambulances don't blow up. That's a well-known fact."

"Yes, indeed." Skull scratched his head and collected a

little sand in his fingernails. "So there's nothing more to be said."

"Oh, the Germans will probably show some wrecked ambulances to the Red Cross and shout atrocity. Usual propaganda humbug. I mean, we all know what happened to those ambulances. They took a wrong turning and got blown up by their own mines."

"Happens all the time, sir," Skull said. "Well-known fact."

"How's Pip Patterson?"

"Quite murderous."

"Good show. Got to keep biffing the Boche."

While they were eating lunch the Kittyhawks arrived. Barton briefed his pilots on the move to LG 250. Only a dozen ground crew would be going, so everyone would have to help with cooking, refuelling, rearming and other chores. Once they had been fed, the ferry pilots flew the Tomahawks out. Air Commodore Bletchley put the wounded airmen in the Brute and took off for Cairo. The bulk of the ground crew, not wanted at LG 250, struck their tents and drove away. Finally, the Bombay and the Kittyhawks got into the air and flew towards the setting sun. That night a section of Italian bombers raided LG 181 and missed by a mile, which was not bad for night bombing in the desert in 1942.

*   *   *

The road from Barce to Benghazi was busy both ways. Schramm joined a stream of empty trucks returning from the front and watched loaded convoys flick past in the opposite lane. Surely Rommel must attack soon. Someone was bound to attack, and if Rommel waited much longer it would be the British. How odd to be a general and draw a large arrow on a map, knowing that it meant the killing of thousands of men, his own and the enemy's. Did the general care? The thought occupied Schramm all the way to the Italian barracks.

He went in, and ten minutes later he came out. Captain di Marco was not in his office, was not in Benghazi. When would he be back? That depended how long he was detained somewhere else. Nobody tried to persuade Schramm to take a seat and have a coffee.

He stood in the sun and thought: bad luck. Immediately he confronted himself: if it was bad luck, why was his nervous system beginning to tingle? Come to that, why hadn't he telephoned di Marco from Barce? Because he didn't want to risk learning that he was not at the barracks, that's why. Schramm got in the car and drove out of the barracks so fast that he sprayed a sentry with gravel. He waved an apology and, driving one-handed, nearly put a wheel in a ditch.

The same bald-headed orderly was reading a different newspaper outside her office. "She's operating," he said fast, before Schramm could hit him.

The operating theatre was off a busy corridor. Schramm was the only person not going somewhere. He stood with his back to the wall and avoided the eyes of the walking wounded, until he found that it made no difference whether he looked or not. The damaged men were interested only in their own pain. He was invisible. And eventually he had seen so many of them that they too ceased to have any individuality. One stained bandage was just like another. They were part of the furnishings, like the stark smell of disinfectant, or the flop of hospital slippers.

His legs grew stiff, so he sat on a windowsill. He felt like a schoolboy, which made him straighten his back, square his shoulders and try to look like a Luftwaffe major; but still he felt like a schoolboy. How odd. Why should that be? He worried about it until his mind almost reached out and touched the answer, and at that moment she came out of the theatre, buttoning her white coat, and saw him.

"Oh, no! Not you." She was shaking her head. "Not now. Not today."

He jumped down. "It's not important," he said. "I'll come back another time."

"Oh, don't be stupid, of course it's important. Why tell lies? It's such a waste. You can walk me to my office." She took his arm. "Why do you tell such lies?" she said again; only now she sounded weary instead of angry.

They walked to her office. Halfway there, her hand slipped down his sleeve and gripped his wrist. He was too pleased to speak.

"A bottle of the good white wine," she told the orderly. He handed her a sheaf of messages. "*Good* wine," she reminded him, "or I won't treat your piles. Give him money," she told Schramm.

They went inside, and she skimmed through her messages. "Thank Christ," she said. "No operations this afternoon. Both cancelled. The patients had the good sense to die. You have brought me luck, Paul Schramm!" She tossed the bits of paper in the air and embraced him. "Ah," he said. "Yes. Good." She kissed him, very firmly and positively. She held him by the ears and looked in his eyes.

"Are we friends?" he asked.

"I have decided to be in love with you for five minutes," she said. "After that, we shall see." She kissed him, lightly, and turned away. "I stink," she said. "All that hacking and chopping, very sweaty. Shower." She took a towel and went into another room.

He had opened and sampled the wine by the time she came out, wearing a white cotton dressing-gown and, from the way it clung, not much else. "That took more than five minutes," he said. "Are we still in love?"

"I'm not sure. D'you think it's wise?" She was back to her old self: composed, controlled, unpredictable.

"It's enjoyable." He gave her a glass of wine. "I'm told I don't enjoy myself enough."

She drank steadily and long. She moved away from him, tipped her head back and stared at the ceiling. "It is possible to know too much human anatomy," she said. "I feel this wonderful wine descend via my pharynx and oesophagus on its journey through my digestive system. It rushes into my stomach now, prompting the gastric glands and the liver into action. Soon, I know, it will make its way into the small intestine, and then . . ." Schramm had crossed the room and was looking out of the window. "I have offended you," she said.

"Not offended. Bored."

"You're not in love with my kidneys?" He shook his head. "You positively dislike my kidneys?" He nodded. "Well, at least that is honest," she said. She poured more wine.

"Look, if you don't want to love me, don't love me," he said firmly. "I lived without you for forty-odd years. I'll survive." He sat on the windowsill, the place she usually took. "Just don't give me all this gibberish. And for Christ's sake cover your breasts."

"About the alleged gibberish I am prepared to negotiate," she said, "but I have just had a hot shower and I am not going to suffer the discomfort of sweaty breasts in order to satisfy your Prussian sense of propriety. *Gesundheit*." She drank.

"I'm not Prussian," Schramm said, "and it's not *Gesundheit*."

"It isn't?" She raised her glass again. "*Donner und Blitzkrieg!*"

He grunted. "You don't hear too much of that sort of thing nowadays, either."

"Well, be patient. Soon the war will wake up."

"And then I shall enjoy myself. Is that right?"

She came over and took his hand; he did not resist. "Listen," she said. Out in the street, a man with an accordion was playing a wistful, jerky little waltz. "He plays that every day," she said. She stepped back and he got off the windowsill, and they began to dance. After a few steps she took him by the arms and shook him. "Relax!" she ordered. The tune was delightful. "He skips a beat now and then," she said. "But so do you, and he never complains." Schramm laughed.

The waltz ended. They stood in the middle of the room, waiting, but there was no more music.

"*Completo*," she said, and gave him a quick hug. "Now it's time for wards." She banged the cork into the bottle.

In three minutes she was dressed; in five they were walking into the first ward. Schramm knew what to expect; the prospect did not worry him. A nurse gave him a white coat. Did she think he was a doctor? He put it on and began to practise the professional stroll, hands behind his back, the expression impartial, tinged with wisdom. He remained three paces behind Dr Grandinetti.

The physical damage did not upset him. He had seen too many wrecks already, dragging themselves along the corridor; by contrast, most of these patients were asleep under sheets that hid the unhappy evidence of a contest between high explosive and flesh and bone. Maria Grandinetti led a hushed bunch of nurses and young doctors from bed to bed, asked questions, checked temperature charts, occasionally peeled back the sheet and scrutinised the repairs.

The next ward was much the same. Occasionally, she turned to him and made a short remark: this patient had been weakened by hepatitis, or that one had a bullet lodged near the spine. Schramm nodded, and the junior doctors looked at him with greater respect.

They moved on. A man in a distant corner was groaning, not expressively but mechanically, the same gloomy sound repeating itself as regularly as breathing. Schramm did not like it. Why couldn't the fellow scream or shut up? He tried to ignore him. He paid attention instead to the patient now being examined and he got a bad shock. It was the young German airman wounded in the Barce raid and Schramm could see that he was much worse. His skin looked bleached and it was creased around his eyes and mouth as if by an effort of concentration. Dried saliva had collected at the corners of his lips. His breathing was so shallow that it scarcely raised his chest. He looked so altered that Schramm turned aside and checked the name on the chart hooked over the bed-rail. *Debratz, Kurt.* Same man.

Maria completed her rounds, and Schramm was glad to get out. The man in the corner was still manufacturing his meaningless groans as they went by.

"I could do with a shower," Schramm said as soon as they were alone.

"I have a better idea," she said. "Let's go for a swim in the sea."

They drove a long way out of Benghazi. She directed him down a rutted lane that went through two farmyards before it became a twisting track. Dried grasses swished and crackled against the car. The air was like a herb-garden and heavy-winged butterflies scouted ahead. He saw a lizard on a great flat rock and before he could blink it had gone. "I'm sure you know where we're going," he said. "The question is, are *you* sure?"

"Have faith."

The track delivered them to a long, flat headland which overlooked a stretch of sand that slipped into the Mediterranean without causing more than a ripple. The water was so clear that they could see the patterned throb of sunlight on the seabed.

"Nobody ever comes here," she said. "It's haunted."

"Who by?"

"Who knows? Nobody ever comes to find out."

They swam, naked. For a middle-aged woman, her body was in good shape and Schramm enjoyed seeing it. But the sight did not excite him. Wrong time and place, he concluded; and then forgot about it in the unrestrained glee of swimming. The water was the only place where he was not a cripple.

They stretched out in the sun to dry, got covered in sand and went back to wash it off. The ripple was in fact a foot or two high, so they lay at the water's edge and let it rush over them. She laughed, got a mouthful of water and spewed it out. "Very, very childish," he said dozily.

"I try to be childish once a day."

They walked along the sand. She had been wrong: somebody did come. A boy brought a herd of goats to the headland, their bells tinkling like small change. He sat on a rock and watched them.

"He thinks we are ghosts," she said, quite untroubled.

"If we don't eat soon he could be right." It was well into the afternoon and the swimming had aroused his appetite.

"Have faith."

"I can't eat faith. And we must be twenty kilometres from civilisation. I need my food, I'm a growing lad. I'm trying to grow a new left leg."

"I like you as you are. Lopsided. Different."

They walked back to their clothes, dressed and climbed up to the car. The boy kept his distance, but he waved when they waved. By now Schramm was too hungry to talk. They jolted back up the track, escorted by the same blithe butterflies or perhaps their relatives, and at the first house Maria told him to stop. "We eat here," she said.

"You know these people?"

"They know me. That's what matters."

A hefty woman in black came out, holding a scythe. They had a conversation in staccato Italian, in which neither seemed to complete a sentence. But within a minute Schramm was sitting in the kitchen with a tumbler of red wine and a bowl of olives. "I treated her brother-in-law's cousin for gallstones," Maria said. "That makes me a member of the family."

It was a simple meal: pasta, salad, fruit. Afterwards, Schramm felt guilty because he could not thank the woman in her own language. Maria read his face. "Don't think about giving money," she said. "Just enjoy."

He drove halfway back to the road and stopped. He turned off the engine. "Look: I did enjoy," he said. "The swim, the walk, the food. It was good." She watched him gravely, her eyebrows raised just a fraction, not quite creasing her brow. "So why did you . . ." He sensed an oncoming stammer and looked away, clenching his jaws. "At first you told me to go," he said. "In the corridor you said *No, not you*, didn't you? *Not you, not now.* That sounds definite. Not much room for doubt, is there?"

She stretched out a hand, and he flinched slightly, but she merely straightened his shirt collar.

"Anyhow, I was ready to go. I mean, what right have I to . . ." For a moment the stammer threatened again, but he beat it down. "That was no good either, was it? You didn't want *that*, and the next thing I know we're in your office drinking your wine and . . . and so on."

"Embracing." Still she watched his face. "We embraced."

"Yes."

"Then say it. Why not?"

"Does it matter? You said you loved me. For five minutes. That was a joke, right? A small joke."

"No, it was true." A blue butterfly flirted with the red bonnet of the car, then quit. "For five minutes it was absolutely true."

"For five minutes you were in the shower."

"You could have been there too." She smiled, and he saw so much imagined pleasure in her smile that he was angry at having lost his chance.

"That's not good enough," he said. "All this emotional

ping-pong, I can't handle that; I'm just a gloomy German, I've got to know how I stand." She pursed her lips a fraction too much. "Don't make a joke about how I stand," he warned. "You make a joke about that and I'll strangle you."

"Let's get out. I'm sticking to my seat."

They strolled to a cluster of olive trees and stood in the shade.

"Bring on the pan-pipes," he said. "All we need is a few nymphs and a couple of satyrs. No, we don't. Cancel that. Feel like a sexual fling?"

"Not in that tone of voice." Her answer was so quick and so calm that it flattened him. *Clumsy idiot*, he told himself. He was swamped by the kind of despair he hadn't felt since he was six and forced to dance with girls at parties.

"You're still in a rage," she said. "You've been angry ever since I came out of the operating theatre and saw you there, looking like a bump on a log. You're always furious, Paul. You're like a man with a trumpet who can only play one note. Experiment, for God's sake! There are lots of other notes."

"Well, so were you angry, too. Angrier than me."

"Listen: I'd just spent several hours groping around inside the guts of one of your countrymen, trying to reassemble him in the order God intended. I'm good but God was better. When I came out, did I want to see you and your problems? No, I certainly did not."

"You didn't have to spell it out."

"Why not? I said what I felt. *You* didn't."

"I tried to —"

"You tried to take all the blame. You felt guilty for what wasn't your fault."

"I didn't want to make matters worse, that's all. You were obviously under pressure and —"

"Oh, pooh. You didn't care a damn about me. What did

you really feel at that moment? Tell me what you really felt."

Schramm felt battered and weary. "Betrayed," he said. He turned away, but she would not allow an easy escape. She stepped round him and grabbed his shoulders. "Louder!" she cried. "What did you feel?"

"Betrayed," he said. She shook him. "Betrayed!" he shouted. "Betrayed!" And this time the word stretched into a howl.

"It's inevitable," she said. "Failure, stupidity, clumsiness, incompetence, pain, unhappiness, betrayal, stupidity, injustice, tragedy: they all happen, so make the most of them."

"You said stupidity twice," he said.

"That's because there is more of it." She kissed him on the mouth. "Don't ask me if I love you," she warned, "or I'll have you sent to the Russian front."

They walked back to the car.

"How can I make the most of feeling betrayed?" he asked. And got no answer.

He dropped her at the hospital and drove to the Italian army barracks. Captain di Marco was there. He studied the aerial photographs and said that he could not make sense of what Major Jakowski was doing, nor where the missing twenty trucks had gone. If they were not on the photographs they must be off the photographs. What was needed was more information. If they were his men, di Marco said, he would *order* them to break radio silence.

"They're General Schaefer's men," Schramm said. "And Schaefer's in Tripoli."

"Send him a signal."

"Saying what? We're worried? He'd blow a fuse. Schaefer works on facts, hard facts."

"I'll give you a hard fact," di Marco said. "Let Major Jakowski make one tiny mistake out there and the desert will make it ten thousand times worse."

Schramm went back to Barce and looked for Benno Hoffmann. He found him watching men installing separate trip-wires around each machine in a squadron of Messerschmitt 109s. The trip-wires used strong black thread, which would be invisible at night. A raider might notice the thread as he broke it, but by then he would have no chance of planting his bomb, which was what mattered.

"Di Marco thinks Jakowski is in dire straits," Schramm said. "He didn't put it so bluntly, but that's what he was thinking."

"Then why hasn't Jakowski signalled for help? He's only been gone a few days. He's got a hundred and fifty men, for God's sake."

They stood and watched the mallets whacking stakes into the ground.

"Maybe I can borrow an aeroplane tomorrow," Hoffmann said. "Fly there and make a search. Find Jakowski and land, if the desert's flat enough. Want to come?"

"Thank you, no," Schramm said. "I nearly killed myself down there once already."

*   *   *

After a long day of cautious driving in low gear, with spells of digging out vehicles that had wandered into soft sand, Lampard's patrol emerged from the Great Sand Sea. Ahead lay a plain of gravel. It was late afternoon.

"Well done," Lampard said. "Time for a little fun, I think. This place looks like a race-course. We'll have some races."

They were all weary, and their skin was gritty and streaked with salt where the sweat had dried. It was a long time since the last meal. Nevertheless, Lampard's decision was right. Too much slow driving had left everyone mentally sluggish.

Lampard matched one jeep against another in straight

sprints until they produced a champion, Corporal Pocock. Then they raced each other round a circle, the jeeps starting back-to-back and passing at mid-point in a test of nerve as to which driver claimed the inside track. Captain Dunn won that. Finally, there was a race to find out who could drive backwards the fastest, swerving in and out of a twisting line of jerricans. Sergeant Davis was best by far. It was all very exhilarating, full of rush and noise and intense competition. "Brilliant idea, Jack," Dunn said.

"Good training, too. You never know when you might have to back out faster than you went in."

They sat in a jeep and watched the sunset. The smell of fried ham began to tinge the air.

"Depending on what we find when we get wherever it is we're going," Lampard said, "there's a possibility I might decide to stay, in which case it'll be up to you to lead the patrol home."

"I don't understand," Dunn said. "Stay? Stay where?"

"Probably in the Jebel. I might hole up somewhere with a sack of bombs and make a nuisance of myself."

Dunn found that prospect too peculiar for words. "I see," he said. Obviously he did not see.

"It's an idea the colonel and I dreamed up over a bottle of whisky," Lampard told him. "It's between him and me. Just an option. I might not do it. Depends on how . . ." He stopped because Dunn had grabbed his arm.

"I can smell a fuse burning." He shoved Lampard. "Get out. Run."

Both men jumped out of the jeep. Lampard shouted; "Any bombs in the back?"

"Yes, yes, dozens." Dunn kept running. A time-pencil-fuse used acid. When the acid was released it burned through a wire until the wire snapped and fired the detonator. If he could smell it the fuse must have been burning for a long time. He looked behind him. Lampard was climbing into the back of the jeep.

"Where are the fuses?" Lampard called.

"In a box, on the left. I think." Dunn watched him shifting the load. "Forget it, Jack. If one goes off, they'll all go off."

"Maybe. Is this it?"

Dunn could not move. He was not standing far enough away. If that box exploded, even if it detonated only one bomb, the jeep would be blown into tiny bits, and the blast and the bits would kill Dunn before he knew it had happened. But as long as Lampard was standing in the jeep, picking out fuses and looking at them and putting them aside, Dunn could not move.

"Here's the little scoundrel," Lampard said. He put the box down and hurled the fuse into the desert. After a few seconds, they heard the hard crack of its detonation, like firewood splitting.

Dunn walked back to the jeep.

"You were right to run," Lampard said. "No point in both of us dying. I wonder how it happened?"

"I expect it was the races. All that zigzagging. The box got chucked about, and it cracked a pencil." Lampard nodded. Dunn hesitated, and then said: "You know, it wouldn't have been the end of the world if you'd left it alone. We can afford to lose a jeep."

"Maybe. But bombs are different, aren't they? Every bomb is another Messerschmitt destroyed. I hate to lose bombs. They're like children to me."

"I never heard such bollocks in all my life." Dunn laughed, and Lampard joined in. But the image that lived in Dunn's mind was of Lampard sorting through the fuses as if he were organising his stamp collection.

*　　*　　*

Midway between Big Cairn and Kufra, with nothing but a flat plain of gravel reaching to the horizon, and with the horizon buckling under the heat, Lampard halted the patrol and announced that they would go for a walk. Quite a long walk, he said: five miles, perhaps ten, even twenty. The going was good, so they might run from time to time. It all depended.

"Are we going anywhere special, sir?" Sergeant Davis asked.

"Towards Kufra, still. I'll leave a driver for each vehicle, plus Corky. Everybody else comes with me. Bring a weapon, a pint of water and a rucksack with a dozen bombs. No fuses. Corky: drive slowly. When we need you, we'll find you."

For the next three hours, Lampard led his men on an erratic course that roughly paralleled the route of the jeeps. He had a long stride. There was no give in the stony surface of the desert. They had to work to keep up with him. The bombs were heavy. Skin chafed under the straps. Sweat soaked through the uniforms, ran into the eyes and blurred the vision with the sting of salt. If a man allowed himself to gasp, his mouth quickly dried and was leather against his tongue.

Lampard paused for five minutes' rest after the first hour. Nobody sat. Once you sat it was twice as hard to get up and go.

He strolled up and down. "Trouble with these patrols is we don't get enough exercise," he said. "Sitting in a jeep's no good to anyone. Suppose you lose your jeep? What d'you do then? Wait for a bus?"

Nobody spoke. The five minutes were soon up.

"Stay awake," Lampard said. "When I whistle, fall flat."

They walked fast for another thirty-five minutes. Trooper Peck was sucking a small stone while counting each pace up to a hundred and then starting all over again in an attempt to dispel an image of cold and sparkling beer that kept drifting seductively into his imagination, when

Lampard blew his whistle and turned. Peck was still falling. Everyone else was flat.

"You're dead, Peck," Lampard said. "Run two hundred yards."

They picked themselves up and brushed bits of gravel from face and hands. Peck ran, his thumbs hooked under the rucksack straps. Soon the scuff and scrape of his boots faded to nothing.

"That looks easy," Lampard said. "We'll do it backwards."

They ran backwards until they caught up with Peck. Lampard turned and strode on. "You won't hear the bullet that kills you, Peck," he called.

"No sir." Peck's chest was still heaving, but he forced his voice to sound as level as Lampard's.

"You're never safe, night or day, not for a minute." Lampard discreetly dropped a thunderflash. It cracked the massive silence of the desert. The noise scattered his men into a wide defensive circle, looking out, weapons cocked. The bang faded and died. "Good," Lampard said. "On we go."

After a few more miles, a few more whistle-blasts, another thunderflash and a couple of short sprints, he led them back to the vehicles. When Dunn took his rucksack off, he felt as if he were floating. The soles of his feet seemed to radiate heat. He had been saving his pint of water; now he took a long swig. His throat was greedy for more.

"Now for the drivers," Lampard said. In a matter of minutes he was leading them into the desert. When they returned, late in the afternoon, he still had that same thrusting pace.

"It's not worth going on," he said. "We'll camp here." Nobody complained.

The meal was tinned ham and tongue and tinned sausages, with the last of the fresh potatoes and cabbage they had bought as they drove out of Cairo; and tinned pears plus a squirt of condensed milk. There was even some stale bread to go with the cheese.

No rum in the tea. The cook took the bottle out and Lampard put it back. Nobody had done anything to justify rum.

All day long an indecisive breeze had come and gone. As the sun set, the wind strengthened and blew steadily from the west. The rush of cool air sent men looking for woollen jumpers or even blankets to drape around their shoulders.

"Smell that!" Lampard told Sandiman. "That's the pure air of the desert. You don't find it near the coast. You've got to get right away from everything. How far are we from Cairo, Corky?"

"As the crow flies? Say five hundred miles. We covered six or seven hundred."

"And where's the next nearest city?"

"Benghazi, I suppose."

"What's south?"

"Oh, south the Sahara goes on forever. A thousand miles or more. I'd have to look at my maps."

"And west?"

"Nothing until you hit Algeria. That's got to be a good thousand, too. Why? Want to buy an evening paper?"

That amused Lampard. "No, I like it here," he said. "I like this wonderful air. I like to think that it's blown across a thousand miles of pure desert to get here, and it will blow over another five hundred of the same before it reaches the stink and the bumf-shufflers of Cairo. God did a good day's work when he made the desert."

"Glad you like it," Davis said, comfortably, "because you can have my share for ten bob, cash, any time."

"It's priceless," Lampard said. "Like freedom."

They had had a hard day. Nobody wanted to debate freedom with the patrol leader, who would win anyway.

They listened to the news bulletin on the BBC. There was nothing about the Western Desert. In the Pacific, Corregidor had surrendered to the Japanese. The RAF had bombed the Skoda munitions factory in Czechoslovakia. The Red Army was fighting hard near Kharkov. It all seemed very remote.

*　　*　　*

Kufra was not like any oasis that Hollywood had conceived. It was sprawling and shapeless, with thousands of dusty date-palms and two salt lakes of brilliant blue. In the town there were two sorts of building: ramshackle, in which the natives lived; and rectangular, which the Italians had put up. The main buildings included a hospital, a school, a cinema (bombed) and a mosque. On the military side there were some stores, a barracks and a small fort. Most had been knocked about in brief struggles between the British and the Italians.

When Lampard's patrol snaked through the date groves and drew up in the square, half the town followed them. Soon a squad of black African soldiers arrived to clear a way for the military commander of Kufra. Major Tickenham was an elderly officer, short and stocky, with a broken nose like a twist of putty. Before Kufra, he had trained recruits for the Sudan Defence Force in Khartoum. His shorts were starched and creased as stiff as boards.

Lampard saluted. "I've brought your reading matter, sir," he said. It was a box of books of all sorts.

"Thank God. D'you know what I'm reduced to? *King's Regulations and Army Law*, which I know backwards, and *How to Learn Welsh in Three Weeks*, with half the pages missing." He plucked a volume from the box. "Zane Grey. Wonderful . . . Look, I've had what used to be the Italian army brothel fumigated since you were last here. Your

376

chaps might like to use it as their billet. Come and see. It's rather special."

The building was bullet-pocked but otherwise intact. "I put in new beds and had everything whitewashed," Tickenham said as they entered, "but I left the propaganda. It has a certain quaint charm."

Each wall carried a different slogan. Tickenham pointed at one: *Il Duce ha sempre ragione.* "Imagine trying to buck up the British army with signs that said 'Churchill is always right'," he said. "Your average Tommy would immediately fear the worst."

They strolled into another room. "*Credere, Ubbidire, Combattere,*" Lampard read aloud. "Trust, Obey, Fight. My goodness. What a way to run a knocking-shop." He prodded a mattress. "Luxury indeed. I'm most grateful to you, sir."

"I believe I counted three officers. Four including yourself. I look forward to your company at dinner. Six o'clock?"

Lampard enjoyed the rest of the day. He took a jeep and drove Dunn, Gibbon and Sandiman out to the lakes for a swim. The water was so dense with salt that they floated effortlessly. Swimming was a wasted effort; they lay in the water and drifted as the breeze caught them; it was the complete rest-cure. They drove back to their billet and showered the salt away. There was ample time for a leisurely shave and a long drink – Pocock had found a supply of ice somewhere – before they dressed in fresh khakis and walked through the deepening dusk to Tickenham's headquarters. "I approve of this," Lampard said. "Any fool can be uncomfortable. It takes a certain skill to go to war and enjoy oneself, don't you agree?"

Tickenham met them at the entrance.

"Hot from the fleshpots of Cairo, as you are," he said, "you chaps don't realise what a pleasure this is for me. Come in. You'll have a drink first, won't you? Good, good

... Just go through there, you'll find the others waiting ..." Lampard went first, into a large room that was bare except for a few cane chairs and some vivid rugs hanging on the walls. A smiling Sudanese soldier, black as boot polish, held a tray of drinks. A bearded man in the garb of a Catholic priest stopped talking and turned towards the arrivals. The man he had been talking to was Henry Lester.

Lampard felt like a man who has trodden hard on a stair that isn't there. For a moment nothing connected, everything was misplaced, and he was standing naked in the bedroom of Mrs Joan d'Armytage. The shock was such that he actually felt naked: his skin crawled, and his genitals shrank in panic. Then he recovered.

Lester was being introduced by Tickenham. "Yes sir, that's my baby," Lester said. "I don't think you know my friend Malplacket." Lampard shook hands and said the right things, but he knew that Lester had seen the bewilderment in his eyes.

News from Cairo, even if it was rumour, was welcome in Kufra. Conversation was brisk. Dunn noticed that Lampard was not giving it his full attention. As they went in to dinner, he said: "Corky says the Pope got married again."

"Good for him."

"Wake up, Jack."

"What? Oh. Sorry." Lampard took a deep breath, and forced a smile. "I was thinking about the Black Cat Club."

"What about it?"

"Nothing. Came into my mind, that's all."

Dinner was curried goat, enlivened by a range of side dishes: chopped coconut, sliced bananas and dates, roast peanuts, small boiled eggs, diced onion, grated cheese, and sour goat's milk sprinkled with herbs and lime juice. Lampard recovered his confidence as he satisfied his appetite. Towards the end of the meal he asked Lester if he had had a pleasant trip to Kufra.

"We flew here," Lester said. "Took four hours and thirty-five minutes in an RAF Hudson. Just enough time to read the Cairo papers, eat a sandwich and have a snooze. I recommend it. It's the only way to travel."

"For the privileged few, yes."

"Fortunate rather than privileged," Malplacket said. "Lester has an American friend in Transport Command. He arranged it."

"The seats were going spare," Lester said. "We didn't do the war effort any harm. Besides, Malplacket's part of the war effort. He's in charge of gung-ho."

"And you? What brings you here?"

"Strictly hush-hush. Tell you later."

"I may not be here later."

"Oh, we have time to talk. Are you an early riser? I like to see the sun come up. Care to join me? It's scheduled for dawn."

"Why not?" Lampard said. He shrugged, and Lester smiled, and Major Tickenham looked on with approval. He liked his guests to hit it off.

*　　*　　*

Malplacket drank too much coffee at dinner. It was made Arab-style, thick and black and strong, and it guaranteed that he had a restless night.

When Lester woke him he was too groggy to get dressed. He pulled on a jellabah, the loose cloak worn by the natives, which he had bought in the market. "I'll do the talking," Lester said. "My dear chap," Malplacket mumbled, "I am incapable of speech and intend to remain so for the indefinite future, so please talk all you wish."

Lampard was waiting in a jeep. He drove them to the

edge of the oasis. They sat and watched the sunrise. "Hot stuff, eh?" Lester said.

"Blindingly obvious," Lampard said.

"I make that fifteen-all," Malplacket said. They looked at him. "Never mind," he said. "It would take far too long to explain, and I honestly haven't the strength."

"You want to know why we're in Kufra," Lester said. "You want to know the score. OK. I'm an accredited war correspondent for the Chicago *News*. You can see my documents if you want. The SAS seems to me to be the only outfit that's doing any actual fighting. I want to go with your patrol and watch you do your stuff, whatever it is. Simple as that."

"If it's so simple," Lampard said, "why didn't you obtain permission through the usual channels in Cairo?"

"Two reasons. One, if I went through the usual channels I wouldn't make first base. Two, if by some miracle they let me go with you, they'd make damn sure they censored the bejesus out of everything I wrote."

"I like the censors," Lampard said. "They keep the enemy guessing."

"Guessing what? Guessing that you guys keep raiding their airfields and blowing up their Messerschmitts? I found out about that, so it's probably reached Rommel too."

"That's still no reason to give the entire game away."

"What game? Long before my story hits the streets, your war will have changed completely. It's campaign season! Time for another battle! Soon the Front will be at the back, or vice versa, and this entire set-up will be history. Meantime," Lester said, "yours is the best story of the desert war, and I want to tell it the way it deserves to be told, not gutted by some fat blue pencil. I could make you the new Lawrence of Arabia, you know that? You should be very happy with me."

Lampard thought about it. "And where do you fit in, Mr Malplacket?" he asked pleasantly.

"Um . . ." Malplacket had not been listening; he had heard it all before. He had been thinking about the way the leaves of the date-palms kept up a leathery creaking in the breeze. He thought it sounded like the cautious mating of elderly elephants; then he dismissed that as a frivolous notion; and finally he wondered if he was fundamentally a frivolous person, a question that called for serious examination, but not before breakfast . . . "Let's see, now," he said. "My role runs parallel with that of Lester. I too am in the market for a dashing exploit. To boost morale back home, you see. Churchill told Blanchtower to find some gallant feat of arms, and Blanchtower sent me to look in the desert."

"Blanchtower's his old man," Lester said. "He's a lord."

"A dashing exploit," Lampard said. "Well, we certainly do our share of dashing." He was wearing a revolver in a webbing holster. He took the gun out and held it between his knees.

"Oh no," Lester said. "You're not that stupid."

Lampard spun the chamber. He cocked the gun. "You're very cocky," he said. "For someone who's an awfully long way from home."

"Don't even think of it," Lester told him.

Malplacket said, "What should he not even think of?"

"Killing us like he killed that Aussie major." Lester got out of the jeep and kicked a tyre, not in anger but for something to do. "Malplacket here may look like a lampshade, but his father really is in the British war cabinet. Lord Blanchtower lights Winston Churchill's cigars. Me, I'm just a hack from the Windy City but I didn't fly here without insurance. Before I left Cairo I wrote up your killing, and it didn't look like self-defence to me, it looked like murder. If I'm not back there within a month, that statement goes straight to the British Army Provost-Marshal."

Lampard let his head fall back until he was staring at

the sky. "Wild accusations from a missing American civilian," he said. "The Provost-Marshal will file it and forget it."

"My lawyer didn't think so. And he drew up the affidavit."

Malplacket said to Lampard, "The sequence of events would appear to be: you kill us, and the army hangs you."

"In a nutshell," Lester said.

Lampard was silent.

"Difficult to detect any benefit to anyone in that arrangement," Malplacket said. "But of course I may have overlooked something."

Lampard put the gun away. "I won't take you on the raids," he said. "You can join the patrol, but raiding is dangerous and it calls for skills and fitness which you two do not possess. You would almost certainly get hurt, you would quite definitely put my men at greater risk, and I won't allow it. But you'll get your story, after the raid." He started the jeep.

"You won't regret this," Lester said.

"D'you know," Malplacket said, "I think I could persuade Blanchtower to authorise a cinema film about your patrol. David Niven, Trevor Howard, Cary Grant."

"Not Cary Grant," Lampard said.

"No, perhaps not. Errol Flynn as Rommel? Rather audacious casting, don't you think?"

After breakfast, Lampard called his men together and told them that two observers would be going with them, both civilians. Nobody was surprised. It was assumed that Lester and Malplacket were spies, to be left in the Jebel. That sort of thing had happened before.

Lampard dismissed the men. The officers remained.

"We're early," Lampard said, "we stay here tomorrow, clean weapons and so on, move out the next day."

"A signal just came in," Sandiman told him. "For you. I had to decode it, of course."

The choice of words, his tone of voice, made Dunn and Gibbon glance at him.

"Of course," Lampard said. He took the piece of paper. He read the message. His head sank, but only briefly. "Change of plan," he announced. "We move out tomorrow, early."

"Cairo want a reply, sir," Sandiman said.

"No reply needed. Don't even acknowledge, in fact don't send *anything* to *anyone* until I say so. Understood?" Lampard strode away, looking as grim as a general. His right fist was clenched. The signal was crushed inside it.

"Golly," Dunn said.

"Better tell us," Gibbon said to Sandiman.

"Can't do that."

"Look: Mike needs to know everything. If Jack gets hit, Mike takes over."

"Sorry," Sandiman said. "No can do. Classified secret."

"Was it an order to move tomorrow?"

Sandiman hesitated. "This isn't fair," he said, and left them.

They watched him go. "So it wasn't an order to move," Dunn said, "but Jack's moving anyway, fast, and nobody's to know. Pick the bones out of that, if you can."

"Looks like a skeleton to me," Gibbon said gloomily; but then, Gibbon said almost everything gloomily.

*　　*　　*

Streams of tracer pumped themselves up from the desert in brilliant red-and-green streaks, climbing easily, almost lazily, until they got a whiff of their target, when they seemed to race and bend towards it.

I shall be killed, Paul Schramm thought, *and all because Maria Grandinetti couldn't answer the telephone.*

The tracer reached the peak of its trajectory and fell away, perhaps a couple of hundred yards short. "Awkward," Benno Hoffmann said. "If I get any closer they'll hit us. If I don't get any closer they'll never identify us."

"What's wrong with using the radio?" Schramm asked.

"The valves are broken."

Hoffmann was flying an RAF Lysander captured in the last British retreat from Benghazi. The Lysander was a high-wing monoplane with a rugged undercarriage, including spats on the wheels, and it was an excellent aircraft for low-level reconnaissance, bigger and far better (in Hoffmann's opinion) than the Luftwaffe's Storch. The trouble was it didn't look anything like a Storch, which was why Jakowski's column was trying hard to destroy it.

He had found the Lysander only the previous night, on a fighter field at Beda Fomm, south of Benghazi. The fighter pilots kept it hidden at the back of a hangar, because it was thoroughly unofficial. They had painted it bright yellow with oversized swastikas, and they used it to shuttle pilots to and from Tripoli when their leave came up. The station commander at Beda Fomm was an old friend of Hoffmann's. He agreed to lend the Lysander in exchange for two cases of Scotch whisky. In the morning someone explained the Lysander's controls and instrument panel, and sat beside Hoffmann while he did a few circuits and bumps. Then he flew her back to Barce.

"Biggest canary in Libya," he said proudly. "Want to come? I'm just waiting for di Marco."

"You're playing with your toys again, Benno," Schramm said. "When are you going to grow up?" He went off to telephone the hospital.

She did not answer. He stood and listened to the phone chewing mechanically at the silence in her office, but nobody answered. After a while his ear hurt, so he switched the instrument to the other ear. "Come on, come on, come on," he muttered, and he was still muttering it when the switchboard decided enough was enough and cut him off. He hung up so hard that he banged his fingers. *All I want is a damned appointment*, he told himself. He made the call again and failed again. All he wanted was to hear her voice.

The Lysander was ticking over, and Hoffmann was talking to Captain di Marco. Schramm joined them. "All right," he said. "I'll go."

"Good man!" Hoffmann said. "You can help push her home if anything breaks."

They refuelled at Jalo. With di Marco navigating and using the aerial-reconnaissance photographs, they flew on and found a cluster of trucks deep in the Sahara. Schramm, through binoculars the size of beer-bottles, saw Afrika Korps markings; but he was looking down, out of the sun, whereas they were looking up, into the midday glare. Hence the tracer.

"Drop a message," di Marco suggested. They did.

Five minutes later Hoffmann put the Lysander down alongside the trucks. Captain Lessing and Lieutenant Fleischmann came to meet them. "Where's Jakowski?" Hoffmann asked.

"He's not here, sir," Lessing said. "He took twenty trucks and went to intercept an enemy unit in the Calanscio. That was four days ago."

They moved out of the sun and under a canvas sheet that had been rigged up to make some shade. After the coolness of the Lysander's cabin the heat of the serir was like a foundry at full blast. Schramm's eyes were swamped with sweat, and the salt stung.

Hoffmann spread the photographs on a table. Lessing summarised events since the column left the Jebel al Akhdar. "Accurate navigation has caused us a lot of difficulty," he said. "That may explain Major Jakowski's late return. On the other hand, he may still be engaged with the enemy."

"Anything's possible, I suppose," Hoffmann said. He looked at di Marco.

"May I talk to the navigator?" di Marco said.

Sergeant Voss brought his maps, but di Marco gave them only a glance. "Your compass?" di Marco said. Voss said it was in his truck.

"Fetch it," Lessing ordered.

"With your permission," di Marco said, "let us go to the compass."

They walked to the truck. Schramm could smell cordite hanging in the air.

Voss pointed out the compass, attached to the centre of the dashboard. Di Marco tipped it slightly and they watched the gimbal mounting make it level and steady again. "Standard Luftwaffe magnetic compass," Hoffmann observed.

"Standard rubbish," Lessing said. He turned to Hoffmann. "With all due respect, sir."

"Please start the truck," di Marco said to Voss.

The engine roared and the compass trembled. Di Marco took the wheel and carefully turned the truck until it was pointing north and south. North on the compass disc was exactly in line with the radiator cap. "Now we need a marker fifty metres to the north of here and another marker five metres to the south," he said.

Two jerricans were produced and placed as he asked.

Di Marco turned the truck to the left, stopped, and backed it until it stood on the same spot, but at a right angle to its previous position. He checked the compass. "North has apparently moved approximately fifteen degrees to the west," he said. "May we have another marker, please?"

In order of rank, starting with Oberstleutnant Hoffmann, they got into the cab and peered at the compass. North no longer pointed at the first jerrican. That jerrican was now a long way to its right.

"Ha!" Schramm exclaimed. Somebody had to say something.

The new marker was put in place. "Now we move in the opposite direction," di Marco said. He turned the truck through a half-circle to the right and manoeuvred it onto its original spot. "North is now fifteen degrees to the east," he said. "Or, if you compare it with the second bearing, *thirty* degrees to the east."

Sergeant Voss hurried off to place another marker.

"So north is there, or there, or there," Lessing said. "Every time you move the compass it changes its mind."

"Every time you move *the truck* the compass changes its mind," di Marco said. "If I might have, say, four or five heavy machine guns?"

The weapons were brought. Di Marco leaned them against the centre of the dashboard. The compass jumped as if it had been stung.

"North has gone west," Schramm said.

"Wait a minute," Hoffmann said. "We have the same sort of problem in our aircraft, don't we? Things like chunks of metal and electrical circuits attract the compass needle, they pull it sideways and give you a false reading. You've got to adjust the compass to compensate."

"Not all metals," di Marco said. "Not aluminium, for instance, and aircraft contain a lot of aluminium. But iron or steel will disturb a magnetic compass, and this truck is made largely of iron and steel."

"Especially the engine," Sergeant Voss said before he remembered to shut up.

"The compass is immediately behind the engine," di Marco said. "Point the truck north and the engine attracts the compass needle forward, so we get an accurate reading, more or less. Point the truck west and the engine is now to the left, so it pulls the compass needle left. Point the truck east, it pulls it right."

"Simple as that," Lessing said emptily.

Schramm saw di Marco hesitate. "There's more?" he asked.

"The load also may exert a magnetic effect," di Marco said. "Different engine speeds can make a difference too. And if another truck is driving alongside, or just ahead . . ." He shrugged one shoulder.

"So the compass is good after all," Lieutenant Fleischmann said.

"The compass is excellent," di Marco told him. "It is useless, but apart from that, quite excellent."

They went back to the canvas shade. Schramm felt limp from the heat, and Hoffmann's shirt was soaked in sweat to a deep chestnut brown. Di Marco, Schramm noticed with weary envy, seemed quite comfortable, but then di Marco had once made his home in this dreadful place.

Each man got a mug of lime juice and water, and a mess tin of dates. There was a bowl of salt for anyone who felt the need.

"That explains it," Lessing said. "That explains why we've been zigzagging all over the damn desert."

"How do the British do it?" Schramm demanded. "They travel about the Sahara as if they were taking a taxi across London. How do they do it?"

"I suppose a magnetic compass is reliable if it's not in a truck," Lieutenant Fleischmann suggested. "Take it, say, twenty or thirty metres away and—"

"Stop-start, stop-start. I can't see an SAS patrol jumping out every five minutes to check its bearings. Can you?"

Benno Hoffmann took a fat pinch of salt and washed it down. "Captain di Marco knows," he said.

"The sun compass is what you should have," di Marco said courteously. "It is the reverse of a sundial. A sundial tells you the time according to the position of the sun. A sun compass tells you the position of the sun according to the time. If you know the time, you can very quickly find north."

There was silence while they got their minds around this idea.

"Sorry," Captain Lessing said. "I don't follow that last bit."

Di Marco took a pencil, drew a circle on a sheet of paper, and marked north, south, east and west. "Imagine that this is a compass face, divided into 360 degrees," he said. He stood the pencil upright in the centre. "The sun makes a shadow which is always moving. We know the exact angle of the sun for every hour of the day, every day of the year."

"Do we?" Lessing said. "I don't."

"There are tables which give this information. Using these tables, we find the known angle – the azimuth, as it is properly called – for the present time and we rotate the compass, so, until the shadow falls on the given bearing. The compass is now set. Its north points to true north. You can navigate accurately anywhere at any time of day. Except noon, when there is no shadow."

"Has the enemy got sun compasses?" Lessing asked.

"Yes," di Marco said.

"And no problems with magnetism," Fleischmann said. "No."

It was time to think about getting airborne. Hoffmann had no authority over Lessing, but his advice was to pack up and go home immediately. Jakowski was almost certainly lost and incapable of making the rendezvous. He was two days overdue already and his radio truck was silent. It would be suicidal to send men into the Sand Sea to look for him. Lessing's best course now was to cut his losses and get out before his water supply ran dangerously low.

Lessing listened in silence and said he was staying. He had his orders. Major Jakowski might turn up at any time, might be just over the horizon at this very minute, might arrive needing help, water, firepower, who knew what? Lessing couldn't leave. Not yet.

"If you wish," di Marco said, "we could carry out a

reconnaissance, now. We could fly halfway to the edge of the Calanscio and then make a wide circle around this position. If Major Jakowski and his men have left the Calanscio, we should be able to see them." Lessing accepted the offer.

"I'm not sure what the fuel consumption of this machine is," Hoffmann told him, "and I don't want to take any chances. So unless we have some news for you, don't expect us to come back."

The yellow Lysander took off. They reached five thousand feet and searched in every direction and found nothing. Captain di Marco gave Hoffmann the course for home. When they were still a long way south of Jalo they saw two vehicles that might have been the pair that Jakowski had ordered to rendezvous with the water-tanker. On the other hand, they might not. The war had left plenty of broken vehicles scattered about the desert. Hoffmann circled, going lower and lower until finally he buzzed the trucks, but nobody emerged to wave. Schramm thought he saw a body lying in deep shadow. He said nothing. The ground was thickly dotted with boulders. No place for a landing.

Back at Barce, what everyone wanted was beer, chilled beer. They drank, and ate salt peanuts, and ordered more beer.

"He took a mobile bakery," di Marco said. "Did you see it? A mobile bakery in the Sahara."

"In the last war the French had mobile brothels," Hoffmann remarked. "Or so my father claimed."

"The British had mobile cinemas," Schramm said. "Join the army and see Charlie Chaplin."

"I haven't thanked you for all your help," Hoffmann said.

"My pleasure," di Marco told him.

"God help me, I believe you. You actually *like* it down there, don't you?"

"The Sahara is clean and strong and very beautiful, yes."

"It's the arsehole of Africa," Schramm muttered.

"Even the arsehole is beautiful in God's eyes," di Marco said. "Try living without one and I am sure you would soon come to desire it keenly."

"Not stuffed with sand, I wouldn't."

The mess windows vibrated as a 109 pilot tested his engine.

"Look: you're better qualified than either of us to make a judgement," Hoffmann said. "What do you reckon Jakowski's chances are?"

Di Marco sucked beer from his upper lip. "Surely you mean Lessing's chances."

"No. Lessing? We just saw Lessing. I mean Jakowski."

"Jakowski is dead."

"You can't possibly know that."

"I have met him. He was as brave as a lion and he did not believe in the possibility of failure. To survive in the desert one must always believe in every possibility of failure. Courage is not enough. There are no lions in the desert."

"Lessing believes Jakowski will turn up."

"Yes, well . . ." For once, di Marco was slightly uncomfortable. He watched the 109 take off, climb and bank towards the sea. "Of course it is easy for me to talk. Jakowski's operation is not my responsibility. I can offer an objective view, an informed opinion. I may be wrong. Even if I am right, it is you Germans who must make the difficult decisions."

"Go ahead," Hoffmann said. "We'd like to hear what you think."

"Very well. If you will forgive me: Lessing is a good German soldier. He is like the Roman sentry who stayed at his post when the volcano erupted and poured lava over him. Lessing will go on finding reasons not to disobey Jakowski's order, even though he knows that Jakowski led

391

his men into the Sand Sea with insufficient water, faulty navigation and no expert knowledge of the most difficult and dangerous part of the Sahara. Let us be optimistic and say that Jakowski has one chance in ten thousand of surviving. Captain Lessing's chances?" He thought as he finished his beer. "Less than fifty-fifty."

Schramm said goodbye; he had to check any signals that might have come in during his absence. As he sat at his desk, flicking through pieces of paper, it suddenly struck him that Jakowski really was dead. That bustling, hustling, ambitious man who never listened and never gave up was now stiff and silent and still. In fact, half his force were probably dead and the rest were facing death. For a moment Schramm could not swallow and his heart began to race. Death in battle he could understand and accept, but this was just wastage, pointless random wastage, and that he could not accept. He walked up and down the room a few times, sucked in some deep breaths and felt strong enough to put through a call to the hospital. Amazingly, she answered after the first ring. "Ah," she said. "I have been thinking of you."

"I've got a problem," he said.

"So have I, alas. Three problems, and they are all shaved and prepared and waiting to be operated on, now."

"*Blast*," he said furiously, and heard her laugh. "I can't compete with that, can I?"

"No," she said. "You can't. Goodbye." And she hung up.

CHAPTER SIX

Pluck and Dash

An old, broken-backed Hurricane sat on the edge of LG 250. Its propeller blades had been peeled back like dying petals, its wings showed ragged holes where the machine guns used to be, and its rudder wagged sadly whenever the wind caught it.

Ostanisczkowski tried first. He fell from the formation and was still picking up speed as he crossed the opposite edge of the landing-ground, fifty feet above the sand and nose-down. Tiny corrections brought the target into the centre of his prop-disc. He levelled out at twenty feet, released his bomb and simultaneously pulled up hard and right as if the bomb had weighed a ton. In fact it was a two-hundred-and-fifty-pound dummy.

The adjutant, the doctor and the intelligence officer sat and watched from a safe distance. The dummy bomb bounced twice and went high over the Hurricane. "No coconut for Sneezy," Skull said. Uncle made a note. The bomb slid to a distant halt. An inevitable rush of dust marked its end.

Kit Carson tried next. He came in even faster, dropped his bomb earlier, and was wide by three lengths. Again, it skidded far into the desert. "Just like playing ducks and drakes," the doc said.

Pip Patterson, circling with Hooper and the CO, had watched these failures. He made his approach very low and left his release very late, the instant before he lost sight of the wreck. But the Kittyhawk had a long wedge of an engine that blocked the pilot's forward view. Pip's dummy bomb fell short, bounced high, and flew with the fighter over its target. "God Almighty!" Kellaway breathed.

"No, he's last," Skull said.

Hick Hooper's attack was much steeper than anybody else's. He bombed half a second before he pulled out, at three hundred feet, and missed by a lot.

"Target's in the wrong place," the doc said. "Obviously."

Fanny Barton had his own idea. He swung across the LG in a high-speed curve, his Kittyhawk steeply banked so that he could always see the ruined Hurricane ahead, right up to the final moment when he flattened out and bombed, and missed.

"Nearly hit my cookhouse!" Skull complained. "Damned hooligans."

"Put your cookhouse in the Hurricane, Skull," the doc said. "You'll be safe there."

There were no jokes when the pilots met beside Barton's machine. Bombing from a fighter was a completely new technique to them. The Kittyhawk had been adapted to carry bombs, but that didn't make it a bomber. If they approached the target at height they couldn't see it when they were over it: the Kittyhawk's wings stuck out on each side of the cockpit. Bombing became guesswork. If they came in low they could see the target ahead, but the bomb was travelling at the same speed as the Kitty, and it bounced and skipped far past the target. A slow approach would reduce the skip-factor, but nobody suggested flying slowly over an enemy airfield.

Skull joined them. "What did it look like to you?" Barton asked, not much interested in the answer. He hadn't wanted Skull to come to LG 250, but Air Commodore Bletchley had made it plain that he wanted an independent mind to make out the combat analyses and summaries, so Barton agreed and then put Skull in charge of the cook-house too. The doc pointed out how appropriate it was to have a Skull in a skeleton crew. Barton put the doc in charge of latrines. That left Uncle. Barton put him in charge of airfield defence. There was no airfield defence, but the adjutant was happy enough, and apparently quite sane. It was Bletchley's idea to include him in the LG 250 party on the grounds that he would recover his wits more quickly with familiar faces around him. The doc watched him closely and tried to keep him out of the sun.

"It looked unpromising and unprofitable," Skull said. "Thanks and goodbye."

"There must be a way," Kit Carson said. "I mean, bloody hell, they wouldn't put bomb shackles on a Kitty just for fun."

"I suppose you've considered dive-bombing?" Skull asked.

"You can't dive-bomb a Kittyhawk," Hick said. "It's a P-40. P for pursuit. Curtiss made it because the US Army Air Corps wanted something to pursue the enemy. Fact."

"Surely it can be persuaded to dive?" Skull made vague diving gestures. "Like a Stuka?"

"Be your age, Skull," Pip said. "You've been around long enough to know a Tommy or a Kitty doesn't need *persuading*. The kite dives like a block of flats. The problem is pulling out. Stukas have air brakes. See any air brakes around here? That's four tons of aeroplane, for God's sake."

"I heard of a guy who got a P-40 up to five hundred m.p.h. in a dive," Hick said. "Took him ten thousand feet to pull out. Minus half his engine cowling."

"Goodness me," Skull said.

"What's to eat?" Barton asked him.

"One must assume the air commodore was mistaken." Skull turned to leave.

"What?"

Skull stopped and scratched at the stiff darkness of the bloodstain on his faded blazer. "Baggy told me that some hotshot Australian pilot had succeeded in dive-bombing with a Kittyhawk," he said. "Piece of cake, apparently, when you know how."

"And did he?"

"Alas, no. Baggy didn't know how." Skull strolled away, still scratching.

Barton picked up his flying helmet and knocked the sand out of it. "If I rip the wings off, Pip, you're CO."

His engine was still hot. It fired first time. Ten minutes later his Kittyhawk was at fifteen thousand feet, a speck of silvery dust that produced an occasional soft echo of a dull rumble.

"One thing I forgot to mention," Skull told Uncle. "There is a school of thought which believes that, at certain angles of dive, the bomb when released may strike the propeller." Uncle was silent. "Too late now," Skull said.

All the way up, Barton worried at the problem of dive-bombing. It was a vertical business, or as near to vertical as you could get. By aiming the bomber, you aimed the bomb. It was like strafing downwards. Dive a Kittyhawk vertically and it would build up speed so fast that when you were close enough to the target to be sure of hitting it, you were far too low to pull out. Pull out earlier and you were far too high to be sure of hitting the target.

Tricky.

He checked the sky and eased the stick forward. Assume the target is two thousand feet below. Assume you want to bomb at five hundred feet. He watched the altimeter unwind and felt his straps grip as the desert floor swung up to face him. Almost at once his right arm was exerting a lot of left thrust on the control column to stop the fighter rolling to the right. Automatically he put on trim, his left hand working the toggle switch that activated the electric trim-tabs: thank God for Yankee know-how. "Bomb now!" he said aloud, and tried to pull her out of the dive, heaving on the stick, vision browning out a little, feeling the nose come up slowly, grudgingly and not enough. He was still counting off the height in hundreds as the Kittyhawk smashed through what would have been the desert floor. As she recovered she rolled sturdily to the left and both his arms were busy, one reversing the trim and the other working the stick, just to keep her straight. What a bitch.

He fooled about with near-vertical dives on imaginary targets for five more minutes, crashed (in theory) three times, and even so knew he would not have bombed within a hundred yards of anything smaller than a cathedral. What a stinking bitch.

Low-level attacks missed. Vertical attacks crashed and missed. Which left what?

At least he had learned one thing. Try to dive-bomb in a Kittyhawk and she rolled hard to the right. Pull out, she rolled hard left.

Barton nudged the nose down and tested the strength of the right-hand roll. When the dive reached an angle of forty-five degrees and he could feel her itching to run away, the roll was still containable. At fifty-five or sixty degrees he had to brace his right arm against his leg in order to fight the roll. At seventy or eighty degrees he was losing the fight, the kite was juddering, the desert was a yellow swirl, and the powered trim-tab was giving him all the help it could. He quit while he was still just ahead, pulled out, browned out, and fought the opposite roll all over again as the Kittyhawk swooped back up to level flight.

Sixty degrees was about as steep as you could dive and get away with it.

What could you see at sixty degrees?

Barton spiralled down to about two thousand feet and stooged around the LG until he reckoned he'd arrived. He shoved the nose down to sixty degrees and was rewarded with a perfect view of the ruined Hurricane. Sixty degrees wasn't vertical, but that wreck hung in front of the

Kittyhawk's nose like a picture on the wall. He resisted the roll, never took his eyes off the target and bombed from what he guessed was five hundred feet. Perhaps less, because the desert rushed up hungrily as he pulled out. But it didn't get him.

Sand sprayed the target. "Spot-on!" Kellaway said. "Tickety-boo!"

Barton landed. "Piece of cake," he told his pilots.

Lunch was bully-and-biscuit pie, an invention of Skull's. The squadron practised sixty-degree dive-bombing all afternoon, and by the end the Hurricane wreck was impressively battered. Barton was pleased. "Take off one hour before dawn tomorrow," he said. "We'll hit the Luftwaffe repair field at Benina. Won't they be surprised?"

Skull said nothing. He went away and studied his maps. Then he found Barton when he was alone. "My guess is they won't be in the least surprised," he said. "Benina's between Benghazi and the western end of the Jebel al Akhdar. That whole area's stiff with enemy. It's lousy with landing-grounds. I can't think of a more dangerous target."

"Well, we'll see," Barton said. "What's for dinner?"

"Curried Geraldo. Aren't you going to tell me anything?"

"Certainly. I'll tell you everything when we get back."

"You might not get back."

"Jesus! What a fucking *worrier* you are, Skull. You keep worrying that we might get killed. Relax, for Christ's sake. *Of course* we're going to get killed. It's a racing certainty. You can't be a fighter pilot without getting killed sooner or later. Does it matter? No, it doesn't matter a tiny toss. Feel better now?"

Skull felt that he was being patronised and he resented it. "In that case, nothing matters. Life and death are trivia, so why bother about anything? Defending democracy, liberating Europe, all the rest of it — who cares?"

"Well, I don't," Barton said. "Fuck democracy, fuck

Europe." He yawned and stretched. "Give me a nice juicy target and see me blow it to buggery and back." He smiled the smile of a healthy lunatic who has the keys to the asylum.

That smile disturbed Skull. He tried to describe it to the doctor, but got nowhere. "If you think you can make sense of the mind of a fighter leader, you're seriously ill," the doctor said. "Take two aspirin and lie down for a couple of months."

Skull retired to his tent and his Al Bowlly records. 'Easy Come, Easy Go' seemed like a suitable number. He wound up the gramophone.

*   *   *

Paul Schramm couldn't sleep. He got up at four a.m. and walked around the airfield with the duty NCO in charge of sentries, until his leg tired him and he limped over to the signals block to ask if any radio messages had come in from Captain Lessing. None had. He went to the flight operations room and looked at the activity on their general situations map, a thing as big as a small room, which showed the area for a hundred kilometres around. Little was happening. An occasional transport plane came in to Berna airfield at Benghazi. The map stopped at the southern side of the Jebel, just where the Sahara began. "What happens if somebody flies down there?" he asked the duty officer. "Off the map?"

The duty officer shrugged. "He goes straight to hell, sir, I suppose."

"I flew down there yesterday."

"What was it like?"

"Hellish."

"Ah." The duty officer waited but that was evidently the end, so he went back to his crossword puzzle.

The cookhouse was coming to life. Schramm got a pot

of coffee and took it to the station commander's quarters. Hoffmann did not welcome being woken up. "For the love of God," he groaned when he saw who it was. "Go and get married, Paul. Spare me these moments of bliss."

Schramm was taken aback. It was the last remark he had expected. "My profound apologies," he said stiffly. "I should have known better than to disturb you over a matter of life or death."

"Is that all it is? Pour me a bucket of that muck." Hoffmann got out of bed. His face had collapsed in the night: he looked like his own death mask. "Who's dead? Apart from me."

"Lessing's men will be soon, if something isn't done about them."

Hoffmann groaned again and drowned the groan in coffee. "We did something," he said. He let his eyes close. After a while, coffee spilled from the cup onto his toes and he opened his eyes. "What do you want?" he asked. "Prayer? Good, I just prayed."

"Call General Schaefer. Get him to order Lessing out of there."

"You call him. It's your idea." Hoffmann picked up a phone and asked for General Schaefer in Tripoli. "Help yourself to coffee, if that's what it is," he said, and went out. Soon he could be heard singing in the shower.

He was still singing when the switchboard rang and Schramm was connected with Schaefer. He knew what he wanted to say and he said it competently.

"That's all very interesting," the general said. "Now let us consider the facts. Jakowski took enough fuel, food and water for three weeks. He has been gone less than a week. You say he's lost but that's not a *fact*. All it means is you can't find him. Maybe Jakowski doesn't *want* to be found. Maybe he's shadowing a British incursion. There is such a thing as camouflage, remember. And his radio silence is planned and deliberate. We know that enemy patrols use that area, don't we? That's a fact. It's why Jakowski went there in the first place. Captain Lessing's orders are clear. If I pull him out now I abandon Jakowski. I trust my commanders, major. I trust Jakowski. I trust Lessing. Thank you for your concern. Don't call me again. Goodbye."

Hoffmann was standing in the doorway, towelling his hair. "It's only a world war," he said. "Don't take it to heart."

Schramm went to the mess and ate breakfast, and then checked the teleprinter to see if there had been any SAS activity. A German road convoy had been mined near Cirene, and an ammunition dump at Bir Semander had exploded. He telephoned the Luftwaffe intelligence officers at a few nearby airfields – Slonta, Derna, Soluch, Berka – and heard nothing of value.

There was nothing more that he could do, so he drove into Benghazi to get a haircut. He had just had a haircut. If they took any more off he would be cropped like a convict. *Why must life be so damn complicated?* he demanded. By the time he reached the city, his left foot throbbed with pain so there was no question of getting a haircut, in fact it was just as well he could drive straight to the hospital. He hobbled in, wincing slightly, determined to get this foot put right, here and now, for good and all.

*   *   *

Barton got the five Kittyhawks airborne while the night was still as black as a cellar. A string of petrol flares on the perimeter created a weak and flickering hint of a horizon, but mainly the pilots let the aeroplane tell them when it was ready to come unstuck.

They climbed to twenty-five thousand feet and cruised north-west. For nearly an hour there was nothing to see except stars and exhaust flames. Patterson had never flown so deep into enemy territory before and he was impressed by the vast emptiness below. LG 250 was at least a hundred miles behind enemy lines, not that there were any lines to be behind, and it was a long way from the Med, so far south that it was almost on the northern edge of the Calanscio Sand Sea. It all added up to a lot of emptiness.

They watched Barton. When at last he dived, they dived. They made a long, unhurried descent. The formation slid down as smoothly as if it were on rails. The engines were throttled back to little more than a powered glide.

It was all so peaceful and pleasant that Hick Hooper began to think they might reach the target undetected. He could actually see it. The sun had not yet risen, but its light was leaking over the horizon, just enough to give a misty, black-and-white impression of the terrain. Soon the runways were as obvious as a grey cross on a faded flag. Something moved against the flag. Hick lost it, found it again, saw it enlarge, and recognised a Messerschmitt 110, climbing hard. Probably just taken off. Its course took it away from the Kittyhawks, but not for long. When it suddenly swung towards them, he knew they had been spotted. Searchlights poked holes in what was left of the night. Flak splattered the sky ahead with sepia blots.

"Good luck," Barton said. "Have fun." They were the first words he had spoken since take-off. The formation, already loose, fanned out. The dive steepened to sixty degrees.

Benina was a big field, one of the biggest Luftwaffe bases in Libya. Aircraft were parked all around it, some in anti-blast pens, most not. Kit Carson chose a target, aimed the four sleek tons of Kittyhawk at it and began counting the seconds aloud. *Pointless*, he told himself. *Why do it?* But he kept counting until he released his pair of two-hundred-and-fifty-pound bombs and enjoyed the lightness of the kite now she was free of her luggage. Then he was pulling out of the dive, reversing the trim-tabs with his left hand to combat the roll, trying to force his brain to stay awake as blood drained to his legs and centrifugal force tried to drag his stomach into his bowels and turn it into quick-setting concrete. Strings of bright beads criss-crossed his foggy vision. A control tower rushed at him, fell away, and now he could see again. Three other fighters were visible. Something exploded on the fringe of his vision and sent out jagged streaks of orange flame like cartoon electricity. By then the four Kittyhawks were wheeling away and sprinting for safety.

The explosion was Sneezy's fighter plunging into a line of German aircraft. He had been holding it in a perfect dive, sixty degrees, no roll, no wobble, target exactly where he wanted it, when a line of flak rippled across his path and hacked open the fuselage below his feet. Shrapnel slashed the control cables, and the stick was loose and useless: it flopped about as if he were stirring paint. There was nothing to do. He folded his arms and wondered why he did, and then sneered at himself for wasting his last few seconds on something so meaningless. In the final instant before the aeroplane destroyed itself and its bombs and its pilot and two or three 110s, his eyes were wide open. Ostanisczkowski had bought his ticket. He was entitled to see all of the show.

If there was any pursuit, the 109s were scrambled too late and sent the wrong way. The 110 had vanished, frightened by flak. Barton led the Kittyhawks up into the Jebel and flew down a series of wadis until they emerged into the desert. They returned to LG 250 at zero feet in a formation so loose that it was spread over half a mile.

Skull debriefed them. At the end, he added up their claims. "Ten probables," he said. "Which, being translated, means ten possibles." He sounded like a school-teacher announcing poor exam results.

"Possibles?" Hick Hooper had landed happy. Now he

was hot with anger. "We hit the bastards! Bombed 'em between the eyes! We fly five hundred miles and you give us *possibles*?"

"Nobody saw a bomb-strike," Skull said. "Everyone was pulling out of the dive, facing up and away. You didn't see it, I can't give it."

"I saw my explosion," Pip said. "I told you that."

"You told me you saw a great cloud of dust and smoke."

They all stood around and hated Skull. He was fireproof. He had been hated by many pilots before.

* * *

The Arabs constantly moved. Greek George never knew why. They never stayed in one place more than two days. If it was a difficult journey they put him on a camel, but he was getting stronger now; he could usually walk. He made himself useful when they reached a new campsite, helped put up the goatskin tent, gathered twigs for the fire, even helped to make tea. This became his special job. He was first assistant tea-maker to the serious little girl.

Arab tea-making, she taught him, was an important ceremony, and he had to watch her do it several times before she would let him touch anything. A small enamel teapot was heated on the fire until the water – with a fistful of tea already in it – boiled over. She filled the tea glasses, which were as small as egg-cups, and emptied them back into the teapot, then boiled the tea again and repeated the process with the tea glasses twice more; tasted it; gave it a final boil, and served it. George saw that froth was considered a desirable part of Arab tea. He became skilled at holding the teapot high above the glasses when he poured. Everyone approved.

In return he tried to teach the little girl how to make a cat's-cradle. Very graciously, she refused to learn; and he realised that to learn the trick would be to destroy the magic. She preferred to keep him as the magician in her life. He liked her even more after that.

Early one morning everyone was sitting on a hillside, watching the animals graze, when four Kittyhawks in line astern came racing down the wadi, twisting and bending to stay inside it. George jumped up and waved. It was a wonderful sight. Then they were gone. The Arabs, all grins and shouts, applauded and congratulated him. All he could do was nod and smile.

From then on he was always planning how to get back to his squadron. He was as dark as an Arab, and his feet were so hard he could walk without shoes. Maybe he could walk home. Others had. They were given a little silver lapel-badge, a winged flying-boot. He thought hard about it.

*   *   *

She was not in the hospital. She was in an Italian cellar-bar around the corner, eating a second breakfast. As soon as he limped through the doorway she called to the owner to make more coffee. Half a dozen civilians, regulars by the look of them, were sitting around her, enjoying her conversation, but she sent them away with a long stage-whisper in husky Italian that made them laugh and glance at him sideways. "What was that about?" he asked.

"I said you are the most demanding lover I have ever known and if your lusts are not satisfied at least three times a day you become uncontrollable and shoot a British prisoner-of-war."

"I don't know how to be uncontrollable," he said. "I never learned."

He sat opposite her. They watched each other while she ate. She spread butter on a fresh bread roll and slid the plate across the table. "You look tired," she said. "You look as if you made love seventeen times last night and didn't like any of it."

He chewed on the roll. "It was a bad night, but not for that reason." Fresh coffee arrived, and two thimble-glasses of brandy. They drank a silent toast to each other. "Why are you so pleased with yourself?" he asked.

"Two amputations before breakfast. Look what I found hiding in the kidneys." She fished in her pocket and tossed a ragged little chunk of shrapnel onto the table. "And the day has scarcely begun."

Schramm put the shrapnel on his palm and rolled it about. Its tiny spikes prickled his skin. "Business is brisk," he said. It was the ugliest thing he had seen all year. "What caused the amputations? Gangrene?" He didn't really care. It was just conversation.

"No, not gangrene. Something far more rapid. High explosive. At Benina." She could see from his face that he didn't understand. "Benina got dive-bombed this morning, at dawn. Hadn't you heard? Obviously not. Luftwaffe Intelligence knows nothing."

"*Dive*-bombed? The enemy hasn't got a dive-bomber. At least not one with enough range to hit Benina."

"Not my problem, Paul. All I know is ambulances, wounded, cut, stitch, dressing, next patient please. The last time we spoke, you sounded troubled. Is there a problem? I noticed when you came in, your foot —"

"My foot is fine." He was still thinking of the raid on Benina. To rid his mind of it, he took her hand. "I'm in great shape," he said. "Would you like to dance?" Foolish question, in a bar, at breakfast. So what? He had a right to be foolish too. She kept his hand and linked fingers. "Alfredo!" she called, and spoke in Italian. After a moment, a hidden accordion wheezed as someone picked it up and began to play that familiar, quirky little waltz. They got up and danced. Sometimes a customer unhurriedly used a foot to hook a stool out of their way. The old man emerged from a back room and stood playing until the barman gave him a chair to sit on. He hadn't shaved in a month, his flies were undone and he weighed slightly less than the accordion.

The waltz ended. "Give him some money," she said. Schramm tucked a note into one hand and shook the other. The skin felt like parchment.

In the street, she took his arm; his confidence took another leap upwards. "How about dinner tonight?" he said. "We should make the most of the Garibaldi while we can. Yes?" It would be a good place to ask her to marry him, which was still a preposterous idea, but he was growing more accustomed to it all the time. "Can you get us a table?"

"Not tonight. General Schaefer's coming back today."

"Oh." That was a blow. "Oh dear."

"Don't you know *anything* in Intelligence? No wonder you're losing the war."

"Are we?"

"You mean nobody told you?" That was a joke, and they both knew it. They walked in silence as far as the hospital entrance. "One day someone's going to bomb this place," she said. "And then all our worries will be over." She checked her watch. "If you're desperate for entertainment, you could come with me while I do wards. Lots of new blood this morning."

Schramm hesitated. He had slept badly, he really didn't feel like looking at smashed bodies. "I don't think so," he said. "If I see that poor bloody Gefreiter from Barce once more I might resign."

"You needn't worry. Gefreiter Debratz has gone."

"Oh." Schramm was ashamed of his relief and therefore felt the need to cover it with words. "Just a boy, wasn't he? What a waste . . . What was the cause of death, in the end?"

She looked at him, soberly and seriously. "If it is important for you to know, I killed him, in the end."

That made no sense. His mind could not accept it. "Something went wrong?" he said. "You made a mistake?"

"No. It was no mistake. His body had failed to recover, but it was also refusing to die. Life was of no value. So I killed him."

"No value?" Schramm's heart was suddenly thumping. "Who says? Who says no value?"

"I do. I could see in his eyes that he was sick of hanging on. His life was agony and filth and despair." She spoke calmly. "Struggling to keep him alive was a cruel waste, so I killed him last night at ten-thirty with an injection. He slipped away like that." She clenched her fist and slowly opened it.

"You've done this before," Schramm said. The back of his neck crawled.

"Yes. You should not imagine Debratz was the only hopeless case the hospital ever had."

"How many?"

She didn't even try to think. "Twenty, thirty. Does it matter?"

"Christ, no, of course not. You're only a doctor, you've only been killing off your patients, why should it matter? Jesus . . ."

His anger and sarcasm failed to touch her. "Now I've spoiled your day," she said. "Now you've really got somebody to hate."

"You know what you're doing?" he demanded. "You're playing God."

"Well," she said, "somebody's got to." Before he could stop her, she kissed him on the cheek and went into the hospital.

Schramm spent the rest of the morning walking around Benghazi. His shoulders were slumped and his head was down. He made no attempt to disguise his limp. The image that kept recurring was Maria Grandinetti's face, sober and serious, as she looked straight at him and said *If it is important for you to know, I killed him.* None of it could be forgotten. His mind might drift sideways into another subject, something unimportant, a memory of Germany, perhaps, or a comment di Marco had made, and abruptly her statement would shoulder everything aside and give him an almost physical jolt. *I killed him.* Well, he would have died sooner or later, Schramm tried to tell himself, and got the answer: We're all going to die sooner or later but nobody has the right to . . .

To what? To kill? You killed Corporal Harris. Remember?

That was duty. No choice. Him or me.

But you got a kick out of it, didn't you?

That's war.

She's in the same war, isn't she?

"I don't care," Schramm said aloud. "I don't care, I don't care, I don't care."

He left the main streets for the back alleys, where he could put his hands in his pockets and he wouldn't have to keep returning salutes. He walked until he was weary and he thought he had exhausted his anger. Max had been right: love is a form of madness, what the army calls a self-inflicted wound. Open your heart to someone and they stick a knife in it.

Schramm saw a glint of turquoise blue and walked down to the harbour. He sat on a block of masonry that had fallen from a bombed building and he enjoyed the breeze off the sea. Two freighters were being unloaded, very fast, before the enemy could bomb them. It was pleasant to rest the body and brain while others worked so hard.

Schramm dozed. His mind was let loose. It could wander where it wished. Nothing was banned. Eventually it strayed into an area so rich with excitement that his head jerked and his eyes opened wide.

It was mid-afternoon when he parked his car at the Hotel

Garibaldi. General Schaefer, they told him, was in a meeting. After that? Another meeting. When that ended he was due to leave for a tour of inspection. His schedule was very tight and he was running thirty minutes late. Major Schramm could wait if he wished, but . . .

Schramm waited.

After an hour someone brought him iced tea.

After another hour a white-haired colonel came in and introduced himself: von Mansdorf, the general's left-hand man. "Awfully sorry to keep you hanging about," he said. "Um . . . You wouldn't be the Major Schramm who telephoned the general rather early this morning?"

"Yes."

"I see. Well, full marks for courage, Major. The Jakowski operation is really none of your business, is it? Is that what you want to see him about?"

"No."

"Ah. In that case I suggest you tell me, and when I get a chance I'll tell him. Otherwise you could be here for a week."

"It's about air superiority," Schramm said. "The British are using SAS patrols and now, so I hear, dive-bombing raids to destroy our fighters before they even get into battle. Well, I have a plan to destroy *their* fighters before they even get into battle. My plan is to attack the Takoradi Trail."

"Let us go into the map room," von Mansdorf said.

He found a large map of North-East Africa and unrolled it, placing glass ashtrays on the corners. "Refresh my memory," he said.

"The port of Takoradi is actually just off this map," Schramm said. "It's on the coast of Nigeria. That's where they assemble their Hurricanes. First stop is Kano." He found Kano. "Then they fly them virtually due east, right across Africa, to Khartoum. Then down the Nile, to Cairo. The vulnerable stretch of the route is here, in the middle, between Kano and Khartoum. The Hurricanes must land to refuel at Maiduguri, Fort Lamy, Geneina and El Fasher. All those landing-grounds are remote and exposed, and easily attacked. I doubt if they are even defended."

"Except by Hurricanes, of course," von Mansdorf said.

"No, sir. The Hurricanes are assembled at Takoradi without guns, to save weight. Their guns are fitted in Cairo."

"That makes sense."

"Cut the Takoradi Trail and –"

"And you would get several large medals," von Mansdorf said. "Now explain how it can be done."

"The same way the SAS operates. They've been raiding north against us. We raid south against them."

Von Mansdorf looked at him, expecting more. Then he looked at the map. "It has the merit of simplicity," he said. "From Benghazi to the Takoradi Trail is about two thousand kilometres." He measured it with a series of hand-spans, just to be sure. "That's in a direct line. It's like driving from Paris to Moscow without roads, and with nowhere to get fuel or food, in fact with nothing but sand, heat and flies. Isn't that something of a tall order?"

"Normally yes, sir. But there's an Italian officer called di Marco who led expeditions across the Sahara before the war –"

"Have you consulted him?"

"Not yet."

"Excuse me."

When von Mansdorf came back, he said, "I've had a talk with Captain di Marco and he says it can't be done."

Schramm was bewildered. "Just like that?" he said.

"It's three times as far as the longest unbroken journey the SAS patrols make. Below Kufra the going is bad, very bad. To carry enough fuel and water you would need a huge column of vehicles. The operation would be highly visible. The Takoradi Trail runs through Chad, which is French. The French would be hostile."

Colonel von Mansdorf walked with Schramm to his car. "Be kind to yourself," he advised. "Don't try to see General Schaefer again. You'll find yourself on the Russian Front, honestly you will."

Schramm drove back to Barce. There was a message on his desk. It said that a signal had been received from a stay-behind agent the Italians had left at Kufra. Captain Lampard's patrol had come and gone.

*   *   *

When the patrol stopped for a midday meal, Lampard opened his sealed orders. He read them twice and called for the other officers: Dunn, Gibbon and Sandiman. "Primary target is Beda Fomm," he told them.

Gibbon had his maps ready. "Ninety-odd kilometres south of Benghazi, just east of the coast road."

"Beda Fomm is a big airfield," Lampard said. "Very juicy."

"German or Italian?" Dunn asked.

"German. Two squadrons of 109s, so I'm told. Don't tell the men anything. I'll brief them later. And certainly don't tell our distinguished passengers."

Lester and Malplacket were relatively content. They had escaped from Kufra; unknown adventures lay over the horizon; and in the meanwhile everything was holiday. All their decisions were made for them. Food was rich and plentiful. Travel was not too uncomfortable, and when it stopped there were amusing soldiers to talk to.

By the end of the first day the patrol had manoeuvred its way across the narrow neck of the Calanscio Sand Sea. It would have made more progress if one truck had not lost its steering. There was tinned steak and fresh eggs from Kufra for supper, with fried potatoes and tinned carrots, followed by tinned pineapple. The sunset was as spectacular as ever. Lester lay in his blankets and watched the staggering display put on by the stars until he felt giddy. He closed his eyes and began writing in his head. *Deep in the merciless Sahara we advanced stealthily . . .* Soon he fell asleep.

*   *   *

"Is it a good idea? I don't know whether it's a good idea, Paul. Did you talk it over with di Marco? After von Whatshisname?"

"No."

"Well, that's brilliant, isn't it? You nominate di Marco to lead your astonishing expedition, but you don't discuss it with him."

"It's pointless now. He killed it."

Hoffmann grunted, and the top of his cigar glowed in the night. "Sounds like it was dead to start with." They were strolling around the airfield. Strictly speaking he was breaking his own blackout regulations, but in his opinion any British bomber pilot who could see a cigar two miles below him deserved a direct hit.

"Schaefer's got no imagination," Schramm said. "He can't see the possibilities. Takoradi is the Achilles' heel of the Desert Air Force."

"Two thousand kilometres away."

"Ever heard of fuel dumps?"

"Over some of the worst terrain in Africa. Keep your voice down."

They were a couple of hundred yards from a row of 109s. The night was so black that the fighters were lost in its darkness, but Hoffmann knew where he was. He and Schramm stepped slowly and cautiously. Their approach seemed to take an age. Towards the end, Schramm felt ill with the tension of expectation. The sentries were armed.

413

At any instant the night might be ripped apart. So might he. Ripped and smashed. He remembered what the bodies of the deserters had looked like.

Hoffmann tripped the alarm first: he felt a tiny pressure on his leg and immediately called out: "Don't shoot! Station commander."

Three spotlights dazzled them. Nobody spoke. The spotlights went out. Schramm relaxed his fists.

As they walked back to their quarters, he said, "I don't know why I suggested doing that. Ludicrously dangerous."

"See what happens when you fall in love? All of a sudden you want to live forever. Fatal, old chap, fatal."

Schramm didn't want to think about love, or women, or anything that suggested Italian lady doctors, life, death, or waltzes on the accordion. "What went wrong at Benina?" he asked.

"Oh, sheer bad luck. Endless trouble with the radar. All night long it kept producing phantom aircraft until finally everyone just ignored it. So inevitably five genuine plots appeared, dive-bombed the field and departed. We lost five or six machines on the ground, plus ten dead and twenty wounded. Flak got one of theirs."

"Yes? What type?"

"Nobody knows. The pilot's thirty feet underground, splashed all over his engine. Flak gunners reckon they were P-40s. Tomahawks or Kittyhawks."

"That's not possible. They haven't got the range."

"Tell Benina. They'll be very relieved."

*   *   *

LG 250 was even more austere than LG 181. A few tents; a couple of packing-cases where spares and tools were kept; a canvas cover under which people ate; and a latrine screen: that was it, all bleached white by the sun and scoured by the endless wind, and lost in a rippling infinity of sand. The adjutant came out from behind the latrine screen, late in the morning, and squinted into the glare. Tents floated like fishing boats on lakes of trembling heat. An aeroplane distorted and shrank until it seemed that nothing connected the tail unit to the fuselage. A man walked, but his limbs were blobs. Kellaway found the whole scene thoroughly unsatisfactory.

He set off for the orderly room and could not find it. It seemed to have been removed. This was getting worse and worse.

A corporal-armourer walked by, dressed in boots and shorts and with belted ammunition draped around his neck. "Not Wednesday, is it?" Kellaway asked.

"Beats me, sir. Dunno the month, let alone the day."

"In this squadron, sports afternoon is Wednesday, corporal. If this isn't Wednesday then you're improperly dressed."

"Sir." The corporal looked around for help.

"If I had my way, you'd be on a 252 and inside the guardroom in double-quick time," Kellaway said. "Trouble is, all the 252s are kept in the orderly room and somebody's moved it." He looked everywhere. "Don't tell me they've taken the guardroom too!" he exclaimed.

"Sir, I think the doctor wants you."

"Where?" The doctor was not in sight. "By God, have they taken the bloody doctor?" Kellaway was indignant. He stamped up and down, shaking his head. "Turn your back for five minutes," he muttered, "this is what happens."

The corporal saw Skull, and waved. "I expect Mr Skelton knows all about it, sir," he said.

"He'd better. Don't see how we can carry on like this."

Skull opened his golf umbrella and came over. "Something troubling you, Uncle?"

"No, no. Nothing of any consequence," the adjutant

said with heavy sarcasm. "It's just that I don't see how we can possibly have a CO's parade without a flagpole, do you?" He folded his arms and tightened his jaw: the very picture of a hardworking staff officer who has done his utmost and got absolutely no co-operation from anyone.

"A flagpole," Skull said. "Where did you see it last, Uncle?" He nodded to the corporal, who marched off, ammo belts swinging.

"Where it always was: right there, in front of the admin block. Where I had my orderly room. Don't suppose I shall see *that* again. Guardroom's gone, too. And the camp cinema. Airmen's ablutions. Sickbay. Cookhouse. All gone."

"Not the cookhouse, Uncle," Skull said. "We still have a sort of a cookhouse." He pointed.

"Nonsense. Cookhouse should be over *there*, next to the airmen's mess. Then the NAAFI, stores, transport section, squash court, officers' mess. Now we haven't even got a flagpole. The whole squadron's gone to pot."

The doctor came hurrying across the sand. "Didn't I tell him to stay out of the sun?" he complained.

"He thinks he's back at Kingsmere," Skull told him. "That's where the squadron was based before the war. It's in Essex."

"Are you going on leave?" Kellaway demanded.

"No, Uncle," Skull said sadly. "I'm not going on leave."

"Then why aren't you in uniform? Customs of the Service say that an officer wears mufti only when he's outside the camp. And mufti means a dark suit with a tie. That's not a dark suit."

"No, Uncle. It's a rowing blazer."

"But today isn't Wednesday." By now the adjutant was trembling with distress. "In this squadron, sports afternoon is on a Wednesday!"

"Come with me, Uncle." The doctor took his arm and

led him away. "Customs of the Service," Kellaway said. "That chap's wearing *suede boots*. An officer does not appear in public in suede boots, for God's sake . . ."

＊　　＊　　＊

Half an hour later, Barton briefed the three pilots. Skull listened. The target was a Luftwaffe landing-ground at the eastern end of the Jebel, called Bir Dagnish. They would make a high approach, taking advantage of the poor visibility at midday, bomb the place and beat it for home. Barton was giving them radio frequencies and compass bearings in case anyone got lost, when the adjutant could be heard, shouting. Then they saw him attacking the doctor with a folding canvas chair. A wild swing made the doctor jump and stumble. A lucky thrust caught him in the stomach and he went down. The adjutant trod on him firmly, folded up the canvas chair, went back and trod on him again, and finally set off for Barton and the pilots.

"He's got to go," Barton said.

"No, no. He's only winded," Skull said. "He'll recover."

Kellaway marched over to them.

"Jolly good," he said. "Just wanted half a minute with the chaps before you all toddled off, if I may, sir." Barton nodded.

They all watched carefully. Uncle, in this state, was like an elderly dog that could wag its tail and bite simultaneously.

"That fool of a doctor wanted me to drink his rum," he said. "I told him, an officer does not 'stand drinks' to a brother officer in the mess. Just not done. Customs of the Service. He wouldn't listen. Kept insisting. Not the sort of thing a chap can take sitting down." He opened the canvas chair, shook it, closed it, and looked at Skull. "What?" he said.

"Of course you know he's Irish," Skull said.

"Yes? Drink a lot of rum in Ireland, do they? Anyway . . . That's not the point. The point is Takoradi. Now I know you chaps think you're here to hammer the Hun and thus avoid getting sent to Takoradi, wherever that is. But such is not the case. You can forget Takoradi."

"Yeah? Who says?" Barton asked.

"Baggy Bletchley. He told me they don't need ferry pilots for Takoradi any more. Someone found a bunch of ferry pilots. They fell down the back of a filing cabinet. Typical HQ cock-up. Anyway, that's not the point." He did his trick with the folding chair again.

"I don't want to hurry you, Uncle," Pip Patterson said, "but we've got an airfield to blow up."

"Exactly," Uncle said. "That's the thing. That's what all this strafing and bombing's been about. Fanny was going to get the chop."

"Oh, shit," Barton said wearily.

"You mean sacked?" Skull said. "Fired? Posted?"

"Another cock-up, obviously," Uncle said. "But Fanny foxed 'em, didn't you, Fanny?" Loyalty and friendship shone in his eyes. "We all knew the squadron would die without Fanny, so Fanny fixed it with Group that he could stay if we strafed like billy-ho, and . . . and . . ." Uncle looked at the little group. "And here we are."

"We few," Skull said. "We happy few."

"Sure, sure," Kit said. He was bored with all this talk.

"I had to tell you," Kellaway said, "because Fanny's too modest."

"For Christ's sake belt up, Uncle," Barton said.

"You foxed 'em," Kellaway said. "He foxed 'em," he told the others. He saw the doc approach, holding his stomach and wheezing. "You're not fit," he told him accusingly. "It's not Wednesday. How dare you wear suede boots in the face of the enemy?" He suddenly swung the folding chair at the doc's feet and whacked an ankle. The doc cried in pain and punched the adjutant in the mouth.

Kellaway ended up on his hands and knees, dribbling blood. "Take yourself off to your tent, you loony!" the doc roared. Kellaway crawled a few yards, then got up and walked.

"Was that strictly necessary?" Skull asked. "The poor chap's doolally."

"That's his bad luck," the doc growled. "I don't know how to treat insanity. I probably missed that lecture." He massaged his ankle. "I expect I was drunk or fornicating or playing rugby. Split lips are different, I went to that lecture, I know all about them. I'll do a grand job on his face, you watch. By the way, he knocked over our last bottle of rum, the idiot."

"Go and sock him one for me," Barton said. The doc limped away.

"I have to tell you this," Skull said. "There are two Luftwaffe fields within five minutes' flying time of Bir Dagnish. Abiar bu Seeia is west of it and Mechili is south. There must be at least ten more fields within fifty kilometres to the north."

"I know. We'll fox 'em." Barton signalled to his ground crew: start up.

The three pilots set off for their aircraft.

"Look what you've done to the squadron," Skull said. "This isn't going to win the war."

"War? What war?" Barton flung his arms out sideways, palms up, and turned in a full circle. "I don't see any war. This is just a bloody good scrap. What's it about? I don't know! And I don't care. I'll fight anyone who fights me." The Kittyhawk engines were coughing and crackling.

"It's not as simple as that," Skull said.

"It's *twice* as simple as that," Barton said, "but you wouldn't understand. Intelligence never understands. Go and cook something, Skull. Make us some nice angel cakes for tea."

From fifteen thousand feet the long olive-green hump of

the Jebel was soon visible. Hick Hooper gave his neck muscles no rest. He scanned the colossal sky like a young man whose girlfriend is late for a date, never tiring of the search. And in the end, when the hunt paid off, he felt the same lover's jolt of recognition. A flicker of silver glinted high above. "Hornet leader," he called. "Bandits five o'clock high." Barton raised a hand. Hick realised the CO had seen them long ago.

The Kittyhawks cruised on, in the formation which the RAF had borrowed from the Luftwaffe, the 'finger-four', so-called because the aircraft made the same pattern as the fingertips of an outstretched hand: Hooper, Barton, Patterson, Carson. Hick could not take his eyes off the enemy. The silver glints were falling, taking shape, growing tiny fins. Peculiar things happened to his body: his toes clenched, his hands prickled, the skin from his scalp to his neck crawled. He was frightened. This was the first time an aeroplane, several aeroplanes, five or six, had dropped out of the sky intent on killing him. He took his left hand off the throttle and punched himself in the face. Real pain drove out fear.

Kit Carson was muttering to himself: "Lumberjack, Lumberjack. Razorblade, Razorblade." They had practised this manoeuvre often enough. Me109s liked to dive, fire, break away, climb. Barton would fly straight and level. When the 109s reached a point four hundred yards behind the formation he would call, "Lumberjack, Lumberjack." Or "Razorblade, Razorblade." The first codeword meant break hard left, the second meant break hard right. L for left, R for right. Get it wrong and you'd fly smack into another Kitty.

Barton looked up and back and watched the 109s falling like swimmers in an endless swallow-dive. He could make out their camouflage: a spatter of colours called sand and spaghetti. Now he saw the shimmer of prop-discs. *Wait.* Dirty great cannons in the middle of those discs. One shell could knock a Kitty sideways. *Wait, wait, wait.* His head was pulled hard around to the right. *Wait.* His eyeballs were screwed up as far as they'd go. *Wait.* The trick was to break exactly one second before the enemy fired. *Wait. Wait.* Now! "Razorblade, Razorblade!" he shouted, and threw the machine into a steep right turn.

Everyone went with him. Pip had broken hard a thousand times before, but the bombs under the wings made the Kittyhawk fly like a runaway fairground ride, redoubling the centrifugal force until he felt as if something hideously heavy was being rammed down inside him and trying to thrust his guts out at the other end. But his foggy brain ordered his hands and feet to hold the turn as tight as possible. With those bombs under the wings, it was like trying to run while carrying suitcases. When he straightened out, the formation had completed a circle and the 109s had overshot, just as Barton had known they must. They were dots on the horizon, climbing.

The Kittyhawks pressed on, faster now. The 109s came at them again. Barton left it very late. He saw tracer before he called "Lumberjack, Lumberjack!" Again the 109s overshot, again the Kittyhawks covered more ground before the third attack was made. This time the 109s came down in a long, extended stream, and the last two had time to alter their dive and fire before they hurtled through the circle. It was the briefest of snap shots and they missed.

"Going down," Barton said. "Follow me, girls."

It was like Benina all over again. First a shallow dive, then a sight of the target, with its crossed runways looking like old sticking-plaster on the wrinkled terrain, then the nose steadily down and the speed steadily up. The Kittyhawk's controls usually responded to a nudge or a twitch; now they demanded a heavy boot and hard muscle. Gradually the finger-four spread apart. The 109s had vanished. At that speed their controls would have locked solid, as if cast in bronze. Not many 109 pilots had tried to catch a P-40 in a full-blown power-dive, and those who had tried too hard were so many stains on the desert floor.

Pip Patterson knew everything was wrong, long before Barton spoke. No flak. No tracer. No movement on the ground. Bir Dagnish was empty.

"Do not bomb," Barton said. "Do *not* bomb. Shit and corruption! Stay with me. We'll scrounge something."

They levelled out at four hundred feet above the hills, belting north, three hundred and fifty on the clock, black smoke streaming from the exhaust stubs. It was strange to fly over trees and bushes, fields, herds of sheep and goats. Hick even saw birds.

Barton flew with one eye on the Jebel while he read the map strapped to his thigh with the other.

The nearest Luftwaffe fields were on the coast. Apollonia, Cirene, El Qubba, Derna, many more. Barton didn't want to go near any of them. The 109 leader must have alerted their defences. The flak batteries would be waiting to pump their filth all over the sky. But Barton hated to jettison and run home.

The problem solved itself. A road came at them, twisting and curling, a big wide road, a tribute to Italian engineering, and thick with trucks. Barton whooped: the Martuba Bypass! Then it was behind them. He broke hard right and curled left in a wide turn that reversed their course. "Line astern," he said. "We'll clobber this convoy."

No need to worry about bomb-skip. Each bomb could skip all it liked: it still ended up on or near a target. Kit Carson, flying last in the line, saw trucks getting blown off the road, exposing their undersides in a curious slow-motion. Trucks charged into ditches and overturned. Trucks burned furiously. Trucks collapsed and skidded broadside into other trucks. It was like a monstrous mechanical temper-tantrum. Kit dropped his bombs and climbed to escape their shock waves.

Scramble klaxons must be blaring on nearby Luftwaffe

fields: Barton had no doubt of that. On the other hand it was difficult to track low-flying intruders over the Jebel. The hills fogged the German radar screens with permanent echoes, and the wadis offered escape routes in various directions. Barton guessed that the defence would expect him to take the shortest way out by flying north, over the Med, where there was no flak and he could wheel right and eventually swing back, behind the Allied lines. He planned to fox them by flying south and going out the same way he came in.

Barton guessed wrong.

The Kittyhawks were attacked as soon as they reached the desert. Four 109s came in on the left flank, firing from such a ridiculous range that Patterson knew the pilots were inexperienced. Their tracer fell away, wasted, as Barton hauled his formation squarely around to face them. *Turn and face, turn and face*: everyone had told Hick to turn and face an attack. They couldn't prepare him for the startling speed of the interception that followed. The 109s flashed past while he was still trying to get his guns on a target. All he could remember was a blur of wings and cockpits and spirals of smoke left by bullets. "Stick with me, Hornet Two," Barton said. Hick was grateful to follow his leader and guard his tail. That, at least, was simple.

For a while, both formations circled and climbed, winding themselves up to three or four thousand feet. Barton knew the 109s wanted height for their standard attack of dive, hit and run. He wanted height because he reckoned a dive would give the Kittyhawks the lead in the marathon sprint back to LG 250. The 109s would give chase, but a long pursuit deep into the desert would soon discourage them. The 109 was not at its best at ground level. At least that was what he hoped. His earphones filled with the roar of somebody else's cockpit noise. It was Kit Carson. "I'm in the shit, Fanny," he said. "The engine's overheating. The oil gauge is in the red. Christ, I can smell it!"

"Throttle back, throttle back," Barton told him; but Kit had already taken so much power off the engine that it was soon waffling along, at little above a stall. The 109s noticed and edged closer. "Can you land?" Barton asked.

"Will they let me?" Kit asked, and laughed. Bloody silly question. Dark smoke was streaming back from the engine.

"Try to land. We'll scare them away." But the enemy had seen their advantage and were making an attack. For a few seconds the sky was a flurry of twisting, chasing fighters around the one that slid as helplessly as a glider. Most of the 109s missed. One hit. Kit's tailplane was shredded. The Kittyhawk wallowed and skidded drunkenly. "That's it!" Kit shouted. "I'm baling out!"

"Stay near the wreck," Barton ordered. "We'll come back and get you."

Kit had never baled out before. He wanted now to do it fast, before the 109s returned and killed him. He released the canopy; it whirled away and bounced off the shattered rudder. The Kittyhawk hated that and threatened to stall. For an instant he panicked. But the Kitty recovered, and he did what he had done countless times. He raced through the ritual of the pilot who lands and gets out: a sequence as automatic and unthinking as unbuttoning his shirt. He unplugged the radio lead and he snapped out the oxygen tube. As one hand released the cockpit-straps, the other hand gave the parachute-harness buckle a quarter-turn clockwise and whacked it against his stomach. The four straps popped out. The Kittyhawk skidded and flung him sideways. Nothing held him secure: he felt naked. He knew what he had done and he shouted his despair. He snatched at the vanishing straps, hoping to shove their ends back in the buckle. Both leg-straps fell to the floor. As he groped for them he felt the shoulder-straps slide down his back, and this time he screamed at the stupidity of it all. The

Kittyhawk lurched and he grabbed the rip cord for no reason at all except it was the only bit of parachute left to grab. Then the aircraft rolled and out he went, snatching at the cord, hoping for a miracle. The silk streamed and blossomed with a soft bang. Kit Carson dropped away from it, still holding the metal ring.

It was four thousand feet to the desert. The empty parachute took more than twenty minutes to wander and drift all the way down. It spread itself a few hundred yards from Kit Carson. Three miles away, the wreck of his Kittyhawk was burning. More than a hundred miles away, Barton, Patterson and Hooper were coming in to land.

Barton told Skull what had happened: the good, the bad, and the inexplicably horrible. "At least we got the Luftwaffe off its backside," he said.

"I'll tell Wing," Skull said heavily. "Wing will tell Group, Group will tell HQ, and HQ will tell the whispering grass but the whispering grass won't tell the breeze 'cos the breeze don't need to know. Have I missed anything?"

"Was that meant to be a joke?" Patterson asked. His goggles had scored great rings around his eyes. They made him look fevered.

"I liked Kit," Skull said. "Kit was a good type."

"Yes," Barton said. "Got something tasty for supper?"

Supper was bully-beef stew. Afterwards Skull went off to his tent and wound the portable gramophone.

Empty guns, covered with rust,
Where do you talk tonight?
Empty saddles in the old corral
My tears would be dry tonight.
If you'd only say I'm lonely
As you carry my old pal –
Empty saddles in the old corral.

"Maudlin tosh," the doc said. "I wish he'd break it."

"I like it," Barton said. "Catchy tune."

* * *

The second day out from Kufra was not exciting. In the morning a few vehicles bogged down in soft sand and everything came to a halt while shovels and sand-channels were used to ease them onto hard ground. For Lester and Malplacket there was little to see and nothing to do. Corky Gibbon explained how a sun compass worked. It was interesting but Lester couldn't see any headlines in it.

Mike Dunn was getting his breath back after some hard shovelling when Sandiman strolled over to him. "You might as well know what was in the signal," he said quietly. "Can't do any harm now, can it?"

Dunn grunted agreement. There was sand in his ears.

"To tell the truth, I'm a bit worried," Sandiman said. "You see, the signal recalled Captain Lampard to Cairo immediately. I mean, it was a direct order."

They looked at the man. Lampard was laughing at something Sergeant Davis had said. He seemed completely at ease, utterly sure of himself. "Who from?" Dunn asked.

"Well, GHQ Cairo gave the order. The regiment sent the signal but GHQ want him."

"Could mean anything. Promotion, posting . . ." But Dunn knew that it would take more than that to turn the heavy wheels of GHQ and drag Lampard back to Cairo in mid-patrol. Sandiman knew it too.

"I think I recognised the ident for the source at GHQ where the signal originated," Sandiman said. "I think it was the Provost-Marshal's office."

Dunn picked up his shovel and gave the Sahara a couple of angry whacks. "It can't be that scrap at the Black Cat," he said. "They'd have to recall the whole patrol for that.

Anyway, since when did anyone give a damn what goes on at the Black Cat?"

"Thought you ought to know."

"The army always catches up with you," Dunn said. "Jack must know that." He wished Sandiman hadn't told him.

After the soft sand they had to negotiate an awkward stretch of rock. Erosion had sharpened its edges and although the drivers trundled gently in bottom gear, there were two punctures. While the wheels were off, Malplacket asked Dunn what would happen if enemy aircraft caught the patrol like this. Dunn said he supposed they would be killed. Malplacket stopped watching the sky.

On the third day, rocks gave way to serir. The patrol put on speed and cruised comfortably until noon, when Gibbon's sun compass lost its shadow and they stopped for lunch: pilchards, beetroot, cheese and pears, all out of tins. Henry Lester took his mess tin and sat next to Dunn. "This is flatter than Kansas," he said. "And I never thought I'd say *that*."

"Bloody good going."

"I feel like a bug on a tennis court. How much more?"

"A fair bit. Calanscio Serir's about two hundred miles long."

"That's like New York to Boston." Lester ate a bit of pilchard. "Anything interesting likely to happen?"

"Shouldn't think so." Dunn chewed as he thought. "Of course, the place to go for excitement is Benghazi. Well . . . Not *excitement*, perhaps, but . . . Benghazi's sort of different. So they say, anyway."

"Wait a minute. Benghazi . . . The Germans have Benghazi."

"Yes. Didn't stop Stirling and Churchill and Maclean having a dirty weekend there, not so long ago. You never heard? I thought everyone knew."

"I heard a rumour," Lester lied. "Tell me more."

Dunn told him. The Prime Minister's son, Randolph Churchill, had persuaded David Stirling to let him join an SAS patrol. Also in the party was a tough ex-diplomat called Fitzroy Maclean. Stirling's patrol drove into Benghazi with the aim of planting mines on enemy ships. The plan failed, but they bluffed their way past Italian sentries and walked the streets openly and freely. Then they drove out again.

"Wearing what?" Lester asked.

"British army uniform. Same as this. Nobody gave them a second glance, so they said."

"That's amazing."

"And on the way home, Stirling put the car in the ditch and they all ended up in hospital." Dunn laughed.

At the same time, Malplacket was talking to Gibbon. "Extraordinary terrain," he said, gesturing at its utter flatness. "Seemingly innocuous, rather like the open sea, yet who knows what menace lurks just over the horizon?"

"What, over there?" Gibbon aimed a chunk of cheese in the same direction. "Anyone who does any lurking over there is a damn fool. Over that horizon is the Sand Sea. Not a place to take your holidays."

"All the same, one feels oneself part of the English buccaneering tradition. Confounding the king's enemies by slipping ghost-like through these arid wastes as once our ancestors held sway over the high seas. The same blood throbs in your veins, surely?"

"Dunno about that. My family have been in the paint trade for generations."

"Ah." Malplacket drank some pear juice. "The Scarlet Pimpernel, perhaps? They seek him here –"

"Yeah, I saw the film, in Cairo. Leslie Howard. He was wearing *lipstick*. You could tell."

While the fuel tanks were being topped up and the tyres checked for damage, Lester took Malplacket aside. "Did you ever hear a story about Randolph Churchill walking through Benghazi? In British uniform? With Stirling and the rest of a patrol?"

"I believe Blanchtower may have mentioned it. Why?"

"*Why?* The Prime Minister's son, strolling around Benghazi? Being saluted by krauts and wops?"

"I suppose it has a certain style. Blanchtower said the Cabinet were quite amused when they heard."

"Hell of a story. *Hell* of a story."

Dunn made sure his jeep was ready to move and walked over to Lampard. "Well, I told him," he said. "It was like giving a lump of sugar to a horse. Now tell me why you told me to tell him."

Lampard shrugged. "Does it matter?"

"No, I'm just curious. Why didn't you tell him yourself?"

"Was he interested?"

"Fascinated. Nearly spilt his pilchards."

"Yes. I thought it might appeal to him . . . Thank you, Mike. Let's move on, shall we?"

The patrol drove northwards over the gravel plain all afternoon. Nothing changed except the power of the sun and the angle of the shadows it cast. The noise of engines never varied and there was a huge superabundance of utterly empty sky to look at. Lester and Malplacket had seen more than enough of it already. They dozed off.

At about four o'clock the vehicles drifted to a halt. Nobody got out, which was unusual. Lester and Malplacket stood up. Everyone was looking ahead, where a stick of black smoke stood on the horizon like a factory chimney.

Lampard sent Dunn and Trooper Peck in a jeep to reconnoitre. Everyone else had a brew-up and a rest.

Gibbon did some calculations, and then went in search of Lampard. He found him cleaning the interminable dust and grit from his tommy-gun. "There's something interesting you ought to see," Gibbon said.

Lampard followed him to his maps.

"There's nothing interesting for you to see," Gibbon said. "I just wanted to make an idiot of myself in private." He was quite serious.

"Is this about that signal I got at Kufra?"

Gibbon sighed. "I don't know, Jack. Maybe it is. Look: I'll tell you, and then you can tell me. Tell me to go to hell, if you want." He raked his fingers through his beard, which was already long enough to hide his expression. "I don't know where to start."

"Try the beginning." Lampard seemed completely composed.

"OK. The beginning was Harris. How he died. And where. Then Waterman. How *he* died, also where. And *when*, too, if it comes to that." Gibbon wasn't enjoying this, but he soldiered on. "All the details – precisely what killed them, and who saw it happen, if anyone."

"You've been talking to Captain Kerr."

"He's been talking to me," Gibbon said sharply.

"Of course. I apologise, Corky." Lampard made a crooked grin, irresistibly boyish. "I should know better. You don't get an MC by chatting with the adjutant, do you? Forgive me. So . . . Kerr wanted chapter and verse on our last patrol, did he? Well, he's entitled to play devil's advocate. After all, there's the little matter of decorations to be considered. Is that all?"

Gibbon looked at the horizon. It told him nothing. He felt the pressure to stop now, to say it was none of his business, but that would be a lie; it was the business of them all. "From the adjutant's questions," he said, "it was pretty obvious that the official version of the way Harris and Waterman died was a long way from the . . ." He was about to say *the truth*. "From the facts."

"Extraordinary," Lampard said, and cocked his head.

"Officially, it seems, Harris got stabbed by a sentry and Waterman got Stuka-ed."

"But that's ludicrous."

"You mean your report didn't say that?"

"Certainly not. Did the adjutant tell you it did?"

"Not in so many words, no. But –"

"Corky," Lampard said. "Forget it. Some arsehole in Cairo has garbled the whole affair. I expect a typist mixed up two separate reports from two different patrols. Anyway, it's all history. What matters is *now*. Agreed?"

Gibbon hesitated. This wasn't what he was good at; he was a navigator, for Christ's sake. "And that signal at Kufra?" he said.

"My little secret," Lampard told him, and winked. "Don't believe everything you hear. All is not what it seems."

Trooper Peck drove the jeep slowly and cautiously. He and Dunn made frequent use of their binoculars. After ten miles, they could see that the smoke came from a burning oil drum, and this was odd enough to make them even more cautious. It was Trooper Peck who noticed a wink of light from far to the west, the dying gleam of a chance reflection from a windscreen caught by the setting sun. They worked towards it and eventually picked out a sprinkle of dots on the horizon. They left the jeep and walked for an hour: a calculated risk that brought them five miles closer, near enough for their binoculars to reveal a cluster of trucks. The blaze of light behind the trucks washed out all detail.

* * *

Captain Lessing knew that placing a smoke marker for Jakowski to home in on was dangerous: anything that attracted Jakowski's men might attract others. But he had no choice. Captain di Marco had underlined what was already obvious, that Jakowski's navigation was a mess; and Lessing could think of no other way to help guide his commanding officer towards the rendezvous.

Meanwhile, he ordered more trenches to be dug and organised a permanent watch, one man guarding each side of the camp, changed every two hours. After sundown the change was every hour. Staring into the desert at night was wearying work. Even the best sentry lost concentration.

Lessing discussed tactics with Lieutenant Fleischmann. "What do we do if a British force attacks us?" he asked.

"By day? Let them get within range of our mortars and see how many trucks we can knock out, for a start."

"They may have mortars too."

"True. All right, we disperse our trucks and –"

"So now we've got no means of moving our mortars quickly, unless you intend to carry them on your shoulders at the double."

"No."

"The men would admire and respect your amazing devotion to duty."

"I think not, sir."

"Neither do I. So we keep a couple of trucks to enable us to shift our firepower. What if they attack at night?"

Fleischmann hunched his shoulders. "All depends," he said. "Do we know how strong they are?"

"Do they know how strong *we* are?"

They stared at each other, and suddenly both men laughed.

"If it's bigger than an armoured brigade it's not fair," Fleischmann said, "and I shan't play." They settled down to work out fields of fire for the heavy machine guns.

*   *   *

The burning oil drum was a mystery, and Dunn refused to guess at the identity of the trucks. Lampard spent ten minutes alone. When he came back he had decided to attack. There was total silence from the other officers.

"Nobody is cheering," he said.

432

"I just don't see the point, that's all," Gibbon said. "We know precisely where they are. I can steer us well clear of them in the dark. Even if they hear us they won't interfere. Not in the dark."

"There's no other SAS patrol in this area," said Sandiman, "but that doesn't prove it's Jerry, does it? And if it *is* Jerry and his radio op gets a message out, it'll be Stukas tomorrow, a pound to a penny."

Lampard tugged his left ear-lobe and looked at Dunn.

"You're the boss, Jack," Dunn said.

"You're against it too."

"Beda Fomm is our target."

"Oh, we'll hit Beda Fomm. I don't like the idea of a Hun ambush waiting for us on our way back." Lampard could see they were not impressed by this argument. "Besides, it's time the chaps had a bit of fun." That made Gibbon stare and Sandiman sniff, but Lampard didn't care. He had made up his mind. He sent for the men and began his briefing.

*　　*　　*

Lessing, Fleischmann and the senior NCO took it in turns to supervise the watch throughout the night. At four a.m. Fleischmann accompanied the new sentries as they replaced the old. Nothing had happened. The moon was down and the blackness was absolute.

The new sentry on the northern side was a twenty-one-year-old Berliner called Manfred. He took over the light machine gun, acknowledged Fleischmann's sharp reminder to stay alert, and for seven or eight minutes he did just that. Then his girlfriend Tania slid into his imagination as sweetly as she had once slid into his bed, and after that his military duty was always on the losing side.

Her real name was Hannah. Tania suited her much better. She was built like a dancer, but a dancer with real breasts instead of the flat blisters which most dancers had.

Manfred had first seen her in a leotard at the gymnasium where he trained, and it was her outspoken nipples that made him gasp. They gave point to breasts that were firm, neat and circular, like her buttocks. A little later he discovered a stunning pair of legs at one end and a delightful face at the other. Manfred was a shy, handsome boy, very good on the horizontal bars, but hopeless at making small talk with any goddess who had outspoken nipples, so he made friends with her brother, Adam, instead. Adam was a cheerful lad and very keen on table tennis.

Months passed. Manfred had been silently in love with Tania for so long that the pain was now part of his everyday life. One weekend his parents went away to attend a funeral and he arranged to stay at Adam's house. That was when Tania slipped into his room and into his bed and stole his virginity, using a combination of sweetness and savagery topped with a small packet of nitro-glycerine that sent skyrockets ricocheting between his ears. When he got his breath back she kissed him. To his amazement, he detected gentle affection. She was in love with him. What a brilliant coincidence!

He sat cross-legged on the sand, stroked the light machine gun, and remembered all the places where they had made love. In the summerhouse. In the attic. Deep in a pine forest, stark naked, while squirrels watched and an oblivious breeze made the tree-tops sigh. In a shower-cubicle, as the hot spray plastered their hair down and made her breasts squeak against his chest. On the back seat of her cousin's car. Under a bandstand in a deserted park. In a sleeping-bag. Behind somebody's garage. In a field of buttercups, rich tall yellow buttercups that gave her skin a buttery sheen. That had been a good one; she had said so, tucking an arm behind her head and looking at him with huge shared satisfaction. Manfred inhaled powerfully through his nose and held his breath while he stared at the stars and listened to the tiny howl of life in his ears. Corporal Pocock wrapped his left hand over Manfred's mouth and cut his throat so expertly that he died in a few seconds.

The sentry on the western side sat huddled in a blanket until the pressure on his bladder became uncomfortable. He draped the blanket over the machine gun and wandered away. Dunn found a shape that was fractionally darker than the darkness and was about to stab it when he heard a splash and a grunt of pleasure, so he backed off. The trickle ceased. The man returned, took some dates from his pocket and started to chew. Guided by the sound, Dunn moved in and whacked him on the head with a spring-loaded cosh. He caught the body at the armpits.

Pocock spent far more time listening than moving. In that way he found a man asleep in his blankets, gently lifted a blanket and pressed it over his face as he killed him with a stab under the ribcage to the heart. Or, if not the heart, the aorta. It was a big knife, and double-edged; it was bound to find something vital.

Dunn smelt the heavy aroma of diesel fuel and carefully traced it to a truck. A man was asleep in the back, snoring sporadically. Dunn tried to climb in. A chain rattled and he froze, right leg in mid-air. Now he could hear *two* sets of breathing. Too dangerous. He lowered himself, inch by inch. One of the men sat up and asked something in blurred and bleary German. "Uh-huh," Dunn muttered. He lost himself in the night and waited until his heart stopped kicking itself to death.

He moved again and his luck ran out. Somebody had a nightmare.

Lieutenant Fleischmann knew who it was. The same man had a nightmare every night at this time, more or less, so Fleischmann was ready for it. He was sitting in the cab of a truck. He switched on the spotlight, swung it towards the panicking screams and caught Dunn in the beam: black of face and bright of knife.

Dunn ran. Fleischmann shouted, chased Dunn with the beam and grabbed with his other hand at the Luger in his belt. He briefly caught Dunn, but Dunn was dodging like a rabbit and he vanished again. Fleischmann fired a shot in the air, then dropped the Luger so that he could switch on the headlights. Corporal Pocock opened the passenger door, leaned across and shot Fleischmann through the head.

At once there was machine-gun fire from the desert. It came from the south, five or six weapons, widely spaced, sending arcs of tracer pulsing towards the German unit.

Captain Lessing did a smooth job of organising the defence. He switched off the headlights and the spotlight. He told the rifles and light machine guns to cease fire: the enemy was out of their range. Then he stopped the heavy machine guns blasting away non-stop. Finally he got the mortar crew assembled. Nevertheless there was much shouting and dashing about; and enough enemy fire came ripping through the canvas hoods of the trucks and flinging up streaks of sand to make the scene very lively and noisy. One machine-gun crew had a stoppage; they were cursing softly and hitting the weapon. Corporal Pocock found a rifle and hid by the wheel of a truck. During the next rattle of fire, he shot both the crew in the back. For a moment nobody noticed. Then he heard shouts, orders, whistles. Two men scuttled across and dragged the bodies from the gun. Pocock briefly considered shooting them too. No. Not wise.

Captain Lessing had had a terrible thought. "What if that's Jakowski out there?" he said to the senior NCO. They were lying in a shallow slit trench.

"Why would Major Jakowski attack us?"

"Christ knows. Why would the British attack us? They could sneak past and be over the horizon long before dawn. Why look for trouble?"

"Major Jakowski always looked for trouble," the NCO said.

More tracer brightened the night. Dunn, lying on his stomach, saw a machine-gunner outlined only ten feet away. He raised his pistol and shot him. Then he shot his loader.

"What the hell was that?" Lessing demanded. "What maniac's using a pistol?" Before the NCO could answer there was a throaty bang: the mortar crew had fired. "Find out what range they're using," Lessing said. The NCO heaved himself up and ran. The mortar crew were reloading. One held a flashlight: mortars were tricky, and they had never operated at night before. As the loader dropped the shell in the tube and ducked away, Corporal Pocock shot him. The NCO saw the muzzle-flash. He knocked the flashlight to the ground and used his Schmeisser to spray the area where Pocock had been standing. One bullet took off Pocock's left kneecap and he collapsed. The NCO rammed on another clip and sprayed again. This time he hit Pocock in the throat and legs. He wasted a third clip, but then he was a good NCO. He always made sure.

Lessing heard the Schmeisser and it made no sense. He counted to three and sprinted to the radio truck. The operator was sitting inside, waiting for orders. "See if you can raise Jakowski," Lessing told him. "That may be Jakowski out there. Try him, call him up." The operator chose a frequency. The light over his set made it easy. Dunn crept to the door, shot Lessing, shot the operator, smashed the valves and called it a night.

He walked in a wide half-circle that took him back to Lampard's assault party. "Not many left," he said. In fact only the senior NCO and three men survived, one of them wounded. In the flat, tired twilight before dawn, the senior NCO surrendered.

The Germans buried their dead and the SAS buried Pocock. Most of the bodies went into trenches they had been running towards when Lampard's machine guns cut them down. The last shovel tidied the last grave as the sun swelled and floated clear of the horizon. Everyone ate breakfast, including Lester and Malplacket, who had been allowed to inspect the scene of the action.

"All I heard was a lot of shooting." Lester said. "What exactly happened here?"

"We infiltrated their position and shot them in the back," Lampard said.

"They were looking the other way, you see," Dunn explained. "Towards Jack."

"Well, now you've seen some action," Lampard said. "Is it any use to you?"

Malplacket hesitated. "To be absolutely truthful, I was hoping for more dash," he said. "More dash and pluck."

"You don't see David Niven playing the part of Pocock?" Lampard said. "Creeping up on German sentries and cutting their throats from ear to ear? No, perhaps not."

"What were these guys doing, out here in the desert?" Lester asked.

"I expect they were up to no good, just like us," Lampard told him cheerfully. "The difference is we're rather better at it, aren't we?"

*　　*　　*

Many people knew about Greek George. He could tell by the way other Arabs glanced when they met up with his Arabs. Many such meetings took place. The foothills of the Jebel seemed empty, but they gave a living to a great network of families, always on the move, always meeting and exchanging news. Greek George was no secret in the Jebel.

This did not worry him; after all, the Arabs had already shown him great kindness. In any case they knew he was planning to walk back to the Allied lines. One day they brought him a pair of desert boots, calf-length: probably taken from an Italian officer. Also an army water-bottle.

Sometimes German patrols passed nearby, on foot or in half-track personnel-carriers. George did exactly what the others did: he stood and watched. The more often it happened, the safer he felt. He was just another Arab.

*   *   *

Schramm's fears for Lessing's safety were not entirely wasted. They prompted General Schaefer's staff to signal Lessing and order him to report by radio twice a day, at six a.m. and six p.m. Jakowski's policy of radio silence was overruled.

When there was no six a.m. transmission, Colonel von Mansdorf telephoned Oberstleutnant Hoffmann and asked him to make a reconnaissance flight in the yellow Lysander. Hoffmann asked Schramm to come along and navigate.

"All right. Provided you tell Schaefer to go and piss in his hat."

"For the love of God!" Hoffmann said impatiently. "You're in a permanent temper nowadays, Paul. What is it? Piles?"

"No, it's worse than piles. It's the knowledge that I wasted so much time on that stupid wop bitch."

Later, as they were strapping themselves into the cockpit of the Lysander, Hoffmann said, "She may be a wop, and she may be a bit of a bitch, but she's not stupid."

"I don't care," Schramm said, "I don't care, I don't care."

"The more you say it, the less I believe it. And if you really think she's stupid, you're in bigger trouble than I thought. Anyway, that's your problem. Let's go."

The flight was routine.

Schramm had the binoculars on the little cluster of trucks as soon as it came out of the haze on the horizon. "Half of them have gone," he said.

Hoffmann made a wide approach and circled. "Nobody there," Schramm said, but Hoffmann could see that for himself. Then Schramm found the row of graves. Hoffmann landed.

Already the sun had baked the bloodstains black and cracked their surface like old paint. Weapons lay about, smashed and useless. Ammunition and empty cartridge-cases made small heaps.

"Nowhere to retreat," Hoffmann said, "and nothing to hide behind. A very short chapter in the history of war."

"This wasn't a chapter," Schramm said. "It wasn't even a paragraph. It wasn't even a footnote. It was a spelling mistake in a grammatical error in a footnote to a footnote that nobody's ever going to read anyway." He went off to count the graves.

They landed at Benina to refuel. While Hoffmann went to a telephone and called von Mansdorf, Schramm looked at the damage from the dive-bombing. Most of the craters had been filled but one was still being excavated. It was enormous. A young Luftwaffe pilot leaned on the barrier, looked down twenty feet and watched dirt being shovelled away from a sixteen-cylinder engine.

"This is the one that didn't get away," Schramm said.

"Yes sir."

"It comes to us all, in the end. I've just helped to bury a few friends. Not as deep as this, of course. I was a pilot once, you know." The other man glanced, and was polite enough to suppress his surprise. "Different war," Schramm said. "Just as messy, though. I'm surprised you feel the need to study the gruesome remains."

"Just killing time. Besides, it's only strawberry jam, isn't it?" He chewed at a bit of tough skin on a finger. "When you go in at full bore with a pair of bombs in your armpits, even the strawberry jam doesn't have any pips."

A sling of steel rope was being manoeuvred under the engine. A crane driver inched his machine nearer the crater.

"What do you fly?" Schramm asked.

"Gustavs, out of Beda Fomm." The Gustav was the 109G. "I'm just waiting to pick up a replacement."

He looks about sixteen, Schramm thought. Probably nineteen or twenty. Ruthless little thug. "Scored yet?" he asked.

The young man nodded. "Five confirmed kills. Two Hurricanes, a Blenheim and a couple of MC200s."

The crane revved, its cable tightened, the engine came out of the earth with a slow, wet, sucking sound, and gently revolved.

It was not unknown for the enemy to capture aircraft and fly them. Transports usually, not fighters; but anything was possible in war. Schramm pulled a splinter off the barrier and tossed it in the pit. "That's an Italian machine," he said, "the MC200."

Again the young man nodded. "Their *squadriglia* gave us some grief. They jumped a bunch of our Gustavs and shot holes in them. Deeply apologetic. Poor visibility, mistaken identification. They thought we were Spitfires. Next day, *we* jumped *them*. Two down in flames. Problem solved."

The crane had hauled the engine up to ground level. "Excuse me," Schramm said, and walked around the crater. Men were hosing dirt off the twisted metal. He soon saw what he was looking for: the manufacturer's name, Allison. That meant it had to be a P-40. The hose washed off something that was not dirt.

*   *   *

The adjutant went over to Kit Carson's tent and cleared it out. That didn't take long. He put Kit's belongings on his bedroll and rolled everything up. Everything except his notebook. Kellaway sat on the folding bed and let the notebook fall open.

The CO ran away from home when he was a kid, so Mick O'Hare says. Uncle told him. Mick ran away from home too. I know Tiny Lush and Billy Stewart got kicked out of school, like me, except I got kicked out twice. Pinky was an orphan, at least that's what he says, but you can't believe everything Pinky tells you. Sneezy and Greek George are like refugees, so most of the squadron has no home to go to. Makes you think. Dunno what it means, but it makes you think.

Kellaway skipped a few pages.

Big joke. Butcher force-landed in the desert and got his Tomahawk towed back to the LG by a couple of camels. Turned out he needn't have force-landed anyway. He forgot to switch over fuel tanks, so he thought he ran out of petrol when he didn't. Butcher reckoned he deserved a gong but Fanny fined him two weeks' pay for being such a berk. Butcher said it cost him a month's pay to hire the camels. Fanny asked the Arabs to give the money back, in exchange for an IOU they could take back to Desert Air Force HQ. The Arabs said OK, they'd give the money back, but only after they'd towed the Tommy with Butcher in it back where they'd found it. Big joke.

Kellaway skipped some more.

Billy Stewart sits outside his tent and watches flies. Why?

And some more.

Dreamt about T. I wish he'd go away. It's over a year since he bought it. Everyone knew he was going to buy it, he was such a bloody awful pilot. Poor bugger.

He skimmed to the last entry.

Uncle's gone doolally again. I suppose that's what happens when you get old. Not for me, I hope.

It was Kit's last entry. Kellaway discovered that his eyes were crying. He was not overwhelmed with grief for Kit, but evidently his eyes felt otherwise. He let them cry, wiped his face, picked up the bedroll and the notebook and trudged off to see the doc.

"Next time I go batty," he said, "kick me out."

"All right. It's only the desert, you know."

"I know."

"If you spend too long in the blue and you don't go mad, there's something seriously wrong with you."

The adjutant thought about that. "Billy Stewart used to spend all his spare time watching flies," he said.

"He did indeed. Come on, we'll take ourselves over to the mess. The Bombay brought some beer in."

Supper that night was fried eggs and potatoes, also flown in on the Bombay.

"Why did Billy Stewart watch flies all day?" the adjutant asked.

"He was exercising the muscles of his eyes," Barton said. "He reckoned that if he could count the corns on the feet of a fly at ten paces, he could easily spot a 109 at five miles."

"Billy had terrific eyesight," Pip said.

"He was a good type."

"I've been thinking about Kit," Pip said.

"Any beer left?" Hick asked. Barton tossed him a tin.

"What about Kit?" the adjutant asked.

"I watched him fall. It was all wrong. The parachute popped open, but he kept going. It didn't check him at all. Ever heard of a parachute strap breaking?" Nobody had. "They're made to carry an elephant."

"Maybe the buckle bust," Hick suggested.

"Buckle's twice as strong," Barton said. "Two elephants couldn't bust a buckle."

"I think he undid it," Pip said.

There was silence while the pilots reviewed the routine of leaving a cockpit, of leaving it in a tearing hurry, of the flurry of acts while smoke gushed by, the kite skidded, the enemy squirted tracer and panic made the hands accelerate.

"Force of habit," Pip said.

"Look," the doc said to Skull, "I hope you're not going to play that bloody dirge again tonight."

"'Empty Saddles'?" Hick said. "National anthem of the American West."

"The potency of the homely metaphor," Skull said, and sang:

> Empty boots covered with dust,
> Where do you walk tonight?
> Empty guns covered with rust,
> Where do you talk tonight?

"You can't beat the simple declarative sentence in English prose," he said. "It goes right back to Chaucer."

"I wish it would," the doc said grimly. "I'd pay its bloody fare."

*   *   *

There were some good vehicles in Lessing's camp. Jack Lampard picked out two Mercedes-Benz and a Fiat, all of them tough-looking trucks with fat tyres and reinforced springs, and had them loaded with German fuel, water and food. Lester saw what was going on and came over. "Risky, isn't it?" he said. "We might get shot up by the Desert Air Force."

"They'd shoot us up if these were Swiss ambulances," Lampard said. "They shoot up anything they see."

"Bastards."

"Tell you what," Lampard said. "If they shoot us up, we'll shoot 'em down. That'll make a good story, won't it?"

Malplacket had been less than honest with Lester about his knowledge of Randolph Churchill's weekend in Benghazi. Before Malplacket left England, Blanchtower had made it very clear to his son that this was an example of

444

the kind of daring that he expected him to uncover in the Middle East. "It's all part of the English buccaneering tradition, Ralph," he told him. "Just as our ancestors held sway over the high seas, so Randolph and Fitzroy slipped ghost-like through those arid wastes."

"You're looking awfully tired, father," Malplacket said, hopefully. "You're not overdoing things, are you? At your age —"

"Pluck and dash. That's what the man in the street wants. That's what Winston wants."

"Mmm."

"Confusion to the king's enemies."

"Well, I'll try. That sort of thing's bound to be awfully hush-hush."

"Of course it is. No rose without a thorn. You must take risks. Don't think of me. Britain is at war. Your life is a sacrifice I must be prepared to make, if necessary."

"I see."

"Pluck and dash, Ralph. The blood of English buccaneers throbs in your veins, remember."

Malplacket had agreed enthusiastically because he knew he would never be expected to duplicate Randolph's mad exploit. Now, however, that was what Lester constantly talked about. The idea of strolling around Benghazi obsessed him. Lampard wouldn't take them on a raid, but to walk around a German-occupied city was a far better story. He discussed it with Dunn. Then he came back and discussed that discussion with Malplacket, who could not be as discouraging as he wished, but who played devil's advocate. The major obstacle, he pointed out, was transport. Lampard would never give them a jeep.

"We could walk," Lester said stubbornly.

"My dear fellow, we could skip, hand in hand, singing quaint old English folk songs as we went. But it will probably be twenty-five miles there and the same distance back. When did you last walk fifty miles?"

Lester grudgingly agreed that walking was out of the question; but this setback only made him more determined. The rasp of triumph was in his voice when, in the aftermath of the firefight, he found Malplacket doing a little looting and he said, "Did you know that Lampard's taking some of these kraut trucks? You realise what that means?"

Malplacket was trying on various German hats. He looked inside a soft, peaked cap, much worn. "A Hauptmann Lessing owned this ... No, I don't. What does it mean?" He had found Lessing's mirrored sunglasses on the ground, beside the cap. He tried them on and gazed invisibly at the American.

"For one damn thing," Lester said, annoyed by Malplacket's blandness, "it means if we bump into any Beaufighters you'll never become Lord Blanchtower the Second."

"Fifth, actually."

"Whatever. And more important, it means if I can find a truck that works, we've got transport into you-know-where. Also some German clothing to wear."

Malplacket tried on the cap. "Just a hint of the Chelsea Arts Ball, don't you think? But I'll take it. Have you asked Lampard?"

"On my way now. You'd better come too."

Thus it was that Malplacket, without ever being given the luxury of making a choice, tacitly agreed to go with Lester to Benghazi. *Why am I getting involved in anything so foolhardy?* he wondered. *Is it to please Blanchtower? Or is it to spite him, since the odds are that I shall be shot as a spy, leaving him with neither a son nor a propaganda victory? Is it that I can't abandon Lester? Or has Lester manipulated me into this recklessness, like a schoolboy dare?* As he trudged through the African heat, polishing Lessing's sunglasses with his shirt tail, Malplacket felt that perhaps the real reason was that he simply didn't care. His life had gone on long enough. It was an overcrowded planet. Time to step aside.

He listened while Lester told Lampard what they planned to do, and what they needed. "I assume you're taking your patrol into the Jebel. During your operation, whatever it is, we can be doing a Churchill and Maclean in Benghazi. We get what we want. From your point of view, if we're killed or captured you're not responsible, and you'll be free of us. If we get out, we just tag along behind you until you get home, and we vanish. I sort of fancy that olive-green Fiat station-wagon over there."

"Bloody dangerous." Lampard's voice was as blank as his face.

"You reckon? Listen, if Malplacket walked through Cairo dressed like that, what would happen?" Lester tipped Lessing's cap to a more rakish angle.

"He'd get a few salutes and lots of offers of dirty postcards."

"There you are, then."

"I'll think about it."

He thought about it for five minutes. "All right," he said. "Take the station-wagon. But I want something in return. I'm not having my career prejudiced just because you two go playing silly-buggers in Benghazi. If you get killed, and I think you will, that affidavit of yours must be destroyed, unopened. I want a letter to that effect, to your lawyer. Tell him to burn the bloody thing, in my presence."

"I'll do it now."

"Do it later. We're leaving now." Lampard climbed onto his jeep. "Start up!" he shouted.

He had put the prisoners in the captured vehicles. The patrol drove in a widely scattered formation in case Stukas arrived from the north. But no aircraft appeared. Gibbon navigated them through the Jalo Gap during the midday haze, and they crossed the Tariq el 'Abd in late afternoon. Lampard was pleased. He found a familiar wadi on the edge of the Jebel and they camouflaged the trucks with camel-thorn. They had covered the best part of two hundred miles without incident, without even a puncture. The men walked back towards the desert, smoothing out the tyre tracks with bunches of fern. There was rum and lime-juice for everyone. "I can smell Hun," Lampard said. His whole nervous system felt boosted.

"That's jolly useful," Malplacket said. "What does it smell like?"

"Hard cheese," Lampard said instantly. It wasn't a joke; he just said the first thing he thought of; yet it made them laugh, so he smiled and took the credit. They were good men, his patrol. For an instant his tired mind strayed, and he wondered why Pocock wasn't present. Then he remembered. Hard cheese on Pocock.

*   *   *

Paul Schramm was not forty-four. He was twelve, and naked, and running to catch a train that might leave at any second. The station was crowded and he was horribly ashamed of his nakedness, but all his clothes were on the train. He kept shouting at everyone to get out of his way. Nobody listened. The harder he ran, the slower his legs moved. He had to force each pace. Then, to make it worse, he couldn't run straight because his left leg was too short. He was struggling, the train was leaving, and now the station was deep in a thick, syrupy fluid that trapped his legs and made him wade laboriously, exhaustingly. That was when he found the knife in his hand. It hadn't been there before, but now he had it and he struck out at the idiots who wouldn't get out of his way because they didn't care, they weren't going to catch the train, they were too ugly to go anywhere. So he hacked and stabbed and slashed furiously with his rubber knife, and he was helpless, useless because his wrists were firmly held by Benno Hoffmann.

Later, much later, after his batman had given him a wet towel to rub his face and body, followed by a dry towel and fresh pyjamas, and had stripped the bed of the sweat-soaked sheets and remade it, and had finally gone away, Schramm stopped trembling. He summoned up all his twelve-year-old strength and asked: "What time is it?"

"Four-forty," Hoffmann said.

"Oh." Schramm took a deep breath, so deep that his chest shuddered when he let it out. "Christ, that was a madhouse. I've never been *there* before. Did I get you out of bed?"

"That's all right, I had to get up. Somebody was having a nightmare. I could hear it all the way down the hall."

"I couldn't catch the train. I was wading in blood." He gave Hoffmann a sorry smile. "What a feeble cliché: wading in blood. I ought to do better than that, at my age." Then he remembered how young he had been, and he got the shakes again. His face seemed to cringe; the skin felt as if it were being touched by fine cobwebs.

Hoffmann put a blanket round his shoulders. "You look like a wreck," he said. "Feel free to cry, if it helps."

"I haven't got the strength to cry. I might manage a drink."

They each had a stiff Scotch. The RAF had left quite a lot behind when they made their hurried exit from Barce, but Hoffmann was running low and he saved it for special occasions.

"What a total madhouse," Schramm said.

"You're not the first, you know. I've been on bases where the pilots' quarters sounded like an audition for the Berlin Opera. Get into bed before you spill that."

Schramm slept late. He awoke with a slight headache and a keen appetite, a very unusual combination for him. He showered and shaved. When he walked to the mess his muscles ached pleasantly, as if he had climbed a small, simple mountain. The dream was sharp in his mind. Its memory retained a tinge of panic and fury.

He was making steady headway through his paperwork, letters to be answered, forms to be completed, telephone calls returned, when a corporal tapped on his door. Station commander's compliments, and could Major Schramm spare him a few minutes?

This was all very formal. Usually Benno just picked up the phone, or strolled down the corridor. A sudden dread took Schramm by the throat. Enemy bombers raided Benghazi harbour every night. Maybe last night they missed and hit somewhere else. He buttoned his tunic.

It wasn't the bombing, thank God. It was Colonel von Mansdorf, sipping Hoffmann's coffee and looking more than ever as if he had shrunk a little in the wash and then been immaculately starched and pressed.

"I'm here to apologise, major," he said. "On behalf of General Schaefer, but also for myself. You were right and we were wrong. I'm sorry."

Schramm nodded. He wanted to smile with relief, but he made himself look sombre.

"Goodbye, Jakowski," Hoffmann said.

"A couple of his men turned up at Jalo," von Mansdorf said. "They were the lucky ones: they'd been driving a truck and a water-tanker. The rest seem to have scattered all over the Sahara. We know about the problem with the compasses, but even so . . ." He shrugged. "Africa wins again, I'm afraid."

"It wasn't Africa that killed Lessing and his men," Schramm said.

"No. They were overwhelmed by a superior force."

"Major Schramm has been tracking an incoming SAS patrol," Hoffmann said.

"I have agents in Cairo and Kufra," Schramm said. "I know where that patrol was, and when. The timing is right for the attack on Lessing."

"Of course there's more than one British patrol skulking about," von Mansdorf said. "A maximum of five or six, so I'm told. Some coming, some going, some just snooping."

"We have a special interest in this one," Hoffmann said. "It's that same lot that hit Barce. Led by a man called Lombard."

"Lampard," Schramm said. "He's back in the Jebel, I'm sure of it."

"That's like saying he's in Belgium. The Jebel goes a long way."

"He'll come here. I know him, I met him, I made a fool of him. He'll come here just to get even."

"Perhaps you'd like to see our new airfield defence system, colonel," Hoffmann said. He made a couple of quick phone calls, and they all went downstairs to his car. As they drove around the perimeter, he said, "We began with a trip-wire rigged up to sentries in the cockpits, but our Engineering Officer dreamed up an improvement." He stopped near a line of 109s. "Here is a bomb." He handed von Mansdorf a pocket German-Italian dictionary. "You are this British desperado, Lombard. It is black night. Do your worst."

"Lampard," Schramm said.

"Relax, Paul. They both look the same in the dark."

Von Mansdorf walked towards the fighters. Hoffmann and Schramm followed, a short distance behind. "No sentries?" von Mansdorf asked. "No dogs?"

"Not needed," Schramm said.

"Intriguing." He was about twenty-five yards from the nearest 109 when a machine gun shattered the quiet with its explosive stutter. Red-and-yellow tracer flicked gracefully in a high arc that cleared the nearest 109 and fell to earth in a deserted part of the airfield. The racket startled von Mansdorf and he jumped back. The gun stopped. "Step forward again," Hoffmann said. Von Mansdorf did so, cautiously, and the gun barked as if he had stood on its tail. He stepped back. It stopped. Now he could see it,

451

tucked away behind sandbags. "Infra-red beam," he said. "That's clever."

"Pure black magic," Hoffmann said. "It baffles me. Paul understands it, though."

"We installed a series of beams so that they each made a box round the aeroplanes," Schramm said. "Each beam is electrically linked to a machine gun whose line of fire is about a foot above the beam. Break the beam and it shoots you. Fall down and it stops."

"For demonstration purposes," Hoffmann said, "the line of fire has been slightly adjusted."

"I'm grateful. And impressed."

They strolled back to the car. "It can be switched off during the day," Schramm said, "so it doesn't interfere with operations. The trouble with the trip-wire was you had to rig it and de-rig it every dusk and dawn. And people kept snapping it."

"One small point," von Mansdorf said. "I take it you intend to allow the raiders to approach the aircraft."

"An airfield is virtually impossible to seal off at night," Hoffmann said. "It would take a regiment to guard the perimeter. Two regiments. We've never had enough barbed wire. Frankly, I've given up on wire. Since the enemy is going to get in anyway, and since we know his object is to plant bombs on the aircraft, this is a simple way of killing him in the act."

"I congratulate you."

They drove von Mansdorf back to Hoffmann's office. While they were waiting for his car to arrive, he said: "By the way: I met a friend of yours last night. Dr Grandinetti. We were guests at a dinner party." Schramm said nothing. He flicked at a fly that was annoying him. "A brilliant surgeon, so I'm told," von Mansdorf remarked.

"She gets results," Schramm said. "She definitely gets results."

They watched the car drive away. "Take some leave,

Paul," Hoffmann said. "It's overdue, you're falling apart, I can get you a place on a plane this afternoon, you'll be skiing in Austria tomorrow. Get out of here."

"Not now. Too much to do."

"Says who? Come back in three weeks, nothing will have changed. Believe me."

Schramm shook his head. "Too much to do," he said.

* * *

Lampard had four hours' sleep and got up at midnight. He left Dunn in charge and set off with Sergeant Davis in one of the captured trucks. If they failed to return by noon, Dunn was to take command.

Corky Gibbon watched them go. "Let's talk," he said to Dunn. They went and sat in the station-wagon, with the doors shut. The leather seats were cool and comfortable, there was sand on the floor and the sweet memory of hot diesel in the air. It reminded Dunn of being driven home from the seaside when he was a boy. "Sandiman told me what was in that signal," Gibbon said.

"Me too."

"I asked Jack about it."

"What did he say?"

"Not much. Tried to laugh it off. That bothers me, Mike. It shouldn't be any of my business, so why didn't he tell me to go and run up my thumb? And another thing. The adjutant —"

"Harris and Waterman. I got cross-examined too."

"Jack's report of that patrol was all balls," Gibbon said. "You know and I know that Harris got killed because of a cock-up, and as for poor old Waterman . . ."

"God alone knows what Jack thought he was up to then," Dunn said flatly.

"On the bloody spree, that's what he was up to. On the razzle."

Dunn was silent. He remembered Lampard on Barce airfield, collecting unused bombs as the pencil-fuses burned, seeking fresh targets, manic, unstoppable, when he should have been leading everyone back to the Jebel at high speed. He'd got away with it then. Jalo had been the same sort of lunacy only far more needless, and in broad daylight too; and Waterman had paid the price.

"Oh well," he said. "The adj saw through him, didn't he? Clever bloke, the adj. Nothing we can do about it now." He was feeling sleepy. Gloomy talk usually did that to him.

"It's your neck," Gibbon said. "It's your funeral."

"Meaning what?"

"I think the man's an addict. He's got to have his dose of glory. If anything goes wrong, if he cocks it up, he's got to have a double dose. He made a cock-up over Harris and that's why he took us into Jalo, chasing the Luftwaffe, for God's sake."

"It might have worked." But there was no passion in Dunn's loyalty.

"So now he's got two cock-ups to make up for. What's worse, he lied about them and he got found out. That's *three* cock-ups. What d'you think he'll do next?"

"Hit Beda Fomm," Dunn said. "As ordered. What else can he do?" Gibbon merely shook his head. "He's the CO, Corky. What he says, goes."

"I think his brakes have failed," Gibbon said. "I think he can't stop himself."

* * *

It was at least fifty kilometres to Beda Fomm and the first twenty-odd would be over twisting, dipping tracks, so Lampard drove with the headlights on. He knew this part of the Jebel fairly well. It was likely that there were enemy patrols about, so the faster he moved, the better. This was like dashing through a rainstorm to miss the drops: it wasn't logical, it didn't always work, but what was the alternative?

They came out of the last slopes of the Jebel without having alarmed anything more than a couple of herds of goats.

The plain south of Benghazi was criss-crossed with farm tracks and camel trails. Lampard let Davis drive, while he tried to pick out a route towards Beda Fomm. Twice they almost blundered into military camps – first an infantry unit, to judge by the sea of tents, and then a squadron of tanks, black and motionless as cattle – and each time Davis had to back out. An hour of this wandering wore out Lampard's patience. He could hear the rumble of heavy traffic only a few kilometres away. He aimed for the noise.

Davis found the coast road. It was busy. They waited until a long column of supply trucks roared by southbound; then Davis accelerated hard, slammed briskly through the gears, and added himself to the end of the line.

The column drove fast. After seven or eight minutes, Davis shouted and pointed to the right. Lampard saw an Me110 dimly illuminated in the shielded lights of a vehicle. Men moved, as flat as shadows. Probably a nightfighter, probably being serviced. "That must be Al Maghrun," Lampard said. "Beda Fomm's about ten kilometres, on the left." But as he spoke, the column slowed down. And stopped.

Checkpoint.

Up ahead, flashlights flickered alongside the leading vehicle. Hurricane lamps, striped barriers, machine guns on tripods. Davis began to reverse. "Hang on, hang on," Lampard said. He jumped down. The truck in front had a red lamp hooked to its tail-gate. He removed it and hooked it on the back of his own truck. "That makes us official," he told Davis. "Now let's see if they check everyone or just the leader of the band."

The column moved off, and it was still picking up speed as the tail-end vehicle went through the checkpoint. Lampard waved slackly at a guard who was counting the trucks. "Pick the bones out of that, Hans," he said.

Davis saw a turn-off where Beda Fomm ought to be and he drove down it. He parked and killed the engine. A wind had got up, bringing a strange, sharp smell. Davis took a good sniff. "Margate sands," he said. "Bank holiday." It was the smell of the sea.

The soil was sandy and it seemed to grow nothing but stunted pines and needle-sharp cactus. Lampard was convinced he knew which way the airfield lay, but after walking for forty minutes the night was still full of pines and cactus; and the slow, shuffling pace of their progress had become wearying. What's more, dawn wasn't far off.

"Stop," Lampard said. "Chocolate." He broke off two big chunks and gave one to Davis. As they stood and ate, a double row of warm yellow lights sprang into life and illuminated Beda Fomm. The perimeter was only fifty yards away. It was like a gift from the gods. The lights were runway beacons. After a while a Junkers Tri-Motor dropped out of the darkness and touched down. The beacons went out, but as the Junkers taxied to its arrival area the pilot used a spotlight, and the spotlight swept over a flock of 109s, widely dispersed.

On their way back, the captured truck broke down in the Jebel. Lampard and Davis hid it and walked home. They reached the camp just after eleven a.m., soaked in sweat, and ravenous. "Beda Fomm's on," Lampard told Dunn. "Briefing at sixteen-thirty, then we eat, then we go." He looked around. "Where are the prisoners?"

"Gone. Sandy managed to signal an LRDG patrol that's going home and they said they'd take the prisoners provided we threw in a case of tinned pears, so we did."

"Commercial travellers," Lampard said. "What else can you expect?"

*   *   *

Fanny Barton surprised Skull by asking him to select an enemy airfield for the next dive-bombing attack.

"Why?" Skull said. "You've always picked your own targets. What's happened? Writer's block? Brewer's droop? Dropped your crayons?"

"I just thought you ought to earn your pay."

"I see." Skull searched the CO's face and found nothing but serious intent. "There is no suitable target for three Kittybombers," he said. "Not unless you count the field at Berka, which is very handy for the British War Cemetery outside Benghazi."

"You'll find something. If there's nothing suitable, give me the least unsuitable. Teatime OK?"

Skull went off to his tent and fished out his maps. He read all the latest intelligence bumf that had come in on the Bombay. The Luftwaffe had plenty of airfields and thickets of flak batteries around each of them. How could men fly into targets like that? And yet he knew that Pip Patterson and Hick Hooper would follow Barton without hesitation, wherever he led. He knew they were conscious of the danger: he had seen fear in their eyes, during the pre-op briefings. Nevertheless, as combat approached, the pilots became intensely alive in a way that Skull could always recognise but never understand.

The doc appeared in the tent doorway and sat on his haunches. "I'll give you five English pounds for that mawkish bit of sentimental slush," he said. "This isn't a joke. I don't make jokes on such a lavish scale."

Skull picked up the gramophone record of 'Empty Saddles'. "This?"

"It's rancid. The very words make me retch."

"I like it. This is the voice of the common man you hear."

"It's a godawful dirge. We can't avoid the dying but do we have to put up with the dirge?"

"The pilots like it too. Ask them. Ask Fanny."

The doc's face twisted as if he had toothache. "Play something else, can't you? What's on the other side?"

Skull turned the record over. "'I'm Headin' For the Last Round-up'," he said. "Another gem."

The doc snatched the record from him and smashed it on his knee. "I should have done that long ago," he said harshly. He turned and walked away.

*　　*　　*

What convinced Greek George was his reflection. One day the serious little girl brought him a small mirror, much cracked. It was the rear-view mirror from an aeroplane. Not his own. Wrong shape. For the first time since the crash he could see what he looked like. He looked like an Arab. The sun had burned him black and his hair, which was naturally black, was matted and tangled. He had a long nose, slightly bent in the crash, and hollow cheeks which seemed to push his cheekbones up. George was amazed at how Arabic he looked and he decided it was time to leave.

The old man was not happy when George got his message across. There was a lot of rapid talking amongst the party. The old man came back. He used some of the simple words that George had learned, plus some mime and a few symbols drawn in the sand. What it added up to was: not yet. Too many German patrols. Too risky. George nodded, and the serious little girl nodded too. Why take chances? There was time. When God made time, He made plenty of it.

*　　*　　*

"About your affidavit, old chap."

"I've given him the letter."

"I know, but . . . Did you use an Egyptian or an English lawyer?"

"Who cares?"

"The point is, Egyptian affidavits aren't recognised by a British court-martial."

"OK, so my lawyer was Anglo-Egyptian. Guy named Kelly, Muhammed Kelly, very smart fellow. Satisfied?"

On the other side of the camp, one of the cooks was singing *We'll meet again, don't know where, don't know when* . . .

"There never was an affidavit, was there?"

"Just shut up about it. What Lampard doesn't know won't hurt us."

"I merely asked, old chap. Merely asked."

*   *   *

Paul Schramm was a fair man. He gave other people the same chance that he gave himself, which was one chance and no more. Either you succeeded or you failed. When he failed, he condemned himself. When people failed him, he wrote them off. He had written off Dr Maria Grandinetti. She had let him down and so, in his mind, he had wiped her out: eliminated all emotional value she might have had for him. An act of destruction like that was not achieved without heat, and after she had told him, with such appallingly casual frankness, that she had ended the life of Kurt Debratz and several other casualties, Schramm's rage had been intense. Now he believed it had burned itself out. He could walk away from her. Limp away, at least. If he felt frozen, that was just what you would expect when rage went cold. It came as no surprise. It was an old, familiar feeling.

Meanwhile, thank God, there was work to be done.

In the middle of reading a thick report on the Allied jamming of Luftwaffe radio frequencies and Luftwaffe countermeasures to evade such jamming, he suddenly thought of the Takoradi Trail again. Why drive? he asked himself. Just because the SAS drive everywhere, must we always copy them?

He pulled down some technical volumes and checked some figures. He found a large-scale map of the Sahara and studied it. Then he telephoned Captain di Marco.

"Suppose we put extra fuel tanks in a Heinkel one-eleven bomber," he said, "and flew it at its most economical cruising speed, would that put the Takoradi Trail within its range?"

"It depends. From where to where, exactly?"

"From an airfield near Benghazi to . . . um . . . Fort Lamy in Chad."

Schramm heard the faint swish of an overhead fan as di Marco thought about it. "Probably yes," di Marco said. "In fact definitely yes." Exultation worked on Schramm like a strong drug. "Of course the machine would not be able to bomb Fort Lamy when it got there," di Marco said, snatching the drug away.

"Why not?"

"Because if you were to add bombs to such a load of fuel, the machine would be too heavy to take off."

"Oh." Schramm felt foolish. "I should have thought of that."

"There is an alternative. It would mean establishing a landing-ground deep in the desert, for instance at Defa. The Heinkel could refuel there. That would save weight. There has been a landing-ground near Defa in the past. I have used it."

"Look," Schramm said, "I have no authority to ask this, but would you be willing to act as navigator? If I can get a Heinkel?"

"I might."

"It would be something, wouldn't it? If we could bring it off."

Di Marco did not comment. "It would be best if I spoke to Colonel von Mansdorf, I think," he said. Schramm agreed. "Bear in mind," di Marco added, "that I have no authority either, and that General Schaefer may not be in the mood to take risks. The last risk he took did not pay off particularly well, did it?"

Schramm tried to get back to work on Allied jamming. He was not a radio expert, but it was important for anyone in Intelligence to understand at least the basics of all things connected with air combat. He slogged on through the report and he was skimming its conclusions when the phrase *garbled signal* tripped a circuit in his brain and abruptly swamped his memory with the desperate struggle to wade through a bloody-minded railway station for a train he could never catch. The whiff of desperation was so strong that he had to put down the book, get up, walk around the room. The scene was as sharp and clear in his mind as a film in a cinema, a black-and-white film, because the train was white. All white. An all-white train.

He went down the corridor to the lavatory and washed his face. Something felt wrong: either the water was too slippery or his skin was oily; whichever it was, his hands seemed remote from his face. He went back to his office and wrote *Hospital train* on a piece of paper. The only white train he had ever seen had been a hospital train. Why had he been so hell-bent on getting on a hospital train? He tore up the paper and burned the scraps in an ashtray. He threw the ashes out of the window. He put the ashtray inside a desk drawer. He was thinking of washing his hands when he heard a faint flicker of laughter that made him stop breathing. It came from somewhere in the building and it could not possibly be anyone but Dr Grandinetti.

It was not repeated, and soon his lungs demanded more air. He was excited — by fear, anger, delight, revenge? He

461

didn't know which. Maybe some, or all, or none; maybe something else altogether. It was foolish to stare at a wall, so he went into the corridor. Empty. He ran to one end and listened hard. Nothing. He ran to the other end. Someone's telephone rang. Someone answered it. Otherwise, the day was a vacuum.

The outside doors swung open and Max came in. "Hallo!" he said. "We tried to find you but you weren't in your office." He came closer and cocked his head. "There's a bar in Bremen that makes a drink called a Suffering Bastard," he said, "and you look as if you could do with about seven of them."

"What's going on? What's she doing here?"

"Came to say goodbye. They're sending her back to Italy to run a new hospital in Milan. If you hurry you might –"

Schramm hurried. She was not outside the building and he ran as fast as his idiot leg would let him. It was fast enough. She was around the corner, talking to Hoffmann. Her car was nearby, the red open-top Alfa tourer. He went and sat in it.

Eventually Benno kissed her, a brotherly-sisterly kiss on each cheek, and she got into the car.

He risked one long, direct, eye-to-eye look. Same old Maria. Same old speculative glance. Same old almost-smile. If she went to Milan this might be the last time they would ever meet. There was, of course, no possibility that she might embrace him: not here, not in uniform, not in public. Even for her to take his hand was more than he could expect; what if some passing airman observed them? So she was a doctor; so what? How could she possibly know that he was wading in blood from a self-inflicted wound? He had one chance to say that meeting her had been the most astonishing experience of his life, to say that love was obviously futile and irrelevant in wartime, to say that simply knowing her was astonishing and exciting. Damn. He'd used 'astonishing' twice. "Killed anybody today?" he asked.

"Have you?"

"None of your business."

"Same here."

"Look . . ." He was shocked by what they had said. "I'm not really angry with you."

"Of course you're not." She leaned across and used her fingers to smooth his brow. "Stop frowning. It makes you look like a walrus. Why are you so bad-tempered, Paul?"

Schramm gave up. He slumped in his seat. "God knows," he said. "You've been playing God lately. You tell me."

"All right, listen. You're angry because you know you're wrong. You keep denying this, but you're too honest to get away with it. Last time we met you weren't just angry, you were *furious*. You were in a rage with me. Why? Because I did what you had always wanted to do."

"Kill helpless patients? Not me, doctor. Not me."

"You wanted to be rid of Kurt Debratz. I saw it in your face. Kurt Debratz disgusted you. He was squalid, stinking, maimed, deteriorating, hopeless, useless, and full of pain, and he wasn't dying fast enough for you. You wanted to kill him. Isn't that the truth?"

"It wasn't my job," Schramm muttered. "He wasn't my responsibility."

"No, but he upset you, didn't he? Believe it or not, I ended his life because I loved him. I did what you wanted to do, but you couldn't admit that to yourself. In fact you hated yourself for wanting it, so you turned your anger on me instead. You couldn't afford to hate yourself, so you hated me. Simple, isn't it?"

Schramm felt pummelled. "We've been through all this before, haven't we?" he said.

"We have."

"Do I really want to kill people? Have I got such an *appetite* for death?"

"Don't ask me. Ask yourself. That's where the answer

is. That's where it's always been. And consider yourself lucky there's a war on so you can find the truth without getting hanged for murder." She started the car. "That will be fifty thousand lire. You can buy me lunch and then we'll go swimming."

*　　*　　*

Malplacket found a shady spot in the wadi and sat down to write his will.

He had little to leave: a small house in London, slightly blitzed; a few paintings, now being looked after by a cousin in Anglesey and therefore almost certainly mildewed; an Aston-Martin on blocks in a garage in Devon, where it had run out of petrol. In any case, his wife would automatically inherit everything. Still, it gave him quiet pleasure to send a few kind words from beyond the grave. 'To my wife,' he wrote, 'without whose mind-numbing conversation I would never have been driven to travel so widely; without whose grudging access to her loins I might have exhausted myself in lust; and without whose few but stupefyingly tedious friends the rest of the world would have seemed to me only half as colourful, I leave everything, confident in the knowledge that my children will grow up to be inept, inane, ungrateful and greedy.' That wasn't right. "Henry," he called, "what's a good two-dollar word that means 'greedy'?"

"Covetous."

"Perfect." He made the alteration. "Many thanks."

"What are you doing?"

"Making my will. Perhaps you would be so kind as to witness it."

Lester came over and signed it. "Maybe I should change mine," he said. "Ah, who cares? She'll get everything, whatever I do. The hell with it."

They were not allowed to attend the briefing at four-thirty p.m.

"Beda Fomm," Lampard told his patrol. "It's a big operational airfield. Not training, not transport, not repairs. Operational. Sergeant Davis and I saw at least one squadron of Me109s and given the size of the place there could well be two. We discovered how to get in and, more important, how to get out afterwards. There are only two approaches to Beda Fomm: one is overland, using tracks and trails. That's hopeless at night. We'll use the other way, the coastal road." Gibbon had the map spread out. Lampard took them over the route. "Study it, memorise it. Any one of you might end up in command. Now the whole point of this raid is *speed*. I want to be in and out in twenty minutes. All your pencil-fuses will be long — sixty minutes. By the time the balloon goes up, we'll have vanished, be back in the Jebel, I hope. We'll take five vehicles. Three jeeps, the Mercedes and the Ford. Splash plenty of mud on it. There are lots of captured Fords on the roads back here. Clear so far? Good. That's the broad outline. Now here's the detail."

Lampard talked for ten minutes. There were few questions. The patrol had rehearsed this kind of raid many times.

"Grub," Lampard said. "Eat hearty. You never know when you'll get another chance."

Malplacket took his loaded mess tin and sat beside Lester.

"Are we absolutely convinced that we want to go ahead with this?" he asked. "I mean, are we quite certain of its merits?"

"I am. This is my big crack at the Pulitzer. 'I Walked into Hitler's Desert Fortress'. Isn't that a headline you'd kill for? *Life* magazine will beat me senseless with their chequebooks." He batted the flies away and ate a chunk of Spam, fast, before they regrouped.

"On the other hand," Malplacket said, "there's no point in taking unnecessary risks, is there?" He pointed his fork at the German pistol tucked into Lester's belt. "That's purely decorative, I hope."

"Don't worry. Any shooting I do will be with a camera." He ate some baked beans. "You never know, I might get a close-up of Rommel."

"Blanchtower would be thrilled, I'm sure," Malplacket said.

Corky Gibbon, Sandiman, the doctor and two fitters stayed at the camp. The rest — Lampard with twelve men in five vehicles — set off just before sunset. Malplacket and Lester went with them, driving their bit of booty. Lester was whistling 'Yes Sir, That's My Baby'. "Try not to do that in Benghazi, old chap," Malplacket said.

*   *   *

Skull showed Barton a list of all the Luftwaffe airfields and landing-grounds within range of LG 250. There were fifty-four in all. The one he considered least unsuitable as a target was an advanced landing-ground called Gadd el Ahmar.

"Convince me," Barton said. He took the list and began tearing it into small pieces.

Skull did a thorough, professional job on Gadd el Ahmar. It was relatively isolated, being forty miles behind the Gazala Line and forty-five miles south of the Mediterranean. The nearest Luftwaffe field, Mechili, was a long way to the west; Tmimi was far to the north. Gadd el Ahmar was relatively close to LG 250, so the Kittyhawks could carry a light load of fuel, thus improving their performance. It was a temporary field, so flak would be minimal and radar probably non-existent: the SAS had blown up a mobile radar at Gadd a month ago and there was no sign that it had been replaced.

Barton nodded and tore.

On the other hand, Skull said, Gadd was often quite

busy. The Luftwaffe used it to refuel Ju88s on reconnaissance missions over Egypt. Recently a squadron of Stukas had trained around Gadd. Engine failure, or navigational error, or bad weather, forced German aircraft to land there. The pickings were promising. Above all, Allied territory was within easy reach if anything went wrong.

"All things considered, then, you reckon Gadd el Ahmar is the obvious target," Barton said.

"Yes, I do."

"That's exactly why I'm not going there. Hold your hand out." Barton scooped up all the bits of paper and flung them into the air. They fluttered down. Some landed on Skull's head and shoulders. One piece fell on his palm. "What have you got?" Barton asked.

Skull turned it over. "Beda Fomm," he said.

"Lovely. That's what we'll hit."

"You're mad," Skull said. "You've gone doolally."

"Not a bit!" Barton cried cheerfully. "If I don't know what I'm doing next, how can the enemy possibly know?"

It was late in the afternoon when the three Kittyhawks took off. Barton led them in a circuit and then brought them down in line abreast to beat up the field. Skull, Uncle and the doc stood and watched. It was useless speaking until the thunder had passed and faded to a drone as the formation climbed westward.

"I apologise for breaking your gramophone record," the doc said. "It was an uncivilised thing to do in the middle of a war."

"Think nothing of it."

"You broke 'Empty Saddles'?" Kellaway said. "Damn clumsy of you. That was Fanny's favourite."

"It was a necrophiliac dirge, Uncle. Pretentious, syrupy guff. Even so, I had no right to break it."

"Don't concern yourself," Skull said. "As it happens, I have another copy in my tent."

"Mother was right," the doc said. "I should never have left Ireland."

The choice of Beda Fomm may have been a matter of chance, but to every other aspect of the raid Barton gave the closest possible thought.

Success hinged on timing their arrival just as the last fat slice of sun slid below the horizon. Sunset happened fast in Libya: day turned to night without the long English compromise of dusk. However, at ten thousand feet the Libyan day lasted a little longer: a pilot still saw the rim of the sun when men below him were in darkness.

The Kittyhawks flew north-west from LG 250, climbing hard, and levelled out at twenty thousand feet. At this time of day the average Luftwaffe fighter pilot would be heading for home: the 109, with its knock-kneed undercarriage and its tendency to crab at the moment of touchdown, was not an easy machine to land in the dark. Barton saw a few metallic glints at great distance. They all faded to nothing.

The Kittyhawks cruised watchfully for almost an hour. Over the Jebel they circled while the sun edged lower and lower until it silently collided with the end of the world and seemed to flatten a little on impact. They made one more circuit and then Barton led them down.

Beda Fomm was clear to see. South of Benghazi the coastline bulged out and then in. Beda Fomm sat in the centre of that inward curve. Its runways made a distinctive pattern, a slanting cross, as if someone had slammed a rubber stamp on the scruffy countryside. It was a tiny cross, but the last, blazing, horizontal rays of the sun made it shine. Soon it was no longer tiny and it no longer shone, and then it was lost in the gloom as the sun vanished. The Kittyhawks were diving at an ever-steeper angle, picking up speed like skis on ice, plunging into darkness. Barton had slipped into his usual stoic, fatalistic frame of mind. Nothing could be changed, so there was no point in worrying. Patterson was not yet frightened, but knew he soon would be and he dreaded it; meanwhile he was a small god about to blast a small enemy and as always the prospect gave him huge excitement. Hooper, too, was enjoying himself. He felt like the hand guiding a giant firearm. The bombs under the wings were bullets. Soon he would fling them at the target and go. Then flak began exploding and he began to shake. His left thigh trembled violently. He whacked it with his fist, but still it shook.

The flak became a storm. Often the smoke obliterated the ground. Barton stopped looking for Beda Fomm: if all this muck was coming up, the target must be down there. He watched the altimeter unwind and he blinked repeatedly as his Kittyhawk smashed through the tortured, blackened air. A dim familiar pattern took shape below and he bombed it, felt the aeroplane shift as it lost its load, and heaved the stick into his stomach.

Nobody escaped undamaged.

They flew home as low as possible, only fifty or sixty feet above the desert. This was to baffle the radar, which would be confused by echoes from the dunes, and to hide from the nightfighters. Barton knew how difficult it was to pick out a low-flying aircraft by day, let alone at night. Yet a pair of Me110 nightfighters bounced the Kittyhawks, bursting out of the blackness with a thumping, dazzling barrage of fire. The Kittyhawks broke hard towards the attack and for a few seconds there was a cursing chaos of near-collisions. The 110s' speed carried them many miles away. They hunted doggedly and caught the Kittyhawks again. Patterson took several hits. But Barton kept his little formation down on the deck, they lost the 110s, and eventually they reached LG 250.

It had a flare path, of sorts: tins full of sand soaked with petrol. They gave a feeble outline to the runway.

"You go first, Pip," Barton said.

"Do my best."

The ground crew were waiting, armed with axes, pick-handles, fire-extinguishers, metal-cutters, buckets of sand. Patterson made his approach like an accident looking for somewhere to happen: left wing down, nose high, speed falling too fast. Far too fast. He knew all this, but he could do nothing to alter it. What he didn't know was that only one wheel had come down. The other was stuck. There were cockpit signals to tell the pilot the state of his under-carriage, but Patterson was in no shape to look at cockpit signals.

The aeroplane fell apart when it hit the ground. Four tons of machinery travelling at well over a hundred and twenty miles an hour is very unforgiving. The Kittyhawk shed its wings, the fuselage screamed and bucketed along until it had snapped off its tailplane, and what was left performed a long, grinding pirouette down the strip, gradually exhausting itself against the unfeeling desert.

The ground crew got Patterson out in a tearing rush. The stench of petrol urged them on. They staggered and stumbled away with him. As the doc knelt in the sand the engine flickered and caught fire with a roar like a trapped animal. "Let it burn," he said. "I need the light."

The fire helped Barton and Hooper too. They picked their way between the lumps of wreckage and landed safely.

"Busy night?" the doc said, without looking up from his work.

"We got bounced by some 110s. How is he?"

"If the kite took as much of a beating as the pilot, it's a miracle he got it down at all." By now Skull and Kellaway were there too. They all formed a loose circle around the stretcher. A pressure lamp added its pure light to the yellow flames.

"What's the score?" Patterson asked. He was very hoarse: the crash-landing had flung his head about so violently that he could scarcely swallow.

"Shut up, you. It's long past your bedtime."

"I want –"

"Lie still and behave."

"I want the song." Patterson looked around until he found Skull. "'Empty Saddles'."

"For the love of Christ!" the doc said. He slid a needle into Patterson's arm. "Is there no taste left in the world? I'm surrounded by the droolings of dross."

"Dross can't drool," Skull said. "Dross is mineral."

"Play the record," Barton told Skull.

"He can't hear it," the doc said. "He's out."

"I don't care. Play it."

The stretcher was carried away. They all trudged alongside it. "Where did he get hit?" Hick Hooper asked.

"Right leg, made a mess of his calf. Left hand, two fingers gone. Shell splinters down his left side. Right eye isn't working. Right shoulder's dislocated, deep cut on the arm, left leg's broken, but I think that all happened in the crash. Probably some other damage I'll discover in due course."

There was a long silence. They were impressed.

"I'll put a new needle in the gramophone," Skull said. "I think we can afford it." He went off to his tent.

"Give us some rum," Barton said. The adjutant was holding the bottle.

"Did we hit anything?" Hick asked. "I couldn't see."

Barton took the glass and drank. "I don't know," he said. "I have a feeling some of the bombs didn't go off." Fifty yards away a dance band began to play.

CHAPTER SEVEN

The Easy Bit

Lampard saw a German foot-patrol. Ten or twelve men were sitting round a fire on a distant hillside. They all stood up when the vehicles went by. Lampard had put his captured Mercedes truck at the front and Malplacket's Fiat station-wagon at the tail, and he hoped the dust would obscure what was in between. He waved, and a couple of Germans waved back. Lester saw them, and he too waved. "Bunch of krauts back there," he said. He amazed himself by his bravery.

Later they passed another foot-patrol. "Bip your horn," Lampard said. The driver did, twice, and almost everyone waved. "All a matter of confidence," Lampard said.

It was dark when they stopped near the coast road. Lampard walked to the rear. "Parting of the ways," he told Lester and Malplacket. "Turn right and Benghazi's twenty kilometres up the road. We'll wait at the rendezvous until forty-eight hours from now, not a minute longer." The rendezvous was a grid reference in the desert. "If anyone stops you, tell them you're staff officers. Shout at them. That's quite effective sometimes, so I'm told. Good luck."

They shook hands. Malplacket drove his Fiat past the patrol and disappeared.

The three armed jeeps were hidden in some scrub.

The raiding party got into the Mercedes and the Ford trucks. A red light was hung on the Ford's tail-gate. They moved up to the road and waited.

Thirty minutes later they were still waiting. A few vehicles had passed, but they were all heading north.

Nothing went south. For most of the time the night was silent.

Lampard got out and strolled back to Dunn in the Ford. "Last night we couldn't cross the road for the traffic," he said. "I wonder what's up?"

"Bridge down somewhere, maybe. Or it could be just an old-fashioned pile-up. Accidents happen, even in a war."

They waited. The tang of some wild herb hung in the air: rosemary perhaps. After a while someone snored softly, then grunted as he got a dig in the ribs. Lampard was not surprised; on his first raid he himself had dozed off while the enemy barbed-wire was being cut. It was a curious response to extreme danger. Maybe the body reacted to heavy stress by switching off, or maybe it was just the phlegmatic British character expressing itself . . . Dunn clicked his fingers. Something was coming. Lampard hurried back to the cab. Engines were started.

It was a big road convoy and it was travelling fast. Lampard searched the darkness, trying to see where the convoy ended. It was painfully long and the *whomp-whomp-whomp-whomp* of tyres seemed endless. Then it ended. "Go!" he shouted and his driver made the truck jump forward. "Stop!" he bawled. "Stop, stop!" His driver trod violently on the brakes. Lampard got flung against the windscreen. "Well done," he said. His temple was bleeding.

Dunn appeared at the window. "Flak wagon." Lampard said. "Their last vehicle was a flak wagon. I couldn't sit behind a lot of Huns with guns staring at me."

"Don't blame you. Enough to put a chap off his grub."

After ten minutes the blood had congealed. No more traffic had appeared.

Lampard waited another five minutes and then called everyone together. "This is hopeless," he said. "We could wait here all night. We'll have to go alone, and if things get sticky at the checkpoint we'll shoot it up and press on. No grenades. I don't want shrapnel in the tyres."

They drove south, without lights. Lampard knew roughly how far it was to the checkpoint. As he counted the kilometres slowly clocking up on the dashboard he tried to think of a way to avoid a firefight at the checkpoint, assuming it was still there. Al Maghrun airfield drifted by on the right. One thing was certain: his German wasn't good enough to fool the thickest sentry.

"Go slow," he said. "It should be near here." The Mercedes lost speed until it was crawling. In the end they both saw it at the same time: a small red light, a fleck of blood in the blackness. "Pull over," he ordered. "Switch off."

They sat and looked at it.

"Right," Lampard said, and got out quietly. He found Sergeant Davis in the back of the Ford. "Take two bombs," he said, "and plant them on the other side of the road, as near that roadblock as you can get. We've got some short fuses, haven't we? Good. You'll have to work out the timing. The point is, I want you back here so we can drive there and arrive just as they explode."

"Ah. Not too near the roadblock, then," Davis said. "You don't want us to get blown up. It's a whatsit."

"Distraction."

"That's the word. Destruction." Davis stuffed bombs inside his battledress blouse, picked out some pencil-fuses, and disappeared into the night as if he had fallen down a well.

He was back in six minutes, breathless and pleased. "Five-minute fuses," he said. He checked his watch. "I set them exactly . . . um . . . three minutes ago . . . *now*. You don't need to start yet. Give it a minute."

"Have some chocolate," Dunn said.

They got back into the trucks. "They're listening to the bloody radio," Davis said. "Lili bloody Marlene again."

Lampard watched the second hand nibble its way around the dial. "Go," he said. "Nice and steady."

A guard came out of the hut, carrying a hurricane lamp, as the Mercedes trundled up to the barrier pole and stopped. Two more men followed. All were armed. One had a clipboard. He put a boot on the step of the cab and asked a question. Lampard began scrabbling through a bundle of papers he had found clipped to the dash, and muttered an answer, but the pencil gripped between his teeth turned it to gibberish. When the man said something else, Lampard turned to the driver and made an incoherent enquiry. The driver looked at him and shrugged. Lampard almost handed the bundle of papers to the guard, changed his mind halfway, and went back to scrabbling and muttering. Saliva dripped from the pencil. The guard banged impatiently on the door with his fist. The first bomb exploded with a blinding crack that swayed the truck on its springs. The guard fell on his backside. Lampard was briefly stunned and deafened so that he couldn't hear himself. More guards poured from the hut. A machine gun opened up but its rattle was lost in the second explosion. At last Lampard heard his voice shouting, "Drive drive drive." The Mercedes was already moving. The barrier pole snapped like a breadstick and bits flew everywhere.

The guards let them go. The place was under attack — bombs, mortars, shells, who the hell knew what? — and the safest place for two German trucks was obviously elsewhere. As the Ford charged after the Mercedes, Dunn saw in his wing mirror a spurt of tracer fire. It was not aimed at them, and he watched with interest until it was lost behind a bend. ·

After all that, Lampard missed the turn-off to Beda Fomm.

He knew it as soon as he heard the wheels rumble over the metal planking of a bridge. There had been no bridge between the roadblock and the turn-off. "We've overshot," he said. The driver made a U-turn and the bridge rumbled again. Lampard was puzzled: how could he have made such a mistake? He must have been daydreaming. "Go slow," he said.

A side road appeared, a soft and dusty grey-white in the blackness, and they pulled over. It didn't look right. Lampard took Sergeant Davis and went to investigate. The others sat in the trucks and kept silent.

After a couple of minutes a truck howled past, towing a small piece of artillery. An army ambulance followed. The guards had called for help. A car raced by, evidently trying to catch up. It braked hard and stopped. It reversed fast, the gearbox whining like a violin, and parked in front of the Mercedes.

A German officer got out. He was big; bigger than any man in the patrol. He shone a flashlight at the trucks and shouted at them. It was the voice of a man who is accustomed to being obeyed.

Dunn got out of the Ford and did his best to look like an Italian soldier who has just woken up. "*Buona sera, signor*," he mumbled. He saluted and did up his buttons at the same time. "*Italiano militari*," he said, bobbing his head deferentially. "*Benghazi regimento*." He saluted again. He had exhausted his Italian. Now it was up to the other man.

The German shone his light on Dunn's face and saw a week's growth plus a lot of dirt. He said something which sounded more like a comment than a question, so Dunn merely grinned and saluted. The light travelled over his uniform, and that definitely provoked a question. Dunn saw a pistol in the other hand. "*Inglesi!*" he said, suddenly inspired. "*Inglesi, signor*." He scratched at a stain on his sleeve. "*Spaghetti*," he said apologetically. This wasn't working. He could smell suspicion. He could also smell his own sweat.

The German poked him with the pistol. They walked to the back of the truck. As the German parted the canvas cover, Trooper Smedley's large hands seized his throat and strangled him. The weight of the body pulled Smedley down until he was kneeling. Dunn held the German by the armpits. "Bye-bye, birdie, bye-bye," Smedley said. He took his hands away. Dunn lowered the body, found the pistol, turned off the flashlight. "You could have used your knife," he said. "Would have been just as quiet."

"I wasn't sure it was him," Smedley said. "It might have been you."

"How could you tell it wasn't?"

"Wrong collar size. He must be seventeen-and-a-half, at least."

Lampard and Davis returned and examined the body.

"Oberst," Lampard said. "Equivalent to a colonel. Well, I hope that teaches him a lesson."

"What?" asked Davis.

"Real colonels don't play at being policemen, do they? That's blindingly obvious. Real colonels *delegate*. They tell someone else to ... to ..."

"Get strangled."

"Exactly. Right, chuck him in his car. You drive it, Smedley. This is the wrong turning. Let's go."

They found the right turning and hid the vehicles. There was sporadic traffic going to and from Beda Fomm, and Lampard was glad to get off the road. Now that the hard work of the journey had been done it would be a relief to get some exercise. Dunn made a final roll-call. Davis checked that each man had a rucksack of bombs, a pocketful of fuses, benzedrine tablets, a full water-bottle and a loaded weapon. He had checked all this before they left the Jebel, but Davis was a good NCO.

The evening was pleasant. Lampard led. He walked between the pines and the cactus as if he were out for a stroll round his estate after dinner. He rarely heard a footstep behind him: hard training and rubber-soled boots paid off. Once, when he stopped suddenly, just to keep the men alert, he looked back and saw nobody; nobody at all;

which pleased him. And the knowledge that at any moment a German sentry might blow one's head off added a certain spice to the whole experience.

They were perhaps ten minutes from the edge of the airfield when he first began to think there was something wrong.

It was too noisy, and the noise was not aircraft engines. The stolid chugging, the intense revving of big diesels, the bass throb: it all signalled heavy machinery at work. Then he noticed a glow in the sky. When the patrol reached the perimeter, Beda Fomm was floodlit. Not the entire field, but the working area: the hangars, buildings, aircraft. The racket came from caterpillar tractors, dump trucks, mobile cranes, generators, earthmovers, winches. Men were everywhere, more men than Lampard could count. "Oh dear," he said. "They've got the builders in."

Sergeant Davis had a pair of Zeiss binoculars, looted from the kit of Captain Lessing. He found a wrecked hangar, still smoking. He found the broken carcases of several aeroplanes, now unidentifiable. He found large holes in the ground. "Look at those blokes with the big tripod in front of the control tower," he said.

Lampard focused. The workers were doing things to a block and tackle over a small crater. "Unexploded bomb," he said.

"Blindingly obvious," Davis said. "Especially if they don't get their finger out."

"We've been fucked," Trooper Peck said. "Fucked by the fucking Desert Air fucking Force."

"Well, I'm fucked," Smedley said.

"Didn't you make a reservation?" Dunn asked Lampard. "You know what it's like on a Saturday night."

"Today's Tuesday," said Davis.

"Fuck me, we're four days early," Peck said. "No wonder the place isn't ready."

"Hopeless," Lampard said. "Quite, quite hopeless."

They walked back to the vehicles. Everyone felt the flat fatigue of anti-climax. In an hour it would be midnight. They'd come all this way for nothing. The useless load in their rucksacks felt heavier and they were glad to stack them in the trucks. A dull rumble of thunder reached them from the north. It might have been naval guns, or mines, or bombs, or even thunder. Nobody cared. It was somebody else's problem.

Lampard and Dunn sat on the ground, leaning back-to-back, and ate some malted-milk tablets. "What's our secondary target?" Dunn asked.

"Mersa Brega. Know it?"

"No."

"Neither do I. It's about a hundred kilometres south of here, if you go by the coast road. Too far. We'd have to do a recce, then lie up tomorrow, raid it tomorrow night and get back here again."

"Another hundred kilometres."

"Not by road. We'd hit Jerry roadblocks every five minutes."

Dunn pondered the problem, but it was insoluble. Lampard would not raid without reconnoitring the target first. Beda Fomm was out. Mersa Brega was out of range. "What about Al Maghrun?" he said. "That's close. We could go and take a look, at least."

"Yes. I suppose so." For a moment Lampard seemed slumped in lethargy. "Nothing to lose." Still he did not move. "Maghrun," Lampard said. "Doesn't sound very thrilling. Sounds like a disease of sheep. Still . . . Nothing to lose." At last he got up, stiffly. "Old age," he said.

Sergeant Davis did not like the idea of going back up the coastal road and bluffing or shooting their way through the roadblock.

"They'll remember these trucks," he said. "They'll be all of a doodah because of the bombs, and they'll see these trucks and they'll think 'ullo-'ullo-'ullo."

Lampard was silent.

"And you know what that'll mean," Davis said. "It'll mean Auf Wiedersehen."

Smedley began to speak, but Dunn poked him in the ribs and he shut up.

"You're right," Lampard said. "But the only other way is dirt tracks and camel trails, and you remember what a bastard that was."

"We only tried the tracks on *this* side of the coast road. The Beda Fomm side. Maghrun's on the opposite side. I bet I can find a way through on that side."

He sounded supremely, disturbingly confident. "Why should that side be any better?" Lampard asked.

"Because it can't be any worse."

"I see." Lampard tried to read Davis's expression in the night and failed. "Well, this will either be an outstanding cock-up or you'll get a large medal. Take Blake with you, see what you can find, come back here. Use that staff car. Better not take the Oberst. You've got an hour."

The dead officer had been left sitting behind the wheel and had begun to stiffen in that position, so he was carried to the front seat of the Ford. Davis was relieved to see that his eyelids had fallen until they had almost closed. Strangulation was all very well, but it played merry hell with the eyeballs. Davis was not squeamish; it was just that, given a choice, he preferred people to keep their eyeballs to themselves.

The staff car left. Everyone had something to eat: slabs of bully on biscuit. Lampard was a great believer in eating whenever you could.

A breeze had sprung up, rustling the trees. It was possible to talk softly.

"I didn't realise you had such strong hands," Dunn said to Trooper Smedley.

"It's all in the thumbs," Smedley said. "I used to tear

480

telephone books in half as a sort of party trick." He spoke mildly.

"Anyone can do that," Peck said.

"Not three books at a time." That silenced Peck. "People got tired of it, so I used different things," Smedley said. "I tore up tarpaulins, sheets of plywood and rolls of lino. You can tear up anything if you've got the hands. I tore up a complete set of the Encyclopedia Britannica once. It's all in the thumbs. After a while it comes natural, but you got to practise. If you want to be good at anything, you got to stick at it."

"Rome wasn't burned in a day," Peck observed.

"Corporal Harris once told me he'd killed a full-grown sheep when he was a boy," Dunn said.

"With his bare hands?" Smedley asked.

"No. He said he used a knife."

They waited for Smedley's reaction. "That's all very well," he said, "but what's he going to do when he hasn't got a knife?"

"Harris always had a knife," Lampard announced. "Harris killed two sentries with it on our last raid, perhaps more. Unfortunately one of them stabbed him in the stomach. He concealed his wound in case it slowed down the patrol. A rough diamond, but a very gallant soldier." Lampard swallowed. "The desert is his grave," he added.

Nobody was going to argue, but total disbelief hung in the air like static electricity. "Bit of bully left," Dunn said swiftly. "Anyone want the last bit of bully? Shame to waste it. Peck, have a bite." The danger passed.

At twenty minutes past midnight the staff car returned. "Dead easy," Davis said.

Lampard let him lead. There were salt marshes on the seaward side of the coastal road and Davis had found a causeway that flanked them. It was narrow and in many places broken, so the trucks went very slowly. The best part of an hour had passed before Davis turned right, into a wandering track that eventually found the perimeter of Al Maghrun airfield. It was big and black. The only noise was the distant rumble of traffic on the coastal road.

Lampard sent Dunn and Peck to recce. "No bombs," he said. "If you get bumped off I don't want them to know why you're here. Make it snappy."

The snappiest they could make it was thirty-five minutes, by which time they had searched Al Maghrun and found it empty of aircraft. "There's some blokes asleep in a billet and a lot of oilstains on the grass," Dunn said. "That's all."

Another disappointment. Sometimes a raid seemed to be jinxed; sometimes a leader seemed cursed with ill-luck. Lampard sensed a slump of spirits and responded instantly with the British army's answer to all misfortune. "Time for a brew-up, sergeant," he said. Long experience had shown that there was no reverse that did not look better after a mug of hot tea. When the operation was a shambles and the situation seemed hopeless, it was time for a brew-up.

They had brought the makings with them. The desert stove – a tin of petrol-soaked sand – was placed where it was hidden between the trucks. There was still a risk of its being seen, but Lampard reckoned that if Al Maghrun really was not operating the risk was worth taking. "We should be flattered," he said. "Obviously the enemy's moving his planes from place to place to try and baffle us."

Nobody said anything. What they were not saying was quite clear: tonight the enemy had succeeded.

The water boiled. A handful of tea was thrown into it. The brew foamed and seethed.

"I suppose there's nothing to stop us going back to camp now and trying again tomorrow night," Dunn said.

"I hate to do that," Lampard said.

Dunn immediately thought: *His brakes have failed. He can't stop himself.*

A tin of condensed milk and half a pound of sugar got stirred in. The result was strong, sweet, hot and immediately cheering.

"Dawn in four hours," Dunn said. "Not much time to recce somewhere else and raid it and still get into the Jebel."

"Of course there's one place we don't need to recce," Lampard said. "We've been there before."

"Barce," Davis said.

They finished their tea in silence; not because they disliked the suggestion but because it was the patrol leader's idea and his decision. "What d'you think?" he asked Mike Dunn.

For the first, and last, time, Dunn did not answer him.

"Hullo?" Lampard said. "Anyone at home?"

"Does it matter what I think?"

"How can I tell till I hear what you've said?"

"All right." Dunn threw his dregs into the dying fire. "I think we should return to camp and try again tomorrow night. I think we ought to recce Barce first because the defences have almost certainly changed since the last time. I think if we try to hit Barce tonight we'll run out of darkness before we're safe."

"Ah. Any more?"

"And I think I'm wasting my breath because you've made up your mind." Some of the men laughed at that, although the harshness in Dunn's voice was surprising.

"As to being safe," Lampard said, "we're never going to be that. We left our calling card on the enemy with those bombs at the checkpoint. Also he's missing one large colonel. And Barce is the ideal target because they'll never expect another raid so soon."

"You're guessing," Dunn said.

"If you want to live by a timetable, old chap, you should have joined the GWR, not the SAS." Lampard spoke gently, and won more laughter. "I'll give you one cast-iron certainty. If we hit Barce twice, the Hun will definitely wet his knickers."

"Not half," said Trooper Smedley.

"How far is Barce from here?" Lampard asked Dunn.

"Couple of hours."

"We'll dump these trucks and take the jeeps. Off we go, then."

As they dispersed to the vehicles, Peck nudged Blake and muttered, "What's up with old Dunn, then?"

"Time of the month."

"Don't be so bloody daft."

"Well, don't ask such bloody daft questions."

Davis navigated them around the perimeter of Al Maghrun until they reached the coastal road; then Lampard took over. He decided he wanted the corpse of the Oberst beside him, in the passenger seat of the staff car. It was fetched from the Ford, the tunic was removed, and the body was lashed to the seat with a length of cord under its armpits. The tunic was slit up the back and replaced on the body, all buttoned-up and tucked-in so the cord was invisible. With its cap on and its hands in its lap, the corpse looked very convincing.

Davis noticed some stiff triangular pennants in the back of the car. Lampard chose two and fitted them into sockets on the wings. Meanwhile Dunn had discovered a briefcase, forced the lock and found various official papers and quite a lot of money. Lampard took charge of it all. "You never know," he said.

He reckoned it was about fifteen kilometres to where the jeeps were waiting and he hoped to cover the distance without meeting a roadblock. But quite soon he saw the familiar solitary red light in the middle of the road; and simultaneously he felt the double action of fear and excitement: a sudden tightening of the stomach muscles and a lively surge of blood to the head and neck. This roadblock must have been added since the supposed bomb attack on the other post. It would be interesting to see how alert the guards were.

They were very alert, and very respectful when they saw the pennants flying on the wings.

A sergeant hurried forward and clicked his heels. He saluted. Lampard made a languid acknowledgement, more papal than military. He let the sergeant get out two or three words and then said, "Sh-sh-sh." He put his finger to his lips, and nodded towards his passenger. The sergeant bent at the knees until his head was level with theirs. He began whispering. Lampard shushed him again. Using his hand to hide his words from his passenger, he said, slowly and softly: "Oberst . . . Max . . . von . . . Rommel." The sergeant's eyes widened. Lampard nodded. He could see the sergeant thinking: I never knew Rommel had a son in the army, but then maybe it's not his son, maybe it's a nephew or a cousin, anyway he's still a Rommel, I'd better watch my step . . .

Lampard made a show of looking at his watch. He frowned and inched the car forward. But now the sergeant had a clipboard, and he needed information for it. While he whispered his question, Lampard leafed through the bundle of official papers, chose the two most impressive, added some of the money, and handed it to him. In exchange he took the clipboard and scribbled something illegible. "Heil Hitler," he whispered. He aimed a finger at the pole-barrier and gestured upwards. "Heil Hitler," the sergeant whispered as he took back the clipboard. There was six months' pay in his hand. This had never happened before. Lampard inched the car further forward. Greed and duty fought for the sergeant's soul. Duty lost. The barrier rose. The car and the trucks accelerated into the night, the same night that concealed the sergeant as he stuffed the money in his pocket, telling himself that Rommel knew best.

At two-twenty the patrol reached the jeeps, transferred

the rucksacks of bombs, hid the trucks and the car, and set off for Barce. Lampard took the corpse of the Oberst as a good-luck token.

By three a.m. they were back in familiar terrain, the western foothills of the Jebel. Lampard wanted to be above Barce by four, which was absurd, and so he set an absurd pace, or tried to, racing along the wandering and rocky trails with headlights full on, skidding and slithering around S-bends in blind faith that he could cope with anything he found when he emerged. Once he failed completely: steering hard right, he could not stop the jeep drifting broadside left, over the edge and down a long, steep patch of rattling scree. Just a little steeper and the jeep would have rolled, bent the Vickers twin machine guns and probably broken a couple of necks. As it was, a few degrees saved them from anything worse than brief terror. The other crews helped manhandle the jeep up to the track. Lampard roared on.

Yet they paid for his impatience. The scree had ripped a tyre; within minutes the jeep was thrashing that wheel to death. He forced himself to sit on a rock, in silence, while others changed it. They were far more competent. As soon as the final wheel nut was tightened, he started up and men scrambled aboard. It was three-fifty. Mike Dunn kept a constant check on the time. He had said very little since they left the airfield at Al Maghrun. Everyone else, including Sergeant Davis, followed Lampard without question; Dunn felt that he had said his bit and if nobody listened there was no point in saying it again. He experienced a sense of fatalism that kept fear at bay. Jack was the boss. Maybe Jack knew best, after all.

And for a time, things went right: for long spells it was like a night exercise, careering round the hills, steering by the stars, trying always to avoid losing height. Things also went wrong. Twice they drove slap into an Arab camp. The first was small, they reversed out and found a way around it, dodging sleepy Arab children who were dazzled by the headlights which, to them, had arrived with all the sudden mystery of meteors. The second was big. Lampard saw a tent jump at him, swerved, and found himself in a sea of sheep. They panicked, which meant the whole night was full of angry Arabs chasing their property. The patrol sat motionless for three minutes until the chaos eased. Sergeant Davis gave the oldest Arab he could see two pounds of sugar and a big packet of tea. They shook hands. The old man seemed well pleased.

Sometimes the trail faded out and they had to search for another; sometimes there were too many trails. Lampard halted at a five-way crossroads and had to guess. While he was guessing, Dunn's jeep reported a puncture. The jack kept slipping; in the end, half the patrol held the jeep up while the wheel was changed. Lampard had gone on: he was exploring the right-hand trail. It led up a wadi and the wadi led nowhere. Dead end. He heard firing behind him and knew his luck had finally run out. You couldn't dash about the Jebel without meeting a German patrol, sooner or later.

Headlights off, he went back down the wadi in an anxious crawl, the firing getting steadily louder. He crept around a bend and saw it: flying needles of red and yellow bouncing off rocks in a confusion of directions, like sparks in a steel mill. All the fire was coming from the enemy. Lampard approved. If they thought they'd won, they might quit.

Meanwhile there was nothing he could do except watch. It was four-twenty. He sat on the warm bonnet of the jeep to comfort his backside, which had taken a beating from too many rocks recently.

Dunn walked out of the night and sat beside him. "I reckon five machine guns and a dozen rifles," he said. "We've got the jeeps behind some boulders."

"This is a dead end."

"Ah. Well, come and join us."

"If I drive down there, they'll clobber me."

"Not if we keep their heads down. We blaze away, you make a dash for it."

"No. Too exposed." Lampard drummed his heels against the radiator. "Why haven't they outflanked us?"

"They tried. Made a hell of a noise. We sprayed a few rounds their way and they made even more noise going back. I think they're pretty new at this game."

"Huns?"

"Sounds like it."

"Right. Tell you what. *We'll* outflank *them*."

"We're not strong enough."

"They don't know that. Pick four men, send two to each side of the enemy position with a couple of Stens and some grenades. While they're making nuisances of themselves I'll sneak down. Then they rejoin and we withdraw."

"OK." But Dunn did not go. "There's another way, Jack. We can just leave this jeep here."

"I'm not going to abandon a vehicle."

That was that. Dunn hurried back to the patrol, explained Lampard's plan and began selecting men. "Walters and Connors," he said. "Smedley and . . . um . . ."

"Me," said Peck.

Dunn hesitated.

"Yeah, Peck's best," Sergeant Davis said.

"Is that a fact?" Smedley said to Peck. "You never told me." He was picking out weapons.

"Why keep a dog and blow your own trumpet?" Peck said. He stuffed extra grenades in his pockets.

Lampard released the brake as soon as he heard the fierce crack of the first grenade. He let the jeep coast down the wadi until he was sure the German gunners had swung round to answer the attacks on their flanks. Then he took his foot off the clutch. The engine fired. He drove half-standing, peering ahead, straining to see rocks that often were gone before he could twist the wheel. At least one rifleman tried to stop him: bullets made firefly-sparks as they struck the ground, and one or two stung the jeep. The wadi widened and ended. He turned square into the trail, all four wheels spitting stones until they gripped and rocketed him towards the elephant-sized boulders beyond which the patrol waited. An enemy machine gun searched with short, probing bursts. It ruined the face of a boulder but it couldn't find Lampard. He was safe.

Walters came back, sweating and pleased. Connors came back with a dislocated finger and without his Sten; it had gone flying when he tumbled down a gully. Smedley came back with a bloody face: stone splinters had sliced his cheek open. Sergeant Davis snatched Connors's hand when he wasn't looking, straightened his finger with a clean jerk and caught him as he fainted. Peck did not come back.

They waited three minutes. Lampard had the body of the Oberst placed at the side of the trail, pistol in hand, facing the enemy. As an afterthought he scattered the remains of the money all about. "Should give them something to think about," he said.

Still no Peck. Enemy fire had tailed off. Only an occasional bullet fizzed by.

"It's four-forty," Dunn said. "You can forget Peck."

"What d'you reckon?" Lampard asked Smedley.

"Dunno, sir." His words were weakened by the hole in his cheek. "We split up. He was firing, running about, making them think there was ten of him." He shrugged. "Dunno, sir."

The jeeps retreated at speed behind spurts of covering fire, and stopped after a quarter of a mile.

'You can bet your boots that Jerry patrol has raised the alarm," Dunn said. "There's still time to reach camp before dawn." This night seemed to have lasted a week.

"Jolly good," Lampard said. Dunn felt he had been

talking to himself. "Sergeant Davis!" Lampard called. "Casualties?"

"One bullet through the leg. Some cuts from rock splinters. Smedley's face you know about. That's all. The jeeps are OK. We lost a bit of petrol from the jerricans. You can smell it."

"That's all right, then." Lampard walked to the edge of the track and stared into the night. "Barce is down there. You can see the road from Benghazi."

Dunn saw nothing but blackness. "Even if we got inside, the sun would be up before we could plant half the bombs," he said. "Barce is a bloody big airfield. You remember." Lampard said nothing. "It's four-fifty," Dunn said. "We simply haven't got the time."

"Bags of time. And won't they be surprised?"

Lampard took the patrol out of the Jebel by the simplest possible means: he let gravity do the steering. As long as the jeeps were going downhill he knew they must be heading more or less north or north-west, towards the road that linked Barce and Benghazi. Often gravity was not a safe guide and he had to turn and drive along the contours until he found a track that the jeeps could skate down without falling out of control. Nevertheless, the night was full of the howling of gearboxes and the bellow of engines and the clash of metal on stone. *This is insane*, Dunn said to himself, over and over, until the word *insane* lost all meaning and became just a noise in his head.

They reached the bottom at five past five. Lampard did not pause. He bucketed across the fields and mounted the road at five-fifteen. That was when he stopped for a briefing.

"We're not going to bomb their aircraft," he announced. "No time. We'll machine-gun them. Strafe 'em. First we leave bombs alongside this road, all the way to the airfield. Thirty-minute fuses. Save a few for the checkpoint at the gate. Short fuses there. We drive into Barce like the clappers of hell, shoot the daylights out of it and leave the same way." He described his plan in detail, giving each jeep its position in the attack and each man his task. "All understood? Good. Off we go."

*   *   *

An airman shook Paul Schramm awake at four fifty-five a.m. and gave him a piece of paper. It was a teletype. The message came from the headquarters of an infantry regiment based eight miles away, towards Benghazi. It was a copy of a signal received by the regiment from one of its patrols in the Jebel. Schramm had asked the regiment to inform him immediately if a patrol made contact with the enemy. Now, it seemed, one had. That was what the teletype said. Any normal person could have understood it in ten seconds. Fifteen, if he needed to find his reading glasses. Schramm was not normal at four fifty-five a.m. His eyes might be open but his brain was made of congealed fog.

He washed his face and read the teletype again. Then he put on his reading glasses again and this time it made some sense.

Time. What was the damn time? He found his watch and it said eleven-thirty. Impossible. Idiot watch was upside-down. Two minutes to five. Dawn in an hour. The SAS never raided just before dawn, it was crazy, how could they get away?

He telephoned the station duty officer, the duty NCO in charge of airfield defence and the ops officer in the control tower, each with the same message: risk of raid, stay alert. They did not sound alarmed. They had heard it before.

Next he telephoned the duty officer at Regimental HQ. "Any developments?" he asked.

"The shooting's over. They pulled back. Our men are looking for bodies."

"I see." Schramm tried to imagine what it was like, clambering about the Jebel, searching for something that might not exist, in a very black night, with a lethal enemy somewhere in the darkness. "Look . . . No offence intended, but how sure are you that the unit your men ran into really was British?"

"It was armed, it had vehicles. What are the alternatives? Arab guerrillas? Deserters? Escaped prisoners of war? No. This outfit was too well organised. We took losses, major."

"You're not going to like this," Schramm said.

That amused the duty officer. "Well," he said, "if it's too painful I shall just burst into tears, like we always do."

"Maybe it was another German patrol, working in the opposite direction," Schramm suggested. The duty officer said nothing. "You're biting your lip," Schramm said. "I can smell the blood."

"Actually I'm eating a rather gruesome frankfurter. Well, I won't say it's never happened. Nothing benevolent about friendly fire. However, I can assure you that we have only one patrol operating in the Jebel right now. Just one."

Schramm got dressed. His mouth tasted foul so he brushed his teeth. When he turned out the lights and opened a window there was still no hint of dawn. Well, the aircraft were safe, that was the great thing. In fact, he rather wished the SAS would have a go at them, just to prove the infra-red beam. Not that it needed proving: it had been thoroughly tested by local paratroops and they had always set it off, even when they knew it was there and tried to crawl under it. The telephone rang.

"I don't quite know how to tell you this." It was the regimental duty officer again.

"I promise to be brave," Schramm said.

"Here it comes, then. Our patrol in the Jebel has just found a body, and it's an Oberst in his best uniform with a pistol in his hand. He wasn't shot and his pistol is fully loaded. I expect you'd like to know how he was killed."

"Please."

"Strangled. Also there was money everywhere."

"Strangled." Schramm thought hard. Was this some kind of gruesome SAS trick? If so, what did it achieve? He could think of nothing. It was a mistake to see the SAS everywhere. "It could be part of a black-market racket," he said. "Maybe this officer of ours was doing a deal with some Italians, they ran into your patrol, assumed it was a trap, killed him and left at top speed. I bet you that's what it was."

"Strangled," the duty officer said. "That's a funny way to murder a German officer in the middle of a gunfight."

"Mafia, probably. I expect strangulation is full of old-fashioned symbolism. You know what they're like."

"Fortunately not." The brutal crump of an explosion rattled Schramm's window. "Hullo!" the duty officer said. "Need help?"

"No," Schramm said. Heavy machine-gun fire broke out. "Yes!" he shouted, and dropped the phone.

*　　*　　*

Guard duty was just killing time. Night guard duty was killing time that had died while you weren't looking and so it went on forever. Eventually the body adjusted to this eternity. The heartbeat slowed, the eyes stopped searching, and the brain avoided all strenuous thought until it was barely ticking over.

People who never had to do it kept saying how important guard duty was. People like the station commander kept on about vigilance. You never saw him at five in the morning, so how did he know what he was talking about? The trick of doing guard duty was very simple. Take it as it comes. That's how you get through the night. Very, very slowly. You don't try and work it to death. That can't be done, because there is no work. You relax and you let the night set its own sweet pace. You can't change it, so you take it as it comes.

The two men on guard duty at Barce airfield main gate had been on their feet since two a.m. and they ached, literally ached, to sit down. Better yet, lie down. Their leg muscles were stiff, their knees hurt, their shoulders resented the weight of their rifles. Twenty minutes ago the NCO had opened the guardhouse door, told them to keep their eyes open, and shut it. Now he had his feet up, lucky bastard.

Only one vehicle had gone through since two a.m. Barce was dead. The guard was due to be relieved at six. Best not to think about it. Best not to think about anything. Just take it as it comes. That was the only way to treat the war: take it as it comes. Thus the two men on guard duty were not excited by the unhurried approach of a pair of dimmed headlights. One man yawned, the other rubbed his eyes. The vehicle slowed, made a turn of more than ninety degrees, and stopped. Evidently it was about to return the way it came. "*Schramm?*" the driver said. "*Herr Major Paul Schramm?*"

"*Ja, ja,*" one of the guards said.

Lampard reached out and gave him a rucksack. "*Heil Hitler!*" he said, and drove away. His presence had lasted seven seconds.

The NCO emerged and wanted to know what was going on. The guards told him it was a delivery for Major Schramm. The NCO squatted on his heels and tried to open the rucksack, but its drawstring had been tightly knotted. The bombs inside were on a one-minute fuse. He was still worrying at the knot when they exploded. The three bodies got hurled away with their arms outstretched in a caricatured gesture of surprise.

Lampard's jeeps rushed the gate as soon as the flash lit up the night, but when they reached it the gate and the wooden guardhouse had gone, were in small pieces, many

494

of them still tumbling from the sky. As he passed, Dunn pointed to another small building and his gunner gave it a four-second blast that knocked it flat. Perhaps it contained more guards, perhaps not. Either way, it was no longer a threat. For the first time all night, Dunn felt good.

Lampard knew this road. He had driven it before. The three jeeps enjoyed the luxury of a perfect surface; quite quickly they were up to fifty, sixty miles an hour and still gaining. Lampard saw lights coming at them, head-on. "Don't slow down!" he shouted. A flashing red was added. A siren wailed. The headlights blazed. It was a fire truck, ten times as big as a jeep and not about to give way. Lampard's driver knew this and he acted fast. The jeep left the road and was fishtailing violently through a stretch of gravel as the fire truck thundered by. Lampard looked back at the cloud of dust and screwed up his face, waiting for a crash that never came. The other two jeeps appeared, they all found the road, they picked up speed.

The road swung sharp left. "Straight on," Lampard ordered. Now they were on the actual airfield. Somewhere behind them a giant klaxon was letting off angry blasts. The other jeeps pulled up and drove alongside Lampard, all their headlights full on, searching for aircraft. They found patches of mist, a stack of oil drums, a small broken glider, more mist, but no aircraft.

The patrol changed direction, and their beams swept over another barren area. Lampard was furiously trying to remember the layout at Barce. They changed direction again, and again the night was empty. The place was so bloody *big*. What if they'd parked their planes in a far corner? What if Barce was another Maghrun? Two searchlights came on, brilliant sticks of light, prodding the sky. Once again the three jeeps swung and searched a fresh, dead spot. Flak began to be pumped up one searchlight beam: bombs meant bombers. In the jeep on Lampard's left, Sergeant Davis fired a brief burst and his driver steered,

495

making his headlights follow the tracer. Lampard saw a row of fighters, 109s, a dozen at least. He shouted with delight.

That burst finally convinced somebody in airfield defence. A light machine gun opened up, then another. Lampard's driver switched his headlights off. The others copied him. Now that they knew where the target was they could drive blind.

Paul Schramm was a spectator to all this. He stood on the narrow balcony outside his bedroom, listened to the rise and fall of jeep engines, saw the sweep of headlights and the pulse of tracer. He felt detached, almost remote. There was nothing he could do.

Benno Hoffmann joined him. "How did they get in?" he asked.

"Through the main gate. They just blasted their way in. I've sent for help. The army's on its way."

"Can't we hit them with something? Mortars, or . . ."

"Too late, Benno. We'd be just as likely to hit our own aircraft now."

"Yes, of course." Hoffmann made himself comfortable in a chair. "Might as well enjoy the show, I suppose."

Lampard guessed the distance, reached across and hit the horn, and all the headlights came on. For a glorious second or two he was entranced by the spectacle of rows and rows of bright, clean Messerschmitt 109s, yellow at nose and wingtip, their canopies gleaming, perched on their undercarriages like well-trained hounds. Then the jeeps changed formation from line abreast to single file and the gunners swung the barrels to the flank and opened up.

The effect was cruel in its savagery: even Lampard was taken aback by the sheer intensity of this devastation. Each jeep carried four Vickers K machine guns, mounted in pairs: two at the front, two at the back. Each Vickers K fired a thousand rounds a minute. The three jeeps cruised parallel to the German aeroplanes and blasted twelve thousand rounds a minute into them. Some burst into flames at once: headlights were no longer needed. The noise was frightening: the night seemed to be battered to bits. The bullet-streams scythed through the undercarriages and the fighters crashed on their bellies. Petrol tanks ignited, blew machines apart, sprayed blazing fuel over other fighters. The jeeps reached the end of the row and one German squadron lay wrecked. Their flames lit up a second row and the jeeps turned on it. The gunners hosed bullets up and down these fresh targets, and as they too exploded it was inevitable that flying debris would fall through the infra-red beams and trigger Schramm's defensive system. His fixed machine guns blazed loyally at the empty air, their voice drowned in the huge roar of the Vickers Ks. It was a scene of mechanised and professional madness. Dunn's mouth was open so long that it dried inside and he could not swallow or salivate. He blinked as one of the searchlights came down and added its beam to the bonfire. Sergeant Davis swung his Vickers. His eyes were squeezed shut but the blinding glare penetrated them. He aimed where the glare was worst and kept firing until it went out. For a long time after that, luminous blossoms of changing colour swamped his vision.

The raid had lasted four minutes and now it was over. The jeeps raced for the empty end of the airfield. The time was five-forty.

The infantry regiment performed miracles: it got two truckloads of troops on the road to Barce only seven minutes after Schramm had asked for help. Halfway there, the commanders saw bombs begin to explode on the road ahead of them, many bombs, a seemingly endless string of bombs, all terrifyingly accurate. They stopped and waited until this air raid had passed. Getting killed wouldn't help Barce. By the time the trucks charged past the airfield's shattered gates, dawn was starting to outline the eastern Jebel.

Schramm's telephone rang.

"You asked to be kept informed," the regimental duty officer said, "and I have some more information. Our patrol has found another body. This one is quite definitely a British soldier. Probably SAS. So we got at least one. How many did they get?"

"They got . . ." Schramm began, and had to stop because he heard himself sound so unconcerned. "They got twenty-four Me109s and they also got clean away."

"Ah."

"Never mind. The sun is up. They've had their fun. Now we'll have ours."

*   *   *

It was broad daylight when the jeeps climbed into the Jebel.

This was the greenest part of the Green Mountain, the northern slopes where most of the rain fell and the trees grew thickly. The patrol had not seen such lushness since they left Cairo; the oasis at Kufra was a thin and dusty affair by contrast. Here, crops grew in tiny fields of red earth, and flocks of sheep or herds of goats were usually in sight. There was a bouncy sense of exhilaration. The night had been a triumph; now the day was a delight. They waved at Arab children, who put down their loads of firewood or goatskin water-bags to wave back. At the same time the patrol watched the sky. Delight died at six thirty-eight a.m. when the first enemy aircraft appeared from the west.

Six Italian CR42 biplanes cruised along the Jebel in a wide formation, only five hundred feet up, obviously searching. The jeeps immediately drove under the nearest cover and stopped.

"I was hoping they'd send 109s," Sergeant Davis said. "These buggers are too slow for my liking."

"109s have got cannon," Dunn said. "These haven't."

"Yeah, but your 109 can't fly slow, can it? Also your 109 pilot's got a lousy view looking down."

They watched the biplanes growl overhead and fly on.

"They'll be back," Dunn said. "They're going to be a pain in the arse all day." He didn't care. He was still drunk on havoc.

"That's why I was hoping for 109s. Not that it makes a lot of difference. If they find us this place is going to be like Gandhi's Inferno anyway."

They drove on but only made half a mile. The CR42s had split into pairs and were flying lower, searching more carefully. Again the jeeps had to find cover. They sat under it for a long time. Steadily, Dunn's sense of intoxication wore off, until he felt flat, used-up, weary. He had no wish to look back on the raid. Nor to look forward. He knew it would be a hard slog back to the camp and the only way to do it was a bit at a time.

*   *   *

No time for breakfast. Schramm ate a fried-egg sandwich in the back of the yellow Lysander as Benno Hoffmann flew him to Berka Main, the biggest Luftwaffe base at Benghazi. Hoffmann landed prettily – he was getting to like this machine – and taxied behind a small truck in which an airman held up a board reading FOLLOW ME, until they got to a Heinkel 111 whose propellers were already spinning. Schramm scrambled down, hurrying as fast as his shrunken leg would let him, and was helped aboard the bomber. It was moving before the hatch was banged shut. "Sit down," Captain di Marco told him. "Fasten your straps." He had to shout because the engines were working up to take-off power.

Schramm waited until the Heinkel was airborne and on course, and the pilot had throttled back to a steady thunder. "When did all this start?" he asked.

"About six o'clock. Just after von Mansdorf told General Schaefer about the raid on Barce. That was when the general decided it was time to retaliate."

Schramm shoved back the sleeve of his flying-suit and found his watch. Five to seven. "It's all rush-rush-rush nowadays," he said. "Never time to sit and enjoy the paper."

"Since it was originally your idea, I suggested it might be a courtesy to invite you to accompany us."

"Many thanks." Schramm looked out at the desert, flat and brown. He looked at the inside of the aeroplane, hard and grey and functional. "What now?" he said.

"First we fly to the advanced landing-ground at Defa. I must navigate." He handed Schramm a newspaper. "Relax," he said.

"I bet you haven't got any coffee."

Di Marco gave him a vacuum flask. Schramm shook his hand. He suddenly wished Dr Grandinetti could see him. He'd get ten out of ten for enjoyment.

*　　*　　*

The Italian CR42s failed to find any of the jeeps. When they finally droned away, Lampard hustled his patrol out of cover and took some chances, sprinting the vehicles across open spaces. The biplanes landed at Barce, refuelled, and heard of the discovery of fresh wheel-tracks across the plain below the Jebel, probably made by the raiding party. Coming out or going in? Nobody knew. But clearly, that part of the Jebel was worth a closer search.

They caught the jeeps on the very top, where the tree line faded out and the hills had been polished by time to smooth domes with fringes of scrub around the edges. But the great thing about the Jebel was there was always a wadi if you looked hard enough. The Italian pilots chased the jeeps, swooping and machine-gunning. Lampard's drivers weaved and dodged, scattered and spread, while their gunners fired snap bursts. It was amazingly difficult to hit a jeep from the air when it was being danced expertly about. And in the end a wadi appeared, a narrow, twisting gap that could protect them. Sergeant Davis's jeep bolted into it. Lampard's jeep zigged and zagged and then dashed into the black shadow. Mike Dunn's jeep had the longest race and it lost. The pilot of a CR42 saw where it was heading and he dived. His bullet-stream pecked at the ground, kicking up little fountains of dust. He eased back the stick and the nose came up and the jeep slid into his gunsight. He fired, and every man in it was knocked over. The impact clubbed the driver, made him drag the wheel down and attempt a sudden right-angled turn, an impossible manoeuvre at that speed, and the jeep somersaulted, shedding bodies. The next CR42 hammered the wreck. It burst into flames.

*　　*　　*

The Bombay flew in with food, fuel and Baggy Bletchley.

He asked Barton to assemble everyone, the officers and the other ranks. While this was being done he said, "The party's over, Fanny. My orders are to evacuate LG 250 immediately."

"The Kittyhawks won't fly before this afternoon, sir. They took a bit of a beating last night."

"So I see." The wreckage of Pip's machine had been dragged to the edge of the runway. "Well, semi-immediately, then."

The men formed a half-circle. Barton introduced the air commodore, and stepped back.

"I'm here to tell you this operation is complete and you're pulling out," he said. "This has been another bright page in the squadron's annals. You might not think so, to look about you. Only two kites on the strength, and both a bit shop-soiled. But think of the havoc you have wrought amongst the enemy. As it says in the Bible, 'Saul hath slain his thousands, and David his ten thousands'. England is proud of you. This has been a vital step on the long road to victory."

While they were loading Patterson into the Bombay, Skull murmured to Bletchley, "I must say I liked that line about Saul and David, sir."

"I thought you might."

"It raised the whole tone of the occasion."

"Let's say it helped. Frankly, there's not a hell of a lot one can say at times like this. Ah . . . many thanks." Bletchley smiled and accepted a mug of tea from an airman. "Who was Saul?" he asked.

"First king of Israel. Fought the Philistines, quarrelled with the high priest, went off his head, killed himself."

"Doolally, I expect. The desert doesn't change much, does it?"

The Bombay flew out with Bletchley, Kellaway, the doctor and all but a very few ground crew. That left Barton, Hooper, Skull and the signals officer, Prescott. Prescott asked Skull why he stayed. "For the sake of the children, of course," Skull said. Prescott stared.

Bletchley had brought a new gramophone record: Geraldo and his orchestra, with Sam Brown singing 'A Foggy Day in London Town'. They all stood around and listened. "Crap," Barton said. He took the disc and sent it spinning into the desert. "Play Bowlly," he ordered. "Play 'Empty Saddles'. That's real music."

*   *   *

Defa's oasis came over the horizon exactly where di Marco had promised it would be. There was no need for the Heinkel pilot to alter course; he simply let the nose sink and eventually he flew the bomber onto the airstrip and made a perfect three-point landing. One piece of professionalism deserved another.

The oasis was just a fistful of dusty palms and a well, with a couple of camels sneering at the new arrival. The camels had already seen two Junkers Tri-Motor transport planes come in, so they were not impressed by a Heinkel 111.

Everyone got out of the Heinkel and stretched their legs. "Nice piece of navigation," Schramm said to di Marco.

"That was the easy bit," the pilot said. "That was like taking a tram across Hamburg."

Already, crewmen from the transports were refuelling the Heinkel from jerricans. The stink of petrol drifted with the breeze and Schramm took a stroll to escape it. Not far. After the coolness of cruising at eight thousand feet, Defa was a swamp of heat. He sat under the wing of the nearest Junkers and did his sweating privately. The flies soon got wind of it and arrived to taste a new vintage.

The pilot and di Marco came and joined him.

"She doesn't look big enough," Schramm said. The Heinkel 111 had two engines and a fuselage like an expensive cigar, curved and streamlined from end to end. "How big is she?"

"Not big enough," the pilot said. "But you don't want to worry about that because she's actually bigger inside than she is outside."

"That's clever."

"It's brilliant."

"All right, it's brilliant. How did Dr Heinkel do it?"

"He didn't. We did. We dumped all the junk the Luftwaffe keeps stuffing into these poor beasts. We threw out all the guns and ammo, all the armour-plating, the oxygen bottles, the heater."

"Also the parachutes," di Marco said.

"You threw out the parachutes?"

"Certainly," the pilot said. "You know how much a

parachute weighs? Ten kilograms. We lost the navigator's table, the gunners' seats, several black boxes and the aviator's thunderbox, so if you haven't moved your bowels today you'd better do it now. We also cut the crusts off the sandwiches and took the pips out of the oranges."

"Amazing," Schramm said. "So how far will she fly now?"

"God knows. Normal loaded weight is twelve thousand kilograms. When they've finished topping up all the extra tanks she'll be well over the maximum permissible over-loaded weight, which is fourteen thousand kilograms. About two thousand kilograms of that is bombs."

"Maybe she won't fly at all. I mean, if she's heavier than the maximum permissible *overloaded* weight then how do you —"

"You're right, I don't." He helped Schramm to his feet. The ground crew were screwing on the fuel caps.

"I'm surprised you agreed to take me," Schramm said. "I'm just useless weight."

"Well, the general insisted on an observer and you can fly her for a bit. It's going to be a long day. Besides, you're fairly thin and you've had a haircut."

They stopped by the starboard wheel. He unzipped his flying overalls. "This is the place recommended by the manufacturer's manual," he said. Schramm unzipped and they pissed on the wheel. "Every little helps," the pilot said.

He taxied to the very end of the airstrip and ran up the engines until the bomber was shaking and the props were screaming. Even so, when he waved the chocks away the Heinkel seemed to waddle forward and there was no eagerness in the way it worked itself up to a fast trundle. Half-way down the strip the tail came up, grudgingly, like a nagged husband, and now the wings were slicing the air with some efficiency. Yet for all the lift they created, they were dragging a load that the Heinkel had never been designed to carry. The throttles were wide open. The exhaust stubs were pumping smoke. It was not the greatest airstrip in Libya and the pilot's teeth clenched every time his wheels thumped a ridge. It wasn't the longest airstrip either. As the Heinkel ate up the final few yards the pilot said silently *Goodbye Mama* and eased the control column back. Maybe the wheels bounced her off a bigger ridge than usual, or maybe she was ready to fly, or maybe God reached down and changed the laws of science. The pilot didn't know and he didn't care. The bomber flirted with the desert for a mile or two as he retracted the wheels. After that she climbed like a pregnant duck. It was thirty minutes before he told himself he could relax and an hour before his jaws completely unclenched.

*　　*　　*

The two jeeps sat in a dark corner of the twisting wadi. The sound of the engines of the Italian biplanes rolled around the sky like an endless echo. The survivors of Lampard's patrol ate dates, sipped water, cleaned weapons, filled petrol tanks and treated the wounded. Apart from the man with a bullet-hole in his leg, two men had been hit by the CR42s: one in the arm, one in the stomach. The arm was broken. The stomach wound was very bad.

Lampard and Sergeant Davis walked back to the entrance to the wadi, keeping in the hard shadow all the way. The burning jeep lay in clear view, on its side, sending up smoke as rich as black velvet. They counted three bodies, none moving. Davis thought he could see the leg of the fourth man sticking out from a patch of camel-thorn, but Davis had banged his head on one of the Vickers when his jeep swerved sharply and he got double vision if he looked at things too hard.

"They'll see us if we go out there," he said.

"Somebody might be alive," Lampard said. "I hate to just leave them."

"Even if he's still alive he'll be half-dead. Best let the German medics have him. They can't be far away, can they?"

They walked back to the jeeps. No need to discuss the situation. It was all too stark. Impossible to move while the Italian aircraft were overhead; yet every minute they waited brought enemy infantry nearer, guided by the marker of smoke.

*   *   *

"How interesting," Skull said. "How *very* interesting." He read on. "My goodness," he said. In the distance a Kittyhawk's engine turned over, coughed and died. "Yes indeed," he said, with a suppressed chuckle, and turned a page. "All too true." He read on, eyebrows up, spectacles down. An overheated breeze came out of the desert, rattled the canvas sunscreen like a bad-tempered child seeking attention, and moved on, ignored. "Mmmm," Skull said.

"Some of us are trying to sleep," Prescott muttered.

"What's that?" Hooper asked Skull.

"This? Oh . . . nothing special. Pinky Dalgleish's diary. I took it off Uncle when he was doolally, because it seemed to upset him. Mind you, I can see why." He began reading again.

The Kittyhawk coughed, started, lost interest, died.

"Why?" Barton asked.

Skull finished reading a sentence and looked up reluctantly. He took a long time to find Barton. He pushed his spectacles up his nose and frowned. "Oh, you wouldn't be interested," he said, and turned back to the diary.

"Yes I bloody would," Barton said.

Skull sighed, and turned back a page. "Let's see . . . Here

it is. *Fanny, through sheer determination, has become the perfect fighter leader.*"

They waited. "Is that it?" Prescott asked.

"What? Oh no, there's more. *He doesn't care who he kills. If he can't find an enemy he invents one. To defend decency and freedom he has become a thoroughly unscrupulous bastard. If he couldn't fly for us I'm sure he'd be perfectly happy in the Luftwaffe.*"

"Bollocks," Barton said.

"Pinky had some funny ideas," Prescott said. "I remember —"

"Utter bollocks!" Barton said. "Crap, turds and bollocks! It's all pure bollocks."

"Of course it's just one man's opinion," Skull said. "I'm sure if you were to ask the rest of the squadron . . ." He broke off, and shook his head. "What am I saying?" he murmured.

"He can write what he likes," Barton growled, "it's bollocks from start to finish."

"Anything there about me?" Hooper asked.

"As it happens, yes, I did come across a remark." Skull searched the pages. "Just a line: *Hooper is a typical American. He believes God invented the gun, and vice versa.* Quite terse."

"God did invent the gun," Hooper said. "America is God's own country and the gun is God's own weapon. It says so in the Bible."

"Bollocks," Barton said doggedly.

"Well, if it doesn't, it ought to."

"What's wrong with those kites?" Barton stood up and glared at them. "Come on, Hick. I want to get weaving." He and Hooper walked towards the aircraft.

"Let's have a look at that," Prescott said.

"Oh . . . it's awfully tedious," Skull said. "Not worth the effort."

"Didn't sound tedious to me."

"And classified, strictly speaking. Top secret. I'd better lock it up."

Prescott, who was tall and muscular, took the diary from him. He skimmed through it. After a couple of minutes he said, "Where's all that stuff about Fanny?"

"Nowhere. I invented it. And the bit about Hick, too. Quite good, wasn't it, for the spur of the moment?"

"Look." Prescott tossed the diary back to him. "I like Fanny. I respect him. I don't go much on this sort of practical joke."

"No joke," Skull said. "Deadly serious. I meant every word."

Prescott was shocked and offended. "You honestly think Fanny would fly for the Luftwaffe?" he demanded. "That's insane."

"Of course it's insane. Fanny forgot which side he's on long ago. There aren't any sides in his war. There's just the desert and the enemy. He doesn't want to *win*, for God's sake. He wants to fly and fight for ever. This desert is fighter pilots' heaven."

"Not much of a heaven for Pinky Dalgleish." Prescott was still angry.

"That's the pity of it," Skull said. "You can't have a Fanny Barton without a Pinky Dalgleish. Don't tell him I said so. He'll hit you."

*   *   *

The Arabs had learned a new word: jip. They were proud of it, and when George the Greek showed no enthusiasm they were disappointed. One of them drew a picture in the sand. It was a box on wheels. "Jip," the man said.

"Oh, *jeep*," George said. The Arab nodded wisely and held up three fingers. "Jip-jip-jip," he said, and much more.

George got the message. There were three jeeps somewhere in the Jebel and these jeeps would carry him home to his friends. Until this could be arranged he must be patient. The idea of walking home was out. Too many Germans in the area.

This he believed, for he saw German patrols almost every day. Once, he even sold some eggs to a foot-patrol that came by at the end of the afternoon, looking very weary. They treated him exactly like the other Arabs. When he tried his few words of Arabic on them, they shrugged or looked away. The soldier who gave him sugar for the eggs, snapped "Imshi!" when the deal was done. Literally it meant 'fast' or 'speedy'; there was a British fighter ace in the desert called 'Imshi' Mason. But every Allied soldier used 'Imshi!' to mean 'Get out!' or 'Buzz off!'. George was amused to hear it from a German in the Jebel, but he did not smile. He imshied.

It was late in the morning and he was sitting on a rock, picking the last flaking traces of dead scabs off his ribs, when a German truck came round a bend and drove up to the camp. It was in no great hurry, and the troops who got out of it took their time assembling the dozen or so Arabs. No force was used; indeed the soldiers were quite courteous. They merely pointed where they wanted every-one to go, which was into the big tent. There was just enough room for them all to sit in a semi-circle, facing the door.

After a while a young German officer came and stood in the entrance. He looked to be about twenty-three. He had freckles. George noticed this because he hadn't seen any freckled men until he left Greece. Freckles usually went with very fair skin. He wondered how this man survived the desert sun.

The man appeared to be waiting. He said nothing and did nothing. He just stood, looking calm and pleasant, and waited.

The tent got hot. It would be hot in any case, of course, with the sun almost directly overhead, but now the body-heat from a dozen people pushed the temperature even higher.

This was no great problem for the Arabs. They never allowed heat to disturb them. They accepted it, suffered it passively, survived it. George had learned the trick. He simply sat and let time pass. If the flies could tolerate it so could he.

The officer stood and waited. Occasionally he shifted his weight from one leg to another. George looked at the officer's boots until they gently went out of focus. It was a restful way to do nothing.

Ten minutes passed. Or it could have been twenty. Or thirty. Nobody moved. The flies made the rounds of hands and feet and faces. Flies were eternal optimists. They landed on ears or eyelids or lips or nostrils as if they were the first explorers and hidden treasure awaited them. Then they flew away. They never learned, and they never gave up.

George became drowsy. Falling asleep might be dangerous, he warned himself, but it was impossible not to be drowsy in this bakehouse atmosphere. For some reason a memory surfaced in his sluggish mind. It was Billy Stewart, back in LG 181, sitting in the sun outside his tent, motionless, watching the flies. Billy could sit like a statue and watch and watch and watch until suddenly . . . *clap*. He never missed. Good old Billy. George brushed the flies off his lips. The officer straightened up. "*Hier ist der Mann*," he said.

A soldier came in, took George by the arm and helped him up. His legs were stiff and he wobbled a bit as he was led out. "You are a spy," the officer said in English. "An English spy." George pretended not to understand. "You are not an Arab," the officer said. "An Arab never does this." He brushed his fingers across his lips. "The flies gave you away," he said.

As they put him in the truck he looked back and saw the serious little Arab girl standing by the tent. Nobody else had come out. George raised his hands and created something that only she could recognise: an imaginary cat's-cradle. She nodded. It didn't mean anything. It was just something they shared.

Later that day he was taken to Benghazi and for a week he was interrogated, sometimes brutally, sometimes not. There was little he could tell them, and nothing about spies or raids or sabotage or intelligence. At the end of a week they shot him. First he had been tried and found guilty. It was all perfectly legitimate.

*　　*　　*

Lampard decided to make a run for it. His patrol was down to seven men and three of them were wounded. Some of the others had taken a few knocks.

Before he could tell them his decision, the CR42s left. Their engines faded; within seconds it was hard to hear them.

"No stamina," someone said. "Gone to lunch."

"Let's go," Lampard said.

He drove the first jeep, not fast, always approaching the bends with caution in case the enemy had somehow sneaked into the wadi. Its narrow walls reflected the rumble of the jeeps and revealed only a narrow strip of sky; which was why none of the patrol heard or saw the Stukas until the first bomb fell. It created a high brown fountain of earth somewhere ahead, followed by a thundercrack of a bang, and then, much later, a shove of air as the blast found its way up the wadi. Lampard stopped. He looked up, and saw the Stuka soaring as if it were performing at an aerobatic show.

Sergeant Davis appeared beside him. "Now what are the buggers up to?" he said.

They waited, and caught a glimpse of a second Stuka in its dive, and they heard the steady scream of its air-brakes. Again, the explosion was far ahead.

"They're bombing that end of our wadi," Lampard said. "They're trying to box us in. They can't see us but they know we're in here."

"Stukas this end, troops the other."

"If they're bombing that end, it means there are no Hun troops in front of us," Lampard said. "It also means the air's going to be thick with dust, I hope. It's worth a try, anyway."

They drove hard, and saw the mouth of the wadi just as another Stuka pulled out of its dive and they could actually watch its bomb continue the plunge until it vanished into a fog of dust and smoke. The explosion radiated dirt and debris around a sullen flash of red, and its blast made the jeeps rock on their springs. Lampard counted to five and charged into the muck before another Stuka could drop its load.

The exit was not blocked: no bomb had toppled its walls; but it was badly cratered. Davis lost sight of Lampard's jeep almost at once. He squared his wheel to dodge a rock the size of an anvil and ended up slithering into a crater that steamed with a choking chemical stink. The other side looked too steep but he charged it, and it was too steep. The jeep got halfway and spun its wheels. "Out and shove!" he bawled. They manhandled the jeep, its tyres smoking with effort, and it climbed out of the hole. Another crater came out of the dust. He swung away from it and his wheels began bouncing off rocks. There seemed to be a hundred. But his double vision was now permanent, so maybe there were only fifty. Too many, anyway. He backed up and tried the other side of the crater. Both craters. And they both had two edges. So what? He had four hands. He chose the wrong edge and felt the jeep lurch and wander like a drunk. He stamped on the brake, set the handbrake, got out. "You drive!" he shouted. The jeep was teetering, as ready to fall as to stay. He joined the manhandlers, twice as powerful now with his four hands, and they coaxed the thing back onto safe ground. By now they were outside the wadi, and there was more space to work in. They ran alongside the jeep, pointing at rocks and potholes ahead. Davis heard an old familiar scream in the sky. "Get in!" he shouted. They were already scrambling aboard. The driver glanced back once and put his foot to the floor. The fog of dust was thinning. The bomb-blast seemed to urge the jeep on its way.

Lampard's jeep was waiting under the inevitable, the invaluable acacia trees. Thank God for acacias. They were like military umbrellas: high enough to get a jeep under, low enough to hide it. The jeeps moved from patch to patch of cover and the Stukas seemed not to notice. The jeeps found a stretch of cliff face and used its black shadow to hide in. They fled, separately, across a bare plateau and met up in a mile-wide wadi where they hid in some scrub. It had been hard driving: hard on the jeeps and even harder on the casualties. The man with the stomach wound was dead.

*　　*　　*

"Skull's never flown," Barton said. "Skull's a fucking penguin. What does he know?"

He was still stiff with anger. He had a rifle, and he fired three rounds at the ancient wreck of the Hurricane. The last bullet hit the rudder and knocked it silly.

Hick Hooper sat on a stack of ammunition boxes and watched. The Kittyhawks were not yet airworthy: fitters and riggers were still at work on them.

"Funny thing about nationalities," Hooper said. "I mean, Churchill's half-American. And Hitler's not really German at all, he's Austrian. Come to that, the King of England's pretty damn German himself."

"Cock." Barton banged off two more rounds and hit the prop. "Who told you that?"

"Skull. He said the royal family's surname is Saxe-Coburg."

Barton scoffed. "That's Intelligence for you! It's Windsor. Even I know that."

"He said it was Saxe-Coburg until 1917. They changed it because —" Barton fired again and cut him off. There was silence while Barton reloaded. "Who gives a damn anyway?" Hooper said. "I'm half-German, if it comes to that." Barton glanced sideways. "My mother was born in Cologne," Hooper said. "Where the eau comes from. We nearly went back there during the slump. I was about thirteen, I guess. How about that? I might have ended up in the Luftwaffe. I might have been flying one of those nightfighters, trying to —"

"Here!" Barton tossed the rifle to him. The conversation made him uncomfortable. He watched Hooper work the bolt and take aim. "Anyway, they bloody well started it," Barton said. "I had a cousin killed in the London blitz. Never met her, but I saw a photograph. Pretty little girl and they blew her to bits." He blinked as Hooper fired. "They're all shits as far as I'm concerned. They don't know the meaning of humanity and decency and fair play. I shan't be sorry if every German gets his stupid fucking head blown off."

"Well, you've certainly done more than your share," Hooper said.

"It's the only way we'll ever get back to a normal civilised kind of living," Barton said, "by ripping their German arms off and beating their German brains in with the bloody German stumps. Blokes like Skull can't understand that. They're too busy filling their fountain pens. Are you going to fire that thing or fondle it all day?" Hooper put three shots through the RAF roundel.

*   *   *

A lot of the Sahara was once seabed. You can pick up fossilised fish bones five hundred miles inland. This is one reason why so much of Libya and Egypt is so flat. Although Defa airstrip was nearly two hundred miles from the Mediterranean it was only three hundred feet above sea-level, and the Heinkel 111 flew south for another couple of hundred miles before the desert floor climbed to twice that height. It was a very gradual, unexciting geography: one beige brown after another. Paul Schramm soon grew tired of it.

With di Marco sitting beside the pilot, the only place left in the cockpit was the bomb-aimer's position, lying face-down in the Perspex nose. Schramm tried it for a while, dozed off, and woke up when the sun began to bake him. He squeezed past the pilot and sidled along the catwalk in the middle of the bomb-bay, to the space where the air-gunners usually lived. There was nothing to look at there, but there was nothing to look at anywhere.

He sat propped against a bulkhead and tried to make sense of his situation. He was a more or less superfluous passenger in a smallish, oldish, twin-engined bomber designed to raid targets a few hundred kilometres away which was trying to reach a target that was two thousand kilometres from its base. Below, for almost the entire flight, was a desert that was so lethal you might as well shoot yourself and get it over with. Assuming, of course, you survived a forced landing in a machine so overloaded with fuel that it was a flying tanker. Schramm found himself listening to the throb of the engine-roar, frightening himself with imagined hiccups or hesitations. That was absurd. The whole damned operation was absurd. He made himself reread the newspaper and he fell asleep.

Di Marco shook him awake. "We are crossing the border between Libya and Chad," he said.

Schramm looked out of a window. Brown desert stretched to the horizon. "Should I care?" he asked.

"Now look out the other side."

Schramm did, and saw mountains that climbed like cathedral spires. They were dangerously, suicidally close. The peaks were several thousand feet above the Heinkel: he had a sick feeling that a breeze could blow the aircraft against those sheer sides at any moment. Then he took a breath and looked harder. The mountains were a mile away.

Di Marco suggested he sit in the cockpit. The view was even more stupendous from there: everything was bigger, clearer, more jagged, more magnificent. Schramm looked at the map and identified the Tibesti Mountains. They reared out of the desert like a gesture of defiance, pushing up and up, until the empty wasteland of sand was left a huge and giddy distance below.

The pilot let him enjoy the view. When it was behind them he said, "My backside's numb. You take her for a bit. We're halfway. She's trimmed to fly hands-off. Just sit here and look confident. Steer one-nine-five and don't touch any of the knobs."

*   *   *

The man with the stomach wound was Walters. They buried him in the scrub. The ground was hard, so his grave was just a scrape in the soil with a lot of rocks heaped on top. "Rest in peace," Lampard said, and that was enough. Nobody was in a mood for funeral rites. The faint noise of German military vehicles kept their nerves on edge; and occasionally the crash of mortar shells reached them from some distant and futile attempt at flushing out.

Lampard itched to get on and get out. They had thirty-odd miles to go. He disliked this wadi: it was too broad, too shallow; there was nowhere to put look-outs; the scrub was so thin that a shufti-kite would spot the jeeps; he felt exposed. But they could not move. Davis's jeep had a puncture. What's more, all the spare tyres were holed. It would be madness to go on when a wheel couldn't be changed in a hurry. Reluctantly, Lampard agreed.

"Time for some grub, too," Davis suggested. Lampard agreed to that. Hunger didn't add to efficiency. Everyone had bully, biscuit and water. The men examined the jeeps as they ate, and found damage caused either by the racketing drive across the Jebel or the attacks by the CR42s; it didn't really matter which. Springs had cracked or snapped, a jerrican of petrol was bullet-holed, the steering on Lampard's jeep was buckled, Davis's jeep was trickling oil. It could all be patched, but patching took time. Lampard watched them work.

"In case I haven't said it," he said, "I want you to know that we put on an absolutely brilliant show last night."

Nobody replied, perhaps because everyone was still eating, perhaps not. Lampard went away and cleaned his tommy-gun.

At last Davis came and told him the jeeps were as ready as they ever would be.

"Good. These blasted flies are all over me."

"Wog flies," Davis said. "Not English. Don't know how to queue."

The branches got thrown off the jeeps and the engines were started. They had travelled perhaps fifty yards when a shufti-kite came dribbling over the skyline and they had to swerve under cover again.

It was a Fieseler Storch, as slow as a bicycle. They sat motionless while it made lazy S-bends, all down the valley. "Now go away and bother someone else," Lampard said. Instead it circled. Five minutes later it was still circling. "What's it found?" he wondered. "What's so important?"

Davis volunteered to go and see. While they discussed this, the Storch flew away. "Still worth a recce," Davis said. "You never know what's waiting down there. NAAFI van, panzer division, herd of elephants, could be anything."

Lampard sent him, on foot, with one other man. Half an

hour later the man returned. "It's a bloody great German wireless truck," he said. "Big radio mast. Sarnt Davis thinks the shufti-kite was reporting to it. He reckons the krauts in the truck are in charge of the search."

"Take me to him," Lampard said.

They found Davis hiding in the collapsed stonework of an old well.

"We could destroy that thing in ten seconds," Lampard said, "but then the Hun would turn up and destroy us in five minutes."

They had to wait for two roasting, fly-tormented hours until the truck dismounted its aerial and drove off. "My God, this war can be boring," Lampard grumbled.

*　　*　　*

Every time they started up Barton's Kittyhawk it fired for ten seconds and died. Dirty petrol. They washed the carburettors and cleaned the fuel lines but still the aeroplane would not come alive. They would have to drain the tanks, filter the petrol and start again.

Barton got fed up with potting at the wrecked Hurricane and he went in search of scorpions to shoot, turning over stones with his boot while he held the rifle ready. He found none and gave up. He noticed a butterfly. It was a Painted Lady, the only sort of butterfly the squadron saw in the desert, a delicate little creature whose wings were mottled a pale buff and red. Presumably it was migrating across the Sahara, a task so huge it was scarcely credible. Barton chased it and tried to shoot it down. He ran a hundred yards and exhausted his ammunition before he gave up, cursing. The Painted Lady fluttered south. It looked good for another thousand miles.

"What the hell's wrong with him?" Prescott asked Skull. "Has he gone doolally too?" They were sprawled in the shade of the canvas roof of the mess.

"He's normal. Fighter pilots exist in one of two states: torpid or rabid. Right now Fanny is rabid. He's quite harmless as long as you don't go near him. Excuse me." Skull got up and strolled over to Barton, who was cleaning the rifle. "Decorations," he said. "Have you done anything about recommending anybody?"

"Piss off. None of your business."

Skull converted his sun-umbrella into a shooting-stick and perched on it. "The bravest pilot I ever knew should have got a DSO and probably a Victoria Cross," he said. "Instead he got nothing, because his CO got killed before he put in any recommendations. No CO, no gong."

"I'm not going to get killed."

"Pip deserves something. Even I know that."

Barton shut one eye and squinted down the barrel. "You do it," he said. "Make a list."

"Don't be absurd, Fanny. I wasn't there. You were."

"That's right, I was." He oiled the breech and worked the bolt. "Well, I don't remember seeing anything special. A few blokes got the chop, but that's not unusual, is it?" He aimed at the sky and squeezed the trigger. "Giving them gongs isn't going to make any difference."

"It might acknowledge their courage."

"Brave because they got the chop? Don't talk balls. You don't need courage to get killed. You need to be unlucky, that's all."

"I see. The squadron gets virtually wiped out and it's just bad luck."

"You've got it, Skull! Well done!" Barton tossed the rifle high in the air and caught it. "At last you've got it. Half of war is luck and the other half is cock-up. I had an uncle got killed at Gallipoli. Now what difference did Gallipoli make to anything?" He stared Skull straight in the eyes. "None. None! All those big brave Anzacs got the chop at Gallipoli and it didn't change anything, not in the slightest! Of course, nobody knew that at the time." Barton scratched his stubbled chin. "My uncle didn't get a medal when he got killed," he said. "He was very annoyed about that, my uncle was."

"This isn't Gallipoli," Skull said.

"I'll recommend everyone for a DSO," Barton said. "Satisfied now?" He walked away before Skull could answer.

*　　*　　*

Schramm liked flying the Heinkel. Even overloaded with fuel she was still responsive and her great sail of a rudder made for good stability. He had no need to change the throttle settings. He just kept her on course, checked the gauges now and then, and when a lump of hot air came bubbling up he did his best to anticipate the bumps and hollows they flew through.

From seven thousand feet – presumably the most efficient cruising height – the ground looked bleak and baked. The foothills of Tibesti had been rust red. An hour's flying changed the colour to a bleached yellow and the texture to an infinity of ripples. Later still, the ground looked as if it had been trampled by the tiny hooves of a mighty herd: for as far as Schramm could see, it was imprinted with a pattern of crescent shapes, all pointing in the same direction. He realised these must be dunes, millions of dunes. He had once suggested driving over this terrain. He breathed deeply and felt hugely grateful to di Marco.

Two hours after Tibesti, five hours after Defa, six and a half hours after Berka, the pilot relieved him. "Many thanks," the man said.

"My pleasure. She was a perfect lady."

"That was the easy bit," the pilot said.

Schramm stood behind di Marco, whose lap was full of charts and notebooks, slide-rules and dividers, and plugged into the intercom. "Where are we?" he asked.

Di Marco showed him. "Lake Chad is the next land-mark. You see? It's about the size of Luxembourg. We should cross the eastern tip of it and then pick up this river, the Chari, which flows into Lake Chad. We fly up the Chari. The Chari goes through Fort Lamy. The airfield is on the left." He made it sound as if he were telling a stranger in town how to find the public library.

The crescent dunes changed to flat scrub, nothing but acacia from horizon to horizon. The acacia gave way to palms. Schramm began to feel hungry, but he felt it was the wrong time to say so. They were steadily losing height: when the palms thinned out and the country became more like wooded parkland, he saw cattle grazing on every side.

Lake Chad came up precisely when and where di Marco had calculated it should. It was a glittering blue, fringed with hundreds of islands of intense green. Waterbirds in their thousands took off and swirled in clouds of flickering white and pink. After the aridity of the desert it was like a huge, costly, choreographed welcome. Black men standing in fishing boats waved. Nobody in the cockpit spoke.

The river Chari was twice as wide as an autobahn. Its banks were lined with grass huts, all arranged in neat rows according to the tidy mind of some French colonial admin-istrator. Fort Lamy was in sight. Di Marco put his charts away and moved down to the bomb-aimer's position. Schramm took his seat. "On schedule," he said. "Con-gratulations."

"That was the easy bit," the pilot said.

*   *   *

As they walked back to the jeep, Lampard and Davis dis-cussed what next.

Davis was all for lying up until nightfall and then driving

the last thirty miles to base camp. It might take most of the night, but they had plenty of time. They could move slowly and continuously, and there would be no shufti-kite to worry about.

Lampard wanted to go now. If they drove in the dark it would have to be without headlights. Too many Hun patrols were out looking for them. So they'd probably miss the track, drive into rocks, bust the jeeps. And they'd certainly get lost.

Davis said he was sure he could navigate from here to base camp in the dark.

Lampard said the trouble with night-driving was you couldn't see the ambush until it was too late.

After that they walked in silence.

Lampard called everyone together. "The good news is that Jerry is obviously rather annoyed by our raid on Barce," he said. "The bad news is the Jebel is now swarming with enemy patrols. However, the good news is the Jebel is a very big place, with ten thousand wadis, and they can't search them all, or even a fraction. Now, we can either wait here until dark and crawl back to base, or we can make a dash for it with our eyes wide open. My decision is to make a dash for it. We go *now*."

As they dispersed, Connors said to Blake, "The bad news is I got the pox. The good news is you can have it if I get killed."

"Charming," Blake said. "Fucking charming."

Lampard led. Battered as they were, the jeeps were remarkably quick and surefooted and he made them go fast. At the same time he showed proper caution. When he came up against a blind bend or a narrowing defile he stopped and sent a man ahead to recce. Davis approved.

They were moving south-west, against the grain of the Jebel. It meant making a series of long zigzags. Often they crossed the marks of half-tracks: the enemy had been here recently. Twice they saw foot-patrols on distant skylines.

Lampard quickly put the jeeps out of their sight and hoped for the best. After an hour they had covered fifteen miles. Now they were over the high ground of the Jebel and the gradient was helping them. No sign of the shufti-kite.

The landscape was starting to look familiar, and when he recognised the mouth of a wadi, Lampard knew they were less than a dozen miles from base camp and a brew-up. This was a good wadi: scoured smooth by flash-floods which had rolled all the boulders against its walls. Furthermore, there were no tyre tracks in the sand. Lampard accelerated. The sooner they got in, the sooner they got out. Halfway through the wadi his jeep took a bend and nearly hit a pair of German trucks speeding in the opposite direction. Before he could shout, a fire-fight was raging.

There was neither time nor space for tactical subtlety or skilled manoeuvre. It was simply a matter of who fired first and who fired longest. The two pairs of Vickers Ks in the second jeep swamped the first German truck, killed the driver, killed the troops, sent the truck headlong into the stone wall of the wadi. As that happened the second German truck turned the corner and a machine-gunner on its cab found the jeep and sprayed it very thoroughly. The jeep had no protection, no armour, nowhere to hide. Sergeant Davis, Trooper Connors, Blake the fitter, all died. This was completed in a matter of a few seconds.

Lampard had overshot the action. In his desperation to reverse he found the wrong gear, bashed a wheel against a rock, found reverse, sent his jeep sprinting backwards. There was a very brief point-blank battle between the double pair of Vickers Ks in his jeep and the machine-gunner in the second truck, aided by a dozen rifles. The German soldiers had been well drilled: they got off a useful volley of shots and the machine-gunner fired over their heads. But the Vickers Ks erupted with a blast of two hundred bullets in five seconds. They had been designed to destroy aeroplanes. They wiped out the second truck. It was a mismatch, the dream of every soldier, to find the enemy exposed and out-gunned and to overwhelm him, kill him ten times over; give him not the fraction of a chance. The fight was over in the time a man might hold his breath. The echoes bounced from wall to wall of the wadi like a ball game. The second truck caught fire. Its fuel tank exploded with a gentle, almost apologetic, *boom*.

The mismatch had not been complete. Of the three men with Lampard in his jeep, one – a gunner called Sharp – was dying, hit by a bullet in the chest. Another, Menzies, had a broken jaw, smashed by a spinning ricochet. He was in great pain; he could barely spit out the fragments of teeth that threatened to choke him. Trooper Smedley was untouched, although the hole in his cheek had started to bleed again. Lampard had been largely protected by the gunners alongside and behind him. A bullet had struck his right ear and left it flapping; blood coated his face and neck. The jeep would not start.

While Menzies and Smedley carried Sharp away, Lampard ran back and looked at Sergeant Davis's jeep. The three men in it were sprawled or twisted in the uncomfortable attitudes of most battlefield corpses. He took their identity discs. This was a messy business: it left his hands sticky with blood. Already the flies had begun to feast. It would be a great day in fly history. He spread pieces of clothing over the dead faces. "Rest in peace," he said. This jeep would not start either. The shimmer of spilled petrol hung around its broken tanks.

Menzies and Smedley were kneeling beside Sharp. His chest was a mass of sodden field-dressings and his eyes were almost closed. Lampard kneeled and gripped Sharp's hand. Tiny pink bubbles kept forming and breaking and reforming at Sharp's mouth. The bubbles got smaller and fewer, and he died. Lampard took his identity disc. "Rest in peace," he said. "The jeeps are kaput. We'll have to walk. Bring water and a weapon."

* * *

Fort Lamy seemed like a very pleasant town. The streets were broad and lined with shade trees. Schramm saw a square with a fountain playing. A restaurant had tables outside it. The food in Fort Lamy would be a lot better than in Benghazi: trust the French to export the best part of their culture to the colonies! "Nice place to sit out the war," he said.

"If there's just one fighter with loaded guns here you won't be going home to Barce," the pilot said.

"Relax. They arm the Hurricanes in Egypt."

"So you say." The pilot was nervous. He had never made such a low, slow approach to a target in broad daylight. He could see people down there pointing up at him. If the airfield had just one anti-aircraft gun it could scarcely miss.

"Left a little," di Marco said. He had already seen aerodrome buildings ahead. The pilot adjusted.

"Tell me when you want a smoke marker," he said. By dropping a marker he could discover the wind strength and direction.

"Not necessary," di Marco said. Smoke from chimneys was rising almost vertically. He lay face-down in the nose, looking through the bomb-sight.

Schramm saw the Hurricanes before the Heinkel crossed the boundary. They were lined up, wingtip to wingtip, as if on parade. He counted twenty-three. "Left, left," di Marco said. "More . . . more . . . more . . . No, that's not good. We're off-target. Make another approach, please."

As they flew over the Hurricanes, Schramm realised that there was no flak, no tracer, and nobody was taking off. The whole scene was placid. A few men looked up. One ran.

Their second approach was better, and di Marco bombed after only a few corrections. They all felt the Heinkel bounce a little when the load detached. Schramm turned and looked back as the Heinkel banked and climbed. Di Marco's aim had been precise. One instant the Hurricanes stood like perfect reproductions of each other; the next instant the stick of bombs rapidly flowered along their line, so quickly that it looked like a magician's trick, a string of silent blossoms of energy destroying the fighters and flinging the bits high in the air.

"Well done," Schramm said. It seemed inadequate.

"Make a circuit," di Marco said.

More people were out on the airfield now; quite a crowd. Schramm thought he could see men with rifles, but of course the range was hopeless. Smoke and dust were thinning over the Hurricanes' graveyard. Recognisable pieces lay all around: wingtips, wheels, rudders, propellers. Several wrecks were burning.

They flew around the field. "I think I see some machines inside that hangar," the pilot said.

"Not fighters," di Marco said. "There is a fuel dump in the north-eastern corner of the field. We should bomb that."

They made their approach. Schramm saw a stack of square tins that looked as big as a small house. "Right . . ." di Marco said. "Steady. Right . . . Steady. Now left . . . Steady. Good. Good. Good. Bombs gone." Again the Heinkel bucked a little.

The stick straddled the fuel dump. It set off a series of explosions, each greater than the last, each pumping a rush of flame that burst like a balloon to release a bigger, fiercer upsurge. Rich black smoke boiled into the sky. Within a minute it was twice as high as the bomber. Schramm had nothing to say. This was more than a fire. It was an act of God. It was beyond words.

The pilot made half a circuit so that di Marco could take

photographs. Then he put the nose down, crossed the field low and flat out, and beat up the crowd. Most of them ducked; Schramm did not blame them. The Heinkel climbed steeply over the hangars and cruised away. "Steer zero-two-zero," di Marco told him.

"I know," the pilot said.

"Well, that was fairly successful," Schramm said.

"That was the easy bit," the pilot said. "That was like going to the bar on the corner for a beer."

"How much fuel have we got?"

"Not enough," the pilot said. "But we all knew that before we left, didn't we?"

*   *   *

The first signal reached Cairo while the Fort Lamy fire crew was still hosing down the remains of the Hurricanes.

There was nothing they could do about the fuel dump. The heat was so intense that you could make toast a hundred yards from the flames, if you were stupid enough to stand there. Much of the fuel had been stored underground. The fire was only beginning when the bomber left the scene. Sixty thousand gallons of aviation fuel takes a lot of burning.

News of the raid hit Middle East HQ like a fox in a chicken house. Quite senior officers were seen running in its corridors. Even more senior officers were tracked down to Shepheard's, or the Gezira, or a seat in the stalls for *Gone with the Wind*, and rushed back to their offices.

At first some people refused to believe the report. *Fort Lamy bombed? Don't be absurd. Some radio operator's got himself blotto on the local hooch.* Signals bounced back and forth. The raid was confirmed, clarified, expanded, personally witnessed and endorsed by the Fort Lamy station commander. A solitary Heinkel had taken out twenty-three Hurricanes and three months' fuel supply.

A brash young squadron leader, freshly arrived from England to fetch and carry for an air vice-marshal, couldn't see what all the fuss was about. "It's a bit cheeky, I agree, sir," he said, "but we often lose more than that to the U-boats in a single convoy, so . . ."

"Don't be a bloody idiot all your life," the air vice-marshal growled. They were pounding along a corridor to a suddenly urgent meeting. "The Takoradi Trail's an artery. In fact it's *the* artery, there isn't another, and we've been getting fifty Hurricanes a week pumped up it. Now this cocky Hun stooges across from God knows where and chops the artery! There's blood all over Chad, and our hopes of air superiority up the blue have gone down the bog! Got it now?"

"Yes sir." The squadron leader put on a spurt and opened the door to the room inside which sudden urgency was already loud.

The meeting made some fast decisions. Within minutes, signals went top secret, top priority, to the station commanders at Maiduguri, Geneina and El Fasher – stages on the Takoradi Trail to the west or east of Fort Lamy – ordering all aircraft to be dispersed immediately. Ditto fuel supplies.

By now an expert on the Heinkel 111 had been found and the meeting was pretty confident that the raider must have refuelled somewhere in the desert. There was much stabbing of index fingers at various spots on the map of North Africa, and a short shock when it was realised that to the north of Nigeria lay the French province of Niger. Unlike Chad, Niger had remained loyal to the Vichy Government in France. Niger was therefore stiff with collaborationists, and if the Luftwaffe had set up a refuelling airstrip inside Niger, that would put the field at Kano within easy range. Warning signals went to Kano, in Nigeria. Also to El Obeid and Khartoum, in Sudan. Christ Almighty, if one obsolescent Heinkel could knock out Fort Lamy, nowhere on the Trail was safe.

Meanwhile, somebody had been talking to the Heinkel expert about the bomber's speed.

"Well," he said, "given a pair of good engines, properly serviced, and assuming no headwind, I'd say a decent pilot might crank two hundred and fifty miles an hour out of her. But this chap won't be doing that, of course. He'll be cruising at the most fuel-efficient speed, which is somewhere in the region of a hundred and eighty miles an hour. Perhaps a hundred and eighty-five as time goes by and his tanks get lighter."

They returned to the map. Assuming he was flying back to Libya – and that made more sense than going by northern Niger, which was nothing but sand seas and rocks, an enormous distance from anywhere, and therefore not an easy place to stockpile jerricans of petrol – assuming he was trudging home to Libya, where was he now?

South of the Tibesti Mountains, that's where.

For the first time, the meeting brightened up.

The bugger still had something like seven hundred miles to go. At a hundred and eighty miles an hour. There was time to find him and bust him. It wouldn't help Fort Lamy, but it might make the Luftwaffe think again.

*   *   *

The smoke from the burning truck must attract attention. Lampard led Menzies and Smedley down the wadi at a steady jog-trot. They had done this sort of thing in training many times; however, none of them had done it with a smashed jaw. The jolt of each pace caused Menzies mounting waves of pain, pain so great that it swamped his senses. He said nothing, and they were still jogging when he fainted. He fell on his face, and this damaged his injuries even more.

They rolled him onto his back and sat him up. Lampard held his head while Smedley picked bits of dirt out of his mouth. A tooth looked so loose that they thought Menzies might swallow it and choke, so Smedley plucked it out. That provoked quite a lot of blood, and they sloshed some water in his mouth to rinse it out. After all this, Menzies was still unconscious. Lampard hoisted him carefully and carried him over his shoulder. A steady splatter of blood soaked into Lampard's battledress.

They got out of the wadi and walked fast for a mile. The hillside was thick with boulders. This made good cover but slow going.

It occurred to Lampard that the intelligent thing to have done would have been to shift two of the bodies from Davis's jeep to his own jeep. Then the Germans might think the whole patrol had been killed.

Too late now.

No shufti-kite. That was encouraging.

Smedley had been watching Menzies's upside-down face; he said he thought they should give him water. Lampard walked to the next patch of scrub, which was very spindly but it would have to do, and put him down. The limbs were slack, the eyelids were thick and heavy, the head lay where it flopped. Menzies looked dead. Smedley searched hard before he found a pulse.

What amazed Lampard was the amount of blood Menzies had lost. Lampard's battledress was drenched; it clung to his skin. "That's because his head's hanging down," Smedley said. "We've got to keep his head up. I don't think he's been breathing right, either."

Lampard decided to carry him piggyback-fashion. He ripped a long strip from his shirt and tied Menzies's arms in front, at the wrist. He looped the arms over his head and picked him up by the legs. Smedley shifted Menzies's head so that it was not on the same side as Lampard's tattered ear. They walked on.

Smedley was now carrying three weapons and two water bottles. He was a big man; nevertheless there were times when the pace that Lampard set had him gasping. Lampard had a stride like a ploughman's. He saw the obstacles coming and stepped over them. In order to keep Menzies's head in a safe and steady position he had to lean forward slightly and tilt his shoulders to the side. The flies had been bad before; now they were an army of occupation, claiming their tribute of blood and sweat. Menzies did not notice them. Lampard let them wander where they liked, unless it was into his mouth. Then he spat a small bundle of saliva-coated fly into the dust.

They heard the shufti-kite, once, but it was far behind them. They heard the clatter of half-tracks, once, but it was faint and grew fainter. They met an Arab herding a dozen goats. He pointed to the north and said: "*Tedeschi*," which meant Germans. Lampard and Smedley were going south of west, but they thanked him all the same. He looked sadly at Menzies's shattered face and murmured a Muslim prayer.

Almost twenty-four hours after his patrol had left it, Lampard carried Menzies into the wadi where the base-camp party should have been waiting. It was empty.

Smedley helped him to lift Menzies down and lay him out. Lampard's hands were locked into the shape of hooks: the fingers refused to relax. But his body felt as if it was floating.

"And here I was, looking forward to a brew-up," Smedley said. "Just goes to show. You never can tell." His voice sounded thin and husky; nevertheless it brought one of the fitters running down the wadi. He had been keeping look-out from a nearby cliff top, and had somehow missed their approach. Gibbon and Sandiman, he said, had decided to move base camp to another wadi when this one began to attract too many curious Arabs.

The doctor drove a truck around, treated Menzies where he lay, then drove him back to the new camp. Lampard and Smedley rode in the truck. Corky Gibbon had a brew-up ready for them. "Just the two of you?" he said. He added rum.

"Just the two of us," Lampard said. "And Menzies, but he's not drinking."

Gibbon was startled and dismayed, but he hid his feelings and he knew better than to ask questions. There was plenty of tea to go around. Lieutenant Sandiman had an urgent signal for Lampard to read; however, he decided to let him get a good drink inside him first. The day's work was not over yet.

CHAPTER EIGHT

Most Urgent

The order came down the chain of command at Desert Air Force, gaining force at every stage like a ball bouncing down a staircase, until it landed at LG 250. Prescott decoded it in two minutes. Barton read it aloud. "Movement order cancelled," he said. "Operation imminent. Bletchley will brief." He cheered up enormously. "See, Skull? The game's never over till it's over."

"I'll write that in Kit's book," Skull said. "I think there's room."

Baggy Bletchley flew in half an hour later, in the Brute.

"By a remarkable stroke of luck, Fanny," he said, "you're in exactly the right place at exactly the right time."

"Luck is very important, sir," Barton said. "Some have it, some don't. Let me carry those maps."

They went to the mess tent. Hooper, Prescott and Skull were already there. "I thought you'd gone," Bletchley said to Skull.

"I do the cooking and some light dusting. My bully fritters are well spoken of."

Bletchley was not listening. He unrolled a map and said, "The most extraordinary thing happened a few hours ago. A Heinkel 111 flew down to Fort Lamy and cut the Takoradi Trail, just like that." He snapped his fingers. "Not only did the rascal destroy a whole lot of brand-new Hurricanes, he also set fire to so much aviation fuel that we shan't be able to get another Hurricane through Lamy for weeks. Very imaginative, thoroughly courageous, and he cannot be allowed to survive. You're nearest. Go and kill him."

ere is he, sir?" Barton asked.

e know where he's going. Or rather, we know where he'd like to get to. Defa." Bletchley circled it on the map. "Little Luftwaffe airstrip. That's where he refuelled on the way out."

"Defa." Barton cocked his head and looked from Defa to LG 250 and back again. "Three hundred miles."

"We have reason to think he will never reach Defa. Two reasons, in fact. One is he simply hasn't got enough fuel. Normal range of a Heinkel 111 is sixteen hundred miles, by which time it's flying on fumes. From Defa to Fort Lamy and back is twenty-two hundred miles. If you put enough fuel in the machine to fly that distance it would be so heavy, it could never take off."

"Especially with a load of bombs."

"Exactly."

"You said there were two reasons, sir."

"I did indeed. The second is a headwind which the pilot is now facing on his return leg. Out of the north-west, twenty to thirty miles an hour. Just what he doesn't want."

"Presumably the pilot knows all this," Skull said. "And presumably the Luftwaffe knows it too."

"We must assume that," Bletchley said.

"So they're waiting for him to come down in the desert," Barton said, "and then they'll go and pick him up."

"Not if you get there first. Our Signals Intelligence people are listening for his transmissions. The instant they get a map reference they'll flash it to you, here, and you can be on your way."

Prescott went off to sit beside his wireless set. Barton and Hooper talked to the ground crew. Both fighters were airworthy again: the fuel problem had been solved. The guns were armed, the windscreens cleaned, the radios checked, the entire skin polished with dusters. An unclean aircraft could cost five miles an hour.

"What sort of range has your Kittyhawk got?" Bletchley asked.

"According to the book, nearly six hundred miles. That's at three hundred miles an hour. If we flew slower I suppose we'd go further."

"You must get there as fast as you can," Bletchley said. "You must kill the crew of that Heinkel. The Luftwaffe must not get a taste for the Takoradi Trail, or the whole desert war could be in jeopardy."

"If you put it like that, sir," Barton said, "I suppose we'd better get weaving."

But Prescott still sat in his tent. Bletchley had brought some bread: a rare luxury in the blue. They ate jam sandwiches and waited while the shadows lengthened.

"I've been thinking, sir," Hooper said. "Presumably the map reference locating this Heinkel pilot will apply to a Luftwaffe map. What I mean is, the Luftwaffe grid may not be the same as ours."

"It's not," Bletchley said. "I brought Luftwaffe maps."

"Oh."

Skull came over with a jug of tea. Barton felt thirsty, but he was worried about drinking just before a long flight. Hooper drank a pint, and Barton worried about that. Then he remembered that the Kittyhawk cockpit equipment included an exit tube for the pilot's relief. Trust the Yanks to think of that. He filled a mug and drank.

"In the circumstances," Skull said thoughtfully, "it rather looks as if Signals Intelligence has broken the Luftwaffe code, sir."

"I try not to speculate," Bletchley said. "That way madness lies."

"Really, sir? You're missing half the fun." Skull went away with the empty jug.

"Awkward sod," Barton said.

"Yes. He makes a good brew-up, though. How does he keep the sand out?"

"Strains it through his socks, I think."

"Ah." Bletchley took another sip. "Touched by the foot of God," he said. "Hullo, we're in business."

Prescott was hurrying towards them with a slip of paper. On it was a six-figure grid reference. When Barton plotted it on the map, his finger ended up a long way south of Defa. "Start up!" he shouted. Hooper was already running to his Kittyhawk. An engine turned over, a propeller jerked. "No, I'm afraid not," Bletchley said.

Barton turned and stared.

"It's not on, Fanny," Bletchley said. "We're about fifteen minutes late. Before you get there the sun will have gone down and you'll never find him in the dark. Work it out for yourself."

"It's worth a try," Barton argued.

"It's not worth a failure. Forget tonight. Try at dawn tomorrow."

The engines died. The evening breeze sent the usual colonies of snakes of sand skittering across the landing-ground. The ground crew tied dustsheets around the noses of the Kittyhawks and locked the rudders. Skull began opening tins of bully.

*   *   *

Lampard was sitting on a box, having his ear stitched together by the doctor, when he saw Sandiman watching him. "Any signals come in?" he asked.

"Yes."

"Tell me, then."

Sandiman took out a piece of paper. "I got this a couple of hours ago. It's marked 'Most Urgent' but there was nothing we could do until —"

"Just tell me what's in it."

"It's an order to move immediately and with all speed to a map reference deep in the desert where we'll find a Heinkel bomber that's come down. We're to capture or kill the crew."

Lampard laughed, hurt his ear severely, apologised to the doctor, and sent for Gibbon. "How soon can we get there?" he asked him.

"It's a hell of a long way, Jack. Halfway to Kufra and off to the west. If we leave now, and if we don't have any tyre trouble ... We might make it some time tomorrow morning. That's provided we don't get Stuka-ed on the way."

Lampard thought, while the doctor made the last stitches and knotted the silk and trimmed the ends with his scissors. He looked at the sun: it hung heavily in the west. An hour to dusk. "If we go now," he said, "you can get us through the Jalo Gap before midnight, can't you?" Gibbon shrugged, but he did not argue. "Then we'll be in the serir," Lampard said. "The serir's really fast. Maybe we can find this Heinkel before dawn."

"Maybe. I can try. What's the tearing hurry?"

"Corky, if *we* want the aircrew, that means they're important, so you can bet the Luftwaffe wants them too."

"Yes." Gibbon scratched his beard with his usual ferocity. "You've just had two rough nights, and a bloody rough day too, by the look of it. You sure you're up to this?"

"No." Lampard stood, but his head was twitching and one hand was trembling. Gibbon had never seen that before. "I didn't expect it would be like this, Corky," he said. "I thought I'd get killed first. This isn't how I expected it at all." Gibbon shrugged.

The trucks were already loaded. Lampard got into the back of the one where Menzies was lying. Smedley got into the other. Sandiman sat next to him. "What went wrong?" he asked quietly.

"Not for me to say, sir," Smedley said.

The trucks moved off.

* * *

The pilot had not been joking when he said the crusts had been cut off the sandwiches. There was ham, cheese, or egg mayonnaise; also an apple each; and iced coffee. The atmosphere in the cockpit was one of well-earned celebration.

"When did you learn to be a bomb-aimer?" Schramm asked.

"Yesterday," di Marco said. "If General Schaefer said yes, I wanted to be ready."

"Very professional."

"When you can fly low, and there is no wind and no flak, it is not difficult."

"What about me?" the pilot said.

"You were very professional too," Schramm said.

"I was, wasn't I? We didn't collide with anything, not even those enormous mountains. That's the first thing they tell you at flying school: don't collide with the mountains."

"Watch out," Schramm said. "Here they come again."

In fact the Tibesti range was still more than two hours away. When it came in view the pilot said he needed another break, and Schramm took over the controls. The peaks looked even more magnificent as they slid past the left wing.

"Good climbing in those mountains," di Marco said. "Many gazelle." During the next hour he gave Schramm several slight changes of course, always nudging the Heinkel towards the north-west. "Headwind," he said. "It keeps pushing us eastward."

"Bad for fuel consumption."

"Not good. But the machine has lost much weight."

"Good for fuel consumption."

"Not bad."

The fuel gauges told their own story, and long before the pilot squeezed his shoulder and Schramm slid out of his seat, he knew the bomber would never make Defa. He plugged in his intercom just in time to hear the pilot say, "How long have we got?"

"Fifteen minutes," di Marco said. "Twenty at most."

"As soon as I find a promising bit of desert I'll go up and circle," the pilot said. "You'll need some height to help the signal on its way."

The rest was routine. The Heinkel climbed and circled, and then spiralled down to the desert floor, which turned out to be flat and smooth. They landed without a bounce and rolled to a stop.

"That's the easy bit," the pilot said.

They got out and walked about. Simple exercise was a huge pleasure. There were some high dunes in the far distance to the west; otherwise the Sahara reached emptily to all the horizons. After a day of constant engine-roar, Schramm found himself listening for a sound, any sound. His ears craved noise. The silence was so greedy that it was painful. When he spoke his voice seemed puny. "What next, d'you think?" he asked di Marco.

"Our Desert Rescue Unit should come out and get us."

"Aircraft?"

"Trucks." He looked at the setting sun. "But not, I think, today."

"They're jokers," the pilot said. "They couldn't find the hangar floor if they fell out of the aeroplane."

*　　*　　*

Barton was up and dressed a good two hours before dawn, which was just as well because his Kittyhawk was stone dead when the troops tried to warm her up.

For forty minutes he sat in the mess tent, hunched over

a pint of tea, and heard the engine kick and die, kick and die.

Skull came in. "Sand," he said. "Sand in the piston-chambers."

"What d'you know about it?"

"Just speculating."

"Well don't. Shut bloody up."

Skull poured himself some tea. He added condensed milk with the flourish of a great chef. Barton watched grimly.

Prescott joined them. "Morning," he said. Skull nodded, Barton grunted. Fifty yards away, his Kittyhawk kicked and died. "Gremlins," Prescott said.

"It's not sodding gremlins," Barton growled.

"Sorry. Figure of speech."

"Stuff it up your chuff. Use it to keep the bullshit in."

"Yes, sir." Prescott took his tea to a dark corner.

Nobody spoke until Bletchley walked in with a cardboard box. "Completely forgot about these," he said. "Real eggs and bacon." He gave the box to Skull and sat opposite Barton. "What's up with your kite, Fanny? Gremlins?"

Barton shook his head. "Christ knows, sir."

"I have it on good authority that it's not sodding gremlins, sir," Skull said. "Thus one sub-species is completely eliminated."

"Go and cook, Skull," Barton said.

When, eventually, the engine fired and crackled and settled into a solid thunder, Hooper came into the mess tent. He had been watching the ground crew's efforts. "What was it?" Prescott asked him.

"Electrics. Damp in the electrics."

"Crap!" Barton said. "They don't know what it was. They just made that up." Skull brought in a tray of fried eggs and bacon. Suddenly Barton felt much better. His future was full of good grub and violence. "Gremlins," he said. "That's what it was, bloody Cambridge-educated gremlins, vicious little buggers, isn't that right, Skull?" He helped himself to bacon.

"Buggery is not yet part of the curriculum at Cambridge," Skull remarked, "although I believe its appeal is second only to plagiarism at Oxford."

Barton and Hooper ate hungrily; they were eager to get in the air. The meal was soon over. Bletchley walked with them to their aircraft. "This Heinkel pilot could be the single most dangerous man in the Luftwaffe," he said. "If he gets back to Benghazi, he'll show them how to do it better and they'll raid the Takoradi Trail seven days a week."

"There may be other crewmen in the target area," Hooper said. "Which one's the pilot?"

"Kill 'em all. No survivors. Take no chances. Kill everyone."

"Yes, sir." Hooper felt more comfortable. He preferred simplicity. Air combat was no place to start picking and choosing.

Airmen were standing on the Kittyhawks' wings, topping up the fuel tanks, right until the very last minute. The glow-worm flare path had been lit, but the brightest things in the night were the flames jetting out of the exhaust stubs as Barton and Hooper took off. Quickly the flames shrank to pinpoints of yellow and were lost to sight. The double drum roll of the engines took much longer to fade.

"Is that true, what you said about Oxford?" Bletchley asked.

"Probably not. I suspect that they were boasting," Skull said. "They have so little to boast about, poor creatures."

*　　*　　*

Noise and jolting did not wake Lampard. Stillness and silence did. He woke up as if someone had flipped a switch and found himself lying beside a man whose face was covered in bandages. For a moment nothing made sense. He sat up and saw an outrageous flush of colours in the eastern sky: reds, greens, yellows, mauves, pinks. Dawn.

He jumped over the tail-gate and ran to the cab. Both trucks had stopped. They were facing a Heinkel 111 that was sitting in the middle of nowhere, apparently intact. It was about a mile away. It seemed no bigger than a tie-pin. "What's wrong?" he asked.

"Nothing's wrong." Gibbon had his binoculars on the bomber. "It's just that your average Heinkel 111 has half-a-dozen guns pointing in various directions. I could drive up, you could demand surrender, we could all be dead in ten seconds."

Lampard took the binoculars. "I don't see any guns," he said. "Get closer."

They advanced cautiously to within half a mile, then a quarter of a mile. Now it was plain that the Heinkel's gun turrets were empty. "Wait here," Lampard said. He took a tommy-gun and walked forward. The air was pleasantly cool, and he felt fresh and strong.

The fuselage door was open. He looked inside and saw three men sleeping on the floor. This was a strange situation for Lampard; usually when confronted with the enemy, asleep or awake, he killed them without delay. Now he intended to capture them, but first he would have to wake them up. What to say? *Wake up* seemed civilian, almost suburban. *Hände hoch!* smacked of the cinema. *You are my prisoners* was awfully formal, and they might not understand English. While he was worrying about it, one man raised his head and stared. It was Paul Schramm. Lampard flinched with shock.

"Jack Lampard," Schramm said. The other two men awoke. "I don't suppose you're alone," he said.

"Of course I'm not bloody alone." Lampard was struggling to catch up.

"One never knows with you chaps." Schramm heaved

himself up and rested on an arm. "You lead such irregular lives. Any chance of some breakfast?"

"You're very frisky," Lampard said, "for a prisoner-of-war with a gammy leg and no boots." They both laughed, very briefly.

"Well, you know me," Schramm said. "I try to enjoy my war."

"So you should. What else can you do with it?"

Schramm pulled on his flying boots and spoke to the others. They all got out, and he introduced them to Lampard. "He's frightfully nervous," he told them, in English. "He may shoot you, just to calm his nerves."

By now the trucks had arrived. The prisoners were searched, and the Heinkel was searched, and no weapons were found.

"Breakfast," Lampard decided.

"The food is awfully good here," Schramm told di Marco in English. "Except for the tea. My advice is to avoid the tea."

"Cheeky bugger!" Smedley said.

"Take that man's name, sergeant," Schramm said; but his remark caused a sudden silence and stillness. He looked around for the cause, and saw no sergeant. "Ah," he said. "My apologies." They got on with their jobs.

"What was that about?" the pilot asked.

"Death in action. They must have suffered losses. I said something rather thoughtless."

"You seem on good terms with that tall officer," di Marco said.

"We have a lot in common. He bombed our best aircraft, I killed one of his best men." Schramm immediately felt slightly ashamed. Killing was nothing to brag about. "I'll tell you later," he said. "There will be plenty of time for conversation, I'm afraid."

The patrol knew how to cook quickly. Bacon, sausages, potatoes, mixed vegetables, all went into one great fry-up and then were spooned into mess tins. They all ate standing up. There was biscuit, margarine and jam for those still hungry. Everyone was. In a very few minutes the meal was finished, the equipment reloaded, the trucks restarted.

Lampard took a sack of bombs from a truck and beckoned to Smedley. "You deserve a treat," he said. "Five-minute fuses." Working together, they planted bombs in the cockpit, on the wing-roots, inside the fuselage, on the tailplane. "If only they were all as easy as this," Lampard said.

"If only." Smedley's voice was as flat as the desert. "I know what you're thinking," Lampard said. "Why you? Why me? Why are we alive when they're dead?" That was not what Smedley was thinking, but he said nothing. "It's not your fault," Lampard said, "and you have no cause to feel guilty." Smedley did not feel guilty, and the words made him stare. "Think of it this way," Lampard said. "War is like boxing. If you want to hit the other man really hard, you've got to get close enough so there's a risk he'll hit you. See what I mean?"

"He hit us yesterday all right," Smedley said. "By Christ, did he hit us."

The trucks moved off to a safe distance and everyone watched except the pilot. The bombs on the wing-roots exploded first. The wings detached, taking the undercarriage with them, and the bomber fell on its belly. The nose exploded, the tail got blown to pieces, the fuselage was shattered. When the pilot looked up there was nothing to see but a patch of smoke drifting away.

"Kufra," Lampard told Gibbon. "And quite quickly, please."

Gibbon led. Lampard drove the second truck. He had asked Schramm to sit beside him. "Tell me," he said, "what have you been up to since we last met?"

"Oh . . . work. Shuffling . . . um . . . what do you call it? Bumf? Is that right?" Lampard nodded. "Routine stuff,"

Schramm said. "Mainly what it consisted of was going around sweeping up after your chaps."

That pleased Lampard. "I'm afraid we are a bit untidy," he said.

"Yes." Schramm made his voice wooden. "Yes . . . Well, I grew rather tired of that, so I organised a trip down to Fort Lamy."

Lampard thought he had misheard. "Fort *Lamy?*" he said. Schramm nodded. "That's in Chad," Lampard said. "Isn't it?"

"What's left of it is in Chad. We bombed it." Schramm spoke modestly, but the words gave him enormous satisfaction.

"You *bombed* Fort Lamy?"

"Yes. We blew up twenty-three new Hurricanes."

Lampard was silent, while he tried to take it all in. Then he said: "You flew to Chad and back. For God's sake, that's a colossal distance!" When Schramm merely smiled and shrugged, he said, "I can't believe it. How far is it?"

"About three hundred kilometres too far, I'm afraid," Schramm said wistfully.

That killed the conversation for a few miles. The desert was blank: the only thing that moved was the other truck, and its shape and size never changed. There was nothing to do but drive and think.

"By the way," Schramm said, "Mrs d'Armytage has moved to Alexandria."

"Hey!" Lampard protested. "That's below the belt."

"Is it? I thought you would prefer to know. It might avoid disappointment when you got to Cairo."

"Blast your eyes." Lampard scowled at the dust from Gibbon's wheels until he realised his right foot was thrusting harder and harder. He relaxed it and the truck dropped back. "Why Alexandria?" he demanded.

"The military police were a nuisance."

"Oh."

"Never mind. The Australian is buried now."

"Uh-huh."

"The latest information I have is that Mrs Challis is free and —"

"Pack it in! Look, you stay out of my love-life and I'll stay out of yours."

Schramm looked out of the window. "The strange thing is that you made my love-life happen. I cut my feet so badly running away from you on the Jebel that I needed treatment and she was the doctor."

"I don't want to hear about it," Lampard said.

"The war brought us together and now the war has broken us up," Schramm said. "Long live the war."

"I don't care," Lampard said. "I don't care about Joan d'Armytage or Elizabeth Challis or your lady doctor or anyone else. All I care about is my patrol."

"What patrol?" Schramm asked. "Where?"

"Shut up or I'll bash you." The right foot went down so hard that Schramm's head was jerked back. He shut up.

*　　*　　*

Barton had had all night to think about this job, and he had changed his mind about the way it should be done.

If the Heinkel was down where Signals Intelligence said it was, it lay at the extreme range of the Kittyhawk. But Barton didn't trust those fixes on forced landings. Direction-finding stations had to work very fast on poor signals from remote aircraft. They were lucky to get three bearings, and when they did, the three lines never met at one definite, unanimous point. They came together and crossed, and what they made was a small triangle. Then the operator usually split the difference and put the fix in the centre of the triangle. It was the best he could do and it might be a long way from the truth of the matter: twenty, thirty, fifty miles from it. Barton had seen it happen. He had no confidence that Luftwaffe DF stations were any better than RAF ones.

If he had to go hunting for the Heinkel, Barton wanted plenty of leeway. He decided not to fly to the target area at three hundred miles an hour, which was a high cruising speed that drank the juice without thought for the morrow. Instead, he decided they would take off early, and fly slowly, and arrive with their tanks a damn sight more than half-full.

That was his plan, and it was why everyone was up two hours before dawn. Then came the gremlins.

When at last the Kittyhawks got off the ground, he climbed gradually to ten thousand feet and settled down with the airspeed indicator at two hundred miles an hour, a nice round figure which would get them there and, God willing, get them home again. Bletchley had promised the Commanding Officer of the Desert Air Force and the C-in-C Middle East and the Prime Minister and the King and Roosevelt and Stalin and the Mormon Tabernacle Choir that Fanny Barton and his intrepid Yankee wingman would race the Luftwaffe across the Sahara, destroy their bastard Heinkel, save the Takoradi Trail and win the war, even if it killed them. Well done, Baggy. You gave, and you did not stop to count the cost. You stayed behind and did not have to worry about returning.

Barton suddenly remembered Baggy saying: *What a hypocritical young thug you are, Fanny, you don't give a tiny toss for Takoradi, do you?* It was true. So what did he care about? The squadron. Nothing else mattered. Uncle had once said the squadron never died, chaps came and chaps went, but the squadron never died. By God, never a truer word was spoken. To Barton, strapped tightly into his Kittyhawk, seemingly balanced and motionless at the top of a night sky, those men lived as vividly as if they sat in the cockpit. Greek George, for instance, had come into the mess and said, "Nobody stuffs Geraldo, Geraldo is my friend." What had that been all about? Barton couldn't remember. People said peculiar things in the mess. Who was it said he'd never seen a fly land on Butcher Bailey? Mick O'Hare, that's who. Fighter pilots were such individuals, you never knew what they were going to say next. That night they were drinking rum, Pip Patterson had said, "I'm definitely going to murder my wife." Was he serious? He'd sounded serious. Pip had always been serious. The great thing about the squadron was it didn't matter if somebody didn't make sense all the time. A chap was entitled to his funny ways and as long as he did his job properly, who cared? *Four strafes in six days*. Someone had said that. Who? Fido Doggart? Tiny Lush? Didn't matter. Only the squadron mattered.

It was full daylight when they reached the map reference. The Luftwaffe DF stations had done quite well: the wreck was only five miles away. It stuck out like a dead fly on a white carpet.

They went down and buzzed it. Nothing moved. It was the most ripped-up, torn-apart wreck that Barton had ever seen.

Hooper saw the wheel tracks. "Heading east," he said.

"Jerry got here first," Barton said.

Following the tracks was child's play: from a hundred feet they were as clear as tramlines. The trucks appeared on the horizon as soft blobs of black. Soon they began to make feathery tails of dust. Then the details emerged: wheels, canvas tops, cabs. Someone saw or heard the fighters coming, for suddenly the trucks turned away from each other. It was all too late. Barton strafed one, Hooper strafed the other. It was an old familiar routine and the streams of tracer chased and found their targets as if the trucks were magnets that wanted to be hit.

Both trucks were on fire after the first pass. The Kittyhawks came back and killed all the men who were running away. Some were aircrew, some were not. Hooper wasn't concerned to distinguish. He had three .50-calibre machine guns in each wing and he gave the area a thorough hosing. If they were running, he killed them. If they were lying, he made sure they were dead. Barton did the same. Twelve machine guns killed everyone on the ground several times over. Towards the end, one of the trucks exploded. Hooper was not impressed. He had seen ambulances blow up with far greater effect.

CHAPTER NINE

Chaps Come and Go

The Benghazi blackout was less than perfect. Malplacket began to see specks of light perforating the night far ahead. He drove the Fiat off the road and stopped. "I need to pee," he said.

"Again?"

"You have an objection?"

"Hell, no, you go ahead. Who am I to stand between a man and his bladder?"

When Malplacket came back he said, "We should have a plan. We're sure to meet some kind of barrier. What do we say then? Who do we claim we are?"

"What do we look like?"

"Two middle-aged German officers in dirty uniforms."

"Then that's what we are. We play it by ear, my friend. That's our plan. You got a better one?" Lester reached across and turned the ignition key. For the first time in years he was free. Life was an adventure. He wanted action.

Malplacket eased the car back on the road and cautiously put on speed. He was driving, not because he was a good driver, but because he was sure that Lester would be a reckless one. The headlights were dimmed with metal grills and their beams made only a small dent in the darkness. He was afraid of running into something: a truck parked without lights, a squad of soldiers on the march, he didn't know what. His feet danced gingerly on the pedals. In the end, something nearly ran into him. A blare like a monster foghorn erupted close behind the Fiat and both men jumped as if stung. Malplacket's foot slammed and the rear wheels spun, gripped and flung the car away from this deafening threat. Lester turned and looked back. "It's a truck," he said. "Jesus, it's big as a goddamn house." Malplacket said nothing. Soon his fingers ached from squeezing the wheel. Once, he almost ran out of road and the wheels jolted and bounced on broken tarmac. "Hey, hey!" Lester complained. His voice shook like jelly.

"I can't see him." Malplacket's eyes were flickering to and from the wing mirror. "Is he still behind us?"

"Slow down. Pull over, let him pass, for Christ's sake."

"I can't pull over, not at this speed. What's *that*?"

Lester turned and looked at the road ahead. He saw a small red glow, magnifying rapidly. "Tail light!" he shouted, and snatched the handbrake. Malplacket was flung forward. His face whacked the top of the steering wheel. The Fiat drifted crabwise across the road leaving four tracks of hot rubber. It bucketed up the bank and stalled with a crush of bushes choking the chassis.

"Oooh," Malplacket said. "Ow." The sounds were juvenile, they could not describe his serious pain, but they were the best his voice could do. "Oh, oh." It sounded like somebody else's voice. He wished it were somebody else's pain.

Lester found a flashlight.

"You took a smack on the hooter, looks like." Blood was rippling down Malplacket's upper lip and chin. "That great schnoz of yours is a couple of sizes bigger than it was."

Lester got out and began freeing the front wheels. "Some skid, eh?" he said. "Handbrake special. One of Capone's men taught me."

"I don't care if I never see Benghazi." Malplacket lay face up on the front seats and breathed through his mouth. "Benghazi is not worth a tenth of that frightful experience. Not a tenth of a tenth."

"It's just a bloody nose. It's nothing."

"Indeed? Bring your nose here and I'll show you how painful nothing can be."

"Listen, don't get mad at me, fella. You were the guy who was driving like a maniac. I was the one who saved our skins."

"Tosh," Malplacket said heavily. "Total transatlantic tosh."

"I like that. I can use that. As we diced with death on our way into the Forbidden City, Malplacket, showing typical English phlegm, dismissed the risks as tosh. *Reader's Digest* is gonna love that."

"Never mind English phlegm. It's gore I'm losing."

"Oh boy. *Gore*. I got to get this stuff down before I forget it."

It was a long time before Malplacket's nose stopped bleeding and he was able to stand. "I can't possibly drive," he said. "My head feels like a pumpkin."

"This is war, Hans. Ve must all sacrifice ourselfs for ze Muzzerland. It's your job to drive. I'm a captain, you're only a lousy leutnant. Sieg Heil!"

Malplacket stared at his silhouette. "Lester: have you been taking benzedrine, or something?"

"*Nein, nein, mein Wagenführer*. Look, we gonna stand around and talk all night, or what?"

Malplacket drove. The Fiat seemed undamaged. The moon was up, and he could see much more of the road now. The flow of traffic carried him smoothly along. More and more, the countryside was dotted with small white farmhouses, homes of Italian colonists. After twenty minutes the traffic began to slow. Ahead they could see a modern triumphal gateway, a tall concrete arch in the massive Fascist style. Lights flickered beneath it where troops were operating a checkpoint.

"This is the beginning and the end," Malplacket said. "They will take us out and shoot us." His nose itched. He held his breath and shut his eyes, but that did no good. He sneezed violently. Blood gushed from his nostrils again. "Hell and damnation," he said thickly.

"Keep your mouth shut," Lester told him. "You're just a lousy leutnant, remember?"

The traffic moved. The station-wagon inched forward. An Italian corporal came over and asked a question. Lester ignored him and Malplacket was looking at the floor. The corporal asked it again. Lester suddenly roused himself, in a blazing rage. "Who the fuck you think you are, asshole?" he rasped. The raw violence in his voice took the soldier aback. He said something that sounded apologetic. Lester turned sideways, grabbed Malplacket's face with one hand and thrust it towards the Italian. "Get a load of this gore!" he shouted. Blood trickled over his splayed fingers, and Malplacket saw the man wince. "*Deutschland über Alles*," Lester snarled. "Ain't that a fact?" He released Malplacket and aimed a bloody finger forward. "Move it!" The barrier went up. They drove through.

*   *   *

Half an hour's driving left them hopelessly baffled.

At night, Benghazi was like any other well-fought-over town. The blackout combined with bomb damage to make driving difficult. If you didn't know exactly where to go, you ended up going in long, confused circles. The second time they drove past the cathedral, Lester said, "Hold it. This is getting us nowhere."

"Where do you want to go?"

"I told you: wherever the action is. See if you can find the harbour. That should be good for a few laughs."

Malplacket tried, but the streets wandered hither and yon, and ten minutes later the Fiat was back at the cathedral. "Shit," Lester said. "No disrespect, God . . . Look, let's at least find a bar."

"Certainly. What does a Benghazi bar look like?"

"Just drive. Pick a new route. Anywhere at all. I'll look."

Eventually Lester found a place that might have been a bar. A large and furious fight was taking place outside it. Malplacket slowed long enough to see *feld polizei* whacking skulls and kicking ribs, and then he accelerated away. Neither of them spoke.

The street they were on merged with a wider road of gleaming white concrete. Malplacket made good speed. The suburbs slipped behind them; now the countryside was largely farmland. "So much for Benghazi," Malplacket said. He pulled over and stopped.

"What's so special about this bit?" Lester asked.

"There's a roadblock ahead." A red light glowed, perhaps a quarter of a mile away. It was hard to be sure. Malplacket rested his head against the side window and closed his eyes. "Furthermore, I am quite, quite exhausted."

"I'm not sleeping here! No sir." Lester pointed at the dim, square shape of a house. "Get us up there. Must be a drive or a track or something."

There was a drive. When Malplacket stopped at the top, Lester whacked the horn. "Me, sleep in a car? I'm a captain in the goddamn Waffen SS, for Christ's sake! Watch me use my powers of requisition."

They found the front door and he beat on it with the butt of his pistol until an upper window opened. "*Afrika Korps*," he snapped. "*Rommel Panzer Luftwaffe Blitzkrieg Gezundheit*, so get your ass down here fast."

She was middle-aged, Italian and alone. Lester saluted, clicking his heels. She did not seem frightened or even surprised, and she immediately set about cooking a meal for them.

"See, it's all in your tone of voice," Lester said. "People expect to be kicked around. Just shout, and half the world jumps. You want to know why? Because half the world feels guilty for being alive, that's why."

Malplacket watched Lester drum his fingers on the arm of his chair. His cap rested on one knee. One boot was propped on the toe of the other. He was more like an officer of the Third Reich than the real thing. Malplacket looked away.

They ate spaghetti. "You got to be a wop to cook this stuff right," Lester said. "My wife, the way she served it up, it tasted like string."

"That's exactly what it means. Spaghetti is Italian for string."

"So what?"

Malplacket carefully placed his fork on his plate. He wiped his mouth, and dislodged some flakes of blackened blood. They fell on the table. He brushed them onto the floor with his hand. "Since you are absolutely determined to find fault with everything and everyone," he said, "I suggest we abandon conversation for the present."

Lester stared while he chewed his pasta. He washed it down with wine. "You know your trouble?" he said. "You give up too easily, that's your trouble. My old man –"

Far away, a siren growled and climbed and wound itself up to a high wail. The Italian woman stopped washing a pot and crossed herself.

"Action!" Lester said. "This I gotta see." He crammed spaghetti into his mouth, found his cap and the car keys, and hurried out.

A dozen searchlights were fumbling and groping for the incoming bombers. Lester stood by the Fiat and tried to pinpoint the rumble of engines, but the noise was too high and too vague. Soon the harsh bark of flak batteries overwhelmed it. He backed the car down to the road and drove towards the centre of town.

The first stick of bombs marched across the harbour area. The explosions cracked the blackness with their brilliance and the thunderclaps followed almost as an afterthought. Lester realised that he was looking down on

Benghazi; this was as good a view as he was going to get. He pulled over and began making notes.

The searchlights found a bomber. It was so high that all he could see was a glowing speck trapped in the cone. Then he saw bursts of flak in the beams; they resembled little smuts of soot. He recorded that. When the bomber began to burn it left a tail of flame, similar to a comet. It did not dive straight down: it fell in a long spiral, patiently tracked by the searchlights. When it crashed, the violence was so great that he felt it through his feet. Bombs still on board, he thought. Either that, or they hit the gasworks.

He counted eighty-four bomb-bursts. The flak tailed off, the searchlights quit, the sky was empty. Benghazi was quiet again, except for the distant, tinny clang of ambulances and the tireless barking of every dog in town. They should be used to the bombing by now, Lester thought. He made a note of it. Dogs were always good copy.

*   *   *

Next morning Malplacket woke up to the life-giving aroma of coffee. He had slept well, his nose had healed, and nobody was trying to kill him. Despite himself, he began to feel cheerful. Perhaps this mad act of derring-do would turn out for the best after all. And by eleven-fifteen that morning, when he was photographing Lester walking past a building festooned with large Nazi flags, he felt as happy as a boy on his first bicycle.

While he and Lester had shaved and showered and breakfasted, the Italian woman had sponged and pressed their uniforms. She was touchingly grateful when Lester gave her some paper money, so he added another couple of notes.

"Where on earth did you get all that?" Malplacket asked him.

"I looted those bodies in the desert. Some of it's a bit bloodstained. She didn't seem to mind that, did she?" He bowed from the waist and kissed her hand.

They drove into Benghazi and hid the Fiat inside a villa that looked as if, long ago, it had been shelled or bombed. The roof had gone and one end-wall was missing. Bushes had invaded the rooms; they filled the gaps that had once been windows with foliage and blossom.

Lester took the distributor cap. "Lotta shady characters about this sorta town," he said.

They walked down the street. Malplacket noticed that Lester had acquired something of a strut; also, he kept his left thumb hooked inside his belt. Coming the opposite way were three German soldiers; they stopped talking as they approached, and saluted. Lester's salute hit the peak of his cap and flew outwards as if on springs. Malplacket saw a soldier smirk.

When they were out of earshot, he said: "Don't salute like that, old chap. It's not done."

"That's how they do it in the movies."

"Forget Hollywood. You gave the impression that you were trying to swat a rather dull wasp. Come with me." They went into an alley, where some Arab children were playing. "Bring your hand the long way up, and let it fall the short way down. Like this." He demonstrated. "It's a mere acknowledgement, you see. Not physical training." Lester practised. So did the Arab children. "Casual, huh?" he said.

"Of course. You are an officer." They went back into the street. "And try not to goose-step, old chap," Malplacket said. The children were following them, saluting hard. He turned and stamped. They fled.

That was the turning point for Malplacket. Suddenly he felt in command. "From what little I saw last night," he said, "the custom here is that officers who are out for a stroll walk arm-in-arm."

Reluctantly, Lester linked arms. "Where I come from, this means we're as good as married."

"Yes? How quaint."

"You ditch me, my brothers break your legs."

They sauntered through the town, merging with the crowds of servicemen. Lester counted a dozen different uniforms in a wide range of colours. He saw carabiniere, and Luftwaffe aircrew, and black soldiers, presumably recruited from the far corners of Mussolini's empire. He returned every salute as if it were the easiest thing in the world. Then they walked into a square and he saw the wreckage of a crashed fighter.

It was stacked on a recovery vehicle, with its wings folded alongside its fuselage. The RAF roundels stood out like bullseyes. "I gotta get a picture of that thing," Lester said hungrily.

He showed Malplacket how to use his camera, and he posed, hands on hips, in front of the wreck. He was not alone. Other cameras were capturing the scene.

"That's gonna be worth a thousand bucks," he said.

"Goodness. Money for old rope, isn't it? We should seek to enlarge your portfolio."

Malplacket shot Lester drinking coffee at an outdoor café, surrounded by bronzed German officers. He shot him standing with his arms folded in front of an 88 mm anti-aircraft gun. He shot him shading his eyes as he watched the gunners of a German navy patrol-boat detonate a British mine, creating a tower of white water. He had used up half the film when they chanced upon a building that could only have been a military headquarters. Despatch riders came and went, and clusters of officers stood on the steps, talking. Swastika flags drooped from the upper windows and a swastika banner – long and pointed – billowed elegantly from the balcony. Machine guns on tripods flanked the door. A screen of sentries checked everyone who entered. Lester and Malplacket stopped and studied the place from a distance. "No," Lester said. "That's pushing our luck too hard."

"All you need do is walk past. I'll take the picture from here. No one will notice."

Lester laughed and turned his back on the scene. "You're getting to be crazier than me."

Malplacket offered him the camera. "Very well. You take the picture and I'll go."

Lester plucked at his fly and laughed again, nervous as a bridegroom. "Go to hell," he said. He turned and walked away. His shoulders were hunched. He looked as if he might be holding his breath.

Malplacket let him cross the street and come back, and he got a nice, busy shot of him passing in front of the machine guns. He wound the film on and shot him waving away an Arab who was trying to sell fly-whisks.

"Let's beat it." Lester was walking so fast he was almost running.

Malplacket went with him. "Is there a problem?"

"I think I should've saluted somebody back there, a general or something. Somebody shouted at me."

Malplacket glanced behind them. Nothing had changed. A couple of German officers on the steps were laughing at whatever a third officer was saying. Lester scuttled round the first corner he reached. Malplacket hurried after him and grabbed his arm.

"Come on, let's go, let's go," Lester urged.

"Nobody is following us. Nobody is interested in us, I assure you." Malplacket was amused by Lester's jumpiness. "Do try to get a grip of yourself, old chap. If you persist in looking as horribly guilty as this, we shall both end up in the clink." Lester scowled. Malplacket photographed him, scowling. "I thought you Americans were made of sterner stuff," he said. "How you conquered the West if you went to pieces every time a Cherokee cleared his throat, I can't imagine. That sort of attitude wouldn't have done in India. Not enough English phlegm, that's your trouble. Now if —"

"OK," Lester said. "Enough."

Malplacket gave him the camera. "I don't intend to be left out of your scoop," he said. "Be sure I'm in focus."

They returned to the street. Malplacket strolled past the military headquarters and turned. He saluted as he walked by the steps; a senior officer paused in conversation and returned the salute. *Perfect*, Malplacket thought. *And if he missed that shot I shall strangle him*. He crossed the street. Lester was not in sight.

Around the corner, twenty yards away, Lester was nodding and frowning as a pair of German naval officers spoke to him. They seemed very young and very friendly. Malplacket dashed forward. "Wilhelm!" he shouted. "Wilhelm!" They all turned. Malplacket made an urgent show of tapping his wristwatch. Lester backed away from the Germans, gesturing his helplessness. Malplacket took his arm and hurried him off.

They lost themselves in the crowd. "What on earth did they want?" Malplacket asked.

"Beats me. Maybe they thought they recognised me. I kept on coughing and shaking my head . . . Listen, I've had enough of all this. My ulcer's burning."

"Did you take my picture?"

"Yeah, yeah, I took your lousy picture." Lester's voice had become weak and thin, and it kept on breaking up. "Let's get back to the goddamn car."

It was a long walk and by now the day was very hot. Twice, Lester had to stop and rest. When they reached the ruined villa, and the Fiat was still there, he let out a long sigh of relief.

"I suggest a siesta," Malplacket said. It sounded peculiar. They laughed.

"Feel free, friend. Suggest a siesta to Lestah." That sounded utterly absurd. Lester laughed until his stomach muscles hurt, and he had to lean against the car. "I got news," he said when he stopped gasping for breath. "There's a guy upstairs."

Malplacket thought it was a joke until Lester took out his pistol. He moved alongside Lester and looked up. Half the ceiling had collapsed when the roof caved in. Upstairs, in the tangle of broken beams and planks, just visible at the fringe of destruction, was an army boot with some bare leg attached.

"Whoever he is, he's not doing us any harm," Malplacket said. He felt slightly sick: too much tension, too much heat. "Why don't we just leave him alone?"

"He's hiding. He's probably a deserter." Lester's voice was cracking up again. "Might be dangerous. Might be armed."

"I'm sorry, old chap, I simply can't handle another crisis before lunch. Just fix the car, quickly, so that we can go."

"Sure." As Lester moved forward, the boot moved back. It dislodged a dribble of stones. Lester stopped. Nobody spoke. Plaster dust sifted slowly through bars of sunlight. There was more movement above. More rubble fell.

"For Pete's sake," Lester said miserably. The pistol hung from his fingers like a dead thing.

A man crawled to the edge and looked down at them. He was young and small and thin. All he wore was shorts and boots. He spoke in German: the words meant nothing to them.

"You never saw us, kid," Lester said. "And we never saw you. Now crawl back into your hole."

With one hand the young man gripped the splintered end of a beam and he swung into space. It was a fall of about eight feet and he landed badly. He was weeping with pain, but he stumbled to his feet and raised his arms in surrender. One arm would not go all the way up. It was broken or dislocated or maybe both. Lester had not seen anyone so thin and filthy since China. What made it worse was the young man's voice. Throughout the weeping he kept chanting the same shrill German phrase, over and over again. Lester recognised the sound of the mentally ill, a noise so full of hurt that it was unbearable. Sooner or later it would be stopped by a punch in the mouth.

Lester's hands were shaking as he replaced the distributor cap. "Try the engine!" he called. The Fiat whirred and grumbled and would not start. Lester crossed himself. "You hypocritical bastard," he whispered. The Fiat coughed and fired and roared, drowning out the German's manic gabble. Lester scrambled into the car. "What's wrong with a bit of hypocrisy, anyway?" he said.

"What?"

"Forget it. Wait!" He opened the door and threw a fistful of money. The young German expected a blow: he staggered back, tripped and fell. "Let's go!" Lester cried.

*   *   *

Malplacket drove carefully through the town. "You've got your story now, haven't you?" he said. "We can leave, can't we?" Lester nodded.

They were old Benghazi hands. Finding the way out was easy. Nobody wanted to stop them. They were waved through the roadblock under the triumphal gateway. After that, it took remarkably little time to reach the turn-off where they had parted company with Lampard's patrol. Malplacket drove into the Jebel and parked under some trees.

They ate lunch: biscuit and bully-beef. An Arab boy appeared and sold them fresh goat's milk. "It ain't Groppi's," Lester said, "but it'll do . . . Jeez, I'm tired. We did it. I can't believe we did it." He photographed the boy, who smiled.

"I hope you took my picture when I was saluting."

"Yeah, sure," Lester shrugged. "I think I did."

"If you missed that salute I shall never forgive you. Neither will Blanchtower."

Gibbon had drilled them in the route to the rendezvous. It was simple: they drove through the foothills of the Jebel until they picked up the main camel trail that went south. It crossed the Tariq el 'Abd at a point marked by the skeletons of three camels and the fresh grave of a German soldier. From there they set the sun compass to one hundred and eighty degrees and drove on that bearing for precisely fifty kilometres into the Sahara. They reached the rendezvous by mid-afternoon. It looked just like the rest of the desert, and it was just as empty.

"I guess we're early, or he's late," Lester said. "Or a bit of both." They had a box of tinned food and two jerricans of water. That should be enough.

*   *   *

Towards sunset Malplacket built a fire as he had seen the patrol do it – fill a large can with sand and soak it with petrol – and he made a stew.

By then Lester had finished his story. He had been writing it in his head ever since they had left Benghazi, so putting it down on paper was easy. Malplacket read it as they ate.

"Splendid. Spiffing, in fact. Congratulations."

"You really like it?"

"Yes, indeed. And Chicago will find it irresistible."

"It zips along."

"I enjoyed your moments of irony. Very refreshing."

"Yeah?" Lester took the pages back. "Huh." He flicked through them. "This is just a first draft, of course. Still kinda rough in spots."

"Don't lose those ironic moments, old chap. They are the little leaven that leavens the lump." Lester raised his eyebrows. "First Corinthians, chapter four," Malplacket said. "Feel free to use it. It's out of copyright."

"Thank God you're not judging the Pulitzer. You'd give it to *Fanny Farmer's Cookbook*."

They had one blanket each, and it was not enough. They awoke, shivering, long before dawn, as a scouring wind blew sand into their hair and ears and nose and mouth.

Tea was hot but gritty. They took shelter in the Fiat and listened to the whine and moan. When the sun came up, they watched the desert floor shift and twist as the wind hustled it elsewhere.

"Goddamn weather," Lester said. "I just hope it doesn't louse up Lampard's navigation."

"Gibbon knows his job. He won the MC, remember."

"Maybe Gibbon got wounded. Or captured."

"In England it is a criminal offence to spread alarm and despondency. You are not only spreading it, you are digging it in."

"I got sand in my crotch."

Malplacket sighed. "*Everyone* in the desert has sand in his crotch. Some have more than others. Corporal Pocock, for instance, has a very great deal of it."

Lester had nothing to say about that. He climbed into the back seat and began to rewrite his story.

The wind dropped at about ten o'clock. Breakfast was another stew; afterwards, Malplacket was so tired that he slept in the shade of the car.

The midday sun awoke him. He felt grubby and stained, and he took a short walk to revive himself. That was a mistake. The desert looked bigger and emptier than ever.

Later, he read Lester's second draft. "Excellent," he said. "A vast improvement."

Lester waited. "I took out all that ironic crap," he said. "You notice?"

"Yes, I did." Malplacket returned the pages. "Very wise."

Lester stuffed them into his back pocket.

"The new satirical undertones are far more telling," Malplacket said.

"Horseshit."

Malplacket recoiled slightly. "My dear fellow. You do yourself an injustice."

"Where? Show me where."

"It runs throughout. The merest undertones. Your satire is never rampant. One of the qualities I most admire in your work is its satirical restraint."

"Sure. And this heat's fried your brains."

An hour before sundown Malplacket cooked another meal. "I'm afraid it's stew again," he said. "However, I put in some prunes for variety."

Lester was standing on the roof of the Fiat, searching the northern horizon. "Forty-eight hours," he said. "They should be here by now." He climbed down. "I've been thinking. We never would have got into Benghazi without your nosebleed. That was a truly gutsy nosebleed."

"Thank you. And your performance at the Italian lady's villa was outstanding."

"Yeah, I thought so. I've always wanted to beat on a door with the butt of a pistol."

"Gratifying?"

"I found it so." Lester walked around the car, kicking the tyres. "Listen: I know how you feel about alarm and despondency and so on, but . . . Let's not kid ourselves. This is beginning to look not so good, isn't it?"

"A fair summary."

The night was cold again. The dawn was brilliant, but it revealed an empty desert.

"If we don't go back to the Jebel now," Malplacket said, "by tomorrow we shall be out of water." But the Fiat would not start. The more they tried, the more they ran down the battery. Winding the starting handle made noise and blisters, but the engine remained dead.

They cleaned every part that was cleanable, and achieved nothing. The sun was brutal. They got into the car to escape it.

"Just tell me one thing," Lester said. "Honest answer, OK? Did I really put any irony in that first draft?"

"None."

"How about the second?"

"I invented the satirical undertones."

"Now tell me why –"

"A joke," Malplacket said. "All a joke."

Lester hunched his shoulders and stared at the trembling horizon.

"Hell of a time to make jokes," he said.

"It was irresistible, I'm afraid."

"I leave irony to Hemingway. I put irony in a story, it gets spiked."

"I apologise. In any case I'm afraid that the joke may have been on me. The real irony is all around us, isn't it? The desert gave us our adventure and now, thanks to the desert, we can't report it."

Lester got out and tried the starting handle again. It felt like winding up a diesel locomotive. He soon quit.

"I was going to do a third draft," he said. "You know, add some more colour."

"I wouldn't bother, old chap. What you've done is fine."

Lester picked at his blisters. "Anyway, the story's not over yet, is it?"

"Good point. Who knows what the morrow may bring?"

When the moon rose, they began walking north. Lester carried a jerrican with about three pints of water in it. Malplacket had calculated that it was roughly a hundred kilometres to the edge of the Jebel, to food and water, provided they kept a straight course. The trouble with walking at night was they couldn't use the sun compass.

"Plenty of stars up there," Lester said. "I don't suppose you know how to steer by the stars?"

"Oddly enough, they failed to teach me that at Eton," Malplacket said. "Very remiss of them, wouldn't you say?" The three pints of water sloshed back and forth with every pace.

*   *   *

It took a long time, but details of the strafing of Lampard's trucks trickled through to SAS headquarters, via the International Red Cross, and Captain Kerr was able to write to the next-of-kin. Colonel von Mansdorf and Oberstleutnant Benno Hoffmann got their information much sooner, of course. A German Desert Rescue column had reached the scene while the wreckage was still smoking and brought all the bodies back to Benghazi. Benno Hoffmann escorted Dr Grandinetti to Schramm's funeral. He was distressed when she cried during the service, but it was only a little, and he cheered up when she smiled at him.

"Poor Paul," she said. "Poor me. Poor us."

Afterwards, he took her for a drink at the Officers' Club. "The first time we went out for dinner, this was where he wanted us to go," she said. "For a romantic, Paul had very little imagination."

"I never thought of him as a romantic," Hoffmann said. "Of course he wanted to marry you, so . . ." He relaxed: the funeral had taken more out of him than he had expected. "Was that ever going to be possible?" he asked.

"He thought so. He thought he had earned it. Paul believed that pain was payment. He'd suffered, so now he deserved to be happy."

"Well, you made him happy," Hoffmann said. "Or at least you made him less unhappy."

"Did I? I helped him to stop feeling sorry for himself and to stop being angry with everyone else. And I showed him a lot of dying men, so he could see that war is not adventure and that pain is not payment, because it buys nothing. He didn't believe me," she added.

"He really shouldn't have gone on that raid," Hoffmann said. "It was bound to be dangerous."

"Oh well. Isn't that why he went? Men are always killing themselves to prove their manhood."

"What Max would call a self-inflicted wound," Hoffmann said sadly.

"At least Paul made a thorough job of it," she said. "At least he didn't come back and expect me to help him finish it for him. He was kind enough to spare me that."

Her words sounded strangely flat. Hoffmann looked, and saw that her eyes were drenched with tears. He felt clumsy and inadequate; he searched for a helpful answer and found none, so in the end he said what he thought. "You loved him, didn't you?" he said.

"He was such a middle-aged child. I shall always miss him."

She finished her drink. They parted and went back to work. Two days later she left Benghazi for Milan.

There were no more raids on the Takoradi Trail. Fanny Barton got made up to wing commander, but he did not get a DSO; he went to Rhodesia and took over a Flying Training School. Hick Hooper returned to the US Army Air Force and enjoyed his war. Pip Patterson survived. Skull got posted to a bomber squadron in Egypt; after all, he knew something about bombers.

Hornet Squadron was re-formed with a fresh batch of pilots. Kellaway had recovered his wits so he stayed on as adjutant. "Chaps come and go," he told the new Intelligence Officer, "but the squadron never dies."

That was in May 1942. One month later, Rommel's advance had carried him so deep into Egypt that he was within a day's drive of Cairo when he was finally checked at El Alamein. By November 1942 the German army had been soundly defeated there. It began a retreat that was to cover more than a thousand miles, through Egypt and Libya, to Tunisia. In May 1943 the last German soldiers in North Africa surrendered. On 4 September 1943, Italy was invaded and Allied armies were on the mainland of Europe. The Desert Air Force and the SAS went with them. They fought until the war was won, on 7 May 1945.

THE END

AUTHOR'S NOTE

A Good Clean Fight is fiction built around fact. I reckon the reader is entitled to know which is which. In brief: the characters are invented, while the history and the geography are as accurate as I could make them.

The Luftwaffe did have airfields around the Jebel (at Barce, for instance) that were attacked by the SAS; and SAS patrols did drive hundreds of miles via Kufra Oasis in order to raid behind enemy lines. Kufra was not the only desert base that the SAS used, and I have juggled the dates slightly so as to make Kufra their main staging-post in the spring of 1942, a time when there was a lull in the ground war and the Gazala Line separated the two sides.

The Desert Air Force never stopped fighting. It had a lot of Curtiss Tomahawks and Kittyhawks. Many Allied pilots liked these aircraft, but without doubt the higher they flew, the less well they performed. (A New Zealand pilot told me that his Kittyhawk had once been outclimbed by a Liberator – a four-engined bomber. Admittedly, the bomber had dropped its load.) However, as a ground-strafer the Tomahawk or Kittyhawk was a great success.

My description of the work of the SAS – the fact that they drove vast distances in order to outflank the enemy; that they hid up in the Jebel; raided airfields by night either silently, with bombs, or loudly, with armed jeeps; and then made the long return journey through the desert – is broadly accurate. So is the scale of the damage they inflicted. For instance, one patrol bombed thirty-seven aircraft at Agedabia airfield; another blew up twenty-seven at Tamit; a third destroyed thirty at Barce. David Stirling led no fewer than eighteen armed jeeps onto a German aerodrome known as LG 12 and in the space of a few minutes machine-gunned rows of Me109s, Stukas, Heinkel 111s and Junkers 52s. In all, the SAS destroyed more than two hundred and fifty enemy aircraft between December 1941 and August 1942.

It was daring work, and the motto of the SAS is, of course, *Who Dares Wins*. They did not always win without loss. Usually they struck hard and escaped fast – the German army was curiously reluctant to retaliate and, as far as I know, Major Jakowski's force had no counterpart in reality. But any SAS patrol that got caught in the open by Stukas or Me109s was likely to suffer badly.

Special operations called for special qualities. Those who served in the SAS were not wild men, but there can be no doubt that some had more than a touch of recklessness. One of the most remarkable was Captain Paddy Mayne, a big, quick-thinking Ulsterman who had been an Irish rugby international before the war. Mayne was apparently quiet, even reserved, but he had an explosive temper. On rugby tours he had been known to throw fellow players out of hotel windows for no particular reason. When Stirling began to recruit officers, he had to get Mayne out of close detention (he had knocked out a superior officer as a means of settling an argument) and the Irishman made it clear that he was interested in only one thing: fighting.

Mayne inspired huge faith in the men he led. One famous story describes how he ran out of bombs and so he ripped the instrument panel from a Messerschmitt in order to disable it. When not on operations he could be moody and bloody-minded to the point of irresponsibility. (Those who drank with him learned to be very wary.) When Stirling left him at base with orders to train some new recruits while Stirling went raiding, Mayne felt snubbed. He built himself a large bed and lay on it, reading, for days on end.

Stirling came back and was furious at Mayne's negligence. Mayne was only good for combat. At that he was superb: before the war was over he had been awarded four Distinguished Service Orders. To win one DSO is a great achievement; to win four is phenomenal.

All the characters in *A Good Clean Fight* are invented, and certainly Jack Lampard is not based on Paddy Mayne. However, when I was writing the story I was aware that there was room for powerful individuals inside the SAS, and that quirks of behaviour were acceptable so long as the individual got results. (Mayne survived the war, but never settled in civilian life; he died in December 1955 when he drove his car into the back of a parked lorry.) Incidentally, as far as I know, Department SU in Cairo did not exist.

As for the unpleasantness at the Black Cat Club: I made it up. This is not to say that troops on leave in Cairo never misbehaved. Men of the Special Forces certainly relaxed in their own way. In *Long Range Desert Group* (Collins, 1945), Captain W. B. Kennedy Shaw recalled certain incidents involving that unit "which ended in the Military Police barracks at Bab el Hadid". For instance, the LRDG was proud of its skill at sand-channelling, the technique of placing steel channels under wheels to extricate a vehicle stuck in soft sand, and one patrol "insisted on sand-channelling their way down the length of Sharia Suleiman Pasha" – a main street in Cairo – "to the fury of the police and the dislocation of the traffic". There were other incidents (one involved a bath and a lift-shaft) and friction developed when men not in the LRDG were found wearing its shoulder patches because these "were always good for a few free drinks". I borrowed this act of dangerous larceny and applied it to the white berets of the SAS instead – an item of clothing which did in fact provoke confrontations in Cairo, until Stirling changed its colour.

There was no Hornet Squadron in North Africa, but

anonymous airstrips such as LG 181 were in fact dotted all across the Western Desert. At one time the Desert Air Force used LG 125, which was well behind enemy lines; I doubled it for luck and called it LG 250. Air Commodore Collishaw's policy of foxing the Italian air force was a reality, but it was not such a total success as some historians have suggested. Like Barton, Collishaw sometimes pushed his luck too far and his squadrons took heavy punishment. Like Barton, Collishaw tolerated no questioning of his orders. On one occasion he sent a squadron of Blenheims to attack the same target for the fourth day running. The squadron commander pointed out that this really was asking for trouble. Collishaw insisted the raid was the last thing the enemy would expect. "We're going to fox 'em," he said. The squadron commander still protested. Collishaw asked: "Are you trying to tell me that you haven't the guts to do your job?" The squadron took off and was swamped by enemy fighters over the target. Only two of its nine Blenheims survived. For once, the enemy had not been foxed.

The manner of Kit Carson's dying is based on the experience of a fighter pilot in North Africa, who told me how easy it was, in the haste of baling-out, to release the parachute harness – simply from force of habit. He himself very nearly did it; and he is convinced that a member of his squadron really did do it.

The episode involving Butcher Bailey's return to LG 181 on the back of a German motorcycle combination is based on an actual incident in the desert. Similarly, Hick Hooper's encounter with exploding ambulances was suggested to me by the experience of a friend who was ground-strafing over northern France in 1944 when he saw a German ambulance blow up spectacularly. Thereafter, he said, he strafed every German ambulance he saw; most of them exploded. He believed they were carrying ammunition. The presence of an American pilot in the desert was not unusual. Many squadrons were made up of pilots from several countries, and by 1942 there were two American fighter squadrons in the Middle East.

The Takoradi Trail is fact. So is the Luftwaffe's raid on Fort Lamy. The Trail covered 3,697 miles and the journey took six days. The first two thousand miles were the worst: "where the weather was uniformly unaccountable and forced landings offered an agreeable choice between impenetrable forest and empty wilderness," as the historian Philip Guedalla observed. One machine in ten failed to complete the journey. Nevertheless, over five thousand aircraft took the Takoradi route to Egypt, and Air Chief Marshal Sir Arthur Tedder said of the men who made possible this steady transfusion, "without their loyal, ever-willing, and tireless assistance our recent successes would have been impossible." Air superiority preceded ground victory.

The Luftwaffe knew this. As Francis K. Mason has described in *The Hawker Hurricane*, a Heinkel 111H took off from a remote airstrip called *Campo Uno*, deep in the south of the Libyan desert, at eight a.m. on 21 January 1942. Its crew included a German explorer, Hauptmann Blaich, and an Italian desert expert, Major Count Vimercati. The Heinkel reached Fort Lamy at two-thirty p.m., bombed the airfield, destroying eight Hurricanes and eighty thousand gallons of fuel, and headed back the way it had come. At six-thirty p.m., after ten and a half hours in the air, it ran out of fuel and made a forced landing in the desert.

Eventually the Luftwaffe Desert Rescue Flight found the Heinkel and refuelled it. It was flown home. Meanwhile the Takoradi route was closed for lack of fuel for several weeks. We can only assume that the Luftwaffe did not realise how much damage this one raid had done: they never repeated it.

The 'thermos' bombs on the Trigh el 'Abd existed, and

the hazards of dune driving were all too real (although it is unlikely that any column would have been quite so lemming-like as Jakowski's men). Sun compasses were essential for long-range travel in the desert. Details of food, of water rations, and of the 'sand-happy' state called 'doolally' are as accurate as I could make them.

The episode in which a time-pencil-fuse accidentally starts burning in the back of a jeep was suggested by an incident involving Stirling, Mayne and others as they drove across the Jebel after a raid. They jumped out only seconds before the fuse – still attached to a bomb – went off and the jeep was blown to bits.

There is a scene in which the Chief Censor in Cairo refers to some ill-timed BBC news bulletins about the fall of Benghazi. In fact those bulletins concerned the fall of Tobruk later in 1942. I rearranged the event in order to help my narrative.

No such adjustment was necessary to describe the risk that a unit operating far behind enemy lines might be attacked by 'friendly' aircraft. Kennedy Shaw reports one occasion when a patrol was thoroughly strafed by Beaufighters of the Desert Air Force. This hazard was inseparable from the work of the LRDG and the SAS.

The curious visit of Malplacket and Lester to Benghazi is similar to one that was actually carried out by Stirling, Randolph Churchill and Fitzroy Maclean in May 1942, although the latter made a much more conspicuous entry and exit. The front wheels of their car had developed a loud, high-pitched, two-tone screech. "We could hardly have made more noise if we had been in a fire engine with its bell clanging," Maclean wrote later. However this racket did not disturb the enemy.

No account can do full justice to the courage, skill and determination of the men of the SAS and the Desert Air Force. Theirs was a hard and lonely war, often fought in desolate conditions. Especially, I am aware that my description of life in the desert is inadequate. You had to be there to know how grim and brutally unpleasant (and yet sometimes how clean and beautiful) the desert could be. Erik de Mauny was there, and in *Return to Oasis* (Shepherd-Walwyn, 1980) he wrote: "Flies descended in plagues of biblical proportions, heavy chlorination made the water ration almost undrinkable, and when the *khamseen* blew, its fine dust infiltrated the body's most intimate recesses, setting up colonies of desert sores." There were always two enemies to be fought 'up the blue'. The desert was the other, and it never lost.